GAMBLE

Books by Dick Francis and Felix Francis

DEAD HEAT
SILKS
EVEN MONEY
CROSSFIRE

Books by Dick Francis

THE SPORT OF QUEENS (autobiography)
DEAD CERT
NERVE
FOR KICKS
ODDS AGAINST
FLYING FINISH
BLOOD SPORT
FORFEIT
ENQUIRY
RAT RACE
BONECRACK
SMOKESCREEN
SLAY-RIDE
KNOCK DOWN
HIGH STAKES
IN THE FRAME
RISK
TRIAL RUN
WHIP HAND
REFLEX
TWICE SHY
BANKER
THE DANGER
PROOF
BREAK IN
LESTER: The Official Biography
BOLT
HOT MONEY
THE EDGE
STRAIGHT
LONGSHOT
COMEBACK
DRIVING FORCE
DECIDER
WILD HORSES
COME TO GRIEF
TO THE HILT
10-lb PENALTY
FIELD OF 13
SECOND WIND
SHATTERED
UNDER ORDERS

GAMBLE

A Dick Francis Novel

by

FELIX FRANCIS

MICHAEL JOSEPH
an imprint of
PENGUIN BOOKS

MICHAEL JOSEPH

Published by the Penguin Group
Penguin Books Ltd, 80 Strand, London WC2R 0RL, England
Penguin Group (USA) Inc., 375 Hudson Street, New York, New York 10014, USA
Penguin Group (Canada), 90 Eglinton Avenue East, Suite 700, Toronto, Ontario, Canada M4P 2Y3
(a division of Pearson Penguin Canada Inc.)
Penguin Ireland, 25 St Stephen's Green, Dublin 2, Ireland (a division of Penguin Books Ltd)
Penguin Group (Australia), 250 Camberwell Road,
Camberwell, Victoria 3124, Australia (a division of Pearson Australia Group Pty Ltd)
Penguin Books India Pvt Ltd, 11 Community Centre,
Panchsheel Park, New Delhi – 110 017, India
Penguin Group (NZ), 67 Apollo Drive, Rosedale, Auckland 0632, New Zealand
(a division of Pearson New Zealand Ltd)
Penguin Books (South Africa) (Pty) Ltd, 24 Sturdee Avenue,
Rosebank, Johannesburg 2196, South Africa

Penguin Books Ltd, Registered Offices: 80 Strand, London WC2R 0RL, England

www.penguin.com

First published 2011
6

Set in 11.5/16 pt Sabon LT Std
Typeset by Jouve (UK), Milton Keynes
Printed in Great Britain by Clays Ltd, St Ives plc

A CIP catalogue record for this book is available from the British Library

ISBN: 978-0-718-15665-7

www.greenpenguin.co.uk

For my granddaughter
Sienna Rose

With thanks to my cousin
Ned Francis
financial adviser

and the offices of
Calkin Pattinson and Company Limited

and to ***Debbie,***
as always

I

I was standing right next to Herb Kovak when he was murdered. *Executed* would have been a better word. Shot three times from close range, twice in the heart and once in the face, he was almost certainly dead before he hit the ground, and definitely before the gunman had turned away and disappeared into the Grand National race-day crowd.

The shooting had happened so fast that neither Herb nor I, nor anyone else for that matter, would have had a chance to prevent it. In fact, I hadn't realized what was actually going on until it was over, and Herb was already dead at my feet. I wondered if Herb himself had had the time to comprehend that his life was in danger before the bullets tore into his body to end it.

Probably not, and I found that strangely comforting.

I had liked Herb.

But someone else clearly hadn't.

The murder of Herb Kovak changed everyone's day, not just his. The police took over the situation with their usual insensitive efficiency, cancelling one of the world's major sporting events with just half an hour's notice and requiring the more than sixty thousand frustrated spectators to wait patiently in line for several hours to give their names and addresses.

'But you must have seen his face!'

I was sitting at a table opposite an exasperated police detective inspector in one of the restaurants that had been cleared of its usual clientele and set up as an emergency incident room.

'I've already told you,' I said. 'I wasn't looking at the man's face.'

I thought back once again to those few fatal seconds and all I could remember clearly was the gun.

'So it was a man?' the inspector asked.

'I think so,' I said.

'Was he black or white?'

'The gun was black,' I said. 'With a silencer.'

It didn't sound very helpful. Even I could tell that.

'Mr … er.' The detective consulted the notebook on the table. 'Foxton. Is there nothing else you can tell us about the murderer?'

'I'm sorry,' I said, shaking my head. 'It all happened so quickly.'

He changed his line of questioning. 'So, how well did you know Mr Kovak?'

'Well enough,' I said. 'We work together. Have done for the past five years or so. I'd say we are work-friends.' I paused. 'At least, we were.'

It was difficult to believe that he was dead.

'What line of work?'

'Financial services,' I said. 'We're independent financial advisers.'

I could almost see the detective's eyes glaze over with boredom.

'It may not be as exciting as riding in the Grand National,' I said, 'but it's not that bad.'

He looked up at my face. 'And have you ridden in the Grand National?' His voice was full of sarcasm, and he was smiling.

'As a matter of fact, I have,' I said. 'Twice.'

The smile faded. 'Oh,' he said.

Oh, indeed, I thought. 'And I won it the second time.'

It was unlike me to talk much about what I now felt was a previous life, and bragging about it was even more uncharacteristic. I silently rebuked myself for my indulgence, but I was getting a little irritated by the policeman's attitude not only towards me but also towards my dead colleague.

He looked down again at his notes.

'Foxton,' he said, reading. He looked up. 'Not Foxy Foxton?'

'Yes,' I said, although I had long been trying to give up the 'Foxy' nickname, preferring my real name of Nicholas, which I felt was more suited to a serious life in the City.

'Well, well,' said the policeman. 'I won a few quid on you.'

I smiled. He'd probably lost a few quid too, but I wasn't going to say so.

'Not riding today, then?'

'No,' I said. 'Not for a long time.'

Had it really been eight years, I thought, since I had

last ridden in a race? In some ways it felt like only yesterday, but in others it was a lifetime away.

The policeman wrote another line in his notebook.

'So now you're a financial adviser?'

'Yes.'

'Bit of a comedown, wouldn't you say?'

I thought about replying that it was better than being a policeman but decided, in the end, that silence was probably the best policy. Anyway, I tended to agree with him. My whole life had been a bit of a comedown since those heady days of hurling myself over Aintree fences with half a ton of horseflesh between my legs.

'Who do you advise?' he asked.

'Anyone who will pay me,' I said, rather flippantly.

'And Mr Kovak?'

'Him too,' I said. 'We both work for a firm of independent financial advisers in the City.'

'Here in Liverpool?' he asked.

'No,' I said. 'The City of London.'

'Which firm?'

'Lyall and Black,' I said. 'Our offices are in Lombard Street.'

He wrote it down.

'Can you think of any reason why anyone would want Mr Kovak dead?'

It was the question I had been asking myself over and over again for the past two hours.

'No,' I said. 'Absolutely not. Everyone liked Herb. He was always smiling and happy. He was the life and soul of any party.'

'How long did you say you have known him?' asked the detective.

'Five years. We joined the firm at the same time.'

'I understand he was an American citizen.'

'Yes,' I said. 'He came from Louisville, in Kentucky. He used to go back to the States a couple of times a year.'

Everything was written down in the inspector's notebook.

'Was he married?'

'No.'

'Girlfriend?'

'None that I knew of,' I said.

'Were you and he in a gay relationship?' the policeman asked in a deadpan tone of voice, his eyes still on his notes.

'No,' I said, equally deadpan.

'I'll find out, you know,' he said, looking up.

'There's nothing to find out,' I said. 'I may have worked with Mr Kovak but I live with my girlfriend.'

'Where?'

'Finchley,' I said. 'North London.'

I gave him my full address and he wrote it down.

'Was Mr Kovak involved in a gay relationship with anyone else?'

'What makes you think he was gay?' I asked.

'No wife. No girlfriend. What else should I think?'

'I have no reason to believe Herb was gay. In fact, I know he wasn't.'

'How do you know?' The policeman leaned towards me purposefully.

I thought back to those rare occasions when Herb and I had spent any time together, sometimes in hotels where we would be staying overnight at financial conferences. He had never made any sort of pass at me, and he had occasionally chatted up the local girls and then boasted about his conquests over breakfast. It was true that I'd never actually seen him in a sexual situation with a woman, but I hadn't seen him with a man either.

'I just know,' I said weakly.

'Hmm,' said the inspector, clearly not believing me and making another note in his book.

But did I really know? And did it matter?

'What difference would it make, anyway?' I asked.

'Lots of murders have a sexual motive,' said the detective. 'Until we know differently, we have to explore every avenue.'

It was nearly dark before I was finally allowed to leave the racecourse, and it had also started raining. The courtesy shuttle service to the distant park-and-ride car park had long since ceased running and I was cold, wet and thoroughly fed up by the time I reached my Mercedes. But I sat for some while in the car before setting off, once more going over and over in my mind the events of the day.

I had picked Herb up from his flat at Seymour Way in Hendon soon after eight in the morning and we had set off to Liverpool in great good humour. It was to be

Herb's first trip to the Grand National and he was uncharacteristically excited by the prospect.

He had grown up in the shadow of the iconic twin spires of Churchill Downs racetrack, the venue of the Kentucky Derby and spiritual home of American Thoroughbred racing, but he had always claimed that gambling on the horses had ruined his childhood.

I had asked him to come to the races with me quite a few times before but he had always declined, claiming that the memories were still too painful. However, there had been no sign of that today as I had driven north on the motorway, the two of us chatting amicably about our work, our lives, and our hopes and fears for the future.

Little did we know then how short Herb's future was going to be.

He and I had always got on fairly well over the past five years but mostly on a strictly colleague-to-colleague level. Today had been the first day of a promising deeper friendship. It had also been the last.

I sat alone in my car and grieved for my new-found, but so quickly lost, friend. But still I had no idea why anyone would want him dead.

My journey back to Finchley seemed to be never ending. There was an accident on the M6 north of Birmingham with a five-mile tailback. It said so on the radio, sandwiched between endless news bulletins about the murder of Herb and the cancellation of the

Grand National. Not that they mentioned Herb by name, of course. He was just referred to as 'a man'. I assumed the police would withhold his identity until his next of kin had been informed. But who, I wondered, were his next of kin? And how would the authorities find them? Thankfully, I thought, that wasn't my problem.

I came upon the back of the traffic congestion just south of Stoke, the mass of red brake lights ahead of me shining brightly in the darkness.

I have to admit that I am usually an impatient driver. I suppose it is a case of 'once a racer, always a racer'. It makes little difference to me if my steed has four legs or four wheels, if I see a gap, I tend to take it. It was the way I had ridden during my all-too-short four years as a jockey and it had served me well.

But, that evening, I didn't have the energy to get irritated by the queues of near-stationary cars. Instead I sat quietly in the outside lane as we crawled past an upturned motor home that had spread its load of human and domestic clutter across half the carriageway. One shouldn't look at others' misfortune but, of course, we all did and thanked our lucky stars it wasn't us lying there on the cold tarmac receiving medical assistance.

I stopped at one of the motorway service areas and called home.

Claudia, my girlfriend, answered at the second ring.

'Hello, it's me,' I said. 'I'm on my way home but I'll be a couple of hours more at least.'

'Good day?' she asked.

'Have you seen the news?'

'No. Why?'

I knew she wouldn't have. Claudia was an artist and she had planned to spend the day painting in what she called her studio but what was actually the guest bedroom of the house we shared. Once she closed the door, turned up the music in her iPod headphones and set to work on a canvas it would take an earthquake or a nuclear strike to penetrate her bubble. I had been quite surprised that she had answered the phone.

'The National was cancelled,' I said.

'Cancelled?'

'Well, there's talk of them holding the race on Monday, but it was cancelled for today.'

'Why?' she asked.

'Someone was murdered.'

'How inconvenient of them.' There was laughter in her voice.

'It was Herb,' I said.

'What was Herb?' she asked. The laughter had gone.

'It was Herb who was murdered.'

'Oh my God!' she screamed. 'How?'

'Watch the news.'

'But Nick,' she said, concerned. 'I mean – are you OK?'

'I'm fine. I'll be home as soon as I can.'

Next I tried to call my boss – Herb's boss – to warn him of the coming disruption to business, as I was sure there would be, but there was no answer. I decided against leaving a message. Somehow voicemail didn't seem the right medium for bad news.

I set off southwards again and spent the remainder of the journey as I had the first part, thinking about Herb and wondering why anyone should want to kill him. But there were so many questions and so few answers.

How did the murderer know Herb would be at Aintree today?

Had we been followed from London and stalked around the racecourse?

Had Herb really been the target or had it been a case of mistaken identity?

And why would anyone commit murder with sixty thousand potential witnesses in close attendance when surely it would be safer to lure their victim alone into some dark, quiet alley?

I'd said as much to the detective inspector but he hadn't thought it particularly unusual. 'Sometimes it is easier for an assailant to get away if there is a big crowd to hide in,' he'd said. 'Also it can pamper to their ego to do it in a public place with witnesses.'

'But it must make it more likely that he would be recognized, or at least allow you to get a good description.'

'You'd be surprised,' he'd said. 'More witnesses often mean more confusion. They all see things differently and we end up with a description of a black white man with straight curly hair, four arms and two heads. And everyone tends to look at the bleeding victim rather than the perpetrator of the crime. We often get a great description of the corpse, but nothing about the murderer.'

'But how about CCTV?' I'd asked him.

'It appears that the particular spot behind the grandstand where Mr Kovak was shot is not in view of any of the racecourse security cameras and was also not visible from any of the cameras brought in by the television people to cover the event.'

The assassin had known what he was doing in that respect. It had clearly been a professional hit.

But why?

Every line of thought came back to the same question. Why would anyone want to kill Herb Kovak? I knew that some of our clients could get pretty cross when an investment that had been recommended to them went down in value rather than up, but to the point of murder? Surely not?

People like Herb and me didn't live in a world of contract killers and hit men. We simply existed in an environment of figures and computers, profits and returns, interest rates and gilt yields, not of guns and bullets and violent death.

The more I thought about it the more convinced I became that, professional as the hit may have been, the killer must have shot the wrong man.

I was hungry and weary by the time I pulled the Mercedes into the parking area in front of my house in Lichfield Grove, Finchley. It was ten minutes to midnight and just sixteen hours since I had left here this morning. It felt longer – about a week longer.

Claudia had waited up and she came out to the car.

'I watched the television news,' she said. 'I can't believe it.'

Neither could I. It all seemed so unreal.

'I was standing right next to him,' I said. 'One moment he was alive and laughing about which horse we should bet on and the next second he was dead.'

'Awful.' She stroked my arm. 'Do they know who did it?'

'Not that they told me,' I said. 'What did it say on the news?'

'Not much, really,' Claudia said. 'Just a couple of so-called experts disagreeing with each other about whether it was as a result of terrorism or organized crime.'

'It was an assassination,' I said firmly. 'Plain and simple.'

'But who on earth would want to assassinate Herb Kovak?' Claudia said. 'I only met him twice but he seemed such a gentle soul.'

'I agree,' I said, 'and the more I think about it the more certain I become that it must have been a case of mistaken identity. Perhaps that's also why the police haven't yet revealed who was shot. They don't want to let the killer know he hit the wrong man.'

I walked round to the back of the car and opened the boot. It had been a warm and sunny spring day when we had arrived at Aintree and we had decided to leave our overcoats in the car. I looked down at them both lying there, Herb's dark blue one on top of my own brown.

'Oh God,' I said out loud, suddenly becoming quite emotional again. 'What shall I do with that?'

'Leave it there,' said Claudia, slamming the boot shut. She took me by the arm. 'Come on, Nick. Time to put you to bed.'

'I'd rather have a stiff drink or two.'

'OK,' she said with a smile. 'A couple of stiff drinks first, then bed.'

I didn't feel much better in the morning, but that might have had something to do with the few more than a couple of stiff drinks I'd consumed before finally going to bed around two o'clock.

I had never been much of a drinker, not least as a need to keep my riding weight down when I'd been a jockey. I had left school with three top grades at A level and, much to the dismay of my parents and teachers, I had forgone the offered place at the LSE, the London School of Economics, for a life in the saddle. So, aged eighteen, when many young men going up to university were learning how to use their new-found freedom to pour large amounts of alcohol down their throats, I'd been pounding the streets of Lambourn in a sweat-suit or sitting alone in a sauna trying to shed an extra pound or two.

However, the previous evening, the shock of the day's events had begun to show. So I had dug out the half bottle of single malt whisky left over from Christmas and polished it off before climbing the stairs to bed. But, of course, the spirit didn't take away the demons in my head and I had spent much of the night troubled and awake, unable to remove the mental image of Herb growing cold on a marble slab in some Liverpool mortuary.

The weather on Sunday morning was as miserable as I was with a string of heavy April showers blowing in on a bracing northerly breeze.

At about ten, during a break in the rain, I went out for a Sunday paper, nipping up to the newsagent on Regent's Park Road.

'A very good morning to you, Mr Foxton,' said the shop owner from behind the counter.

'Morning, Mr Patel,' I said in reply. 'But I'm not sure what's good about it.'

Mr Patel smiled at me and said nothing. We may have lived in the same place but we did so with different cultures.

All the front pages on the shelves had the same story: DEATH AT THE RACES read one headline, MURDER AT THE NATIONAL read another, GUN HORROR AT AINTREE ran a third.

I glanced quickly at them all. None gave the name of the victim and, to me, there appeared to be far greater coverage about the aggravation and inconvenience suffered by the crowd rather than any commiseration or condolence towards poor Herb. I suppose some conjecture was to be expected as the reporters had so little real factual information from which to make a story, but I was surprised at their apparent lack of sympathy for the target of the assassin.

One paper even went so far as to suggest that the murder was likely to have been drug related and then went on to imply that everyone else was probably better off with the victim dead.

I bought a copy of the *Sunday Times* for no better reason than its headline – POLICE HUNT RACE-DAY ASSASSIN – was the least sensational and the story beneath it didn't immediately assume that Herb had probably deserved to be killed.

'Thank you, sir,' said Mr Patel, giving me my change.

I tucked the heavy newspaper under my arm and retraced my tracks home.

Lichfield Grove was a fairly typical London suburban street of mostly 1930s-built semi-detached houses with bay windows and small front gardens.

I had lived here now for the past eight years yet I hardly knew my neighbours other than to wave at occasionally if we happened to arrive or leave our homes at the same time. In fact, I knew Mr Patel the newsagent better than those I lived right next to. I was aware that the couple on one side were called Jane and Phil (or was it John?) but I had no idea of their surname or what either of them did for a living.

As I walked back from the newsagent, I thought how strange it was that members of the human race could live here so cheek-by-jowl with their fellow beings without any meaningful reaction between them.

But at least it made a change from the rural village life I had experienced before, where everyone took pains to know every other person's business, and where nothing could be kept a secret for long.

I wondered whether I should make more of an effort to be more community minded. I suppose it would depend on how long I intended to stay.

Many of my racing friends had thought that Finchley was a strange choice but I had needed a clean break from my former life. A clean break – that was a joke! It had been a clean break that had forced me to stop race riding just as I was beginning to make my mark in the sport. The clean break in question was to my second cervical vertebra, the axis, on which the atlas vertebra above it rotated to turn the head. In short, I had broken my neck.

I suppose I should be thankful that the break hadn't killed or paralysed me, either of which could have been a highly likely outcome. The fact that I was now walking down Lichfield Grove at all was due to the prompt and gentle care of the paramedics on duty at Cheltenham racecourse that fateful day. They had taken great pains to immobilize my neck and spine before I was lifted from the turf.

It had been a silly fall, and I had to admit to a degree of carelessness on my part.

The last race on the Wednesday of the Cheltenham Steeplechase Festival is what is known as the Bumper – a National Hunt flat race. No jumps, no hurdles, just two miles of undulating rich green grass between start and finish. It is not the greatest spectacle the Festival has to offer and many of the large crowd had already made their way to the car parks, or the bar.

But the Bumper is very competitive and the jockeys take it very seriously. Not often do the jump boys and girls get to emulate Willie Shoemaker or Frankie Dettori. Judging the pace with no jumps to break up the rhythm is an art, and knowing where and when to make your final challenge to the finish can make all the difference to the outcome.

That particular Wednesday, just over eight years ago, I had been riding a horse that the *Racing Post* had rather kindly called 'an outsider'. The horse had just one speed – moderate – and absolutely no turn of foot to take it past others up the final climb to victory. My only chance was to go off fairly fast from the start and to try to run the 'finish' out of the others.

The plan worked quite well, up to a point.

At about half way, my mount and I were some fifteen lengths in front of the nearest challenger and still going reasonably well as we swung left-handed and down the hill. But the sound of the pursuers was getting ever louder in my ears, and six or seven of them swept past us like Ferraris overtaking a steamroller as we turned into the straight.

The race was lost, and it was no great surprise to me, or to the few still watching from the grandstands.

Perhaps the horse beneath sensed a subtle change in me – a change from expectation and excitement to resignation and disappointment. Or perhaps the horse was no longer concentrating on the task in hand in the same way that his jockey's mind was wandering to the following day's races and his rides to come.

Whatever the real cause, one moment he was galloping along serenely, albeit one-paced, and the next he had stumbled and gone down as if shot.

I had seen the television replay. I'd had no chance.

The fall had catapulted me over the horse's neck and head-first into the ground. I had woken up two days later in the neurosurgery and spinal-injuries department of Frenchay Hospital in Bristol with a humdinger of a headache and a metal contraption called a halo brace surrounding and literally screwed into my skull.

Three uncomfortable months later, with the metal halo finally removed, I set about regaining my fitness and place in the saddle only for my hopes to be dashed by the horseracing authority's medical board, who decided that I was permanently unfit to return to racing. 'Too risky,' they had said. 'Another fall on your head could prove fatal.' I had argued that I was prepared to accept the risk and pointed out that a fall on the head could prove fatal even if you hadn't previously broken your neck.

I had tried at length to explain to them that all jockeys risked their lives every time they climbed aboard half a ton of horse and galloped at thirty miles per hour over five-foot fences. Jockeys were well used to taking risks and accepted the consequences without blaming the authorities. But it was all to no avail. 'Sorry,' they said. 'Our decision is final.'

So that had been that.

From being the new kid on the block, the youngest winning jockey of the Grand National since Bruce Hobbs in 1938 and widely tipped to be the next Champion, I was suddenly a twenty-one-year-old ex-jockey with nothing to fall back on.

'You will need an education for when your riding days are over,' my father had once said in a last futile attempt to make me take up my place at university instead of going racing when I was eighteen.

'Then I'll get my education when I need it,' I'd replied.

And so I had, applying again and being accepted once more by the LSE to read for a combined degree in government and economics.

And hence I had come to live in Finchley, putting down a deposit on the house from the earnings of my last successful season in the saddle.

Finchley Central Underground Station, round the corner from Lichfield Grove, was just ten stops up the Northern Line from the LSE.

But it hadn't been an easy change.

I had become used to the adrenalin-fuelled excitement of riding horses at speed over obstacles when winning was the thing. Winning, winning, winning – nothing else mattered. Everything I did was with winning in mind. I loved it. I lived it. It was like a drug, and I was addicted.

When it was snatched away from me, I suffered badly from withdrawal symptoms. An alcoholic with the DTs had nothing on me.

In those first few months I tried hard to put on a

brave face, busying myself with buying the house and getting ready for my studies, cursing my luck and telling everyone that I was fine; but inside I was sick, shaking and near suicidal.

Another shower was about to fall out of the darkening sky as I hurried the last few yards along the road to my house with the newspaper.

In keeping with many of my neighbours, I had arranged, early on, to concrete over my small overgrown front lawn, converting it into an off-road parking space that was now occupied by my ageing Mercedes SLK sports car. I had excitedly bought the car brand new with my percentage from the Grand National win. That had been ten years and more than a hundred and eighty thousand miles ago and, in truth, I was well past needing a change.

I opened the boot and looked down at the two coats lying there. The previous evening the sight of Herb's blue cashmere had almost been too much for me to bear, but now it appeared as just an overcoat without a home.

I picked them both up, slammed the boot shut, and hurried inside as the first large drops of rain began to wet my hair.

I hung my coat on one of the hooks behind the front door and wondered what I should do with Herb's. He wouldn't be needing it now but I supposed it belonged to his family and would go back to them eventually.

In the meantime, I hung it up next to mine in my hallway.

I am not quite sure why I went through the pockets. Maybe I thought that he might have left his flat key there as he had been wearing the coat when he had locked his door the previous morning.

There was no key but there was a piece of paper deep in the left-hand pocket. It had been roughly folded over and screwed up. I flattened it out on the wall.

I stood there in disbelief reading the stark message written on the paper in black ballpoint:

YOU SHOULD HAVE DONE WHAT YOU WERE TOLD. YOU MAY SAY YOU REGRET IT, BUT YOU WON'T BE REGRETTING IT FOR LONG.

Did that mean Herb had been the real target? Had the assassin actually shot the right man? And if so, why?

2

I spent much of Sunday morning reading and re-reading the message on the paper, trying to work out whether it actually was a prediction of murder or just an innocent communication with no relevance to the events at the Grand National the previous afternoon.

> YOU SHOULD HAVE DONE WHAT YOU WERE TOLD. YOU MAY SAY YOU REGRET IT, BUT YOU WON'T BE REGRETTING IT FOR LONG.

I dug out the business card that I had been given at Aintree by the detective: Inspector Paul Matthews, Merseyside Police. I tried the number printed there, but he wasn't available. I left a message asking him to call me back.

I wondered what it was that Herb should have done, what he had been told to do. And for what, and to whom, had he expressed regret?

I gave up trying to work it out and read the many reports about the murder in the *Sunday Times*. I thought again about calling my boss, but he would also read about it in the papers and he would find out soon enough that the victim had been his senior assistant. Why spoil his Sunday lunch?

I knew all too well from my time as a jockey that

one should never believe what one reads in newspapers but, on this occasion, I was surprised how accurate they were as far as the factual information was concerned. The *Sunday Times* correspondents clearly had good links direct to Merseyside Police headquarters, but not so good that they could actually name the victim. And they had little or no information about any motive but that didn't stop them from speculating.

'Such a clinical assassination has all the hallmarks of a gangland organized crime "hit".' It went on to suggest that a reason the name of the victim was being withheld was possibly because he was a well-known criminal and the police didn't want potential witnesses to feel it wasn't worth coming forward.

'That's rubbish,' I said out loud.

'What's rubbish?' Claudia asked.

I was sitting in our small kitchen with the newspaper spread out across the kitchen table while Claudia was baking a cake for her sister's birthday, her long black hair tied back in a ponytail.

'This in the paper,' I said. 'They're suggesting that Herb was a criminal and probably deserved to be killed.'

'And was he?' Claudia asked, turning round.

'Of course not,' I said firmly.

'How do you know?' she asked, echoing the detective inspector.

'I just do,' I said. 'I worked at the next desk to him for the past five years. Don't you think I'd have noticed if he was a criminal?'

'Not necessarily,' Claudia said. 'Do you think those

who worked next to Bernie Madoff realized he was a crook? And how about that doctor, Harold Shipman? He murdered two hundred of his patients over more than twenty years before anyone suspected him.'

She was right. She usually was.

I had met Claudia during my second year at the LSE. We actually met on the London Underground, the Tube, an environment not usually renowned for introducing strangers. That particular evening, nearly six years ago, I had been going into college for an evening event and I was sitting next to Claudia when the train came to a halt in the tunnel. Twenty minutes later the driver came through the train explaining that there was a signal problem at Euston due to an electrical fire. Another twenty minutes after that we moved slowly forward to Kentish Town, where everybody was required to leave the train.

I never did get to the evening event at the LSE.

Claudia and I went to a pub for supper instead. But it was not a romantic liaison, it was strictly business. I was finding life as a student far more expensive than I had budgeted for, and Claudia was in need of digs close to the Byam Shaw School of Art where she was studying.

By the end of the evening we had a deal. She would move into the guest bedroom in my house as a lodger and pay a contribution towards the mortgage.

By the end of the same month she had moved out of the guest bed and into mine as full-time girlfriend, while she still went on renting the guest bedroom as her studio.

The arrangement still existed although, since our student days, the rent she paid had decreased steadily to nothing as my earnings had risen and hers had remained stubbornly static at zero.

'Making your mark as an artist is not about commercial sales,' she would wail whenever I teased her about it. 'It's all to do with creativity.'

And creative she was, there was no doubt about that. Sometimes I just wished that others would appreciate her creations enough to write out a cheque. As it was, the third bedroom of the house had so many finished canvases stacked against the walls there was no longer space for a bed.

'One day,' she would say, 'these will all sell for tens of thousands and I'll be rich.' But the main problem was that she didn't actually want to part with any of them so she didn't even try to sell them. It was as if she painted them solely for her own benefit. And they were definitely an acquired taste – one I would call dark and foreboding, full of surreal disturbing images of pain and distress.

With the exception of a small life study in pencil, drawn during her Byam Shaw days, none of her work was hung on our walls and that was because I found them impossible to live with.

And yet, surprisingly, I was able to live happily with the artist.

For a long while I had worried about her state of mind but it was as if Claudia placed all her dark thoughts into her paintings, and there they stayed, leaving her to exist outside her work in a world of brightness and colour.

She herself had no real explanation for why she painted as she did and denied that it was due to the sudden death of her parents when she'd been a child. She said it was just how things turned out when her brushes stroked the canvas.

I had often thought of taking a selection of her weirdest paintings to be seen by an analyst to see if there might be some sort of psychological disturbance present but I hadn't liked to do so without her consent and I'd been too apprehensive to ask, in case she had objected.

So I had done nothing. I had always tried to avoid personal confrontation, not least because I had grown up with it all around me from my parents, who had fought each other tooth and nail for more than thirty years until they had finally divorced in their late fifties.

'But it says here,' I said to Claudia, pointing at the newspaper, 'that the murder had all the characteristics of a gangland killing. Now surely I would have known if Herb had been involved in that sort of thing.'

'I bet my friends have all sorts of skeletons in their cupboards we'll never hear about.'

'You're such a cynic,' I said, but she did have some strange friends.

'A realist,' she replied. 'It saves being disappointed.'

'Disappointed?'

'Yes,' she said. 'If I believe the worst of people then I'm not disappointed when it turns out to be accurate.'

'And do you believe the worst of me?'

'Don't be silly,' she said, coming over and stroking my hair with flour-covered hands. 'I know the worst of you.'

'And are you disappointed?'

'Always!' She laughed.

But I began to wonder if it was true.

I arrived at the offices of Lyall & Black on the fourth floor of 64 Lombard Street at 8.15 a.m. on Monday morning to find the door blocked by a burly looking police constable in full uniform complete with anti-stab vest and helmet.

'Sorry, sir,' he said in an official tone as I tried to push past him, 'no one is allowed into these offices without permission from my superior officer.'

'But I work here,' I said.

'Your name, sir?' he asked.

'Nicholas Foxton.'

He consulted a list that he had removed from his trouser pocket.

'Mr N. Foxton,' he read. 'Very well, sir, you may go in.' He moved slightly to one side while I passed, but then he stepped quickly back into his former spot as if expecting to prevent a rush from those not on his list.

The offices of Lyall & Black had never seen such activity so early on a Monday morning.

Both the senior partners, Patrick Lyall and Gregory Black, were in the client waiting area leaning on the chest-high reception desk.

'Oh, hi Nicholas,' said Patrick as I entered. 'The police are here.'

'So I see,' I said. 'Is it to do with Herb?'

They nodded.

'We've both been here since seven,' Patrick said. 'But they won't let us along into our offices. We've been told not to go beyond here.'

'Have they said what are they looking for exactly?' I asked.

'No,' Gregory said, sharply and with irritation. 'I presume they are hoping to find some clue as to who killed him. But I'm not happy about it. There may be sensitive client material on his desk that I wouldn't want them to see. It's highly confidential.'

I thought it was unlikely that the police would accept that anything was in the least bit confidential if it could have a bearing on unmasking a murderer.

'When did you find out he was dead?' I asked them. I knew that Herb's name had finally been included in the late news on Sunday evening.

'Yesterday afternoon,' said Patrick. 'I received a call from the police asking us to meet them here this morning. How about you?'

'I did try and call you on Saturday but there was no reply,' I said. 'I was actually with Herb when he was shot.'

'My God,' said Patrick. 'That's right. You were going to the races together.'

'And I was standing right next to him when he was killed,' I said.

'How awful,' Patrick said. 'Did you see who killed him?'

'Well, sort of,' I said. 'But I was looking mostly at his gun.'

'I just don't understand it.' Patrick shook his head. 'Why would anyone want to kill Herb Kovak?'

'Dreadful business,' said Gregory, also shaking his head. 'Not good for the firm. Not good at all.'

It wasn't too hot for Herb either, I thought, but decided not to say so. Lyall & Black, although very small, had risen to be one of the significant players in the financial services industry solely due to the single-mindedness of both Patrick Lyall and Gregory Black. Where Lyall & Black led, others usually followed. They took an innovative approach to their clients' investments, often recommending opportunities that more traditional advisers might classify as too risky.

All independent financial advisers are required to determine and grade their clients' attitude to risk. Low-risk investments, such as fixed-interest bank accounts or triple-A-rated government bonds, tended to give only a small rate of return but the capital sum was safe. Medium-risk might include stocks in major companies or unit trusts and mutual funds, where the return should be greater but there was a chance of losing some of the capital due to a drop in the stock market price. High-risk investments, including venture capital trusts and foreign currency dealings, gave the opportunity to make big returns but could also result in large losses.

Lyall & Black, however, also advised on investments for which the risk level could only be described as extreme, such as the financing of films or plays, buying shares in wine funds, in foreign property portfolios or in works of art. Returns could be vast, but so were the chances of losing everything.

It was the attitude that had first attracted me to them.

Kicking a horse hard in the belly to ask it to lengthen its stride, to make it right for a jump, was also an extreme-risk strategy that could so easily result in a crashing fall. An alternative, safer approach might be to take a pull, to ask the animal to shorten and to put in an extra stride. It may have been safer, but it was slower, much slower. A great deal better in my mind to crash to the turf trying to win than to be satisfied with second place.

'How much longer are they going to keep us waiting here?' Gregory Black demanded. 'Don't they realize we have work to do?'

No one answered.

One by one, all the other staff had turned up and the client waiting area was now full to overflowing. For the most part, they had only heard of Herb's demise as they had arrived, and the last thing they wanted to do was to start work. The two ladies who doubled as receptionists and admin assistants were both in tears. Herb had been popular and much loved, and not least because he'd been a change from the usual rather straight-laced, pin-stripe-suited City financier.

Herb had loved being the American abroad, turning up on the 4th of July with gifts of candy sticks and apple pie, hosting an office Thanksgiving lunch of turkey and all the trimmings in November, and drawling 'yee-haw!' at the top of his voice like a cowboy when he'd managed to lasso a new client. Herb had been fun, and life in the office was going to be a lot less cheerful for his passing.

Finally, around nine thirty, a middle-aged man in an ill-fitting grey suit came into the reception and addressed the waiting faces.

'Ladies and gentlemen,' he began formally. 'I am Detective Chief Inspector Tomlinson of the Merseyside Police. Sorry for the inconvenience but, as you will be aware, my colleagues and I are investigating the murder of Herbert Kovak at Aintree Races on Saturday afternoon. I expect we will be here for some time and I ask for your patience. However, I must ask you to remain here as I will want to speak to each of you individually.'

Gregory Black didn't look pleased. 'Can't we work in our offices while we wait?'

'I'm afraid that won't be possible,' replied the policeman.

'And why not?' demanded Gregory.

'Because I do not want any of you,' he looked around the room, 'having any access to your computers.'

'But that's outrageous.' Gregory was building up a head of steam. 'Are you accusing one of us of having something to do with Mr Kovak's death?'

'I'm not accusing anyone,' Chief Inspector Tomlinson replied in a more conciliatory tone. 'I just need to cover every avenue. If evidence does exist on Mr Kovak's computer then I am sure you will all understand that it has to be free from any possible contamination due to any of you accessing the files through the company server.'

Gregory was hardly placated. 'But all our files are remotely saved and can be viewed directly as they were at any time. This is completely ridiculous.'

'Mr Black.' The policeman turned to face him directly. 'You are wasting my time and the sooner I get back to work, the sooner you will be able to get into your office.'

I looked at Gregory Black. I suspected that no one had spoken to him like that since he was at school, if then. There was absolute silence in the room as we all waited for the explosion, but it didn't come. He just muttered something under his breath and turned away.

But in one respect Gregory was absolutely right: the restriction on using our computers was ridiculous. Our system allowed for remote access so that certain members of the firm could access the company files from their laptops when away from the office. If any of us had wanted to 'contaminate' the files since Herb's death, we'd had most of the weekend to have done so.

'Can we go out for a coffee?' asked Jessica Winter, the firm's Compliance Officer. The photocopy room, which also doubled as the small kitchen where we made all our hot drinks, was beyond the offices and hence currently out of bounds.

'Yes,' said the chief inspector, 'but not all of you at once. I will be starting the interviews soon. And if you do go, please be back by ten o'clock.'

Jessica stood up quickly and made for the door. Half a dozen more made a move in the same direction, including me. Clearly none of us exactly relished the prospect of being confined in close proximity to Gregory Black for the next half hour.

I had to wait until after eleven before I was interviewed and, much to Gregory Black's annoyance, I was second on the policeman's list after Patrick Lyall.

I don't know whether the policeman did it on purpose to further antagonize Gregory, but the interviews were carried out in *his* office and across *his* desk, with Chief Inspector Tomlinson sitting in the high-backed leather executive chair in which Gregory usually rested his ample frame. That wouldn't go down well, I thought, especially during a certain Gregory Black's interview.

'Now then, Mr Foxton,' said the chief inspector while studying his papers, 'I understand you were at Aintree Races on Saturday afternoon and were interviewed there by one of my colleagues.'

'Yes,' I replied. 'By Detective Inspector Matthews.'

He nodded. 'Have you anything further you wish to add to what you said in that interview?'

'Yes, I have,' I said. 'I tried to call Inspector Matthews yesterday. In fact, I left a message for him to call me back, but he didn't. It was about this.'

I removed from my pocket the folded piece of paper I had found in Herb's coat and spread it out on the desk, rotating it so the chief inspector could read the words. I knew them now by heart: YOU SHOULD HAVE DONE WHAT YOU WERE TOLD. YOU MAY SAY YOU REGRET IT, BUT YOU WON'T BE REGRETTING IT FOR LONG.

After quite a few moments, he looked up at me. 'Where did you find this?'

'In Mr Kovak's coat pocket. He'd left his coat in my car when we arrived at the races. I found it only yesterday.'

The chief inspector studied the paper once more but without touching it.

'Do you recognize the handwriting?' he asked.

'No,' I replied. But I wouldn't, the note had been written carefully in capital letters, each one very precise and separate.

'And you have handled this paper?' I assumed it was a rhetorical question as he had clearly seen me remove the paper from my pocket and spread it out. I remained silent.

'Did you not think this might be evidence?' he asked. 'Handling it may jeopardize the chances of recovering any forensics.'

'It was screwed up in his coat pocket,' I said in my defence. 'I didn't know what it was until I'd opened it up and by then it was too late.'

He studied it once more.

'And what do you think it means?'

'I've no idea,' I said. 'But I think it might be a warning.'

'A warning? Why a warning?'

'I've spent much of the night thinking about it,' I said. 'It's clearly not a threat or it would say "Do as you are told or else" and not "You should have done what you were told".'

'OK,' the policeman said slowly, 'but that doesn't make it a warning.'

'I know,' I said. 'But think about it. If you wanted to kill someone you'd hardly ring them up and tell them, now would you? It would do nothing except put them on their guard and make it more difficult for you. They might even ask for police protection. There is absolutely nothing to be gained and everything to lose. Surely you would just do it, unannounced.'

'You really have thought about it,' he said.

'Yes,' I said, 'a lot. And I was there when Herb was killed. There was no "You should have done so and so" from the killer before he fired. Quite the reverse. He shot so quickly, and without preamble that I reckon Herb was dead before he even knew what was happening. And that is not in keeping with this note.' I paused. 'So I think this might have been a warning from someone else, not from the killer. In fact, I believe that it's almost more than a warning, it's an apology.'

The chief inspector looked up at me for a few seconds. 'Mr Foxton,' he said finally. 'This isn't a television drama, you know. In real life people don't apologize for murdering someone before the event.'

'So you're saying I'm wrong?'

'No,' he said slowly, 'I'm not saying that. But I'm not saying you're right either. I'll keep an open mind on the matter.'

It sounded to me very much like he thought I was wrong. He stood up and went to the door and presently another officer came in and removed the piece of paper, placing it carefully into a plastic bag with some tweezers.

'Now,' said the chief inspector as the door closed. 'Do you know of anything in Mr Kovak's work that might help me understand why he was killed?'

'Absolutely not,' I said.

'Mr Lyall told me that you and Mr Kovak worked closely together.' I nodded. 'So what did he do exactly?'

'The same as me,' I said. 'He worked mostly for Patrick Lyall as one of his assistants but he also had some clients of his own. He –'

'Sorry,' said the chief inspector, interrupting, 'I'm a little confused. Mr Lyall didn't mention that Mr Kovak was his personal assistant.'

'But he wasn't like a secretary or anything,' I said. 'He assisted in the monitoring of the investments of Mr Lyall's clients.'

'Hmm,' he said, pausing and not appearing to be any the wiser. 'Could you describe to me exactly what you do here, and also what this firm does?'

'OK,' I said. 'I'll try.'

I took a breath and thought about how best to explain it so that DCI Tomlinson would understand. 'Putting it simply, we manage people's money for them.

They are our clients. We advise them where and when they should invest their capital and then, if they agree, we invest their money for them and then we monitor the performance of the investments, switching them into something else if we believe there is a better return elsewhere.'

'I see,' he said, writing some notes. 'And how many clients does the firm have?'

'It's not quite that simple,' I said. 'Even though we are a firm, the advisers are all individuals and it's they who have the clients. There are six qualified and registered IFAs here, at least there were before Herb got killed. I suppose there are now five.'

'IFAs?'

'Independent Financial Advisers.'

He wrote it down.

'Are you one of those?' he asked.

'Yes.'

'And you have clients of your own?'

'Yes,' I said. 'I have about fifty clients but I spend about half my time looking after Patrick's clients.'

'And how many clients does Mr Lyall have?'

'About six hundred,' I said. 'Apart from Herb Kovak and myself there are two other assistants that help look after them.'

'Are they also IFAs?'

'One is,' I said, 'although she's just recently qualified and has no clients of her own yet. And the other isn't.' I gave him their names and he found them on the list of all the firm's staff.

'How can you be *independent* if you work for a firm?'

It was a good question and one that I was asked often.

'Independent in this case means we are independent of any investment providers and we are therefore free to advise our clients about all investment opportunities. If you go to see your bank about investing some money, an adviser there will only sell you something from that bank's investment portfolio even if there are better products elsewhere. They may be excellent financial advisers but they are not independent.'

'So how do you make your money?' he asked. 'I'm sure you don't do this for free.'

'No,' I agreed. 'We make our money in one of two ways, depending on the client. Most of them nowadays opt to pay us a fixed fee, which is a small percentage of the total we invest for them, and others choose that we collect the commissions from investment providers on the products we advise them to buy.'

'I see,' he said, but I wondered if he did. 'How much money do you look after in total?'

'Lots,' I said flippantly, but he didn't laugh. 'Some clients have just a few thousand to invest, others have millions. I suppose the firm as a whole looks after hundreds of millions. Most of our clients are high earners or they have considerable family wealth, or both.'

'And these clients trust you with large sums of their money?' He sounded surprised.

'Yes,' I said. 'And they trust us because we have masses of safeguards and checks to ensure that none of it goes missing.'

'And do these safeguards and checks work?'

'Absolutely,' I said, trying to sound affronted that he should even question it.

'Could Mr Kovak have been stealing from his clients?'

'Impossible,' I replied instantly, but I couldn't help thinking about what Claudia had said the previous afternoon about not knowing if someone was a crook. 'Everything we do is subject to spot-check inspections by the financial services regulatory authorities, and we have someone called a Compliance Officer in the firm whose job is to scrutinize the transactions to ensure they are done according to the rules. If Herb had been stealing from his clients the Compliance Officer would have seen it, not to mention the regulator.'

He looked down at the staff list. 'Which is the Compliance Officer?'

'Jessica Winter,' I said. He found her on the list. 'She was the woman who asked you earlier if we could go out for a coffee.'

He nodded. 'How well did Mr Kovak know Miss Winter?'

I laughed. 'If you're suggesting that Herb Kovak and Jessica Winter conspired together to steal from his clients, you can forget it. Herb thought that our dear Compliance Officer was an arrogant little prig, and she thought he was a bit of a maverick. Jessica was the only person in the firm who didn't like Herb.'

'Maybe that was just a front,' said the detective, writing a note.

'My, you do have a suspicious mind,' I said.

'Yes,' he said, looking up. 'And it's surprising how often I'm right.'

Could he really be right? Could Herb and Jessica have been fooling the rest of us all this time? And could anyone else at the firm also be involved? I told myself not to be so silly. At this rate I would soon be distrustful of my own mother.

'And do you also think Mr Kovak was a bit of a maverick?'

'No,' I said, 'not really. He was just a flamboyant American in a business where people have a bit of a reputation for being boring.'

'And are you boring?' he said, looking up at me.

'Probably,' I said. I was certainly more boring now than I had been as a jockey. But maybe it was better being boring and alive than flamboyant and dead.

I returned to the reception area after my interview to join the other fifteen members of the firm squashed into the client waiting area that had been designed for just a small coffee table and two armchairs.

'What did they ask you?' Jessica said.

'Not much,' I said, looking at her and trying not to let her see in my face the questions about her that the chief inspector had triggered in my mind. 'They just want to know what Herb did here and why I thought anyone would want to kill him.'

'Surely he wasn't killed because of his work.' Jessica looked shocked. 'I thought it must be to do with his private life.'

'I don't think they have the slightest idea why he was killed,' said Patrick Lyall. 'That's why they're asking about everything.'

There was a slight commotion outside in the lobby as someone not on the company staff list tried to gain access. He was being barred by our rather overbearing uniformed guard. I could see through the glass door that the would-be visitor was Andrew Mellor, the company solicitor. Lyall & Black was too small to have a full-time company lawyer of its own, so we used Andrew who worked in a legal practice round the corner in King William Street.

Patrick saw him as well and went over to the door.

'It's all right, officer, Mr Mellor is our lawyer.'

'But he's not on my list,' said the uniformed policeman adamantly.

'It was I who provided that list and I forgot to add Mr Mellor.'

Reluctantly the policeman stood aside and allowed the visitor to enter.

'Sorry, Andrew,' said Patrick. 'It's all a bit of a nightmare here at present.'

'Yes, so I can see.' Andrew Mellor looked around at the sea of faces. 'I'm so sorry to hear about Herb Kovak. Unbelievable business.'

'And bloody inconvenient too,' interjected Gregory,

who had been mostly quiet since his altercation with the chief inspector earlier. 'But I'm glad you're here.' I wondered if Gregory had asked Andrew to come round to be present during his interview. 'We'll have to talk outside.' Gregory began to ease himself up from one of the armchairs.

'Actually, Gregory,' said the lawyer, putting up a hand to stop him, 'it's not you I have come to see. I need to talk to Nicholas.' Fifteen pairs of eyes swivelled round in my direction. 'Do you mind?' he said to me, holding out his arm towards the door.

I could almost feel the stares on my back as I went outside into the lobby with Andrew. We went past the lifts and round a corner so that the prying eyes in Lyall & Black could no longer see us through the glass door, and the policeman on guard couldn't hear our conversation.

'Sorry about this,' he said, 'but I have something to give you.'

He pulled a white envelope out of his jacket inside pocket and held it out to me. I took it.

'What is it?' I asked.

'Herb Kovak's Last Will and Testament.'

I looked up from the envelope to Andrew's face.

'But why are you giving it to me?' I asked.

'Because Herb named you in it as his executor.'

'Me?' I said, somewhat taken aback.

'Yes,' Andrew said. 'And you are also the sole beneficiary of his estate.'

I was astonished. 'Has he no family?'

'Obviously none that he wanted to leave anything to.'
'But why would he leave it to me?' I asked.
'I've no idea,' Andrew said. 'Perhaps he liked you.'
Little did I realize at the time how Herb Kovak's legacy would turn out to be a poisoned chalice.

3

On Tuesday I went to the races – Cheltenham Races, to be precise. But this was no pleasure outing, it was work.

Racing can be a funny business, especially amongst the jockeys.

Competition is intense. It always has been. Before the advent in 1960 of the racing patrol films to aid the stewards in catching the wrongdoers, stories abounded of jockeys who would cut off a rival, giving them no room and literally putting a horse and rider through the wings of a fence in order to help their own chances of winning. And riding whips have not always been employed solely to strike the horse but have left their mark on jockeys too. On one famous occasion at Deauville in France, Lester Piggott, having dropped his own whip, pinched one from another jockey actually during the race, to help him ride a tight finish.

But once the race is run, whatever the result, there exists a camaraderie between these men and women who risk their lives five or six times an afternoon for the entertainment of others. And they look after their own.

Such it was with me.

My erstwhile opponents who, during my riding days, would have happily seen me dumped onto the turf if it meant that they could win a race, were the first to express their concern and support when I'd been injured.

When I had been forced to retire at the ripe old age of twenty-one it had been a handful of my fellow jocks who had arranged a testimonial day for me at Sandown Park to raise the funds needed to pay my university tuition fees. And it had been the same individuals who had clamoured to become my first clients when I'd qualified as an IFA.

Since then I had acquired a bit of a reputation as horseracing's very own financial adviser. Nearly all my clients had some connection with racing and I had a near monopoly within the jockeys' changing room that I believed had much to do with a shared view of risk and reward.

So I now regularly spent a couple of days a week at one racecourse or another, all with Patrick and Gregory's blessing, making appointments to see my clients before or after, and occasionally during, the racing.

Cheltenham in April has a touch of 'after the Lord Mayor's Show' about it – rather an anticlimax after the heady excitement of the four-day Steeplechase Festival in March. Gone were the temporary grandstands and the acres of tented hospitality village. Gone, too, was the nervous energy and high anticipation of seventy thousand expectant spectators waiting to cheer home their new heroes.

This April meeting may have been a more sedate affair in the enclosures but it was no less competitive on the course, with two of the top jockeys still vying to be crowned as the Champion for the current season that concluded at the end of the month. Both were my clients and I had arranged to meet one of them, Billy Searle, after racing.

Part of the government's anti-money-laundering requirements was that financial advisers had to 'know their clients', and Lyall & Black, as a firm, reckoned that a face-to-face meeting with every client should occur at least annually, in addition to our regular three-monthly written communications and twice-yearly valuations of their investments.

I had long ago decided that expecting racing folk to come to a meeting in the London offices was a complete waste of time. If I wanted them as clients – and I did – then I would have to come to see them, not vice versa. And I had found that seeing them at their place of work, the racecourses, was easier than chasing after them at home.

I had also discovered that being regularly seen at the races was the best way to recruit new clients, which was why I was currently standing on the terrace in front of the Weighing Room warming myself in the midday April sunshine more than ninety minutes before the first race.

'Hi, Foxy. Penny for your thoughts? What a lovely day, eh? Did you see the National yesterday?' Martin Gifford was a large, jovial, middle-ranking racehorse trainer who always joked that he had never made it as a jockey due to his large feet. The fact that he stood more than six feet tall and had a waist measurement that a sumo wrestler would have been proud of seemed to have escaped him.

'No,' I said. 'I missed it. I was stuck in the office all day. I just saw the short report on the television news. But I'd been at Aintree on Saturday.'

'Bloody rum business, that was,' Martin said. 'Fancy postponing the Grand National just because some bastard got themselves killed.'

He had obviously been reading the papers.

'How do you know he was a bastard?' I asked.

Martin looked at me strangely. 'Because it said so in the paper.'

'I thought you knew better than to believe what you read in the papers.' I paused, deciding whether to go on. 'The person murdered was a friend of mine. I was standing right next to him when he was shot.'

'Bloody hell!' shouted Martin. 'God, I'm sorry. Trust me to jump in with both feet.'

Trust him, indeed. 'It's OK,' I said. 'Forget it.'

I was suddenly cross with myself for even mentioning it to him. Why hadn't I just kept quiet? Everyone in racing knew that Martin Gifford was a five-star gossip. In an industry where there were many who believed that there was no such thing as a private conversation or a secret, Martin was the past master. He seemed to have a talent for knowing other people's private business and passing it on to anyone who would listen. Telling Martin that the murder victim had been a friend of mine was akin to placing a full-page spread in the *Racing Post* to advertise the fact, except quicker. Everyone at Cheltenham would probably know by the end of the afternoon, and I was already regretting my indiscretion.

'So was the National a good race?' I asked, trying to change the subject.

'I suppose so,' he said. 'Diplomatic Leak won easily in the end but he made a right hash of the Canal Turn first time round. Nearly ended up in the canal.'

'Were there many people there?' I asked.

'Looked pretty full to me,' he said. 'But I watched it on television.'

'No runners?' I asked, but I knew he hadn't any.

'I haven't had a National horse for years,' he said. 'Not since Frosty Branch in the nineties and it was the death of him, poor fellow.'

'Any runners today?' I asked.

'Fallen Leaf in the first and Yellow Digger in the three-mile chase.'

'Good luck,' I said.

'Yeah. We'll need it,' he said. 'Fallen Leaf probably wouldn't win if he started now, and I don't rate Yellow Digger very highly at all. He has no chance.' He paused. 'So who was this friend of yours who got killed?'

Dammit, I thought. I'd hoped he would leave it, but I should have known better. Martin Gifford hadn't earned his reputation for nothing.

'He was just a work colleague, really,' I said, trying to sound indifferent.

'What was his name?'

I wondered if I should I tell him. But why not? It had been in all of yesterday's papers.

'Herbert Kovak.'

'And why was he killed?' Martin demanded.

'I've no idea,' I said. 'As I told you, he was only a work colleague.'

'Come on, Foxy,' Martin said in an inviting tone. 'You must have some inkling.'

'No. None. Nothing.'

He looked disappointed, like a child told he can't have any sweets.

'Go on,' he implored once more. 'I know you're holding something back. You can tell me.'

And half the world, I thought.

'Honestly, Martin,' I said. 'I have absolutely no idea why he was killed or who did it. And if I did, I'd be telling the police, not you.'

Martin shrugged his shoulders as if to imply he didn't fully believe me. Too bad, I thought. It was true.

I was saved from further inquisition by another trainer, Jan Setter, who was everything that Martin Gifford wasn't – short, slim, attractive and fun. She grabbed my arm and turned me round, away from Martin.

'Hello lover-boy,' she whispered in my ear while giving me a kiss on the cheek. 'Fancy a dirty weekend away?'

'I'm ready when you are,' I whispered back. 'Just name your hotel.'

She pulled back and laughed.

'Oh, you're such a tease,' she said, looking up at me beguilingly from beneath her heavily mascaraed eyelids.

But it was she who was the tease, and she'd been doing it since we had first met more than ten years ago. Back then I had been an impressionable eighteen-year-old, just starting out, and she was an established trainer for whom I was riding. I hadn't really known how to react, whether to be flattered or frightened. Apart from anything else, at the time she'd been a married woman.

Nowadays she was a mid- to late-forties divorcée who seemed intent on enjoying life. Not that she didn't work hard. Her stables in Lambourn were full with about seventy horses in training and, as I knew from experience, she ran the place with great efficiency and determination.

Jan had been one of my clients now for three years, ever since she had acquired a substantial sum from her ex during a very public High Court divorce case.

I adored her, and not just for her patronage. Perhaps I should accept her invitation to a dirty weekend away, but that would then have changed everything.

'How's my money?' she asked.

'Alive and kicking,' I replied.

'And growing, I hope.' She laughed.

So did I. 'How was the preview?'

'Fabulous,' she said. 'I took my daughter, Maria, and a friend of hers. We had a really wonderful time. The show was terrific.'

At my suggestion, Jan had invested a considerable sum in a new West End musical based on the life of Florence Nightingale set during the Crimean War. The true opening night was a week or so away but the previews had just started, and I'd read some of the newspaper reports and pre-reviews. They had been somewhat mixed but that didn't always mean the show wouldn't be a success. The *Wizard of Oz* spin-off musical, *Wicked*, had been panned by the *New York Times* after its opening night on Broadway, but it was still running there more than seven years and three thousand performances later, and it was breaking box-office records all round the world.

'Some of the pre-reviews are not great,' I said.

'I can't think why,' Jan replied with surprise. 'That girl that plays Florence is gorgeous, and what a voice! I think she'll make me a fortune. I am sure the proper reviews after the first night will be fabulous.' She laughed. 'But I'll blame my financial adviser if they aren't and I lose it all.'

'I hear he has broad shoulders,' I said, laughing back.

But it wasn't necessarily a laughing matter. Investing in the theatre had always been a high-risk strategy and fortunes had been lost far more often than they'd been won. Not that investing in anything was certain. It was always a gamble. I had known some seemingly cast-iron and gold-plated investments go belly-up almost without warning. Shares in big established companies were usually safe, with expected steady growth, but even that was not always the case. Enron shares had fallen from a healthy ninety dollars each to just a few cents within ten weeks, while Health South Inc., once one of America's largest health care providers, had lost ninety-eight per cent of its value on the New York Stock Exchange in a single day. Both those collapses had been due to fraud or dodgy accounting practices inflating their revenues and profits, but business catastrophes can have the same effect. BP shares fell in value by more than fifty per cent in a month when an oil platform exploded in the Gulf of Mexico, even though the costs associated with the explosion, and the subsequent oil clear-up, represented far less than half the company's assets.

Could such a calamitous loss have resulted in Herb's murder?

I couldn't believe it was possible.

Patrick Lyall held regular meetings, usually on a Monday, when investment plans for our clients were discussed. All his assistants were present and that had included Herb and myself. We were expected to research the markets and put forward investment suggestions – for example the new musical that I had recommended to Jan Setter – but the firm's rule was clear and simple: none of our clients' money could be invested in any product without the prior approval of either Patrick or Gregory.

Our exposure to BP losses had been mostly through personal pension schemes and, bad as it was, the risks had been well spread with no individuals actually losing their shirts, or even as much as a tie. Certainly not enough, I thought, to murder their adviser.

'You should come and ride out for me,' said Jan, bringing my daydreaming back to the present. 'First lot goes out at seven thirty on Saturdays. Come down on a Friday and stay the night. You'd enjoy it.'

Now, was that an invitation to a dirty weekend, or not?

And yes, I would enjoy it. The riding, that is. At least I think I would have, but I hadn't sat on a horse in eight years.

I could remember so clearly the devastation I had felt when told I couldn't be a jockey any more. I had been sitting at an oak table in the offices of the Jockey Club in High Holborn, London. Opposite me were the three members of the medical board.

I could recall almost word for word the brief announcement made by the board chairman. 'Sorry, Foxton,' he had said almost before we were all comfortable in our chairs, 'we have concluded that you are, and will permanently remain, unfit to ride in any form of racing. Consequently, your jockey's licence has been withdrawn indefinitely.' He had then started to rise, to leave the room.

I had sat there completely stunned. My skin had gone suddenly cold and the walls had seemed to press inwards towards me. I had expected the meeting with the Board to be a formality, just another necessary inconvenience on the long road to recovery.

'Hold on a minute,' I'd said, turning in my chair towards the departing chairman. 'I was told to come here to answer some questions. What questions?'

The chairman had stopped in the doorway. 'We don't need to ask you any questions. Your scan results have given us all the answers we need.'

'Well, *I* have some questions to ask *you*, so please sit down.'

I could recall the look of surprise on his face that a jockey, or an ex-jockey, would talk to him in such a manner. But he did come back and sit down again opposite me. I asked my questions and I argued myself hoarse, but to no avail. 'Our decision is final.'

But, of course, I hadn't been prepared to leave it at that.

I'd arranged to have a second opinion from a top specialist in neck and spinal injuries to help me win my case. But he only served to confirm the medical board's findings, as well as frightening me half to death.

'The problem,' he told me, 'is that the impact of your fall occurred with such force that your atlas vertebra was effectively crushed into the axis beneath. You are very lucky to be alive. Extraordinarily lucky, in fact. Quite apart from the main fracture right through the axis, many of the interlocking bone protrusions that helped hold the two vertebrae together have been broken away. Put in simple terms, your head is balanced precariously on your neck and the slightest trauma might be enough to cause it to topple. With that neck, I wouldn't ride a bike, let alone a horse.'

It hadn't exactly been encouraging.

'Is there nothing that can be done?' I'd asked him. 'An operation or something? How about a metal plate? I still have one in my ankle from a previous break.'

'This part of the neck is a difficult area,' he'd said. 'Far more complicated than even an ankle. There are so many planes and degrees of movement involved. Then there is the attachment of the skull, not to mention the inconvenience of having the nerves for the rest of your body passing right through the middle of it all, indeed the brain stem itself stretches down to the axis vertebra. I don't think a metal plate would help and it would certainly be another problem you could do without. In normal life, your muscles will hold everything together and your neck should be fine – just try not to have a car crash.' He'd smiled at me. 'And, whatever you do, don't get into a fight.'

For weeks afterwards I had hardly turned my head at all and, for a while, I'd gone back to wearing a neck brace to sleep in. I remember being absolutely terrified to sneeze in case my head fell off, and I hadn't even been near a horse, let alone on one's back. So much for being a carefree risk taker. The Health and Safety Executive had nothing on me when it came to my neck.

'I'd love to come and watch your horses work,' I said to Jan, returning once again to the present. 'But I'm afraid I can't ride one.'

She looked disappointed. 'I thought you'd love it.'

'I would have,' I said. 'But it's too much of a risk with my neck.'

'What a bloody shame,' she said.

Bloody shame was right. I longed to ride again. Coming racing every week was a pleasant change from spending all my time in a London office but, in some ways, it was a torment. Each day I chatted amicably to my clients as they wore their racing silks and I positively ached to be one of them again. Even after all this time, I would sometimes sit in my car at the end of a day and weep for what I had lost. Why? Why? Why had this happened to me?

I shook my head, albeit only slightly, and told myself to put such thoughts of self-pity out of my mind. I had much to be thankful for and I should be happy to be twenty-nine years old, alive, employed and financially secure.

But, oh, how I wanted still to be a jockey.

I watched the first race from a vantage point on the grandstand, the vivid harlequin-coloured jackets of the jockeys appearing bright in the sunshine as they cantered down to the two-mile hurdle start.

As always, the undiminished longing to be out there with them weighed heavy in the pit of my stomach. I wondered if it would it ever go away. Even though Cheltenham had been the scene of my last, ill-fated ride, I held no grudge towards the place. It hadn't been the racecourse's fault that I had been so badly injured. In fact, it was only due to their paramedics' great care after the fall that I wasn't paralysed, or dead.

Cheltenham had been the first racecourse I had ever known and I still loved the place. I had grown up in Prestbury village, right alongside the course, and I'd ridden my bicycle past it every morning on my way to school. Each March, as the Steeplechase Festival approached, the excitement surrounding not only the racecourse but the whole town had been the inspiration for me: first to ride a horse, then to pester a local trainer for holiday jobs, and finally to give up a planned future of anodyne academia for the perilous existence of a professional jockey.

Cheltenham was the home of jump racing. Whereas the Grand National was the most famous steeplechase in the world, every racehorse owner would rather win the Cheltenham Gold Cup.

The Grand National was a handicap so the better horses carried the greater weight. The Handicapper's dream was that all the horses would cross the finish line in a huge dead-heat. But it was a bit like making Usain Bolt run the Olympic 100 metres in wellington boots to even up the chances of the others. However, in the Cheltenham Gold Cup, other than a slight reduction for female horses, all the participants carried the same weight, and the winner was the true champion.

I had only ridden in it once, on a rank outsider that'd had no chance, but I could still recall the tension that had existed in the jockeys' changing room beforehand. The Gold Cup was not just another race, it was history in the making and one's performance mattered even if, as in my case, I had pulled up my horse long before the finish.

Away to my left, at the far end of the straight, the fifteen horses for the first race were called into line by the starter. 'They're off,' sounded the public address, and they were running.

Two miles of fast-paced hurdle racing with the clatter-clatter from hooves striking the wooden obstacles clearly audible to those of us in the grandstands. The horses first swept up the straight towards us, then turned left-handed to start another complete circuit of the course, ever increasing in speed. Three horses jumped the final hurdle side by side and a flurry of jockeys' legs, arms and whips encouraged their mounts up the hill to the finish.

'First, number three, Fallen Leaf,' sounded the public address system.

Mark Vickers, the other jockey in the race to be the Champion, had just extended his lead over Billy Searle from one to two.

And Martin Gifford, the gossip, had trained the winner in spite of his expressed lack of faith in its ability. I wondered if he had simply been trying to keep his horse's starting price high by recommending that other people should not bet on it. I looked down at my race-card and decided to invest a small sum on Yellow Digger in the third race: the other runner Martin had told me would have no chance.

I turned to go back to the Weighing Room, looking down at my feet to negotiate the grandstand steps.

'Hello, Nicholas.'

I looked up. 'Hello, Mr Roberts,' I said in surprise. 'I didn't realize you were a racing man.'

'Oh, yes,' he said. 'Always have been. In fact, my brother and I have horses in training. And I often used to watch you ride. You were a good jockey. You could have been one of the greats.' He pursed his lips and shook his head.

'Thank you,' I said.

Mr Roberts – or, to use his full title, Colonel The Honourable Jolyon Westrop Roberts MC OBE, younger son of the Earl of Balscott – was a client. To be precise, he was a client of Gregory Black, but I had met him fairly frequently in the offices at Lombard Street. Whereas many clients are happy to leave us to get on with looking after their money, Jolyon Roberts was one of those known to have a 'hands-on' approach to his investments.

'Are you on your day off?' he asked.

'No,' I replied with a laugh, 'I'm seeing one of my clients after racing, you know, the jockey Billy Searle.'

He nodded, then paused. 'I don't suppose . . .' He paused again. 'No, it doesn't matter.'

'Can I help you in some way?' I asked.

'No, it's all right,' he said. 'I'll leave it.'

'Leave what?' I asked.

'Oh, nothing,' he said. 'Nothing for you to worry about. It's fine. I'm sure it's fine.'

'What is fine?' I asked with persistence. 'Is it something to do with the firm?'

'No, it's nothing,' he said. 'Forget I even mentioned it.'

'But you didn't mention anything.'

'Oh, right,' he said with a laugh. 'So I didn't.'

'Are you sure there is nothing I can help you with?' I asked again.

'Yes, I'm sure,' he said. 'Thank you.'

I stood there on the grandstand steps for a few seconds looking at him but he made no further obscure reference to whatever was clearly troubling him.

'Right then,' I said. 'No doubt I'll see you sometime in the office. Bye now.'

'Yes,' he replied. 'Right. Goodbye.'

I walked away leaving him there, standing ramrod straight and looking out across the course as if in deep thought.

I wondered what that had all been about.

Mark Vickers won twice more during the afternoon, including the big race on Yellow Digger at the relatively long odds of eight to one, giving Mark a four-winner lead over Billy Searle in the championship race, and me a tidy payout from the Tote.

Billy Searle was not in the least bit happy when he emerged from the Weighing Room after the last race for our meeting.

'Bloody Vickers,' he said to me. 'Did you see the way he won the first? Beat the poor animal half to death with his whip. Stewards should have banned him for excessive use.'

I decided not to say that I actually thought that Mark Vickers had been rather gentle with his use of the whip in the first race, and had in fact ridden a text-book finish with his hands and heels to win by a head. Perhaps, in the circumstances it wouldn't have been very diplomatic. I also chose not to mention to Billy that Mark was a client of mine as well.

'But there's still plenty of time left for you to catch him,' I said, though I knew there wasn't, and Mark Vickers was bang in form while Billy was not.

'It's my bloody turn,' he said vehemently. 'I've been waiting all these years to get my chance and now, with Frank injured, I'm going to bloody lose out to some young upstart.'

Life could be hard. Billy Searle was four years older than me and he'd been runner-up in the championship for each of the past eight years. Every time he'd been beaten by the same man, the jump-jockey recognized by all as the best in the business, Frank Miller. But Frank had broken his leg badly in a fall the previous December and had been out of action now for four months. This year, for the first time in a decade, it would be someone else's turn to be Champion Jockey, but, after today's triple for Mark Vickers, it seemed likely that it wouldn't be Billy. And time was no longer on Billy's side. Thirty-three is getting on for a jump jockey and the new crop of youngsters were good, very good, and they were also hungry for success.

It was obvious to me that Billy was in no real mood to discuss his finances even though it had been he, not me, who had called the previous afternoon asking for this urgent meeting at Cheltenham. But I'd come all the way from London to talk to him, and I didn't want it to be a wasted journey.

'What was it that you wished to discuss?' I asked him.

'I want all my money back,' he said suddenly.

'What do you mean, back?' I asked.

'I want all my money back from Lyall and Black.'

'But your money is not with Lyall and Black,' I said. 'It's in the investments that we bought for you. You still own them.'

'Well, I want it back anyway,' he said.

'Why?' I asked.

'I just do,' he said crossly. 'And I don't need to tell you why. It's my money and I want it back.' He was building himself into a full-blown fury. 'Surely I can do what I like with my own money?'

'OK. OK, Billy,' I said, trying to calm him down. 'Of course you can have the money back, but it's not that simple. I will need to sell the shares and bonds you have. I can do that tomorrow.'

'Fine,' he said.

'But Billy,' I said, 'some of your investments were bought with long-term growth in mind. Just last week I acquired some thirty-year government bonds for you. If I have to sell them tomorrow, you are likely to sustain a loss.'

'I don't care,' he said. 'I need the money now.'

'All right,' I said. 'But, as your financial adviser, I have to ask you again why you need your money so quickly. If I had more time to sell you might get a better return.'

'I haven't got more time,' he said.

'Why not?'

'I can't tell you.'

'Billy,' I said seriously, 'are you in some sort of trouble?'

'No, of course not,' he said, but his body language gave another answer.

I could remember most of the details of the investment portfolios of most of my clients, and Billy Searle was no exception. His was rather smaller than one might imagine after so many years at the top of his profession, but Billy had always been a spender rather than a saver, driving expensive cars and staying in lavish hotels. However, as far as I could recall, he had a nest egg of around a hundred and fifty thousand growing nicely for his retirement, certainly more than he would prudently need just for a new car or a foreign holiday.

'OK, Billy,' I said. 'I'll get on with liquidating everything tomorrow. But it'll take a few days for you to get the cash.'

'Can't I have it tomorrow?' He looked desperate. 'I need it tomorrow.'

'Billy, that simply isn't possible. I need to sell the shares and bonds, have the funds transferred into the company's client account, and then transfer it to your own. Banks always say to allow three days for each transfer so overall it might take a week, but it will probably be a little quicker than that. Today's Tuesday. You might have it by Friday if you're lucky, but more likely it will be Monday.'

Billy went pale.

'Billy,' I said, 'are you sure you're not in any trouble?'

'I owe a guy some money, that's all,' he said. 'He says I have to pay him by tomorrow.'

'You will just have to tell him that's impossible,' I said. 'Explain to him the reasons. I'm sure he'll understand.'

Billy gave me a look that said everything. Clearly the guy in question wouldn't take excuses.

'I'm sorry,' I said. 'But I can't do it any quicker.'

'Can't your firm lend me the money until everything's sold?' he asked.

'Billy,' I said, 'it's a hundred and fifty thousand pounds. We don't have that sort of cash lying around.'

'I only need a hundred,' he said.

'No,' I said firmly. 'Not even a hundred.'

'You don't understand,' he said in desperation. 'I need that money by tomorrow night.' He was almost crying.

'Why?' I asked him. 'Why do you owe so much?'

'I can't tell you.' He almost screamed the words at me and the heads of a few other late-leaving racegoers turned our way. 'But I need it tomorrow.'

I looked at him. 'And I cannot help you,' I said quietly. 'I think I'd better go now. Do you still want me to sell your portfolio and liquidate the money?'

'Yes,' he said in a resigned tone.

‘Right,’ I said. ‘I’ll get the office to send you a written authority. Just sign it and send it straight back. I’ll try and get the cash into your account by Friday.’

He was almost in a trance. ‘I hope I’m still alive by Friday.’

4

I sat in my car in the members' car park and thought through my recent conversation with Billy Searle. I wondered what I should do about it, if anything.

As he had said, it was his money and he could do what he liked with it. Except that he clearly didn't like what he was doing with it.

He'd also told me that he owed some guy about a hundred thousand, and had implied that his life would be in danger if he didn't repay it by the following evening. I would have usually dismissed such a threat as melodramatic nonsense but now, after the events at Aintree the previous Saturday, I wasn't so sure.

Should I tell someone about our conversation? But, who? The police would probably want some evidence, and I had none. I also didn't want to get Billy into trouble. Jockeys who owe money would always be suspected of involvement with bookmakers. Perhaps Billy's need for urgent cash was completely legitimate. Maybe he was buying a house. I knew that estate agents could be pretty determined in their selling methods, but surely they didn't threaten murder to close a deal.

I decided to do nothing until I'd had a chance to discuss it with Patrick. Besides, I would need to inform him before I could start the process of liquidating Billy's assets.

I looked at my watch. It was already past six o'clock and the office would be closed. I'd have to speak to Patrick about it in the morning. Nothing could be done now anyway, the markets in London were also long closed for the day.

Instead, I went to stay with my mother.

'Hello, darling,' she said, opening her front door. 'You're far too thin.'

It was her usual greeting and one that was due to her long-standing pathological fear that I was anorexic. It had all started when I'd been a skinny fifteen-year-old who had been desperate to be a jockey. I'd never been very short so I had begun starving myself to keep my weight down. But it hadn't been due to anorexia, just willpower. I had always loved my food but it seemed that my body, and my mind, had now finally trained themselves to stay thin.

As a rule, I never really thought about food and, if left to my own devices, there was little doubt that I would have become undernourished through neglect. But my mother saw to it that I didn't. She would send food parcels to Claudia with strict instructions to feed me more protein, or more carbohydrate, or just more.

'Hello, Mum,' I said, ignoring her comment and giving her a kiss. 'How are things?'

'So so,' she replied, as always.

She still lived near Cheltenham but not in the big house in which I had grown up. Sadly, that had had to be sold during my parents' acrimonious divorce proceedings in order to divide the capital between them. My mother's current home was a modest whitewashed cottage, hidden down a rutted lane on the edge of a small village just north of the racecourse with two double bedrooms and a bathroom upstairs, and a single open-plan kitchen/diner/lounge downstairs, the levels connected by a narrow, twisting, boxed-in staircase in the corner, with a lever-latched door at the bottom.

The cottage was an ideal size for her enforced solitary lifestyle but I knew she longed still to be the charming hostess in the grand house, a role in which she had excelled throughout my childhood.

'How's your father?' she asked.

Her enquiry was a social nicety rather than a true request for information. She probably thought that I'd appreciate her asking.

'He's fine,' I replied, completing the duty. At least, I assumed he was fine. I hadn't spoken to him for more than a fortnight. We really didn't have much to say to each other.

'Good,' she said, but I doubt that she really meant it. I thought she would almost certainly have also replied 'good' if I'd told her he was on his death bed. But at least she had asked, which was more than he ever did about her.

'I've bought you some fillet steak for dinner,' she

said, turning the conversation back to my feeding habits. 'And I've made some profiteroles for pudding.'

'Lovely,' I said. And I meant it. As usual, when coming to stay with my mother, I hadn't eaten anything all day in preparation for a high-calorie encounter with her cooking and, by now, I was really hungry.

I went up to the guest bedroom and changed out of my suit and into jeans and a sweatshirt. I tossed my mobile onto the bed. As always, the closeness to Cleeve Hill, and the phone-signal shadow it produced, rendered the thing useless. But at least I'd have a rest from its constant ringing.

When I came down, my mother was standing by the stove with saucepans already steaming on the hob.

'Help yourself to a glass of wine,' she said over her shoulder. 'I've already got one.'

I went over to the antique sideboard that had once sat in the dining room of the big house and helped myself to a glass of Merlot from the open bottle.

'How is Claudia?' my mother asked.

'Fine, thank you,' I said. 'She sends her love.'

'She should have come with you.'

Yes, I thought, she should have. There had been a time when we couldn't bear to be apart even for a single night, but now that longing had seemingly evaporated. Perhaps that is what happens after six years.

'High time you made an honest woman out of her,' my mother said. 'Time you were married and raising children.'

Was it?

In spite of what had happened to my parents, I'd always believed that someday I would marry and have a family. A few years ago, I'd even discussed the prospect with Claudia but she had dismissed the notion, saying that marriage was for boring people, and that children were troublesome and not for artists like her who were busy pushing the boundaries of existence and imagination. I wondered if she still felt the same way. There had certainly been no recent hints about rings on the finger, or brooding over other people's babies but, if there were, would I still have welcomed them?

'But you and Dad are hardly a great advertisement for marriage,' I said, possibly unwisely.

'Nonsense,' she said, turning round to face me. 'We were married for thirty years and brought you into the world. I would call that a success.'

'But you got divorced,' I said in disbelief. 'And you fought all the time.'

'Well, maybe we did,' she said, turning back to the pans. 'But it was still a success. And I don't regret it.' I was amazed. She must be getting soft in her old age. 'No,' she went on, 'I don't regret it for a second because otherwise you wouldn't exist.'

What could I say? Nothing. So I didn't.

She turned back to face me once more. 'And now I want some grandchildren.'

Ah, I thought. There had to be a reason somewhere. And I was an only child.

'You should have had more children yourself, then,'

I said with a laugh. 'Not good to put all your eggs in one basket.'

She stood very still and I thought she was going to cry.

I placed my glass down on the kitchen table, stepped forward, and put my arm around her shoulder.

'I'm sorry,' I said. 'I shouldn't have said that.'

'It's all right,' she said, reaching for a tissue and dabbing her eyes. 'You never knew.'

'Knew what?' I asked.

'Nothing. Forget it.'

It clearly wasn't nothing if it reduced her to tears all these years later.

'Come on, Mum,' I said. 'Something's obviously troubling you. Tell me.'

She sighed. 'We wanted more children. We wanted lots. You were the first, although you were quite a long time coming as we'd been married for nearly eight years by then. I was so happy you were a boy.' She smiled at me and stroked my cheek. 'But something had gone wrong with my insides and we couldn't have any more.'

It was I who was almost crying now. I had always so wanted brothers and sisters.

'We tried, of course,' she said. 'And once I did become pregnant but the baby miscarried at three months. It nearly killed me.'

Again, I didn't know what to say, so, once more, I said nothing. I just hugged her instead.

'It was the real reason behind so much unhappiness in our marriage,' she said. 'Your father gradually became so bitter that I couldn't have any more babies, stupid man. I suppose it was my body's fault, but I couldn't do anything about it, could I? I tried so hard to make up for it, but . . .' She tailed off.

'Oh, Mum,' I said, hugging her tight again. 'How awful.'

'It's all right,' she said, pulling away from me and turning back towards the stove. 'It's a long time ago, and I'll overcook these potatoes if I don't get to them now.'

We sat at the kitchen table for dinner and I ate myself to a complete standstill.

I felt bloated and still my mother was trying to force me to eat more.

'Another profiterole?' she asked, dangling a heaped spoonful over my plate.

'Mum,' I said, 'I'm stuffed. I couldn't eat another thing.'

She looked disappointed but, in fact, I had eaten far more than I would have normally, even in this house. I had tried to please her, but enough was enough. Another mouthful and my stomach might have burst. She, meanwhile, had eaten almost nothing.

Whereas I had ploughed my way through half a cow, along with a mountain of potatoes and vegetables, my mother had picked like a bird at a small circle of steak, much of which she had fed to an overweight grey cat that purred against her leg for most of the meal.

'I didn't know you'd acquired a cat,' I said.

'I didn't,' she said. 'It acquired me. One day it just arrived and he has hardly left since.'

I wasn't surprised if she regularly fed it fillet steak.

'He sometimes goes off for a few days, even a week, but he usually comes back eventually.'

'What's his name?' I asked.

'I've no idea,' she said. 'He isn't wearing a collar. He's a visitor, not a resident.'

Like me, I thought. Just here for a good meal.

'Are you going to the races tomorrow?' she asked.

The April meeting at Cheltenham ran for two days.

'Yes, I'll go for the first few,' I said. 'But I have some work to do here in the morning. I have my computer with me. Can I use your phone and your broadband connection?'

'Of course you can,' she said. 'But what time do you plan to leave? I don't want to rush you away but I have the village historical society outing tomorrow afternoon.'

'The first race is at two o'clock,' I said. 'I'll be off around twelve.'

'Then I'll get you some lunch before you go.'

The thought of yet more food was almost unbearable. And I knew she would have bought the makings of a full English breakfast as well.

'No thanks, Mum,' I said. 'I'm meeting a client there for lunch.'

She looked sideways at me as if to say she knew I'd just lied to her.

She was right.

*

'I don't like it, but we have to do as he asks,' said Patrick when I called him at eight in the morning using my mother's phone in the kitchen. 'I'll get Diana on it right away.' Diana was another of his assistants, the one who had just qualified as an IFA. 'Are you at Cheltenham again today?'

'Yes,' I said. 'But I'll probably just stay for the first three.'

'Try and have another word with Billy Searle. Get him to see sense.'

'I'll try,' I said. 'But he seemed pretty determined. Scared, even.'

'All sounds a bit fishy to me,' Patrick said. 'But we are required by the regulator to do as our clients instruct, and we can't go off to the authorities every time they instruct us to do something we don't think is sensible.'

'But we have a duty to report anything we believe to be illegal.'

'And do you have any evidence that he wants to do something illegal with the funds?'

'No.' I paused. 'But I wonder if breaking the Rules of Racing is illegal?'

'Depends on what he's doing,' said Patrick. 'Defrauding the betting public is illegal. Remember that case at the Old Bailey a few years back.'

I did indeed.

'Billy told me he owed a guy some money,' I said. 'Seems he needs a hundred grand. That's a very big debt. I wonder if he's got mixed up with a bookmaker.'

'Betting is not illegal,' Patrick said.

'Maybe not,' I agreed, 'but it is strictly against the rules for a professional jockey to bet on horseracing.'

'That's not our problem,' he said. 'And if you do ask Billy any questions, for God's sake try and be discreet. We also have a duty to keep his affairs confidential.'

'OK, I will. I'll see you in the office tomorrow.'

'Right,' said Patrick. 'Oh, yes. Another thing. That policeman called yesterday asking for you.'

'He didn't call my mobile. It was on all day, although the damn thing doesn't work here. My mother lives in a mobile-phone-signal hole.'

'No, well, that wouldn't have mattered anyway because it seems he was rather rude to Mrs McDowd so she refused to give him your number. She told him you were unavailable and not to be contacted.'

I laughed. Good old Mrs McDowd, one of our fearless office receptionists.

'What did he want?' I asked.

'Seems they want you to attend at Herb's flat. Something about being his executor.' He gave me the policeman's number and I stored it in my phone. 'Call him, will you? I don't want Mrs McDowd arrested for obstructing the police.'

'OK,' I said. 'See you tomorrow.'

I disconnected from Patrick and called Detective Chief Inspector Tomlinson.

'Ah, Mr Foxton,' he said. 'Good of you to call. How are you feeling?'

'I'm fine,' I replied, wondering why he would ask.

'Is your toe OK?' he asked.

'Sorry?'

'Your toe,' he repeated. 'Your receptionist told me about your operation.'

'Oh, that,' I said, trying to suppress a laugh. 'My toe is fine, thank you. How can I help?'

'Was Mr Kovak in personal financial difficulties?' he asked.

'In what way?' I said.

'Was he in debt?'

'Not that I am aware of,' I said. 'No more than any of us. Why do you ask?'

'Mr Foxton, are you well enough to come to Mr Kovak's home? There are quite a few things I would like to discuss with you, and I also need you, as his executor, to agree to the removal of certain items from his flat to assist with our enquiries. I can send a car if that helps.'

I thought about my planned day at Cheltenham Races.

'Tomorrow would be better.'

'Of course,' he said. 'How about eight a.m.?'

'Eight tomorrow is fine,' I said. 'I'll be there.'

'Do you need me to send a car?'

Why not, I thought. 'Yes, that would be great.'

I'd have to develop a limp.

Billy Searle was in no mood to explain to me why he suddenly needed his money.

'Just put the bloody cash in my bank account,' he shouted.

We were standing on the terrace in front of the Weighing Room before the first race and heads were turning our way.

'Billy, for goodness' sake calm down,' I said quietly but determinedly.

It didn't work.

'And what the hell are you doing here anyway?' he shouted back. 'You should be at your desk getting my bloody cash together.'

More heads turned.

So much for Patrick's instruction to keep things discreet.

'Billy, I'm only trying to help.'

'I don't need your fucking help!' He curled his lip and spat out the words, spraying me with fine drops of spittle.

The racing journalists were moving ever closer.

I dropped my voice, leaned forward and spoke directly into his ear. 'Now listen to me, you little creep. You clearly need someone's help and I'm on your side.' I paused. 'Call me when you've calmed down. The money will be in your bank by Friday.'

'I told you I need a hundred grand by tonight,' he was shouting and almost crying. 'I need my money today.'

We were now the centre of attention for half the Cheltenham crowd.

'Sorry,' I said quietly, trying to maintain some level

of dignity. 'That's impossible. It will be there by Friday, maybe by Thursday if you're very lucky.'

'Thursday will be too late,' he screamed at me. 'I'll be fucking dead by Thursday.'

There was no point in us standing there arguing, with all the racing world listening to every word, so I simply walked away, ever conscious of the hacks gathering around us like vultures, their pencils now scribbling ferociously in their notebooks. At least there was no sign of Martin Gifford, the five-star gossip, but he'd no doubt know every detail by the end of the day.

'Why are you trying to murder me?' Billy shouted after me at full volume.

I ignored him and continued over towards the relative privacy of the pre-parade ring, where I called the office to check how the liquidation of Billy's assets was progressing.

Mrs McDowd answered. Patrick and Gregory didn't like automated telephone answering and faceless voicemail. 'Our clients need to know they are dealing with real people,' they said. Hence we employed Mrs McDowd and Mrs Johnson, to answer the telephones.

'What on earth did you say to that policeman?' I asked her. 'He's being uncommonly nice to me.'

'I told him you were having an ingrowing toenail removed.'

'Why?'

'Because he was bloody rude to me,' she said with indignation. 'Spoke to me as if I was the office cleaner, so I told him you couldn't be reached. The trouble was, he wanted to know why you couldn't be reached, so I told him you were unconscious having an operation. Seemed like a good idea at the time, but the damn man was persistent, I'll give him that. Demanded to know what you were having done so I told him it was an ingrowing toenail. I could hardly make it something more serious, now could I? Not with you up and about, like.'

'Mrs McDowd, if I ever need someone to make up an alibi, I promise I'll call you,' I said, never thinking for a second that I would need an alibi much sooner than I realized. 'Can I speak to Miss Diana please?'

She put me through.

The sale of Billy Searle's assets was progressing smoothly, albeit with a sizable loss on some of my recent bond purchases. But did I care? No, probably not. Billy deserved it. I chided myself a little for such non-IFA thoughts, but I was only human. I thanked Diana and disconnected.

'Hello, lover-boy,' said a voice close behind me. 'On the phone to my competition?'

'Please stop,' I said with mock indignation. 'People will talk.'

Jan Setter cuddled herself up to my back.

'Let them talk,' she said while giving me a tight hug, pressing her whole body against mine. 'I want you.' She said it into my ear, with passion.

This was the second time in two days she had made a pass at me in public, and there was nothing casual and light-hearted about this one. Perhaps she really was serious, and that could be a problem. I had always rather enjoyed my flirtatious friendship with Jan, but that was because I had believed we were both just having a bit of verbal fun with no prospect of any actual physical contact. Now, it seemed, the stakes had been raised quite a few notches.

I pulled her arms away from my waist and turned round.

'Jan,' I said firmly. 'Behave yourself.'

'Why should I?' she asked.

'Because you must.' She turned down the corners of her mouth like a scolded child. 'For a start,' I said, 'I'm too young for you.'

'Oh, thanks a lot,' she said crossly, stepping back. 'You really do know how to make a woman feel wanted.'

There was no mock indignation here, she was angry, and hurt.

'Look,' I said. 'I'm sorry, but I never intended this to get out of hand.'

'Nothing has got out of hand,' she said. 'Things are just as they have been before. Nothing has changed.'

But we both knew it had, and there would be no going back to as we had been before.

'Great,' I said.

She smiled at me ruefully. 'But you will let me know if you change your mind.'

'OK.' I smiled back at her. 'What do you have running?'

'Nothing,' she said. 'Most of mine have finished now

for the summer.' She paused. 'I only came today because I hoped you would be here.'

I stood silently for a moment and looked at her.

'I'm sorry,' I said.

'Yeah,' she replied with a sigh. 'So am I.'

Colonel The Honourable Jolyon Westrop Roberts MC OBE, younger son of the Earl of Balscott, was waiting for me in the same place on the grandstand where I had met him the previous day.

'Ah, Nicholas,' he said as I made my way up to watch the first race. 'I was hoping you might be here again today.'

'Hello, sir,' I said. In spite of calling himself plain Mr Roberts, I knew he liked his formality. 'How can I help?'

'Well,' he said with a slight laugh. 'I hope you can help. But there may be nothing to help about. If you know what I mean?'

'No, sir,' I said. 'I don't know what you mean. You haven't told me anything.'

He laughed again, nervously.

'As I explained to you yesterday,' he said, 'there may be nothing to worry about. In fact, I expect there isn't. I'm probably only wasting your time. And I wouldn't want to get anyone into trouble, now would I?'

'Sir,' I said with some determination. 'How would I know if you won't tell me? What is it exactly that is worrying you?'

He stood for a few seconds in silence looking out over my head towards the racecourse as if deciding whether he should go on.

'Gregory,' he said finally. 'I'm worried about Gregory.'

'What about Gregory?' I asked. At times we had all been worried about Gregory. He ate far too much and didn't do any exercise that we were aware of, other than to walk to the end of Lombard Street for a substantial lunch five days a week.

'It's probably nothing,' Jolyon Roberts said again. He stamped his feet and looked uncomfortable. 'Best forget I ever said anything.'

'Are you worried about Gregory's health?' I asked.

'His health?' Mr Roberts repeated with surprise. 'Why would I worry about Gregory's health?'

'Then what is it about Gregory that you are worried about?'

Jolyon Roberts drew himself up to his full six-foot three, the ex-Guards colonel who had won a Military Cross for gallantry as a young subaltern in the Falklands War.

'I'm worried about his judgement.'

My planned early departure from Cheltenham was put on hold as I steered Mr Roberts into a quiet corner of the seafood bar for a discussion away from the ears of others. When a client, especially one with such a large investment portfolio as the younger son of the

Earl of Balscott, questions the judgement of one of the senior partners, it is no time to hurry away home.

'Now, sir,' I said when we were each settled with a plate of prawns in Marie Rose sauce with smoked salmon. 'In what way do you question Gregory Black's judgement? And why are you telling *me*?'

'It's probably nothing,' he said again. 'He has been so good to me over the years, very good. In fact, I'm sure it's nothing.'

'Why don't you let me be the judge of that?'

'Yes,' he said slowly. 'I think you might be a good judge. You always were on a horse. It was me who recommended you to Lyall and Black in the first place, don't you know?'

No, I didn't know. And I was flattered. No wonder there had been such a welcoming open door when I'd applied for a job.

'Thank you, sir,' I said. 'I didn't know.'

'Oh, yes,' said Mr Roberts. 'I've had my eye on you since you were eighteen years old and won on my cousin's horse at Chepstow. Remarkable piece of riding. Told my cousin then that you would be Champion Jockey one day. Bloody shame you got injured.'

Yes, I thought once more, it was a bloody shame.

'But tell me about Gregory Black,' I said, trying to get back to the matter in hand.

'It's probably nothing,' he said once more.

'Sir,' I said. 'Colonel Roberts, you must see that you have to tell me now that you have questioned his judgement. I promise you that I will treat what you say in the strictest confidence.'

At least, I *hoped* I could treat what he told me with confidence. Independent financial advisers were governed by the financial regulator. We were expected to act in a manner that always reflected the highest principles of behaviour. I would not be able to suppress information of wrongdoing solely because it would embarrass another IFA, even if he were my boss.

He was still reluctant to start.

'Is it about one of your investments?' I asked.

Still nothing.

'Do you disapprove of something Gregory has asked you to do?'

He absent-mindedly ate some of his prawns, the cogs in his mind turning over slowly.

'He may be mistaken,' he said finally.

'Who might be mistaken? Gregory Black?'

Mr Roberts looked up at me. 'No,' he said. 'My nephew, Benjamin.'

I was becoming more confused.

'How might your nephew be mistaken?' I asked.

'He visited the site and he tells me there are no houses, no factory and no building work being done on it. In fact, he said it was just waste ground with a large amount of heavy-metal pollutants sitting there in stagnant pools. A local government official apparently told him that the cost of removal of the toxic waste would be far greater than the actual value of the land.'

'I'm sorry,' I said. 'But what has this to do with Gregory Black?'

'He advised me to invest in the project.'

'What project?' I asked.

'A Bulgarian property development project,' he said. 'Houses, shops and a new factory making low-energy light bulbs.'

I vaguely remembered the project being discussed several years ago at one of Patrick's weekly meetings but, as far as I could recall, it had been rejected as too risky an investment for us to recommend to our clients. But that didn't mean that Gregory hadn't thought it a sound investment. Patrick and Gregory may have had both their names on the company notepaper but they valued their independence, even from each other.

'Are you sure it's on the same site that your nephew visited?'

'He says so. He says there is no mistake. The site where there should be a factory and hundreds of new homes and shops is nothing but an industrial waste-land. There is even talk of it having being used as a dump for nuclear waste during the Soviet era.'

'How much have you invested in the scheme?' I asked him.

'Not that much,' he said. 'The family trust has invested about five million into the project as a whole. The factory is named the Balscott Lighting Factory after my father. I've seen pictures of the development. The project is designed to be a great social experiment for one of the most deprived areas of the European Union. A lot of EU money has gone into it.'

Five million may not be that much to Jolyon Roberts and his family trust, but it was a fortune to most people.

'Do these pictures show a factory and new homes?'

'Yes they do, and they show more houses under construction,' he said. 'Gregory Black showed them to me. But what am I to believe, the photos or my nephew?'

'There must be a simple explanation,' I said. 'Why don't you go and ask Gregory about it? I am sure he will have invested your money wisely.'

'I've already approached him and he just told me not to be so silly, of course the factory has been built. But Benjamin is adamant. He says that no Balscott Lighting Factory exists anywhere in Bulgaria.'

'So what do you want me to do?' I asked him.

'Find out the truth.'

'But why me?' I asked. 'If you think there is a fraud being perpetrated then you should go to the police, or to the financial services regulator.'

He sat and looked at me for a moment.

'Because I trust you,' he said.

'But you hardly know me.'

'I know you much better than you might realize.' He smiled. 'I've been watching your career every step of the way since you first rode that winner for my cousin. And I normally pride myself on being able to spot the good'uns from the bad'uns. That is why I am so concerned about this project. After all, it was me who persuaded my brother, Viscount Shenington, that the family trust should invest in something that appeared so worthwhile. I just need to know what is going on.'

'Sir,' I said. 'I am under an obligation to report it if I find that there is a fraud, or even if there is misrepresentation in advertising an investment.'

'Mmm, I see,' he said, stroking his chin. 'My brother and I are most concerned that the good name of the Roberts family should not be dragged through the courts. He is in favour of simply writing off the investment and saying nothing. However . . .' He stopped.

'You feel responsible?' I asked.

'Exactly,' he said. 'But I would prefer it if you could be very discreet. If this *is* a scam, well, to be honest, I would rather not have everybody know that I've been a fool.'

'Especially your brother.'

He looked me in the eye and smiled. 'Trustworthy, and wise.'

'But I will have to talk to Gregory about it,' I said.

'Can you not have a little look at things first without telling anybody? I am sure that someone with your keen nose for a good investment will be able to spot a rotten egg pretty quickly if there's one to find.'

I laughed. 'I think you have the wrong person. My nose isn't that keen.'

'Oh, I think it is,' Jolyon Roberts replied. 'I have a friend who's forever telling me about all the money you've made for her in films and theatre.'

'I've just been lucky,' I said.

'Yes,' he said, smiling. 'You and Arnold Palmer.'

I looked at him quizzically.

'You're too young,' he said, laughing. 'Arnold Palmer the golfer.'

'What about him?' I asked.

'When a reporter once asked him why he was so lucky in golf, he famously replied, "It's a funny thing, the harder I practice the luckier I get."'

But my luck was about to run out.

5

True to his word, Detective Chief Inspector Tomlinson sent a car to collect me from home on Thursday morning, and he was waiting at Herb Kovak's flat when I arrived at eight a.m. sharp.

'Ah, good morning, Mr Foxton,' he said, opening the front door and offering his hand. 'And how is your toe today?'

'It's fine,' I said honestly. 'It doesn't hurt at all.'

And I'd forgotten to limp.

'Nasty things, ingrowing toenails,' he said. 'Had one myself years ago. Hurt like hell.'

'Luckily, I'm a quick healer,' I said. 'Now, how can I help?'

He stepped to the side and I walked past him and into the hallway of Herb's flat. I still thought of it as Herb's flat although, I supposed, it was now technically mine, or it would be in due course.

'Are you certain Mr Kovak was not in personal financial difficulties?' the chief inspector asked while closing the front door.

'No, I'm not certain, but I have no reason to think he was. Why do you ask?'

He waved a stack of papers towards me.

'What are they?' I asked.

'Credit card statements,' said the chief inspector.

'So?'

'Mr Kovak appears to have had more than twenty credit cards and, according to these statements, at his death, he owed nearly a hundred thousand pounds on these cards alone.'

I could hardly believe it. Not only because Herb was in so much debt, but also because his debt was on credit cards. If anyone knew how expensive it was to borrow on plastic, then a financial adviser would. Even with interest rates historically low, the annual percentage rate on credit cards was typically between sixteen and twenty per cent, with some even as high as thirty. Borrowing money on credit cards was a mug's game. The interest charges alone on a debt as big as that would be around fifteen hundred a month. That was about half what Herb was taking home in salary, after the usual deductions for tax and National Insurance.

If Herb had owed nearly a hundred thousand on credit cards, then his flat must surely be mortgaged to the hilt. It certainly wouldn't end up being mine, more likely the bank's.

And yet he'd always had plenty of money in his pocket. He was extravagant, even, in his spending, always wearing new clothes and dining out as the norm. It didn't make sense.

'Can I have a closer look at those?' I asked the chief inspector, reaching out for the papers.

He handed them over and I skimmed through the first three or four statements. There was no doubt that the outstanding balance on each was very large and, in some cases, close to the maximum limit, but that did not show the full picture, not by a long way. I looked through the rest. They were all the same.

'Didn't you notice something unusual about these?' I asked.

'Notice what?' said the chief inspector.

'There are no interest payments from previous months. All these charges, on all of these statements, they're all new.'

I turned a statement over to look at the detailed breakdown and to see what Herb had spent a hundred thousand pounds on in a month and was shocked again. There were no purchases, as such, just payments to and from a plethora of internet gambling and online casino sites. Masses of them. I looked through all the statements and they were the same. Many of the payments were quite modest but one or two ran into the thousands. Quite a few of the betting sites had actually paid money back to the accounts, but most showed a deficit. Overall, Herb had been a loser not a winner, nearly a hundred-thousand-pound-a-month loser.

All the statements showed clearly that the previous month's balances had been settled in full by the due date. I mentally added them up. As well as still owing almost a hundred thousand, Herb had paid nearly the same amount in gambling debts to the cards during March alone. Where had he obtained that sort of money? And how on earth had he had the time to gamble on so many different sites with so many different credit cards while working full-time at Lyall & Black? It sure as hell didn't make any sense.

As Claudia had said, you never really knew what even your closest friends were up to. Could this compulsive online gambling somehow be the reason that Herb was killed? The totals may have been large but the individual entries on the statements were modest, and surely not big enough to initiate murder.

'There are some other things I would like you to have a look at,' said the chief inspector. 'You may be able to help me understand them.'

He turned and walked down the hallway, turning left through a door. I followed him.

Herb's living room was in true bachelor-pad fashion, with half of it taken up by a single deep armchair placed in front of a large wall-mounted flat-screen television. On the far side of the room was a large desk with a laptop computer, a printer and three piles of papers in metal baskets.

It was some of the papers that the chief inspector wanted me to look at.

'We need your permission, as Mr Kovak's executor, to remove certain items that we believe may help with our enquiries. These for example. But we would like your opinion on them first.'

He handed me two sheets of paper covered entirely on both sides by handwritten lists with columns of what appeared to be dates with amounts of money alongside, together with a further column of capital letters. 'Could they have something to do with Mr Kovak's work?'

I studied the lists briefly.

'I doubt it,' I said. 'They are handwritten and we do everything on computer. I think these could be amounts of money.' I pointed at the centre two columns. 'And these look like dates.'

'Yes,' he said. 'I worked that much out. But do you know what they are?'

'Do they correspond to the amounts on the credit cards statements?' I asked.

'No. I looked at that. None of the figures are the same.'

'How about last month's statements?' I said. 'Most of these dates are last month.'

'We have been unable to locate any statements other than those you have seen. But some of the dates on this list would have been for the statements we have, and none of the amounts match.'

'Then I'm afraid I can't help you,' I said. 'I don't recognize any of the amounts and, individually, most are far too small to be anything to do with Mr Kovak's work. We always work in thousands, if not tens of thousands. Most of these are hundreds.' I looked once more at the lists. 'Could that third column be people's initials?'

The chief inspector looked. 'It might be. Do you recognize any of them? For example, do they match any of your work colleagues?'

I scanned through the list. 'Not that I can see.'

'Right,' he said suddenly, as if making a decision. 'With your permission we will take these papers away, together with the credit card statements, Mr Kovak's laptop computer, and these other things.'

The chief inspector waved a hand towards a box on a side table near the door. I went over and looked in. The box contained various bits and pieces including Herb's American passport, an address book, a desk diary and a folder full of bank statements. It was all rather sad.

'It's fine by me,' I said. 'But you do know that his computer won't give you access to Mr Kovak's work files?'

'So I believe.'

'He would have been able to access the office files and e-mails through his laptop but no records of them would have been stored on it. The laptop would have merely been acting as a keyboard and a screen for the firm's mainframe computer in Lombard Street.'

'Nevertheless,' said the chief inspector, 'it is our policy to search through such a device for any correspondence that might have a bearing on his death. I trust you are happy with that.'

'Absolutely,' I agreed.

'Good,' he said, folding the computer flat and placing it in the box with the other things.

'But can I make copies of that credit card stuff before you take it away. I do know that one of the first tasks for executors is to close the bank accounts and pay the debts of the deceased but goodness' knows where I will get a hundred thousand to do that. How much did he have in the bank?'

'Not that much,' said the chief inspector.

'Do you mind if I look?' I asked.

'Not at all,' he said. 'I understand from Mr Kovak's lawyer that it will be yours anyway.'

I pulled the folder of bank statements out of the box and looked at the most recent ones. The balance was quite healthy but, as DCI Tomlinson had said, it didn't run to anything like a hundred thousand. More like a tenth of that. I unclipped the last statement from the folder and made a photocopy using the printer/copier on the desk. I then photocopied all the credit card statements, and both sides of the two sheets of handwritten figures, before handing them all back to the policeman.

'Thank you,' he said. 'I just need your signature on this form to give us permission to remove these items, and I have a receipt for them to give you.'

He handed me the form, which I signed, and the receipt, which I put in my pocket.

'Bloody paperwork,' he said, taking back the form. 'These days we have to be so damn careful to do everything exactly according to the book or some clever-dick defence lawyer will claim that any evidence we find is not admissible in court. I can tell you, it's a bloody nightmare.'

Although better, on the whole, I thought, than the police marching in anywhere they liked in their size-twelve boots taking away any stuff they wanted without permission, and for no good reason.

He packed his paperwork into the box along with the other things. 'Now, Mr Foxton,' he said, 'could you just wander around the flat to satisfy yourself that we have left the place in reasonable order, and also to check that nothing appears out of place or is missing.'

'I'm happy to have a look,' I said, 'but I've never been in here before so I don't know what it looked like before you arrived.'

'Please, anyway,' he said, putting his hand out towards the door.

He followed me as I went round the flat, looking briefly in each of the two bedrooms, the bathroom, and the well-fitted kitchen. Nothing to my eye appeared out of place but, of course, it wouldn't.

'Have you searched everywhere?' I asked.

'Not a proper forensic search,' he said. 'We haven't taken the floorboards up or knocked holes in the walls, that sort of thing. But we had a reasonable look around to see if there was anything that could assist us in determining why he was killed. Mr Kovak was the victim of the crime, not the perpetrator.'

'How did you get in?' I asked as we went back along the hallway. 'The front door doesn't seem to have been forced.'

'The key was in Mr Kovak's trouser pocket.'

I thought again about Herb lying silent and cold in some morgue refrigerator.

'How about his funeral?' I asked.

'What about it?' he said.

'I suppose it's my job to organize it.'

'Not before the coroner has released the body,' he said.

'And when will that be?' I asked.

'Not just yet,' he replied. 'He hasn't been formally identified.'

'But I told you who he was.'

'Yes, sir,' he said with irony, 'I know that. And we are pretty certain we know who he is because you told us, but you are not his next of kin and, to be fair, you have only known him for five years. He could have told you that he was Herbert Kovak while not actually being so.'

'You're showing that suspicious mind of yours again, Chief Inspector.'

He smiled. 'We are still trying to trace his next of kin but, so far, without success.'

'I know he lived in New York just before he came to England,' I said. 'But he was brought up in Kentucky. In Louisville. At least, that is what he said.'

Did I now doubt it?

'Yes,' said the chief inspector. 'We have been in touch with our counterparts in New York and Louisville but, so far, they have been unable to contact any members of his family. It would appear that his parents are deceased.'

'Can you give me any idea of when a funeral can be held?'

'Not at present,' he said. 'I imagine it won't be for a few weeks at least. Maybe his remains will need to be sent back to the United States.'

'Don't I decide that, as the executor of his will?' I asked.

'Maybe,' he said. 'Depends on the formal identification. But I'll leave that up to the coroner. In the meantime, if you think of anything else that might help us with our enquiries, please call me.' He dug in his inside pocket for a card. 'Use the mobile number. It's usually on all the time, and you can leave a message if it's not.'

I put the card in my wallet and Chief Inspector Tomlinson collected the box of possible evidence.

'Can I offer you a lift home?' he asked.

'No, thank you. I think I'll have a look around here first. I can catch the bus.'

'Don't overdo it with that toe,' he said. 'That's what I did with mine and it took weeks to get right.'

'I'll be careful,' I said with an inward smile. I would, in fact, be going in to the office and not home when I left here. 'Now, how do I lock up?'

'Ah, yes,' he replied, digging into his coat pocket. 'I had another key cut. We would like to hang on to one for the time being just in case we need to pop back to look through his things further.'

'Right,' I said, taking the offered key. 'Are you based down here, then? I thought you were Merseyside Police.'

'I am,' he replied. 'But I'm working on this case out of Paddington Green all this week. I will be going home on Friday.'

'And you'll let me know when I can start making funeral arrangements?'

'The Liverpool coroner will be in contact with you

in due course,' he said, rather unhelpfully, and then he departed, carrying his box of potential treasures under his arm.

I sat for a while at Herb's desk looking again at the credit card statements.

There were between twenty and thirty internet gambling or online casino websites on each statement. Half of them I didn't recognize but their names showed what they were. One was called www.oddsandevens.net and another www.pokermillions.co.eg. It didn't take a genius to work it out.

Not every statement had all the same sites, but some were on all of them, and all appeared at least half a dozen times. I started adding up. In total there were twenty-two different credit cards and five hundred and twelve different entries on the statements. The total owed was ninety-four thousand, six hundred and twenty-six pounds and fifty-two pence.

Some of the entries on all of the statements were credits but, overall, the average loss per entry was a fraction under a hundred and eighty-five pounds. I checked the actual amounts against those on the handwritten lists but, as the chief inspector had said, not one of them matched.

It wasn't so much the amount of money that amazed me, even though it did, it was the number of different entries. Again I wondered how Herb had had the time to play or gamble online with five hundred and twelve different log-ins. I did some more mental arithmetic. Without work, eating or sleeping, and spending every moment of the day for a whole month at the computer would have given him just an hour and a half on each account. It was impossible.

I stood up and went into the kitchen.

My mother always maintained that one could learn most about a person by looking in their fridge. Not with Herb. His fridge was starkly empty with just a plastic carton of skimmed milk and a half-full tub of low-fat spread. His cupboards were almost equally bare, with a couple of boxes of breakfast cereal and half a loaf bread, gone stale. On the worktop were a jar of instant coffee, and two round tins with TEA and SUGAR printed on their outsides and with some teabags and granulated sugar on their insides.

I filled the electric kettle and made myself a cup of coffee. I took it back to the desk in the living room and went on studying the credit card statements.

I spotted that there was something else slightly odd about them.

They didn't all have the same name or the same address at the top.

Some of them had this flat's address and others the Lyall & Black office's address in Lombard Street. Nothing too unusual about that. But the names on them also varied. Not very much, but enough for me to notice.

I looked through them again, carefully making two piles on the desk, one for each address.

There were eleven statements in each pile, and eleven

slight variations in Herb's name: Herb Kovak, Mr Herb E. Kovak, Herbert Kovak Esq., Mr H. Kovak, Herbert E. Kovak, Mr H. E. Kovak, H. E. Kovak Jr., H. Edward Kovak, Bert Kovak Jr., Herbert Edward Kovak, and Mr Bert E. Kovak.

No two statements had the same name and address.

Now, why did I think that was suspicious?

I heard the key turn in the door and thought that DCI Tomlinson must have forgotten something. I was wrong.

I went out into the hallway to find an attractive blonde-haired young woman struggling through the front door with an enormous suitcase. She saw me and stopped.

'Who the hell are you?' she demanded in a Southern American accent.

I'd been about to ask her the same thing.

'Nicholas Foxton,' I said. 'And you?'

'Sherri Kovak,' she said. 'And where's my damn brother?'

There was no easy way to tell Sherri that her brother was dead, but it was the nature of his death she found most distressing.

She sat in the big armchair and wept profusely while I made her a cup of hot, sweet tea.

In between bouts of near hysteria, I discovered that she had arrived early that morning on an overnight flight from Chicago. She had been surprised, and rather annoyed, that Herb had not been at the airport to meet her as he had promised, but she had eventually made her own way to Hendon by train and taxi.

'But how did you have a key to get in?' I asked her.

'Herb gave me one when I was here last year.'

Herb hadn't mentioned to me last year that his sister was visiting, or even that he had a sister in the first place. But why would he have? We had been work colleagues rather than close friends. He also hadn't mentioned to me that he was a compulsive online gambler.

I wondered if I ought to inform DCI Tomlinson that Herb Kovak's next of kin had turned up. Probably, but then he'd be back round here with a list of awkward questions when it was clear to me that, after a night of sitting upright on an aeroplane, what she needed most was a good sleep. I'd call the chief inspector later.

I found some fresh bed linen in an airing cupboard and made up the bed in the smaller of the two bedrooms. I then guided the over-tired and still-crying Miss Kovak from the living room to the bed, and made her take off her shoes and lie down.

'You sleep for a bit,' I said, covering her with a blanket. 'I'll still be here when you wake.'

'But who are you exactly?' she asked between sobs.

'A friend of your brother's,' I said. 'We worked together.' I decided not to mention to her, just yet, that her brother had left his entire estate to me and not to her. And I wondered why that was.

Sherri Kovak was almost asleep before her head reached the pillow. I left her there and went back to Herb's desk and the credit card statements.

It was gone nine o'clock and I called the office number on my mobile. Mrs McDowd answered.

'It's the man with the ingrowing toenail calling in sick,' I said.

'Shirker,' she announced with a laugh.

'No, really,' I said. 'I won't be in the office until later. Please tell Mr Patrick that I'm sorry but something has come up.'

'Trouble?' she asked.

'No,' I said. 'No trouble, but something that I need to deal with.'

I could almost feel her wanting to ask what it was. Mrs McDowd liked to know everything about the goings-on of her staff, as she called us. She was always asking after Claudia, and she seemed to know more about my mother than I did.

'Tell me, Mrs McDowd,' I said in a friendly tone, 'did you know that Herb Kovak had a sister?'

'Yes, of course,' she said. 'Sherri. She lives in Chicago. She and Mr Herb were twins. She visited him last summer.'

'Did you proffer this information to the policeman when he interviewed us all on Monday?'

'No,' she said firmly. 'I did not.'

'Why not?' I asked her.

'He didn't ask me.'

Mrs McDowd clearly didn't like the police very much.

'Please tell Mr Patrick that I'll see him later today,' I said.

'Right, I will,' she said. 'It's a good job you're not here now anyway. Mr Gregory is angry fit to burst.'

'What about?' I asked.

'You,' she said. 'He's absolutely livid. Claims you've brought the whole firm into disrepute. He wants your head on a stick.'

'But why?' I asked, rather worried. 'What have I done?'

'Don't you know?'

'No,' I said.

'Read the front page of the *Racing Post*.'

I went along the hall to check on Sherri. Her long blonde hair was obscuring her face so I waited in the doorway for a few seconds listening to her breathing. She was sound asleep. Best thing for her, I thought. Sadly, the horrors of real life would still be waiting for her when she woke.

As quietly as I could, I slipped out the front door and walked down towards Hendon Central in search of a newsagent.

I could see the problem even before I picked up the paper. The inch-high bold headline read:

FOXY FOXTON AND BILLY SEARLE IN £100,000 GAMBLE?

I bought the paper with shaking hands and stood reading it in the shop.

In addition to the headline there were photographs of Billy and me, mine taken during my racing days wearing racing colours and cap.

The article beneath was as damning as the headline:

Leading National Hunt jockey Billy Searle was observed in a heated argument at Cheltenham Races yesterday with former fellow jockey Nick (Foxy) Foxton. The topic of their acrimonious exchange? Money.

According to the Racing Post *correspondent at the course, the amount under discussion was in excess of a hundred thousand pounds, with Searle demanding instant payment of this amount, which he claimed he was owed by Foxton. At one point Searle was heard to ask why he, Foxton, wanted to murder Searle. Could this all be connected with Foxy's new job at City financial firm Lyall and Black, where he gambles daily with other people's money on the stock markets?*

Well-known trainer, Martin Gifford, stated that Foxton had informed him on Tuesday that Herbert Kovak, the man whose murder last Saturday led to the postponement of the Grand National, was Foxton's best friend and a fellow stock-market speculator who had also worked for Lyall and Black. Gifford implied that Foxton may have known more about the killing than he was telling.

Not surprisingly, people yesterday were asking if Foxton's argument with Searle could have had some sinister connection to the Aintree murder. The Rules of Racing clearly ban gambling by professional jockeys but no such restriction applies to former jockeys. The Racing Post *will endeavour to keep its readers up to date with this story.*

The article cleverly didn't actually accuse Billy Searle or me of any wrongdoing, it merely asked leading questions. But there was little doubt that the tone of the piece was designed to imply there was a criminal conspiracy between us, which also had something to do with the death of Herb Kovak.

No wonder Gregory Black was steaming round the office fit to burst.

I was surprised my phone wasn't ringing off the hook.

Bugger, I thought. What should I do now?

I called Patrick on his mobile. I didn't fancy using the office number just in case Gregory himself answered, as we all sometimes did if the receptionists were busy on other calls.

'Hello, Nicholas,' said Patrick. 'I thought I told you to be discreet. I hear that Gregory's after your blood. I'd keep your head down if I were you.'

'I will,' I said. 'But it's all a pack of lies.'

'You know that, and I know that. But, unfortunately, Joe Bloggs in the street will believe what he reads in the paper.'

'But they have completely distorted the truth. It's so unfair.'

'Tell that to the politicians.' He laughed. 'I have already told Gregory not to believe what he reads but he says, quite rightly, that you shouldn't have been having a public argument with a client in the first place. He's pretty mad.'

'It wasn't an argument,' I claimed in my defence. 'Billy Searle just started shouting and swearing at me for no reason.'

'Don't worry about it,' Patrick said. 'It'll all blow over in a couple of days.'

I wish he'd been right.

6

I walked back to Herb's flat hardly feeling my feet on the pavement.

What a bloody mess.

I could imagine that Billy Searle wasn't too happy about it either. I thought the last thing he'd want would be the racing authorities asking him questions about why he needed a hundred thousand pounds so urgently.

I let myself in through Herb's front door and went to check again on Sherri. She hadn't moved and was still sound asleep. I left her alone and went back to the living room, where I sat at Herb's desk wishing I'd brought my laptop with me. It was lying on the kitchen table in Finchley and I was tempted to go home to fetch it. Instead I called Claudia.

'Hi, it's me,' I said when she answered.

'Hi, you,' she replied.

'Could you bring my computer over to Herb's flat?' I said. 'His sister has turned up and she didn't know he was dead. She's sleeping now but I don't feel I can leave her for long. I'll stay and work here, but I do need my laptop.' I decided against mentioning, as yet, the unwelcome coverage in the *Racing Post*.

There was a slight pause.

'OK,' Claudia said in a slightly irritated tone.

'It's not very far,' I said encouragingly. 'Use the car. You won't need to park or anything, just drop it off.'

'OK,' she said again, lacking enthusiasm. 'But I was just going out.'

Bloody hell, I thought. It wasn't very much to ask.

'Where are you going?' I asked.

'Oh, nowhere,' she said. 'Just to have coffee with a friend.'

'Who?'

'No one you know,' she said evasively.

Probably one of her artist friends. I didn't know them, and I didn't really want to. Some of them were as weird as her paintings.

'Please, Claudia,' I said firmly. 'I need it here so I can do my job.' And to bring in the money so you can live rent free, I thought, but didn't say.

'OK,' she said once more, resigned. 'Where is the flat?'

I gave her the address and she promised she would bring the computer right over.

While I waited I went through the piles of papers on Herb's desk, those remaining after the chief inspector had taken his box away.

There were the usual clutter of utility bills and debit card receipts, interleaved with financial services' magazines, insurance documents and some personal letters. I glanced through them all but nothing gave any clue to who would want Herb dead, or how he came to gamble away a hundred thousand pounds a month on the internet.

I didn't expect them to. I assumed that the police would have removed anything of interest.

Next I went through the desk drawers. There were three on each side and the ones on the left contained such exciting items as a stapler with spare staples, various-sized brown envelopes, paper and ink cartridges for the printer, a pack of permanent markers in bright colours, a plastic tub of large paper clips, and a calculator.

Those on the right were only partially more interesting with a large pile of paid bills, various income tax papers, a copy of Herb's United States tax return, a rubber-band-bound stack of received Christmas cards, and a plastic folder containing monthly pay slips from Lyall & Black.

I was curious to see that Herb had been paid somewhat more than I was, no doubt due to his three years' prior experience at J.P. Morgan Asset Management in New York before moving to London. Now that I was Patrick's most senior assistant, I would have to have a discussion with him about a raise.

I flicked through the bills but there was nothing that appeared to shine out like a lighthouse to guide me to his killer, although I did notice that Herb had been what my mother always described as a 'free-spending spirit'. It was a term she used for those she considered to squander their money on lavish, unnecessary purchases instead of prudently saving it for a rainy day, as she had always done.

Two separate invoices from a local travel agent showed

that Herb's free spending had run to at least two British Airways first-class round-trip tickets across the Atlantic at eight thousand pounds each, one of them dated only the previous month for a planned, but not yet taken, trip in May. He may have been earning more than me but there was no way he could have financed those out of his income from Lyall & Black, even without the online gambling debts he had run up on the credit cards.

I wondered if he had inherited a large sum from his dead parents. I thought it unlikely as he had always claimed that his father had gambled away most of his family's money. But perhaps Herb had been busy spending and gambling away the rest.

But where had he kept it?

I looked again at the photocopy I had made of his last bank statement. I had only made it to have a record of Herb's account number and sort code. I would need them when I contacted the bank to inform them of his death. The latest balance was a little under ten thousand pounds but there were no entries on the statements that appeared to be payments for the credit card accounts, and certainly no eight thousand pounds to the travel agent the previous month.

Herb had to have had another bank account, but there was no sign of it anywhere in his desk.

I looked at my watch. I had called Claudia nearly half an hour ago and the journey should have taken her only ten minutes from Lichfield Grove, Finchley to Seymour Way, Hendon. I went to the door to see if she was outside somewhere but there was no sign of her, or the Mercedes.

I waited in the doorway for five further minutes with slightly increasing irritation. I didn't really want to call her again, but she was beginning to try my patience.

Once, I would have been so excited by the prospect of seeing her, I wouldn't have minded if she had been half a day late arriving. On one occasion I had been at Heathrow Airport at least two hours before her flight was due to land, just to be sure not to miss her arriving through customs.

But now, and not for the first time, I wondered if our relationship had run its course.

She finally arrived some thirty-five minutes after I had called. She stopped in the middle of the road and put down the passenger window. I leaned through it and picked up my computer from the seat.

'Thanks,' I said. 'See you later.'

'OK,' she said, and drove off quickly.

I stood in the road waving but, even if she could see me, she didn't wave back. There had been a time when we never parted without us waving vigorously until we were completely out of sight of each other.

I sighed. I had invested so much of my emotional capital in my relationship with Claudia and the thought of being single again, having to start out once more, did not fill me with any joy. And I wasn't at all sure I wanted it to end.

Claudia still excited me, and the sex was good, albeit somewhat rarer than it once had been. In fact, sex had been non-existent over the last couple of weeks with Claudia always making some excuse. So what had gone wrong? Why was she suddenly not so loving towards me?

I wondered if she was seeing someone else. But who? Surely not one of her artistic layabout friends from her time at art college. The thought of her being intimate with one of them was enough to make me feel ill, and not a little bit angry.

Miserably, I went back into Herb's flat and sat down again at his desk but, even with my computer, I couldn't concentrate on any work due to thinking about the article in the paper, and also about Claudia. After about half an hour I called her mobile but it went straight to voicemail. I didn't leave a message because I didn't know what to say.

Instead, I logged on to the internet through Herb's router and checked my office e-mails, many of which were junk from various finance firms offering rates of return that were well above the norm for the market.

Nestled amongst the trash were three work e-mails from this morning: one from Diana confirming the sales of all Billy Searle's assets and the impending transfer from the firm's client account to his bank, one from Patrick asking me to research a new personal pension plan being offered by one of the leading providers in the light of new pension legislation, and the third from Jessica Winter advising me to wear a bulletproof vest if I was planning on coming into the office.

I thought it a particularly insensitive comment

considering what had happened to Herb only five days previously.

I looked again at all the junk mail.

If a promised return appeared to be too good to be true, then it invariably was just that, too good to be true.

I thought back to my conversation with Jolyon Roberts at Cheltenham the previous day. Had the promised return on the Bulgarian property development project been too good to be true? Not as far as I could remember. It had not been the level of return that had been the concern, rather the distance away and the potential difficulty in acquiring accurate and up-to-date information on the progress of the project. In fact, just the problem that Mr Roberts believed to be the issue.

I started to type 'Roberts' into the company client index but thought better of it. The office mainframe computer kept a record of all files accessed, so any of us could see who had been looking at each file. It wasn't particularly designed to spy on us or to prevent us accessing files, indeed it made it easy to keep a record of files visited. I could expect my files to be accessed by Patrick on a fairly random but regular basis, and the company files as a whole were regularly scrutinized by Jessica Winter, our Compliance Officer.

Whenever any of us opened a file it clearly showed, in the top right hand corner of the computer screen, a list of the five people in the firm who had accessed the file most recently, together with the date and time of their access.

As one of the IFAs, I had authority to look at any of the company files but I might have had difficulty explaining to Gregory why I had accessed those of one of his clients without his knowledge, especially a client as important as the Roberts Family Trust, and especially now.

I told myself that I should go straight to Gregory and Patrick, and probably to Jessica as well, and tell them about my conversation with Jolyon Roberts and get the matter looked at by them. But did I really want to go and accuse Gregory of misleading one of his clients, and on today of all days?

Then I would truly need that bulletproof vest.

Unlike in the United States where the Securities and Exchange Commission, the SEC, employs a prescriptive rule-based regime, the United Kingdom authorities had moved to a principles-based regulatory system. The onus was now on me to act in a manner that upheld the highest principles of honesty, openness and integrity, and to prove it.

It was difficult to decide which system was the better. Experience had shown that neither was fraud-proof. Indeed, the SEC had investigated Bernie Madoff several times without unearthing the biggest individual fraud in American history. Talk about the asylum being run by the lunatics, Madoff served three times as chairman of the NASDAQ stock market. And that was many years after he had started his fraud, and even after the first failed SEC investigation into his company's activities.

And he'd just had to be called Madoff, hadn't he? He'd 'made off' with sixty-five billion dollars – yes, billion. And all because he'd been able to fraudulently circumvent the fixed US regulatory rules. Whereas in the UK, it was not just the letter of the law I had to follow, but also its spirit.

But was I, in fact, following the spirit of principles-based regulation not to mention immediately to my superiors, and to the Compliance Officer, that a client of the firm was questioning the judgement of one of the senior partners?

Probably not.

And I would mention it to them, I thought, just as soon as Gregory had calmed down a bit. In the meantime, I would do a bit of discreet investigating just as Jolyon Roberts had asked.

First I tried 'Bulgarian development projects' in the Google search engine but this turned up some fifty-five million hits, the first two pages of which appeared to have nothing to do with the development project I was looking for. Next I tried 'Balscott Bulgarian development project' and this turned up just two hits but neither of them had any connection whatsoever with a low-energy light-bulb factory on either side of the Danube.

Next I tried 'Europa', the official European Union website, but that was more difficult to navigate through than the continent itself.

It was all a bit of a dead end without accessing the firm's Roberts Family Trust computer file to see with whom and where the contact had been made in Bulgaria or with the EU. And I daren't do that.

I decided instead that I'd try to have a quiet look through the paper records we kept at the office. Shares and bonds may have increasingly been bought and sold online but the digital deals were still all backed up with physical paperwork, and we were required to keep the papers for a minimum of five years. The office was consequently stacked high with boxes of transaction reports and somewhere amongst them would be the Roberts Family Trust paperwork for their five-million-pound investment in the Balscott Lighting Factory.

I sat back in the chair and thought about Claudia. I tried her mobile again but, as before, it went straight to voicemail without ringing. I wished now that I had told her about the article in the *Racing Post* when she had brought over my computer. I tried her number once more and, this time, I did leave a message.

'Darling,' I said. 'Could you please give me a call when you get this? Love you. Byeee.' I hung up.

I looked at the clock on Herb's desk. It was only a quarter to eleven. I had been here for nearly three hours but it seemed like much longer.

I wondered what Claudia could be doing at a quarter to eleven in the morning, and with whom, that required her to have her phone switched off.

I sighed. Perhaps I didn't want to know.

In my role as Herb's executor, I used the account number and sort code on his statement to send an e-mail to his bank informing them that Mr Kovak was deceased, and would they please send me details of all his accounts, and especially the balances.

Somewhat surprisingly I received a reply almost immediately thanking me for the sad news and advising me that they would need various pieces of original documentation before they could release the information I had asked for, including the death certificate, a copy of the will, and a grant of probate.

And how long would it take to get that lot?

I heard Sherri go along the corridor to the bathroom.

At least my troubles with Billy Searle were minor compared to hers.

I took the front cover sheet off the *Racing Post* and folded it up, as if not being able to see the damning words would in some way limit their damage to my reputation and career. I put the offending piece in my pocket and went to throw the rest of it into the waste bin under Herb's desk.

The bin had some things in it already and, I thought, as I've looked everywhere else, why not there?

I poured the contents of the bin out onto the desk.

Amongst the opened envelopes, the empty Starbucks coffee cups and the screwed-up tissues were lots of little pieces of paper about an inch square. I put the cups, envelopes and tissues back in the bin leaving a pile of the paper squares on the desk. It was fairly obvious that they were the torn-up remains of a larger piece so I set about trying to put them back together. It was a bit like doing a jigsaw puzzle, but one without the picture on the box to guide me.

I quickly established that the pieces had not been from one larger piece but three. I slowly built up the originals in front of me. They were each about six inches by four, printed forms with words written on them in pen, similar forms but each with different writing. I stuck the bits together with sticky tape.

'What are you doing?' Sherri asked from the doorway.

She made me jump.

'Nothing much,' I said, swivelling the desk chair round to face her. 'How are you feeling?'

'Dreadful,' she said, coming into the room and flopping down into the deep armchair. 'I can't believe it.'

I thought she was about to cry again. I wasn't sure whether the dark shadows beneath her eyes were due to tiredness or her tear-smudged mascara.

'I'll get you some more tea,' I said, standing up.

'Lovely,' she said with a forced smile. 'Thank you.'

I went through to the kitchen and boiled the kettle. I also made myself another coffee and took both cups back to the living room.

Sherri was sitting at the desk looking at the pieces of paper, so I sat down on the arm of the big armchair.

'Do you know what they are?' I asked her.

'Of course,' she said. 'They're MoneyHome payment slips.' She sipped her tea. 'One for eight thousand, and two for five.'

'Pounds?' I asked.

She looked at them.

'Dollars. Converted into pounds.'

'How do you know?' I asked.

She looked at me.

'I use MoneyHome all the time,' she said. 'It's a bit like Western Union only cheaper. They have agents all over the world. Herb sent me the money for my air fare via MoneyHome.'

'Are any of these slips from that?'

'No,' she said with certainty. 'These are the slips you get when you collect money, not when you send it.'

'So Herb collected eighteen thousand dollars' worth of pounds from MoneyHome?'

'Yes,' she said.

'When?' I asked.

She looked at the reconstructed slips carefully. 'Last week, but not all on the same day. Eight thousand on Monday, and five each on Tuesday and Friday.'

'Who from?' I asked.

'These only tell you which MoneyHome office it was collected from, they don't say who sent the money.' She drank more of her tea. 'What's all this about?'

'I don't know,' I said. 'I just found those torn-up sheets in the waste bin.'

She sat drinking her tea, looking at me over the rim of the cup.

'But why are you here, anyway?' she asked.

'I was a friend of Herb's, and a work colleague,' I said, giving her one of the business cards from my wallet. 'He made me the executor of his will.' I decided again not to mention that he had also made me the sole beneficiary.

'I didn't know he even had a will,' Sherri said, reading from my card, 'Mr Nicholas Foxton, BSc, MEcon, DipPFS.'

'He made it five years ago when he first arrived at Lyall and Black,' I said, ignoring her reference to my qualifications. 'Everyone in the firm has to have a will. The senior partners are always saying that we can hardly advise our clients to plan ahead if we aren't prepared to do the same. But I have absolutely no idea why Herb chose to put me in his. Maybe it was just because we sat at desks next to each other. He'd only just landed in the country and perhaps he didn't know anyone else. And none of us really expect to die when we're in our twenties anyway. But he should still have named you as his executor, even if you were in the United States.'

'Herb and I weren't exactly talking to each other five years ago. In fact, I'd told him by then that I never wanted to see or hear from him again.'

'Wasn't that a bit extreme?' I said.

'We had a flaming row over our parents.' She sighed. 'It was always over our parents.'

'What about them?' I asked.

She looked at me as if deciding whether to tell me.

'Our mom and dad were, shall we say, an unusual couple. Dad had made a living, if you can call it that, acting as an unlicensed bookie round the back-side of Churchill Downs. He was meant to be a groom but he didn't do much looking after the horses. He spent his time taking bets from the other grooms, and some of the trainers and owners too. Sometimes he won, but mostly he lost. Mom, meanwhile, had worked as a cocktail waitress in one of the swanky tourist hotels in downtown Louisville. At least that's what she told people.'

She paused, and I waited in silence. She'd say it if she wanted to.

'She'd been a prostitute.' Sherri was crying again.

'You don't have to tell me,' I said.

She looked at me with tear-filled eyes. 'I've got to tell someone,' she gulped. 'I've bottled it all up for far too long.'

Between bouts of tears she told me the sorry saga of her and Herb's upbringing. It amazed me that I had sat next to Herb for all those years without realizing the hurdles he'd had to overcome to be a financial adviser.

Herb and Sherri's father had been an abusive drinker who had seemingly treated his children as unpaid slave labour. Both of them had excelled at school but their father insisted that they drop out, aged sixteen, to go to work, Herb as a groom in the Churchill Downs stables, and Sherri as a chambermaid in one of the tourist hotels where her mother had plied her trade.

Herb had rebelled and run away to Lexington, where he had secretly applied for, and won, a free place at a private high school. But he'd had no accommodation, so he'd slept on the streets. One of the trustees of the school had found him there and offered him a bed. The trustee had been in financial services and hence Herb's career had been decided.

He'd stayed in Lexington after high school to attend the University of Kentucky on a scholarship, before landing the top graduate job at J.P. Morgan in New York.

I wondered how such a high flyer had come to move from one of the global-asset-management giants to a firm such as Lyall & Black, a relative tiddler in the financial pond. Had he somehow queered his pitch in New York?

Sherri, meanwhile, had been good at her job, and bright with it, and she had been spotted by the management of the hotel for further training. That was ultimately how she came to be in Chicago, where she was currently assistant-housekeeper in a big hotel of the same chain.

I didn't see how all this information was going to be of any use to me, but I sat quietly and listened as she unburdened her emotions.

'How come you and Herb fell out?' I asked in one of the frequent pauses.

'He refused to come home from New York for the funeral when Dad died. I told him he should be there to support Mom, but he refused and he said he wouldn't come to her funeral either if she dropped down dead tomorrow. Those were his exact words. And Mom heard him say them because she and I were in my car and the call was on speaker-phone.' She paused and more tears ran down her cheeks. 'I still think it's the reason why she did it.'

'Did what?' I asked.

'Swallowed a whole tub of Tylenol Extra. A hundred tablets.'

'Dead?' I asked.

She nodded. 'That night. I found her in the morning.' She sat up straight and breathed in deeply through her nose. 'I accused Herb of killing her, and that's when I told him I never wanted to see or hear from him again.'

'How long has it been since your parents died?'

'About six years, maybe seven.' She thought for a moment. 'It'll be seven years in June.'

'When did you change your mind?'

'What? About contacting Herb?'

I nodded.

'I didn't. It was he who contacted me, about two years ago.' She sighed. 'Five years was a long time not to speak to your twin brother. I had wanted to be in touch with him much sooner but I was too proud.' She paused. 'Too stupid more like. He wrote to me at the hotel company and we arranged to meet in New York. Then last summer he invited me to come to England and stay with him for a holiday. It was great.' She smiled. 'Just like old times.' The smile faded and the tears began again. 'I just can't believe he's dead.'

Neither could I.

I finally arrived at the office at twenty past one, a time when I reckoned Gregory should be just sitting down to his substantial lunch at the far end of Lombard Street. However, I approached number sixty-four from the opposite direction to the one he took to his usual restaurant in order to minimize the chances of running into him if he was late.

I ignored the lift, sneaked up the emergency stairway to the fourth floor, and put my head around the glass entrance doors. 'Has Mr Gregory gone to lunch?' I whispered to Mrs McDowd, who was sitting at the reception desk.

'Ten minutes ago,' she whispered back.

'And Mr Patrick?' I asked.

'Went with him,' she replied. 'Both gone for an hour and a quarter at least, probably longer.'

I relaxed and smiled at her. 'Maybe I'll just stay for an hour.'

'Very wise,' she said with a grin from ear to ear. 'Now, tell me, is it true what it says in that newspaper?'

'No, of course not,' I said.

She gave me one of her 'I don't believe you' looks. 'You must have done something or it wouldn't have been on the front page.'

'Mrs McDowd, it's nothing. I promise you.'

She curled down her mouth as if she was a spoiled child who had failed to be given an ice cream. I ignored her, walking past the reception desk and down the corridor beyond. As I passed by, I glanced through the ever-open door of the compliance office, but Jessica Winter was not at her desk. Jessica was one of those who always went out for her lunch hour, as Herb had done, though in his case it was not to eat but to work out at a local gym.

I went on and into my office, not that I had it completely to myself. There were five desk cubicles crammed into the small room, one of which was mine. Herb had been next to me, both of us close to the window, while Diana and Rory, Patrick's other assistants, occupied the two cubicles nearer the door. The fifth cubicle was no one's specific personal domain but was used by any visiting staff, usually an accountant for two days a week, and Andrew Mellor, the lawyer, if he needed a desk. Today it was empty.

Diana was out to lunch, as usual, while Rory was sitting at his desk typing with one hand on his computer keyboard while holding a half-eaten sandwich in the other.

'My God,' said Rory with his mouth full. 'The invisible man returns. Gregory's been looking for you all morning. You're in real trouble.' He sounded as if he was rather pleased about it, and I could see a folded copy of the *Racing Post* lying on his desk. It had probably been he who had showed it to Gregory.

'You haven't seen me, all right!' I said.

'Don't involve me in your sordid little affairs,' he said rather haughtily. 'I'm not putting my career at risk for you.'

Rory could be a real pain sometimes.

'Rory,' I said. 'When, and if, you ever qualify to be an IFA, you can then start talking about your career. Until then, shut up!'

Rory knew that I knew that he had failed his

qualifying exams twice and he was now in the Last Chance Saloon. He sensibly kept quiet.

I took off my suit jacket and hung it on the back of my chair. Then I sat down at Herb's desk and pulled open the top drawer.

'What are you doing?' Rory asked somewhat arrogantly.

'I'm going through Herb's desk,' I said. 'I'm his executor and I'm trying to find the address of his sister.' He wasn't to know that Herb's sister was in Hendon. Rory ignored me and went back to his one-handed typing.

There was no sign of Sherri's address but there were two more of the MoneyHome payment slips lurking in a drawer and, this time, not torn up into squares. There was also another of the sheets with handwritten lists on both sides, just like the one Chief Inspector Tomlinson had shown me in Herb's flat. I carefully folded them all up and put them in my pocket.

Apart from that, the desk was almost too clean. No screwed-up sweet papers or chocolate bar wrappers.

I wasn't surprised. In fact, I was amazed there had been anything at all. I would have expected the police would have stripped it completely bare on the Monday after his death.

I looked around me at the cubicle. Some of the staff personalized their noticeboards with family pictures or souvenir postcards sent by friends on holiday, but there had never been any such personal items pinned to Herb's, not even a picture of Sherri. There was only the usual mandatory internal company telephone directory and a small key, pinned to the board with a drawing pin. I looked at it closely but left it where it was. A key without a lock wasn't much use.

And there was nothing of interest in his waste bin either, which was completely empty. It would be. Even if the police hadn't emptied it, the office cleaners had been in since Herb had last sat at this desk on the previous Friday afternoon.

I walked along the corridor and put my head right into the lion's den.

Now Gregory, as a senior partner, did qualify for an office of his own but, fortunately for me, this particular lion was still out to lunch. I sat down in his chair and looked at his computer screen. As I had hoped, he hadn't bothered to log out from his session when he went to lunch. Most of us didn't. The office system was great when it was working, but it took so long to boot up that we all tended to leave it on all day.

I typed 'Roberts Family Trust' into Gregory's computer and it instantly produced the details of the file on his screen with the date of the original investment prominently displayed at the top. The access list in the right-hand corner showed me that Gregory himself had looked at the file only that morning, at 10.22 a.m. precisely, no doubt in a lull from searching the offices for me. I just hoped he wouldn't notice that his computer had accessed it again at 1.46 p.m.

However, it was one of the other names on the recent-enquiry list I found most interesting. The list showed that Herb Kovak had accessed the file just ten days previously. Now why had Herb looked at one of Gregory's client files? It would have been most improper, just as it was for me to be looking at it now. Perhaps Herb had also had some suspicions about the Bulgarian investment. I wondered what they had been. It was too late to ask.

I would have loved to print out the whole file but, unfortunately, the office server used a central printing system that recorded who had asked for what to be printed, and when. How could I explain away an apparent request from Gregory when he was out to lunch? More to the point, how would I explain away sitting at Gregory's desk and using his computer if he returned unexpectedly early?

I instinctively looked at my watch. It was ten to two. I reckoned I should be safe for at least another twenty minutes but I had no intention of being even half that long.

I flipped through the pages of the file trying to find the names of the Bulgarian agents involved in the project but it was a nightmare with pdf scans of the relevant documents all in the local Cyrillic script. It might as well have been in Chinese. I couldn't read any of the words, but I could read what I thought was a telephone number written in regular digits. I copied it down on the back of one of Herb's MoneyHome payment slips. It began +359, which I knew from looking at the internet earlier was the international code for Bulgaria.

I looked again at my watch. Two o'clock.

I opened Gregory's e-mail inbox and did a search for 'Bulgaria'. There were six e-mails, all from September two years ago. I glanced through them but nothing seemed amiss. They were about European Union money and they were all from the same source. I copied down the e-mail address of the sender uri_joram @ec.europa.eu, and also that of the recipient, dimitar .petrov@bsnet.co.bg. Gregory had been copied into the correspondence but there was no sign of any replies. I took a chance and forwarded the e-mails to my private e-mail address, then I deleted the forwarded record from Gregory's 'sent' folder. I wished I could have e-mailed myself the whole Roberts file but our security system wouldn't allow it.

I reluctantly closed Gregory's inbox and the Roberts Family Trust file and checked that the screen appeared the same as when I had first arrived.

I slipped out into the corridor and no one shouted a challenge or questioned what I had been doing in Gregory's office.

As everywhere in the offices, the corridor outside was lined with cardboard document boxes holding the paper transaction reports. I searched for the box containing those for the date at the top of the computer file.

Mrs McDowd may not have liked policemen very much, and she was definitely too nosey about the staff's lives and families, but she was very methodical in her filing. All the boxes were in chronological order with dates clearly written in thick marker pen on the ends.

I lifted up the box with the correct date and dug through its papers until I found the Roberts Family Trust transaction report and associated paperwork. I pulled them out, folded them, and stuffed them in my trouser pocket alongside Herb's MoneyHome payment slips, before putting the box carefully back in the same place I'd found it.

I glanced at my watch once more, twenty past two. Where had those twenty minutes gone? Time I was away. But why did I suddenly feel like a thief in the night? I'd done nothing wrong. Or had I? Maybe I should just go and see Jessica straight away when she returned from lunch. But the client, Jolyon Roberts, had specifically asked me to have a discreet look rather than initiate a possible fraud investigation that would, as he put it, drag the good name of the Roberts family through the courts.

Nevertheless, whatever else I might do, I didn't want to be in the offices when Gregory returned from the restaurant.

I went back into my office to collect my jacket.

'Leaving already?' said Rory sarcastically. 'What shall I tell Gregory?'

I ignored him.

As I walked down the corridor towards the reception area I realized with a heavy heart that I'd left it too late. I could hear Gregory and Patrick talking. I would just have to face the music.

'Ah, there you are, Foxton,' Gregory announced at high volume. 'I've been looking for you all morning.'

I was so mesmerized by Gregory that I hardly took any notice of a man standing to the side of him, next to Patrick, but the man suddenly stepped forward, right in front of me.

'Nicholas Foxton,' the man said. 'I arrest you on suspicion of the attempted murder of William Peter Searle.'

7

I spent the afternoon waiting in an eight-foot-by-six holding cell at Paddington Green Police Station not quite knowing what to think.

The man in the office had identified himself as another detective chief inspector, this one from the Metropolitan Police.

I'd missed his name. I hadn't really been listening.

I did, however, remember him advising me that I didn't have to say anything, with the proviso that it might harm my defence if I didn't mention something when questioned that I later relied on in court. I'd been too shocked to say anything anyway. I had just stood there with my mouth open in surprise as a uniformed policeman had applied handcuffs to my wrists and then led me down in the lift to a waiting police car.

William Peter Searle, the chief inspector had said when I was arrested.

That had to be Billy Searle.

So, Billy had been right about one thing.

Thursday had been too late.

I suppose I couldn't really blame the police for arresting me. Hundreds of witnesses had heard Billy shouting the previous afternoon at Cheltenham. 'Why are you trying to murder me?' had been his exact words, even if the *Racing Post* had distorted them somewhat.

I hadn't been trying to murder him, but I hadn't taken him seriously either.

But to whom could Billy have owed so much money? Clearly, someone who was prepared to try to kill him for non-payment by the Wednesday-night deadline.

I sat on one end of the cell's fixed concrete bed and went on waiting. But I wasn't particularly worried. I knew I had nothing to do with Billy's or anyone else's attempted murder and surely it would be only a matter of time before the police discovered that.

First Herb Kovak, and now Billy Searle. Could the two be connected?

Thursday afternoon dragged on into early evening, and I was left alone in the cell, still waiting.

For the umpteenth time I looked at my wrist to check the time and, for the umpteenth time, saw no watch.

It had been removed when I was 'checked in' to the custody suite by the custody sergeant, along with my tie, my belt, my shoelaces and the contents of my pockets, including Herb's MoneyHome payment slips and the transaction report from the box outside Gregory's office.

The cell door opened and a white-shirted policeman brought in a tray that held a covered plate and a plastic bottle of water.

'What time is it?' I asked.

'Seven o'clock,' he said without looking at his watch.

'How much longer am I going to be kept here?' I asked.

'The DCI will see you when he's ready,' replied the policeman, who then placed the tray down next to me on the concrete bed and went out. The door clanged shut behind him.

I looked under the cover – fish and chips – and quite good too.

I ate the lot, and drank the water. It took about five minutes.

And then I waited some more, counting the bricks in the walls of the cell in an attempt to alleviate the boredom. It failed.

The detective chief inspector finally opened the metal door long after the barred and frosted-glass window had turned from day-light to night-black.

'Mr Foxton,' he said, coming into the cell. 'You are free to go.'

'What?' I said, not quite taking it all in.

'You are free to go,' the detective said again, standing to one side of the door. 'We will not be charging you with any offence.' He paused as if not being quite able to say the next bit. 'And I'm sorry for any inconvenience that may have been caused.'

'Sorry!' I said. 'Sorry! I should bloody well think you are sorry. I've been treated like a common criminal.'

'Mr Foxton,' the chief inspector replied, somewhat

affronted. 'You have been treated exactly in accordance with the laid-down regulations.'

'So why was I arrested?' I demanded.

'We had reason to believe you were responsible for the attempted murder of the jockey, William Searle.'

'So what's happened that now makes you so sure I'm not responsible for it?' I was purposefully making myself appear angry. It might be the only chance I would have of asking the detective for some answers and I wanted to take advantage of his defensive position.

'I am persuaded that you could not have been present when Mr Searle was attacked. You have an alibi.'

'How do you know?' I said. 'You haven't asked me any questions.'

'Nevertheless,' he replied, 'I am satisfied that it was not possible for you to have committed the attack. So you are free to go.'

I didn't move.

'How are you satisfied that I couldn't have done it?' I asked with persistence.

'Because it is physically impossible for you to have been in two places at the same time. That's what having an alibi means. *Alibi* is a Latin word meaning "somewhere else", and you were somewhere else when the attempt was made on Mr Searle's life.'

'So where was this attack?' I asked. 'And when?'

The chief inspector looked uncomfortable, as if he didn't particularly like answering questions. No doubt he was more relaxed when asking them.

'Mr Searle was deliberately knocked off his bicycle

on the road outside his home in the village of Baydon in Wiltshire at exactly five minutes past seven this morning. He is currently in a critical condition at the Great Western Hospital in Swindon.'

'And how are you so sure I was somewhere else at five minutes past seven this morning?' I asked.

'Because you were at 45 Seymour Way in Hendon exactly fifty-five minutes later,' he said. 'You were interviewed at that address at precisely eight o'clock by Detective Chief Inspector Tomlinson of the Merseyside Police. There is no way you could have travelled the seventy-two miles from Baydon to Hendon in fifty-five minutes, and especially not at that time of the morning during the rush hour.'

'And why didn't you work this out before I was arrested?' I was beginning to sound rather self-righteous, even to my ears.

'We were simply acting on a request from the Wiltshire force,' he replied, neatly passing the blame elsewhere.

'Well, then they should have checked,' I said, trying to maintain a look of rightful indignation. 'Maybe I'll sue you for wrongful arrest.'

'I think, sir,' he said very formally, 'that you will find that attempted murder is an arrestable offence, and that we had reasonable grounds for an arrest. Just because it turned out that you couldn't have been the perpetrator doesn't give you grounds for claiming false arrest.'

'Hmm,' I said. 'So I am now free to go, just like that?'

'Yes,' he said.

'No questions? No police bail?'

'No, sir,' he replied. 'An alibi is a complete defence. It doesn't mitigate a crime, it proves innocence. So there would be no point in charging or bailing you. However, I am sure that the Wiltshire force will want to ask some questions about your argument with Mr Searle at Cheltenham Races yesterday. No doubt they will be making an appointment in due course. You are free to go home now,' he said. He waved a hand towards the doorway as if trying to encourage me on my way.

I'd had enough of this cell and I didn't need his encouragement to leave it.

The custody sergeant sneered at me as he returned my watch and mobile phone, my tie, belt and shoelaces, and the previous contents of my pockets. He clearly enjoyed booking prisoners in far more than letting them go.

'Sign here,' said the sergeant without any warmth, pointing at a form on the desk.

I signed.

'Thanks for the supper,' I said cheerily.

The sergeant didn't reply.

'Which way out?' I asked, looking around at various doors, none of them with a convenient 'EXIT' sign above it. Perhaps it was designed that way to confuse any escapees.

'That way,' said the sergeant, pointing at one of the doors. He pushed a button on his desk and the lock on the heavy steel door buzzed. I pulled it open and walked out into the police station reception area as the door closed automatically behind me with a loud clunk.

Claudia was waiting there, sitting on an upright tubular-steel chair that was bolted to the floor. She jumped up when she saw me and rushed over, throwing her arms round my neck and hugging me tight. She was crying.

'Oh, Nick,' she sobbed into my neck, 'I've been so frightened.'

'Come on,' I said, hugging her back. 'Let's go home.'

We walked out into the night, hand in hand, and hailed a passing black cab.

'I didn't think you'd be here,' I said to Claudia as we sat down.

'Why ever not?' she said. 'I've been here ever since I found out where they'd taken you. It's been bloody hours.'

'But how did you know I'd been arrested?' The police had allowed me only one call and I'd made that to the company's lawyer, Andrew Mellor.

'Rosemary called me,' Claudia said. 'She was in floods of tears.'

'Rosemary?' I asked.

'You know,' she said. 'Rosemary McDowd. She's such a dear.'

I had worked at Lyall & Black for five years and, for all that time, I'd had no idea that Mrs McDowd's name was Rosemary. The receptionists were always referred to as Mrs McDowd and Mrs Johnson, because that's what they called each other. Only the other staff had first names, Mr Patrick, Mr Gregory, Miss Jessica,

Mr Nicholas and so on, and we were only addressed in that way because, again, that was how the Mesdames McDowd and Johnson did it.

'How did Mrs McDowd have your number?' I asked.

'Oh, we speak quite often.'

'What about?' I asked.

Claudia didn't reply.

'What about?' I repeated.

'You,' she said.

'What about me?' I asked.

'Oh, nothing,' she said evasively.

'No. Come on,' I said. 'Tell me. What about me?'

Claudia sighed. 'I sometimes call her to find out what sort of mood you're in when you leave the office.'

More likely, I thought suspiciously, to check that I was actually in the office, or when I'd left it.

'So what did Mrs McDowd tell you today?' I asked, purposely changing the conversation's direction.

'Between sobs, she told me that you had been arrested by the police for attempted murder. I thought it must be to do with Herb Kovak but she said it was about someone else.'

I nodded. 'Billy Searle was attacked this morning. He was a top jump jockey, and also a client of mine.'

'What the hell's going on?' Claudia said.

That's what I wanted to know.

It had been nearly eleven o'clock by the time I'd been released and I'd asked the taxi driver to go to the newspaper kiosk on the Edgware Road, where I knew they received the early editions of the daily newspapers the night before.

Claudia stayed in the cab as I went to buy copies of all they had, including the *Racing Post*, which arrived in a van as I was paying for the rest.

If its previous day's front-page headline had been vague and set as a question, this one pulled none of its punches:

BILLY SEARLE ATTACKED – FOXTON ARRESTED FOR ATTEMPTED MURDER

And the article beneath gave no comfort to me either:

Further to our exclusive report in yesterday's Racing Post *concerning a heated argument at Cheltenham Races on Wednesday between top jump jockey Billy Searle and ex-jock turned financial wizard Nicholas (Foxy) Foxton, we can exclusively reveal that Foxton was yesterday arrested for Searle's attempted murder.*

Billy Searle was taken to the Great Western Hospital in Swindon from the scene of an horrific incident in Baydon, near Lambourn, early yesterday morning when it appears he was deliberately knocked from his bicycle. Doctors at the hospital state that Searle's condition is critical with a broken leg and serious head injuries.

Foxton was arrested yesterday at 2.25 p.m. on suspicion of attempted murder at the Lombard Street offices of City financial services firm Lyall and Black, and he is currently being held for questioning at Paddington Green Police Station.

Remarkably accurate, I thought, except for the bit about currently being held at Paddington Green Police Station, and that had been right until about twenty minutes ago. Beside the article was another picture of Billy Searle, this time all smiles and wearing a business suit, and a photograph of the cordoned-off village of Baydon. Overlaid across the top right-hand corner of this photo was a smaller head-and-shoulders shot of me positioned, to my eye, as if to imply my presence in Baydon High Street.

Gregory was going to have a field day in the morning. It wouldn't just be my head he would have on a stick, it would be my career as well. Who would trust a financial adviser who was on the front page of a national newspaper having been arrested for attempted murder?

Not me, for one.

I climbed back into the cab with the papers and showed the *Racing Post* to Claudia.

'It so bloody unfair,' she said, reading the headline. 'How can they mention your name when you haven't even been charged? You should sue.'

'Over what?' I asked. 'They haven't said anything that wasn't true.'

'But why do the police give out names before they charge someone?'

I suspected that the information had not come from

the police but from a source much closer to home. The time and place of the arrest were too precise, and too accurate. The police would have only said something like 'A twenty-nine-year-old man has been arrested and is helping with our enquiries'.

My money would be on Rory to be the office mole, although what he hoped to gain by it was anyone's idea. He couldn't have my job without passing his IFA exams first, and even I didn't believe he would have murdered Herb for the cubicle close to the window. It would have been Diana's anyway.

I looked at all the newspapers before I went to bed and all of them had front- or back-page reports about the attack on Billy Searle. None of them had the full facts but each still managed to mention me by name and imply my guilt.

Oh, God, I thought, my mother would see them in the morning, and it was far too late to call and warn her now.

I switched on the television and watched the latest news on one of the 24-hour news channels. They had a report live from Baydon.

'It appears,' said the reporter, 'that the jockey Billy Searle was leaving his home to ride his bicycle to Lambourn as he did every morning. He was due to ride horses at morning exercise. He was being waved away by his girlfriend when a car, which had seemingly been waiting in the street, suddenly accelerated into the bicycle, knocking Searle violently to the ground, before being driven away at speed. Billy Searle was taken to hospital in Swindon where he is in a critical but stable condition with head and leg injuries. Police are asking anyone who may have any information concerning the incident to come forward. A man, who we believe to be the ex-jockey Nicholas Foxton, was arrested in connection with the attack but he has since been released without charge.'

'Well at least they said you'd been released,' said Claudia.

'I'd rather they hadn't mentioned my name at all,' I said. 'You watch. Most people will think I'm guilty. They will already have me tried and convicted in their minds. Being released will make little difference. What I need is for the police to catch the real attacker and for him to confess. Even then there will be plenty of people who'll still believe I did it.'

'It's so unfair,' Claudia said again.

Indeed it was, but complaining about it wasn't going to help. I just hoped that they arrested the real culprit soon.

Claudia and I went upstairs to bed but I couldn't sleep. I lay awake in the darkness going over and over everything in my head.

Last Saturday morning my life had been so settled and predictable, and my career path mapped out to success and riches, even if it was a little boring. But the last five days had seen so much change. I had witnessed one murder at close range and been arrested for attempting another; I'd begun to doubt my relationship with Claudia, even suspecting that she might be having an affair with someone else; and I'd gone behind the back of my superior at work to access his personal e-mails to try to determine if he was complicit in a multimillion-pound fraud.

Not to mention becoming the executor and beneficiary of someone that I hardly knew, who then turned out to have a twin sister. And then, to top it all, I'd been propositioned for sex by a woman nearly twenty years older than me, and I'd also discovered the real heartbreaking reason for my parents' unhappy marriage.

It was enough to keep even the most tired of men from sleeping.

I tossed and turned for hours as I mulled over what I should do next, and also over whether I would still have a job to go to in the morning.

I woke late after a restless night, the space in the bed next to me already empty and cold.

I rolled over and looked at my bedside clock. It was gone eight o'clock and I was usually on the Tube by now.

The phone beside the clock started ringing loudly. I decided I didn't want to talk to anyone so I didn't pick it up and eventually it stopped when Claudia answered downstairs.

I turned on the television for the news. Billy Searle's

attempted murder had been downgraded from the top story by a government U-turn on schools' policy, but it still warranted a report from Baydon village, and they still managed to mention me by name and show my picture, in spite of my release.

At this rate the whole bloody world would believe me guilty.

Claudia came into the room. 'It's your mother,' she said.

I picked up the phone. 'Hello, Mum,' I said.

'Darling,' she said. 'What the hell's going on? You're in all the papers and on the TV.' She sounded very upset, as if she was in tears.

'It's all right, Mum,' I said. 'Calm down. I didn't do anything and the police know it. Otherwise they wouldn't have released me. I promise you, all is fine.'

It took me about five minutes to calm my mother down completely. I knew when I'd managed it because she told me to get up and have a good breakfast. Eventually I put the phone down and laid my head back on the pillow.

'Aren't you going to the office today?' Claudia asked, coming back into the bedroom carrying two cups of steaming coffee.

It was an innocent enough question so why did I straight away wonder if she was checking on my movements in order to plan her own?

'I don't know,' I said, taking one of the cups from her. 'What do you think?'

'Things could be worse,' she said. 'You could still be

in that police station, or in court. Let's look on the bright side.'

'What plans do you have?' I asked.

'Nothing much,' she said. 'I might go shopping later.'

'For food?'

'No,' she said. 'I need a new dress for the show next week.'

'Oh,' I said. 'I'd forgotten about that.'

The thought of attending the opening night of a new West End musical with all the associated press coverage did not now fill me with great joy. Claudia and I had accepted an invitation from Jan Setter to join her at the star-studded event, and at the after-show party. I wondered if, after my clumsy brush-off at Cheltenham, Jan would now be so keen for me to be there, to say nothing of my subsequent arrest.

Look on the bright side, Claudia had said. Things could indeed have been worse. I could have still been stuck in that unwelcome cell, or I might have been lying in a Liverpool mortuary refrigerator like Herb, or in a Swindon hospital intensive care bed like Billy. Things could have been a lot worse.

'Right,' I said with determination. 'It's time to show a defiant face to the world. I'm going to get up and go in to work and bugger what anyone thinks. I'm innocent and I'm going to act like it.'

'That's my boy,' said Claudia with a huge grin. 'Bugger the lot of them.'

She lay down on the bed and snuggled up to me, slipping her hand down under the sheets in search of me.

'But do you have to go immediately? Or . . .' She grinned again. 'Can you wait a while longer?'

Now I was really confused.

Had I been reading the signals incorrectly?

'Hmm, let me think,' I said, laughing with joy as well as expectation. 'Work or sex? Sex or work? Such difficult decisions.'

Not really.

Sex won – easily.

I didn't go into the office until after lunch but that was not solely due to having fun and games in bed with Claudia. It was because I went to Hendon on the way to check on Sherri and to collect my laptop that I'd left on Herb's desk.

'What happened to you?' she said, opening the door. 'I thought you were coming back yesterday afternoon.'

'I was,' I said. 'But I was detained elsewhere.' I decided not to elaborate. 'What have you been up to?'

'I've started going through Herb's things in his bedroom,' she said. 'I got fed up doing nothing, and it somehow seems to help.'

'Did you find anything of interest?' I asked as I followed her down the corridor to the bedroom.

'Only this,' she replied, picking up something from the bed. 'It was at the back of his wardrobe, hanging on a hook behind his coats.'

She handed me a small blue plastic box with a clip-on lid. Inside the box, all neatly held together by a rubber band, were twenty-two credit cards. I rolled off the band and shuffled through them. As far as I could tell, they matched the statements, right down to the variations in Herb's name.

'Why would anyone have so many credit cards?' Sherri asked. 'And why would they all be in a box hidden in his wardrobe? They all look brand new to me.'

And to me, I thought. Herb hadn't even bothered signing them on the back. These cards had been obtained solely for use on the internet. But I knew that. I'd seen the statements.

Underneath the cards were four pieces of folded-up paper similar to the ones that Chief Inspector Tomlinson had shown me the previous morning. I looked at the lists of numbers and letters. The first columns on each side were definitely dates but they were written in the American way with the month first and then the day so 2/10 was the tenth of February. All the dates on these pieces started 1, 2 or 12, so were from January, February or December.

Sherri was sitting on the floor busily looking through a chest of drawers, lifting out neat piles of T-shirts and stacking them on the bed. I left her and went out of the bedroom, along the corridor and into the living room.

The handwritten lists I had photocopied yesterday were still on the desk next to my computer along with the photocopied bank and credit card statements. The dates on those lists all started with a 3, for March.

I took them back to the bedroom.

On all of the lists, the second and third columns definitely looked like amounts of money. And the fourth column was a list of capital letters, possibly initials. I counted them. There were ninety-seven different sets of letters.

'What are you looking at?' Sherri said.

'I don't know exactly,' I replied. 'Lists of numbers and letters. Have a look.' I handed her the sheets. 'I think the first column on each side are dates and the next two are probably amounts of money.'

'In dollars or pounds?' she asked.

'I don't know,' I said slowly. Was that why, I wondered, the amounts on the credit card statements didn't match the amounts on the sheets. Were one lot in dollars and the other in pounds?

I left Sherri studying the lists while I went back to the desk for the statements and Herb's calculator.

'What's the exchange rate for the US dollar to the pound?' I asked coming back into the bedroom.

'About one-point-six dollars to one pound,' Sherri said. 'At least it was last week but it changes all the time.'

I multiplied some of the amounts on the credit card statements by 1.6 and tried to match the new figure against any on the handwritten lists. It was a hopeless task. I didn't know the exact exchange rate and there were over five hundred different entries on the twenty-two statements. Some of the amounts were close but none were exactly the same. The best I could say was that they might have been related.

'Do you recognize any of the initials on the lists?' I asked Sherri.

'Is that what they are?' she said.

'I don't know, but they look like it.'

She shook her head.

'Did you know that Herb liked to gamble?' I asked.

She looked up at me. 'Of course,' she said. 'Don't all men? Herb had always been one for an occasional flutter on the horses. Just like his father had been. It must be in the genes.'

'Did you know how much he gambled?' I asked.

'Never very much,' she said. 'He may have liked the odd bet but I know he believed that gambling had ruined our childhood. He would never have staked more than he could afford to lose. I'm absolutely sure of that.'

'And how much could he afford to lose?' I asked.

'What are you getting at?' Sherri said.

'Herb gambled a lot on the internet,' I said. 'A huge amount.'

She was shocked. 'Are you sure?'

I nodded. 'He must have spent hours every day gambling on internet betting sites and playing poker on the virtual tables in online casinos. And he lost. He lost big time.'

'I don't believe it,' Sherri said. 'How do you know?'

I held out the photocopies of the credit card statements to her. 'Herb lost more than ninety thousand pounds last month alone. And the same the month before.'

'He can't have done,' she said with a nervous laugh. 'Herb didn't have that sort of money.'

'Look for yourself,' I said, handing her the statements.

She looked at them for a moment but, I could see, she was crying again.

'Do you think that's why he was killed?' she asked.

'I don't know,' I said. But I thought it quite likely.

She cried some more.

'I wish he'd never come to England,' Sherri said sadly. 'Herb wouldn't have been able to gamble like that at home. Internet gambling is illegal in most of the United States.'

So it was.

I remembered reading about the head of an internet gambling website who'd been arrested when he'd arrived at a US airport and charged with racketeering, simply for allowing Americans to gamble on his website, even though it was based in England. It had all been about accepting credit card accounts with a United States address.

I looked again at the handwritten lists of dates, amounts of money and initials. And I pulled from my pocket the MoneyHome payment slips I had found in Herb's office cubicle.

Only last week, according to the torn-up payment slips I'd found in his waste bin, Herb had received three large amounts of cash, two equivalent to five thousand dollars and one to eight thousand.

Suddenly, all of it made complete sense to me.

It hadn't been Herb who had lost ninety thousand pounds last month, it had been the people whose initials were to be found on Herb's lists, the ninety-seven people who were responsible for the five hundred and twelve different entries on the credit card accounts. And I'd like to bet they were all Americans.

If I was right, Herb had been running a system to provide ninety-seven Americans with a UK-based credit card account in order for them to gamble and play poker on internet betting and casino sites.

But why would that have got him murdered?

8

To say my arrival at the offices of Lyall & Black about an hour after lunch caused a bit of a stir would be an understatement.

'Get out of these offices,' Gregory shouted at me almost as soon as I walked through the door on the fourth floor into the reception area, and he wasn't finished then. 'You are a disgrace to your profession and to this firm. I will not have you here contaminating the other staff.'

I had made the mistake of not sneaking in while he was at lunch.

Mrs McDowd looked positively frightened by the outburst. I probably did as well.

'Gregory,' I tried to say, but he advanced towards me bunching his fists. Surely, I thought, he's not going to hit me. He didn't, but he grabbed me by the sleeve of my suit and dragged me towards the door.

He was surprisingly strong and fit for someone whose only workout was the walk to and from the restaurant on the corner.

'Leave me alone,' I shouted at him. But he took no notice.

'Gregory. Stop it!' Patrick's deep voice reverberated round the reception area.

Gregory stopped pulling and let go of my sleeve.

'I will not have this man in these offices,' Gregory said. 'He has brought the firm of Lyall and Black into disrepute.'

Patrick looked at the reception desk, and at Mrs McDowd and Mrs Johnson who were sitting behind it.

'Let us discuss this in your office,' Patrick said calmly. 'Nicholas, will you please wait here.'

'Outside the door,' Gregory said, pointing towards the lifts and not moving an inch towards his office.

I stood there looking back and forth between them. Everyone in the firm knew of Gregory's temper, it was legendary, but I had rarely seen it laid bare and so raw, and at such close quarters.

'I will go out for a coffee,' I said. 'I'll be back in twenty minutes.'

'Best to go home,' Patrick said. 'I'll call you later.'

Gregory turned towards Patrick. 'I told you that we should never have taken him on in the first place.'

'In your office, please, Gregory!' Patrick said, almost shouting. He had a pretty good temper in him, too, although it was usually slow to rise.

I waited while Gregory reluctantly moved off down the corridor with Patrick. I would have adored being a fly on the wall during their discussion.

'You had better go,' said Mrs McDowd firmly. 'I don't want you upsetting Mr Gregory any more. His heart can't take it.'

I looked at her. Mrs McDowd, who saw it as her business to know everything about everyone in the firm. She probably knew Gregory's blood pressure, and his heart surgeon.

'Tell me, Mrs McDowd, do you think Herb gambled much?'

'You mean on the stock market?' she asked.

'On the horses.'

'Oh, no,' she said. 'Mr Herb didn't like betting on the horses. Too risky, he said. So much better to bet on a certainty, that's what he always told me.'

Death was a certainty.

Benjamin Franklin had said so: death – and taxes.

I did go home, but not immediately.

Before I left Hendon I had looked up the locations of MoneyHome agents near to Lombard Street. I was amazed at how many there were, at least thirty within a one-mile radius of my office, the nearest being just round the corner in King William Street.

'This didn't come from here,' said the lady sitting behind a glass screen. 'It hasn't got our stamp on it.'

I had somehow expected the MoneyHome agency to be like a bank, or a money exchange, but this one was right at the back of a convenience store.

'Can you tell me where it did come from?' I asked the lady.

'Don't you know?' she asked.

'No,' I said with declining patience. 'I wouldn't have asked if I knew.'

She looked at me through the glass, then down at

the payment slip. I had brought with me one of those I had found in Herb's desk rather than the torn-up squares, which were still at Herb's flat anyway.

'Sorry,' she said. 'I don't recognize the stamp. But I know it's not ours.'

'Can you tell who sent the money?' I asked.

'No,' she said.

'What do you need to produce in the way of identification to collect money from a MoneyHome transfer?'

'The recipient's name and the MTCN.'

'What's that?'

'There,' she said pointing at the payment slip. 'It's the Money Transfer Control Number.'

'And that's all you need to collect the money,' I said. 'No passport or driving licence?'

'Not unless it's been specially requested by the sender,' she said. 'Sometimes there's a question I have to ask and then you'd have to give the right answer. It's a bit like spies and such.' She smiled.

'So, in fact,' I said, 'you have no way of knowing who has sent the money, or who has collected it?'

'The recipient's name is on the slip.'

The recipient's name on the slip I had shown her was Butch Cassidy. The names on the others I had were Billy Kid, Wyatt Earp, Jessie James and Bill Cody.

'That isn't his real name,' I said.

'No,' she said, looking. 'I suppose not. But it's their money. As long as they've paid us our fee, it's not our business who they really are.'

'Does the amount make any difference?' I asked.

'MoneyHome's head office doesn't allow us to accept transfers of more than the equivalent of ten thousand US dollars as that breaks the money-laundering rules. Other than that, the amount doesn't matter, although we here have a payout limit of four thousand pounds without prior notice. You know, so we can get in the cash.'

'Are your transfers always in cash?' I asked.

'Yeah, of course,' she said. 'That's what we do. Cash transfers. Lots of the immigrant workers round here send cash home to their wives. Poles mostly. And we do a special deal on transfers to Poland, up to a thousand pounds for just twenty quid.'

Overall, it wasn't very helpful. Herb had clearly set up a system that would be difficult, if not impossible, to unravel. From what I could tell from the lists and the MoneyHome payment slips, it was clear that he'd received large sums of cash from multiple sources, money he must have then used to pay the monthly balances on the twenty-two credit cards.

Herb had collected eighteen thousand dollars' worth of pounds sterling only the previous week, five thousand of it just the day before his death. Some of that cash must still be hidden somewhere.

My problem was that, while I had the statements showing the ninety-four thousand pounds outstanding and, as his executor and beneficiary, I was liable for the debt, I hadn't yet found the stash of readies to pay it.

*

Claudia wasn't at home when I arrived back at three thirty. I tried her mobile but it went straight to voicemail.

I wandered round the house wondering what had gone wrong with our relationship.

I didn't really understand it. The sex that morning had been as good as ever but Claudia had been uncharacteristically quiet during, and afterwards, as if her mind had been elsewhere.

I asked myself what I really wanted. Did I want to continue or was it time to draw a line, and move on? Did I love her enough? How much would I miss her if she left?

Claudia and I had been together now for almost six years. I was twenty-nine, and she was three years my junior. Apart from my real concern about her weird paintings, I found the set-up comfortable and fulfilling. And I was happy as things were.

Was that the trouble? Did Claudia want something more from our relationship than I did? Did she perhaps now want that ring on her finger? Or maybe she had changed her view about children? But then surely she would have told me. I would have been delighted.

So, I concluded, it had to be me that was the problem. Claudia must have tired of me, and perhaps there was someone else already lined up to take my place. It was the only conclusion that made any sense.

I tried her mobile again but, as before, it went straight to voicemail.

The house suddenly felt very empty and I realized

that I was lonely without Claudia here. I wandered round looking at familiar things as if it was the first time I had seen them.

I went up to Claudia's studio and looked at the painting she was working on and also at two or three others leaned against the wall waiting for the paint to dry and harden.

As always, they were dark and, to my eye, somewhat disturbed. One of them was full of bizarre flying monsters with bird-like bodies and human heads, each head with a huge open mouth full of fearsome-looking pointed teeth.

I shuddered and covered the image with another painting, this one of several identical and very beautiful women all dressed in blue ball gowns. A pretty enough sight one might think, except these women had feet that were, in fact, eagle claws ripping apart the naked body of the man on whom they were standing.

Was the man meant to be me? And were the women all representations of Claudia herself? Was this how our relationship would end, with Claudia ripping me apart? I doubted it would happen quite so literally as in the picture, but emotionally, she had me half-way to the funny farm already.

Once again I asked myself how such a sweet girl could paint such strange images. And I was sure they had become more bizarre and much more violent in recent months. Was there a whole side to Claudia's character that I remained totally unaware of? But, on the whole, I believed that it was better for her to find an outlet for such strange thoughts than to keep them bottled up inside her head, with the pressure ever building towards explosive levels.

The house phone rang and I went through to our bedroom to answer it, hoping it would be Claudia.

It wasn't. It was Patrick.

'I'm sorry for Gregory's outburst earlier,' he said. 'He and I had a discussion, and he's now calmed down a lot. He was just upset by what had been written in the papers.'

Not as upset as me, I thought.

'So can I come back into the office?' I asked.

'Not today,' he said rather too quickly. 'Maybe on Monday, or later next week. Let the dust settle for a few days.'

'I'll work from home, then,' I said, 'using the remote-access facility.'

'Right,' Patrick said slowly. 'But I agreed with Gregory that you would not be representing the firm for the immediate future.'

'And how long exactly is the immediate future?' I asked.

'Until he and I agree,' he said.

'Are you telling me I'm fired?'

'No, of course not,' he said. 'Just that it might be better for you to take some paid holiday until the police sort out who really did try to murder Billy Searle.'

'What if they never do?' I asked.

'Let's hope that is not the case,' he said. 'I'll call you next week. In the meantime I must ask you not to use the remote-access facility, and not to contact anyone at the firm.'

Patrick disconnected without saying goodbye, no doubt pleased to have got through the conversation without me shouting at him.

I felt like shouting at someone. Everything that had been fine just a week ago was suddenly going down the tubes. I sat down on the edge of the bed feeling more miserable than I had since the day I had been told I couldn't ride again.

I decided that feeling sorry for myself wasn't going to achieve anything, so I went downstairs and sat down at the kitchen table with my laptop computer.

I spent a fairly unproductive half hour looking at the six e-mails that I had forwarded to my inbox from Gregory's, concerning the Bulgarian property development.

They were all from the same man, Uri Joram, and the first two were about the grants available to disadvantaged parts of the European Union for industrial developments that would assist in the regeneration of sites previously occupied by state-subsidized factories. Many such factories had quickly gone bust when the communist regime had collapsed and free-market competition had arrived in its place.

As far as I could make out from Mr Joram's rather poor grasp of written English, the EU money would only be forthcoming if there was some private investment in the project on the basis that two euros would be granted for each one euro invested privately. Jolyon Roberts had told me that his family trust had invested five million pounds so that alone could have attracted a further ten million from the European tax coffers.

But that was not all, not by a long way.

The four remaining e-mails were about funding for the homes to be constructed close to the factory to house the workers. This was to come from a different source, the EU Social Housing Fund, and required no similar two-for-one arrangement. It appeared that the new factory alone was sufficient to trigger the hundred per cent grant for the housing, which was in the region of eighty million euros.

If, as Jolyon Roberts's nephew had implied, no houses and no factory had been built in Bulgaria, then someone somewhere had likely pocketed nearly a hundred million euros, most of it public money.

I looked closely at the e-mail addresses. The e-mails had been sent by uri_joram@ec.europa.eu to dimitar.petrov@bsnet.co.bg with Gregory Black being copied in. The ec.europa.eu domain indicated that Uri Joram worked in the offices of the European Commission, probably in Brussels, and I could deduce that Mr Petrov must be in Bulgaria from the .bg extension.

It wasn't a huge help.

I also looked at the telephone number I had copied from the Roberts Family Trust file on Gregory's computer. I wondered if I should call it. But what good would it do? I couldn't speak Bulgarian and, even if whoever answered could understand English, they were most unlikely to give me any information that would answer my questions.

What should I do?

It may very well have been a simple mistake made by Mr Roberts's nephew. He might have gone to the wrong place in Bulgaria, with the factory and the houses existing elsewhere. Surely there would have been checks made by the European Union officials running the EU Social Housing Fund to confirm that their eighty million euros had been spent properly on bricks and mortar.

I decided that, having been asked by Jolyon Roberts to look into it, I couldn't just do nothing so I sent a short e-mail to Dimitar Petrov asking him to send me the names and addresses of the directors of the Balscott Lighting Factory, if he had them.

By the time I realized that sending the e-mail was possibly not such a good idea if Mr Petrov himself was one of those involved in the potential hundred-million-euro fraud, it was well on its way and there was no bringing it back.

It couldn't do any harm, could it?

I closed my computer and looked at the clock. It was a quarter to five so I made myself a cup of tea.

I couldn't help but notice that Claudia had left her latest mobile phone bill lying on the worktop right next to the kettle. And I also couldn't resist the temptation to look at it.

I suppose I was looking for numbers I didn't recognize that she had called regularly. There was one, with calls almost every day for the past two weeks, and often more than once a day.

Now what did I do? Did I call the number and demand to know who had been talking so often to my girl? No, of course I didn't. But I copied the number into my mobile phone, just in case I changed my mind.

Claudia arrived home at five thirty and I resisted the temptation to ask her where she had been, and why her phone had been switched off.

'Why aren't you at the office?' she asked.

'Patrick sent me home,' I said. 'Gregory seems to think I've brought the company into disrepute. Patrick thinks it would be best for me to have some time off, to stay away from the office, just to let the dust settle.'

'But that's ridiculous,' she said. 'The police let you go. You have a cast-iron alibi.'

'I know that, and you know that,' I replied crossly. 'But you know what most people are like, they believe what they read.'

'Those bloody newspapers,' she said with feeling. 'They shouldn't be allowed to give out people's names before they're charged.'

Or even convicted, I thought. But I also knew the police were secretly quite keen for the names of those accused to be released early so that potential witnesses would come forward.

'Patrick says it will all blow over in a few days,' I said. 'He thinks people will forget.'

'I hope he's right,' she said.

So did I.

'Did you get your dress?' I asked.

'What dress?' she said.

'Come on, darling,' I said, slightly irritated. 'You know. The one you were going to buy for the opening night on Wednesday.'

'Oh, that,' she said, clearly distracted. 'Perhaps I'll go tomorrow. Something came up this afternoon.'

I didn't like to think what, so I didn't ask.

'How long did Patrick say you had to stay away from the office?' Claudia asked into the silence.

'Maybe a week,' I said, wondering if she was asking for reasons other than worries over my reputation and career. 'Perhaps I'll go to the races instead.'

'Great idea,' she said. 'Give your mind a rest from all those figures.'

Perhaps it was time to start looking at figures of a different kind.

9

On Saturday afternoon I put on my thick skin and went to Sandown Park Races on the train from Waterloo.

'Bloody hell,' said Jan Setter. 'I didn't expect to see you here. I thought you'd been sent to the Tower.'

'Not quite,' I said.

I was standing on the grass close to the parade ring, near the statue of the horse Special Cargo.

'Did you do it?' Jan asked in all seriousness.

'No, of course I didn't,' I said. 'The police wouldn't have let me go if they still thought I'd tried to kill Billy. I have an alibi.'

'Then who did do it?'

'I don't know,' I said. 'But it wasn't me.'

'Blimey,' she said. 'Then there's still a would-be murderer out there on the loose.'

'Lots of them,' I said. 'Not just Billy's but Herb Kovak's too.'

'Who's Herb Kovak?' she asked.

'Chap who was shot at Aintree last Saturday,' I said. 'He was a colleague of mine at work.'

'Did you kill him, then?'

'Jan,' I said forcefully, 'I didn't kill anyone, or try to. OK?'

'Then why were you arrested?'

I sighed. People, even good friends, really did believe what they read in the papers.

'Someone told the police that Billy had shouted at me at Cheltenham demanding to know why I was going to murder him. They put two and two together and made five. That's all. They got it wrong.'

'So why did Billy shout at you?'

'It was to do with his investments,' I said.

Jan raised a questioning eyebrow.

'It's confidential,' I said. 'You wouldn't want me telling everyone about your investments, now would you?'

'No,' she agreed. 'But then I haven't been deliberately knocked off my bike.'

'That's a fair point, but confidentiality rules still apply,' I said. 'Severely injured or not, he's still my client.'

Mind you, I thought, there was a limit to confidentiality.

The Wiltshire Police had called me on Friday evening to make an appointment, and I had spent time with two of their number earlier, going over in minute detail all the events of Tuesday and Wednesday at Cheltenham Races with particular reference to Billy Searle's investments.

'Was it true that you owe Mr Searle over a hundred thousand pounds?' one of them had asked me as his opening shot.

'No,' I'd replied calmly. 'Not personally. I'm a financial adviser and Billy Searle is a client of mine, which means I manage the investment of his money. In total, he has about a hundred and fifty thousand invested through me and he told me on Tuesday that he urgently wanted all his money out in cash. He became very distressed and angry when I told him it would take a few days to realize the cash through the sale of his stocks and shares.'

'Why do you think Mr Searle needed such a large sum so quickly?' the other policeman had asked.

'He told me he owed some guy a hundred thousand and he needed to pay it back by Wednesday night at the very latest, or else.'

'Or else what?' they'd both asked in unison.

'Billy seemed frightened and, when I told him that his money wouldn't be in his bank until Friday, he said he hoped he would still alive by Friday.'

'Those were his exact words?'

'Pretty much,' I'd said.

'Did he give you any indication who this guy was?'

'None, but he was clearly terrified of him. Why don't you ask Billy?'

'Mr Searle is in a critical condition,' one of them had replied. 'He has severe head injuries and it is far from certain yet whether he will ever recover consciousness.'

How dreadful, I thought. Billy had survived all those racing falls over all those years, only to have head injuries due to someone knocking him off his bike. It didn't seem fair.

'I wouldn't have thought that knocking someone off their bicycle was a very sure way of killing them,' I'd said. 'How would someone know he would be riding his bike at that time?'

'Mr Searle rode his bicycle to Lambourn every day at the same time. Apparently it was part of his fitness regime, and well known. And the car seems to have struck him with considerable force.'

'Yes, but even so, it is not as certain as a shooting.' I had been thinking of Herb the previous Saturday. 'Are you sure it was attempted murder?'

'We are treating the attack as attempted murder,' one of them had replied rather unhelpfully.

Yes, I'd thought, but that didn't necessarily make it so.

'Can we go back to this man to whom Mr Searle owed money? Are you sure that Mr Searle gave you no indication who it was?'

'Positive,' I'd said. 'All Billy told me was that he owed the money to some guy.'

But why would you try to kill someone because they owed you money? Then there would be no chance of getting it back. Maybe the attack had been meant as a warning, or a reminder to pay up, and had simply gone too far. Or had it been a message to others: pay up or else – just as Billy had been afraid of.

'The *Racing Post* seems to have implied it was a bookmaker.'

'I think that was probably speculation on their part,' I'd said. 'Billy never mentioned anything like that to me. In fact he said that he couldn't tell me why he owed the money.'

'So why did he claim that it was you who was murdering him?'

'I now realize that he must have believed he might

be murdered because I couldn't get his money together by Wednesday night, and it would therefore be my fault if he was killed. But, obviously, I didn't think that at the time.'

The two policemen had then effectively asked me the same questions over and over again in slightly different ways, and I had answered them each time identically, with patience and good grace.

Eventually, after more than an hour, they had been satisfied that I had nothing else to tell them and had gone away, but not before they'd had a close inspection of my car to see if there were any dents or scratches caused by Billy Searle's bicycle. So much for my alibi.

As soon as they had gone, I had rushed away from home, just making it to Sandown in time for the first race. I'd had to endure a few stares on my way into the racecourse, together with a few indelicate and abusive comments but, even so, it felt good to be in a familiar environment, as well as free in the fresh air.

It would have been better still if I'd been riding.

'Do you have any runners today?' I asked Jan. At least I could be certain that, this time, she hadn't come to the races just to see me.

'One in the big chase,' she said. 'Ed's Charger. Not much chance but the owner insisted.' She rolled her eyes up into her head and I laughed. 'Still got your sense of humour, then?'

'Why shouldn't I have?' I asked.

'Seems everyone you talk to gets themselves murdered or attacked. I hope it doesn't happen to me.'

So did I. She might have indeed been just about old enough to be my mother, but she was still a very attractive woman. Had I been a tad too hasty, I wondered, in turning down her offer?

Jan went into the Weighing Room to find the jockey who was riding her horse, while I leaned on the rail of the paddock and looked up Ed's Charger in the racecard. I noticed it was to be ridden by Mark Vickers, my client, and now, with Billy Searle out of the running, the Champion Jockey in waiting.

Billy's attempted murder had certainly been convenient for Mark's championship ambitions but I didn't really believe that the attack in Baydon had been arranged for that purpose. True, there had been the infamous incident when one Olympic ice skater had allegedly arranged for the leg of her rival to be broken, so as to better her own chances, but attempted murder was surely a step too far, if indeed that was what it had been. And there was the unanswered question of the hundred thousand pounds and, in particular, to whom it had been owed by Billy, and why.

'Hi, Foxy. Penny for your thoughts?' said a voice behind me and I groaned inwardly. Martin Gifford was the last person I wanted to see.

I turned round and forced a smile at him. 'Just working on my next murder,' I said. 'Do you fancy being the victim?'

Martin looked really worried for a fraction of a second before he realized I was joking.

'Very funny,' he said, regaining his composure. 'Tell me, what was it like being arrested?'

'A laugh a minute,' I said. 'And you didn't bloody help by telling the *Post* you thought I knew more about the Aintree killing than I was letting on. And why did you tell them that Herb Kovak was my best friend when I specifically told you he was only a work colleague?'

'I only told them what I believed to be true,' he said self-righteously.

'Bastard,' I said. 'You made it all up, and you know it.'

'Now, come on, Foxy,' he said. 'You weren't being completely honest with me. The truth, remember, the whole truth and nothing but the truth.'

'Bollocks,' I said forcefully. 'We were not in court, and what makes you think you have a divine right to know everything about everybody, anyway? You're the most indiscreet man on a racecourse. You couldn't keep a secret if your life depended in it.'

I knew as soon as I'd said it that it had been a mistake. Martin Gifford was all I'd said he was, but he was also the sort of person one needed to keep on one's side, and I'd probably just lost him as an ally for ever. But I didn't care. I'd had my fill of him over the years, and I looked forward to him not coming up every time he saw me and offering me a penny for my thoughts.

'Well, if that's what you think,' he said haughtily, 'you can bugger off.' And, with that, he turned and walked away with his nose held high. It had been a fairly weak riposte but no less accurate for that.

Jan came back out of the Weighing Room and over the grass to where I was standing. I watched her walk towards me with slightly renewed interest. She saw me looking at her and wiggled her hips.

'Changed your mind, then, lover-boy?' she said quietly as she came up close to me.

'No,' I said. But had I?

'Pity,' she replied. 'Are you sure you won't come over to my place for a ride?'

'I told you I couldn't. I can't take the chance with my neck.'

'Not that sort of ride, silly.' She smiled. 'I'd give you a ride where it wouldn't be your neck that would have to take its chances.' She leaned forward suggestively over the paddock rail, rubbing her bottom up against my leg.

'Jan, behave yourself!' I said.

'Why should I?' she asked, laughing. 'I'm a rich divorcée remember. By definition we're not meant to behave ourselves. Fancy a fuck?'

'Jan!' I said. 'Please stop it.'

'My,' she said, abruptly standing bolt upright next to me. 'I do believe you're embarrassed. What an old-fashioned strange boy you are.'

I was certainly old fashioned, but was I really strange?

Maybe I was, but did that mean I wanted Jan as a lover?

No, I suddenly decided, it did not.

I wanted Claudia.

My real reason for coming to Sandown had been to see Jolyon Roberts.

According to the morning paper, one of the horses running in the third race was owned by Viscount Shenington, and I hoped it was one of those he co-owned with his brother.

I looked out for Colonel Roberts on the grandstand during the first and second races but, unsurprisingly, I couldn't see him. The fine weather had helped to bring out a good Saturday crowd at Sandown for one of the very few mixed meetings of the year, that is where both flat and jumping contests were scheduled side-by-side on the eight-race card. Indeed, the first race of the day was a special one-mile flat race where jockeys from both codes raced against each other in a sort of Flat versus Jumping championship.

I went down to the parade ring before the third race and, sure enough, Jolyon Roberts was there, standing on the grass in the centre with a group of three other men and two ladies, none of whom I recognized.

I manoeuvred myself next to a gap in the rails through which I assumed the Roberts party would eventually need to pass, and waited.

He saw me when he was about five strides away and, if he was shocked or surprised, he didn't show it.

However, I did detect a very slight shake of the head as he looked me square in the eye.

As a true gentleman he stepped to the side to allow the others in his party to pass through the exit first.

'Chasers Bar after the sixth,' Jolyon Roberts said quietly but distinctly, and straight at me as he went through the gap, not breaking his Guard's step. I stood still and watched as he caught up one of the ladies and took her arm. He didn't look back at me. His words may have been softly spoken but his message had been crystal clear – 'Don't stop me now, I'll speak with you later, in private.'

I was in the Chasers Bar well ahead of him. In fact I watched the sixth race on one of the wall-mounted television sets so as to ensure I could get a table discreetly situated in the corner furthest from the door, and away from the bar.

I sat watching the entrance with two glasses of wine in front of me, one red and one white.

Jolyon Roberts appeared, stopped briefly to look around, then strode purposefully over and sat down opposite me.

'Sorry about this, sir,' I said. 'But I had no other way of contacting you.'

'What do you have to tell me?' he said.

'Drink?' I asked, indicating the wine.

'No thank you,' he said. 'I don't. Never have.'

'Something soft?' I asked.

'No, nothing, thank you.'

'What a shame about your horse,' I said.

It had fallen at the second hurdle and broken a leg.

'These things happen,' he said. 'My wife was more upset about it than me. To be honest it solved the problem of what to do with the damn thing. It couldn't have won the race if it'd started yesterday.' He chuckled loudly at his own joke, a habit I found slightly irritating. 'Now, tell me what you've found.'

'Nothing much, I'm afraid,' I said, taking a large sip of the white wine. 'Except that, if it is a fraud, it's a much bigger fraud than either of us thought.'

'In what way?' he asked.

'The factory project would seem to be only the key to a much bigger enterprise,' I said. 'The factory was to have cost about twenty million euros with your family trust putting in just over six million and getting European Union funding at the rate of two euros for each one of yours.'

He nodded. 'That's right,' he said. 'It was about five million pounds.'

'Yes,' I said. 'But it was the funding of the factory that triggered the grant for the housing project. And that was a whopping eighty million euros, without the need for any further private finance. So it was your investment that was the key to it all.' I paused. 'How did you hear about the investment opportunity in the first place?'

'I can't really remember,' he said. 'But it must have been through Gregory Black. Almost everything the trust invests in, other than the family estate, is done through Lyall and Black.'

'So was the naming of the factory Gregory Black's idea?'

'Oh, I can't remember,' he said. 'What does it matter? The important thing is whether or not the factory exists. That's what I'm most concerned about.'

'I haven't yet managed to find that out. Is there any chance I could speak with your nephew?'

Mr Roberts looked doubtful.

'I'd just like to ask him where he went and what he saw, or not as the case may be.'

'He's up at Oxford,' he said.

'Oxford University?' I asked.

Jolyon Roberts nodded. 'At Keble. Reading PPE. Thinks he wants to change the world. Bit full of himself, if you ask me.'

PPE was philosophy, politics and economics. I'd thought of applying for it myself but had opted instead for a degree course at the LSE.

PPE at Oxford was often seen as the first step on the political ladder to real power, both in British and foreign governments, and elsewhere. Alumni included such diverse members as three UK Prime Ministers, including David Cameron, the Nobel Peace Prize winning Burmese pro-democracy campaigner Aung San Suu Kyi, the media tycoon Rupert Murdoch, and the convicted IRA bomber Rose Dugdale. Even Bill Clinton had studied with the Oxford PPE class for a while when he was at the university as a Rhodes Scholar.

If Jolyon Roberts's nephew wanted to change the world he was starting at the right place.

'Do you have a telephone number for him?' I asked.

Jolyon Roberts seemed rather hesitant. 'Look,' he said, 'I'd much rather he wasn't involved.'

'But, sir,' I said, 'he is involved. You told me he was the one who started your concerns in the first place by visiting Bulgaria.'

'Yes,' he said, 'but my brother, his father, has told him to forget it.'

'Does your brother have any idea you have spoken to me?'

'Good God, no,' replied Mr Roberts. 'He'd be furious.'

'Sir,' I said formally, 'I think it might be best if I left you to sort out any further questions you might have with Gregory himself. I have rather gone out on a limb here to find out the small amount I have but I think it's time to stop. The Roberts Family Trust is our client in this matter and your brother is the senior trustee. I really should not act behind his back.' Nor behind Gregory's, I thought.

'No,' he said. 'Quite right. I can see that.' He paused. 'Sorry. Should have realized. I'll give Gregory Black a call about it on Monday.' He paused again. 'Right, matter closed as far as you're concerned. I'll trouble you no further.' He stood up, nodded at me briefly and walked out of the bar.

I sat there for a while longer and transferred my allegiance from white wine to red.

Had I done the right thing?

Definitely.

I was a financial adviser not a fraud investigator.

But what if there really was a hundred-million-euro fraud going on? Had I not a responsibility to report it to someone? But to whom? Perhaps I should send an e-mail to Uri Joram at the European Commission. But did I care?

I finished the red wine and decided it was time to head home.

Going home to Claudia had always filled me with excitement, raising the pulse a fraction and causing things to stir down below. But now, I was hesitant, even frightened of what I might find, of what I might hear, of what I might see.

Claudia was at home when I arrived back, and she'd been crying.

She tried to hide it from me but I could always tell. The slight redness of the eyes and the streaky mascara were dead giveaways.

'You could have phoned me,' she said crossly as I walked into the kitchen. 'You should know better than to sneak up on a girl.'

I'd hardly sneaked up, I thought. This was my home and I was arriving back from the races at six thirty on a Saturday evening.

'You can't phone on the Tube,' I said.

'You could have phoned on the train from Sandown.'

That was true, but the reason I hadn't was because I didn't want my call to go straight to voicemail again. That alone sent my imagination into overdrive. It was much better not to know if Claudia's phone was turned off.

'Now, darling, what's the matter?' I said, putting an arm round her shoulders.

'Nothing,' she said, shrugging me off. 'Just my back hurts. I'm going up to have a bath.'

She walked briskly out of the kitchen leaving me standing there alone. She had complained of backache a lot recently. Probably from too much lying on it, I thought somewhat ungraciously.

I mixed myself a large, strong gin and tonic. Not really a great idea after two glasses of wine at Sandown, but, who cares, I wasn't trying to make a riding weight for the next day's racing, more's the pity.

I could hear her bath running upstairs and, quite suddenly, I was cross. Did she think I was a fool? Something was definitely not right in this household and, painful as it might be, I had a right to know.

I thought about charging upstairs and confronting her in the bathroom, but I was frightened. I didn't want to lose her. And I'm not sure I could bear it if she said she was leaving me for someone else.

I walked through into the sitting room and flicked on the television but I didn't watch it. Instead I sat in an armchair feeling miserable, and drank my gin.

In due course, I heard the bathwater drain away and, presently, Claudia came downstairs and went into the kitchen, closing the door.

I really didn't know what to do. Did she want me to go in to her or not? Not, I thought, or she would have left the door open.

I stayed where I was in the sitting room and finished my drink. According to the clock on the mantelpiece it was twenty past seven.

Was it too early to go to bed?

I sat in the armchair while some teenage stick insect warbled away on the screen in a TV talent show, going over and over in my head what I needed to say to Claudia. Doing nothing was no longer an option.

If our relationship was dead, so be it. Let me mourn. Anything was better than remaining in this state of limbo with my imagination running wild, and my emotions in turmoil. I loved Claudia, I was sure of it. But, here I was, angry and hurt, accusing her in my mind of deceiving me and sleeping with another. It was time for the truth.

When I walked into the kitchen she was crying openly and with no pretence this time that she wasn't. She was sitting at the kitchen table in her blue towelling dressing gown, her elbows on the table, a glass of white wine in one hand and her head in the other. She didn't look up as I went in.

At least, I thought, she's not leaving me with a dismissive wave of the hand and not a single glance back. This break-up was going to be painful for both of us.

I went over to the worktop beside the fridge and poured myself another stiff gin and tonic. I was going to need it.

'Darling, what's the matter?' I said, but without turning round.

Perhaps it would be easier for her to talk if she couldn't see my face.

'Oh, Nick,' she said, her voice quivering slightly. 'There's something I have to tell you.' She gulped. 'And you're not going to like it.'

I turned round to face her. Maybe I didn't want to make it too easy for her after all.

She looked up at me.

'I'm so sorry,' she said.

I could feel the tears welling up in my own eyes. All I wanted to do was to hug her.

'I'm so sorry,' she said again. 'I've got cancer.'

10

How could I have been so wrong? And so stupid?

'What?' I said.

'Cancer,' she repeated. 'I've got ovarian cancer.'

'How?' I said foolishly. 'I mean . . . when?'

'I've sort of known for about two weeks, but I found out for certain on Thursday.'

'So why didn't you tell me?' I asked.

'I was going to but, to start with you were so busy at work. Then I was going to tell you on the night of the Grand National but there was all that Herb Kovak business. I thought you had enough of your own troubles. Then on Thursday . . .' She gulped. 'Thursday was an awful day. When I left the hospital after the doctor confirmed everything, I was sort of numb, couldn't feel anything, didn't even know where I was going.' She paused and wiped a tear from her cheek with the sleeve of her dressing gown. 'It was while I was walking aimlessly down Tottenham Court Road that Rosemary called to tell me you'd been arrested. It was all dreadful. Then you were so angry at having your name in the papers that, somehow, I couldn't tell you that night and . . . well, yesterday seemed so fraught between us and I thought it best to leave it because you had so much else on.'

'You silly gorgeous girl,' I said. 'Nothing is more important to me than you.'

I went round behind her and put my hands on her shoulders and rubbed them.

'So what do we do now?' I asked.

'I've got to have an operation on Tuesday.'

'Oh,' I said. Suddenly this was very real, and very urgent. 'What are they going to do?'

'Remove my left ovary,' she said, choking back more tears. 'And they might have to remove them both. Then I'll never be able to have a baby.'

Oh, I thought. Too real, and too urgent.

'And I know how much you want to have children,' Claudia said. 'I'm so sorry.'

The tears flowed freely again.

'Now, now,' I said, stroking her back. 'Your current health is far more important than any future children. You always said children were troublesome anyway.'

'I've been desperate,' she said. 'I thought you'd be so cross.'

'Don't be so silly. The only thing I'm cross about is that you didn't tell me straight away. It must have been dreadful for you, bottling it all up with no one to talk to.'

'My doctor has been wonderful,' she said. 'He gave me the name of a cancer counsellor.' She produced a crumpled business card from the pocket of her dressing gown. 'And she's been an absolute rock. I've called her so many times now, I know her number by heart.'

I looked at the business card. The number was the

much-called one I had copied from her mobile phone bill.

How, I asked myself again, could I have got things so wrong?

'Tell me,' I said. 'What did the doctor say?'

'I first went to my GP because I didn't feel very well and I could feel that my tummy was bloated.' She smiled. 'I actually thought I might be pregnant, but I'm on the pill, and I'd just had my period.'

'And?' I prompted.

'He asked me if I had any back pain, and I said yes, so he sent me to see a cancer specialist who did some scans and other tests and they came back positive.'

Back pain.

I inwardly chastised myself for my earlier thoughts.

'So what is actually wrong with your ovaries?' I asked.

'I have a tumour in the left one,' she said. 'It's what is apparently called a germ cell tumour.'

'Is it malignant?' I asked, dreading the answer.

'Yes, I'm afraid it is,' she said. 'But it's fairly small, about the size of a peanut.'

That didn't sound that small to me. I thought whole ovaries themselves were not much bigger than that.

'And the oncologist is hopeful that it hasn't spread. But he will find out for sure about that on Tuesday.'

'Where are you having the op?' I asked.

'University College Hospital,' she said. 'It's where I've been seeing the oncologist and having tests all this last week. I was there most of the day yesterday having

MRI scans so they know exactly to the millimetre where the cancer is and how big, ready for the operation.'

With her phone turned off.

'Overall, I've been lucky they found it so soon. Apparently it's quite usual for such tumours to go undetected until it's too late because many GPs dismiss the symptoms or confuse them with other problems.'

'What can I do to help?' I asked.

'Nothing,' she said. 'Just be here.' She smiled. 'I love you so much.'

I felt a fool, and a charlatan. How could I have been so stupid?

'I love you so much more,' I said, kissing the top of her head. 'Do you need to go to bed?'

'I'm not feeling ill,' she said, turning and looking up at me with a smile. 'Or were you thinking of something else?'

I blushed. It must have been the gin.

'I wasn't,' I said. 'However, I could be persuaded. But, I mean, are you all right?'

'For sex?' she said. I nodded. 'Absolutely. The oncologist told me on Thursday that it wouldn't make any difference.'

It made a difference to me.

I lay awake in the dark of the small hours trying to get my head round this new problem.

I had feared so much the thought of losing her to

another man that the news of the cancer had almost been a relief, a reprieve. But this was now a much more serious battle with the unthinkable outcome of losing her altogether if the fight was lost.

Claudia had gone to sleep around ten o'clock and I had then spent the next couple of hours at my computer researching ovarian cancer on the internet.

My initial results had been far from encouraging.

Overall, ovarian cancer five-year-survival rates were only about fifty per cent.

That was not good, I thought. It was like tossing a coin. To live, you had to correctly call 'heads'.

However, Claudia had said that the oncologist thought that the cancer hadn't spread. For Stage 1a ovarian cancers, those that were confined within the affected organ and which hadn't spread to its surface, the survival rate was nearly ninety-two per cent.

That was better.

Throw two dice: score eleven or twelve and you die, anything else you live.

For germ cell cancer the rates were even better. Women with only Stage 1a germ cell tumours had a near ninety-seven per cent chance of survival at five years.

Throw those dice again: you are dead now only with a double-six.

Slightly worse than the statistical survival rate for a space shuttle flight (ninety-eight per cent), much better than for a heart transplant (seventy-one per cent at five years).

I could hear Claudia's rhythmic breathing on the pillow next to me.

Funny, I thought, how it often takes a crisis to reveal one's true feelings. Since coming home from the races I had been through the whole gamut from resentful anger to perilous joy, with apprehension, fear and overwhelming love coming in late on the side.

I was exhausted by it all, but still I couldn't sleep.

How close had I come to making a complete fool of myself?

Too close. Much too close.

Sunday morning dawned bright and sunny, both in terms of the weather and my disposition.

I looked at Claudia soundly asleep beside me and, in spite of the uncertainty of her future treatment, I thanked my lucky stars. True, I had been tempted by Jan's extraordinary behaviour, but I had resisted. In fact, it had been Jan's very behaviour that had strengthened my resolve to sort out a problem with Claudia that, in the end, hadn't existed.

Suddenly the other problem, the coming battle against the cancer, while not easy, somehow seemed now manageable. Especially as Claudia and I would both be fighting on the same side.

I got up quietly, leaving her sleeping, and went downstairs to the kitchen, and to my computer.

I pulled up the e-mails from Uri Joram onto the screen

and read them again. I wondered what I should do about them.

A hundred million euros was an awful lot of money but it was a mere drop in the ocean compared to the European Union total budget of more than a hundred and twenty-five billion. But if the European Court of Auditors, the body that had refused to sign off the annual audit of the EU budget for each of the past umpteen years, had themselves been unable to make a single major fraud charge stick, what chance did I have?

I decided that it simply wasn't my fight. Claudia and I now had more pressing things on our minds. If Jolyon Roberts needed to ask any further questions about his investments, then he'd have to speak directly to Gregory.

I, meanwhile, turned to other matters, in particular, the copies of the statements from Herb's twenty-two credit cards.

I sorted them into date order and noticed that four of them were due for payment in the coming week. I wondered what the law was on outstanding credit card debt at death. One thing I was absolutely certain about was that none of the banks would, out of the kindness of their hearts, cancel their debt. But it was the interest that I was most concerned about. Ninety-four thousand, six hundred and twenty-six pounds and fifty-two pence would, if left unpaid, attract a substantial interest charge each month, not to mention late-payment fees, and it might take many months before probate was granted and I was able to pay off the debts from other assets in Herb's estate.

I had to find the cash.

Even the eighteen thousand he collected from the MoneyHome agents the week of his death would not be enough to pay off the four most urgent ones.

And that would not be all.

The ninety-seven separate individuals who were using Herb's accounts for their internet gambling and casino playing probably didn't know Herb was dead. If their past form was anything to go by, they would be racking up further charges.

All gambling requires a degree of trust, but surely Herb must have required an upfront cash advance from each of the ninety-seven in order to allow them to operate the system. That meant the debt of ninety-four thousand, six hundred and twenty-six pounds and fifty-two pence that existed on the credit cards statements may have only been the start of it. How much more did he owe?

I had to find the cash.

I decided that the very first thing I had to do was to cancel the cards so that no more charges could be made on them.

Each of the statements had a phone number on the back and I set about calling them. Many of them did not answer because they were not open on Sundays, and those that did were mostly in India and, in truth, could have been more helpful.

As soon as I said that Mr Kovak was dead, they all

required me to contact them in writing enclosing an original death certificate.

'Fine,' I said to one man called Ashwin, making a mental note to ask the police chief inspector for twenty-two originals of Herb's death certificate. 'But could you, in the meantime, make a stop on any future charges?'

'Cut up the cards,' Ashwin said, 'and then there can't be any more charges, can there?'

How, I wondered, should I explain to him that the cards themselves hadn't actually been present when any of the charges on the statements had been made?

'There are some regular payments,' I said. 'Where the card is not actually present for the transaction. Can't you stop those?'

'You will have to contact the payee,' he said unhelpfully.

All five hundred and twelve of them, I thought.

Next I tried impersonating Herb to cancel one card, but this didn't work either as I didn't have the card – it was in Hendon – and I had no idea of the expiry date, or the pin number. Anyway, I was firmly told, I couldn't cancel a card until I had paid off the outstanding balance.

Dead end.

I just had to find that cash.

Claudia came downstairs in her blue dressing gown.

'What are you doing?' she asked.

'Oh, nothing,' I said, closing the lid of my laptop onto the credit card statements. 'Nothing for you to worry about, anyway.'

'Look here,' she said, putting on a stern face, 'I told you my troubles so now you have to tell me yours.'

'It's just something to do with Herb Kovak,' I said. 'In his will he appointed me as his executor.'

'And what does that mean exactly?' she asked.

'It means,' I said, 'that I have to sort out all his bloody affairs when I should be looking after you.'

'Quite right,' she said, coming over and sitting on my lap. She put her arms round my neck. 'Naughty boy.'

I smiled.

Life was back to normal – or almost.

During the afternoon I called Detective Chief Inspector Tomlinson on the mobile number he had given me.

'Hello,' a voice said, sounding sleepy.

'Chief Inspector Tomlinson?' I asked.

'Hello, yes?' he said, this time more alert.

'Sorry to wake you,' I said. 'This is Nicholas Foxton.'

'Just resting my eyes,' he said. 'How can I help you?'

'I think it's me who's going to help you,' I said. 'Herb Kovak's sister has turned up.'

'Really,' he said. 'When?'

'Well, actually, on Thursday morning not long after you'd left his flat. But so much has been happening since then that I forgot to tell you.'

'Yes,' he said. 'I did hear that you've been kept rather busy.'

'Yes,' I agreed. 'Thank you for giving me an alibi.'

'You don't have to thank me,' he said. 'I simply told

them there was no way, short of using a helicopter, that anyone could travel the seventy miles from Baydon to Hendon in fifty-five minutes at that time of day. Especially someone who'd just had an ingrowing toenail removed. I could hardly walk with mine for weeks.'

I stifled a laugh. Good old Mrs McDowd and her fertile imagination.

'Well, thank you nevertheless,' I said. 'Now, I have some other information for you.'

'Yes?' he said.

'I think I may have solved the riddle of the credit cards.'

'Go on,' he said.

'I think that Herb Kovak was allowing other people to use his credit card accounts to gamble on the internet, probably fellow Americans because it's illegal to gamble in most states over there.'

'What evidence do you have?' he asked.

'Not much,' I said. 'But I think I'm right. There are five hundred and twelve different entries on those statements. But there aren't five hundred and twelve different individuals because many of them bet or play on more than one internet site.'

'Do you have any idea who these people are?'

'No,' I said. 'But we do have ninety-seven different sets of initials. They're on those sheets you showed me. I think they refer to ninety-seven different people.'

'So you're saying that you think ninety-seven different people, who all live somewhere in the United

States, were using Herb Kovak's credit card accounts to bet on the internet.'

'Yes,' I said. 'And to play online poker. I found some MoneyHome receipts that show Herb collected large amounts of cash during the week before he died. I believe that cash was to pay off some of the credit card debts.'

'And are you telling me this has something to do with why he was killed?'

'Not necessarily,' I said. 'I have no idea why he was killed. I thought that was your job.'

He didn't rise to my bait. There was just silence from his end.

'I've been trying to cancel the credit cards,' I said finally, 'but they all need an original death certificate. Can you get me some? I'll need at least twenty-two.'

'No death certificate has been issued as yet,' he said. 'All unnatural deaths are subject to an inquest, and that would usually follow any criminal trial. The death certificate would be issued only after the inquest was complete.'

'But that will be months, if not years, away,' I said with a degree of exasperation. 'There must be some official piece of paper that shows that he's dead. I need something to show the damn credit card companies.'

'As his executor, you can apply for probate before the death certificate is issued.'

'How?' I said. 'I've got nothing to show he's even dead.'

'The inquest was opened and adjourned last Tuesday,' he said. 'The Liverpool coroner will issue you with a letter. I'll arrange it.'

'Thank you.'

'So where can I find Mr Kovak's sister?' the chief inspector asked.

'At his flat, I think. She was there on Friday afternoon.'

'Right,' he said. 'Does she know her brother was murdered?'

'Yes,' I said. 'I told her.'

'Good. I'll be in touch so she can make an official identification.' Poor girl, I thought. 'Anything else?'

'Yes,' I said. 'Have you any idea who killed him?'

'Not as yet,' he said.

'Any leads at all?'

'No. None. The gunman seems to have disappeared completely.'

At least he was honest.

'How about the note I found in Herb's coat pocket?' I asked.

'Nothing to go on,' he said. 'The paper was just common copy-paper available from any stationer or office supply store, and the only discernible finger-prints were either yours or Mr Kovak's.'

'How could you tell?' I asked.

'We checked yours against the sample set you gave me, and I arranged for Mr Kovak's to be taken from his body.'

I wished I hadn't asked.

'So where do you go from here?'

'I think I had better take another look at those lists,' he said. 'And I want to see those MoneyHome receipts. I'll arrange to have them collected from your office.'

'I may not be in the office this week,' I said. 'Can you collect them from my home?' I thought for a moment. 'In fact, I have two receipts here but the three from last week are still at Herb's flat.'

'I may need to go and see Mr Kovak's sister. I'll call you back later when I know my movements.'

'Sherri,' I said.

'What?'

'Sherri,' I repeated. 'Sherri Kovak. Herb's sister. They were twins.'

'Oh,' he said.

Somehow, being twins made it worse.

Claudia and I went out to dinner at Luigi's, a local Italian restaurant, and managed to spend the whole meal talking without once mentioning the 'c' word.

We both skirted around it on purpose, like a game, but it did mean we discussed all sorts of other things, many of which we had bottled up over the past couple of weeks.

'My mother sends her love,' I said.

'Oh, thanks,' Claudia replied. 'How is she?'

I wanted to say she was in need of grandchildren, but I didn't. My mother would have to take her chances on Tuesday with the surgeon's knife, like the rest of us.

'Fine,' I said. 'She loves her little cottage and she's been busy with the local village historical society.'

'Perhaps we can go down and see her together,' Claudia said. 'After.'

After the operation, she meant.

'I'd better call Jan Setter in the morning and tell her we won't be able to make the opening night on Wednesday.'

'You can go on your own,' Claudia said. 'You'll enjoy it.'

Sitting next to Jan in a theatre all evening, with her hands wandering all over me in the darkness? No thanks.

'No,' I said. 'I'll tell her that neither of us will be there.'

Claudia smiled at me. I knew it was what she really wanted.

'It saved me buying a new dress anyway.'

We laughed.

That was the closest we came all evening to discussing her operation and, presently, I paid the bill and took my girl home to bed.

She had to go into the hospital the following evening ready for the surgery on the Tuesday morning. Hence our lovemaking was passionate and full-on, as if we both realized that this might be our last time together with Claudia as a fertile woman.

11

At nine a.m. sharp on Monday morning I called Patrick in the office.

'Am I forgiven yet?' I asked him.

'Gregory's not here today,' he replied. 'He's been away for the weekend and isn't back until tomorrow afternoon or Wednesday. I think it best if you stay away a while longer.'

I wasn't going to argue. Not having to be in the office over the next couple of days suited me very well.

'Can I now use the remote access facility?' I asked. 'Just to check that I'm not missing something that should be done today.'

The system allowed us to attach reminder notices to client files, for example to alert us to a maturing bond or a rights issue, so that we didn't miss an opportunity to invest the client's money most favourably.

'Of course,' Patrick replied.

Things had clearly mellowed over the weekend.

'So shall I plan on being in again on Wednesday?' I asked.

'Thursday might be better,' Patrick said, seemingly a little undecided. 'I'll speak to Gregory over lunch on Wednesday.'

'Thursday it is, then,' I said. 'Unless I hear from you sooner.'

'Right.' Patrick seemed rather distracted. 'There is a bit of a backlog with both you and Herb not being here. Diana and Rory will just have to cover everything until Thursday. I'll ask them to stay late.'

I smiled. I bet Rory wouldn't like that. There was no extra money for doing overtime in our job.

Detective Chief Inspector Tomlinson had called on Sunday evening to say he was travelling down from Liverpool, and to ask if could I meet him at Herb Kovak's flat at eleven the following morning. Yes, I'd said, I could.

In the end both Claudia and I went over to Hendon together in the Mercedes because she didn't want to be left alone, and I was delighted to have her with me.

The policeman was there ahead of us and he had been interviewing poor Sherri Kovak, who was clearly distressed by the experience. Her eyes were red from crying and she looked pale and drawn. Claudia went immediately and put her arm round Sherri's shoulders, even before they were introduced, taking her off into the kitchen.

'Thank you for coming,' the chief inspector said to me, shaking my hand. 'I'm sorry but I seem to have rather upset Miss Kovak.'

'How?' I asked.

'I told her that I needed her to come back with me

to Liverpool to carry out a formal identification of the body.'

I nodded. 'I feared you might. You would think it wouldn't be necessary to put people through such emotional trauma.' Especially, I thought, as one of the bullets that had killed him had entered through his face.

'I'm afraid the law takes little notice of people's feelings.'

'And you should know,' I said.

'Yes,' he said looking me in the eye. 'I certainly do.'

Claudia came back out into the hallway and I introduced her properly to Detective Chief Inspector Tomlinson.

'So, are you the man who arrested my Nick?' she asked accusingly.

'No, darling,' I said, springing quickly to the policeman's defence. 'This isn't the man who arrested me, this is the one who provided me with an alibi.'

'Oh,' she said. 'All right, then. You may live.'

The chief inspector smiled at her little joke, but he was there strictly on business.

'Now,' he said to me, getting down to it, 'where are these MoneyHome receipts?'

Claudia went back to Sherri in the kitchen while the chief inspector and I went through into the living room. I spread out the stuck-together little squares on Herb's desk. The chief inspector's eyebrows rose a notch.

'I found them torn up like this in the waste bin,' I

said. 'I stuck them together. There are three different payment slips here, one for eight thousand dollars and two for five thousand each.'

'And you say that Mr Kovak collected this money from a MoneyHome agent during the week before he was killed.'

'Yes,' I said. 'That's according to the stamps on them.'

'And do you know who sent him the money?'

'No,' I replied. 'MoneyHome apparently only require the recipient's name and something called the Money Transfer Control Number in order to pay out. The agent doesn't seem to know the sender's name.'

'These bloody money transfer companies,' he said. 'They seem to be absolutely determined to allow people to transfer money around the world completely anonymously. Cash in, cash out, no questions asked. They make it so easy for the villains, especially the drug dealers.'

'Can't you make them tell you who sent the money?' I asked.

'They probably don't know themselves,' he said. 'And if they do get a name it's probably false.'

'Butch Cassidy,' I said.

'Eh?'

'The recipient names on the payment slips,' I said. I added the two from my pocket to the three on the desk. 'Butch Cassidy, Billy Kid, Wyatt Earp, Jessie James and Bill Cody. It's not very difficult to spot they're false.'

'Were they the aliases used by Mr Kovak when he collected the money?' he asked, studying the slips.

'Yes,' I said.

I could see from his expression that the chief inspector immediately cast Herb as one of his villains.

'He wasn't a drug dealer,' I said. The chief inspector looked up at me. 'And he wasn't a crook. He was just allowing his fellow Americans to do what we in England can do quite legitimately every day.'

'Gambling is a mug's game,' he said.

'As maybe,' I agreed. 'But it's legal, taxed and, without it, there probably wouldn't be any horse racing. Certainly not the industry we have today.'

The policeman pursed his lips as if to say he didn't think it would be a great loss. I wondered if all policemen were born puritanical, or did it develop after several years in the job.

'Mr Kovak was still breaking the law.'

'Was he?' I asked. 'Whose law?'

'He was aiding and abetting others,' the chief inspector said with certainty.

I wasn't going to argue with him. I was pretty certain myself that, if the reports of the arrest of the CEO of the internet gambling site was anything to go by, Herb would have faced racketeering charges in the United States if they had known what he was up to.

I also showed the chief inspector the stack of unsigned credit cards but he seemed far more interested in the MoneyHome payment slips.

'So where do we go from here?' I asked.

'I will take these slips and try and get MoneyHome to at least divulge which of their offices the money was sent from. The transfer number should be enough to do that. Then we will have to painstakingly try to find out whose initials are on the sheets of paper.'

'You really think this must have something to do with Herb's murder?' I asked.

'Don't you?' he said. 'We've no other leads to go on. You never know, perhaps Mr Kovak was blackmailing one of his "clients", threatening to tell the US authorities about their illegal gambling. So they killed him.'

'There goes that suspicious mind of yours again, Chief Inspector.'

'Suspicion is all we have at the moment,' he said seriously. 'And there's precious little of that in this case.'

There was a heavy knock at the front door.

'That will be my sergeant,' the chief inspector said. 'He's come to drive Miss Kovak and me to Liverpool.'

Claudia and I watched them go.

'That poor girl,' Claudia said, holding my hand. 'Her family are all dead. She's alone in the world.'

At least she's healthy, I thought. How typical of my gorgeous Claudia to think of others when she had enough of her own troubles to worry about.

'Do you fancy going out to lunch?' I asked.

'Lovely,' she said.

'Luigi's again?'

'It's a bit unimaginative,' she said. 'But, why not? I like it there.'

I drove us home and we again walked round the corner to our favourite restaurant. On this occasion the proprietor, Luigi Pucinelli, was present.

'Ah, Signor Foxton and the lovely Signorina Claudia, *buongiorno*, welcome,' he said, being his usual effusive self. 'Table for two? *Bene*. Follow me.'

He showed us to our favourite table in the window.

'We don't often see you for lunch,' Luigi said in his Italian accent, adding an 'eh' to every word that ended in a consonant.

'No,' I said. 'It's a special treat.'

'*Eccellente*,' he said with a flourish, giving us the menus.

'*Grazie*,' I said to him, playing the game.

Luigi was no more Italian than I was. I had met his mother one night in the restaurant and she had told me with a laugh that Luigi Pucinelli had been born Jim Metcalf in a nursing home up the Tottenham High Road, not five miles away.

But good luck to him, I thought. The food and service at Luigi's were superb, and his restaurant thrived, authentic Italian or not.

Claudia chose the *antipasto* for us to share as a starter, with *saltimbocca alla pollo* to follow, while I decided on the *risotto al funghi*.

We ate the *antipasto* in silence.

'Speak to me,' Claudia said. 'This is not the last meal of the condemned, you know.'

I smiled at her. 'No, of course not.'

But we were both nervous.

Nervous of what tomorrow morning would bring.

I ordered a taxi to take us to the hospital that evening, at seven o'clock.

'Why do you need to go in the night before?' I asked Claudia as we made our way down the Finchley Road.

'Something about wanting to monitor me overnight before the operation so they have something to compare the readings with afterwards.'

'What time is the op in the morning?' I asked.

'The surgeon said it would be first thing, just as soon as he's finished his early-morning rounds.'

That meant it could be anytime, I thought.

In my experience, and I had plenty of it from my racing days, doctors and surgeons were about as good at time keeping as a London bus in the rush hour.

'At least we won't have to wait all day,' I said, smiling at her.

She gave me a look that said she would be quite happy to wait all year.

'It's better to get it done, and then at least we will know what we're up against.'

'I know,' she said. 'But I'm frightened.'

So was I. But now was not the time to show it.

'Everything will be OK,' I said, trying to sound reassuring. 'You said they've found it early, and I've researched everything on the internet. You're going to be just fine. You'll see.'

'Oh, Nick,' she said, grasping my hand very tight. There were tears in her eyes.

I pulled her close to me and we sat in silence as the taxi manoeuvred through Regent's Park and out onto the Euston Road.

It was a difficult evening, and night, for both of us.

Claudia was checked into the hospital by the admissions' staff, for whom it was a regular routine to be completed with brisk efficiency. They didn't mean to be uncaring but, quite a few times, they made us feel uncomfortable and even foolish.

I kept having to wait in the corridor outside her room as nurses and technicians came to perform some action or other. Swabs were taken from inside Claudia's nose and mouth, and others were then taken from more intimate areas. Blood was drawn for this, and urine was tested for that.

After a couple of hours they finally said that she was ready for the morning and they left us in peace. I turned off the bright overhead lights and dimmed the reading light to a much more subdued level. Suddenly everything did not look quite so stark and antiseptic. Much better.

I sat on a chair by her bed and held her hand.

'You ought to go home,' Claudia said. 'I'll be fine.'

'Unless they physically throw me out,' I said, 'I'm not going anywhere.'

Claudia laid her head back on the pillow and smiled. 'Good,' she said.

I still couldn't believe how badly I had read the situation between us. What a fool I had been, and what a greater fool I might have become. Just thinking about it brought me out in a cold sweat.

'You get some sleep now, my love,' I said to her. 'You'll need all the strength you can get for tomorrow.'

'This bloody bed is so hard. It makes my back ache.'

I spent a few minutes using the electric bed control, lifting the head or feet, trying to make her more comfortable. It didn't really work.

'Why can't they have bloody beds that are comfortable to lie on?' Claudia complained. 'You'd think that would be the first priority.'

I recognized what was happening. She was getting irritated by the slightest little thing. It was a sign of the nervous condition she was in. I would just have to smile gently and agree with her.

'Yes, darling,' I said. 'Please try and close your eyes and get some rest.'

'You try resting on this bloody thing,' she snapped, turning herself over once again to face away from me.

In the end she settled and, in time, I could tell from the sound of her breathing that she was asleep. I settled down into the chair and closed my eyes.

One of the nurses came into the room and snapped on the overhead lights.

'Time for your vitals,' she said loudly.

And so it went on through the night, with temperature, pulse and blood pressure being measured at two-hourly intervals, each time accompanied by the

Blackpool illuminations. Hospitals were clearly never designed for relaxation and recovery.

No one told me to go home, so I didn't, although I had to admit, it was not the best night's sleep I'd ever had.

Breakfast wasn't eaten by Claudia, or even offered, there being a large NIL BY MOUTH sign hanging on a hook by the door, so I went down to the hospital lobby at about six a.m. in search of a coffee and a bun for myself, while the patient had a shower.

At about eight thirty Mr Tomic, the surgeon, arrived wearing light blue scrub tunic and trousers, all set for the operating theatre. He brought with him some paperwork and a thick permanent marker pen, which he used to draw a big black arrow on the left side of Claudia below her belly button.

'Don't want to take out the wrong one now, do we,' he said.

It somehow wasn't very encouraging.

'What exactly are you going to do?' I asked.

'I will make two small incisions here and here.' He pointed to each side of Claudia's lower abdomen. 'I will then use a laparoscope to have a good look at all her bits, and then I'll remove the left ovary completely,' he said. 'I also plan to take a wedge biopsy of the right ovary.'

'And what is a wedge biopsy exactly?' I asked.

'A small sample that is removed, like a tiny bite, which is then tested to see if it's clear,' he said. 'Then I will sew everything up and Claudia will be back here before you know it. About two hours in total, maybe a fraction more.'

'And if the biopsy's not clear?' Claudia asked.

'If I can tell that straight away just by looking,' the surgeon said, 'then I'll have to remove that ovary as well, otherwise the biopsy will be sent to the lab for tests. There is a slight chance that I may also need to perform a complete hysterectomy if I find cancer cells attached to the uterus. But I think from the scans that that will be most unlikely.'

Claudia looked at me with rising panic in her eyes.

Mr Tomic spotted it. 'Claudia,' he said, 'I promise you I will do as little as possible. But we have to deal with this. It won't go away on its own. I have to tell you everything that might happen because I need your consent to proceed. You will understand that I can't wake you up half-way through the operation to ask your permission to remove your womb if I need to do it in order to save your life.' He smiled at her. 'But I really don't think it will come to that.'

'Can't you just remove the tumour?' I asked. 'Do you have to take the whole ovary?'

'The tumour will probably have taken over most of the ovary and it is the only way of ensuring it doesn't return.'

'If the second ovary is clear, does that mean it will remain so?' I asked.

'Let's cross one bridge at a time,' he said. 'We'll discuss the future after the operation.'

I took that to mean 'no', it probably wouldn't remain clear.

My mother's wish for grandchildren was not looking too promising.

'Right, then,' said Mr Tomic, 'I need you to sign here.' He pointed. 'And here. And here.'

Claudia looked at me in despair. I pursed my lips and nodded at her. She signed the papers. What choice did we have?

'OK,' said the surgeon, taking back the forms from her. 'I'll see you in theatre in about twenty minutes. Wait here, they'll come for you.'

I wanted to tell him to be careful with my girl, but I didn't. Of course he'd be careful. Wouldn't he?

If the previous evening had been bad, the next twenty minutes were intolerable.

Mr Tomic had left the door open and every time someone walked down the corridor outside, we both jumped.

What was there to say? Nothing. We both just watched the clock on the wall move inexorably round from eight fifty to nine o'clock, then ever onwards to nine five and nine ten.

Claudia held on to my hand as if her life depended on it.

'It'll be all right,' I said. 'You heard what he said, you'll be back in here before you know it.'

'Oh, Nick,' she said miserably, 'if I come out of this with only a tiny piece of an ovary left, let's use it to have kids.'

'OK,' I said. 'You're on.'

'Marry me first?' she asked.

'You bet,' I said.

It was an unusual proposal, but we were in an unusual situation.

At nine fifteen a theatre porter arrived wearing blue scrubs and a J-cloth hat.

'Please be careful with my fiancée,' I said to him as he wheeled her bed out of the room into the corridor. 'She's very precious to me.'

I went with her to the lift, where the porter said he was sorry, but I couldn't come any further. I looked at Claudia's frightened face until the closing lift doors cut off our line of sight, and all too quickly she was gone.

I went back into her room and sat down on the chair.

Never before had I felt so desperate, so helpless, and alone.

In truth, it was not a great start to an engagement.

Claudia didn't come back for nearly three hours, by which time I was almost crawling up the walls of her room with worry.

Sitting alone in that hospital room had been far worse than spending three times as long in a cell at Paddington Green Police Station.

I spent some time going over in my mind what must be happening downstairs in the operating theatre, mentally carving up the clock face into segments. First I tried to imagine how long it would take for Claudia to be put to sleep; then how long to make the incision in her body; next how long to remove the ovary, and so on. I had no idea if I was right or not, or even if I was close, but it seemed to help.

My mental calculations, however, had her coming back to the room in two hours and, when she didn't, my imagination went into overdrive, envisaging all sorts of horrors. While the clock on the wall went on ticking, as if mocking me. And still Claudia didn't return.

By the time I finally heard her being wheeled back along the corridor, I had convinced myself that the whole thing had gone horribly wrong and Claudia had died on the operating table.

But she wasn't dead, she was just cold, and shivering uncontrollably.

I was so pleased to see her but she was not a happy bunny, not at all. She was sore from the surgery and feeling nauseous from the anaesthetic. And she couldn't stop the shivering.

'It's quite normal,' said a nurse curtly when I asked about it. 'She'll be fine soon.'

'Can she please have another blanket?' I asked.

Reluctantly she agreed and, in time, the shivering did abate and Claudia relaxed and, eventually, she went to sleep.

*

Mr Tomic came to see us at about two o'clock while Claudia was still sleeping.

'I have some good news and not quite such good news,' he said to me quietly. 'Firstly, the good news is that I removed only one ovary and the other one looked perfectly fine, although I took a piece for a biopsy and it's currently being assessed in the path lab.'

'And the not-so-good news?' I asked.

'The tumour was not quite fully contained in the ovary as we had thought, and it had erupted on the surface. It's often difficult to tell precisely from the scans.'

'And what exactly does that mean?' I said.

'It means there is every likelihood that there will be some ovarian cancer cells present in the fluid within the abdominal cavity. We will know for sure when the lab tests are complete.'

'And?' I said.

'In order to be sure we've killed off the cancer completely, I think a course or two of chemo will probably be needed.'

'Chemotherapy?' I said.

'I'm afraid so,' he replied. 'Just to be sure.'

'Does that mean I'll lose my hair?' Claudia asked. Her eyes were closed and I hadn't realized she'd been awake, and listening.

'It might,' he said, 'although the drugs are much better than they used to be.' I took that to mean yes, she would lose her hair. 'But even so, it will grow back.'

Claudia's long, flowing, jet-black hair was her pride and joy.

'Does the chemo start straight away?' I asked.

'Within a few weeks,' he said. 'We'll give Claudia time to recover from the surgery first.'

'Will it affect the other ovary?' I asked. 'I read on the internet that some cancer drugs made women infertile.'

'The drugs used are very powerful,' he said. 'They work by attacking cells that divide rapidly, like cancer cells, but they do tend to affect everything in the body to some degree. Am I to assume that preserving fertility is a priority?'

'Yes,' said Claudia unequivocally, still not opening her eyes.

'Then we will just have to be very careful,' he said. 'Won't we?'

At three thirty in the afternoon I left Claudia resting in the hospital while I went home to change and have a shower, taking the Northern Line tube from Warren Street to Finchley Central.

'I won't be long,' I told her. 'About an hour and a half. Is there anything I can get you?'

'A new body,' she said miserably.

'I love the one you have,' I said, and she forced a smile.

The doctor had told us that she would have to stay in hospital for another night but she should be able to go home the following day, or on Thursday at the latest.

The sun was shining as the tube train rose from the dark tunnels into the daylight just before East Finchley

Station. It was always a welcome sign. It meant I was nearly home.

As I walked down Lichfield Grove I could see that there was a man standing outside my house with his finger on the doorbell. I was about to call out to him when he turned his head slightly, as if looking over his shoulder.

In spite of telling the police that I hadn't seen Herb's killer at Aintree, I knew him instantly. Here he was standing outside my front door in Finchley, and I didn't think he was visiting to enquire after my health.

My heartbeat at once jumped to stratospheric proportions and I stifled the shout that was already rising in my throat. I started to turn away from him but not before our eyes had made contact, and I had glimpsed the long black shape in his right hand: his trusty gun, complete with silencer.

Bugger, I thought.

I turned and ran as fast as I could back up Lichfield Grove towards Regent's Park Road.

Lichfield Grove may have been used as a busy short-cut during the rush hour but it was sleepy and deserted at four o'clock in the afternoon with not even any schoolchildren on their way home.

Safety, I thought, would be where there were lots of people. Surely he wouldn't kill me with witnesses. But he had killed Herb with over sixty thousand of them.

I chanced a glance back, having to turn my upper body due to the restricted movement in my neck. It was a mistake.

The gunman was still behind me, only about thirty yards away, running hard and lifting his right arm to aim.

I heard a bullet whizz past me on my left.

I ran harder and also I started shouting.

'Help! Help!' I shouted as loudly as my heaving lungs would allow. 'Call the police!'

No one shouted back, and I needed the air for my aching leg muscles. Oh to be as fit as I once was as a jockey.

I thought I heard another bullet fly past me and zing off the pavement ahead as a ricochet, but I wasn't stopping to check.

I made it unharmed to Regent's Park Road and went left round the corner. Without breaking stride I went straight into Mr Patel's newsagency, pushed past the startled owner and crouched down under his counter, gasping for air.

'Mr Patel,' I said. 'I am being chased. Please call the police.'

I didn't know why, perhaps it was because of his cultural background, but he didn't become angry or question why I had invaded his space. He simply stood quietly and looked down at me, as if in slight surprise at the strange behaviour of the English.

'Mr Patel,' I said again with urgency, still breathing hard. 'I am being chased by a very dangerous man. Please do not look down at me or he will know that I am here. Please call the police.'

'What man?' he said, still looking down at me.

'The man outside the window,' I said. Mr Patel looked up.

Suddenly I remembered that I had my mobile in my pocket. As I dialled 999 I heard the shop door being opened, the little bell ringing once.

I held my breath. I could feel my heart going thump, thump in my chest.

'Emergency, which service?' said a voice from my phone.

I stuffed the phone into my armpit, hoping that the newcomer into the shop hadn't heard it.

'Yes?' said Mr Patel. 'Can I help you, sir?'

The newcomer made no reply and I went on holding my breath, my chest feeling like it was going to burst.

'Can I help you, sir?' Mr Patel said again but more loudly.

Again there was no reply. All I could hear were faint footsteps.

I just had to breathe so I let the air out through my mouth as quietly as I could, and took another deep breath in.

I wished I could see what was happening in the shop. After a few seconds I heard the door close, ringing the bell once again, but was the gunman on the inside or the outside?

Mr Patel stood stock still above me giving me no indication either way.

'He has gone outside,' he said finally, without changing his position.

'What's he doing?' I asked.

'He is standing and looking around,' Mr Patel said. 'Who is he and why is he chasing you? Are you a criminal?'

'No,' I said. 'I am not.'

I remembered the phone under my arm. The operator had obviously got fed up waiting and had hung up. I dialled 999 again.

'Emergency, which service?' said a voice again.

'Police,' I said.

'Police incident room, go ahead,' said another voice.

'There's an armed gunman in the street on Regent's Park Road in Finchley,' I said quickly.

Mr Patel looked down at me.

'Mr Patel,' I said urgently. 'Please do not look down. The man might see you, and come back into the shop.'

'What number Regent's Park Road?' said the voice on the phone.

'Near the corner of Lichfield Grove,' I said. 'Please hurry.'

'Your name, sir?' said the voice.

'Foxton,' I said into the phone. 'Mr Patel, what is the man doing now?'

'He is walking away. No. He has stopped. He is looking back. Oh, goodness gracious, he is coming back this way.'

Mr Patel leaned down, grabbed some keys from a hook under the counter, and walked out of my sight.

'What are you doing?' I called after him urgently.

'Locking the door,' he said.

I didn't have time to think whether it was a good idea or not before I heard Mr Patel turn the key in the lock. Now the gunman would be sure where I was. And I could hear the door being shaken.

'Mr Patel,' I shouted, 'get away from the door. The man has a gun.'

'It is all right, Mr Foxton,' he said with a laugh. 'It is not him shaking the door, it is me. The man has gone past. I cannot see him any more.'

It didn't mean he wasn't there so I stayed exactly where I was. My heart rate may have come down a few notches but, as far as I was concerned, it was still no laughing matter.

'Now, Mr Foxton, why is a man with a gun chasing you? It is like a film, no?'

'No,' I said. 'This was very real life. He was trying to kill me.'

'But why?' he said.

It was a good question. A very good question.

I remained sitting on the floor behind Mr Patel's counter until the police arrived. It took them nearly forty minutes and I had telephoned 999 again twice more before two heavily armed and body-armoured officers finally made an appearance at the shop door. Mr Patel let them in.

'About time too,' I said, standing up from my hiding place.

'Mr Foxton?' one of the officers asked, his machine

pistol held at the ready position with his finger over the trigger.

'Yes,' I said. 'That's me.'

'Are you armed, sir?'

'No,' I said.

'Please put your hands on your head,' he said, pointing his gun towards me.

'It's not me who's the gunman,' I said, slightly irritated. 'It was the man who was chasing me.'

'Put your hands on your head,' the policeman repeated with a degree of menace. 'And you, sir,' he said, pointing his gun briefly towards Mr Patel.

We both put our hands on our heads. Mr Patel smiled broadly as if he thought the whole thing was a huge joke.

The second officer came forward and searched me, making sure he didn't get between my chest and the muzzle of his colleague's weapon. He then did likewise to Mr Patel. Then he went through the shop and out of sight through a plastic curtain into the room behind. He soon reappeared, shaking his head. Only then did they relax a little.

'Sorry about that, sir,' said the first officer, securing his gun across his chest with a strap. 'We can't be too careful.'

I put my arms down. 'What took you so long to get here?'

'We had to seal off the whole area,' he said. 'Standard practice when there's a report of a gunman.' He put his finger to his ear, clearly listening to someone on his personal radio earpiece. 'Now, sir,' he said to me, 'my superintendent wants to know if you have a description of this gunman.' His tone suggested that he didn't altogether believe that a gunman had been stalking the streets of Finchley on a sleepy Tuesday afternoon in late April.

'I think I may have better than that,' I said. 'Mr Patel, does your closed-circuit TV system have a recorder?' I had passed some of my time waiting for the police by looking up at the small white video camera situated above the racks of cigarettes.

'Of course,' Mr Patel replied. 'I need to have it to catch the young scoundrels who steal my stock.'

'Then, officer,' I said, 'please would you kindly inform Detective Chief Inspector Tomlinson of the Merseyside Police that we have the murderer of Herb Kovak caught on video.'

But how had he known where to find me? And why?

12

In the end, it was I who rang Chief Inspector Tomlinson, but not before the Armed Response Team had completed a full debrief of the events in Finchley.

'So you say you saw a man standing outside your front door?' asked the response team superintendent as we stood in Mr Patel's shop.

'Yes,' I said. 'He was ringing the doorbell.'

'And he had a gun?'

'Yes,' I said again, 'with a silencer.'

There was something about his demeanour that said that he, too, didn't really believe me. Mr Patel hadn't seen any gun nor, it seemed, had anyone else.

'He shot at me,' I said. 'As I ran up Lichfield Grove. He shot at least twice. I heard the bullets whizz past my head.'

A team was despatched to search and, in due course, one of them returned with two empty brass cases in a plastic bag.

Suddenly everything became more serious. They believed me now.

'You will have to come to the police station,' said the superintendent. 'To give a statement.'

'Can't I do it here?' I asked.

'I need to reopen my shop,' said Mr Patel anxiously.

'At my house, then?' I asked. 'I need to get back to University College Hospital. My girlfriend had an operation this morning and she's expecting me.'

Reluctantly the superintendent agreed to do it at my house and we walked down Lichfield Grove together. The road had been closed to traffic and about a dozen police officers in dark blue boiler-suits were moving up the road in line abreast, crawling on all fours.

'Looking for the bullets,' the superintendent informed me before I asked. 'Don't touch the door,' he said as we arrived at my house, 'or the doorbell.'

I carefully opened the door with my key and we went into the kitchen.

'Now, Mr Foxton,' the superintendent said formally, 'tell me why a gunman would come calling at your front door.'

It was the question I'd been asking myself for the past hour.

'I'm sure he was here to kill me,' I said.

'That's very dramatic. Why?'

Why, indeed, when he could have done it so easily at Aintree at the same time as he killed Herb. What, I wondered, had changed in the intervening ten days that meant that I needed to be killed now but hadn't needed to be then?

I told the superintendent all about the murder at the Grand National and it was then that I again suggested calling DCI Tomlinson.

'My goodness, Mr Foxton,' the chief inspector said

down the wire with a laugh. 'You seem to be making a habit of being interviewed by the police.'

'I can assure you it's a habit I intend to give up at the earliest opportunity,' I replied.

The two senior policemen then spoke together for some time and it was frustrating for me listening to only one half of the conversation. Mostly they spoke about the video tape that the superintendent had removed from Mr Patel's recorder. The superintendent and I had watched it on the small black-and-white screen in the storeroom behind the shop. Just seeing the grainy image of the man as he had come through the shop door made the hairs on the back of my neck stand upright. He had advanced a couple of paces in and stood there, looking around. Then he had walked down the length of the shop, putting his head through the plastic curtain into the storeroom behind. He then retraced his steps and went out of the door, closing it behind him. Unfortunately the angle of the CCTV camera didn't show what he did next. And none of the images showed his gun, which he must have been holding in his anorak pocket.

I shivered. How close had I come to hiding in the back room? Very close.

'Chief Inspector Tomlinson would like another word,' the superintendent said to me finally, handing over the phone.

'Yes,' I said.

'Can you think of any reason why someone would want you killed?'

'No, I can't,' I said. 'And, if they did, why wait until now? Why not do it at Aintree at the same time as killing Herb Kovak? Something must have changed since then.'

'But what?' he said. 'Have you been trying to find out whose initials are on those sheets?'

'No, I haven't. I did go into a MoneyHome agent and ask about the payslips, but that was last Friday.'

'Leave the investigating to the professionals, Mr Foxton,' said the chief inspector somewhat formally.

I think I was being told off.

'But if I hadn't,' I said in my defence, 'then you wouldn't know that it was other Americans who were gambling using Mr Kovak's credit cards.'

'We still don't know that for certain,' he said.

Maybe not, I thought, but I was sure I was right.

'So how are you going to catch this guy?' I asked him. 'And before he succeeds in killing me?'

'Superintendent Yering will issue an immediate alert to all stations, including the airports and ports, with the man's image from the tape. And we will be approaching the TV stations to run the video clip in their news broadcasts.'

It didn't sound sufficiently proactive to me.

'Haven't you got some mug shots or something for me to look at?' I asked. 'I have to tell you I don't feel very safe with this guy still out there on the loose.'

'You had better ask Superintendent Yering,' he said.

So I did but he wasn't very forthcoming.

'We have literally tens of thousands of mug shots,' he said. 'It would take you weeks to look through them all, and our man may not even be there. We need something else to point us in the right direction first, then it might be worthwhile. Perhaps we'll get a fingerprint from your doorbell. Be patient, Mr Foxton. The video image is good and it should bear dividends when it's shown on the news.'

If I lived that long, I thought.

'Can't you provide me with some police protection?' I asked. 'In a safe house, or something?'

'MI5 might have safe houses but we don't,' he said with a smile. 'You've been watching too much TV.'

'But someone is trying to kill me,' I said in frustration. 'Surely it's your job to prevent that. I need some protection.'

'I'm sorry,' he said. 'We simply don't have the manpower.'

They had the manpower, I thought, to have a dozen officers crawl along the road on their hands and knees looking for a bullet, but not enough to prevent a future murder. It was crazy.

'So what am I to do?' I asked him. 'Just sit here and wait to be killed?'

'Perhaps it wouldn't be sensible to stay here,' he conceded. 'Have you anywhere else to go to?'

My home and my office were now off limits. Where else?

'I'm going to go back to the hospital to see my girlfriend,' I said.

Some of the Armed Response Team agreed to wait in my house while I belatedly had a shower and changed my clothes. I then threw some things into a suitcase, including my computer, and set off for the hospital in the back of one of their police vans.

'It's the least we can do,' they said.

At one point I insisted that the police driver go right round the big roundabout at Swiss Cottage to make sure we were not being followed.

We weren't, of course. What sort of killer would follow a van full of heavily armed police? But what sort of killer would gun a man down with sixty thousand witnesses close to hand? Or try to kill someone on their own front doorstep?

I couldn't help but think of Jill Dando, the British TV personality, gunned down in exactly that way in a Fulham street.

And her killer has never been identified.

Claudia was still resting when I made it back to her room in the hospital. She was neither aware nor surprised that I had been away for nearly four hours, and not the one and a half I'd promised.

I had made it unmolested and alive from the police van outside the hospital main door to her room, but not without a nervous glance at every person I met on the way. I nearly had heart failure when, just as the lift doors were closing, a man jumped through the gap who slightly resembled my would-be killer.

If I went on like this I'd be a nervous wreck in no time.

I closed the door to Claudia's room but, of course, there was no lock on the inside.

It made me feel very uneasy.

I thought it unlikely that the gunman would give up just because he'd lost me once. I imagined he was a professional assassin and, like most professionals, he would take pride in completing his job.

Bugger the police, I thought. I felt so vulnerable. I believed absolutely that I needed some protection or else I'd wind up dead. Maybe I might be killed even if I had a bodyguard, but at least it would make me feel a little safer. However, Mrs Gandhi, the Indian Prime Minister, had been shot dead by one of her bodyguards so armed protection wasn't always the best policy.

What should I do?

I couldn't hide for ever. But what was the alternative? Perhaps I should buy a bulletproof vest.

My main objective had to be to find out who was trying to have me killed and stop them, or at least remove the need, as they saw it, for my life to be terminated.

Easy.

But why would anyone want me dead? It seemed a very extreme solution to any problem.

I must know something, or have something, that someone didn't want me to tell or show to somebody else. Hence I needed to be killed to prevent it.

So what was it that I had, or knew?

The police already had the credit card statements and the MoneyHome payment slips, so surely it couldn't be them. Was there something else I had inherited from

Herb that was so incriminating that murder was the only answer?

Claudia groaned a little and woke up.

'Hello, my darling,' I said. 'How are you feeling?'

'Bloody awful,' she said. 'And really thirsty.'

I poured some water from the jug on her bedside cabinet into a plastic glass and held it out to her.

'Just go easy,' I said. 'The nurse said to drink just small sips.'

She drank several large ones and then handed back the glass.

'I feel so sore and bloated,' she said.

'Mr Tomic said you might. It'll pass in a day or so.'

She didn't seem much reassured.

'Can you help me sit up a bit?' she asked. 'I'm so uncomfortable in this bloody bed.'

I did as she asked, but it didn't really improve matters. Nothing would, I realized, for as long as she was in pain.

'Let's get you some painkillers,' I said and pushed the nurse call bell.

They gave her an injection of morphine that deadened the pain but also sent Claudia back to sleep. It was probably the best thing for her.

I put on the television to watch the news, but I kept the sound down to a minimum so as not to disturb the patient.

The gunman in a London newsagent's was the lead story and, true to their word, the police had convinced the TV company to play the whole video clip of Herb's killer coming into the shop, looking around, and then leaving again. They even showed a blown-up still of the man's face as he had glanced directly up at the camera.

Just looking at his image made me nervous once more.

The news reporter then warned the viewers not to approach the man if they saw him but to report his presence to the police. The man is armed and very dangerous, the reporter said, but he didn't mention anything about Herb Kovak or the killing at Aintree.

Did the news report and the video make it safer for me or not?

I also wondered if it put Mr Patel at risk. After all, he was the one who'd had the best view of the gunman. I suddenly went quite cold just thinking about how much mortal danger I had placed Mr Patel in by hiding behind his counter. But what else could I have done? Stayed out in the street and been killed?

I switched over to another channel and watched the whole thing once more, trying my best to recognize the face staring out at me from the screen. I knew I didn't know him, other than at Aintree and in a Finchley street, but I tried to find some semblance or likeness. There was none.

Thankfully, Claudia slept soundly through both bulletins. She had enough worries on her own plate for the time being without being burdened with something else. After all, there was nothing she could do about it.

While she went on sleeping, I tried to work out

where I could spend the night. I wasn't going back to Finchley, that was for sure, but a second night sitting upright in the chair in Claudia's hospital room wasn't a very attractive proposition either.

As I still had the key in my pocket, I thought of going to Herb's flat in Hendon but I didn't want to turn up there late at night frightening Sherri after her traumatic trip to Liverpool. So, instead, I used my phone to find a cheap room near the hospital in a hotel located round the corner in Euston Square Gardens. They had plenty of availability so I didn't leave my name. I just planned to turn up there when I left the hospital. That somehow seemed safer.

One of the nurses came into Claudia's room to take, once more, her vital signs and to settle her for the night. I took it as my cue to leave.

'Night night, my darling,' I said. 'I'll be back in the morning.'

'What about your job?' she said sleepily.

'I'll call the office and tell them I'm not coming in,' I said. 'The work will have to wait.'

She smiled and laid her head back on the pillow. She looked very vulnerable with her pale face almost matching the slight greyness of the hospital linen. We had to beat this impostor within her body, this cancer that would eat away at our happiness. If chemotherapy was what was needed, so be it. Short-term discomfort for long-term gain, that was what we had to think, what we had to believe.

*

I checked in to the hotel using a false name, and I paid for the room in advance with cash that I had drawn from an ATM in Euston Station. As the superintendent had said, I'd probably been watching too much TV, and I didn't really believe for a minute that the gunman had access to my credit card accounts, but I was taking absolutely no chances.

I had left the hospital by the main door only because there were no dark shadowy corners as there were outside the back entrance, but not before I had stood for a while behind a pillar watching the road, checking for anyone lurking in wait for me with a silenced pistol.

And I hadn't left the building alone, but had waited for a group of cleaning staff going off duty.

No one had fired a shot or come running after me. But would I even know if they did? I was certain Herb had been dead at Aintree before he realized what was happening.

I locked my bedroom door and then propped a chair under the door handle for good measure. I then relaxed a little and ate the takeaway cheeseburger, fries and milkshake that I'd bought from a late-night burger bar in the railway station.

It was the first thing I'd eaten all day. My mother would not have been pleased.

I removed my computer from my bag and logged on to the internet to check my e-mails.

Amongst the usual bunch from various fund managers wanting me to contact them about their latest investment offering was one from Patrick expressing his disquiet over recent happenings both inside and outside the office.

It hadn't been addressed solely to me but had been sent to all the Lyall & Black staff, but it felt like I was the main target.

'Dear colleagues,' Patrick had written, 'At this time of seemingly major upheaval within the firm, it is important for us all to concentrate on why we are here. While we are, of course, greatly saddened by the tragic loss of Herb Kovak, it is our clients who we are here to serve. It is they who pay our salaries and we must not give them cause to look elsewhere for their investment advice. We need to conduct our personal affairs with the highest degree of probity, and not give them any reason to doubt our honesty and integrity. I am sure that you will be asked by clients to speculate concerning the reason for Herb's untimely death, as well as on the nature of it, and on the other unfortunate event that occurred in these offices last Thursday. I ask that you refrain from any comments that may in any way place Lyall & Black in a bad light. If in doubt, please refer the clients to Mr Gregory or myself.'

I assumed that the 'other unfortunate event' referred to was my arrest.

It made me wonder how Billy Searle was faring in hospital and whether the police had made any progress in finding his attacker. Claudia's cancer revelation and her operation, coupled with the minor matter of finding an assassin on my doorstep, had kept my mind somewhat occupied elsewhere.

I went on to the *Racing Post* website.

'Billy Searle,' it said, 'was reported to be making steady progress. In fact, doctors at the Great Western Hospital in Swindon are amazed by the swiftness of his recovery from what were thought to be life-threatening injuries.'

They shouldn't really be surprised, I thought. Jump jockeys were made tough, and a breed apart from normal human beings. Broken bones and concussion were accepted as normal hazards of their employment, to be endured and recovered from as quickly as possible. All jockeys were self-employed – no rides meant no pay. It was a powerful incentive for quick healing.

There was nothing in the report about his attacker other than the stated hope that Searle would soon be able to be interviewed by the detectives investigating the incident about the identity of his assailant.

I wondered, meanwhile, if Billy was getting police protection.

The night passed without incident although I lay awake for much of it half-listening for someone climbing the drainpipe outside my bedroom window with gun in hand, and murder in mind.

I also spent the time thinking.

In particular I spent the time thinking about the note I had found in Herb's coat pocket. I knew the words of it by heart.

YOU SHOULD HAVE DONE WHAT YOU WERE TOLD. YOU MAY SAY YOU REGRET IT, BUT YOU WON'T BE REGRETTING IT FOR LONG.

I had told DCI Tomlinson that I thought it hadn't been so much a warning as an apology, even though he'd pooh-poohed the idea.

However, it did mean one thing for certain: Herb had known his killer, or at least he knew someone who knew he was going to die. That was assuming that the '*won't be regretting it for long*' did, in fact, refer to him dying soon. It could, I suppose, have been from a girlfriend who was dumping him for not doing as he was told, but somehow I doubted it. Notes from girlfriends are never written in stark capital letters without a salutation of some kind, and a name.

What had Herb been told to do that he hadn't done?

Was it something to do with the gambling and the credit cards, or was there something else?

I turned on the bedside light and wrote out the words in full on a notepad:

YOU SHOULD HAVE DONE WHAT YOU WERE TOLD. YOU MAY SAY YOU REGRET IT, BUT YOU WON'T BE REGRETTING IT FOR LONG.

I studied it carefully.

Maybe Herb hadn't *not done* something that he'd been told to do, perhaps he had *done* something that he'd been told not to.

But to whom had he expressed regret for his inaction

or action? And why had he regretted it? Because it had been wrong, or because it had placed him in danger?

Still so many questions and still so few answers.

'Leave the investigating to the professionals,' the chief inspector had said to me. But how long would they take? And would I still be alive by then?

Maybe it was time for me to start poking a few hornets' nests, and hope not to get stung.

I went into the hospital just after seven thirty on Wednesday morning. Claudia was so much improved, sitting up in her uncomfortable bed without as much as a murmur about backache, and she was eating a breakfast of muesli and natural yoghurt.

'Well, look at you,' I said, smiling broadly. 'You obviously had a better night than me.'

'Why? What was wrong with your night?' she asked.

'Lumpy hotel bed,' I said.

'Why didn't you go home?'

Ah, I thought. Careless. Now what do I say?

'I wanted to be nearer you, my darling.'

'But what a waste of money,' she said with mock disapproval of my profligacy. 'If I have to stay in here another night, I insist you go home. I'll be fine.'

Little did she know that there was no way I was going home, and neither was she. It was far too risky.

'You look well enough to run a marathon,' I said. 'I'm sure they'll chuck you out just as soon as Mr Tomic's seen you.'

'The nurse says he's usually here by eight.'

I looked up at the clock on the wall, the one that had driven me mad the previous day when Claudia had been in the operating theatre.

It was ten minutes before eight.

As if on cue, Mr Tomic swept into the room. He had the blue scrubs on but, this time, wore a doctor's white coat over them.

'Good morning, Claudia,' he said, and he nodded at me. 'How are you feeling?'

'Much better than last night,' Claudia replied. 'But I'm rather sore.'

'Yes,' he said. 'That's normal. I had to make incisions in the abdominal wall. They were only small but still painful. Do you think you are up to getting up?'

'I have been,' she said, almost in triumph. 'I went to the loo last night and again this morning.'

'Good,' he said. 'Then I think you can go home today. I'll see you in ten days to check on everything and take out the stitches. Until then, take it easy.'

'Great,' I said. 'She will. I'll see to that.'

'And,' he went on, 'we've had the first results from the tests.'

'Yes?' Claudia said. 'You can tell me.'

'The right ovary seems clear but, as I feared, there were some cancer cells in the peritoneal fluid. Not many, but enough.'

We were all silent for a moment.

'Chemotherapy?' Claudia said.

'I'm afraid so,' said Mr Tomic. 'But maybe just one

course. Two at most. I'm sorry, but it's the best way forward.'

He left us digesting that not-so-tasty morsel, rushing off, no doubt, to cut out bits from another desperate cancer patient. It was not my idea of a fun job.

'Let's look on the bright side, my darling,' I said finally. 'The right ovary is clear.'

'That's true,' Claudia replied, trying to be a little enthusiastic.

'So we might still have kids,' I said.

'If the chemo doesn't make me infertile,' she replied gloomily.

Even the thought of being discharged from hospital didn't cheer her up much, especially when I told her we weren't going home but to my mother's house in Gloucestershire.

'Nick, you've got to be kidding?' were her exact words.

'Nope,' I said. 'And Mum is so looking forward to it.'

'But I want to go home,' Claudia whined. 'I want my own bed.'

'But how would I look after you there when I have to go to work tomorrow?'

'And how, pray,' she asked dryly, 'are you going to go to work tomorrow from Cheltenham?' She paused briefly. 'Come on, Nick, please, let's just go home.'

Now what could I say? I could hardly tell her I was worried we might get murdered on our own doorstep. She probably wouldn't have believed me anyway.

I was convinced that Lichfield Grove was far too dangerous for us, and there was no way I was knowingly going to place my new fiancée into jeopardy. I'd been lucky last time, very lucky, and I'd had to run for my life. There was no way that Claudia would be able to run after having had two incisions through her abdominal wall. And who was to say I'd be lucky again?

And, to live, I had to be lucky every time.

My best chance, surely, was to be where the assassin wouldn't be, and to remain where he couldn't find me. He only had to be lucky once.

So, I decided, returning to Lichfield Grove was completely out of the question.

'My mother is so looking forward to it,' I said. 'And you yourself said it would be nice to go down to see her after the operation.'

'Yes,' she replied, 'but I didn't mean straight from the hospital.'

'Oh, come on, darling,' I pleaded. 'If your mother were still alive we would probably go and stay with her.'

It was a low blow, well beneath the belt, and to someone who was in no state to receive one.

We rarely, if ever, spoke of Claudia's parents. They had left her, aged eight, to spend the day with her grandmother, but they had never come back. Their Ford Escort had been driven off the cliff at Beachy Head straight down to the shingle beach some five hundred feet below.

The inquest had, apparently, returned a misadventure verdict rather than one of suicide. There had been some doubt as to which of the two had been driving at the time, or whether some malfunction of the car had been the cause. But, either way, Claudia blamed them both absolutely for leaving her alone in the world.

I thought it was quite likely the true reason behind all her weird paintings, but it was a topic that I raised rarely, and then with great care and tact.

'Nick, that's hardly fair,' she said crossly.

'I'm sorry,' I said. 'But I do want us to go straight to Mum's.'

'But what about my things?' she said.

'You've got many of them here with you,' I said. 'And I collected a few more yesterday from home.'

'And I definitely can't go to your mother's without my make-up,' she said defiantly.

'I've collected that too,' I said, trying not to sound too triumphant.

We went to my mother's, but not before I'd received another tongue-lashing over my extravagance in hiring a car for the trip.

'And what's wrong with our Mercedes?' Claudia had asked angrily.

'I thought you'd rather have a bit more space after your op,' I said, all sweetness and light. 'The SLK is so cramped for the passenger.'

And rather conspicuous, I thought.

The man at the Hertz car rental centre had tried to get me to hire his 'Car of the Week', a bright yellow Audi convertible with shiny chrome wheels. 'It would suit you, sir,' he'd said eagerly. 'Your sort of colour. Makes a big statement.'

I had opted instead for a bog-standard, four-door, blue saloon with not so much as a 'go-faster' stripe down the side. I wanted to blend into the background, not stand out from it.

I'd make my big statement in another way.

I'd told Claudia that my mother was looking forward to having us to stay, and she was, but only after I had talked her out of going to her regular Wednesday-afternoon whist drive in the village.

'Mum,' I'd said on the telephone, having woken her at ten to seven in the morning, 'I just need to get us away for a few days.'

'But why, darling?' she'd replied. 'What's so sudden that you can't come tomorrow?'

'Please, Mum,' I'd said to her in a tone like a seven-year-old trying to get his reluctant parent to buy him a coveted toy.

'Oh, all right,' she'd said. 'But I'll have to go shopping for some food. And I really don't like letting down the other players.'

'They'll understand,' I'd said. 'Just tell them your son is coming and bringing his fiancée home for the first time.'

She hadn't been able to speak for a few moments. I had waited.

'Oh, darling,' she'd said eventually, her voice full of emotion. 'Is it really true or are you just saying that?'

'It's really true,' I'd replied.

Hence, when we drove down the lane to her cottage, my mother was already outside to welcome us, in tears and almost unable to speak with joy. She hugged Claudia like she'd never done so before.

'What did you say to her?' Claudia asked me quietly as we went inside.

'I told her we were engaged,' I said. 'We are, aren't we?'

'Yes,' she said, smiling. 'Of course we are. But what else did you tell her? You know, about the cancer?'

'Nothing,' I said. 'I'll leave that for you to decide.'

'I think not,' she said. 'Not yet.'

'Fine,' I replied.

We went into the open-plan kitchen/diner/lounge and Claudia sat down gingerly on a chair.

'What's the matter, my dear?' my mother asked with concern. 'You look like you're in pain.'

'I am, Dorothy,' Claudia said. 'I've just had an operation. A hernia. But I'll be fine soon.'

'My dear,' said my mother, 'come at once and put your feet up on the sofa.'

She fussed around her future daughter-in-law like a brooding mother hen and soon had Claudia propped up on a chintz-covered sofa with multiple pillows.

'There,' my mother said, standing back. 'How about a nice cup of tea?'

'That would be lovely,' Claudia said, and she winked at me.

I left them to their bonding session while I took our

things upstairs to the guest bedroom, negotiating the narrow, twisting staircase with our bags.

I sat on the bed and called the office using my mother's cordless phone. Gregory should have returned from his long weekend away by now and, with luck, Patrick would have convinced him over lunch not to hang, draw and quarter me, and even perhaps to let me back into the offices.

Mrs McDowd answered.

'Lyall and Black,' she said in her usual crisp tone. 'How can I direct your call?'

'Hello Mrs McDowd,' I said. 'Mr Nicholas here.'

'Ah, yes,' she said curtly. 'Mr Patrick said you might ring. But it's not your number.'

Mrs McDowd, I decided, was sitting on the fence with regards to me. She was being neither friendly nor hostile towards me. She would clearly wait to see how I fared with the senior partners before committing to an allegiance either way.

'Are Mr Patrick and Mr Gregory back from lunch yet?' I asked.

'They didn't go to lunch,' she said. 'They've gone to a funeral. They'll be gone for the rest of the day.'

'That was rather sudden,' I said.

'Death often is,' she replied.

'Whose funeral is it?' I asked.

'A client of Gregory's,' she said. 'Someone called Roberts. Colonel Jolyon Roberts.'

13

'What?' I said. 'What did you say?'

'Colonel Jolyon Roberts,' Mrs McDowd said again. 'Mr Patrick and Mr Gregory have gone to his funeral.'

'But when did he die?' I asked. I'd been talking to him only on Saturday at Sandown Park Races.

'Seems he was found dead early yesterday morning,' she said. 'Heart attack, apparently. Very sudden.'

'The funeral is mighty sudden too,' I said, 'if he only died yesterday.'

'Jewish,' she said by way of explanation. 'Quick burial is part of their culture, and usually within twenty-four hours. Something to do with the heat in Israel.'

She was a mine of information, Mrs McDowd. The heat in England in April isn't quite as intense as that in a Jerusalem summer but, I suppose, traditions are traditions.

And I'd never realized that Jolyon Roberts had been Jewish. But why would I?

'Are you sure it was a heart attack?' I asked her.

Never mind the chief inspector's suspicious mind, I thought, mine was now in overdrive.

'That's what I heard from Mr Gregory,' said Mrs McDowd. 'He was quite shocked by it. Seems he'd only been talking to Colonel Roberts on Monday afternoon.'

'I thought Mr Gregory was away for a long weekend.'

'He was meant to be,' she said. 'But he came back on Monday. Something urgent cropped up.'

'OK,' I said, 'I'll call Mr Patrick on his mobile.'

'The funeral service is at three,' she said.

I looked at my watch. It was well past two thirty.

'I won't call him until afterwards,' I said. 'Where is it?'

'Golders Green,' she said. 'At the Jewish cemetery, in the family plot.'

I disconnected and sat on the bed for a while, thinking.

Herb Kovak had accessed the Roberts Family Trust file, and the Bulgarian investment details, and, within a week of doing so, he'd been murdered. I'd sent an innocent-looking e-mail to a man in Bulgaria about the same development and, four days later, someone turned up on my doorstep trying to kill me.

And now, Jolyon Roberts, with his questions and doubts about the whole Bulgarian project, conveniently dies of a heart attack the day after speaking to Gregory about it, as I had told him he should.

Was I going crazy, or was a pattern beginning to appear?

A hundred million euros of EU money was a lot of cash.

Was it enough to murder for? Was it enough to murder three times for?

*

I decided to call Detective Chief Inspector Tomlinson, if only to try and get some more information about the death of Jolyon Roberts.

'Are you suggesting that this Colonel Roberts was murdered?' he asked in a sceptical tone.

Suddenly the whole idea appeared less plausible.

'I don't know,' I said. 'But I'd love to hear what the pathologist said.'

'Assuming there was an autopsy.'

'Surely there would be,' I said. 'I thought all sudden deaths were subject to post mortems.'

'But why do you believe he was murdered?'

'I'm probably wrong,' I said.

'Tell me anyway,' the chief inspector said with a degree of encouragement. 'And I promise not to laugh.'

'Murder is pretty uncommon, right?'

'I've seen more than my fair share on Merseyside.'

'But, generally,' I said, 'for us non-homicide detectives, I'd say it was a pretty rare thing to know a murder victim. Wouldn't you agree?'

'OK, I agree. Murder is uncommon.'

'Well,' I said, 'if I'm right and Colonel Roberts was murdered, then I've known two murder victims, and both of them have been killed within the past two weeks, and I nearly became the third.' I paused.

'Go on,' he said.

'So, I looked to see what connection Herb Kovak had with Colonel Roberts, and also with myself.'

'Yes?' he said with greater eagerness.

'Lyall and Black, for one thing,' I said. 'Herb Kovak

and I work for the firm and Colonel Roberts was a client, although not a client that Herb or I would usually have contacted.' I paused. 'But Herb accessed the Roberts file just ten days before he died, in particular looking at the details of a Bulgarian investment that the Roberts Family Trust had made. I saw the record of him having done so on a company computer.'

'And what is significant about that?' the detective asked.

'Colonel Roberts approached me just a week ago over his concerns about that very same investment.'

'Why did he approach you in particular?'

'I'm not really sure,' I said. 'He knew I worked for Lyall and Black and he met me at the races on Tuesday and again on Wednesday. It was a chance meeting the first time but I'm sure it was on purpose the second day. He was worried that the factory he had invested in hadn't actually been built as he had been told it had, but he didn't want a full enquiry as he was worried that he'd been duped and didn't want the whole world to know. So he asked me to quietly have a look and check that all was well with the investment.'

'And did you?' he asked.

'I did a little bit of digging, but I told him on Saturday that I couldn't go searching behind the backs of others at the firm and he should speak to his investment manager about it.'

'Who is?' he asked.

'Gregory Black,' I said. 'Colonel Roberts spoke to him on Monday, only the day before he died.'

'But it's quite a jump to think that he was murdered because of it. And are you telling me you suspect Gregory Black of killing him?'

'No, of course not,' I said. 'Gregory Black may have an explosive temper but he's hardly a murderer.'

Or was he? Could I really tell what went on in his head? Or in anyone else's head for that matter? But Gregory a murderer? Surely not.

'But that's not all,' I said. 'I sent an e-mail to someone in Bulgaria last Friday, and a would-be assassin turned up at my door on Tuesday afternoon.'

'OK,' he said, now firmly interested. 'I'll try and find out if there was an autopsy carried out on this Colonel Roberts. Where did you say he lived?'

'Hampstead,' I said. 'He only died yesterday and he's being buried in Golders Green Cemetery even as we speak.'

'That's very quick,' he said.

'Apparently it's a Jewish tradition to bury the dead as quickly as possible.'

'At least it's not a cremation,' he said. 'No chance of a second look at the body if it's cremated. And I speak from experience.' He laughed.

What a strange occupation, I thought, daily dealings with violent death and its fallout.

'You will let me know the results?' I asked.

'If I can,' he said. 'I'll call you if I get anything.'

'I'm not at home. And my mobile doesn't work where I am.'

'And where is that?'

I was a little reluctant to tell him. The fewer the people who knew, the safer I'd feel. But he was the police, and he had provided me with an unshakeable alibi when I was arrested for attempted murder.

'I'm in a village called Woodmancote,' I said. 'It's near Cheltenham racecourse. It's where my mother lives.' I gave him my mother's telephone number.

'Cheltenham is a long way from your office,' he said in a tone that seemed to ask a question.

'I know. I know,' I said. 'I ran away. Superintendent Yering was unable to provide me with any protection and I felt very vulnerable, so I didn't go home.'

'I can't say I really blame you,' he said.

'So how about you giving me a bodyguard?' I asked. 'Preferably one bristling with guns, and with evil intent towards assassins.'

'I'll see what I can do,' he said. 'Especially if it does turn out that Colonel Roberts was murdered.'

'And another thing,' I said, deciding to get my requests in quickly as the chief inspector seemed to be in a generous mood. 'Can you find out whether Billy Searle has started talking to the Wiltshire Police? And what he's told them.'

'Do you think he has something to do with all this as well?'

'No, I don't,' I said. 'I happen to know where Billy's money was invested because I manage his portfolio, and it was nowhere near Bulgaria. I'm just interested to know what he's told the police. After all, I was arrested on suspicion of trying to kill him.'

'I'll try,' he said. 'But some of these rural detectives can be reluctant to discuss their cases with officers from other forces.'

'Just remind them it was me who gave them the information that Billy Searle owed someone a hundred thousand, and it was you that stopped them from looking bloody foolish by charging me with attempted murder when I had a cast-iron alibi.'

'OK. OK. I said I'd try.'

When I went downstairs, my mother and Claudia were in full flow with wedding plans.

'It was about time he asked you to marry him,' she said to Claudia while looking at me.

'But he didn't,' Claudia replied. 'I asked him.'

My mother was quite taken aback and even rendered speechless for a few seconds. She had always been a stickler for tradition.

'How very unusual,' she said finally. 'But Nicholas always was a funny boy.'

Jan Setter had called me strange.

Was I really funny, or strange?

I didn't think so.

To me I was 'normal', but I suppose everyone thinks they are 'normal', and yet we are all so different. There was actually no such thing as 'normal'.

'Now, darlings,' my mother said, changing the subject, 'would you like some late lunch? I've a shepherd's pie in the oven.'

'Mum,' I said, 'it's gone three o'clock.'

'So?' she replied. 'I thought you might be hungry when you arrived.'

Surprisingly, I was, and I could tell from Claudia's eager look that she was too. I had been so busy trying to make the journey smooth and jerk-free, to keep Claudia as comfortable as possible, that I hadn't even thought of stopping for food.

Consequently the three of us sat down to a very late lunch of shepherd's pie and broccoli, with my mother insisting that I had a second helping.

I called Patrick on his mobile at twenty to six, late enough for the funeral to be over, but early enough for it still to be in the working day.

Claudia was upstairs having a rest and my mother was busying herself by the stove, preparing yet another high-fat, high-protein, chicken casserole for our dinner. I sat on the chintz sofa in the lounge area, facing her, but at the furthest point of the room.

'Ah, yes. Nicholas,' Patrick said, seemingly slightly flustered. 'Mrs McDowd told me you'd called. Sorry I wasn't able to speak to you earlier.'

'And I am sorry to hear about Colonel Roberts,' I said.

'Yes, what a dreadful thing. He was only sixty-two as well. Enjoy life while you've got it, that's what I say. You never know when the Grim Reaper will catch you up.'

Yes, I thought. But I'd outrun him once down Lichfield Grove.

'Have you spoken to Gregory?' I asked, getting to the point of the call.

'Yes, I have,' he said. 'He is still very angry with you.'

'But, why?' I asked.

'Why do you think?' he said crossly. 'For getting arrested and being splashed all over the papers and the television. He believes you brought the firm into disrepute.'

'But, Patrick, his anger is completely misplaced, and he is wrong. It wasn't my fault that I was arrested. The police jumped to a conclusion and it was an incorrect one.'

'Yes,' he said. 'But you did give them reason to draw it.'

'I did not,' I said, getting quite angry myself. 'It was that idiot Billy Searle who shouted out about murder. I did absolutely nothing wrong.'

My mother glanced over at me from the kitchen area.

'Gregory says there is no smoke without fire. He still thinks you must have had something to do with it.'

'Well, in that case, Gregory is more of an idiot than I thought.' My raised voice caused my mother to stand and look at me from across the room, and with a furrowed brow. I paused to calm myself down. I then spoke much more quietly. 'Am I being fired? Because if I am, I'll be taking Lyall and Black to court.'

He did not reply, and I stayed silent. I could hear his breathing.

'You had better come in to the office tomorrow,' he said at last. 'I will tell Gregory to hold his tongue.'

'Thank you,' I said. 'But I may not make it in tomorrow. Claudia is not very well and I'll probably work from home using the remote-access system. I hope to see you on Friday.'

'Right,' he said, sounding slightly relieved that he had at least another day to dampen the erupting Gregory volcano. 'I'll see you on Friday.'

He hung up and I sat for a while wondering about my future, if I still had one with a gun-toting assassin on the loose.

'What was all that about?' my mother asked with concern.

'Oh, nothing, Mum,' I said. 'Just a little problem at work. Nothing to worry about.'

But I did worry about it.

I had really enjoyed working for Lyall & Black over the last five years, but the role of an independent financial adviser was one that necessitated absolute trust, both of the client and of one's colleagues. What sort of future did I have in a firm where one of the senior partners believed me to be involved in an attempted murder and, at the same time, I wondered if he had been involved in a successful one?

The three of us sat at my mother's dining table for dinner, and I ate and drank too much for my own good.

‘What’s happened to your cat?’ I asked, noticing its absence from under the table.

‘It’s not my cat,’ my mother said. ‘He’s just an irregular visitor and I haven’t seen him for days. He’ll probably be back sometime soon.’

No doubt when fillet steak was back on the menu, I thought.

Claudia and I went up to bed early for us, around ten o’clock.

‘You are such a clever thing,’ Claudia said to me as we snuggled up together under the duvet.

‘In what way?’ I asked.

‘Insisting we came here,’ she said. ‘If we’d gone home I would have felt pressured to cook or clean, or do something useful. Here I can relax completely, my phone doesn’t even ring, and your mother is such a dear.’

I smiled in the darkness. Now that was a turn-up.

‘But we can’t stay here very long,’ I said seriously.

‘Why not?’ she asked.

‘Because, if she goes on feeding me as she’s done today, I’ll end up with a waistline like Homer Simpson’s.’

We giggled uncontrollably.

Since we’d left the hospital that morning, neither of us had mentioned anything about the cancer, or the upcoming chemo treatments. It was as if we had left all our troubles behind, in London.

But they were about to come looking for us.

*

I dreamed that I was riding in a race but, like all dreams, it was inconsistent and erratic. One second I was on a horse, the next on an ostrich, or in a car. However, one part of the dream was unvarying: whatever we were riding I was always racing against Gregory. And he was ever-smiling, and aiming a gun with a silencer at my head.

I woke up with a jerk, breathing fast, ready to run.

I relaxed, and lay there in the dark listening to Claudia's rhythmic breathing beside me.

Did I really think that Gregory Black was involved in fraud and murder?

I didn't know, but I was sure interested to hear the results of the post mortem examination on Jolyon Roberts, if there had been one.

I drifted back to sleep but only fitfully, waking often to listen for sounds that shouldn't have been there. Woodmancote was much quieter without traffic, and much darker without streetlamps, than our home in Lichfield Grove but, nevertheless, I slept badly and was wide awake long before the sun lit up the bedroom window soon after six o'clock.

I got up quietly and padded silently downstairs in bare feet with my computer. I had been seriously neglecting my clients over the past two weeks and, if I didn't pull my finger out soon, I'd have no job worthy of the name at Lyall & Black to cry about even if I was fired.

I logged on to the internet.

I had forty-three unread e-mails including a fresh

one from Jan Setter telling me how fantastic the first night of the Florence Nightingale show had been and how crazy I was to have missed it. It was timed at 5.50 a.m. this morning and the show in London hadn't finished until ten thirty last night, not to mention how late the after-show party had gone on. Did she never sleep, or had she sent it as soon as she'd arrived home?

I e-mailed back to her and said how pleased I was she had enjoyed it and how I hoped it would make her lots of money.

Then I went onto the daily newspaper websites to read the reviews. All but one were pretty encouraging, so maybe the show might make some money. Backing shows and films was always a risky business. I usually told my clients that it was far more of a gamble than they would have on the stock market but, as with most risky investments, the potential gains were greater too. But they had to be prepared to lose *all* their money.

One of my clients never expected any financial return from such investments, he just revelled in rubbing shoulders with the stars at the first-night functions, and taking all his friends to see 'his' show in the best seats. 'I know I might lose it all,' he would say, 'but, if I do, I'll enjoy every minute while I'm losing it. And you never know, I might just make a fortune.'

And he had done precisely that the previous year.

At my suggestion, he had backed a small independent film company to make an obscure and irreverent comedy based around the first transportation of convicts from England to Australia in 1787. To everyone's surprise, not least my client's, the film had been a huge international hit. At the box office worldwide it had earned back over two hundred times its production cost, as well as receiving an Oscar nomination for its young star who played the title role in *Bruce: The First Australian*.

But the successes were few, and the disasters many.

It took me over two hours just to answer my outstanding e-mails, by which time I could hear movement above and, presently, my mother came downstairs in her dressing gown.

'Hello, dear,' she said. 'You're up early.'

'I've been down here over two hours,' I said. 'I have work to do.'

'Yes, dear,' she said. 'Don't we all. Now, what would you like for breakfast? I have some bacon and local eggs, and Mr Ayers, my butcher, has made me some wonderful sausages. How many would you like?'

'Just a coffee and a slice of toast would be lovely,' I said.

It was like King Canute trying to hold back the tide.

'Don't be ridiculous,' she said, already placing a frying pan on the stove. 'You've got to have a proper breakfast. What sort of mother would I be if I didn't feed you?'

I sighed. Perhaps Claudia and I would go out for a drive at lunchtime.

I took her up a cup of tea while the sausages and bacon were sizzling in the pan.

'Morning, gorgeous,' I said, pulling open the curtains. 'How are you feeling today?'

'Still a bit sore,' she said, sitting up. 'But better than yesterday.'

'Good,' I said. 'Time to get up. Delia Smith downstairs is cooking breakfast.'

'Mmm, I can smell it,' she said, laughing. 'Now don't you expect that every morning when we're married.'

'What?' I said in mock horror. 'No cooked breakfasts! The wedding's off!'

'We haven't even fixed a date for it yet,' she said.

'Before or after the hair loss?' I asked seriously.

She thought for a moment. 'After it grows back. Give me time to get used to this engagement business first.'

'After it is, then,' I said. I leaned down and kissed her. 'Don't be long or Mr Ayers's sausages will get cold.'

She dived back under the covers and put a pillow over her head. 'I'm staying here.'

'Hiding won't help,' I said, laughing, and leaving her alone.

My mother hadn't lied, the sausages were excellent, but, as always with her meals, they were too big and too numerous, and then there was the mountain of bacon and the scrambled eggs on fried bread, not forgetting the mushrooms and grilled tomatoes on the side.

I felt totally bloated by the time I sat down again at my computer to check through my client files using the firm's remote-access facility.

Claudia, meanwhile, had managed to extract herself from her bed, coming down to join us in a bathrobe, but she ate just a small bowl of muesli and a little sliced fruit. And had grinned at me as she did so. It really wasn't fair.

I spent the morning briefly looking through all the files for my fifty or so personal clients, to check on the reminder tags, ensuring that I hadn't missed reinvesting the proceeds of maturing bonds, or suchlike.

What I really needed to do was to study all the recent stock movements. It was something that I should be doing every day in order to maintain a 'feel' for the markets, to try and be, if not one step ahead, at least in tune with market trends. Not that Lyall & Black invested directly in individual stocks. That proportion of our clients' money put into equities was almost exclusively invested through unit trusts or investment funds that had a broad range of different shares within them. It was a way of spreading risk, of placing one's eggs in many baskets at the same time. But it was still important for me to have a feel for the markets in order to advise my clients which of the hundreds of trusts and funds to buy into.

And, over the past week or so, I had been guilty of serious dereliction of my duty in the study department.

I used my mother's landline to check on my voicemail. There was one new message and it was from Sherri asking me to call her at Herb's flat.

'Hi,' I said when she answered. 'Is everything all right?'

'Fine,' she replied, sounding totally fed up. 'Least I suppose it's fine. Monday in Liverpool was a bit of an ordeal.'

'I'm sorry,' I said.

'Yeah,' she said. 'Well, it's over, anyway.' She sighed audibly down the phone. 'I'm going home tomorrow morning. I'm on a flight at ten forty-five to Chicago. I just called to say goodbye.'

'Thanks,' I said. 'I'm glad you did.'

'A few letters have arrived here for Herb and I had a phone call from his gym, something about Herb not paying them and they want his locker back. Hold on, I've got their number somewhere.' I could hear her rummaging in the background. 'Here it is. Somewhere called the Slim Fit Gym.' She read out the telephone number and I jotted it down on the back of the rental-car agreement.

'Don't you worry,' I said. 'Leave the letters on the desk, I'll deal with them, and I'll call the gym. You look after yourself. I hope you have a safe trip home. I'll let you know about the funeral and such when I know myself.'

'The police said it could be weeks away. That's why I'm going back. I'll lose my job if I stay here much longer.'

Life could be a bugger.

I called the Slim Fit Gym.

'Mr Kovak's direct debit has been cancelled,' someone said. 'So we want his locker back.'

'He died,' I said. 'So take it back.'

'But there's a padlock on it,' the person said.

'Don't you have a spare key?' I asked.

'It was Mr Kovak's own padlock.'

'Can't you cut it off?' I said, somewhat impatiently.

'No.' The person was getting quite agitated 'We must have the key.'

I remembered the one that was pinned to the notice-board above Herb's desk.

'OK, OK,' I said. 'I'll bring it in next week.'

They didn't like it but it was too bad. However, they did insist on having my contact details. I hated giving out my mobile number so I gave them the office one instead.

I disconnected and leaned back in the chair, stretching.

'Do you fancy going out?' Claudia said, coming over and rubbing my shoulders. 'It's a lovely day out there.'

My studying would have to wait.

'That would be nice,' I said, turning round on the chair. 'But are you sure you're feeling up to it?'

'Absolutely,' she said. 'I'm feeling much better today. But let's take the car. I'm not yet ready to yomp around the countryside. Why don't we go to a pub for lunch?' She winked at me.

'Great idea,' I agreed. I stood up and went into the kitchen area where my mother was fussing with the dishwasher. 'Mum,' I said to her, 'Claudia and I thought we might drive to a pub for lunch. Do you want to come?'

'Oh,' she said. 'I have some nice pork chops from Mr Ayers for lunch.'

'Won't they do for this evening?' I said.

'I've got a roast leg of lamb for us tonight.'

Mr Ayers had obviously been busy.

'Leave the chops in the fridge,' I said. 'Give yourself a rest. Let's all go out for lunch.'

And we did, with me looking over the hedge for my would-be assassin as the three of us climbed into the nondescript blue saloon. But, of course, he wasn't there and we made it safely to a local country pub with a big GOOD FOOD sign outside. Claudia and my mother both ordered a glass of white wine and a poached salmon salad, while I just had a Diet Coke and a bag of roasted peanuts.

'But, darling,' my mother complained bitterly, 'you must have a proper lunch, or you'll fade away.'

'Mother, dear,' I said. 'I've done nothing but eat since we arrived. I think fading away is the least of my worries.' But she didn't like it, and I could already feel an extra-large portion of lamb coming on for dinner.

The phone was ringing when we arrived back at the cottage and my mother rushed in to answer it.

'It's for you,' she said, handing over the phone to me.

'Hello,' I said.

'It was definitely a heart attack,' said Chief Inspector Tomlinson down the line. 'While he was swimming in his own pool. Then he drowned as a result. A full post mortem was carried out at the Royal Free Hospital on Tuesday afternoon. Seems Colonel Roberts had a history of heart problems.'

'Oh,' I said. 'Such are the perils of early-morning swimming.'

'It was late-night swimming, apparently, and on his own. And he'd been drinking. Stupid fool. His blood alcohol level was more than twice that for drunk driving.'

'But he wasn't driving,' I said.

'No,' said the detective, 'but he was swimming and, in my experience, alcohol and water don't mix.' He laughed at his own joke, and I found it slightly irritating. But it reminded me of Jolyon Roberts doing just the same thing during our meeting in the Chasers Bar at Sandown Park Races.

'Hold on a minute,' I said, suddenly remembering something else from that meeting. 'Colonel Roberts told me, categorically, that he didn't drink alcohol. And that he never had.'

14

'I'll get back to you,' said Chief Inspector Tomlinson suddenly. 'I need to call in a few favours.'

He hung up, and I was cross I hadn't asked him about Billy Searle. But it would wait.

The phone rang again in my hand.

'Hello,' I said, answering it. 'Did you forget something?'

'Sorry?' said a female voice. 'Is that you, Mr Nicholas?'

'Mrs McDowd,' I said. 'How lovely to hear from you.'

There was a slight pause at the other end as Mrs McDowd worked out that I was being sarcastic.

'I have a message from Mr Patrick,' she said.

'How did you get this number?' I asked.

'He wants you to –' she started, but I interrupted her.

'Mrs McDowd,' I said again loudly. 'How did you get this number?'

'It was on caller-ID when you called in this morning,' she said.

That was rather careless, I thought, for someone meant to be in hiding.

'Anyway,' she said. 'I know that number. You're staying with your mother. How is she?'

Bloody Mrs McDowd, I thought. How does she know so much about me?

'She's fine, thank you,' I said, biting my tongue. 'Now, what does Mr Patrick want?'

'He wants you to call him in the morning before you come into the office. Something about arranging a meeting between you and Mr Gregory.'

'Did he say what the meeting was about?' I asked.

'No,' she said, but I bet she knew. Mrs McDowd knew everything.

'Please tell Mr Patrick that I won't be in the office very early tomorrow.'

'I've already told him that,' she said. 'Not with you being down in Gloucestershire.'

Who else had she told, I wondered.

In particular, had she told Mr Gregory?

I spent much of the afternoon catching up on the changing price of derivatives and futures, and on how a recent fall in the Dow Jones index in the United States had affected markets in the Far East more than those in Europe, and on fluctuations in the value of gold in pounds as a result of changes in the cost of a barrel of oil in dollars.

It was like a balancing act.

Some economies grew and others contracted; stock markets moved at different paces or in opposite ways; some currencies went up and others went down. The trick to winning in the great global financial game was to invest in the things about to go up in real value, while selling those about to go down. Then there were hedge funds and short selling, both designed to make you money when the values went in the wrong direction.

But it was all a bit like gambling with a bookmaker. For you to win, he had to lose. So it was in the markets – there were winners and losers. The winners had big houses and the losers went bust, losing their big houses to the banks, which then sold them to the winners.

The money went round and round but it did not always end up with the same people.

And then there were the fraudsters, those who tried to load the odds in their favour through insider dealing or market manipulation.

Once upon a time insider dealing had been seen as a perk of the job for stockbrokers and company directors, cashing in on prior knowledge of profits and mergers by buying or selling stock before the facts were known to others. Nowadays the courts send them to jail for doing what everyone used to do, and quite rightly too.

But there are always those who think they can beat the system, and many of them do, because betting on a certainty was like having a licence to print money.

Herb Kovak had said to Mrs McDowd that he liked to bet on certainties.

She'd told me.

Chief Inspector Tomlinson called back at five o'clock.

'He'd definitely been drinking,' he said. 'I've seen the full autopsy report. There's no mistake. They tested both his blood and the aqueous humour in his eye. And the stomach contained whisky residue.'

'How easy is it to force someone to drink whisky?' I asked.

'My, my,' he said. 'Now who has the suspicious mind?'

'It's just too convenient,' I said.

'But how could you give someone a heart attack?' he asked, his slightly sarcastic tone clearly indicating that he didn't believe me.

'Hold his drunken head under the surface of his own swimming pool,' I said. 'Either he drowns straight away or, as he has a history of heart problems, he panics, has a heart attack and then drowns.'

'But why the alcohol?' he asked.

'To add confusion,' I said. 'When you knew he'd been drinking, you instinctively believed he had been a stupid fool, and you probably thought he half deserved to die for it.'

'True,' he said. 'I did. But you are only speculating. There's no evidence of foul play.'

'No,' I agreed. 'And what there was has conveniently been buried in Golders Green Cemetery.'

He laughed. 'Story of my life.'

'What about Billy Searle?' I asked. 'What did you find out?'

'He's wide awake and talking,' he said. 'But he's not saying anything.'

'Nothing?'

'Pretty much. He refuses to say if he knew the person

who knocked him off his bike. Says it was an accident. And he denies owing anyone any money.'

I wasn't surprised. If it was a bookmaker, and Billy was involved in some betting scandal, he was hardly likely to admit it. It would be tantamount to handing in his jockey's licence for good.

'Well, thanks for finding out for me,' I said. 'Any news on the gunman?'

'Nothing as yet.'

'Didn't you get any response from the video?'

'Masses,' he said. 'Too much, really. The Met and us are sifting through it all, and cross-referencing with the criminal records bureau.'

That was what worried me the most. If he were a professional hit-man he was unlikely to have a criminal record, so he would never turn up from their cross-reference.

'So how about that bodyguard you promised me?' I asked. 'I can't stay down here for long as it's too far from London, but I don't fancy going home with our friend still out there.'

'I'll talk to my Super,' he said.

'Thanks,' I said, 'And please make it soon.'

We disconnected and I looked at my watch. It was quarter past five. Time to finish for the day.

I leaned back in the chair and pushed the 'get mail' button for a final check on my e-mails. One arrived from Gregory Black.

I sat forward quickly and opened it.

'Nicholas,' he had written, 'Patrick has asked me to write to you to apologize for my outburst of last Friday. So I am sorry. I can also assure you there will be no repetition of my actions when you return to this office after your stay with your mother. Yours, Gregory Black.'

Wow, I thought. My threat of court action had really put the cat amongst the pigeons. I could imagine Gregory absolutely hating having to write that e-mail with Patrick standing over him on one side, and almost certainly with Andrew Mellor, the company's lawyer, on the other, advising them both on employment law.

I may have received a grudging apology from Gregory, but he would resent it for ever. And it wouldn't make my future at the firm any easier.

I also didn't like the fact that Gregory knew that I was staying with my mother.

Mrs McDowd not only wanted to know everything about everyone, she also liked them to know she knew it, by spreading the information. The whole office would now be aware that I was in Gloucestershire, and probably half of Lombard Street too.

At about seven thirty my mother insisted I open a bottle of champagne to properly celebrate Claudia's and my engagement.

'I put one in my old fridge last night,' she said, 'so it should be nice and cold.'

And it was.

I retrieved the bottle and poured three glasses of the golden bubbly liquid, then we each, in turn, made a toast.

'To a long and happy marriage to my Claudia,' I said, and we drank.

'To long life and good health,' Claudia said, looking at me. We drank again.

'To masses of grandchildren,' my mother said, and we all drank once more.

Claudia and I held hands. We knew without saying what we were each thinking. Oh yes, please, to all three of the above. But, with cancer, it was all so scary and unpredictable.

'Have you told your father yet?' my mother asked.

'No,' I said. 'You're the only person that knows.' Not even Mrs McDowd, I thought, knew this little secret.

'Aren't you going to tell him?' Mum asked.

'Eventually,' I said. 'But I haven't spoken much to him recently.'

'Stupid man,' she said.

I knew she blamed him for the break-up of their marriage but, in truth, it had been as much her fault as his. But I didn't want to get into all that again.

'I'll call him tomorrow,' I said. 'Let's enjoy our own company here tonight.'

'I'll drink to that,' said Claudia, raising her glass. So we did.

I thought about my father.

Seven years ago, when my parents had finally divorced and the big house had been sold, he'd taken his share of the money and used it to buy a boring bungalow in Weymouth, overlooking the sea. I'd only been there a couple of times since, although I'd seen him a few times in London for various functions.

We hadn't been very close to start with, and we were drifting further apart day by day. But I don't think it was something that bothered either of us particularly. He hadn't even called me when I'd been arrested and my face had been splashed all over the papers, and on the TV. Perhaps my impending marriage, and the possibility of grandchildren, might help to revitalize our relationship, but I doubted it.

Claudia laid the dining table as my mother busied herself with saucepans of potatoes and carrots, and the lamb roasted away gently in the oven. I, meanwhile, poured us all more champagne and let them get on with it, leaning up against the worktop and enjoying the last of the evening sunshine as it shone brightly through the west-facing kitchen window.

'Bugger,' my mother said.

'What's wrong?' I asked.

'The cooker's gone off,' she said.

'Is it a power cut?'

She tried a light switch, clicking it up and down. Nothing happened.

'Bloody electricity company,' she said. 'I'll call them straight away.'

She rummaged in a drawer for a card and then picked up the phone.

'That's funny,' she said, 'the phone's dead too.'

'Doesn't it need power?' Claudia asked from over by the table. 'Our cordless one does.'

'I'm not using the cordless,' my mother said. 'This is the wired-in landline.'

Oh, shit!

There was a heavy knock on the front door.

'I'll get it,' said Claudia, turning away.

The power was off, the telephone was dead, there was a knock on the front door, and the hairs on the back of my neck were suddenly standing bolt upright.

'Don't touch it,' I shouted at Claudia.

She turned to look at me but she still moved towards the danger. 'Why ever not?' she said.

'Claudia,' I shouted again, 'get away from the door.'

I was already half-way towards her when the knock was repeated. And still Claudia moved towards it.

I grabbed her just as she was reaching for the handle.

'What on earth are you doing?' she said loudly. 'Answer the bloody door.'

'No,' I said quietly.

'Why ever not?' she demanded.

'Keep your voice down,' I hissed at her.

'Why?' she said, but much quieter, with concern. She could probably read the fear in my face.

'Please. Just go over to the kitchen area.' I looked over at my mother, who was staring at us, still holding the useless telephone in her hand.

Something about the urgency of my voice finally got through to Claudia and she went over to join my mother.

They both suddenly looked rather frightened.

I went into the small cloakroom next to the front door and peeked through a minute gap in the net curtains at the person standing outside.

He had on a grey/green anorak with the collar turned up and, this time, he was wearing a dark blue baseball cap, but there was no doubt, it was the same man that I had last seen in the grainy video from Mr Patel's newsagents, the same man who had gunned down Herb Kovak at Aintree, and the same man who had shot at me in Lichfield Grove.

Bugger, I thought, echoing my mother.

I went back into the big room.

The front door had locked automatically when it was closed, with a lock a bit like a Yale latch. It was quite strong, but was it strong enough?

I went quickly across to the kitchen and locked the back door as well, turning the key slowly to keep the noise to a minimum, and sliding across the bolt at the top.

Both my mother and Claudia watched my every step.

We heard the man rattle the front door and they both instinctively crouched down below the worktop.

'Who is it?' whispered my mother.

I'd have to tell them.

'Darlings,' I whispered. 'He's a very dangerous man, and he's trying to kill me.'

Claudia's eyes opened so wide I thought they would pop out of her head. My mother, however, thought I was joking and began to laugh.

'I'm being serious,' I said cutting her off in mid

guffaw. 'It's the same man who killed Herb Kovak at Aintree Races.'

This time they both looked more frightened than ever. And I was, too.

'Call the police,' Claudia said, then she remembered. 'Oh, my God, he's cut the phone line.'

And the electricity.

The broadband connection would have failed with the power, and our mobiles didn't have any signal here.

We were on our own.

'Upstairs,' I said quietly but firmly. 'Both of you. Now. Lock yourselves in the bathroom, sit on the floor, and don't come out until I tell you to.'

Claudia hesitated a moment, but then she nodded and took my mother by the hand. They started to go but then turned back. 'But what are you going to do?' Claudia asked, with huge fear in her face.

'Try to keep him out,' I said. 'Now, go on, go!'

They disappeared up the boxed-in staircase and I heard the bathroom door being shut and locked above me.

And if he did get in and kill me, I thought, perhaps he'd leave them alone and go away, job done. As it was, with all three of us down here, I was sure he would have killed us all.

I looked around for some sort of weapon.

A loaded shotgun would have been nice, but my mother had about as much interest in country sports as I did in origami.

I heard the back door being tried and I instinctively ducked away from it.

The sun went down, the last of its orange rays disappearing from the kitchen window. And it began to get dark, especially indoors with no electric lights to brighten the gathering gloom.

I looked round in desperation for something to use as a weapon. An umbrella stood in a large china pot near the front door, and a walking stick. I grabbed the walking stick but it was a collapsible model, for ease of packing. So I opted for the umbrella, one of those big golf umbrellas with a heavy wooden handle. It wasn't much but it was all there was. How I wished the cottage still had a proper open fire with a big, heavy, metal poker, but my mother had replaced it with one of those gas things with fake coals.

But, at least, I had one advantage over my assailant in so far as I could see him much more easily than he could see me.

It was still quite light outside and I watched him through the windows as he went right round the house. At one point he came close to the kitchen window, cupping his hands round his face and up against the glass in order to peer in. I made sure I was standing to the side of the window, in a dark corner, where he would have had no chance of spotting me.

Perhaps he would go away, I thought.

He didn't.

The sound of breaking glass put paid to any hope I may have had that this was going to end simply and without violence.

My mother's windows were old, in keeping with the

age of her cottage. They were a version of the old leaded lights, small panes of glass held together by a lattice framework of metal strips.

The gunman had broken just one of the little panes in one of the kitchen windows, but it was enough for him to put his gloved hand through the opening and unlatch the whole thing. I watched him do it in the fading light, and the window swung open outwards.

Where could I hide?

Without doubt the best place to be was in the bathroom upstairs with the door locked but I had no intention of joining Claudia and my mother there. I was sure that that would lead, in the end, to the deaths of all three of us.

So, where else was there to hide?

Nowhere.

I concluded that hiding was, in fact, my least-favoured option. It would simply give the advantage to the gunman, who could take his time, all night if necessary, and, eventually, he would undoubtedly find me and then I, too, would get a couple of bullets in my heart and another in my face, just as poor Herb had.

So, if I wasn't going to hide, and I certainly wasn't going to merely stand and wait to be killed, the only other option was to attack, and attack hard and fast.

He started to climb through the window, his gun with its long black silencer entering first.

I stood just to the side of the window and raised the umbrella, holding it by the pointed end so that I could swing the heavy wooden handle.

I used all my strength and brought the handle down hard onto the gun. I had actually been aiming for his wrist but he pulled it back a fraction just at the last second.

The gun went off, the bullet ricocheting off the granite worktop below the window with a loud zing before burying itself in the wall opposite. But the blow had also knocked the gun from the man's grasp. It clattered to the floor, sliding across the stone-quarry tiles and out of sight under my mother's old fridge. That evened things up a bit, I thought, but I would have loved to have been able to grab the gun and turn it on its owner.

'*Ebi se!*' the man said explosively.

I didn't know what he meant, and it sadly didn't stop him coming through the window.

I raised the umbrella for another strike but he was wise to me now and he grabbed it as it descended and tore it from my grasp, tossing it aside as he stepped right through the open window, crouching on the worktop.

I rushed at him but he was ready, pushing me aside with ease so that I stumbled across the kitchen towards the sink.

I turned quickly but the man had already jumped down to the floor. I watched him as he looked around and then withdrew a large carving knife from the wooden block next to my mother's stove. Now why hadn't I thought of that?

I moved quickly to my right, putting the dining table between him and me. If he couldn't reach me, he couldn't stab me either.

There followed a sort of ballet with him moving one way or the other, and me mirroring him, always keeping the table between us. Once we ran round and round the table three or four times with me watching carefully for him to change direction. He pulled out chairs to try to slow me down, but I was quick. I may not be as fit as I was as a jockey but I was still no slouch in the running department. It had fared me well in Lichfield Grove and was doing so again here.

But, for how long?

He only needed to get lucky once.

He changed his tactics, using one of the chairs to climb up onto the table, and then he came straight at me across it.

I turned and ran for the stairs, pulling open the latch door, and bounding up the steps two or three at a time. I could hear him behind me and he was gaining.

Where could I go? I was running out of options.

Panic began to rise in my throat. I didn't want to die.

I turned to face him. At least I would see it coming and I'd be able to make some effort to get away from the thrust of the knife.

He stood at the top of the stairs with me just four feet away in front of him. He advanced a step and I retreated a step, then we both repeated the drill, but my back was now up against the wall. I had no further to go.

He came a step closer to me and I readied myself for his strike, although what I would do when it came, I didn't know.

Die, probably.

Claudia stepped out of the bathroom, just down the corridor to his right.

'Fuck off, you bastard,' she shouted at him with full fortissimo. 'Leave him alone.' She then slammed the bathroom door shut again and locked it.

He turned momentarily towards the noise and I leapt at him, wrapping my right arm round his neck with my forearm across his throat while, at the same time, I tried to gouge his eyes out with the fingers of my left hand.

I squeezed his neck with all my strength.

But it was not enough.

The man was considerably taller and stronger than I and, in spite of my best grip, he simply began to turn himself round to face me. And with both of my arms held up round his head, my abdomen would be totally defenceless to a thrust of the knife.

What had that spinal specialist told me?

'Whatever you do,' he'd said, 'don't get into a fight.'

He'd said nothing about falling down stairs.

I hung on to the man's neck as if my life depended on it, which it probably did, and then I dived head first down the narrow boxed-in stairway, taking the man down with me. It was a crazy thing to do, especially for someone who had precious little holding his head to his body. But it was my only chance.

I twisted as we fell so that I landed on top of the man, his head taking the full force of the heavy contact with the wall where the stairway turned through ninety degrees half-way down. We slithered on to the bottom of the wooden stairs coming to a halt still locked together by my right arm, which I was still pulling as tightly as I could round his neck. We were lying partially through the lever-latch doorway, our legs still on the stairs, with our heads and torsos sticking out into the room below.

Even for me on top, and using the man's body to break my fall, the first impact with the wall had been enough to drive the air from my lungs, but at least my head hadn't fallen off with it.

I pulled my arm from under his neck and jumped to my feet ready to continue the fight, but there was no need. The man lay limply, face down, where he'd come to rest.

I went quickly to fetch my mother's collapsible walking stick, and then I used it to retrieve the gun from beneath her fridge, hooking it out with the handle.

If the man moved so much as an eyebrow, I thought, I'd shoot him.

I stood over him for what felt like a very long time, pointing the gun at his head and watching for any movement.

But the man didn't move. Not even to breathe.

Nevertheless, I still didn't trust him not to jump up and kill me, so I kept the gun pointing at him all the time.

'Claudia,' I shouted as loudly as I could. 'Claudia, I need your help.'

I heard the bathroom door being unlocked and then footsteps on the floorboards above my head.

'Has he gone?' Claudia asked from the top of the

stairs. It was so dark that she couldn't even see the man lying right beneath her.

'I think he might be dead,' I said. 'But I'm taking no chances, and it's getting so dark I can hardly see him.'

'I've got a torch by my bed,' my mother said in a matter-of-fact tone.

I heard her walk along the corridor to her room then she came back shining the torch brightly down the stairwell.

'Oh, my God!' Claudia said, looking down.

In the torchlight we could see that the man's head was lying almost flat against his right shoulder in a most unnatural position. The man's neck was clearly broken, just as mine had once been.

But, on this occasion, there were no friendly paramedics to apply an immobilizing collar, no one to save his life with prompt and gentle care as there had been for me at Cheltenham racecourse all those years ago.

This man's broken neck had bumped on down to the bottom of a wooden stairway, all the time being wrenched to one side by my arm.

And it had killed him.

15

'What the hell do we do now?' Claudia said from the top of the stairs.

'Call the police,' I said from the bottom.

'How?'

'I'll take the car and find somewhere with a signal,' I said.

But there was no way Claudia and my mother were allowing me to go off in the car, leaving them alone in the house with the gunman. Dead or not, they were still very frightened of him, and I can't say I blamed them.

'Pack up our things,' I said to Claudia. 'Mum, pack an overnight bag. No, take enough for a few days. We're going somewhere else.'

'But why?' my mother asked.

'Because someone sent this man here to kill me and, when they find out that he hasn't succeeded, that someone might send another to try again.'

Neither of them asked the obvious question – why was the man trying to kill me? Instead they both quickly went together to pack, taking the torch with them, and leaving me standing in the dark.

In spite of being pretty certain the man was indeed dead, I didn't stop listening, holding the gun ready in case he made a miraculous recovery.

I found I was shaking.

I took several deep breaths but the shaking continued. Perhaps it was from fear, or relief, or maybe it was a reaction to the sudden realization that I had killed a man. Probably a bit of all three.

The shaking continued for several minutes and I became totally exhausted by it. I wanted to sit down, and I felt slightly sick.

'We're packed,' Claudia said from upstairs, the torchlight again shining down the stairway.

'Good,' I said. 'Pass the things down to me.'

I stepped carefully onto the first few stairs, next to the man's legs, and reached up as Claudia handed down our bags and my mother's suitcase.

Next, I guided each of them down in turn, making sure they stepped only on the wood and not on the man.

'Oh, my God. Oh, my God,' Claudia said, repeating it over and over again as she came nervously down the stairs, pressing herself against the side while, at the same time, holding her hands up to ensure she wouldn't touch the man by mistake.

My mother was, surprisingly, much more stoical, waltzing down the stairs as if there was nothing there. In fact, I suspected that she would've liked to have given the corpse a sharp kick for ruining her roast dinner.

The three of us went out to the car, loaded the stuff, and drove away down the rutted lane, leaving the dead man alone in the dark house.

*

I drove into Cheltenham and called the police, but I didn't dial the emergency number. Instead, I called Chief Inspector Tomlinson on his mobile.

'The man who killed Herb Kovak,' I said, 'is lying dead at the bottom of my mother's stairway.'

There was the slightest of pauses.

'How tiresome of him,' the chief inspector said. 'Did he just lie down there and die?'

'No,' I said. 'He broke his neck falling down the stairs.'

'Was he pushed?' he asked, once again demonstrating his suspicious mind.

'Helped,' I said. 'We fell down the stairs together. He came off worse. But he was trying to stab me with a carving knife at the time.'

'What happened to his gun?' he asked.

'He lost it under the fridge,' I said.

'Hmm,' he said. 'And have you told the local constabulary?'

'No,' I said. 'I thought you could do that. And you can also tell them he was a foreigner.'

'How do you know?'

'He said something I didn't understand.'

'And where are you now?' he asked.

'In Cheltenham,' I said. 'The gunman cut the power and the telephone wires. I've had to leave to make a call on my mobile. There's no signal at the cottage.'

'Is anyone still at the cottage?'

'Only the dead man,' I said. 'I have Claudia and my mother with me in the car.'

'So are you going back there now?' he asked.

'No,' I said firmly. 'Whoever sent this man could send another.'

'So where are you going?' he asked, not questioning my decision.

'I don't know yet,' I said. 'I'll call you when I do.'

'Who knew you were at your mother's place?' he asked, always the detective.

'Everyone in my office,' I said. And whomever else Mrs McDowd had told, I thought.

'Right,' he said. 'I'll call the Gloucestershire Police but they'll definitely want to talk to you, and to Claudia and your mother. They may even want you back at the cottage.'

'Tell them I'll call them there in two hours,' I said.

'But you said the line had been cut.'

'Then get it fixed,' I said. 'And get the power back on. Tell them I think my mother has left the stove on. I don't want the place burning down when the power's reconnected. And also tell them I've left the back door unlocked so they won't have to break the front door down to get in.'

'OK,' he said. 'I'll tell them.' He paused. 'Is the gun still under the fridge?'

'No,' I said. 'I retrieved it.'

'So where is it now?'

I had so wanted to bring it with me, to give myself the armed protection that I'd been denied by the police.

'It's outside the front door,' I said. 'In a bush.'

'Right,' he said, sounding slightly relieved. 'I'll tell

the Gloucestershire force that too. Save them hunting for it, and you.'

'Good,' I said.

It had been the right decision to leave the gun behind. I could still claim the moral high ground.

I hung up and switched off my phone. I would call the police on *my* terms, and I also didn't want anyone being able to track my movements from the phone signal.

'Do you really think we're still in danger?' Claudia asked from next to me.

'I don't know,' I said, 'but I'm not taking any chances.'

'Who knew we were there?' she asked.

'Everyone at the office, I expect,' I said. 'Mrs McDowd definitely knew, and she'd have told everyone else.'

And Detective Chief Inspector Tomlinson had known as well.

I'd told him myself.

It was my mother who finally asked the big question.

'Why was that man trying to kill you?' she said calmly from the back seat.

We were on the road between Cirencester and Swindon.

I'd made one more stop in Cheltenham, at one of the few remaining public phone boxes. I hadn't wanted to use my mobile for fear that someone could trace who I was calling. We were going where no one would find us.

'I'm not totally sure, but it may be because I am a witness to him killing a man at Aintree Races,' I said. 'And it wasn't the first time he'd tried.'

Neither my mother nor Claudia said anything. They were waiting for me to go on.

'He was waiting outside our house in Lichfield Grove when I got back there on Tuesday afternoon,' I said. 'Luckily, I could run faster than him.'

'Is that why we came to Woodmancote?' Claudia asked, 'instead of going home.'

'It sure is,' I said. 'But I didn't realize that Woodmancote wasn't safe either. Not until it was too late. I won't make that mistake again.'

'But what about the police?' my mother asked. 'Surely we must go to the police. They will look after us.'

But how much did I trust the police? I didn't know that either. They hadn't given me any protection when I'd asked for it, and that omission had almost cost us our lives. No, I thought, I'd trust my own instincts. The police seemed more interested in solving murders than preventing them.

'I have been to the police,' I said, driving on through the darkness. 'But it will be *me* who will look after you.'

And I would also find out who was trying to have me killed, and the real reason why.

'Well, lover-boy,' Jan Setter said, 'when I asked you to come and stay, I didn't exactly mean you to bring your girlfriend and your mother with you!'

We laughed.

We were sitting at her kitchen table in Lambourn drinking coffee, the said girlfriend and mother having been safely tucked up in two of Jan's many spare bedrooms.

'I didn't know where else to go,' I said to her.

I had briefly thought about going to my father's bungalow in Weymouth but he had only two double bedrooms and, amusing as the thought had been, I could hardly expect my parents to share a bed, not after seven years of divorce, and I certainly wasn't sleeping with the old bugger.

'So what's all this about?' Jan asked finally.

All I had said to her on the phone from Cheltenham had been that I was desperate and could she help by putting us up for a night or two.

'How desperate?' she had asked calmly.

'Life or death,' I'd said. 'Complete secrecy.'

She had asked nothing further but had simply said 'come', and she'd asked no questions when we'd arrived, not until after my traumatized mother and fiancée had been safely ushered up to bed. As it had with me, the shock and fear had manifested itself in them after the event.

In all the years I had known Jan, both as her former jockey and, more recently, as her financial adviser, I had never known her to be flustered or panicked by anything. She was the steady head I needed in this crisis.

But how much did I tell her?

Would she even believe me?

'I know this is going to sound rather overly dramatic,' I said, 'but someone is trying to kill me.'

'What's her name?' Jan asked with a laugh.

'I'm being serious, Jan,' I said. 'Tonight a man came to my mother's cottage to murder me. He had a gun. I promise you, we are extremely fortunate to be alive. The same man has now tried to kill me twice.'

'Let's hope it isn't third time lucky.'

'He won't get a third time.'

'How can you be sure?' she asked.

'Because he's dead. The last time I saw him he was lying on the floor of my mother's sitting room with his neck broken.'

She stared at me. 'You are being serious, aren't you?'

I nodded. 'Very.'

'Have you called the police?'

'Yes,' I said. 'But I need to call them again.' I looked at my watch. It had been at least two hours since I'd spoken to Chief Inspector Tomlinson. But they could wait a little longer.

'So why come here?' she asked. 'Why not go straight to the police?'

'I need somewhere to hide where no one can find me.'

Not even the police, I thought.

'But, if the man's dead, why do you still need to hide?' she asked.

'Because he was a hired killer and I am worried that whoever hired him will simply hire another.'

I could tell from the look on Jan's face that her credulity had reached its limit.

'It's true, I assure you,' I said. 'I'm not making it up, and I think it's all to do with stealing a hundred million euros from the European Union. Now that really is big money. And what's the going rate for having someone killed these days? Twenty thousand? A hundred grand, maybe? Or even half a million? That's still only a half of one per cent of the take. Cheap at twice the price.'

'But what have *you* got to do with stealing a hundred million euros?' she asked.

'Nothing,' I said. 'But I may have asked the wrong question to those that have. And I suspect that somebody believes I need to be permanently removed before I ask some more questions and bring the whole scheme tumbling down round their ears.'

'So what are you going to do?' she said.

'Ask the questions quickly,' I said, grinning at her. 'And then keep my head down.'

Someone answered after just one ring when I called my mother's cottage. I was sitting in Jan's office and using her mobile phone, and I had carefully withheld the number from caller-ID. I hoped it was enough to keep it secret.

'Hello,' I said.

'Is that Nicholas Foxton?' came a man's voice in reply.

'It is,' I said. 'To whom am I talking?'

'Detective Chief Inspector Flight,' he said. 'Gloucestershire Police.'

Not another detective chief inspector, I thought. What's the collective noun for detective chief inspectors? It was a posse of police, so maybe it's an evidence of detective chief inspectors.

'Where are you, Mr Foxton?' asked this particular chief inspector.

'Somewhere safe,' I said.

'And where is that?' he asked again.

I ignored him. 'Who was the man who tried to kill me?' I asked.

'Mr Foxton,' he said. 'I need you to come to a police station to be interviewed. Tonight.'

He was persistent, I'd give him that.

'Have you spoken to DCI Tomlinson from Merseyside Police?' I asked. 'Or Superintendent Yering from the Metropolitan Police Armed Response Team?'

'No,' he said. 'Not personally.'

'Then I suggest you do,' I said.

'Mr Foxton,' he said. 'You are in danger of obstructing the police in the course of their duties. Now, please, tell me where you are.'

'No,' I said. 'Did you watch the television news on Tuesday? The dead man in my mother's cottage is the same man as in the video. And I think he was foreign. He said something I didn't understand. Something like "*ebi se*".'

'Mr Foxton.' Detective Chief Inspector Flight was getting quite worked up. 'I must insist you tell me where you are.'

'And I must insist you speak to DCI Tomlinson or Superintendent Yering.'

I hung up.

That didn't go too well, I thought. Too bad. But I was definitely not going to any police station to be interviewed tonight, or any other night if I could help it. People could get shot at police stations. Ask Lee Harvey Oswald.

I heard Jan leave the house at a quarter to seven in the morning to supervise the exercising of her horses on the gallops. She had asked if I wanted to accompany her up onto the downs to watch, but I had declined, not because I didn't want to, but because I didn't want anyone to recognize me and hence know where I was staying.

It may have been eight years since I was a regular in Lambourn, but there were plenty who had been here longer than that, even amongst Jan's staff, and most would have known me by sight.

I realized it was highly unlikely that news of my whereabouts would then get back to hostile ears, but I didn't want to take any unnecessary risks.

I got up as quietly as I could but Claudia was already awake.

'Don't go,' she said.

I snuggled down again next to her, under the covers.

'When will this all end?' she asked.

'Soon,' I said, but I really had no idea when.

'I was so frightened last night,' she said with tears in her eyes. 'I really thought he was going to kill you.'

I'd thought it too.

'But he didn't,' I said. 'So everything's all right.' I was trying to sound encouraging, even if I was not so sure inside.

'So why have we come here?' she asked. 'Why can't we go home now?'

'There's just a few things I have to do before we can go home,' I said, sitting up on the side of the bed. 'And I don't want to take any chances if we don't need to.'

'I think we should go to the police,' she said.

'I spoke to them last night after you went to bed. They agreed that it was better for us to stay here for a couple of days while they carry out their investigations.'

At least the first bit was true.

'So what is it that you have to do?' she asked.

'Well, first, I have to go to Oxford,' I said. 'And I'm going to do that right now.' I stood up and started to dress.

'I'll come with you,' Claudia said, throwing the duvet to one side and sitting up.

'No,' I said firmly. 'You stay here with Jan and my mother. You need to recover fully from your operation. And I won't be long. You'll be quite safe here.'

I think she was secretly relieved, as she lay down again and pulled the duvet back over her.

'Why are you going?' she asked.

'To see a young man at the university,' I said. 'I want

to ask him some questions about a factory, or rather, about the lack of a factory.'

I stopped on the outskirts of Oxford and turned on my mobile phone to call Detective Chief Inspector Tomlinson.

'DCI Flight of Gloucestershire Police is not happy with you,' he said. 'Not happy at all.'

'Too bad,' I said.

'He's applied for a warrant for your arrest on suspicion of manslaughter.'

'But that's ridiculous,' I said.

'Maybe it is,' he agreed, 'but he's really pissed off. I do think it might be better if you go and see him.'

'Not if he's going to arrest me.' I didn't relish spending another day in a police cell. 'Anyway,' I said, 'I have things to do first.'

'Not investigating again, are you?' said the professional detective. 'I've told you to leave that to the police.'

'But what are you going to investigate?' I said. 'It is me, not you, that believes Colonel Jolyon Roberts was murdered, but there is no evidence for that belief. In fact, quite the reverse. The evidence indicates that he died of natural causes, helped by a dose of stupidity. The police see no crime, so there is no investigation.'

'So what do you want me to do?' he asked.

'Speak to Flight,' I said. 'Get him off my back. Tell him there's no way I'll see him if he's going to arrest me.'

'I'll try,' he said. 'But I still think you ought to at least talk to him.'

'Get me his number,' I said. 'Then I'll call him.'

'How can I contact you?' he asked.

'Leave a message on this phone. I'll pick it up. Flight can do the same.'

'Anything else?' he asked.

'Yes,' I said. 'Can you find out if the dead man in my mother's cottage was Bulgarian?'

I thought about also asking him to get the fraud squad to initiate an investigation into the Balscott factory project but, as I knew from previous experience with a former client, fraud investigations involving foreign investments started with months and months of delving into paperwork before there was any prospect of an arrest. Add to that the complexities of the European Union grants system, and it would take years.

And I'd be dead and buried long before that.

I disconnected from DCI Tomlinson but the phone rang again in my hand almost immediately.

'This is your voicemail,' said an impersonal female voice when I answered. 'You have two new messages.'

One of them was from DCI Flight and, as the other chief inspector had said, he didn't sound very happy. I ignored it.

The other was from Patrick Lyall, who also wasn't pleased with me, in particular because I had left a message on his mobile saying that I wouldn't be coming into the office today.

'Nicholas,' Patrick's voice said, 'I am sorry that you

have decided not to be in the office once again. I think we need to have a talk about your commitment to the firm. I will be writing to you today, formally warning you as to your future conduct. Please would you call me and tell me where to have the letter delivered.'

It sounded to me as if the company lawyer had been advising him again on employment law – written warnings and all that.

I ignored him too.

Did I, in fact, have any future in the firm? And did I really care?

Keble College was on the north side of the city near the Oxford University Museum of Natural History. I parked in Museum Road and walked back to the college.

'Sorry, sir,' said a man in a smart blue jersey intercepting me in the entrance archway. 'The college is closed to the public. Trinity has begun.'

'Trinity?' I asked.

'Trinity term,' he said. 'The students are here.'

It hadn't even crossed my mind they wouldn't be.

'Exactly,' I said to him. 'I've come to see one of the students.'

'Which one?' he asked politely but firmly. He was obviously used to repelling visitors who had no good cause to be there.

'Benjamin Roberts,' I said.

'And is Mr Roberts expecting you?' he asked.

'No,' I said. 'It's a surprise visit.'

He looked at his watch, and I looked at mine. It was just past ten o'clock.

'It might be a bit early for Mr Roberts,' he said. 'I heard he was partying rather late last evening. But I'll try and call him. What name shall I say?'

'Smith,' I said. 'John Smith.'

The porter looked at me somewhat sceptically.

'I get that reaction all the time,' I said. 'Unimaginative parents.'

He nodded, as if making up his mind, and then disappeared into the porter's lodge.

I waited patiently under the arch.

Presently, the porter reappeared. 'Mr Roberts asks if you could come back later, around one o'clock.'

'Could you please call Mr Roberts again and tell him I'm from the Balscott Lighting Factory and I need to see him now.'

Benjamin Roberts appeared in three minutes flat with his long dark hair still unbrushed, bags under his eyes, and with no socks beneath his black leather shoes. He was tall, probably near six-foot four or five, and he towered over me at just five-foot eight.

'Mr Smith?' he asked. I nodded. 'Jarvis here tells me you're from the Balscott factory.'

We were still standing in the entrance archway with students passing us continually in both directions, and with Jarvis, the porter, hovering nearby.

'Is there anywhere quiet we could go and talk?' I asked.

He turned to the porter. 'Thank you, Jarvis, I'll be taking Mr Smith up to the Dining Hall for a while.'

'All visitors have to be signed in,' Jarvis said rather officiously.

Benjamin Roberts went into the lodge for a moment and then reappeared.

'Bloody rules,' he said. 'They treat us like kids.'

We walked along a gravel path down the side of a building and then up some wide steps to the college dining hall, an impressively tall space with three lines of refectory tables and benches running along its full length.

Some catering staff at the far end of the hall were laying up for lunch but Benjamin and I sat down close to the door, across one of the tables from each other.

'Now,' he said, 'what's all this about?'

'Benjamin –' I said, starting.

'Ben,' he interrupted.

'Sorry, Ben,' I said, corrected. 'I was a friend of your uncle Jolyon.'

He looked down at his hands on the table. 'Such a shame,' he said. 'Uncle Jolyon was fun. I'll miss him.' He looked up again at me. 'But what have you to do with the factory?'

'Your uncle Jolyon told me that you'd recently been to Bulgaria.'

'Yes,' he said slowly. 'A group of us from the university skiing club went to Borovets during the Easter vac. It was very good value and great snow. You should try it.'

Not with my neck, I thought.

'But your uncle also said you went to see the factory.'

'There isn't any factory, is there?' he said.

'You tell me,' I said. 'You're the one that went to see it.'

He didn't answer but sat looking at me across the table.

'Who are you?' he said. 'Is Smith your real name?'

'No,' I admitted, 'it is not.'

'So, who are you?' he asked, standing up, and with a degree of menace in his voice. 'And what are you after?'

'I'm not after anything,' I said defensively, looking up at him. 'Except to be left alone.'

'Then why are you here? If you want to be left alone, why don't you just go away?'

'I would, but someone is trying to kill me,' I said, this time without looking up at his face. It was hurting my neck. 'Now, will you please sit down.'

He slowly lowered his huge frame back down onto the bench. 'Who is trying to kill you?' he asked in a tone that indicated disbelief. 'And why?'

'I don't know who,' I said. 'Not yet. But I think I may know why. Your uncle approached me because he was worried that the family's investment in the Bulgarian factory project was a scam. He had been shown photographs of the factory buildings, but you had then told him that they didn't actually exist. So he asked me to look into it, to check that, in his words, it wasn't a rotten egg of an investment.'

He smiled at the use of the words. They were clearly familiar to him.

'And,' I went on, 'I think that it is, indeed, a rotten egg of an investment. Your family money was the key to everything because the private finance for the factory triggered the public funding for all the houses. Someone has been defrauding the European Union out of a hundred million euros by obtaining grants towards the cost of building a light-bulb factory and hundreds of homes that don't actually exist, and never will. And that same someone is trying to kill me before I can prove it, and before I find out who they are.'

I paused and Ben Roberts sat staring at me in silence.

'And,' I said, going on, 'I believe your uncle may have been murdered for the same reason.'

16

'Uncle Jolyon wasn't murdered, he died of a heart attack,' Ben Roberts said unequivocally. 'At least, he had a heart attack and then he drowned.'

Ben looked down again at the table in front of him. Jolyon Roberts had died only four days previously. It was still very recent – very raw.

'Did you know that he was drunk when he drowned?' I asked.

'He couldn't have been,' Ben said, looking up at me.

'The post mortem showed he was.'

'But that's impossible.'

'Why? Because he didn't drink?'

'Never,' Ben said. 'He might have a tiny sip of champagne occasionally, you know, at a wedding for a toast, that sort of thing, but otherwise he never touched any alcohol.'

'Did he ever drink whisky?' I asked. 'Late at night, maybe?'

'Not that I was aware of,' Ben said. 'And I very much doubt it. I tried to get him to have a beer at my twenty-first birthday party but I had no chance. He said that he didn't like booze, so it was no hardship not to have it.'

'Was he teetotal because of his heart condition?' I asked.

'Heart condition?' Ben said. 'Whatever gave you the impression Uncle J had a heart condition? His heart was as strong as an ox. Or, at least we all thought it was until last Monday.'

Perhaps Ben hadn't known about his uncle's heart condition, I thought. After all, it's not the sort of thing people usually advertise about themselves.

'Tell me about your trip to Bulgaria,' I said. 'When you went to see the factory.'

'There's absolutely nothing there,' he said. 'Nothing at all. And the locals know nothing about it. They've never even heard of any plans to build a factory, let alone the houses.'

'Are you sure you were in the right place?' I asked.

He glanced at me with a look that could only be described as one of contempt.

'Of course I'm sure,' he said. 'I took all the details with me so that I would be able find it. My family are so proud of what the Trust does to help those less fortunate than ourselves. That's why I was so keen for the skiing club to go to Bulgaria in the first place, and especially to Borovets. It was close enough so I could spend a day going to see the factory if I wanted.'

'Did anyone know you were going to the factory?' I asked.

'No,' he said. 'I wasn't absolutely sure that I would. It depended on the snow and the weather. To be honest, I'd much rather ski than visit factories but, on one day, the cloud was right down on the slopes so I went, but the factory wasn't there.'

'Where was it meant to be?' I asked.

'Close to a village called Gorni, south of Sofia. But, when I saw the site, it was nothing more than a toxic waste dump left over from the mass industrialization of the country during the Soviet era.'

'So what have you done about it?' I asked. 'Your family has invested a lot of money into the project.'

'Yeah, and lost it all too.' He sounded resigned to the loss.

'Aren't you even going to try to get it back?'

'I don't expect so,' Ben said. 'My father is worried that the family name will be discredited. What he means is that we will be shown up to have been bloody fools – and fools that were easily separated from their money. He is furious about it, but mostly because he was talked into it by Uncle Jolyon and some financial adviser chap.'

'Gregory Black?' I asked.

'He's the one,' he said.

'So your father says to forget it? Forget five million pounds, just like that?'

'It's only money,' he said almost flippantly. 'And money is fairly easy to replace. It's not like one's family reputation. It can take many generations to repair damage to one's family's standing, and sometimes it can never be restored.'

It sounded to me that he was quoting his father.

'But it's not possible to replace your Uncle Jolyon,' I said.

'That's surely all the more reason to forget about

the whole thing. If the stress of this factory business gave Uncle J his heart attack, then we should unquestionably let sleeping dogs lie. Otherwise our foolishness will be shown to have cost the family far more than mere money.'

'But I believe your uncle was murdered,' I said. 'Don't you want justice?'

'Would that bring him back?' he said angrily. 'No, of course it wouldn't. And, anyway, I believe that you are wrong. In fact, I believe you are just here to cause my family trouble.' He stood up quickly, bunching his fists. 'What is it you're really after? Do you want money? Is that it? Money or you'll go to the papers?'

This could get very nasty, and very quickly, I thought. I didn't move but just sat still on the bench, not even looking up at him.

'I don't want your money,' I said calmly.

But what did I want?

Did I really care if some clever Eurocrat in Brussels and a Bulgarian property entrepreneur were conspiring to steal a hundred million euros from the European Union, with or without the help of Gregory Black? Or did I care that the Roberts Family Trust had been duped out of five million pounds?

No, I decided. I didn't care about either of those things.

And was I really bothered whether Jolyon Roberts had died of natural causes, or if he'd been murdered?

No, I suppose I didn't even care about that. He had been a nice enough man, and I was sorry he was dead, but it didn't make any real difference to me how he'd died.

But I did care that someone had killed Herb Kovak, and I cared very much more that they were trying to kill me too.

'So what exactly do you want?' Ben Roberts asked belligerently from somewhere above my eye-line.

'I want what is right,' I said. Whatever that meant.

And, I thought, I want to live a long and happy life with my future wife.

I looked up at his face. 'What is it that *you* want?' I asked back. He didn't answer and I went on looking at him. 'Your uncle told me you wanted to change the world.'

He laughed. 'Uncle J was always saying that.'

'And is it true?' I asked.

He thought for a moment.

'It's true that I want to be a politician,' he said. 'And all politicians hope to be in power. To be in a position to make the changes they believe in, otherwise there'd be no point.' He paused. 'So, yes, I suppose I do want to change the world. And for the better.'

'For the better, as *you* see it,' I said.

'Obviously.'

'So,' I said, 'is it for the better that you value your family's reputation ahead of doing what is right by your late uncle?'

He sat down again and stared at me.

'What's your real name?' he asked.

'Foxton,' I said. 'Nicholas Foxton. I am a financial

adviser with Lyall and Black, the same firm where Gregory Black works.'

'Well, Mr Nicholas Foxton, financial adviser, what is it that *you* really want?' he asked. 'And why have you come here?'

'I need to find out more about your family's investment in the Bulgarian project,' I said. 'I simply don't have enough information to take my concerns to the authorities. They'd probably laugh at me. All I have are some copies of the original transaction report, some e-mails between someone in Brussels and a man in Bulgaria, and a sackful of suspicion. And, now that your uncle is dead, I can't ask *him*.'

'So why don't you go and ask Gregory Black?' he said.

'Because I'm not altogether sure that I trust him.' In fact, I was sure I didn't.

'OK. I'll speak to my father about it,' Ben said. 'But, I can tell you now, he won't like it, and he probably won't talk to you.'

'Ask him anyway,' I said.

'How do I contact you?' he asked.

'Leave a message on my mobile.' I gave him the number, which he stored on his own phone.

'Please speak to him soon.'

'I'm going home tonight for the weekend,' Ben said. 'I'll try to find the right moment to speak to him on Sunday afternoon. He's always at his most relaxed after a good Sunday lunch.'

I hoped it would be soon enough.

*

When I returned to Jan's place in Lambourn at four thirty, I found her, Claudia and my mother sitting round the kitchen table and they were already hard at the vino.

'Bit early, isn't it?' I said, looking at my watch and declining the offered glass of Chardonnay.

'Early?' Claudia said with a giggle. 'We started at lunchtime.'

The others giggled with her.

'Are you sure it's wise to drink so soon after surgery?' I asked. 'Especially on top of your painkillers.'

'Don't be such a killjoy,' Jan said amid more sniggering.

What a fine state of affairs, I thought. I was trying to keep us alive and my mother and fiancée were drunk.

'So what have you done today, other than drinking?' I asked.

'Nothing,' Jan said. 'We've been talking, that's all.'

'I thought you'd be at the races,' I said to her.

'No runners today,' she said. 'But I've got to go now to evening stables.' She stood up with a slight wobble and giggled again. 'Oops, I think I've had a bit too much.'

A lot too much, I thought. But what the hell, it was Friday afternoon, and it had been quite a week.

I left them refilling their glasses and went upstairs to fetch my computer. I then used Jan's broadband to connect to the internet, and checked my e-mails. As always, there were the usual collection from fund managers, but nestling amongst them was one from

Patrick Lyall. It was timed at 3.50 p.m. He had clearly become fed up waiting for me to return his call telling him where to send the letter. I could almost feel the anger as I read it.

'Nicholas,' he had written, 'As you have obviously decided not to reply to my telephone call asking for your whereabouts, I have no option but to deliver the attached letter to you by e-mail. I find the whole situation most unsatisfactory. I hope that you soon come to your senses and start giving the firm the priority it deserves. Patrick.'

I clicked on the attachment. It was a letter from the lawyer, Andrew Mellor, acting on behalf of Lyall & Black. There were no niceties, and the letter was very much to the point.

Mr Foxton,
In accordance with the Employment Act 2008, I am writing to inform you that your employer, Lyall and Black and Co. Ltd, hereby give notice that they consider your recent behaviour to be far below the standard expected from an employee in your position. Consequently, Lyall and Black and Co. Ltd hereby issue you with a formal warning as to your future conduct. Furthermore, and in keeping with the statutory requirements as laid down in the Act, you are requested and required to attend a disciplinary meeting with Patrick Lyall and Gregory Black at the company offices in Lombard Street,

London, at nine o'clock on the Monday morning following the date of this letter.
Yours sincerely,
Andrew Mellor, LLB

It sounded to me that, this time, I really was about to be fired.

Strangely, I didn't seem to care any more. Perhaps that policeman at Aintree had been right all along – becoming a financial adviser had been a bit of a comedown from the thrill of being a jump jockey.

Maybe it was time for me to look for more excitement in my life?

Like being shot at? Or stabbed?

I think not. I'd had enough of that.

On Saturday morning I left the three women nursing their hangovers while I went to visit Billy Searle in the Great Western Hospital in Swindon.

'So who knocked you off your bike?' I asked him.

'Don't you bloody start,' he said. 'The fuzz have been asking me nothing else but that since I woke up.'

'So why don't you tell them?' I said.

'Are you effing stupid or something?' he said. 'I'd rather go on living, thank you very much.'

'So it wasn't an accident?' I said.

'I didn't say that. It might have been.'

'Now who's being effing stupid?' I said.

He stuck two fingers up at me and said nothing.

We were in a single room, hidden away at the far end of one of the wards. It had taken me three separate requests to find him as well as a security escort that had only departed after Billy had vouched for me as his friend, not foe.

'How much longer are you going to be here?' I asked him. He clearly wasn't going anywhere soon as he was firmly attached to the bed by a weights contraption that was pulling on his right leg.

'About another week,' he said. 'At least, that's what they tell me. They need to apply something called a fixator to my leg but they can't do that until the traction has pulled everything straight. Then I'll be able to get up.'

'I thought they pinned and plated broken legs these days.'

'I did too,' he said. 'But the doc here says that this is the best way, and who was I to argue?' He grinned. Both he and I knew that Billy Searle argued all the time. 'Anyway, I was effing unconscious at the time.'

'They thought you were going to die,' I said.

'No bloody chance,' he replied, still grinning.

'And *I* was arrested for your attempted murder.'

'Yeah,' he said. 'So I heard. Serves you right.'

'What for?' I said.

He laughed. 'For being such a boring bastard.'

Was I really boring?

'I'm sorry.'

'You were much more fun as a jock,' Billy said. 'Do you remember that time we all got thrown out of that effing hotel in Torquay after your big win at Newton Abbot?'

I smiled. I remembered it well. 'It was all your fault,' I said. 'You poured champagne into their grand piano.'

'Yeah, well, so maybe I did,' he said. 'But it was a crap piano anyway. And it was you throwing those pot plants around that did for us in the end.'

It was true, I thought. The plants had come out of their pots and the earth had spread all over the new carpet. The hotel manager had not been at all pleased. We had been politely asked to leave, and never to come back, or else he would call the police.

Billy and I laughed together at the memory.

'Those were the days,' he said. 'Carefree and bloody stupid we were.'

'But such fun,' I said, still laughing.

For both of us, it seemed, fun had been on the wane recently.

'So who do you owe a hundred grand to?' I asked. The laughter died in Billy's throat. But he didn't answer. 'Was it the same guy who tried to kill you?'

He still didn't answer. He just looked at me.

'Or was he just trying to give you a gentle reminder to pay up, a reminder that went too far?'

'Did the bloody cops tell you to ask me that?' he said crossly.

'No, of course not,' I said. 'They don't even know I'm here.'

'So why are you so bloody interested in me all of a

sudden?' The bonhomie of just a couple of minutes previously had disappeared completely.

'Billy. I'm just trying to help you,' I said.

'I don't need your fucking help,' he said explosively, just as he'd done outside the Weighing Room at Cheltenham.

'That's what you said to me once before, and you ended up in here. Next time, it might be the morgue.'

He lay back against the hospital pillows and said nothing.

'All right,' I said. 'If you won't tell me who, at least tell me why you owe someone a hundred thousand. Then I can properly advise you about your financial dealings.'

'I can't,' he said, staring at the ceiling. 'Even if I didn't end up dead, which I probably would, I'd have no bloody job left.'

'Against the Rules of Racing,' I quoted, somewhat self-righteously.

He turned his head and gave me a sideways look.

'Actually, no. At least not that time. That's what's so bloody ironic.'

He paused.

'What's ironic?' I prompted.

'Are you sure you're not working for the fuzz?'

'I swear on a bottle of champagne in a grand piano,' I said with a smile.

'And some separated effing pot plants?' he asked, smiling also.

'Them too,' I said, placing my right hand over my heart.

He thought for a while longer, as if still debating whether or not to tell me.

'I won a race I should have lost,' he said finally.

'What do you mean, a race you should have lost?'

'I told him I'd lose, but then I went and bloody won it,' he said.

'That was rather careless of you.'

'No, not really,' he said. 'I did it on purpose. I was so fed up with that bastard Vickers overtaking me in the championship, I was trying to win on everything I rode. Fat lot of good it did me. I've come bloody second yet again.'

'So who was it that you told you'd lose the race?'

He thought for a moment.

'Sorry, mate,' he said. 'I can't tell you that. My effing life wouldn't be worth tuppence.'

'Is he a bookie?' I asked.

'No,' he said with certainty. 'He's a bloody nob.'

I expect, to Billy, anyone who spoke the Queen's English without a liberal scattering of swear words would be classed as a 'nob'.

'Which nob in particular?' I asked.

'I'm not saying,' he said. 'But even if I did you wouldn't effing believe it.'

'And does this nob still want his hundred thousand?'

'I expect so,' he said. 'That's what he claims he lost because I won the race. But I haven't actually talked to him since this little caper. Perhaps I'll tell him to bugger off. A broken leg must be worth a hundred grand at least.'

'Tell him you'll enlighten the cops as to the identity of your attacker if he doesn't leave you alone.'

'Don't be bloody naïve,' he said. 'These sort of guys don't mess about. Telling him that would get me killed for sure.'

'Sounds to me like you're in trouble if you do say who attacked you, and also if you don't.'

'You are so right,' he said. 'Once you say *yes* to them the first time, you're bloody hooked for life. They've got you by the balls, and there's no way out.' He leaned his head back against the white pillows and I thought there were tears in his eyes.

'Billy,' I said. 'There never will be a way out unless you fight back.'

'Well, count me out,' he said adamantly without moving. 'I am not going to be first over the top to be shot down. I value my jockey's licence.'

'So how often have you stopped one?' I asked.

'Too bloody often,' he said.

I was surprised. Billy didn't have a reputation as being a fixer.

'About ten times altogether, I suppose,' he said. 'Spread over the past three years or so. But I decided there would be no more when Frank Miller broke his leg in December, and I finally had the chance to be Champion Jockey.'

'But then young Mark Vickers pops up to beat you.'

'The bastard,' he said with feeling. 'It's not bloody fair.'
Life wasn't fair, I thought. Ask anyone with cancer.

Jan Setter had already left for Uttoxeter Races by the time I arrived back at her house at noon. I would have loved to have gone with her but I was worried that my enemies might have seen us together and worked out where I was staying.

Claudia was beginning to think I was becoming paranoid, but I would rather be paranoid than dead. And I only had to mention the dead gunman for her to agree to almost anything.

'But how much longer do we need to stay here?' she asked. 'I want to go home.'

'I do too, my darling,' I said. 'We will go home just as soon as it is safe.'

I had asked Jan over breakfast how much longer we could stay.

'How long do you need?' she'd asked.

'I don't know. Another few days at least.'

'I'll need you out by next Friday at the latest,' she'd said. 'I've got my sister and her family coming for the weekend.'

By next Friday we would have been here for eight nights.

'I sincerely hope it won't be as long as that,' I'd said. But, in truth, I had no real idea when it might be safe to go home.

'That's a shame,' Jan had said. 'I'm quite enjoying

the company. I get so bored here on my own since my divorce.'

I logged on to the internet and checked my e-mails. There were none – it had to be the weekend. With the exception of dealings on foreign markets, which could extend the working week for a few hours at either end, all financial services in the UK usually went to sleep at five o'clock on a Friday afternoon and awoke again at eight on Monday morning, as if the weekend had never been.

Except, of course, for interest, which was charged daily on loans whatever day of the week it was.

I used online banking to check on my personal accounts.

Things might be going to get quite tight if I did lose my job at Lyall & Black. I had managed to save quite well over the previous five years but much of it had been used to pay off the debts that I'd run up as a student.

While I might regularly handle investments for others of hundreds of thousands, or even millions of pounds, my own nest egg was much more modest.

Historically, the stock market has always outperformed fixed-interest investments such as bank accounts, certificates of deposit, and government bonds. However, stock markets are very susceptible to even minor changes in investor confidence and can fluctuate quite dramatically, especially downwards. For long-term investment, say over ten or twenty years or more, the stock market is considered to be the best but, if you need your money out sooner, the risk that the market may go down suddenly just before you need it would be too great, and more lower-risk assets may be better. Consequently, as an investor gets older, and the time for buying a pension becomes nearer, the balance tends to move away from high-risk stocks and further towards the 'safer' bonds.

In my case, with my expected pension requirement still a long way over the horizon, my savings were almost totally in equities. I would ride the stock market roller-coaster, but hope and expect the underlying trend to be upwards.

If I did get fired from my job, I might need to live off my savings for a while. And then what would I do? Billy had accused me of being boring but it wasn't me that was boring, I decided, it was my job. I needed more excitement in my life, more adrenalin rushing through my veins, but not necessarily due to having a silenced pistol pointed at me.

But what could I do? I was trained and qualified only to be a financial adviser. But what I wanted to be most was a jockey, or a rodeo-rider, or a free-fall sky-diving instructor, or a crocodile fighter, or . . .

Bugger my dodgy neck.

My mother interrupted my depressing thoughts by asking me what I wanted for lunch.

'What have we got?' I asked.

'Jan said we can use whatever we want from the fridge, or from the larder.'

'So what is there?' I said.

'Come and have a look.'

In truth, there wasn't very much to choose from,

just a few low-calorie frozen meals for one in the freezer, with more bare shelves than anything in the larder. Old Mother Hubbard would have felt quite at home.

'Time to go shopping,' I said.

So the three of us piled into the unremarkable blue hire car and went to a huge supermarket on the outskirts of Newbury in order to fill the empty spaces in Jan's fridge and larder. It was the least we could do as uninvited guests.

While Claudia and my mother went from aisle to aisle loading two large trolleys with mountains of food, I was banished by them to the clothing section.

I browsed through the rails of shirts and trousers, jackets and suits, but, sadly, this particular supermarket didn't stock bulletproof vests.

17

Sunday was, indeed, a day of rest.

The trip to the supermarket had almost been too much for Claudia, who was still far from well after her surgery.

'Don't try and do too much too soon,' Mr Tomic, the surgeon, had said. 'Plenty of rest is needed to allow the abdominal wall to mend.'

He hadn't mentioned anything about running up stairs, shouting at gunmen, or food shopping, but he probably wouldn't have approved of any of them.

'You stay in bed today,' I said to Claudia. 'I'll fetch you some breakfast.'

She smiled and closed her eyes again as I went out.

Jan was already downstairs making toast.

'My God,' she said, going into the larder, 'we've even got marmalade!' She turned round and grinned at me. 'I can't remember when I last had so much food in here. I'm completely useless at cooking. All I can do is heat things up in the microwave. But you really shouldn't have bought so much.'

'Consider it our rent,' I said.

'You don't have to pay rent, lover-boy,' she said, coming back out of the larder and opening the marmalade. 'You can pay me in kind.' She laughed. 'Except I now know I have no chance of that.'

'I'm sorry,' I said.

'Don't be,' she said. 'I think Claudia is really lovely. You're a lucky man.' She paused and breathed deeply. 'And I suppose I'd better stop calling you lover-boy.'

There were tears in her eyes. I went over to her and gave her a hug. There was nothing to say, so I didn't speak, I just held her tightly until the moment had passed.

'Life can be so random,' she said, stepping back from me. 'When I was married to Stuart all I wanted was to divorce him and keep half his fortune. Well, I've done that but – and I know this sounds crazy – I miss him. I even miss the godawful rows we used to have. Now, with Maria away at university in London, I'm just a rich, lonely old spinster.'

'But you must have masses of friends,' I said.

She looked at me as she spread the marmalade on her toast. 'I have plenty of acquaintances, but no real friends. Racing is so competitive that I find it difficult to make any true friends with racing people. Of course, I know lots of them round here, other trainers and such, and I see them at the races, but I'm not a member of the village dinner-party set. All my friends were Stuart's friends and, when he went, they went too.'

'Well it's high time you met some more,' I said, trying to lighten the mood.

She laughed again, but only briefly. 'That's not as

simple as it sounds, and finding someone to satisfy one's needs is far from straightforward, I can tell you. You chaps have it made.'

'In what way?' I asked.

'If a man wants sex, he can just go and buy it from some girl on a street corner, or in some lap-dancing club,' she said. 'It's not so easy for a middle-aged woman.'

I stood there slightly dumbstruck. I had always treated her advances as a bit of a joke. I hadn't realized the degree of her desperation.

'Oh, Jan!' I said. 'I'm so sorry.'

'I don't want your pity,' she said, quickly turning away from me and taking the marmalade back into the larder.

No, I thought, she wanted my body.

I took a cup of coffee and some muesli up to Claudia.

'You took your time,' she said, sitting up in bed.

'Sorry. I was talking to Jan.'

'Isn't she lovely?' Claudia said. 'We had a long chat yesterday morning, while you were out.'

'What did you talk about?' I asked.

'Life in general,' she said obliquely. 'Stuff like that.'

'Did you tell her about ... you know?'

Why was the word *cancer* so difficult to use?

'I started to but then your mother came in, and I'm still not sure it's time to tell her yet.'

'But when will it be time?' I said. 'Now seems as good a time as any.'

'I suppose you're right,' she said. 'I just feel . . .' She stopped.

'What?' I said.

'I suppose I feel a failure. And I don't want her to be disappointed in me.'

'Don't be daft,' I said. 'She loves you.'

'Only because she thinks I'm her pathway to grandchildren.'

'That's not true,' I said, but I did wonder if she was right.

'And she won't love me if I marry you and then we find I can't have any babies. She will then see me not as a pathway but as an obstacle.'

She was almost in tears.

'Darling,' I said, 'please don't upset yourself. OK. If you don't want to, we won't tell her. Not yet.'

But we would have to tell her if, and when, Claudia's hair started falling out.

The rest of Sunday seemed to drag on interminably with me forever wondering how Ben Roberts was faring with his father. But, as I was still reluctant to leave my mobile phone switched on, I would have no way of knowing anyway.

My mother, with Jan helping, cooked roast beef for lunch with all the trimmings, the wonderful smells even enticing Claudia downstairs in her dressing gown.

'I can't tell you how long it's been since I had a proper Sunday lunch in this house,' Jan said as we all sat down at the kitchen table. 'Not since Stuart left, that's for sure. He used to do the cooking.' She laughed. 'Can't you stay for ever?'

The lunch was accompanied by a couple of bottles of the supermarket's finest claret, of which I had just one small glass. Someone had to keep their wits about them. I left the ladies to sleep it off on the deep sofas in the drawing room, while I again went to make some calls from Jan's office.

First I used her landline to remotely access my voicemail. There were four new messages. All were from Chief Inspector Flight, and each one threatened me with arrest if I didn't come forward immediately to speak to him. He read out a number where he could always be reached, and I wrote it down on the notepad beside the telephone.

But there was no message from Ben Roberts. Perhaps he hadn't yet found the right moment to speak to his father.

Next, I called DCI Tomlinson's mobile, taking care to dial 141 first to withhold Jan's number from caller-ID.

He answered at the fourth ring, but he sounded as if I'd woken him from a Sunday-afternoon slumber.

'Sorry,' I said. 'I thought you'd have your phone off if you weren't working.'

'I am working,' he said. 'I'm in my office. Just having forty winks on my desk. I was up half the night.'

'Partying?' I asked.

'Something like that,' he said. 'Or what goes for partying round these parts. An abused girlfriend finally had too much and stabbed her boyfriend to death.'

'Nice.'

'No,' he said, 'not really. She stabbed him about thirty times with a screwdriver. He bled to death. It was not a pretty sight, and especially not at four in the morning when I should have been tucked up in my bed.'

'Sorry,' I said.

'Thanks,' he replied. 'But it's sadly too common round here, especially after they've been drinking. I rarely get a full night's sleep on a Saturday.'

I decided against adding 'homicide detective' to my list of possible future careers.

'Do you have any news for me?' I asked.

'What sort of news?' he asked back.

'Anything,' I said. 'How about the dead man? Was he Bulgarian?'

'We don't know yet. His image and fingerprints haven't turned up on anything. Still waiting for the DNA analysis. But I can tell you one thing.'

'Yes?' I said eagerly.

'The forensic boys have been working overtime and they tell me the gun matches.'

'Matches what?' I asked.

'The gun found in the bush outside your mother's cottage was definitely the same gun that killed Herb Kovak, and they're pretty sure the same gun was also used to shoot at you in Finchley. They can't be a hundred per cent certain without the bullets.'

The image of the line of policemen crawling up Lichfield Grove on their hands and knees came into my mind. They obviously hadn't found anything.

'Does that mean that Chief Inspector Flight is now off my back?'

'I wouldn't exactly say that,' he said. 'He's still hopping mad.'

'Yes,' I said. 'I know. He's left messages on my phone.'

'Speak to him,' Tomlinson said. 'That's probably all he wants. He may think you're playing with him.'

'Does he still want to arrest me?' I asked.

'I don't know. Ask him.'

We disconnected.

I looked at the number on the notepad and thought about calling DCI Flight. Ignoring him would only make him madder, and then he might use more of his energies trying to find *me* than discovering the identity of his corpse. But I wasn't going to call him from here. Dialling 141 might be enough to prevent the number appearing on caller-ID but I was sure the police could still obtain it from the telephone company if they really wanted to.

But I'd called Chief Inspector Tomlinson using Jan's phone. What was the difference?

It was a matter of trust, I thought. I trusted Chief Inspector Tomlinson not to go to the trouble of finding where I was from the call. But I didn't trust DCI Flight.

So, at about five o'clock, I drove into the outskirts of Swindon and stopped in a pub car park before switching on my mobile and calling the Gloucestershire detective.

'DCI Flight,' he said crisply, answering at the first ring.

'This is Nicholas Foxton,' I said.

'Ah,' he said. 'And about time too.'

'Have you spoken to DCI Tomlinson and Superintendent Yering?' I asked.

'Yes,' he said slowly. 'I have.'

'Good,' I said. 'So who was the man at my mother's cottage?'

'Mr Foxton,' he replied curtly. 'It is *me* who needs to ask *you* some questions, not the other way round.'

'Ask away,' I said.

'What happened at your mother's cottage last Thursday evening?'

'A man with a gun broke in, we had a fight, and he fell down the stairs and broke his neck.'

'Is that all?' he asked.

'Isn't that enough?' I asked sarcastically. 'Oh yes, and he was trying to stab me at the time he fell down the stairs.'

'We found a knife under the body,' he said. 'But why did he need one? What happened to his gun?'

'It was under the fridge,' I said.

He paused.

'And how did it get under the fridge?'

'I hit it with an umbrella.'

This time there was a lengthy pause from the other end.

'Are you being serious, Mr Foxton?' he asked.

'Very,' I said. 'The man cut the power and the telephone. He then broke a pane of glass in the kitchen to get in and, as he was climbing through the window, I hit him with a golf umbrella. He dropped the gun, which slid under the fridge. He then took a knife from the block and tried to stab me. I managed to get upstairs but the man followed. As he was attacking me, we struggled and both of us fell down the stairs. He came off worse. End of story.'

There was another pause, another lengthy pause, almost as if the chief inspector had not been listening to me.

'Hold on,' I said suddenly. 'I'll call you back.'

I hung up, switched my phone off, and quickly drove the car out of the pub car park and down the road towards the city centre. After about half a mile, a police car with blue flashing lights drove past me, going fast in the opposite direction. Now was that just a coincidence, I wondered.

I went right round a roundabout and drove back to the pub, but I didn't go in. I drove straight past without even slowing down. The police car, still with its blue flashers on, had stopped so that it was completely blocking the pub car park entrance, and two uniformed policemen were getting out of it.

Was that also a coincidence? No, I decided, it was not.

I obviously hadn't needed to ask DCI Flight if he still wanted to arrest me. I'd just seen the answer.

I drove north along the A419 dual carriageway towards Cirencester, in the opposite direction to Lambourn, and pulled over near the village of Cricklade.

I turned my phone on again, and pressed redial.

DCI Flight answered immediately.

'Trust,' I said. 'That's what you need.'

'Give yourself up,' he said.

'But I've done nothing wrong.'

'Then you have nothing to fear.'

I hung up and switched off my phone. Then I started the car and made my way back to Lambourn, being careful not to speed or in any way attract the attention of any passing policeman.

Dammit, I thought. All I didn't need was an overly interfering detective who was more interested in catching me than in anything else. 'Give yourself up' indeed. Who did he think I was, Lord Lucan?

I caught the train from Newbury to Paddington just after seven o'clock on Monday morning, leaving the blue hire car in the station car park.

As the train slowed to a stop in Reading, I turned on my phone and called my voicemail.

'You have two new messages,' said the familiar female voice.

The first was from DCI Flight promising not to arrest me if I came to Cheltenham Police Station to be interviewed.

Why did I not believe him?

The second was from Ben Roberts.

'Mr Foxton, I have spoken with my father,' his voice said. 'He is not willing to meet with you or to discuss the matter further. I must also ask that you do not contact me again. I'm sorry.'

He didn't actually sound very sorry and I wondered if his father had been standing next to him as he had made the call.

My investigating wasn't exactly going very well. Where did I go from here?

I turned off my phone and sat back in my seat as the train rushed along the metal towards London. I watched absent-mindedly through the window as the Berkshire countryside gradually gave way to suburbs, and then to the big city itself, and I wondered what the day would bring.

I had to admit that I was nervous about the disciplinary meeting with Patrick and Gregory.

Lyall & Black had been my life for five years and I had begun to really make my mark. I had brought some high-profile, high-worth clients to the firm and some of my recommendations for investment, especially in film and theatre, had become standard advice across the company.

Over the next few years I might have expected to have expanded my own client base while giving up most of the responsibility of acting as one of Patrick's assistants. I might even have hoped to be offered a full senior partner position when Patrick and Gregory retired, and that would be only five or six years away. That was where the real money was to be made, and when my modest nest egg might start expanding rapidly. Providing, of course, that I was good enough to maintain the confidence of the clients.

However, I was now in danger of missing out completely.

But why? What had I done wrong?

It wasn't me who was defrauding the European Union of a hundred million euros, so why was it me who was attending a disciplinary meeting?

Perhaps the only thing I had done incorrectly was to not go straight to Patrick, or to Jessica Winter, the Compliance Officer, as soon as Mr Roberts had expressed his concerns over Gregory and the Bulgarian factory project. I should never have tried to investigate things behind their backs.

And I would rectify that mistake today.

I caught the Circle Line tube from Paddington to Moorgate and then walked from there towards Lombard Street.

As I walked down Prince's Street, alongside the high imposing walls of the Bank of England, I suddenly started to feel uneasy, the hairs again standing up on the back of my neck.

For the past four days, I had been so careful not to let anyone know where I was staying, yet here I was walking to a prearranged appointment at the offices of Lyall & Black. Furthermore, the appointment was for a meeting with one of those I believed was responsible for trying to kill me.

I really didn't fancy finding another gunman waiting for me in the street outside my office building.

I slowed to a halt on the pavement with people hurrying past me in each direction, late for their work. I was less than a hundred yards away from Lombard Street.

It was as near as I got.

I turned round and retraced my path back up Prince's Street to London Wall, where I went into a coffee shop and ordered a cappuccino.

Perhaps Claudia was right and I was becoming paranoid.

I looked at my watch. It was ten to nine. Patrick and Gregory would be expecting me in ten minutes.

What should I do?

My instinct at my mother's cottage had been absolutely right when I had prevented Claudia from opening the front door to the gunman. But I desperately needed to talk to someone about my suspicions, to set in motion a proper investigation into the Bulgarian affair. Surely then I would be safe, as killing me would then be too late. If Ben Roberts's father wouldn't talk to me, who else should I speak to? It had to be Patrick, if not to save my job, to at least to save my life.

I turned on my mobile phone and rang the office number.

'Lyall and Black,' answered Mrs McDowd. 'Can I help you?'

'Hello, Mrs McDowd,' I said. 'It's Mr Nicholas here. Can I speak to Mr Patrick, please?'

'He's in the meeting room with Mr Gregory and Andrew Mellor,' she said. 'I'll put you through.'

Patrick came on the line. 'Hello,' he said.

'Patrick,' I said. 'Please don't say anything. It's Nicholas. I need to talk to you alone,' I said. 'And without Gregory knowing.'

'Hold on a minute,' he said. 'I'll go to my office.'

There were some clicks on the line and then Patrick came back on.

'What's this all about?' he asked quite crossly. 'You are due to be here now for a disciplinary meeting.'

'I'm sorry,' I said, 'but I won't be coming to the meeting.'

'Nicholas,' he said formally, 'I must insist that you come into the office right now. Where are you?'

Where should I say?

'I'm at home,' I said. 'Claudia still isn't well.'

'I'm sorry,' he said, not sounding it. 'But this meeting is very important.'

So was Claudia, I thought.

'Where can I speak to you in private?' I asked.

'Here,' he said firmly and loudly. 'I will speak to you here, in the office, at the disciplinary meeting.'

'I'm sorry,' I said, 'but I will not be coming to the office today.'

'Listen to me,' he said. 'If you don't come into the

office today, there seems little point in you coming back at all.' He paused. 'Do I make myself clear?'

'Yes,' I said. 'I'll see what I can do.'

'Yes,' he said with ill-disguised anger. 'You do that.'

He hung up.

I could imagine him going straight back into the meeting room and telling Gregory and Andrew that I wasn't coming. I was just glad I hadn't told him the truth about where I was.

I caught the Tube from Moorgate Station, but not back to Paddington. Instead I took the Northern Line to Hendon Central, walked down Seymour Way to number 45 and let myself into Herb Kovak's flat.

Sherri had gone home to America the previous Friday and there were already a few letters lying on the mat. I picked them up and added them to the pile that she had left on the desk.

I sat down on Herb's desk chair and opened his mail.

Amongst other things there were some utility bills and a letter from a building society complaining that the direct debit had been cancelled and they hadn't received the preceding month's interest on Herb's mortgage. It reminded me of the gym that also hadn't been paid due to the bank cancelling the direct debit. I wondered how many others there would be.

There was so much to deal with, and the worst of it was not the domestic bills, troublesome as they were, it was the never-ending stream of demands from the twenty-two credit card companies. About half of them had sent their next statements and not only were the previous month's balances still outstanding, overdue and generating interest, but there were more charges on the accounts.

The American gamblers were still gambling, and still losing. But how could I stop them if I didn't know who they were?

There must come a time, I thought, when the credit card accounts reached their credit limit. That should bring it all to a stop, but at what cost?

I used Herb's landline telephone to call the building society and let them know why the direct debit had been stopped. They were so sorry to hear of Mr Kovak's death but, of course, that did not mean they would stop accruing the interest on the loan. Did they not know the real meaning of mortgage? The 'mort' bit referred to death, like the 'mort' as in mortuary and mortality. A mortgage was originally a pledge to repay the loan outstanding on one's death, not on the never-never thereafter.

Next I called the utility companies and tried to arrange for the gas, electricity and phone to be cut off. I made the mistake of telling them that I wasn't Herb Kovak himself, that he was dead, and I was his executor. They all needed documentary proof that I was acting on Mr Kovak's behalf and, anyway, they needed the bills paid first. I pointed out that if I didn't pay the bills they would cut the services off anyway. It didn't help.

I collected the credit card statements and the other

things together and put them in a large white envelope that I found in Herb's desk. What I really needed was a solicitor to get things moving on the job of obtaining probate. At least I would then be able to cancel the credit cards, but probably not before they were paid off as well. This apartment would also have to be sold, and if the scale of the outstanding interest payment in the building society's letter was anything to go by, there may not be enough capital remaining after paying off the mortgage to cover the other bills. Perhaps I might need to make Herb's estate bankrupt.

All in all, it was not such a fine legacy.

I knew Patrick lived in Weybridge. I knew it because Claudia and I had been to his house for dinner a few times, and also the firm's annual summer party the previous year had been held in his expansive garden.

I also knew that his journey from home to work involved being dropped at Weybridge Station by his wife, catching a train to Waterloo, and then squeezing onto the Waterloo and City tube line to Bank. Everyone in the office knew because Patrick was not adverse to complaining loudly about public transport or, for that matter, his wife's driving, especially if it had made him late for work.

I assumed his return journey would be the same but in the opposite direction, and I planned to join him for some of it.

He usually left the office between six o'clock and

half past but I was at Waterloo waiting by five in case he was early. Even so, I still very nearly missed him.

The main problem was that there were at least six trains an hour to Weybridge and they seemingly could leave from any of the nineteen platforms.

I waited on the mainline station concourse opposite the bank of escalators that rose from the Underground lines beneath. During the peak evening rush hour, two of the three escalators were used for up-traffic and these, together with the stairs alongside, disgorged thousands of commuters every minute onto the concourse, all of them hurrying for their trains.

By twenty-five past six my eyes were so punch-drunk from scanning so many faces that my brain took several long seconds to register that I had fleetingly glimpsed a familiar one and, by then, he had become lost again in the crowd walking away from me.

I chased after, trying to spot him again while also attempting to search the overhead departure boards for trains to Weybridge.

I followed someone right across the concourse towards platform 1 and only realized it wasn't Patrick when he turned into one of the food outlets.

Dammit, I thought. I had wasted precious minutes.

I turned back and looked carefully at the departure boards.

There was a train for Basingstoke, via Weybridge, leaving from platform 13 in two minutes. I would have to take the gamble that Patrick was on it. I rushed right back across the station, thrust my ticket into the grey automatic barrier and ran down the platform.

I leapt aboard the train just seconds before the doors slammed shut. But I hadn't foreseen that it would be so crowded, with more people standing in the aisles than actually sitting in the seats. As the train pulled out of Waterloo Station I began to make my apologies and work my way along the congested carriages.

Eventually, after annoying at least half the train's occupants, and thinking that Patrick must have caught a different one, I spotted him sitting in the relatively empty first-class section. Where else? He was reading an evening newspaper and he hadn't noticed me coming towards him. He didn't even look up as I made my way through a sliding glass door and sat down on the empty seat next to him.

'Hello, Patrick,' I said.

If he was surprised to see me, he didn't particularly show it.

'Hello, Nicholas,' he said calmly, folding his paper in half. 'I was wondering when you would turn up.'

'Yes,' I said. 'I'm sorry about this but I needed to talk to you without Gregory knowing, or listening.'

'What about?' he asked.

'Colonel Jolyon Roberts,' I said quietly, conscious of the other passengers.

He raised his eyebrows a little. 'What about him?'

'He spoke to me nearly two weeks ago at Cheltenham Races and again at Sandown a week last Saturday.'

'You know he died last week?' Patrick asked.

'Yes,' I said. 'I do know. Terrible. I spoke to you after his funeral.'

'Of course you did,' Patrick said. 'He had a heart problem apparently.'

'So I've heard.'

'So, tell me, what did he speak to you about?'

'He was worried about an investment that the Roberts Family Trust had made in a light-bulb factory in Bulgaria.'

'In what way was he worried about it?' Patrick asked.

'Mr Roberts's nephew had evidently been to the site where the factory should be and there was nothing there. Nothing except a toxic waste dump.'

'Perhaps it hasn't been built yet. Or the nephew was in the wrong place.'

'That's what I thought,' I said. 'But apparently Gregory had shown photos of the factory to Mr Roberts, and the nephew is adamant that he was in the right place.'

'You have spoken to the nephew?' Patrick asked.

'Yes, I have,' I said. 'I spoke to him on Friday.'

'And have you approached Gregory about it?'

'No,' I said. 'Gregory was so angry with me last week for all that Billy Searle business that I didn't like to.'

'How about Jessica?' he asked.

'No, not her either. I know I should have done, but I haven't had the chance.'

The train pulled into Surbiton Station and two of the passengers in the first-class section stood up and departed.

'So why are you telling me?' Patrick asked as the train resumed its journey. 'The Roberts Family Trust is a client of Gregory's. You need to speak to him, or to Jessica.'

'I know,' I said. 'I just hoped you could look into it for me.'

He laughed. 'You're not frightened of Gregory, are you?'

'Yes,' I said.

And I was, very frightened indeed.

'Is this what all this being away from the office has been about?'

'Yes,' I said again.

He turned in his seat and looked at me. 'You are a strange man at times, Nicholas. Do you realize that you have placed your whole career on the line here?'

I nodded.

'Gregory and I agreed at the disciplinary meeting this morning, the one you were supposed to attend, that we would demand your resignation from Lyall and Black forthwith.'

So I *was* being fired.

'However,' he went on, 'Andrew Mellor advised us that we were obliged to hear your side of any story before we made such a precipitous decision. So no final conclusion was reached.'

'Thank you,' I said.

'So will you be in the office tomorrow so we can sort all this out?'

'I can't be sure of that,' I said. 'I would much rather

you started an internal enquiry into the Bulgarian investment before I returned.'

'You really are afraid of Gregory,' he said with a chuckle. 'His bark is worse than his bite.'

Maybe, I thought, but his bark had been pretty ferocious. And I also wasn't too keen on his hired help.

'Patrick,' I said seriously. 'I have reason to think that a multimillion-euro fraud is going on here, and that Gregory may be mixed up in it. Yes, I am frightened and I feel I have good reason to be.'

'Like what?' he said.

'I know it sounds unlikely but I believe that the Bulgaria business may have something to do with why Herb was killed.'

'But that's ridiculous,' he said. 'Next you'll be accusing Gregory of murder.'

I said nothing but just sat there looking at him.

'Oh, come on, Nicholas,' he said. 'That's madness.'

'Madness it may be,' I said. 'But I'm not coming into the office until I'm certain that I'd be safe.'

He thought for a moment.

'Come home with me now and we'll sort this out tonight. We can call Gregory from there.'

The train pulled into Esher Station.

Esher was the station for Sandown Park racecourse. Had it really been only nine days since I had alighted here to go to speak to Jolyon Roberts?

And two days later Jolyon Roberts was dead.

'No,' I said, jumping up. 'I'll call you tomorrow morning in the office.'

I rushed through the glass dividing door and then stepped out onto the platform just before the train's doors closed shut behind me.

I didn't want Patrick telling Gregory where I was – not tonight, nor on any other night.

18

By the time I made it back to Lambourn, all three of the ladies were in bed and the house was in darkness save for a single light left on for me in the kitchen. It was only fair, and I had called from a public phone box at Paddington to tell them not to wait up.

I realized I was hungry.

I looked at the clock hanging above the Aga. It was ten to eleven at night and I'd had nothing to eat since a hurried slice of toast at six o'clock in the morning. All day my stomach had been so wound up with worry that I hadn't even thought about food. My mother would not have been pleased.

I raided Jan's fridge and made myself a thick cheese sandwich.

I then sat eating it at the kitchen table, washing it down with a glass of orange juice.

It had been a good day, I decided. I still just had a job and I had finally spoken to Patrick about my concerns. Whether or not he believed me was another matter. But surely he was duty-bound to start an investigation and bring Jessica Winter into the loop, whatever he might think of my cloak-and-dagger tactics.

But would I then be any safer?

If Gregory, or whoever, was trying to kill me in order

to prevent an investigation into the fraud being started, then surely I should be out of danger once it had, because killing me then would only reinforce the need for the investigation to continue. Unless, of course, he felt he had nothing more to lose and killed me out of revenge for uncovering his scheme.

Either way, I was going to lie low for a few more days yet.

Tuesday dawned bright and sunny, which matched my temperament. Talking to Patrick had set my mind more at ease and I really felt I was getting somewhere at last.

In spite of being the final one to bed, I was the first up and downstairs, making myself an instant coffee by the time Jan appeared.

'Are you sure you don't want to come up on the Downs to watch the horses?' she said. 'It's a beautiful day for a change.'

I thought about it.

'I can lend you a hat and sunglasses,' she added with a laugh. 'As a disguise.'

'OK,' I said. 'I'd love to. I'll just take some tea up to Claudia.'

'There's plenty of time,' Jan said. 'First lot doesn't pull out until seven thirty and, even then, I give them a good head start. Be ready by about seven forty-five. We have breakfast afterwards.'

I glanced up at the clock. It was only five to seven.

'Right,' I said. 'I'll be ready.'

I took the tea and coffee up to our room and sat on the bed.

'Morning, sleepyhead,' I said to Claudia, gently shaking her shoulder. 'Time to wake up.'

She rolled over onto her back and yawned. 'What time is it?'

'Seven,' I said. 'And it's a beautiful morning so I'm going up on the Downs with Jan to watch the horses work.'

'Can I come too?' Claudia asked.

'I'd love you to,' I said. 'But how are you feeling?'

'Better every day,' she replied. 'I just wish . . .' She tailed off.

'I know, I know,' I said. 'But everything will be just fine. You'll see.'

I leaned down and gave her a hug and a kiss.

'I do so hope you're right,' she said.

This cancerous Sword of Damocles seemed to cast a shadow over our every waking moment. We were living in limbo and, as far as I was concerned, the sooner she started the chemotherapy the better. These weeks of doing nothing just seemed to invite the cancer to grow within her.

To my mind, there was nothing more revitalizing to the soul than a bright sunny, spring morning on the gallops. My only sadness was that I was watching the horses work from inside Jan's Land Rover rather than from the saddle.

God, how I still ached to ride, to sit again astride half a ton of Thoroughbred racehorse, and to gallop once more at full pelt with the wind in my face.

I watched with envy as Jan's stable staff brought the horses up the hill towards us side-by-side in pairs, some racing flat out and others at half or three-quarter pace. Just to hear the sound of their hooves thudding into the turf was enough to give me goosebumps, and to raise my pulse.

How cruel had been my neck injury to rob me of such delight.

But I supposed I shouldn't be too downhearted. At least my broken neck hadn't killed me, unlike someone else I could think of.

I didn't wear Jan's offered sunglasses, but I did don one of her ex-husband's old trilbies with the brim pulled firmly down and with my coat collar turned up. And I was careful not to get too close to the horses. I could easily recognize some of Jan's long-serving stable staff and I was still wary of them seeing me, if only to prevent DCI Flight from turning up with his handcuffs.

Claudia had no such qualms and walked across the grass to be nearer the horses.

Standing there, I watched her in the sunshine as she shook her hair out of a woolly hat and let it blow free in the wind.

How strange things had been over the previous few weeks. I had thought I was losing her to another man, and now I feared losing her to an illness. There was no doubt that the cancer had brought us closer together. I loved her more now than I had ever done. I would stay alive for her, I promised myself. And she must live for me.

She turned towards me and waved, her long hair blown in streaks across her face. In spite of it, I could tell she was laughing with joy, living for the moment.

I waved back.

In two or three weeks' time all that gorgeous hair would start to fall out, and she would absolutely hate it, but, I suppose, it was a relatively small price to pay for more life, and more love.

After lunch, I took the car out to call Chief Inspector Tomlinson. In the light of the episode at the Swindon pub, I decided that calling-on-the-move was the best policy, hence I started to dial the chief inspector's number as I was travelling at seventy miles an hour eastwards along the M4 motorway between Newbury and Reading. But the phone rang in my hand before I had a chance to complete the number.

'Nicholas Foxton,' I said, answering.

'Hello, Mr Foxton, it's Ben Roberts.'

'Yes, Ben,' I said. 'How can I help?'

'My father has changed his mind. He'd now like to talk to you.'

'Great,' I said. 'When and where?'

'He wonders if you would like come to Cheltenham Races tomorrow evening as his guest. It's the Hunter

Chase evening meeting and he's hired a private box. He says he would like to talk to you at the end of the evening's racing.'

'Will you be there?' I asked.

'I will to start with but I'll have to leave early to get back to Oxford for a club dinner.'

'Can I get back to you?' I said. 'I need to talk to my fiancée.'

'Bring her with you,' he said immediately. 'It's a buffet supper, not a sit-down, so numbers are not a problem. And I'll be leaving before the pudding so there'll be plenty of that left, anyway.' He laughed.

I couldn't help but like Ben Roberts.

'OK,' I said. 'I'd love to.'

'One or two?' he asked.

'One definitely, two maybe.'

'I'll tell my dad. He'll be pleased,' he said. 'We'll be there by five o'clock. See you then.'

We hung up.

I wondered if it was sensible to go back to Cheltenham. It was DCI Flight's home patch and the racecourse would be full of Gloucestershire policemen. But why should I worry? After all, I hadn't done anything wrong.

Next I called Chief Inspector Tomlinson.

'Where are you?' the chief inspector asked. 'There's lots of noise on the line.'

'I'm on the motorway,' I said. 'And this car isn't very well sound-insulated.'

'Which motorway?' he asked.

'Does it matter?' I said evasively.

'Are you using a hands-free system?' he asked.

I didn't answer.

'OK,' he said. 'I'll take that as a no.'

'So what are you going to do about it, arrest me for using a mobile phone while driving?'

'No,' he said. 'I'll just try and keep the call short. What do you want?'

'I want a meeting with you and Superintendent Yering,' I said. 'And DCI Flight, I suppose, if he wants to be there. As long as he doesn't arrest me.'

'Where do you want this meeting?'

'That's up to you,' I said. 'But arrange it for Thursday if you can.'

'What's the meeting for?' he asked.

'So I can tell you why I think Herb Kovak was killed and why our dead gunman was also trying to kill me.'

'What's wrong with today?' he said. 'Or tomorrow?'

'There's someone else I want to talk to first.'

'Who?' he said.

'Just someone.'

'I told you to leave the investigating to us,' said the chief inspector sternly.

'I intend to,' I said. 'That's why I want the meeting with you and the superintendent.'

But I also wanted to learn more about the Bulgarian investment before it.

'OK,' he said. 'I'll fix it. How do I contact you?'

'Leave a message on this number, or I'll call you again tomorrow.'

I disconnected.

I left the motorway at the Reading junction, went round the interchange and joined the westbound carriageway to go back towards Newbury.

I called the office and Mrs McDowd answered.

'Hello, Mrs McDowd,' I said. 'Mr Nicholas here. Can I speak to Mr Patrick, please?'

'You're a very naughty boy,' she said in her best headmistressy voice. 'You mustn't upset Mr Gregory so. His heart can't take it.'

I didn't reply. As far as I was concerned, the sooner his heart gave out the better.

I waited as she put me through.

'Hello, Nicholas,' said Patrick. 'Where are you?'

Why, I wondered, was everyone so obsessed with my whereabouts?

'In Reading,' I said. 'Have you spoken to Jessica?'

'Not yet. I've been reviewing the file myself this morning. I intend to discuss the matter with Gregory this afternoon.'

'Mind your back,' I said.

'Be serious,' Patrick said.

'I promise you I am being serious, very serious,' I replied. 'If I were you, I'd speak to Jessica first and then both of you talk to Gregory.'

'I'll see,' Patrick said.

Patrick and Gregory had been partners for a very long time and I reckoned that Patrick might need quite a lot of convincing that his friend was up to no good. I suppose I couldn't really blame him for checking things himself before he brought in the Compliance Officer.

'You might need someone who can read Bulgarian,' I said.

'Leave it to me,' Patrick replied decisively.

'OK,' I said. 'I will. But I'll call you again tomorrow to see how you're getting on.'

I hung up and glanced in the rear-view mirror. There were no signs of any flashing blue lights, nor of any eager unmarked police cars. I drove on sedately, back to Lambourn.

'I want to go home,' my mother said, meeting me in Jan's kitchen as I walked in from the car.

'And you will,' I said. 'Just as soon as I'm sure it's safe.'

'But I want to go home now.'

'Soon,' I said.

'No!' she stated in determined fashion, putting her hands on her hips. 'Now.'

'Why?' I asked.

'We've been here long enough,' she said. 'And I'm worried about my cat.'

'I didn't think it was *your* cat.'

'He's not, but I'm worried about him nonetheless. And I've got a WI meeting tomorrow night and I don't want to miss it.'

Don't mess with the Women's Institute. Tony Blair, for one, had discovered that.

'All right,' I said. 'I promise I'll take you home tomorrow.'

She wasn't very happy but, short of ordering herself a taxi, there wasn't much she could do. Tomorrow would have to do. I'd take her before I went on to the races.

And there was more unrest in the ranks from Claudia.

'I want to go home,' she said when I went up to our bedroom. She was standing by the bed packing her things into her suitcase.

'Have you been talking to my mother?' I asked.

'Maybe,' she said.

I thought there was no 'maybe' about it.

'Darling,' I said. 'I've arranged a meeting with the police on Thursday to sort everything out. We can go home after it.'

'Why can't you have this meeting tonight or tomorrow?'

'Because I have to talk to someone first and I'm seeing them at Cheltenham Races tomorrow evening.'

She stopped packing and sat down on the bed.

'I don't understand it. If the man who was trying to kill you was himself killed then why are we still hiding?'

'There may be others,' I said. 'And I don't want to take any unnecessary risks. You're far too precious to me.'

I sat down on the bed next to her and gave her a hug.

'But I'm bored here,' she said. 'And I've run out of clean knickers.'

Ah-ha, I thought, the true reason reveals itself.

'I'll tell you what,' I said. 'I've promised Mum I'll

take her back to her cottage tomorrow so why don't I take us all out to dinner tonight, then we'll go back to Woodmancote with Mum around lunchtime, and you can either stay there or come with me to the races in the evening. What do you say?'

'I'm not going to the races.'

'OK,' I said, 'that's fine. You can stay at Mum's cottage.'

'Oh, all right,' she said in a resigned tone. 'Where shall we go for dinner tonight?'

'Some nice quiet pub with good food.'

And preferably where I wouldn't be recognized by any Lambourn locals.

On Jan's recommendation, we went to the Bear Hotel in Hungerford for a sumptuous dinner in their Brasserie, washed down with a bottle of fine wine.

'I'll miss you,' Jan said over coffee. 'It's been great having the house full again. Please can you all come back for Christmas?'

My mother and Claudia toasted her kindness with large snifters of brandy and it seemed to have done the trick as I drove a happy car-load back to Lambourn, and to bed.

'Will the police still be there?' Claudia asked as I drove the last few miles to Woodmancote.

It was the question I had been wondering about ever since I'd agreed to bring my mother home.

'I don't care if they are,' my mother said loudly from

the back seat. 'I'm just so looking forward to being home again.'

'If they are,' I said, 'I'll pretend to be a taxi driver just delivering you two.' I dug in my pocket and gave Claudia a twenty-pound note. 'Here. Give me this and I'll drive away after I've unloaded your stuff. Then I'll call you later, from the races.'

'But they might recognize you,' Claudia said.

'I'll just have to take that chance.'

What I was more worried about was arriving to find the whole place sealed up as a crime scene, with 'Police – Do Not Cross' tape across the porch, and padlocks on the doors.

I needn't have worried. We arrived to find no tape, no padlocks, and no police guard.

The only external signs that anything was different was a new dangling wire that connected the corner of the building to a telegraph pole in the lane – the hasty repair of the cut telephone wire.

My mother let us in through the front door using her key.

It was all, remarkably, just the same as before with no visible evidence to show that a ferocious life-or-death struggle had gone on here less than a week previously. However, none of us could resist staring at the foot of the stairwell, at the place where we had last seen the gunman. There was no white-chalk-drawn outline of a body, or any other such comic-book indication of where the man had lain. Indeed, there was nothing at all to signify that anyone had violently died there.

The police had even secured the kitchen window, fixing a piece of plywood over the broken window pane.

'Fine,' said my mother, trying to show that things were back to normal and that she wasn't as uneasy as she sounded. 'Who'd like a cup of tea?'

'Lovely,' said Claudia, also betraying a nervousness in her voice.

I couldn't blame them. Being once again in that cottage suddenly brought the memory of the terrifying evening back into vivid focus, and none of us had quite realized the effect it would have.

'What time are you leaving for the races?' Claudia asked.

I looked at my watch. It was just past three o'clock and the first of the six races was at half past five.

'In about an hour and a half or so,' I said.

'And what time is your WI meeting?' she asked my mother.

'Seven thirty,' she said. 'But I usually go round to Joan's beforehand. We go to the meetings together.'

'So what time do you leave here?' Claudia asked patiently.

'About six,' she said. 'Joan and I usually have a sherry or two before we leave. Gives us a bit of courage for the meeting.' She giggled like a schoolgirl.

'And what time does it end?' Claudia asked.

'I'm usually home by ten, ten thirty at the very latest.'

'I really don't fancy being here on my own all evening,' Claudia said. 'I've changed my mind. I'm coming to the races.'

19

In the end, Claudia and I dropped my mother off at Joan's house at a quarter to five on our way to Cheltenham Races. It seemed she didn't particularly want to be on her own in the cottage either, which didn't bode well for the morning, when Claudia and I planned to return to London.

'Who is it we are going to see?' Claudia asked as we turned into the racecourse car park.

'A man called Shenington,' I said. 'Viscount Shenington. And he's hired a private box.'

'Very posh,' she replied, making a face.

We might be glad of the box, I thought as we climbed out of the car. The brief sunny interlude of yesterday morning was a distant memory and another weather front had moved in from the west, bringing a return to the thick clouds and rain that had characterized the weather for the majority of the last week. Evening meetings like this one at Cheltenham, with no floodlighting, relied on long bright summer evenings. I reckoned the last race on this particular dank miserable evening might be run in near-total darkness.

'And who is this Viscount exactly?' Claudia asked as we walked to the entrance huddled together under her minute umbrella.

'He's a racehorse owner and the senior trustee of the Roberts Family Trust. They're clients of Lyall and Black.'

'Oh,' she said, seemingly losing interest. Was my job really that boring? 'So why do you need to talk to this man before you see the police?'

I had purposely not told Claudia anything about my suspicions concerning the Bulgarian factory and housing project. She had far too many of her own problems to contend with, without having mine added on top.

'The Trust,' I said, 'has made an investment in something which I think is a front for fraud. I need to learn more about it before I speak to the police. I just have some questions to ask him, that's all.'

'Will it take long?' she asked.

'He wants to speak to me after the racing.'

'Oh,' she said again, this time sounding disappointed. 'So we're here till the bitter end.'

'I'm afraid so,' I said. 'But he has invited us to his box for the whole time, and there'll be food and drink available.'

That cheered her a bit, and she perked up a lot more when she discovered that the box in question was a magnificent glass-fronted affair at the top of the grandstand with a wonderful view over the racecourse.

It was also dry and warm.

Even though we were hardly late at ten past five, the box was already full of guests, none of whom I recognized.

I was just beginning to think we must be in the

wrong place when Ben Roberts came through the door, instinctively ducking his head as he did so.

'Ah, Mr Foxton,' he said, marching over to me with outstretched hand.

'Ben,' I replied. 'How nice to see you again. Can I introduce my fiancée, Claudia?'

'Great,' said Ben, shaking her hand and smiling. 'I'm Ben Roberts.'

Claudia smiled back.

'Come and meet my father.'

He led the way across the room to a group of men standing in the far corner. It was pretty obvious which one of them was Ben's father. He towered above the others by a good five or six inches. The 'tall' gene was clearly alive and well in all the Roberts family.

'Dad,' said Ben during a lull in the men's conversation, 'this is Mr Foxton and Claudia, his fiancée. My father, Viscount Shenington.'

'Delighted to meet you,' I said, offering my hand.

He looked down at me and slowly put forward his hand to shake. It was hardly the most friendly of welcomes, but I hadn't really expected anything else. I knew that even though he was prepared to speak to me, he didn't truly want to.

'Good evening, Mr Foxton,' he said. 'Good of you to come.' He turned slightly towards Claudia. 'And you too, my dear.'

That wouldn't go down too well, I thought. My father always called Claudia 'my dear' and she hated it, claiming that he was an arrogant old git who shouldn't be so patronizing.

'Have a drink,' Shenington said. 'And some food.' He waved a hand towards the impressive buffet table. 'We'll speak later.'

He went back to his former conversations.

'Good,' said Ben with considerably more warmth. 'What would you both like to drink? Champagne?'

'Lovely,' Claudia said.

'Fruit juice for me, please,' I said. 'I'm driving.'

'Yeah, me too,' said Ben, holding up a glass of orange liquid. 'But I'll get a proper skinful later at the Boat Club dinner.'

'Rowing?' I asked.

'Absolutely. Tonight's our home celebration for beating the hated enemy.'

'The hated enemy?' said Claudia.

'Cambridge,' Ben said, smiling broadly. 'In the Boat Race. Beat them by half a length. Dead easy!'

'Were you in the crew?' I asked.

'Certainly was,' he said, pulling himself up to his full six-foot-plus-plus. 'Number four – in the engine room.'

'Well done,' I said, meaning it. 'Are you trying for the Olympics next?'

'No. Not for me. I was good, but not that good. It's time to retire gracefully and get my life back. These last few weeks I've really enjoyed not having to be on the river every morning at dawn, and in all weathers. Now I'm just working hard for my finals.'

'And then what?' I asked. 'Politics?'

'That's the plan,' he said. 'A special adviser and political researcher for the party, at least for a while. Then Parliament.'

Then the world, I thought.

'Commons or Lords?' I asked.

'Commons,' he said with a laugh. 'The power house. There's no place left in the Lords for the likes of us, not any more. And I wouldn't want it even if there was.'

Ben himself was a walking 'power house', and his enthusiasm was infectious. I was sure he'd go far.

'Good luck,' I said to him. 'I personally can't think of anything worse than being a politician. Everyone I know seems to hate them.'

'No, they don't,' he said sharply. 'All they hate is that it's other people who are the politicians, when they want the power for themselves.'

I wasn't going to argue with him, and not least because I had a feeling I would lose, and lose badly. If Ben told me the grass was blue and the sky was green, I'd probably believe him. Except that, this particular evening, the sky wasn't green or blue, it was dark grey.

Claudia and I took our drinks out onto the private balcony and I briefly turned on my phone to check my voicemail. There was a new message from Chief Inspector Tomlinson.

'The meeting is fixed for tomorrow morning, Thursday,' his voice said. 'Eleven a.m. at Paddington Green Police Station.'

Not back in their holding cells, I hoped. I'd had my fill of those.

From our vantage point on the box balcony Claudia and I looked down at the few brave souls rushing around in the rain beneath us.

'It's such a shame,' Claudia said. 'The weather makes or breaks an event like this. Everyone gets so wet.'

'It's worse for the jockeys,' I said. 'They'll not just get wet, they'll get completely covered in mud kicked up from the horses ahead of them. On days like this, being a front-runner is the only sensible option. At least you can then see where you're going, and where the fences are. However, the down side is that, if your horse falls, the rest trample over you as you lie on the ground.'

'At least they're getting paid,' she said.

'Not tonight, they're not. All the races are for amateur riders only.'

'Then they're mad,' she said.

I laughed. 'Not at all. For some of them, tonight is the best evening of their whole year. They've been working hard all winter to qualify their horses for this one meeting, and a bit of dampness isn't going to spoil their party.'

'Well,' said Claudia, 'I'd definitely want a big fee to ride in this rain.'

Not me, I thought. I'd happily do it for nothing. In fact, I'd pay to be able to join them, and handsomely.

'Amateur jockeys do it just for the love of the sport,' I said. 'Indeed, the very word "amateur" comes from the Latin word "*amator*", meaning "lover".'

'You're my *amator*,' she said quietly, turning towards me and cuddling up with her arms inside my coat.

'Not now, darling,' I said. 'And not here. I'm working, remember.'

'Shame,' she said, letting me go. 'Your job is *so* boring.'

That seemed to be the unanimous conclusion.

Claudia and I braved the damp conditions to go down to the parade ring after the second race. We went to support Jan, who had a runner in the third.

'Not much chance, I'm afraid,' Jan said as she emerged from the Weighing Room with a small saddle over her arm. 'The horse is fine but the owner insists his son should ride it and he's only eighteen. He's still just a boy and this mare needs to be held up to the last. She gets lazy if she's in front too soon.'

'But *I* was only eighteen when I rode my first winner for you,' I reminded her.

'Yes,' she replied. 'But you were good, very good. This boy is barely average.' She rushed off towards the saddling boxes to prepare the horse.

Claudia and I waited under cover in front of the Weighing Room and, presently, Jan's mare came into the parade ring, closely followed by her and the horse's owner.

I scanned my soggy racecard to see who it was and, instead, noticed that one of the other runners in the race was owned by our host, Viscount Shenington. I looked around the parade ring and spotted him and some of his other guests huddling under large golf umbrellas at the far end. They were talking to the horse's trainer, the gossip, Martin Gifford.

The jockeys were called from the changing room and the eager mob streamed out onto the grass, their brightly coloured silks in stark contrast to the gathering gloom of the day.

Claudia and I decided to stay down where we were for the race rather than to go back up to the grandstand box. We could watch all the action on the big-screen television, and we wouldn't have to get wet coming down again if Jan's horse won. And also, I thought, I didn't really want to have to talk to Martin Gifford, who would surely go up to the box with his owner to watch their horse run.

But, on that score, I was sadly wrong.

Martin Gifford came to stand on the Weighing-Room terrace right next to me to watch the race on the television.

'Hi, Foxy,' he said. 'Penny for your thoughts?' He seemed to have recovered from, or forgotten, our little spat at Sandown. 'What a horrid day.'

'Yes,' I agreed.

'I'm quite surprised you're here for the hunter chasers,' he said. 'I wouldn't be if I didn't have this damn runner. I tried to talk the owner out of running it but he insisted. It should win, though.'

Now what was I to make of that? Martin Gifford made a habit of saying his horses had no chance, and then they went on to win. I knew that from the last meeting at Cheltenham, when both his horses had won after he'd told me they wouldn't. But was the reverse also true? Was this horse, in fact, a useless no-hoper? Did I even care? I wasn't going to back it either way.

I looked again at my racecard. A rating was printed alongside the details for each horse as a guide to punters. The higher the rating the better the horse was supposed to be, but, of course, it didn't always work out that way. Martin's horse certainly had a high rating for what was otherwise a moderate field of runners. Perhaps he really was telling the truth. I glanced up at an approximate-odds indicator and the public clearly agreed with him. The horse was starting as a very short-priced favourite.

We watched on the television as the horses jumped off very slowly from the start, which was at the far end of the finishing straight. With more than two complete circuits in the three-and-a-half-mile race, and in heavy ground, no one was really prepared to make the running and the fifteen horses had hardly broken into a gallop by the time they reached the first fence.

'Come on, you bugger,' said Martin next to me. 'I could really do with this one winning. Perhaps then the bloody owner will pay me some of his training fees.'

I turned my head towards him slightly. Maybe Martin could be useful after all.

'Slow payer, is he?' I asked.

'Bloody right,' said Martin without taking his eyes from the screen. 'But not so much slow, more like dead stop. I've even threatened to apply to Weatherbys to have the ownership of his horses transferred to me. He owes me a bloody fortune.'

Weatherbys was the company that administered all of British racing, and through which all racehorse registrations were held.

'How many horses does he have?' I asked.

'Too many,' he said. 'Twelve altogether, I think, but only six are with me, thank God, including one he used to jointly own with his brother. He hasn't paid me anything now for months. I tell you, I'm getting desperate.'

'But you'll get your money in the end, surely.'

'I don't know,' he said. 'Shenington claims he hasn't got it. Says he's nearly bankrupt.'

How interesting, I thought. The Roberts Family Trust, it seems, could happily lose five million pounds on an investment in Bulgaria, but the senior trustee couldn't pay his training fees because he was broke.

And how about hiring a private box for this meeting? It wasn't the sort of behaviour I would have expected from someone flirting with the bankruptcy courts. Not unless, of course, he had wanted to maintain a façade of affluence and respectability. Maybe the other guests were his creditors. Perhaps it was not so surprising that Martin hadn't been invited up there to watch the race.

'But Lord Shenington must have pots of money,' I said.

'Apparently, that's not so,' said Martin. 'Seems his father, the old Earl, still keeps his fingers very tightly on the family purse strings. And what money Shenington did have of his own, he's lost.'

'Lost?' I said.

'Gambling,' Martin said. 'On the horses, and at the casino tables. Addicted to it, evidently.'

'And how do you know this?' I asked with a degree of scepticism.

'Shenington told me so himself. Even used it as his excuse for not paying my bills.'

'So why are you still running his horses?' I asked. 'Did he pay the entry fee for this race?'

'No, of course not,' he said. 'I paid it.'

'You're mad,' I said.

'He has promised me all the prize money if it wins.'

We both watched on the screen as the horses swung past the grandstands for the first time. The daylight was now so dismal that, in spite of the different silks, it wasn't easy to spot which horse was which, but they were all racing closely packed and there was still a long way to go. All of them remained in with a chance of the prize money, but that wouldn't be much, I thought, just a few thousand pounds at most. I looked at the race conditions in the racecard. The prize to the winner was just over four thousand, and a month's training fees for six horses would be at least double that. The win would hardly pay off much of what Martin was owed, even if Shenington kept his promise, which somehow I doubted.

By the time the runners passed the grandstand for the second time, their number had been reduced by fallers from fifteen to twelve, and those twelve were no longer closely bunched but spread out over more than a furlong. And if it had been difficult to tell them apart last time round, it was almost impossible to do so now as they raced towards the television camera, each jockey with a uniform mud-splattered brown frontage. Only when the horses swung away onto their final circuit was it feasible to tell them apart by the coloured patterns on the backs of the silks.

Both Jan's and Martin's horses were still in the leading group, although even those appeared tired and leaden-footed as they reached the highest point of the course and then swung left-handed down the hill towards the finishing straight. Three and a half miles was a very, very long way in such heavy going.

Just as Jan had feared, the young jockey on her horse took the lead too soon. Even on the screen, it was clear to see that the horse didn't enjoy being on her own in front and the mare started to falter and weave about, almost coming to a complete stop just before the last fence. She would probably have refused to jump altogether if another horse hadn't galloped past and given her a lead to hop over the obstacle with almost zero forward motion, not that the other horse seemed that keen to win the race either.

That horse, too, swung from side to side as the jockey kept looking round, as if he was wondering where all the other horses had gone. The answer was that most of them had pulled up on their way down the hill, figuring, quite rightly, that they didn't have any chance of winning.

Only three of the original fifteen starters actually

crossed the finishing line with Martin Gifford's horse home first. Jan's mare was second, finishing at a walk and some twenty lengths behind the winner, and then one of the others finally staggered up the hill to be third, and a very long way last.

The rain eased a little and Claudia and I made our way over to the white plastic rails that ran across between the parade ring and the unsaddling enclosure, to watch the exhausted horses come in.

Jan wasn't very pleased. 'She could have won that,' she said, referring to her mare. 'I told the stupid little arse not to hit the front too soon. Certainly not until after the last, I told him, and then what does he do? God help me.' Martin Gifford, meanwhile, was beaming from ear to ear, which was more than could be said for his horse's owner.

Viscount Shenington looked fit to explode with fury, and he gave the victorious rider such a look that I wondered if this young man, like Billy Searle before him, had also won a race which he'd previously agreed to lose, not that he'd had much choice in the matter. Short of pulling up during the run-in, or purposely falling off, he'd had no alternative but to win.

And Lord Shenington was certainly a 'nob'.

Perhaps I would look at the records to see if Billy had ever ridden any of Shenington's horses.

'I'm freezing,' said Jan, coming over to us again after the horses had been led away. 'Either of you two fancy a Whisky Mac to warm up? I'm buying.'

As the rain began to fall heavily once again, the

three of us scampered over to the Arkle Bar on the lower level of the grandstand.

'How well do you know Viscount Shenington?' I asked Jan as we sipped our mixture of Scotch whisky and ginger wine.

'I know of him, of course,' she said. 'But not well enough to speak to.'

'We're guests in his box,' Claudia said.

'Are you, indeed?' Jan said. 'He does seem to have quite a lot of clout in racing, and his father is a long-standing member of the Jockey Club.'

'He's a client of the firm's,' I said. 'But not one of mine.'

She smiled at me. She was *my* client, she was saying but without using the words, and don't forget it.

'Do you know if he's got any financial troubles?' I asked her.

'How would I know anything about his finances?' she said. 'You're the specialist in that department.'

True, I thought, but he wasn't my client, and I could hardly ask Gregory.

We watched the fourth race on a television in the bar, the winner again coming in exhausted and smothered in thick mud.

'They ought to do something when the going's as heavy as this,' Jan said.

'Do what?' Claudia asked.

'Make the races shorter, or reduce the weights.'

'You can't realistically reduce the weights,' I said. 'Half of them are carrying overweight already.' Most amateur jockeys were taller and heavier than the professionals.

'The races should be made shorter, then. Most of these poor horses are finishing half dead. Three and a half miles is too far in this mud.'

She was right, of course, but how could the clerk of the course predict the course conditions when planning the races several months in advance?

'Right,' said Jan decisively, finishing her drink, 'I've had enough of this misery. I'm going home.'

'Can't we go too?' Claudia asked, shivering.

'Not yet,' I said. 'I've still got to talk to Viscount Shenington.'

Claudia looked far from happy.

'I'm sure Jan would take you back to Mum's place, if you'd like,' I said. 'It's only a mile or so down the road from here.'

'No problem,' said Jan.

'Here,' I said, taking my mother's house key from my pocket. 'I'll be back by ten and I'll collect Mum from Joan's on the way.'

Claudia took the key, but slowly as if nervous.

'Jan will see you into the cottage,' I said, trying to be reassuring. 'Then lock yourself in, and only open the door to me.'

Suddenly, she wasn't so sure about going back to the cottage on her own, but I could see that she was very cold, and she was also not yet fully recovered from her operation. If the truth were told, I would be much happier if she went with Jan as I could then concentrate on what I had to ask Shenington, and be quick about it.

'OK,' she said. 'But please don't be long.'

'I won't,' I said. 'I promise.'

Shenington's box was much emptier when I went back up there before the fifth race, and there was no sign of Ben.

'He's had to go back to Oxford,' explained his father as I removed my Barbour and hung it on a hook by the door, the rainwater running down the waxed material and dripping off the sleeves onto the carpet. 'He said to say goodbye.'

'Thank you,' I said. 'He's a very nice young man. You should be proud of him.'

'Yes, thank you,' he replied. 'But he can also be a bit idealistic at times.'

'Isn't that a good thing in the young?' I said.

'Not always,' he replied, staring at the wall above my head. 'We all have to live in the real world. To Ben, everything is either right or wrong, black or white. There's no middle ground, no compromise, and little or no tolerance of other people's failings.'

It was quite a statement, I thought, and one clearly born out of a certain degree of conflict between father and son. Perhaps Ben didn't easily tolerate his father's addiction to gambling.

Shenington seemed to almost snap out of a trance.

'Where's your lady?' he asked, looking around.

'She was cold,' I said. 'A friend has given her a lift to my mother's house. I'll pick her up later. I'm sorry.'

'I don't blame her,' he said. 'It's a cold night, and many of my guests have already gone. The rest will probably go before the last race.'

I ventured out onto the balcony and peered through the gloom as yet another long-distance hunter chase became a test of stamina for the tired and dirty participants. At least this one promised to give the crowd an exciting finish, that was until one of the two leaders slipped while landing over the last fence and deposited its hapless rider onto the grass with a sickening thump. I watched as the miserable jockey sat up holding his arm in the classic 'broken-collarbone' pose, the bane of every rider's life.

I realized that it was at a point not very far from where the jockey was sitting that my own life had changed for ever some eight years previously. How different things might have been if I'd landed on my outstretched arm that day as he had just done, and not on my head; if I'd only broken my collarbone instead of my neck.

As Shenington had predicted, almost all his remaining guests departed after the race, saying their goodbyes and preparing for the dash to their cars in the rain.

Finally, there was just Viscount Shenington, myself, and two other men in rather drab suits remaining. Even the catering staff seemed to have disappeared.

Suddenly I felt uneasy.

But my concern was far too late.

One of the two men stood by the door to ensure no one could come in, while the other advanced towards me. And he had a gun in his gloved hand, together with the ubiquitous silencer.

'Mr Foxton, you are an extraordinarily difficult man to kill,' Shenington said, smiling slightly. 'You usually don't turn up when you're expected, and yet you came here so sweetly, like a lamb to the slaughter.'

He almost laughed.

I didn't.

This time I'd been bloody careless.

20

'What do you want?' I asked, trying to keep the fear out of my voice.

'I want you dead,' Viscount Shenington said. 'So you can stop spreading your silly rumour that my brother was murdered.'

'But he was, wasn't he?' I said.

'That is something you are not going to have to worry about any more,' Shenington said.

'How could you have killed your own brother?' I asked. 'And for what? Money?'

'My brother had no idea what it was like to be desperate for money. He was always so bloody self-righteous.'

'Honest, you mean.'

'Don't give me all that claptrap,' he said. 'Everyone's on the make. I just want my share.'

'And is your share a hundred million euros?' I asked.

'Shut up,' he said loudly.

Why should I? Maybe I should shout as loudly as I could, to attract attention.

I took a deep breath and the cry for help began in my throat. But that was as far as it got. The man with the gun punched me very hard in my lower abdomen, driving the air from my lungs and leaving me lying in a heap on the floor, gasping for breath. And then, just for good measure, the same man kicked me in the face, splitting my lip and sending my blood in a fine spray onto the carpet.

'Not in here, you fool,' Shenington said to him sharply.

That was slightly encouraging, I thought, through the haze in my brain. At least they weren't going to kill me here. It might have been rather incriminating to leave a dead body in the corner of the box amongst the empty champagne bottles.

'It won't do you any good,' I said through my bleeding mouth, my own voice sounding strange even to me. 'The police know I'm here.'

'I somehow doubt that,' Shenington replied. 'My information is that you've also been avoiding them over the past week.'

'My fiancée knows I'm here,' I said.

'Yes, so she does. When I've dealt with you, I'll deal with her too.'

I thought about saying that Jan Setter also knew I was here, but that might have placed her in mortal danger as well.

I kept quiet. I'd opened my big mouth enough already.

I could hear the public address system outside. The last race had started.

'Now,' said Shenington to the men. 'Take him down now while the race is running.'

The two men came over and hauled me to my feet.

'Where are you taking me?' I asked.

'To your death,' Shenington said with aplomb. 'But not here, obviously. Somewhere dark and quiet.'

'Can't we –'

It was as far as I got. The man on my right, the one without the gun who had been standing by the door, suddenly punched me again in my stomach. This time I didn't fall to the floor, but only because the two men were holding me up by my arms. My guts felt like they were on fire and I was worried that some major damage may have been done to my insides.

'No more speak,' said the man who had punched me. English was clearly not his strong point.

'No more speak' seemed a good plan, at least for the time being, so I kept quiet as the two men walked me past my coat, through the door, across the corridor, and into one of the deserted catering stations. The three of us descended to the ground in one of the caterer's lifts. There was no sign of Shenington. I wasn't sure whether that was good or bad. I suppose two against one was marginally better than three to one but, on the down side, I'd have little or no chance of reasoning with these two heavies. Although I doubt if I'd have had any chance anyway, had Shenington been there with us.

The lift stopped and I was marched out of it, and then across the wet tarmac towards the north exit and the racecourse car parks beyond. The facilities at Cheltenham were really designed for the Steeplechase Festival in March, when more than sixty thousand would flock into the course every day. The car parks were therefore huge but, on a night like this with only a small fraction of the crowd, most of them were deserted and, at this time of the evening, they would be dark and quiet.

'Somewhere dark and quiet,' Shenington had said.

I came to the conclusion that my last, brief journey would likely come to an abrupt end in a far corner of the racecourse car park. I tried my best to slow down but I was being frog-marched forward. I also tried to sit down, but they were having none of that. They gripped my arms even tighter and forced me on.

I'd have to shout for help, I thought, and chance another punch, but the commentator's voice was booming out through the public address, so would anyone hear me? There were only a very few people about, hurrying to go home with their heads bowed down and their collars turned up against the rain. Most of the remaining crowd were sensibly under cover watching the race. Only a fool would stand about down here in the wet.

'Horse!' a voice called loudly off to my right in warning. 'Loose horse!'

There is no doubt that horses have a homing instinct. Ask any trainer who has had a horse get loose and lost on the gallops. More often than not, the horse is found happily standing back in the stable yard, in its own box, and is usually home before the search party.

Horses that are reluctant to race, or those that might get loose due to falling, often dive back towards the place where they came out onto the course, as if they were trying to get home, or at least back to the racecourse stables.

This particular loose horse came galloping down the horse-walk and attempted to negotiate the ninety-degree turn to get back into the parade ring. A combination of too sharp a bend and too much momentum, coupled with the wet surface, meant that the horse's legs slipped out from beneath it and it fell, crashing through the white plastic railings and sliding across the ground towards the three of us, its legs thrashing about wildly as it tried to regain its footing.

The men on either side of me instinctively took a step backwards away from the sharp flailing horse-shoes, slightly relaxing their hold on my arms as they did so. But I stepped forward boldly, out of their clutches, and caught the horse by the reins. In one movement, as the animal managed to stand up, I swung myself onto its back and into the saddle.

I needed no second invitation. I kicked the astonished horse in the belly and we galloped back the way it had come, down the horse-walk towards the race-course.

'Hey, stop!' shouted an official who was standing in my way, waving his arms about. I glanced behind me. The two men were in pursuit and one was reaching into his pocket. I had no doubt he was going for his gun.

The official realized at the very last second that I wasn't going to stop and he flung himself aside. I kicked the horse again, and crouched as low as I could to provide the smallest target for the gunman.

I looked ahead. Even though the last race of the day was still in progress, out on the racecourse was definitely the safest place for me to be. Another official saw the horse galloping back towards him and he tugged frantically at the movable rail, closing it across the end of the horse-walk.

But I wasn't stopping. Stopping meant dying and I'd promised myself I wouldn't do that.

A rider communicates with his mount in a variety of ways. Pulling on the reins, either together or separately, is an obvious one, and cajoling with the voice or kicking with the feet are others. But the most powerful messages between horse and jockey are transmitted by the shifting of weight. Sit back and a horse will slow and stop, but shift the weight forward over his shoulders and the same horse will run like the wind.

I gathered my feet into the stirrup irons, stood up, shortened the reins, and crouched forward over the horse's withers. The animal beneath me fully understood the 'go' message. Riding a horse was like riding a bike – once learned, never forgotten.

As we neared the end of the horse-walk I made no move to slow down. In fact, I did quite the opposite. I kicked the horse hard in the belly once more. The animal received the new message loud and clear, and he knew what to do. I shifted my weight slightly again, asking him to lengthen his stride and to jump, and to jump high.

We sailed over the rail with ease, and over the official as well, who'd had the good sense to duck down.

The horse pecked slightly on landing, almost going down on its knees and, for a moment, I feared he was going to fall, but I pulled his head up with the reins and he quickly recovered his balance.

Left or right?

Left, I decided, pulling that way on that reins, away from the grandstand and towards the safe wide-open spaces of the racecourse.

The other horses were coming up the finishing straight towards me, but I was well to the side of them, on what would have been the hurdle course at any other meeting.

My mount tried to turn, to run with the others, but I steered him away and galloped down to the far end of the finishing straight before stopping and looking back.

What remained of the daylight was disappearing rapidly and the grandstand lights appeared unnaturally bright. It was difficult to tell if the two heavies were giving chase but I had to assume they were, joined possibly by Viscount Shenington himself. He must be keener now than ever to remove me permanently from the scene.

I turned the horse again and cantered up the hill, towards the farthest point on the racecourse away from the stands and the enclosures.

What did I do now?

The nondescript blue hire car would be waiting for me in the racecourse car park, but the problem was that its keys, together with my mobile phone and my wallet, were in the pockets of my Barbour, which I presumed was still inconveniently hanging by the door in Shenington's box.

I watched as a vehicle turned onto the racecourse from close by where I had emerged from the horse-walk. I could see the headlights bumping up and down slightly as it worked its way along the grass in the direction that I had come.

Another vehicle followed it onto the grass but turned the other way.

Both vehicles then moved forward slowly, driving round the course. If I stayed where I was then the two of them would close on me in a pincer movement.

But who was in the vehicles? Was it Shenington and his cronies, or would it be the police, or the racecourse security guards? I imagined that the trainer of the horse I was riding would be far from pleased to have discovered that his charge had been horse-napped, and was currently running about the racecourse in the dark.

But I couldn't stay where I was, that was for sure. Not without being seen or captured. And I had absolutely no intention of allowing a vehicle to come up close to me unless, and until, I knew for certain that Shenington and his heavies were not in it.

At Cheltenham, the racecourse, unlike those in America, was not a simple oval track, but was in fact two complete racecourses laid one on top of the other, and with an extra loop down one end. In addition the centre was used for cross-country races. There was no way that these two vehicles would be able to corner me on their own, not unless I was careless, and I had been quite careless enough for one day.

I waited to see which part of the racecourse the car

would choose to move along and then simply rode the horse down the other bit. By this time, the last of the daylight had faded away completely and there was no way the occupants of the vehicle would be able to see me unless I was actually in the arc of the headlights.

However, I watched with some dismay as three more vehicles turned out onto the racecourse, two turning straight towards me and the third starting the long anticlockwise sweep round the course. And worse, in the glow of their lights, I could see some figures walking, spreading out across the centre of the track in search of the horse, or of me.

They couldn't all be Shenington's men. Some of them must be the good guys, the cavalry coming to my rescue. But which ones? I simply couldn't afford to get it wrong.

I decided that my present position was hopeless, and it would be only a matter of time before I would be seen by either someone in the vehicles, or one of those on foot. I trotted the horse over to the very edge of the racecourse property looking for an exit, but the need to keep out the ticket dodgers had resulted in a robust five-foot-high chain-link fence being erected along the whole length.

I supposed I could have tied the horse to the fence and climbed over but the location of the deserted horse would then have given away the fact that I had gone and where, and I feared I would have had Shenington and his mob still on my tail. And I somehow felt safer on the horse because I could outrun those on foot, gun or no gun.

'With that neck, I wouldn't ride a bike, let alone a horse,' the spinal specialist had said to me all those years ago. Yet here I was on horseback galloping around in the dark, but I felt completely safe and at home. I just had to make sure I didn't fall off.

I cantered the horse right along the fence in the hope there might have been a gate. Five feet was too high for any horse to jump, let alone a tired-out hunter chaser that should have been warm in his stable by this time of night. Not that a gate would help much. It would probably be locked and I couldn't ask the horse to jump it in the dark.

The pincer arms of the search parties were moving closer together and, if I didn't move away pretty soon, I was in danger of being caught in their trap. I kicked the horse hard and galloped back along the perimeter fence all the way down to the far northern end of the racecourse and into the extra loop, taking my chances that the horse wouldn't stumble or put his foot in a rabbit hole.

I was still looking unsuccessfully for an exit through the fence. And I was beginning to think that my only option might be to double right round and try to find a way out through the car parks, but the lines of searchers were getting closer, and the opportunities for doing that were being closed off by the minute.

The chain-link fence finally gave way to a hedge,

though not a nice low jumpable hedge but a high impenetrable jungle of hawthorn and blackberry. I trotted on along its length and finally found a gap in the undergrowth. The horse and I went through the gap and into the field that was used as a helicopter landing area during the Festival meeting.

I doubled back, putting the hedge between me and my pursuers. By this time it was an almost completely black night and I didn't now have the reflected light from the vehicle headlamps to help me. The horse and I moved steadily forward at the walk, the blind leading the blind. The animal beneath me must have been as confused as I was as to where we were going but he had been trained well and responded easily to my every command.

'Come on, boy,' I said quietly into his ear. 'Good boy.'

I could see the lights from the houses in Prestbury village. The hedge must be thinner straight ahead.

Suddenly, I thought I heard a man cough. I gently pulled the reins and the horse stopped and stood silently. I listened intently in the darkness.

Had I been mistaken?

The man coughed again. Then he called out, but in a language I didn't recognize. He was on the other side of the hedge, but I couldn't tell exactly how far away. A second man answered, again in a foreign tongue, and he was certainly further away still.

The men had to be Shenington's heavies.

I held my breath and prayed that the horse wouldn't make a noise or jangle the bit in his mouth.

I strained to listen to their conversation and thought I might have heard the nearest man moving, but I was far from sure.

The rain came to my aid.

It had been easing somewhat but now it returned with a vengeance, falling in heavy drops that ran down my neck. But I didn't care. The noise of the rain may have prevented me from hearing anything further of the men's conversation, but, more importantly, it would also mean that they would be unable to hear me moving on.

I made some fairly gentle clicking noises and gently nudged the horse in the ribs with my foot. 'Walk on,' I said to him in his ear.

We eventually came upon a gate, and it wasn't locked.

I dismounted and led the horse through, closing the gate behind us.

A light suddenly came on, flooding the area with brightness and momentarily startling the horse, which whipped round, pulling the reins from my fingers.

Dammit!

'Here, boy,' I said in as calming a voice as I could muster. 'Good boy. Come on.' I held out my hand towards the terrified animal, which tossed his head up and down and neighed loudly. 'Good boy,' I repeated, as I moved towards where he stood quivering by the gate. When I was close enough, I lunged forward and grabbed the reins once more, but not before the horse had neighed loudly a couple of times more.

Had the men heard? Or seen the light?

The light in question was attached to the gable-end of a wooden barn and had a motion sensor below it – a security light.

I looked around. We were in a farmyard with more buildings beyond the barn.

I heard a whizzing sound close to my right.

The sound instantly gave me goosebumps on my arms and made the hairs on my neck stand upright. I knew that noise. I knew it because I'd heard it before in Lichfield Grove. It was the sound of a bullet passing by, and much too close for comfort. A second whizzed past and embedded itself into the wooden planking just a few inches from my face. And I could hear shouting, foreign-language shouting. Time to move, I thought, and quickly.

I pulled the horse forward and we ran around the corner of the barn away from the direction of the shouting. Another bullet whizzed past me and disappeared into the night.

I had intended leaving the horse tied up somewhere, while I made my way to safety alone, but my plans had just changed. If the men were close enough to shoot at me, they would be close enough to catch me if I was on foot. I needed the speed of the horse to escape.

I put my left shoe into the stirrup iron and pulled myself back up into the saddle, gathered the reins, and set off again. More security lights came on as I cantered the horse through the farmyard but the horse was happier now with someone on his back, and he didn't react once. We went right across the brightly lit farmyard and then down a long drive that curved away into the darkness. Soon I could see headlights moving quickly from right to left ahead of us, as a car moved along the Winchcombe road at the end of the drive.

We had now left the security lights well behind, but I had to take a chance in the dark as I kicked the horse forwards as fast as I dared.

I neared the road. Which way should I turn?

I knew that I ought to go to the right towards Prestbury village and Cheltenham. I knew it because I should be on my way to Cheltenham Police Station. I'd be safe there, and DCI Flight would finally get his interview.

I even worked out the best route in my head.

I had grown up in Prestbury village and I knew intimately all the short cuts from there to Cheltenham town centre. I had used them either on foot or on my bicycle for half my life. And I knew all the deserted back-roads and the quiet way through Pittville Park, past the Pump Room that gave Cheltenham its spa status, across the Tommy Taylor's recreation area, and down past the allotments off Gardner's Lane where I had often played as a kid with my school friends. Wherever possible I would keep the horse off the hard surfaces and on the grass, all the way to Swindon Road, not far from the old Cheltenham Maternity Hospital where, nearly thirty years ago, I had been brought screaming into the world.

I could then trot the horse past the railway station

and down the wide, tree-lined avenues around Christ Church to my destination on Lansdown Road.

Yes, I thought, I really ought to turn right towards the police station.

Instead, I turned left towards Woodmancote, and Claudia.

How could I have been so stupid to have told Shenington that she had gone to my mother's? If he had been the one who sent the broken-neck gunman there to kill me, and I had no doubt that it had been, he would know exactly where to find my mother's cottage. It would only be a matter of time before he worked out that he could get to me by attacking Claudia.

I just hoped I would get there first.

Fortunately, at this time on a wet Wednesday, the road was quiet. Only on a couple of occasions did I have to pull off onto the wide grass verges as cars came sweeping past. Neither of them even slowed down. Other than that, I kept to the road. It was much too dangerous for the horse even to walk along the verges at night with the many hidden drainage ditches.

However, the noise of the metal horseshoes clickety-clacking on the tarmac as we cantered along suddenly sounded alarmingly loud in the night air. Which was safer, I wondered, speed or stealth? That same question had been taxing military strategists ever since armies had been invented.

I opted for speed, but I did slow to a walk as we reached the edge of Southam village and, as much as I could, I used the grass there to minimize the noise.

Even though it was late, and still raining, the sound of a horse at such an hour, especially one moving at speed, might bring people out of their houses to investigate, and there was no way I wanted to have to stop and explain what I was doing, not yet.

The horse and I went right through the village of Southam without attracting any unwelcome attention, other than a curious look or two from a cat out on its nocturnal hunt for food.

Southam to Woodmancote was less than a mile and I trotted the horse down the centre of the road using the dotted white line for guidance. At long last the rain was beginning to stop, not that it made much difference to me, I was completely soaked to the skin, and cold with it.

I skirted round the edge of the village towards the lane where my mother lived.

The lane was actually the fourth arm of a crossroads junction and I was just approaching it from straight ahead when a car came along the other road and turned right into it. The car had to be going to my mother's cottage as it was the only house down there.

I kicked the horse forward and followed, keeping to the grass to deaden the noise of the hooves.

Half-way down the lane I slid off the horse's back and tied him to a tree, moving forward silently but quickly on foot. I stayed close to the hedge as I came round the last turn.

I could now see the cottage and Shenington was standing to one side of it as I looked, by the front door, his face brightly lit by the outside light. I crept closer across the grass, towards the gravel drive.

'Viscount Shenington,' he was saying loudly. 'We met earlier at the races.'

'What do you want?' I could hear Claudia shouting back from inside.

'I'm returning Mr Foxton's coat,' Shenington said. 'He must have left it in my box by mistake.' He was holding my coat out in front of him.

Don't open the door, I willed Claudia. PLEASE – DON'T OPEN THE DOOR.

She did, of course. I could hear her turning the lock.

Once Shenington was inside I would have no chance. He could simply put a knife to Claudia's neck, or a gun to her temple, and I would do exactly as he wanted. A lamb to the slaughter it would certainly be.

My only chance was to act decisively, and to act now.

As the front door swung open I ran for him, crunching across the gravel. He turned slightly towards the noise but I was on him before he had a chance to react.

At school, despite my moderate size, I'd been a regular member of the first XV rugby team, and primarily for my tackling.

I caught Shenington just above the knees in a full-blown flying rugby tackle that literally lifted him off his feet.

The two of us crashed to the ground together, the whiplash causing his upper body and head to take most of the impact.

Shenington was in his mid to late sixties and I was

less than half his age, and I had the strength brought on by desperation and anger.

He really had no chance.

I jumped up quickly and I sat on him, twisting my fingers in his hair and forcing his head down into a rain-filled puddle on the drive. How did he like it, I wondered, having *his* face held under water?

Claudia stood, shocked and staring, in the doorway.

'Nick,' she wailed. 'Stop it. Stop it. Stop it. You'll drown him.'

'This is the man who has been trying to kill me,' I said, not releasing my grip.

'That doesn't mean you can kill *him*,' she said.

I reluctantly let go of his hair and rolled him over onto his back. His lips were blue and I couldn't tell if he was breathing or not. I didn't care. One thing was for sure. There was absolutely no way I was going to put my mouth over his to breathe air into his lungs. Even the thought of it made me feel sick.

'He's got a gun,' Claudia said suddenly, the fear clearly apparent again in her voice.

He'd been lying on it.

I leaned down and picked it up by the barrel.

I left Shenington where he lay and went inside to call Cheltenham Police Station.

'Can I please speak to DCI Flight?' I said to the officer who answered. 'I want to give myself up.'

'What have you done?' he said.

'Ask DCI Flight,' I replied. 'He's the one who wants me.'

'He's not here at the moment,' the officer said. 'Some bloody lunatic has stolen a horse up at the racecourse and every spare man is out looking for him.'

'Ah, I might just be able to help you there,' I said. 'The horse in question is tied up outside my mother's house in Woodmancote.'

'What!' he said.

'The horse is right outside where I'm standing now,' I repeated.

'How the hell did it get there?'

'I rode him,' I said. 'I think I'm the bloody lunatic that everyone is looking for.'

21

Detective Chief Inspector Flight was far from amused. He, personally, had spent more than an hour trudging across the dark, muddy racecourse looking for the horse while wearing his best leather shoes and, if that wasn't bad enough, he was also soaked to the skin. As he explained to me at length and rather loudly, his coat was meant to have been waterproof but, on that count, it seemed to have failed rather badly.

'I'm tempted to put you in a cell and throw away the key,' he said.

We were in one of the interview rooms at Cheltenham Police Station.

'How is Viscount Shenington?' I asked, ignoring his remark.

'Still alive,' he said. 'But only just. They're working on him at the hospital. The ambulance paramedics got him breathing again but it seems his heart is now the problem.'

Just like his brother.

'And the doctor is also saying that, even if he does survive, his brain is likely to have been permanently damaged due to being starved of oxygen for so long.'

Shame, I thought. Not!

'You say that you simply rugby-tackled him and

you didn't see that his nose and mouth were lying in the water?'

'That's right,' I said. 'I just thought he was winded by the fall. Only after I'd checked that Claudia was all right did I discover he was face-down in a puddle. Then, of course, I rolled him over onto his back.'

'Did you not then think of applying artificial respiration?' he asked.

I just looked at him.

'No,' he said. 'I can see the problem.'

'Exactly,' I said. 'The man had come there to kill me. Why would I try and save him? So that he could have another go?'

'Some people might argue that you were negligent.'

'Let them,' I said. 'Whatever happened to Shenington was his own fault. You saw the gun. He wasn't there making a social call.'

He looked up at the clock on the wall. It showed that it was well after midnight.

'We'll have to continue this in the morning,' he said, yawning.

'I have to be at Paddington Green by eleven,' I said.

'So do I,' Flight replied. 'We can talk on the way.'

The meeting at Paddington Green Police Station lasted for more than two hours. In addition to me, there were four senior police officers present, Detective Chief Inspectors Tomlinson and Flight, a detective inspector from the City of London Police Economic Crime Department – the Fraud Squad – and Superintendent Yering, who chaired the meeting by virtue of his superior rank.

At his request, I started slowly from the beginning, outlining the events in chronological order from the day Herb Kovak had been gunned down at Aintree, right through to those of the previous evening at Cheltenham racecourse, and at my mother's cottage in Woodmancote. However, I decided not to include the finer details of how I had forced Shenington's head down into the puddle on the gravel driveway.

'Viscount Shenington,' I said, 'seems to have been desperate for money due to his gambling losses and clearly provided the five million pounds from the Roberts Family Trust in order to trigger the grants from the European Union. It appears that he even gave his brother the impression that he had needed to be convinced to make the investment.'

'Perhaps he did to start with,' said DCI Flight, 'until he discovered the availability of the grants.'

'Maybe,' I said. 'But I think it's far more likely that the idea for stealing the EU grants came first and Shenington was simply brought in as the necessary provider of the priming money.'

'So he wasn't the only one involved?' Tomlinson said.

'Not at all,' I said. 'I've seen e-mails between a Uri Joram in the office of the European Commission in Brussels, and a Dimitar Petrov in Bulgaria.'

'How did you see them?' Tomlinson interrupted.

'On Gregory Black's computer,' I said. 'He was copied in on their correspondence.'

'And who is Gregory Black?' asked the detective inspector from the Fraud Squad.

'He's one of the senior partners at Lyall and Black, the firm of financial advisers where I work.' Or where I used to work.

'And what do you think he has to do with this?' he asked.

'I'm only guessing, but I believe that Gregory Black probably found Shenington for Joram and Petrov. They would have needed someone with five million pounds to invest to trigger the much larger sum from the EU. Shenington was a client of Gregory's and who could be better, a man who controlled a wealthy family trust but was himself broke and in dire need of lots of ready money to pay his gambling debts. And Gregory would have known that. Financial advisers are aware of all their clients' most intimate financial secrets.'

'But what has all this to do with the death of Herbert Kovak?' asked DCI Tomlinson. That was *his* major concern.

'Herb Kovak had accessed the file with the e-mails between Joram and Petrov just a few days before he was killed. And Gregory Black would have known he had, because Herb's name appeared on the recently accessed list. I saw it there. Perhaps Herb had asked some difficult questions about the project, questions that got him killed.'

I could see that I was losing them.

'Remember,' I said, 'we are talking about a huge amount of money here. A hundred million euros. Even split four ways, it's a handsome sum, and worth a bit of protecting.'

I could see them doing the simple maths in their heads.

'And,' I went on, 'in the last week or so, every time Gregory Black knew where I was, someone tried to kill me there. I now think that Shenington only changed his mind about wanting to talk to me, then asked me to the races because I hadn't been turning up at my office. He as good as admitted it yesterday. He said I was a difficult man to kill because I usually didn't turn up when I was expected. Well, I was expected at a meeting with Gregory Black on Monday morning, and I'm now certain that I would have been killed if I'd gone to it. I probably wouldn't have even reached the office front door. I'd have been shot down in the street. Murdered in a public place, just like Herb Kovak was at Aintree.'

'I think it's time I spoke again to Mr Gregory Black,' said DCI Tomlinson. 'I remember him from my previous encounter.'

Yes, I thought, and I bet he remembers you.

There followed a brief discussion as to who had the proper jurisdiction to arrest, and on suspicion of what charges. Finally, it was agreed that the honour would fall to DI Batten, the detective inspector from the Fraud Squad – after all, the City of London was his patch. However, we all wanted to be present and a total of three police cars made the trip across London to 64 Lombard Street where we were joined by a fourth from the uniformed branch.

It was quarter past two by the time we arrived at my office. Gregory should be just back from his usual substantial lunch at the restaurant on the corner. I hoped he'd made the most of it. There would be no more *foie gras* and *filet mignon en croûte* where he was going.

'Can I help you?' Mrs McDowd asked as the policemen entered. Then she saw me with them. 'Oh, Mr Nicholas, are these men with you?'

DI Batten ignored her. 'Can you tell me where I might find Mr Gregory Black?' he said rather grandly.

'I'll call him,' she said nervously, clearly slightly troubled by the mass of people crowding into her reception area.

'No,' said DI Batten, 'just tell me where he is.'

At that point Gregory walked down the corridor.

'There he is,' said Mrs McDowd, pointing.

The detective inspector wasted no time.

'Gregory Black,' he said, taking hold of Gregory by the arm, 'I arrest you on suspicion of conspiracy to defraud, and also on suspicion of conspiracy to murder. You do not have to say anything, but it may harm your defence if you do not mention when questioned something which you later rely on in court. Anything you do say may be given in evidence.'

Gregory was stunned. 'But that's ridiculous,' he said. 'I've done nothing of the sort.'

Then he saw me.

'Is this your doing?' he demanded, thrusting his face belligerently towards mine. 'Some kind of sick joke?'

'Murder is never a joke,' said DI Batten. 'Take him away.'

Two uniformed officers moved forward and handcuffed Gregory, who was still loudly protesting his innocence. The policemen ignored his pleas and led him out of the glass door and into the lift.

I knew all too well what that felt like.

'What the hell's going on?' Patrick had appeared in the reception, obviously summoned by the noise. 'What are these men doing here?'

'It seems they are here to arrest Mr Gregory,' said the unflappable Mrs McDowd.

'Arrest Gregory? But that's ridiculous. What for?'

'Conspiracy to defraud, and conspiracy to murder,' DI Batten said.

'Fraud? Murder? Who has he murdered?' Patrick demanded, turning towards the policeman.

'No one,' said DI Batten. 'Mr Black has been arrested on suspicion of *conspiracy* to murder.'

Patrick wasn't to be deterred.

'So who, then, is he suspected of conspiring to murder?'

'Me,' I said, stepping forward.

Patrick said nothing. He just stared at me.

Later in the afternoon, life in the offices of Lyall & Black at 64 Lombard Street returned to some sort of normality, if having one of the senior partners arrested for conspiracy to defraud and murder could ever be considered normal.

I went into my office for the first time in almost two weeks to find that Rory had moved himself into Herb's desk by the window. Diana was still where she had always been.

'By rights that should have been Diana's,' I said to Rory. 'She's the more senior.'

'She had yours until half an hour ago,' Rory replied with a sneer. 'Patrick said you weren't coming back.' His tone implied that he was sorry I had.

Diana, meanwhile, remained silently resentful as I opened the window to let in some of the warm spring day. Perhaps the weather had changed for the better as well.

Maybe Diana wouldn't have to wait too much longer to get back to my desk, anyway. That was, if my desk remained at all. At the moment, I couldn't see Lyall & Black surviving as a firm beyond next week. Once news of a fraud investigation got out, our clients would desert us quicker than rats off a sinking ship. Everything in financial services comes down to client confidence, and confidence in a firm involved in fraud would be close to absolute zero.

The quickest way to create a run on a bank was to publicly warn that there might be one. Depositors would quickly lose confidence in the institution and would queue round the block to get their money back. But, of course, no bank leaves cash lying around in its vaults just in case of such an eventuality. The money will have been lent out to other customers as mortgages and business loans. Hence the bank can't pay. As word spreads that the bank is in trouble, even more depositors come looking for their money and the whole crisis self-perpetuates, and then crashes down like a house of cards. The bank's credibility, which might have taken several hundred years to establish, can be destroyed in as little as a day. As it had been with Northern Rock in the UK and IndyMac in the US, and so would be with us but, in our case, there would be no government bail-out.

Yes, indeed, we had all better start looking for new positions by another firm's window, but what chance would we have with a reference from Lyall & Black? Not much.

There were nearly a hundred unanswered e-mails for me on the company server, plus twenty-eight messages on my office voicemail, including quite a few from irate clients with whom I had missed meetings. There were also two from the Slim Fit Gym reminding me again that they wanted Herb's locker back.

'Where's the key?' I asked Rory.

'What key?' he said.

'The key that was pinned to Herb's desk.'

'Still on it, I expect,' Rory said. 'I swapped the whole desk cubicle.'

I went over to one of the empty cubicles and checked. The key was still pinned to the board. I took it off and put it in my pocket.

I sat down again at my desk and started going

through the mass of e-mails but without really taking in any of the information contained in them. My heart simply wasn't in this job any more.

If and when Claudia beat this cancer, we would do something different, something together.

Something more exciting. But maybe something a little less dangerous.

'I'm going out,' I said to Rory and Diana, as if they cared.

As I walked down the corridor I had to step over some big tied-up polythene bags stacked full of files and computers. The Fraud Squad was busily packing up the stuff from Gregory's office. I was quite surprised they hadn't thrown us all out of the building to pack up the whole firm. That would come later, no doubt, when they had discovered a little more.

The receptionist at the Slim Fit Gym was really pleased to see me.

'To be honest,' she said in a broad Welsh accent, 'it's beginning to smell a bit, especially today in this warm weather. It's upsetting some of our other clients. There must be some dreadfully sweaty clothes in there.'

The key from Herb's desk fitted neatly into the hefty padlock on the locker, and I swung open the door.

The receptionist and I leaned back. It smelled more than a just a bit.

There was a dark blue holdall in the locker with a pair of off-white training shoes placed on top, and I think it was the shoes, rather than the clothes inside, that were the culprits as far as the smell was concerned. Perhaps Herb had suffered from some sort of foot fungal problem that had spread to his shoes, and then they had clearly festered badly over the last three weeks. But whatever the cause, the smell was pretty rank.

'Sorry about this,' I said. 'I'll get rid of it all.'

I tucked the offending shoes into the holdall on top of the clothes and left the receptionist tut-tutting about having to disinfect all the lockers.

I walked back towards Lombard Street and dumped the whole thing, together with all the contents, into a City-of-London-crested street litter bin. I didn't think Mrs McDowd would be very happy if I took that smell back into the office.

I had walked nearly a hundred yards further on when I suddenly turned round and retraced my steps. I had searched everything else of Herb's. Why not that holdall?

Neatly stacked, in a zipped-up compartment beneath the clothes, was over a hundred and eighty thousand pounds wrapped in clear-plastic sandwich-bags, three thousand in twenty-pound notes to each bag. There was also a list of ninety-seven names and addresses, all of them in America.

Good old Herb. As meticulous as ever.

'Mr Patrick would like to see you,' Mrs McDowd said to me as I skipped through the door with the bag of loot over my shoulder. 'In his office, right now.'

Patrick was not alone. Jessica Winter was also there.

'Ah, Nicholas,' said Patrick. 'Come and sit down.' I sat in the spare chair next to the open window. 'Jessica and I have been looking at how things stand. We need to implement a damage-limitation exercise. To seek to maintain the confidence of our clients, and to assure them that it's "business as usual" at Lyall and Black.'

'And is it "business as usual"?' I asked.

'Of course,' he said. 'Why wouldn't it be?'

I thought that was pretty obvious. Members of the Fraud Squad were still in the room next door bagging up evidence.

'No,' Patrick went on, 'we mustn't let this little setback disrupt our work. I will write to all of Gregory's clients telling them that, for the time being, I will be looking after their portfolios. It will just mean we all have to work a little harder for a while.'

But for how long, I wondered.

The maximum sentence for conspiracy to murder was life imprisonment.

'So how about the Bulgarian business?' I asked.

'Jessica and I have just been looking at it,' Patrick said. 'Or what is left to look at after those damn police have been in here taking stuff away.'

'And?' I asked.

'It's rather inconclusive,' Jessica said.

'What's inconclusive?' I asked, somewhat surprised.

'There seems to be no evidence to show if the original investment was obtained by fraudulent means, or whether there was any purposeful deception by anyone in this firm,' Jessica said.

She's covering her back, I thought.

'But how about the European Union grants?' I said.

'They are not our business,' Patrick said sharply. 'Neither Gregory individually, nor Lyall and Black as a firm, can be held responsible for the actions of people in Brussels, those who may have issued EU grants without due diligence. The only matter that affects this firm is the original Roberts Family Trust investment, and then only if we were knowingly negligent in brokering it. As far as we can establish, the investment idea was put forward by the senior trustee of the trust.'

I had to admit, it was a persuasive argument, especially as Viscount Shenington was unlikely to be in any state to refute it. Perhaps I had been a tad premature in writing off the future of Lyall & Black.

But that didn't explain what had happened to Herb Kovak, and it didn't explain Shenington's comment about me being difficult to kill, and not turning up where I was expected. The only place I'd been expected had been the offices of Lyall & Black, and the only people who had known where I'd been expected had been the firm's staff. Gregory must have at least discussed the matter of my murder with Shenington. That alone would have been enough to convict him.

'What about the photographs that Gregory showed to Colonel Roberts?' I said. 'The ones that purported to prove that the factory and houses had already been built.'

'Gregory told me this morning that he'd been sent those by the developer in Bulgaria, and in good faith,' said Patrick. 'He'd had no reason to doubt their authenticity.'

'Not until Jolyon Roberts asked about them,' I said. 'What did he do then?'

'Gregory told me that Colonel Roberts didn't exactly say that he questioned whether the photos were accurate or not. In fact, Gregory said that Roberts kept contradicting himself and changing his mind throughout their final telephone conversation, and he kept apologizing all the time for wasting Gregory's time. In the end, Gregory wasn't quite sure what to think.'

I could believe it. Jolyon Roberts had done exactly the same with me at Cheltenham. I thought it strange that a man who had clearly been so decisive on the battlefield could have been so befuddled and incoherent when it came to accusing a friend of lying, and of stealing from him. I suppose it was all about honour, and not losing face.

'Thank you, Jessica,' Patrick said. 'You can be getting back to your office now.'

Jessica stood up and left. I remained where I was.

'Now, Nicholas,' said Patrick when the door was shut, 'I have decided to overlook your rather strange behaviour over the past three weeks and to wipe the slate clean. Your job is still yours if you want it. To be honest, I don't know how we would manage at the moment if you weren't here.'

So was that a vote of confidence in my ability, I wondered, or a decision born simply out of necessity?

'Thank you,' I said. 'I'll think about it.'

'Don't take too long about it,' Patrick said. 'It's time to put other things out of your mind and get back to work.'

'I'm still not happy about things,' I said. 'Especially the fraud.'

'Suspected fraud,' he corrected. 'If you ask me, it is a shame you ever went to see Roberts's nephew in Oxford.'

'Maybe,' I said.

'Well go now and get on with your work, I have things to do.'

It was a dismissal, so I stood up and went back to my desk.

I was still greatly troubled by Patrick's and Jessica's seeming brush-off of such a serious situation.

Herb had accessed the file and then he was killed.

Shenington and his gunmen knew more about my movements than they could have done without someone in the firm passing on the information.

Something wasn't right. I could tell because the hairs on my neck refused to lie down. Something definitely wasn't right. Not right at all.

I took out a sheet of paper from a drawer and wrote out again a copy of the note I had found in Herb's coat pocket.

YOU SHOULD HAVE DONE WHAT YOU WERE TOLD. YOU MAY SAY YOU REGRET IT, BUT YOU WON'T BE REGRETTING IT FOR LONG.

I wrote it out in capital letters using a black ballpoint pen so that it looked identical to the original.

I picked up my mobile phone and the note, and went down the corridor. I walked into Patrick's office, closing the door behind me.

'Yes?' he asked, showing some surprise at my unannounced entrance.

I stood in front of his desk looking down at him as if it was the first time I had ever seen him properly.

'What did you tell Herb to do?' I asked him quietly.

'What do you mean?' he replied with a quizzical expression.

'You told him that he should have done what he was told,' I said.

I laid the note down on the table, facing him, so that he could read the words.

'What was it you told Herb to do?'

'Nicholas,' he said, looking up at me and betraying a slight nervousness in his voice, 'I don't know what you're talking about.'

'Yes, you do,' I said with some menace. 'It was *you* all along, not Gregory. *You* devised the fraud, *you* found Shenington to put up the five million from his family trust, and *you* saw to it that you weren't found out.'

'I don't know what you're talking about,' he said again, but his eyes showed me he did.

'And *you* had Herb killed,' I said. 'You even wrote this note to him as a sort of apology. Everyone liked Herb, including you. But he had to die, didn't he? Because he had accessed the Roberts file and he'd worked out what was going on. What did you do?

Offer him a piece of the action? Try and buy his silence? But Herb wasn't having any of that, was he? Herb was going to go to the authorities, wasn't he? So he had to die.'

Patrick sat in his chair looking up at me. He said nothing.

'And it was *you* that tried to have me killed as well,' I said. 'You sent the gunman to my house in Finchley and then, when that didn't work, you sent him to my mother's cottage to kill me there.'

He remained in his chair staring at me through his oversized glasses.

'But that didn't work either,' I said. 'So you arranged for me to come here on Monday for a meeting with you and Gregory.' I laughed. 'A meeting with my maker, more like. But I didn't come, although you tried hard to convince me to. Then I saw you on the train and you said, "Come home with me now and we'll sort this out tonight". But I'd have been dead if I had, wouldn't I?' I paused and stared back at him. He still said nothing. 'So then Shenington changed his mind about talking to me and invited me to be his guest at the races in order to complete the job.'

'Nicholas,' Patrick said, finally finding his voice, 'what is all this nonsense?'

'It's not nonsense,' I said. 'I never told you that I'd been to see Mr Roberts's nephew in Oxford. In fact, I'd purposely *not* told you because I didn't want any-one knowing my movements. I just told you that I'd spoken to him. For all you knew, it could have been on the telephone. But Shenington told you that I went to Oxford to meet his son, didn't he? And you repeated it to me just now.'

'You have no proof,' he said, changing his tune.

'Did you know that you can get fingerprints from paper?' I asked, picking up the note carefully by the corner.

He wasn't to know that the original had already been tested by the Merseyside Police forensic department and found to have only my and Herb's prints on it.

His shoulders sagged just a fraction and he looked down at the desk.

'What did Herb say he regretted?' I asked.

'He said he regretted finding out,' Patrick said wistfully with a sigh. 'I was careless. I stupidly left a document under the flap of the photocopier. Herb found it.'

'So what did you tell him to do?' I asked for a third time.

'To accept what he'd been offered,' he said, looking up at me. 'But he wanted more. Much more. It was too much.'

Herb had clearly not been as much of a saint as I'd made out.

'So you had him killed.'

He nodded. 'Herb was a fool,' he said. 'He should have accepted my offer. It was very generous, and you can have the same – a million euros.'

'You make me sick,' I said.

'Two million,' he said quickly. 'It would make you a rich man.'

'Blood money,' I said. 'Is that the going rate these days for covering up fraud, and murder?'

'Look,' he said. 'I'm sorry about Herb. I liked him and I argued against having him killed, but the others insisted.'

'Others?' I said. 'You must mean Uri Joram and Dimitar Petrov.'

He stared at me with his mouth open.

'Oh yes,' I said. 'The police know all about Joram and Petrov because I told them. I told them everything.'

'You bastard,' he said with feeling. 'I wish Petrov had killed you at the same time he shot Herb Kovak.'

Throughout the encounter I'd been holding my mobile phone in my left hand. It was one of those fancy new do-anything smartphones, and one of its functions was the ability to act as a voice-memo recorder.

I'd recorded every word that had been said.

I pushed the buttons and played back the last bit. Patrick sat very still in his executive leather chair listening and staring at me with a mixture of hatred and resignation in his eyes.

'I wish Petrov had killed you at the same time he shot Herb Kovak.'

It sounded rather metallic out of the telephone's tiny speaker, but there was no doubting that it was Patrick Lyall's voice.

'You bastard,' he said again.

I folded the note, turned away from him, and walked

back along the corridor to my desk to call Chief Inspector Tomlinson. But I'd only just picked up the telephone when there was a piercing scream from outside the building.

I stuck my head out through the window.

Patrick was lying face up in the middle of the road, and there was already a small pool of blood spreading out around his head.

He had taken the quick way down from our fourth-floor offices.

Straight down.

And it had been the death of him.

Epilogue

Six weeks later Claudia and I went to Herb Kovak's funeral at Hendon Crematorium, the Liverpool coroner finally having given his permission.

There were just five mourners, including the two of us.

Sherri had returned from Chicago and would be taking Herb's ashes back to the States with her. The previous day, she and I had attended the solicitor's offices of Parc Bean & Co., just off Fleet Street, to swear affidavits in order for the court to confirm a Deed of Variance to Herb's will, making her, his twin sister, rather than me, the sole beneficiary of his estate. It would surely have been what he would have wanted. I, however, was to remain as his executor in order to complete the sale of his flat, and to do the other things that were still outstanding.

I had written to all the American names I had found in Herb's dark blue holdall informing them of his untimely death, and that their little scheme to use his credit card accounts for their internet gambling had died with him. I'd told them that they shouldn't worry about me going to the authorities and they wouldn't be hearing from me again. But I also told them that I had no expectation of hearing from them either, even if they had paid Herb in advance more than they had subsequently lost. Then I'd used the cash from the holdall to pay off all the credit card balances, and used my letter from the coroner to close the accounts.

Detective Chief Inspector Tomlinson had come down from Merseyside for the funeral service and he sat in front of Claudia and me in the chapel wearing the same ill-fitting suit he'd worn when I'd first met him in the offices of Lyall & Black. That had been less than three months ago but it felt like a lifetime.

Lyall & Black and Co. Ltd was no more.

Gregory Black had been quickly released by the police but he had taken early retirement. Without Patrick, he hadn't had the incentive to carry on, and he had heeded his heart doctor's advice to put his feet up in his Surrey garden.

I, meanwhile, had quit before I was fired, walking out of 64 Lombard Street for the last time before the paramedics had even had a chance to scrape Patrick's lifeless corpse from the pavement.

I still didn't know what I would do, so I was currently living off my savings, and looking after Claudia.

We stood up to sing the hymn 'The Lord's My Shepherd' and I took her hand in mine.

The last six weeks had been very difficult for her. She had undergone two sessions of chemotherapy, each for three days, and three weeks apart.

Her hair had fallen out in handfuls immediately after the second treatment and, by now, she was completely bald. Today, as usual, she was wearing a headscarf, mostly to prevent other people from staring at her. Strangely, it had not been the loss of hair on her head that had upset her the most, but the loss of her lovely long eyelashes with it.

However, Mr Tomic, the oncologist, was pleased with her progress and reckoned that the two sessions were enough. As he'd said, 'We don't want to jeopardize your fertility now, do we?'

On that count we would just have to wait and see. With cancer, there were never any guarantees.

The fifth mourner at the funeral was Mrs McDowd, who had arrived just before the undertakers had carried in the plain oak coffin. I wondered how she had known about the funeral but, of course, Mrs McDowd knew about everything.

I stood out at the front to utter a few words about Herb, as it somehow seemed wrong to allow him to go for ever without at least marking his passing.

I tried hard to visualize in my head the features of the man lying in the wooden box beside me. The unravelling of the enigmas of his life had seemingly brought us closer together and, in a strange way, he had become more of a friend to me after his death than he ever had before it.

I didn't really know what I should say so I made some banal comments about his love of life, and his wish to help others less fortunate than himself, but without actually pointing out that the others he helped were law-breaking American internet gamblers and poker players.

In all, the service took less than twenty minutes. Sherri sobbed quietly and the rest of us stood in silence as the priest pushed a hidden button, and the electrically operated red curtains closed round my colleague, my friend, my free-spending greedy friend.

Then the five of us went outside into the warm June sunshine.

Claudia and Mrs McDowd consoled Sherri while the chief inspector and I moved a little distance away.

'The European Union have started an internal enquiry,' he said, 'into the whole Bulgarian light-bulb factory affair.'

'Any arrests?' I asked.

'Not yet,' he said. 'And between you and me, I don't think there will be. There didn't seem to be the slightest urgency at the meeting I had with the administrator from the European Court of Auditors. He seemed to think that a hundred million euros was hardly big enough to worry about. I ask you. A hundred million euros could build us a new hospital in Liverpool, or several new schools.'

'Any news on Shenington?' I asked him.

'No change,' he said. 'And I doubt if there will be. The medics are now saying he has entered what they call a "persistent vegetative state". It's a sort of half-coma, half-awake condition.'

'What's the prognosis?'

'They say he's unlikely ever to make any improvement, and he'll certainly never stand trial. In cases of severe brain damage like this, if patients show no change for a whole year, the doctors usually recommend to their families that artificial nutrition should be withdrawn, to let them die.'

Ben Roberts would clearly have some difficult decisions to make in the months ahead. And I also wondered what effect the actions of his father might have on his planned life in politics. He would surely now become the Earl of Balscott rather earlier than he might have expected.

'Have you managed to identify the dead gunman as Dimitar Petrov?' I asked.

'We're still working on it,' he said. 'It seems that both Dimitar and Petrov are very common names in Bulgaria.'

'Can't Uri Joram in Brussels help you?'

'Apparently he denies any knowledge of anything,' he said. 'Claims his e-mail address must have been used by others.'

'Why am I not surprised?' I said. 'How about Shenington's heavies at Cheltenham?'

'Not a sniff,' he said. 'I expect they vanished into the night as soon as their boss ended up in hospital.'

It reminded me of Billy Searle, who was now, in fact, out of hospital, recuperating at home with the fixator on his broken leg. Officially, he was still denying any knowledge of who had knocked him off his bicycle, but he had confirmed to me privately that the 'nob' responsible had indeed been Viscount Shenington. 'I'm so glad the effing bastard got what was coming to him,' had been his exact words when I'd told him of Shenington's medical condition. And he had giggled uncontrollably, and repeatedly punched the air.

The chief inspector and I rejoined the others.

'Rosemary says she's lost her job,' said Claudia, sounding affronted on her behalf.

'Everyone at Lyall and Black has,' said Rosemary McDowd with bitterness.

Her tone also implied an accusation, and I took it to be towards me. Why was it, I wondered, that the blame often fell, not on the wrongdoer, but on the person who exposed them?

It wasn't me who Mrs McDowd should blame for the demise of Lyall & Black. It was Patrick Lyall, and maybe Gregory Black too, for not being sufficiently diligent in his management of the Roberts Family Trust.

And I surely had more right to be angry with her than vice versa.

After all, it had been she who had told Patrick that I'd been staying at my mother's house, which had then allowed him and Shenington to send a gunman there to try to kill me.

'So what are you going to do now?' I asked her.

'I have absolutely no idea,' she said flatly. 'How about you?'

'I thought I might try my hand at working in the movies, or in the theatre,' I said. 'I've written to a few companies offering my services as a funding specialist, to help them find the production money for films and plays. I think it looks quite interesting.'

'But isn't that a bit of a gamble?' she said.

I smiled at her.

With ovarian cancer, life itself was a bit of a gamble.

Heads you win, tails you die.

Cambridge Studies in Social Anthropology

General Editor

JACK GOODY

12

RESOURCES AND POPULATION

OTHER TITLES IN THE SERIES

1. *The Political Organization of Unyamwezi*
   R. G. ABRAHAMS
2. *Buddhism and the Spirit Cults in North-East Thailand*
   S. J. TAMBIAH
3. *Kalahari Village Politics: An African Democracy*
   ADAM KUPER
4. *The Rope of Moka: Big-men and Ceremonial Exchange in Mount Hagen, New Guinea*
   ANDREW STRATHERN
5. *The Majangir: Ecology and Society of a Southwest Ethiopian People*
   JACK STAUDER
6. *Buddhist Monk, Buddhist Layman: A Study of Urban Monastic Organization in Central Thailand*
   JANE BUNNAG
7. *Contexts of Kinship: An Essay in the Family Sociology of the Gonja of Northern Ghana*
   ESTHER N. GOODY
8. *Marriage among a Matrilineal Elite: A Family Study of Ghanaian Senior Civil Servants*
   CHRISTINE OPPONG
9. *Elite Politics in Rural India: Political Stratification and Political Alliances in Western Maharashtra*
   ANTHONY T. CARTER
10. *Women and Property in Morocco: Their changing relation to the process of social stratification in the Middle Atlas*
    VANESSA MAHER
11. *Rethinking Symbolism*
    DAN SPERBER

RESOURCES AND POPULATION

A Study of the Gurungs of Nepal

ALAN MACFARLANE

Lecturer in Social Anthropology
University of Cambridge

CAMBRIDGE UNIVERSITY PRESS

CAMBRIDGE

LONDON · NEW YORK · MELBOURNE

Published by the Syndics of the Cambridge University Press
The Pitt Building, Trumpington Street, Cambridge CB2 1RP
Bentley House, 200 Euston Road, London NW1 2DB
32 East 57th Street, New York, NY 10022, USA
296 Beaconsfield Parade, Middle Park, Melbourne 3206, Australia

Library of Congress catalogue card number: 75-13448

ISBN: 0 521 20913 7

First published 1976

Photoset and printed by
Interprint (Malta) Ltd

It certainly appears that a superabundant population in an unfertile country must be the greatest of all calamities, and produce eternal warfare or eternal want. Either the most active and the most able part of the community must be compelled to emigrate, and to become soldiers of fortune or merchants of chance; or else, if they remain at home, be liable to fall a prey to famine in consequence of some accidental failure in their scanty crops.

[Turner's Embassy to Tibet, part ii.c.x. p. 351; quoted in T. R. Malthus, *An Essay on Population* (Everyman edn., no date), i, p. 122.]

The distinctive note of Chinese agriculture, he observes, was 'economy of space, economy of materials, economy of implements, economy of fodder, economy of fuel, economy of waste products, economy of everything except of forests, which have been plundered, with prodigal recklessness, to the ruin of the soil, and of the labour of human beings, whom social habits have made abundant and abundance cheap'.

[R. H. Tawney's *Land and Labour in China*, p. 48, quoted in Barrington Moore, *Social Origins of Dictatorship and Democracy* (Peregrine edn., 1969), p. 190].

Contents

Tables and figures

TABLES

In appendices

FIGURES

Figures

Preface and acknowledgements

The fieldwork upon which this book is based was carried out mainly in the village of Thak, some twelve miles north of Pokhara in central Nepal. Perched on a steep ridge at six thousand feet, the village was overshadowed by the Himalayan range known as the Annapurna mountains. The inhabitants largely consisted of a tribe called in Nepali the Gurungs, famous throughout the world as fighting men in the Gurkha regiments of the British and Indian armies. The aim was to carry out an intensive analysis of a particular community, with a stress on the economic and demographic aspects of life. The Gurungs were chosen on the advice of Professor C. von Fürer Haimendorf, my supervisor and a specialist on Nepal. The village of Thak was chosen because it seemed a convenient distance from the market town of Pokhara.

A number of previous and subsequent studies have been made of the Gurungs and these are listed in the bibliography. In the nineteenth century Brian Hodgson collected material on the Gurungs as well as other groups; much of this is unpublished but is deposited at the India Office Library. For most of this century Nepal has been closed to outside investigators, but the flow of army recruits provided army officers with informants. Thus the sketches of Gurung customs made by John Morris, an officer with anthropological training, give us a valuable picture of certain aspects of the culture in the 1920s. There are also useful comments in the general description of the Gurungs by Dor Bahadur Bista. By far the most important contribution to the study of the Gurungs, however, is that made by Bernard Pignède in his work *Les Gurungs* (Mouton: Paris, 1966) and in his unpublished field notes. Pignède spent some seven months among the Gurungs in 1958, the major portion of which time he spent in the village of Mohoriya. Despite his short visit, lack of any previous anthropological training, and tragic death soon after his return, he was able to collect and analyse a very large amount of material, postumously published under the direction of Professor Louis Dumont. Although one is bound to find small mistakes of fact and interpretation in such a long work, my experience with the Gurungs amply corroborated most of his material and underlined its great accuracy and value. Since he covered almost all aspects of Gurung society in considerable detail it is difficult not merely to repeat his work. I have therefore tended to concentrate on particular aspects of the society, especially those which need quantitative data. Although Pignède gave a general account of these topics, a longer period in the field, plus the existence of his prior description as an invaluable framework, enabled me to go into certain questions more deeply. But it should be stressed that the following chapters, although intelligible in themselves, are designed to complement his work. My chapters omit a number of obvious topics, particularly politics, kinship, social structure and religion, and these omissions can be understood only if we realize that Pignède has already covered the ground. Cross-references to his work are frequently made in order to prevent duplication. A short visit to Mohoriya in 1969 and the use of his unpublished field notes has made it possible in a number of cases to see whether Thak is unique in certain respects and also to compare the situation in Mohoriya in 1958 with that in 1969.

Two unpublished theses have also been found helpful. One is by N. J. Allen and is a general account of Nepalese societies. Though based on secondary sources, it has some valuable suggestions concerning the Gurungs, particularly respecting their origin and cross-cousin marriage system. A thesis by D. A. Messerschmidt, based on research among the Gurungs to the east of Thak, came to my attention after this text was completed, but some of the many useful analyses contained in the thesis have been referred to below.

The methods used in fieldwork were basically the 'participant-observation' techniques upon which most anthropological work is based. General surveys and a census were combined with observation and questioning of key informants. Special stress was laid on collecting historical documents, particularly those of landholding. These records are described in the text. Undoubtedly the most interesting aspect of the Gurungs from a purely anthropological point of view is their complex religious life, in which Hinduism, Buddhism, and a local form of animism, derived from old Tibetan *bon* religion, are blended. I observed many propitiatory rituals and with the help of the local diviner (*poju* in Gurung) I was able to collect over sixty myths, of which only a dozen or so had been noted by Pignède. The rituals were often long and complex and extensive notes were taken on these. Material was also collected concerning beliefs about causation, the after-life and other topics including witchcraft.

The fieldwork was financed by the London Committee of the London–Cornell Project for East and South-East Asian Studies (financed jointly by the Carnegie Corporation of New York and the Nuffield Foundation in England). The School of Oriental and African Studies, London, provided a Governing Body Postgraduate Exhibition which made it possible to undertake full-time writing for one year. The Provost and Fellows of King's College, Cambridge, provided further time by an election to a Senior Research Fellowship. Further support was provided in connection with a project entitled 'The Study of Non-Industrial Communities: Three Case Studies', one of which was Thak, financed by the Social Science Research Council. I am deeply grateful to all these institutions for the support without which, of course, this study would have been impossible.

While in Nepal I was assisted by a number of people, especially Mr. M. B. Pant of the British Council Library, Pokhara, and the staff of the Nepal Research Centre, Thyssen House. The research was undertaken in collaboration with Tribhuvan University, Kathmandu, and this made access to central Nepal possible. I am especially grateful to Dr Upraity for his assistance here. Warren and Jessie Glover of the Summer Institute of Linguistics helped us to learn the Gurung language. But, above all, deepest thanks are due to the villagers of Thak and Mohoriya who made us so welcome, especially Bohansing and Prembahadur Gurung and their families. The privilege of living with such tolerant, humourous, relaxed and intelligent people was a very great one.

I am also grateful to Professor Louis Dumont, Professor A. W. Macdonald and the staff of the Centre D'Etudes Indiennes in Paris for their help in locating Pignède's manuscripts and for permission to use them in this work. Professor C. von Fürer-Haimendorf first aroused my interest in Nepal. His wide knowledge of Himalayan peoples has been of constant value and I am most grateful for his sympathetic comments on my thesis. Doctors Lionel and Pat Caplan have added to many kindnesses by reading the whole work and making numerous useful criticisms. Their suggestions on restructuring the argument have been especially valuable. Nicholas Allen has also greatly helped by reading and commenting on the typescript. Chris Langford of the London School of Economics gave time to check the demography. Dr Gerald Turner of the Shining Hospital, Pokhara, helped to carry out a short medical survey and has read the passages on medicine and mortality. Sarah Harrison commented on the whole text and helped check the figures. Professor Jack Goody, Geoffrey Hawthorn, Iris Macfarlane and Dr D. Parkin have also read and commented on the whole manuscript and Dr E. A. Wrigley commented on the final chapter. To all of them, my warmest thanks. My greatest debt, however, is to Gill, who spent fifteen months in a Gurung village with me and helped in the collection and analysis of data. Amoebic dysentery was only part of the price she paid for this help; her support and ideas have influenced me very greatly.

Abbreviations and conventions

All references to rupees (rs.) are to Nepalese currency, unless otherwise stated (for their value see below).

Several Nepalese and Gurung terms are frequently used because there is no real English equivalent; they are italicized. A *poju* (spelt *pucu* by Pignède) is a local diviner and magician. A *panchayat* is the local area of government, roughly equivalent to an English parish. The Gurungs are split into two strata, the *carjat* (four *jat*) and *sorajat* (sixteen *jat*). The words 'class' and 'caste' do not either of them exactly translate *jat* for it contains and omits elements of both. Where possible the word *jat*, meaning an endogamous group with certain restrictions on eating with other *jats*, is employed. Where it is translated as 'class' or 'caste' the misleading nature of such translation should be borne in mind. It should also be stressed that when *sora* and *car jats* are translated as 'upper' or 'lower' in the following pages, this implies nothing concerning their relative status, but only reflects the fact that the *carjat* tend to be wealthier in most Gurung villages.

Throughout, the term Gurung is used, though in the Gurung language itself (*tumul-kwi*) these peoples know themselves as *tumul-mae* (*mae* = a plural suffix). I also write of the village of Thak (pronounced Tark), though it is known in Gurung as Tolson.

All Nepalese and Gurung terms are italicized and, wherever possible, the spelling follows R. L. Turner's *A Comparative and Etymological Dictionary of the Nepali Language* (1931). Gurung words that do not appear in Turner's book have been spelt as they are pronounced. The only stress added in such words is to the letter 'e' when it has the same sound as an é in French.

Castes as opposed to occupations are indicated by a capital letter; thus Blacksmith caste, blacksmith occupation.

As indicated below, a *muri* can be a measure of either area or volume. When it is used as a measure of land area it is written *sa muri* (*sa* = earth).

The word 'rice' is generally used for husked grain; paddy or unhusked grain is described as 'unhusked rice'.

Full titles of all works cited in abbreviated form in the notes will be found in the bibliography.

Weights, measures, and conversion factors

Monetary (Nepalese 1969)

1 mohr	=	½ rupee (rs.)
1 rs.	=	4p (approx.)
24 rs.	=	£1 (approx.)
10 rs.	=	$1 (approx.)

Weight

Tola	=	one third of an ounce (approx.)
Dharni	=	3 kg (approx.)
1 kg	=	2.2046 lb
1 lb	=	0.4536 kg

Metric equivalents of weight, grains (from Nepal, Ministry of Economic Planning, *Physical Input–Output Characteristics of Cereal Grain Production* ... Nepal, 1965/6)

Unhusked rice, 1 *muri*	=	50 kg
Rice (husked), 1 *muri*	=	68.6 kg
Wheat, 1 *muri*	=	67.3 kg
Maize, 1 *muri*	=	62.7 kg
Millet, 1 *muri*	=	67.3 kg

Volume of grain

1 *muthi*	=	handful (closed)
1 *mana*	=	10 *muthi* (about 1 pint or 57 cl)
1 *poti*	=	8 *mana*
1 *muri*	=	20 *poti* (Nep. *pāthi*)

Measures of area

4 *pathi*	=	1 *anna*
16 *anna*	=	1 *ropani*
1 *ropani*	=	0.13 acres
1 *ropani*	=	4 *sa muri*
1 *ropani*	=	0.051 hectares
1 hectare	=	2.4711 acres
1 sq. mile	=	640 acres

There is a parallel system employing some identical terms, the *sa muri* measurements, as follows:

10 *muthi*	=	1 *mana*
8 *mana*	=	1 *pathi*
20 *pathi*	=	1 *sa muri*
(4 *sa muri*	=	1 *ropani*)

I

Demography and anthropology

Few people would now dispute Paul Ehrlich's statement that 'The explosive growth of the human population is the most significant terrestrial event of the past million millenia'.[1] Nor is it easy to argue with McNamara's view that the population problem is 'by half a dozen criteria, the most delicate and difficult issue of our era – perhaps of any era in history. It is overlaid with emotion. It is controversial. It is subtle. Above all, it is immeasurably complex'.[2] At the regional level we have endorsement from Gunnar Myrdal who spoke of the 'population explosion in recent years, which constitutes by far the most important social change in South Asia, overshadowing everything else that has happened'.[3] A brief look at a few well-known figures will remind us of the current situation.

Population figures before about 1650 are notoriously inaccurate, but a rough guess has been made in table 1.1.

There are other ways of putting such figures. Each day world population increases by over 200,000 persons; by the end of this century, on present projections, it will be increasing by 500,000 every day. It took a million years for world population to double, from about $2\frac{1}{2}$ million to 5 million in 6000 B.C. By the end of this century we will be adding such a $2\frac{1}{2}$ million every 5 days. By the year 2000 there are projected to be about $7\frac{1}{2}$ billion human beings on the earth. A number of countries now have 3 % and 4 % annual growth rates, thus

TABLE 1.1 *Doubling times*

Date	Estimated world population	Time for population to double
B.C. 8000	5 million	1500
A.D. 1650	500 million	200 years
A.D. 1850	1000 million	80 years
A.D. 1930	2000 million	45 years
A.D. 1975	4000 million	
Estimated doubling time around 1970: 35–7 years		

Source: *Population, Resources, Environment: Issues in Human Ecology*, 2nd edn., by Paul R. Ehrlich & Anne H. Ehrlich, p. 6. W. H. Freeman & Co. Copyright © 1972.

their population doubles every twenty years or less. A rate of 3 % growth, a little higher than that of current world growth, means a thousand-fold increase over two centuries. Over a longer period, the increases are even more astonishing. If one hundred persons had been alive in 5000 B.C. and had increased at less than *half* current world rates, in other words at 1 % per annum, there would currently be 2.7 billion persons per square foot of land surface on the earth.[4] It is with such principles in mind that we can understand, for example, how Java has grown from approximately 4 million in the year 1800 to roughly 70 million in 1970, and will, at current rates, have some 4 billion in the year 2100; thus roughly equalling the whole of world population at present.[5]

Historians of pre-industrial England have recently recognized the enormous effects of population growth on social and economic institutions. Lawrence Stone has commented that 'Population pressure has replaced the wicked enclosing or rackrenting landlord as the *diabolus ex machina*... It was demographic growth which stimulated the change to a market economy... It was relentless demographic growth which multiplied the number of villagers until the pressure on the land became acute...'[6] Yet we may wonder how such growth compares with that in currently developing countries. It would seem that between 1500 and 1640 English population doubled, an average growth of just 0.5 % p.a.[7] Many countries in Asia and Africa and Latin America are now increasing at over 2 % p.a. and doubling in 35 years rather than in 140. If historians have diagnosed shattering effects from such a relatively small rate of growth, we would except that anthropologists, often doing fieldwork in societies where very much greater changes are occurring, would have noticed far greater repercussions. Furthermore, we might expect that living for a while in societies where birth, marriage and death are so clearly very important would have made observers interested in demography. Extensive analysis of the social framework of reproduction, kinship, marriage and sexual behaviour, did, indeed, emerge. It is one of the most revealing indications of the blinding effects of a theoretical system that fieldworkers should have almost entirely managed to miss the most important social change that was occurring in the society around them. A brief analysis of how this omission occurred throws some light on the current state of anthropological research. It is also necessary, since it may help anthropologists to apply themselves to a task of unparalleled importance. We are rapidly moving towards a population catastrophe which will make past plagues and two world wars seem insignificant by comparison. Any contributions which can be made to mitigate this disaster would be acceptable; it is too late completely to avoid it.

That the anthropological record is unsatisfactory has been pointed out by a number of writers, including anthropologists. Some time ago Myrdal commented that the 'rapidly accumulating village surveys show an astonishing lack of interest in local health conditions, or in demographic changes and their social and economic consequences'.[8] Recently, Geoffrey Hawthorn has written that 'With a small handful of creditable exceptions, social anthropologists have not been given to collecting statistics, or to collecting data over any period of time, and both are necessary for a demographic picture'.[9] The anthropologist Burton Benedict concludes that 'the information we have about population regulation in simple societies is extremely poor. Very few anthropologists have been concerned with this problem ... The quantitative data they have collected on population growth or decline have not been very systematic or complete, nor have the data been collected in such a way as to make comparisons from society to society possible'.[10] The contribution by social anthropologists up to 1968 was disappointing.[11] The voices of the profession indicated little interest: the *Biennial Review of Anthropology*, *Man*, the *British Journal of Sociology*, the *Association of Social Anthropology* collections, none of these included, to that date, more than the most occasional reference to anthropological work on population. It is true that *Notes and Queries in Anthropology* suggested fieldworkers collect 'urgently needed' material 'for the study of the relation between demographic conditions and social institutions'.[12] Yet if we look at more recent textbooks, for example those by Beattie or Lienhardt,[13] we do not find the subjects 'demography' or 'population' in the indexes. It is not surprising, therefore, that when Hauser and Duncan produced an inventory of important work on demography there should be chapters on 'Physical Anthropology and Demography', 'Genetics and Demography', 'Sociology and Demography', but nothing on social anthropology and demography.[14]

If we turn to specific monographs produced by social anthropologists during the last two generations the lack of interest is also apparent. This is openly admitted by fieldworkers. Colin Turnbull has written that 'as a social anthropologist myself I am very aware that our interests have led us in other directions, and that our time in the field tends to be occupied in trying to grapple with problems more directly related to those interests, and that it simply is not possible to devote the time to the kind of minute detail and data collection that would be required for effective demographic study'.[15] Instances of neglect could be multiplied indefinitely, so that it is somewhat invidious to pick on cases, but three examples may be cited. Obeyesekere in his work on Madagama land tenure noted (on p. 305) that there were 79 people in the village in 1911; in 1961, we learn (on p. 8) there were 289. Yet this 400 % increase in fifty years is nowhere discussed.[16] Stirling remarks of his Turkish village that 'population has apparently expanded rapidly in the last generation and is still increasing', yet the causes or effects of this change are not discussed.[17] Bailey admitted that due 'partly to an oversight, while in the field I did not seek past population figures for the village' and explicitly abdicates the right to analyse demographic factors.[18] Other anthropologists have recognized the need for social anthropology and demography to complement each other, but have usually not been able to effect this.[19]

There are a number of exceptions to this picture. Early work by Daryll Forde[20] and Krzywichi[21] in compiling some fairly simple statistics was complemented by the material of Fortes and Richards in Lorimer's collection on *Culture and Human Fertility.*[22] Firth, Borrie and Spillius published useful material on the demography of Tikopia,[23] as did Mitchell on the Yao[24] and Roberts on the Dinka.[25] Nag collected most of the data together from the Cross Cultural Files,[26] and Ardener contributed to the study of infertility.[27] This almost exhausts the list of direct contributions by social anthropologists, the only other major exceptions being Mary Douglas' analysis of 'Population control in primitive groups'[28] and Benedict's summary of speculations on the demography of small-scale societies.[29] During the years since 1968 the population crisis has deepened but, despite a growing spate of work on population, the anthropological contribution has not been considerable. A major intensive community study of family planning, the Khanna project, has been effectively criticized by a young anthropologist.[30] A good deal of time and money has been spent on large-scale conferences.[31] A useful collection of work edited by Harrison and Boyce contains a good critique of family planning in Mauritius by Benedict, some helpful work on the demographic features of the Mbuti and Ik by Turnbull, and a stimulating essay by Kunstadter which I shall discuss later.[32] A number of essays by Goody on inheritance and heirship also have demographic implications.[33]

The major development in the last six years has been in 'ecological anthropology', an approach which has a self-conscious interest in population factors as one of the central features of ecological balance. Outstanding among the contributions here are Geertz's work on Java[34] and work on New Guinea by Rappaport, Clarke, Waddell, Brookfield and Brown.[35] Other pioneering work, particularly by Parrack, Lee, Vayda, Wagley and Sahlins, following the earlier work of Barth, is conveniently collected in the reader edited by Vayda.[36] A somewhat similar approach is adopted in Ekvall's essay in a collection significantly titled *Population Growth: Anthropological Implications.*[37] This collection indicates the growing interest in the subject, as does a collection of essays presented at the second demography seminar at Port Moresby.[38] The subject of the relation between population and resources which preoccupies 'ecological anthropology' is an impetus to more sophisticated demographic work. So is the rapid development of neighbouring disciplines concerned with population, particularly historical demography,[39] genetics,[40] the sociology of fertility,[41] the ecology of animal behavior,[42] as well as 'ecology' as a subject in its own right.[43] Yet, despite this theoretical impetus and the practical necessities forcing a growing interest, there are still very considerable obstacles to major work on social demography on the part of social anthropologists. Until these difficulties are located and removed, progress is unlikely.

For the purposes of argument we may isolate four major obstacles to a union between demography and anthropology. Three out of four of them posed very serious difficulties, which will be apparent in the following discussion of Nepalese demography. The first problem is the basic assumption, implicit in most anthropological work, that population growth is unimportant as a variable. The second is the basic difference between the disciplines of anthropology and demography; one is characteristically static and the other dynamic. Thirdly, anthropology tends to be qualitative and demography quantitative. Fourthly, there is the technical difficulty of establishing ages in many non-literate societies.

The assumption that demographic factors are unimportant, or beyond analysis, is very deep-rooted. It partly stems from the Malthusian premise that economic organization is the determining variable and population growth and structure the dependent one. Anthropologists tend to make the same assumption with regard to social structure and mentality as 'determinants' of population structure. It is no coincidence, as we shall see, that they have contributed more to the analysis of the factors affecting demographic growth than to the analysis of the *consequences* of features of population. This is a self-confirming hypothesis. If little interest is shown in collecting the data for analysing population, demography appears to have little significance. Yet the brief survey which we shall shortly make of some possible causes and consequences of population patterns amply illustrates that they are both a cause *and* a consequence of social structure, economic organization, attitudes. Furthermore, in the models discussed in the conclusion to this work, we shall see that the counter-Malthusians, notably Boserup, have presented a strong case for making us believe that demographic growth is often an independent variable – with economic change as its consequence. If this is more broadly interpreted, it suggests that we should look at population patterns as a determinant of social and mental structure as well as determined by them. Thus population is not an epiphenomena of 'real' features like kinship and marriage and hence of secondary interest. On the other hand it is not an entirely independent variable, biologically determined and without any feed-back from social or economic factors. The interplay between population patterns and the elements more usually analysed by anthropologists is very powerful, though subtle. Although population growth cannot be grasped as *the* explanation of all social, economic or political change, it is clearly one of the most powerful forces shaping the world today. Hence it deserves especial attention from anthropologists. It is susceptible to such attention since the facts of birth, marriage and death are socially determined, and so come within the view of social anthropologists.

As Wilbert Moore, among others, has pointed out, demography is explicitly concerned with change over time.[44] Speculations can only be made when it is possible to see alterations in fertility, mortality, or other demographic phenomena, over a period of time. Most anthropological studies during the last several decades, however, have tended to be static cross-sections of a particular society at the point in time at which the society was visited by a field-worker.[45] The absence of written history seemed to make this a necessity and the functionalist and structuralist approaches make a virtue of this necessity by devising explanations in terms of *present* functions and structure. Again there was a self-confirming element in this process. Historical material was consciously or unconsciously ignored because it was considered unimportant to the theoretical framework. It is likely that interest in the history of non-industrial societies which has grown amongst anthropologists in the last two decades will make it easier for them to incorporate demographic factors into their analysis. Such incorporation will prove to be of great benefit. It is clear that many of the major achievements of anthropology were connected to the functionalist hypotheses, yet such interpretations found it very difficult to deal with change over time. Other, more flexible, models are increasingly needed on which to hang observations of a more historical kind. Some of these can be supplied by demographic investigations which have always been attentive to the time element. Again, Wilbert Moore has made the point: namely that the dynamic element intrinsic in demographic work helps to force anthropology from its static plain.[46]

Yet anthropologists did not fail to contribute much to demographic analysis merely because of outworn theories. There are practical difficulties of a very considerable kind in undertaking good work on non-literate societies, and the shortcomings of the following analysis of the Gurungs illustrate some of these. Serious demographic work requires not only data over a long period, but *quantitative* data over a long period, as well as in the present. The normal fieldwork situation means that evidence gathered from informants tends to be impressionistic and non-statistical. The description is usually either of what *ought* to happen or what *is thought* to happen, rather than what actually, if counted, happens. This deficiency also afflicted economic anthropology, but could be partially overcome by even a single fieldworker who was prepared to undertake a great deal of counting of transactions, assets, relationships.[47] Economic anthropologists also had the advantage that historical records of land and taxation are much more likely to exist than the raw materials for demographic history, namely the registration of births, deaths and marriages, and household censuses. This is reflected, for instance, in the fact that the data in the 'Resources' discussion below is much more extensive than that under 'Population'. Demographic anthropologists rarely find such records and, furthermore, their data is much less concentrated than that of economic or social analysts. In a community of a thousand individuals there will be, on average, only about one hundred vital events, that is births, marriages and deaths, in the one year of an anthropologist's visit. Fluctuations in rates in such a small community are enormous, and professional demographers would place very little reliance on such a small, non-random, sample. Any attempt to break down such events, by age or socio-economic status, would soon make the statistics meaninglessly small. Yet the very foundations of anthropological methodology rest on the intensive, face-to-face, study of very small communities. To take one single aspect, demography, and study it over a much wider area and time span would undermine the foundation of the discipline, the study of the multi-stranded interconnectedness of human life, and dissipate its aims. Yet the concentration on one community makes it impossible, without historical figures, to measure even the most simple demographic features, such as whether a community is growing or declining, and at what speed.[48]

Another practical difficulty is the absence of accurate age-reporting in many non-literate societies. More and more the study of demography requires accurate ages; particularly age at marriage, age-specific fertility and age-specific mortality. The difficulty is highlighted by the various techniques which anthropologists have devised to deal with lack of knowledge. There is the method of constructing a calendar of major events that have occurred in a local community over the last fifty or so years and then attempting to find out how particular vital registration events are related to it.[49] 'Was X born after or before the Great Flood?' for example. Female ages are particularly important; Forde tried to deduce age structure from female age grades[50] and Reining and Richards attempted to estimate age at puberty from the physical growth of breasts.[51] Various tests were developed by demographers to see how accurate any statistics of age were.[52] Sometimes an investigator was fortunate enough to study a society which had some calendar of its own; for example the Lepchas of Sikhim studied by Gorer had adopted the twelve-year Tibetan animal cycle and each individual knew under which animal sign he was born.[53] It was the presence of a similar system among the Gurungs of central Nepal that made it possible to undertake some of the demographic study reported in this work.

The basic demographic data around which the social and economic factors are to be woven might be thought to be out of the reach of social anthropologists.

That this is not entirely the case has been shown by several small but notable studies, for example those by Firth and Mitchell already cited, and another by the demographer Carrier on the Rungus Dusun. Carrier was prepared to limit himself to a tiny sample, only 185 persons in all, yet still expected to obtain worthwhile results by asking how often people had married, how previous marriages had been terminated, the number, sex and age of children still alive of each woman and the age at death of women now dead.[54] The advantages of studying such a small community, even for demographic analysis, are very great. 'Microdemography' can combine some meaningful estimates of general demographic trends with intensive study of the social and economic correlates of such trends, and can still make a very useful contribution to population studies. As the Nashes have observed, the major demographic patterns of a society 'rest on a combination of social, cultural, and psychological factors which can only be uncovered through the intensive methods of the field anthropologist'.[55] The discussion of the relation between resources and population in central Nepal will illustrate some of the severe limitations of demographic work but will also, it is hoped, show that some analysis is possible.

The society analysed below was not specifically chosen because of its potential as demographic fodder. But it does have certain features which make it both easier to investigate and especially worthy of such investigation. Firstly, as noted above, most informants know their ages accurately and this is of enormous importance. Secondly, the Gurungs have traditionally been one of the major tribes recruited into the Gurkha regiments of the Indian and British armies. The absence of a large proportion of adult males and the inflow of cash from the army are likely to have considerable effects on the demographic, social and economic patterns of the society. The consequences of this migratory labour will be one of the central features of the analysis.

Above all, ecology, the study of the relationship between man and his resources in a particular setting, is the general theme. The permanent settlement and proliferation of a hitherto nomadic tribe has altered the whole balance of natural resources in the area. To study this change it has been necessary to make as much use as possible of the meagre historical sources. With their aid it is possible to see that every feature of the society has been changing very rapidly. On the surface, a year's visit gives an impression of stability and permanence. In fact, changes which took many millenia to occur in other parts of the world have been concentrated into the last hundred years in Nepal. The pressures correlated with fertility and mortality are particularly stressed in the following analysis since I believe it is demographic fluctuations which underlie many of the social and economic changes in the area.

In the following chapters we will first survey Gurung economics. The long-term changes which have occurred and the present stocks of land and other resources will be described. The production and consumption patterns of this Himalayan society will be analysed in considerable detail in order to see how labour is allocated and whether households have surpluses or deficits in their ordinary household budgets. Having established the resource basis, we will turn to population growth and some of its causes and consequences. The complex interrelations between social structure, fertility and mortality will be examined in order to see why the Gurungs tend to have somewhat different demographic features from the lowland populations of Nepal. The possible ecological consequences of a doubling of population every thirty years will be discussed. The way in which the Nepalese evidence fits into more general models of demographic change will be discussed in the concluding chapter.

2

The Gurungs of Nepal

The Gurungs are a tribe living at an altitude of between four and seven thousand feet in central Nepal. The location of the tribe and of the villages where intensive study has been conducted is shown in Fig. 2.1.

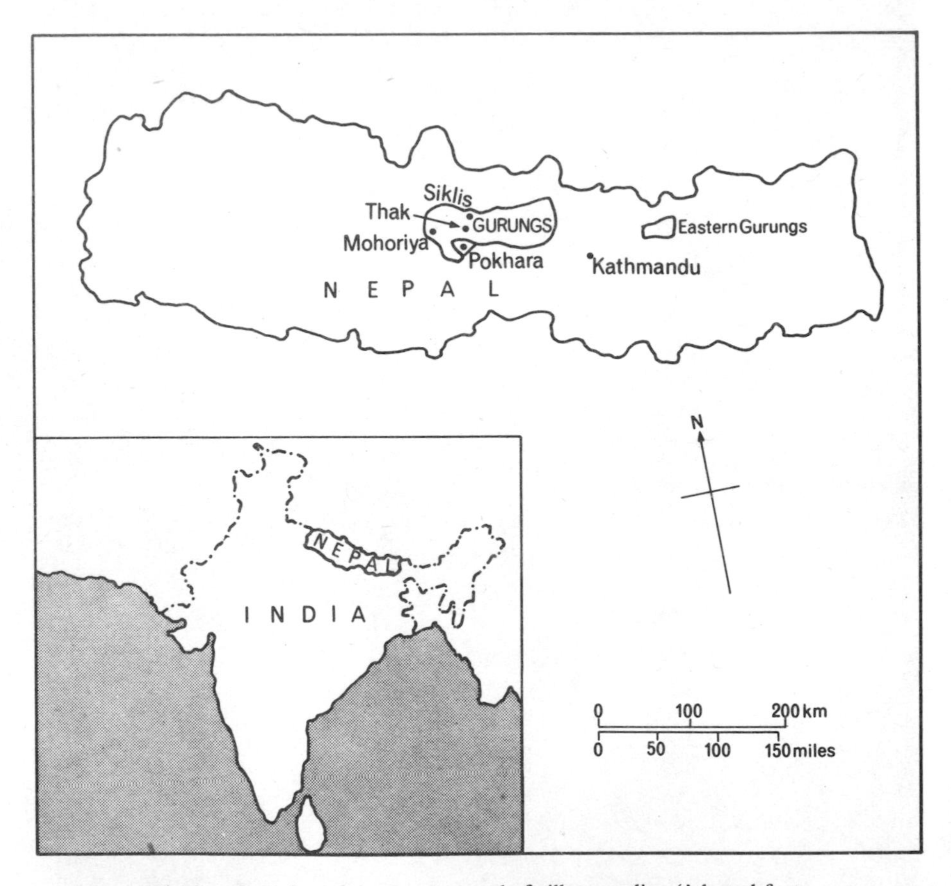

Fig. 2.1. Location of the Gurungs and of village studies. (Adapted from Pignède, *Les Gurungs*, p. 25, fig. 1.)

Fig. 2.2. Rice and maize fields down to the river.

The Gurungs represent only a small part of the Nepalese population. Of a total national population of some $9\frac{1}{2}$ million in the 1961 national census, approximately 158,000 were said to have Gurung as their mother tongue.[1] This is only a rough estimate since spoken language is not a reliable index. The major part of the material upon which the following account is based was gathered in the *panchayat* (Nepali: 'village district') of Thak, which is situated some 12 miles north-west of the second largest Nepalese town, Pokhara. Within the nine 'wards' of Thak, the study was especially concentrated on the main village of Thak and nearby hamlets; these constituted wards 6 and 8. In order to test the sample a visit was made to the village of Mohoriya, previously studied by Bernard Pignède.

The majority of Gurungs live on the north–south ridges that run down from the Annapurna and Dhaulagiri ranges of central Nepal. Once heavily forested, much of the lower slopes down to the river valleys have now been cleared to grow maize, millet, and rice and raise buffaloes, cows, goats and oxen (see Fig. 2.2 and 2.3). The climate changes considerably with season and altitude. The monsoon rains fall during June through to August; the hottest time is just before the monsoon breaks. Thanks to the altitude, the temperature very seldom reaches above 100 °F. There is usually a cold spell, lasting a few weeks and with a little snow, towards the end of January. The hillsides are extremely steep and rocky so that communications are still primitive; almost all travel is done on foot, and during the summer months swollen rivers make it difficult to travel west–east, except near the bottom of river valleys where bridges are being constructed. Almost everything is carried on the human back.[2]

The Gurungs share these hills with many other tribes and groups, though none of these are, by themselves, as numerous as they. The Gurungs themselves are undoubtedly an amalgam of several different peoples who have migrated into this area during the last thousand years. They appear to incorporate elements of both Tibeto-Burman and Indo-Aryan origin. This is especially evident in their religion and ritual, which is a bewildering mixture of Hinduism, Buddhism, and beliefs very similar to the old *bon* religion of Tibet. Their language is, however, predominatly Tibeto-Burman. It seems certain that they overlap in origins and culture with many of the neighbouring tribes, particularly the Tamangs. Therefore, to isolate the 'Gurungs' as an object of study is artificial. It is one approach which has as many advantages and drawbacks as any other artificial demarcation of the community of study.

One particular reason for not isolating them is that for many decades their economy and social system has been partially integrated with that of western

Fig. 2.3. An outlying hamlet.

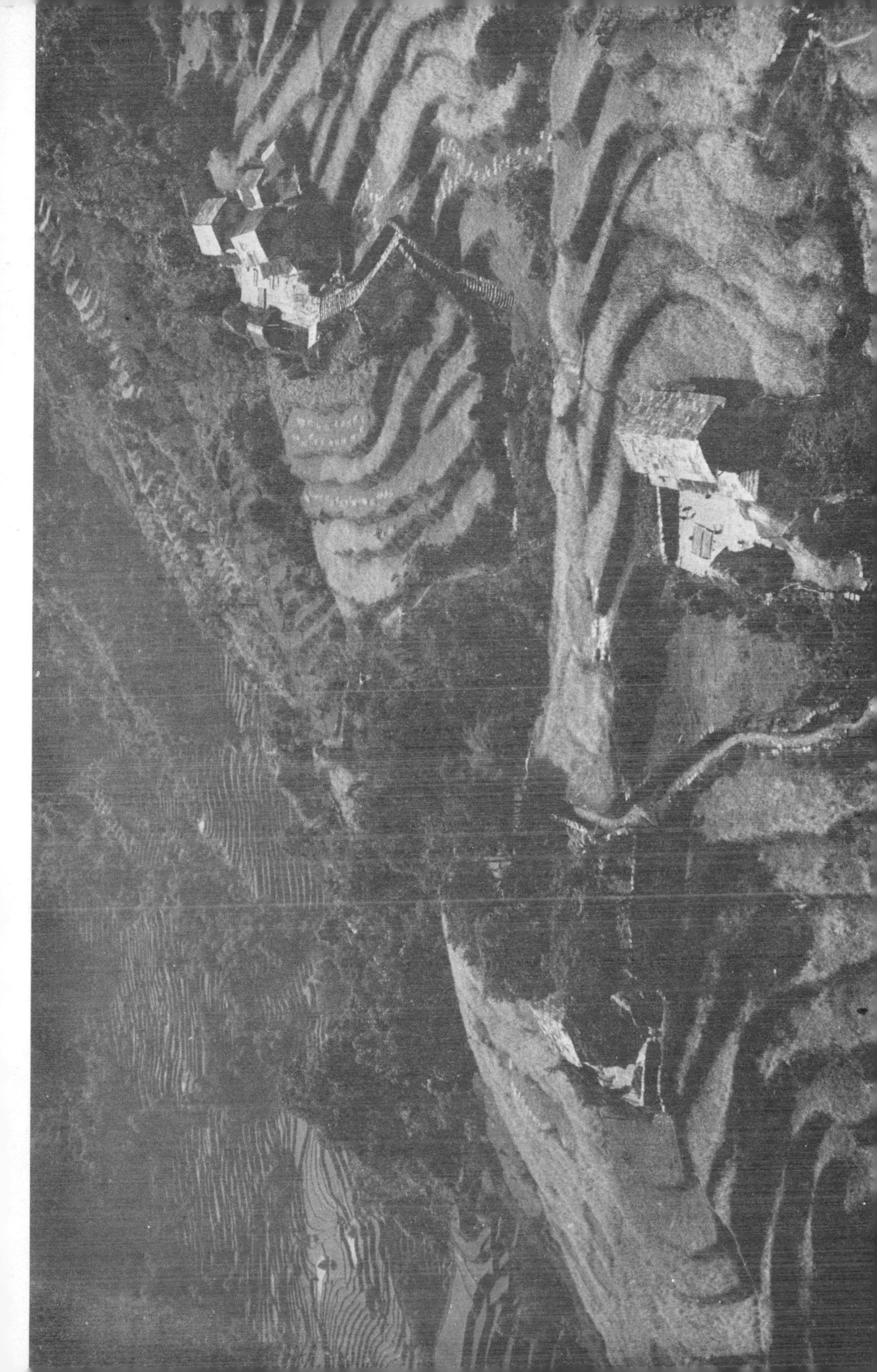

Europe and India. Undoubtedly the most important external influence on the Gurungs has been mercenary recruitment into the army. During the past century many thousands of Gurungs, as well as Magars and other tribal peoples, have been drafted into the British and Indian armies as 'Ghurkas'. The enormous effects of this situation on the indigenous social, economic and demographic situation will be apparent throughout the following chapters. The Gurungs may be looked at, from one angle, as a tribe of migrant labourers, a strange off-shoot of the British Empire set amongst other less affluent and mobile peoples.

OCCUPATIONAL AND CASTE STRUCTURE

The major activity of all those resident in Thak is agriculture. Even for the 'service castes' such as Blacksmiths and Tailors their particular trade is of secondary importance. Yet caste and ethnic differentiation, often overlapping with minor occupational differences, are vital when considering social relations, so that we need to have some idea of the relative size of the major groups with whom the Gurungs co-exist. The distribution in Thak *panchayat* is given in table 2.1. It is based on the population figures collected by the heads of the nine wards (*jana sankhyapharam*). It will be seen that even in a supposedly Gurung *panchayat*, in the centre of Gurung culture, the Gurungs are outnumbered by all other groups combined. It will also be seen that by far the most significant numerical rivals to Gurungs are the Brahmins.

Within Thak a detailed census of one hundred households in wards 5–8 was the real unit of study. Table 2.2 shows how these households were divided.

TABLE 2.1 *Ethnic and occupational groups in Thak* panchayat, *1968–9.*

	Number	%
Gurung	150	44.5
Brahmin	84	24.9
Blacksmith[a]	31	9.2
Thakuri	20	5.9
Tamang	19	5.6
Tailor[a]	12	3.6
Chetri	7	2.1
Magar	5	1.5
Gharti	3	0.9
Leather-worker[a]	2	0.6
Other	4	1.2
	337	

[a] Considered by Gurungs to be lower caste and polluting.

TABLE 2.2 *Ethnic groups in the sample census area, 1969*

	Nos. of households	Nos. of person
Gurung	77	386
Blacksmith	12	61
Tailor	6	38
Tamang	3	26
Magar	2	17
	100	528

Note: Both those temporarily present and those temporarily absent are included in the above table.

It is clear that in the limited area of intensive study Gurungs predominate, while Brahmins are completely absent. By taking the central village where the Gurungs, as the first to arrive, established themselves, the sample is not representative of the whole *panchayat*. The distribution of houses is shown in Fig. 2.4.

HOUSEHOLD AND FAMILY STRUCTURE

The importance of the household unit is very considerable among the Gurungs. There is no local term for the nuclear family as such; a group of parents and children is not distinguished, though the household (*jahan* or *pariwar*, Nep.) is so distinguished. Any persons sharing the same part of a house and, therefore, eating from the same hearth, are of the same *jahan*. This household unit has important functions as a labour, ritual, commensual, and child-rearing group. All members, except servants, also have property rights. There is, however, a major theoretical difficulty in analysing the actual composition of households. Unlike most of the communities of South Asia, the absent male heads of household, away in the army or police, constitute a very considerable proportion of all adult males in the community. This is a particular instance of the long-debated problem of how one is to define a 'joint-family'. A common feature of Gurung villages is the 'joint-family' which is incomplete because one or more of the married males is away on service. It is thus necessary to use not only the normal terms for household analysis, but also the extra term 'stem'.[3] The situation in two Gurung villages is shown in table 2.3.

From the table, and from the more detailed calculations in the appendix, it is clear that the majority of those living in Gurung villages, Gurungs and non-Gurungs alike, live in elementary families of father, mother and children (if we include here those households where the man is away in the army). Joint families are extremely rare. Comparison of the 1969 census of Mohoriya with Pignède's 1958 census notes shows that there has been no decrease in the size

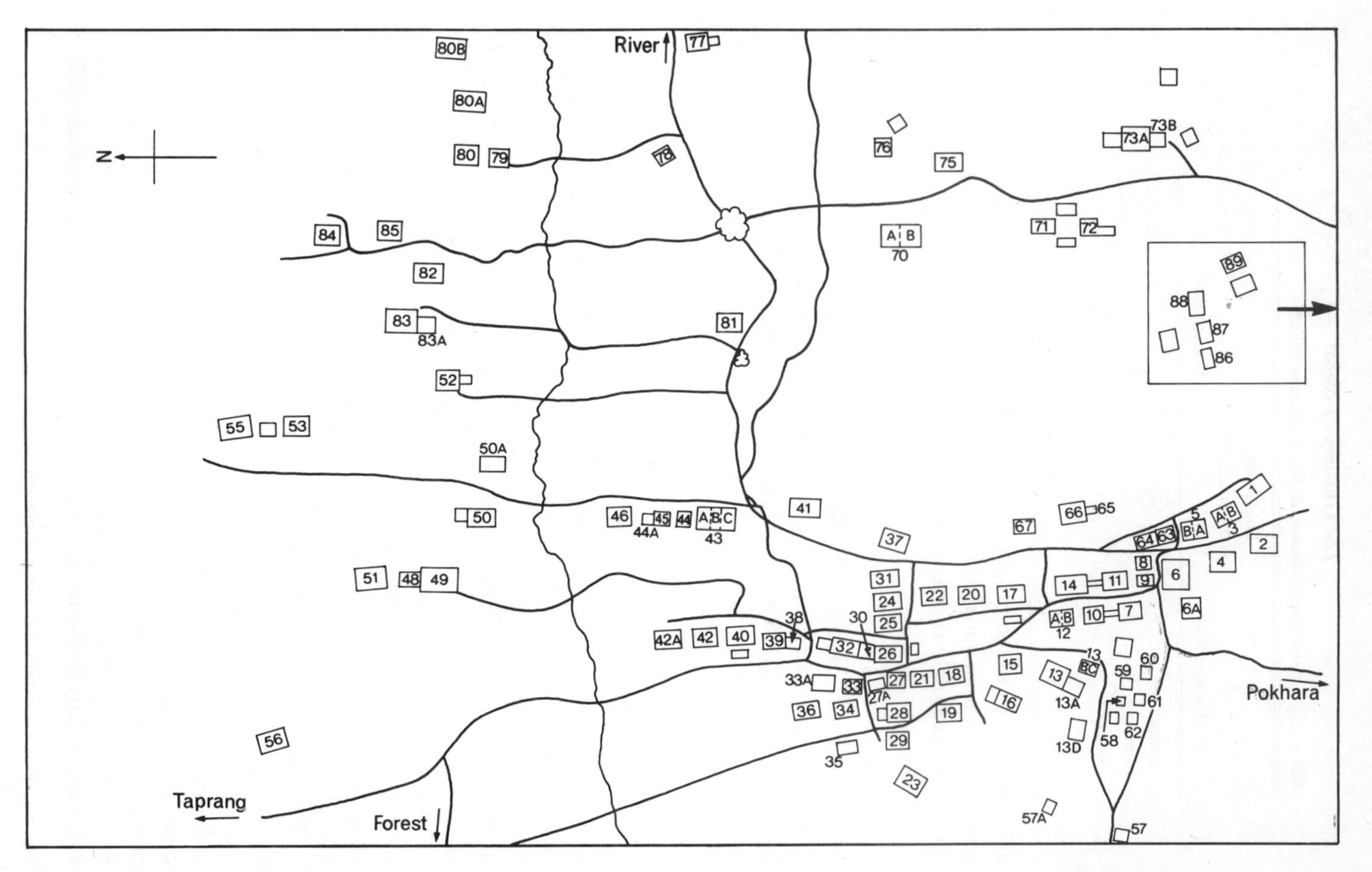
River
Pokhara
Forest
Taprang
N

TABLE 2.3 *Structure of households in two Gurung villages*

Type of household	Thak, 1969 (100 households)	Mohoriya, 1969 (87 households)
	% of households	
Elementary	62	67.9
Stem	24	28.8
Extended	0	0
Joint	1	1.1
Other	13	2.2

of households or in the proportion of joint households. Analysis of the figures gives some impression that wealthier households tend to be larger, because they keep the family together longer.

CLAN AND KIN GROUPINGS

Bernard Pignède describes the Gurungs as having a two-tiered social structure.[4] The upper tier ideally has four patrilineal exogamous clans and is hence known as the *carjat* (Nep. *car* = four; Gurung, *plegi* – *ple* or *pli* = four). The most commonly encountered names and their theoretically permitted marriage relationships are, as Pignède illustrated them, as follows.

ghale ——— *lamme*
kon (ghotane) ——— *plon* (lamechane)

The permitted marriages are shown by arrows; the names in brackets are the Nepali terms. There is some evidence here of a dual system, divided between lords (on the left in the diagram) and priests (on the right). This has undoubtedly been accentuated by recent pressures from Hindu classification systems. It is also an ideal system with only a local coverage. It is believed, for example, in some parts of central Gurung territory that any of the four clans may marry each other.[5] While the theory is upheld in Thak, in practice all the clans do intermarry. Pignède also observed that, in fact, there are more than four named clans, and this was confirmed by my observations.

The other tier consists of several dozen named patrilineal exogamous clans, collectively termed the 'nine *jats*' (*naujat*, Nep.; *kwogi*, Gg.) or 'sixteen *jats*' (*sora* or *sola-jat*, Nep.). Whatever their original number, there are now well over fifty such clans and possibly many more. Small sub-sets of such clans appear to prohibit intermarriage, but, on the whole, there is free marriage between them. Marriages between *carjat* and *sorajat* are theoretically forbidden though they increasingly occur. Sexual or marital relations within a clan are strictly forbidden and occur very infrequently. There is considerable

Fig. 2.4. House location and house numbering in Thak sample.

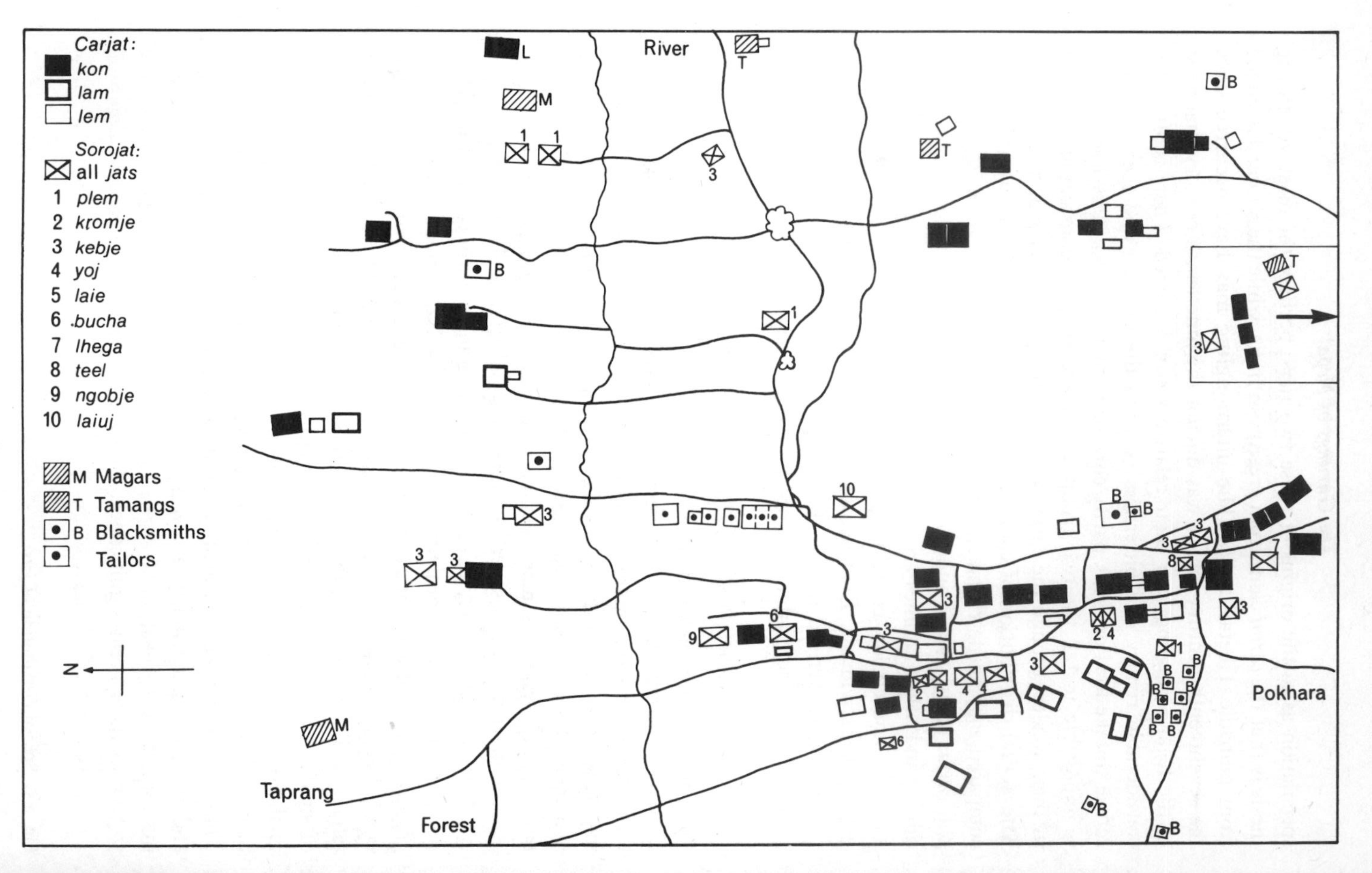

Carjat:
kon
lam
lem
Sorojat:
all jats
1 plem
2 kromje
3 kebje
4 yoj
5 laie
6 bucha
7 lhega
8 teel
9 ngobje
10 laiuj
M Magars
T Tamangs
B Blacksmiths
Tailors
N
River
Taprang
Forest
Pokhara

speculation as to the origins of these two tiers; perhaps the most convincing thesis is that the *carjat* came from pre-Aryan India, while the *sorajat* descended from nomadic Tibetan tribes. The intermingling may have occurred since the seventeenth century and it was during the nineteenth century that most of the legal wrangling over their relative status occurred. There is often still considerable rivalry and bitterness between the two *jats* and the *carjat* still refuse to take food or drink partly consumed by the *sorajat*. Physiologically it is impossible to tell the two groups apart and there is considerable overlap in their wealth, though the *carjat* seem, on the whole, richer in most villages. The actual distribution of clans in the central part of Thak, which may be compared to Pignède's similar map for Mohoriya,[6] is shown in Fig. 2.5. The two *carjat* clans, *konme* and *lamme*, are residentially fairly distinct, while the *sorajat* and other families are scattered round them. There are, in all, some 53 *carjat* households, containing 268 individuals, and 24 *sorajat* households, with 118 individuals. Evidence from the census and land records suggests that the *carjat* arrived first in the village, towards the end of the eighteenth century, and were gradually joined by *sorajat* households.

KINSHIP STRUCTURE AND TERMINOLOGY

Pignède has provided a detailed and usually accurate account of Gurung kinship.[7] The system as he described it is an asymmetrical one, with different terms for kin on the mother's and father's side and a marked preference for marriage with a mother's brother's daughter (matrilateral cross-cousin marriage). There is considerable evidence, however, that both in theory and in practice the system is more symmetrical than he suggests with marriages occurring with father's sister's children just as often and with a mixture of symmetry and asymmetry in the kinship terminology. Within each named clan there are smaller patrilineal lineages, which Pignède described as 'local descent groups'. He assumed that all members of the same clan living in one village would belong to one such group.[8] This was the case in Mohoriya. In the older village of Thak, however, the dominant *konme* clan had broken into a number of smaller named lineages, which recognized that they were linked, but were unable to trace their connection to each other. If a man died without a male heir, and without a will, within such a group, other members would inherit. There is considerable residential unity within each of these minor lineages and they act, particularly at death, as a ritual group. In everyday life, for instance the organization of work or formation of leisure groups, they do not appear to have great significance. There is, in general, a shallow depth of

Fig. 2.5. Spatial distribution of *jats*.

knowledge concerning ancestors among the Gurungs. Most children in Thak did not know the name of even their grandfathers; most adults could not go back further than two generations in their genealogies, and some less. In contemporary genealogical linking, however, there is very considerable interest in female members of the lineage. Although clan membership and property flow through the male line, and hence the society is basically patrilineal, genealogies include those married to male ancestors as well as unmarried daughters and many Gurung rituals, particularly at the major festival of *Dasain*, stress the links with sisters and daughters. Fictive kin links between members of different *jats*, *sorajat* and *carjat* for example, or a Gurung and a Tamang, are emphasized by the institution of 'ritual friendship' which is widespread throughout Nepal, and which, as interpreted in Thak, *must* occur between different *jats*.[9]

OTHER FEATURES OF SOCIAL STRUCTURE

There are a number of other principles, as well as blood and marriage, upon which Gurung society is based. One of these is physical proximity or neighbourhood. The central village of Thak is divided for administrative purposes into two official wards, but it is also conceptually divided into a number of smaller units known as *tol* (Nep. ward) or *naasa* (Gg. a small town or hamlet). These 'maximal neighbourhoods' divide the central part of Thak into eight named sections; within each section there are subdivisions of 'minimal neighbourhoods', groups of neighbours (*ngie-mae* or *chema-gi*) who are recognized as having particularly strong bonds with each other. It is with such 'close neighbours' that Gurungs mainly gossipped, did simple jobs and rituals, and constantly interracted.

Another important principle is age. Although young and old mix freely and Gurung society appears to be the extreme opposite of authoritarian, it is clear that relative age is an extremely important principle of social organization. Gurung kinship terminology, for instance, recognized relative age as an important criterion. The central importance of the *rodi* or young girl's dormitory, which was not just a leisure organization but a focus for work-groupings as well, will become apparent later. It seems clear, however, that the *rodi* were only one feature of a complex age-grade system of which only a part now remains. There appear to have been distinguished age groups in Thak known as *torve* (Gg.), consisting of Gurungs of all types who are roughly of the same age. There are twelve such divisions in Thak, each covering roughly 8–10 years. There were, it seems, no age rites, but groups of age-mates of both sexes would work together as a combined work group in the day, then, having eaten communally or at home, they would congregate to joke, sing, and flirt. Members would all be given nick-names. A child of either sex until about its fifteenth year, in other words until joining the third age group or *chomba torve*, would be called a *kolo*. Then, during the years covered by the next two *torve*, up to about 32 years of age, a man was a *preshi* (related to Nep. *preyasi*, sweetheart?) and a girl a *tsami* (Gg. daughter). Marriage or child-bearing made no differences to such terms. Then from about 33–45 years a person is *adha bainse* (Nep., 'half his years have gone'). Then from about 45 a woman is *maba*, a man *khiba*, or 'old person'. Although the full force of these divisions are rapidly declining, the organization of work and leisure is still as much along age and neighbourhood lines as those of kin and wealth.

The overall impression from living with Gurungs is of a very flexible and fluctuating system. Almost everyone in the village is bound to everyone else by a multiplicity of bonds. These multiple and many-stranded relationships, which are characteristic of village life in most societies, enable an individual to select other individuals from a wide range of alternatives for particular occasions. What appears to be exceptional about the Gurungs is that the various criteria – age, kinship, residence, sex, *jat*, wealth – are so evenly balanced. Consequently the actual groupings into which people form in daily life are extremely fragile, dissolving and re-forming from day to day. The boundaries are not tightly set, the contrasts between old and young, rich and poor, upper and lower *jat*, one neighbourhood and another, are not stressed. Such a situation helps to explain the adaptable nature of the Gurungs, for example their ability to change with their social environment, to become world-renowned for their courage and practicality as warriors when, in their own homes, the men are gentle, somewhat impractical, and extremely unagressive.

PART I

RESOURCES

3

Long-term change in the Gurung economy

The only real evidence we have for the economic situation of the Gurungs up to the beginning of the nineteenth century comes from the myths (*pie*) recited by the *poju*. The *pie* are obviously extremely old, and although it is impossible to be sure whether the situation they describe occurred three or thirteen hundred years ago, it seems likely that they do reflect one early stage of Gurung economy. These myths, and scraps of information from other historical sources, suggest that for many centuries (up to three or four hundred years ago) the Gurungs consisted of small bands of wandering shepherds and hoe cultivators who circled the Himalayan foothills, moving form site to site every few generations. The *pie* give glimpses of this existence. They recount, often in great detail, the various villages and regions through which the tribesmen wandered. Hunting was clearly an important part of the existence. Large scale hunts, in which hunting dogs and beaters were employed in the pursuit of deer, and a full-scale uniform (including special jackets, knives, kilts, bloodcarrying flasks) was worn. Other *pie* describe herding (including the man going off to live by himself in the forest to herd animals) – usually of sheep, goats, chickens, and two long-haired animals (varieties of yak?) called *Yo* and *Pri* in Gurung. Horses are also mentioned, but never plough animals except in one rather exceptional *pie*. In this (*Aba Krolu pie*) the scene is said to be China, rice is referred to as a crop (though it is not mentioned elsewhere in the *pie*) and the plough is drawn by a tiger and a bear. This is the only occasion when ploughing is mentioned. Elsewhere the method of cultivation is always the same; vegetation is set alight and then the land is hoed and sown, usually with millet, maize, buckwheat or rye.

Until a more detailed examination is made of historical sources it is impossible to say when the Gurungs finally began to settle in permanent villages. Our first positive evidence comes at the beginning of the nineteenth century, for Francis Buchanan wrote a description of the Gurungs on the basis of information collected in 1802–3. He wrote thus:[1]

> Near the Magars was settled a numerous tribe named Gurung, whose wealth chiefly consisted in sheep, but whose manners are, in most respects, nearly the same with those of the Magars, except that, in the course of their

> pastoral life, they frequent the Alpine regions in summer, and return to the valleys in winter. The men also employ themselves in weaving blankets; they are a tribe addicted to arms ... The Gurungs cultivate with the hoe and are diligent traders and miners. They convey their goods on sheep, of which they have numerous flocks. The crops they cultivate with the hoe are 1. Barley 2. Uya (?) 3. Maniya or *Eleusine Corocanus* 4. Kangum (*Panicum Italicum*) 5. Phapar (?).

This description is substantially the same as that obtained by Brain Hodgson some thirty years later.[2] Hodgson also provides added details of great interest.

> They make their own clothes of wool, cotton and hemp, of the coarsest kind of Khadi, Panga, Bhangria and Pankhi – the two first of cotton, 3rd of hemp and 4th of wool of their own vast flocks of Burwal sheep ... They are chiefly shepherds but also keep some Chouris or Yaks and of cows and Buffaloes. They dwell mostly in small villages wherein each Cot is quite separate and they are a deal abroad in the Coths or Sheep sheds. They cultivate the ground to a considerable extent growing chiefly Makai (maize) & Kodo (millet). Making Dhero from both & that is their favourite food. They also eat Makai dressed rice-wise & also such of their sheep as die, they do not habitually eat their sheep. They milk them and make Ghee of the milk & shear & make Pankhi & Kamals of the wool, & using them also for carriage over the snows bringing back rock salt of Tibet. They are the traders across the snows, taking hence cotton & rice, & wheat & Dalls & merchants' wares also either on the sheep or on their own backs. They dwell high in the Lekhs ... They are also great Shikarees (i.e. hunters) and serve much as soldiers, having been renowned for hardihood since Prithi Narains time ... their usual custom is to cook in Iron pan – now in these days they cook in Copper & Brass pots & in earthen pot ... They are soldiers & traders as well as shepherds: less agricultural than Magars ... Their herds are often very large 1 or 2,000 sheep ... Gurungs carry & sell salt of Tibet & are, in fact, great traders across the snows with the Bhoteas, all the local trade & mutual wants, of the immediate tribes on this & that side the Himal, being theirs and through them supplied.

These accounts have been quoted at length because they provide such a startling contrast with the situation as I observed it in Thak in 1969. Although there were vague memories of the old system, almost every feature had entirely changed, and there can be no doubt that with this economic transformation the whole social system must also have changed very considerably. Before examining the minutiae of change, it is worth briefly comparing the picture given by Hamilton and Hodgson to that I obtained in Thak.

In the early part of the nineteenth century the Gurungs were a mainly pastoral tribe, grazing huge herds of cows and sheep. The latter, especially, were the mainstay of the economy. In Thak in 1969 no one had any sheep, and there were only a very few households with cows. The methods of carrying goods on sheep-back, still employed by Bhotia traders in West Nepal,[3] is no longer known. Everything was carried on the human back. The importance of the sheep lingered on only in ritual, especially in the funeral (*pae lava*) when two sheep are needed to accompany the dead person's soul to the village of the dead. Now that sheep are gone it is not surprising that villagers do not weave blankets as the old Gurungs used to, nor make their own clothes out of 'wool, cotton & hemp'. Clothes are easily bought in the local bazaar, or fabrics brought from Malaya and India. Only the *renga* or traditional overshirt of men is still made from bark-fibre in the village. It is not certain that villagers in Thak have ever been large-scale shepherds, but certainly they once grazed large herds of cows and buffaloes. I was told that some thirty years ago, a medium-wealth household would have some fifteen or so buffaloes and twice as many cows. Only two households were remembered to have kept small flocks of sheep.

If the Gurungs were ever diligent 'miners', there is no trace of this now. Nor did I see or hear of any deserted mines near Thak or on my walks around Gurung territory.

Trading has also declined in importance among the Gurungs. The description of the way in which Gurungs acted as middlemen, carrying cotton, rice, wheat, lentils and salt across the Himalayas, finds no echo in the present situation in the villages near Thak. Pignède described a relic of this trade in Mohoriya, where the men used to go up the Kali Gandaki valley with grain which they exchanged for salt.[4] The same thing occurred in Thak, and there was a trade up over the pass above Siklis. The bartering of salt against grain ended with the Chinese invasion of Tibet. The journey from Thak, if the route to the west was taken, used to take 10–12 days there and back. If the goods were exchanged at about the level of Tukche, one measure of rice was exchanged for one of salt. After the closing of the Tibetan salt route people went for a few years to Butwal in the Terai, which took about the same length of time. During the last five or six years, however, Gurung villagers in Thak have bought salt at Pokhara. This direct barter of salt for grain may have been a relic of earlier trade, but by the time it reached its close it was very different from the system described by Hodgson in which the Gurungs acted as middlemen.

The crops and manner of cultivating them have also changed very considerably in the last hundred years. The agriculture of this part of Nepal has been roughly divided into two zones, the 'Hindu culture area' where rice, maize and millet are the staples, and the 'Tibetan' area where barley, wheat and buckwheat are the main crops.[5] The description of crops by Hamilton, as well as descriptions in the *pie* and other traditions suggest that about one hundred and fifty years ago the Gurungs lived predominantly in the 'Tibetan' area, in villages at about 8000 feet or above (such as Siklis and Ghandrung). Though they did not live too high to grow maize and millet (as Hodgson's account indicates), they were almost certainly too high for rice. Nor is there mention of potatoes, though the neighbouring *murmilama* (Tamang) people knew of potatoes at the time as we shall see shortly. It is impossible to say when the Gurungs moved low enough to grow wet rice. The land records of Thak show that they were growing it, almost certainly on terraces, in the second half of the nineteenth century. Therefore it seems likely that this critical change over to terraced wet rice cultivation had occurred in some villages by at least the beginning of the nineteenth century.

As the crops changed, so did the methods of cultivating them. Two major changes have occurred, though it is impossible to be certain to what extent they coincided. Firstly, there has been a change over from hoe cultivation to hoe and plough in combination. Hamilton described the Gurungs as cultivating with the hoe, and neither he nor Hodgson mention the existence of the currently used plough animal, the ox. Ploughing is especially important for wet-rice cultivation, and has probably only fairly recently been applied to maize growing also. Therefore it seems likely to have come in when rice began to be grown extensively, towards the middle of the last century.

The second major change is from slash-and-burn, rotating, agriculture, to permanent fields. The *pie*, we have seen, described how forest was burnt down and the seed was planted in the hoed-up ashes. A relic of the system survived in Mohoriya on the very steep slopes where it was impossible to construct terraces. There the vegetation was burnt down and millet sown in the ashes.[6] An informant in Thak said that up to about ten years ago such cultivation was the main method of growing maize and millet in the village. Large fields which have now become the private property of particular families used to belong to the village communally. Every nine or ten years a portion of them would be cultivated by cutting and burning the vegetation. Only in one particularly flat and low-down field (Uli) was the system as it is nowadays, in other words the field is manured and millet is planted after the maize has been harvested in July–August. In the old system, I was told, the undergrowth was cleared and burnt in March–April, the millet planted the following month and harvested before the rice in August–September. Maize or millet grown thus was called *Mokhai* or *nari* 'kode'. Depending on its labour supply, a house could obtain such as much maize and millet as it wanted.

The above description fits in with the normal description of shifting cultivation: 'an economy of which the main characteristics are rotation of fields rather than crops; clearing by means of fire; absence of draught animals and of manuring; use of human labour only; employment of the dibble stick or hoe; short periods of soil occupancy alternating with long fallow periods'.[7] The arrangement of such shifting cultivation among the peoples of the Himalayan region has often been described by observers who could see the system in action. Reading their accounts gives us a useful insight into what Gurung agriculture must have been like over twenty years ago, though we need to bear in mind that Gurungs were also gaining their living from livestock, trade, and the army.[8] There were probably also close resemblances between the situation among the Gurungs and that among the neighbouring *murmi-lamas* (Tamangs) whom Hodgson's informants described thus:

> After two years we cultivate another field because the soil of it is wasted away. And in two years time that field becomes jungle and again after 2 years we cultivate the same field. [The field] which is close to our House we always cultivate. After two years we burn the jungle of the same field and dig it & the ashes becomes manure and as much jungle we can cut down we can cultivate it – on paying to the Durbar from 1 to 10 Rupees (Thek) whether we cultivate large or small ground in the jungle. We sow Mokae (maize) corn twice in a year (one sort small) and in that field any other corn cannot grow – except Mokae, but some times we sow kodae (millet) in it. The field on which potato grows no corn can [not] grow in it – the same potato seed remains for nine years. Corn &c is yearle sown . . . First we plough the field then throw the manure over it & sow the mokai & Kodoe, Thori, Phapur: these are sown only once in a year and suker Kund is produced three times in a year . . . The field that produces strongly is not changed – & other fields are changed after 3 or 4 years.[9]

It seems likely that the Gurungs, who were less dependent on their crops since they had other sources of income, did not cultivate as intensively as this. Thus their rotation appears less frequent and they probably did not 'plough', as the above people were said to do.[10]

Two other sources of income among the Gurungs in the early nineteenth century are described above, hunting and fighting. We are told that they were great 'Shikarees' and this is confirmed by the *poju's pie* already cited. Pignède described their passionate love of hunting and also the hunting methods as they existed until recently.[11] From Thak informants I learnt how the forests used to abound in deer, wild pig (which Gurungs eat), jungle cock and other birds. The rivers were full of fish. These valuable sources of protein have almost dwindled away in Thak. The forest is no longer within easy reach of the village, and one has to travel many miles before reaching areas where most of the game has not been exterminated. One or two villagers were still keen huntsmen, but despite many expeditions only one small deer was shot during our fifteen months in the village. The hunting dogs of which the myths tell are no longer kept, and blunderbusses and shot-guns have replaced bows and arrows. Firearms are expensive to buy and to use; a cartridge cost some $6\frac{1}{2}$ rs. in 1969. At this price it is hardly economical to shoot jungle fowl, since one can buy a chicken for this sum. Rivers and streams near Thak were also a dwindling asset; bombed, poisoned, trapped, the fish were very small and growing scarce.

Even in 1802 the Gurungs had a reputation as a 'tribe addicted to arms' and had had such a reputation since the mid-eighteenth century. It is impossible to know what proportion of the population served as mercenaries at this date, but there seems little doubt that the inflow of cash from this source, if not the total number employed, increased with the expansion of recruitment into the British army in the second half of the nineteenth century. Such recruitment became, along with the cultivation of wet rice, the major foundation for the new Gurung economy.

The descriptions for the early nineteenth-century show a multifarious economy, in which animal husbandry, trading, mining, domestic industry (blankets chiefly), arable farming, hunting, and mercenary service combined to provide a wide range of income. This does not fit in with Pignède's statement that 'the Gurung village has been, for the last 60 years, an almost closed economic unit',[12] unless we take 'closed' merely to mean that the Gurungs were largely self-sufficient as far as clothing and food were concerned. Yet it is possible that despite their trading and army service they were still basically a subsistence, non-cash, economy, turning their profits from trade and war into goods before they reached the village. Thus the main trend in the last hundred years would seem to be away from a predominantly pastoral but many-sided economy, to one heavily dependent on two types of work, arable farming and the army. Even in the 1930s, the Gurungs could be described as 'chiefly a pastoral people',[13] but this would be incorrect now. Even since the Second World War there appear to have been very considerable changes, at least in the two villages I studied. The remnants of communal village land on which slash-and-burn cultivation was practised have disappeared; the salt trade with Tibet has been closed; clothes are no longer made in the village, but almost entirely bought in the bazaar.[14] Although we are told that even in the 1930s some villages had a small shop with kerosene, oil, umbrellas and other goods,[15] there can be no doubt that the retailing of consumer goods has expanded very rapidly. This narrowing of resources and intensification of arable farming means that the Gurungs have a more precarious economic base than in the past. If there are a series of bad harvests, or army recruitment is cut back, or population continues to grow at the present rate, they will then be dramatically exposed to economic hardship.

It seems likely that the changes described above are two-fold, and are more pronounced in some areas than others. Population pressure has had a double effect. On the one hand it has forced the Gurungs to establish new villages lower on the slopes of the Himalayas. The altitude of these settlements is such that new crops, in particular wet-rice, could be grown. The summer grazing for the huge flocks of cows and sheep also became inaccessible. The villages of Thak and Mohoriya, along with the many others at the same level (*c.* 5–7000 ft), are examples of these new settlements, founded with increased frequency since the late eighteenth century. Pignède described the Moḍi valley thus: 'During the second half of the 19th century, the majority of the land below 2400 m. was covered with wood. Great herds of 200 to 300 cows & many thousands of sheep lived there. Gurung economy was much more pastoral than nowadays.'[16] The same is true of the Siklis valley near Thak. Thus we see that a number of Gurungs were moving out of the region of yaks, high Alpine grazing, wheat and buckwheat, down onto the lower ridges where they could exploit the river bottoms for irrigated rice.

The old pattern of trading and pastoralism continued much more in the higher villages from which the settlers had emigrated. Thus even in 1969 Siklis, a big Gurung village to the north of Thak, is much closer to the picture painted by Hodgson than are Mohoriya or Thak. Blankets are still woven, very large herds of sheep are still driven up into the mountains in early summer. The same is true of Ghandrung, to the north of Mohoriya; Pignède described the huge herds of sheep from Ghandrung, but in Mohoriya there were no sheep.[17] If, therefore, the following study had been undertaken in one of the higher Gurung villages, it is likely that the contrast with the nineteenth century situation would not have been so dramatic.

Yet the contrast is not merely between high and low Gurung villages; even within individual villages there have been very marked changes. The case of Thak, to be examined in subsequent chapters, shows how in recent years population pressure has forced an intensification of agriculture and limited the fodder and grazing available for livestock. It seems likely that the same is true of all Gurung territory, though we cannot be certain of this until further research has been undertaken on higher villages. It is well known that shifting agriculture, such as that once practised by the Gurungs, can only bear a certain, limited, density of poplulation. As Clark puts it, 'As population increases, the shifting cultivator has to work on a rather shorter cycle of cutting and burning . . . repeated burning at fairly short intervals, with the consequent destruction of humus, may have a very serious effect on the soil.'[18] It is true that the Gurungs were buffered against the effects of increasing population for a number of years. Large expanses of woodland enabled them to pasture livestock which provided much of their protein and manure; they did not need to produce a cereal surplus and could even afford a slight deficit for they had a cash income from trade and army service. Furthermore, in lower villages, they were already combining slash-and-burn with wet-rice cultivation, and in some higher areas possibly using the potato as a supplementary food. Hence such shifting cultivation could continue until very recently in Thak.

We may wonder how well the disappearance of shifting cultivation fits with theories developed by agricultural economists about the population density such an economy will support. Various estimates have been made as to the population density tolerable before the land deteriorates; these may vary from at least 39 per sq. km for the Hanunoo down to 2 person per sq. km in Northern Rhodesia.[19] The 1961 census gave a population density for the Western Hills of Nepal (the area where most Gurungs live) of 174.7 per sq. mile or 45.21 per sq. km. Even including the large areas of uncultivable mountain peaks, therefore, the density is higher than has ever been reported as sustained by slash-and-burn agriculture. If we confine ourselves to the more limited area of Thak (wards 6–9) it would seem that roughly 700 people are dependent on 4 square miles of field and forest. This is a density almost identical to that for the Western Hills as a whole. Gurung population has been increasing in this area fairly rapidly over the last twenty years. It therefore would seem that villagers in Thak ceased to practise shifting cultivation in the years between 1945 and 1960, when population density was between 30 and 40 per sq. km. The change only occurred in the secondary crops. For over a century, as land records show, irrigated rice had been extensively grown in the lower fields.

The change in methods of cultivating secondary crops emphasizes the most important change now taking place throughout Gurung villages. This is the transition from an economy where land is plentiful and labour is the limiting factor in production to the reverse situation. In the earlier setting 'absolute yield per hectare is less important to the farmer than yield per unit of labour'.[20] Those who own good rice land have an advantage, but any family can obtain maize and millet as long as it has a supply of labour, and it can demand good returns for working on the rice lands of others. The egalitarian society of the Gurungs might well be seen as a product of this situation. In this earlier stage, the most precious capital asset is not land or machinery, but labour, and this is an asset which cannot easily be passed on from generation to generation. The steeply increasing price of land, the dividing up of communal maize fields, the growing surplus of labour except in peak periods of agricultural activity, all these are signs that the situation is changing. Although this is not a necessary result, it seems likely that there will be a growing differentiation in wealth between those who own the increasingly precious asset, land, and those whose labour becomes more and more redundant. This process will be accelerated by the introduction of agricultural machinery or new crops which necessitate heavy outlay on fertilizers or improved drainage.

At present, as we shall see, the agricultural technology remains extremely simple and time-consuming. The Gurungs have a pre-wheel culture in which the human back lifts and moves everything, and the human arm and leg does most of the grinding and pounding. The only non-human power so far utilized is that of oxen in ploughing and residual threshing, and of water mills for a minor part of the grinding. There even appears to have been a loss of power, for sheep are no longer used to carry goods, and horses, once fairly common, are now almost gone. In terms of the power available per person, from non-human sources within the community, the Gurungs are an extremely 'primitive' people. Yet the standard of living is much higher than in most other Nepalese or Asian communities. The way in which this is achieved will be analysed more fully in later chapters. The theme of these chapters will be the way in which population pressure is turning a basically expansive economy, where resources of land, fodder, timber, grazing and wild life are abundant, into an economy where human beings are abundant and resources rapidly diminishing. The enormous effects of this change in altering the distribution of wealth in the community, in precipitating a change from a protein-full to a carbohydrate-based (meat to starch) diet, from a labour-deficient to a labour-surplus community, will also be explored. The chronic unemployment, shortage of cash, poverty and malnutrition which will occur if population growth further presses on limited resources will also be considered.

That the change has already progressed far may be illustrated by one small instance. A Gurung in Thak told me that when he was a young man some thirty years ago, a poor family, including those of the lower castes, would have some four *mokhai suli* (or sections of maize) in front of the house. In 1969, when I went round counting the stacks, a four-section stack was only found in front of middling or rich Gurung houses: the lower castes seldom had as many as two. Though we must allow for wistful exaggeration, this informant said that his own father had had an annual harvest of some 70 *muri* of rice. He thought that his father had not been particularly rich. In 1969 there was only one family in the village that produced over 50 *muri*. This informant himself, his land deteriorated in quality and quantity (through partition), claimed to be harvesting some 22 *muri*. Likewise, as we have seen, there has been a great reduction in the number of livestock per household. What this means in practice is that the time when resources were flexible, expanding with population, is now over. That this should happen to coincide with the introduction of health measures which, if effective, will raise the population growth rate from under 2 % p.a. to anything up to 4 % p.a. is disastrous. With a doubling of population every 20–30 years, the Gurung economy will have to be transformed out of all recognition before the end of the century, merely to feed the new mouths. The possibility of doing this, when the necessary capital is already absorbed by a growing burden of old and young, seems slight.

4
Forest and land resources

The hundred families in Thak which I studied intensively had only limited resources of land, labour, housing, clothing and other capital. An attempt to compile an inventory of such resources in 1969 and to show their distribution in various groups will of necessity be largely based on guesswork. For example, no adequate inventory of forest or mineral resources for the area was undertaken. Nor are the various types of land record satisfactory as indicators of land-ownership, as we shall see. I was only able to obtain detailed inventories of goods and land from a tenth of the hundred families, and extrapolating from these is subject to several types of error. Yet the attempt must be made, for no description of the Gurung economy will be adequate without such analysis, nor will it be possible to assess the effects of population growth, or the future possibility of economic improvement, without having some general cross-section of resources.

For present purposes we will disregard mineral resources in the *panchayat*. Although, as stated in the previous chapter, the Gurungs were said once to have been diligent miners, they are not so now, at least in the areas I visited. The only slight exception is in the quarrying of stone and slate used for house-building. Those villages where slate for roofing is scarce, for instance Siklis, are forced to spend considerable sums of money on buying and transporting corrugated-iron roofing sheets. Thak appears to be well supplied with such stone, though how long the supplies will last under the pressure of current extensive building, I am unable to say.

For convenience sake the natural resources within Thak *panchayat* may be divided into three categories; forest, grazing, and arable land. These are not, obviously, completely separate; the forest, for example, provides fodder for animals and therefore may be termed a grazing area also. Nor does this include every type of natural resource; water, both permanent supplies and monsoon rains, is not considered here. The classification does enable us to examine the changing relationship between different types of land use and the way growing population alters the whole ecological basis of a society.

The area selected for detailed study lies within the *panchayat* of Thak. The boundaries of this *panchayat* and the way in which other villages border on it

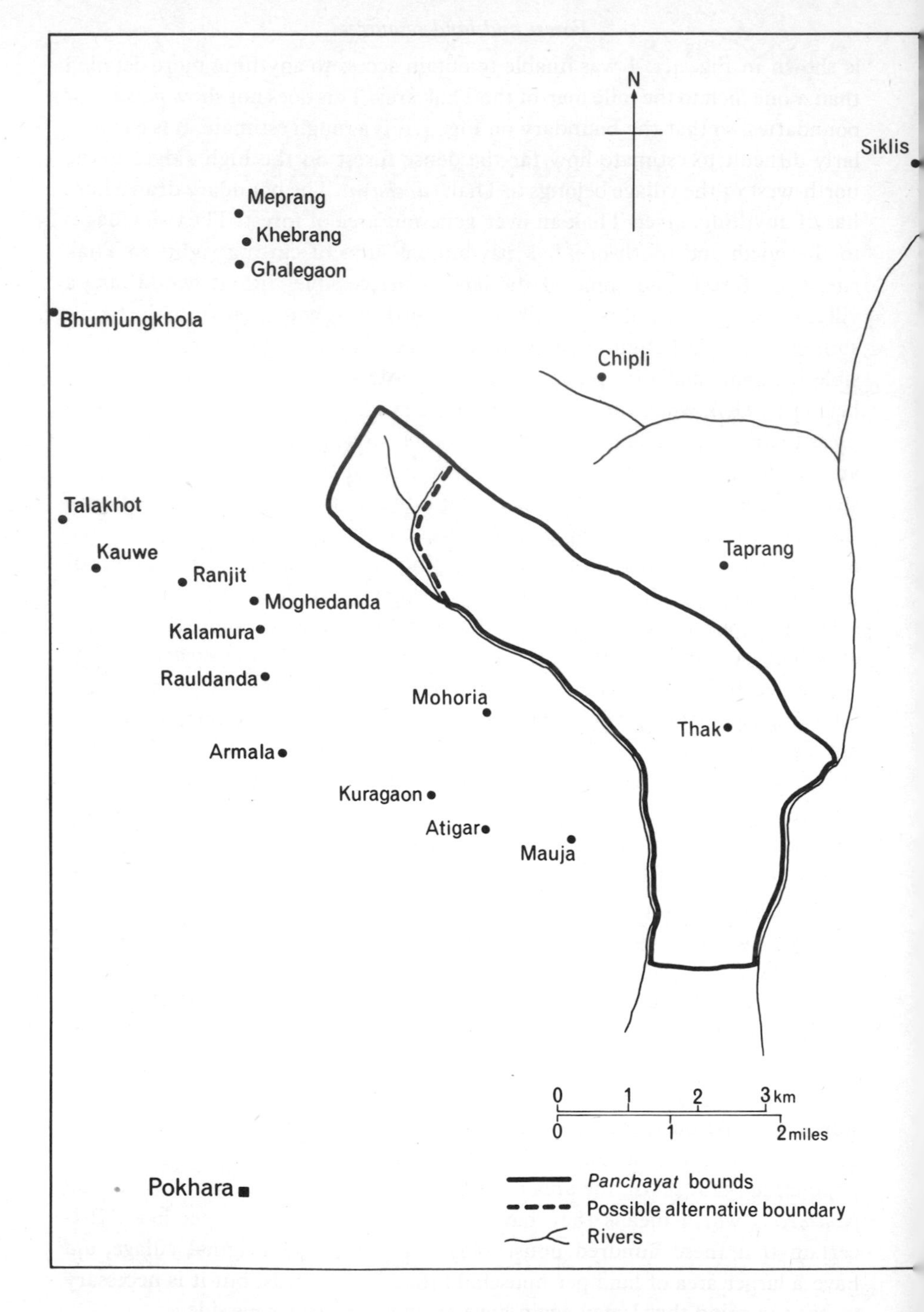

Fig. 4.1. Thak *panchayat* in relation to neighbouring villages.

is shown in Fig. 4.1. I was unable to obtain access to anything more detailed than a one inch to the mile map of the Thak area. This does not show *panchayat* boundaries, so that the boundary on Fig. 4.1. is a rough estimate. It is particularly difficult to estimate how far the dense forest on the high ridges to the north-west of the village belongs to Thak *panchayat*. The boundary drawn here has, if anything, given Thak an over-generous area of forest. The two villages to the north and south of Thak pay annual sums of cutting rights in Thak *panchayat* forest, and some of the land is inaccessible cliff. It would take a villager some 2–2½ hours to walk to this north-west boundary from the township of Thak. Although, at present, the forests further north are also accessible for game and rare plants, it is unlikely that they will be considered to belong to Thak when the demand for wood makes other neighbouring villages press their claims. The forests are also too far to be useful as supplies of wood and fodder for the central village. It will be seen that Thak has a very good share of the surviving jungle in the area. Informants often spoke with pride of the fact that Thak had a very good forest, and it was for this reason that Mauja, Mohoriya and Taprang, already outstripping their woods, paid annually to cut in Thak *panchayat*. It seems likely that in twenty years or so, when every hillside is precious and new settlements have spread out from Moghedanda, Ranjit, Ghalegaon and elsewhere, the effective border of Thak *panchayat* will be considered to be at the alternative line marked on the map. Nevertheless the following calculations will be based on the optimistic assumption that this will not happen. It needs to be borne in mind, therefore, that all the following statistics may be much too high: if the border is really at the alternative line this would subtract nearly a third of the forest resources for Thak, and nearly one-sixth of the land available to the 100 sample families.

The total area of land available in Thak *panchayat* as a whole is approximately 10 sq. miles or 6400 acres.[1] Given the approximate total population of 1810 persons in 1969, this gives a density of 3.53 acres per person. Within the whole *panchayat*, a certain area was the basis for the economy of the sample hundred households. This area can only be roughly demarcated, as in Fig. 4.2. On the north of the *panchayat* a belt of land has to be allowed for the inhabitants of ward 9, who were not included in the sample households (ward 9 consisted of 29 households in 1968). To the south live the inhabitants of wards 1–5. Again these 100 households have probably been given an over-generous allocation of land: although including less than one-third of the population (528:1810), the area on the map constitutes about 4/10 of the total *panchayat*, which means they have an average of 4.85 acres per head. It is certain that these hundred households, centred on the original village, *did* have a larger area of land per household than other wards, but it is necessary to bear in mind that I may again have erred on the generous side.

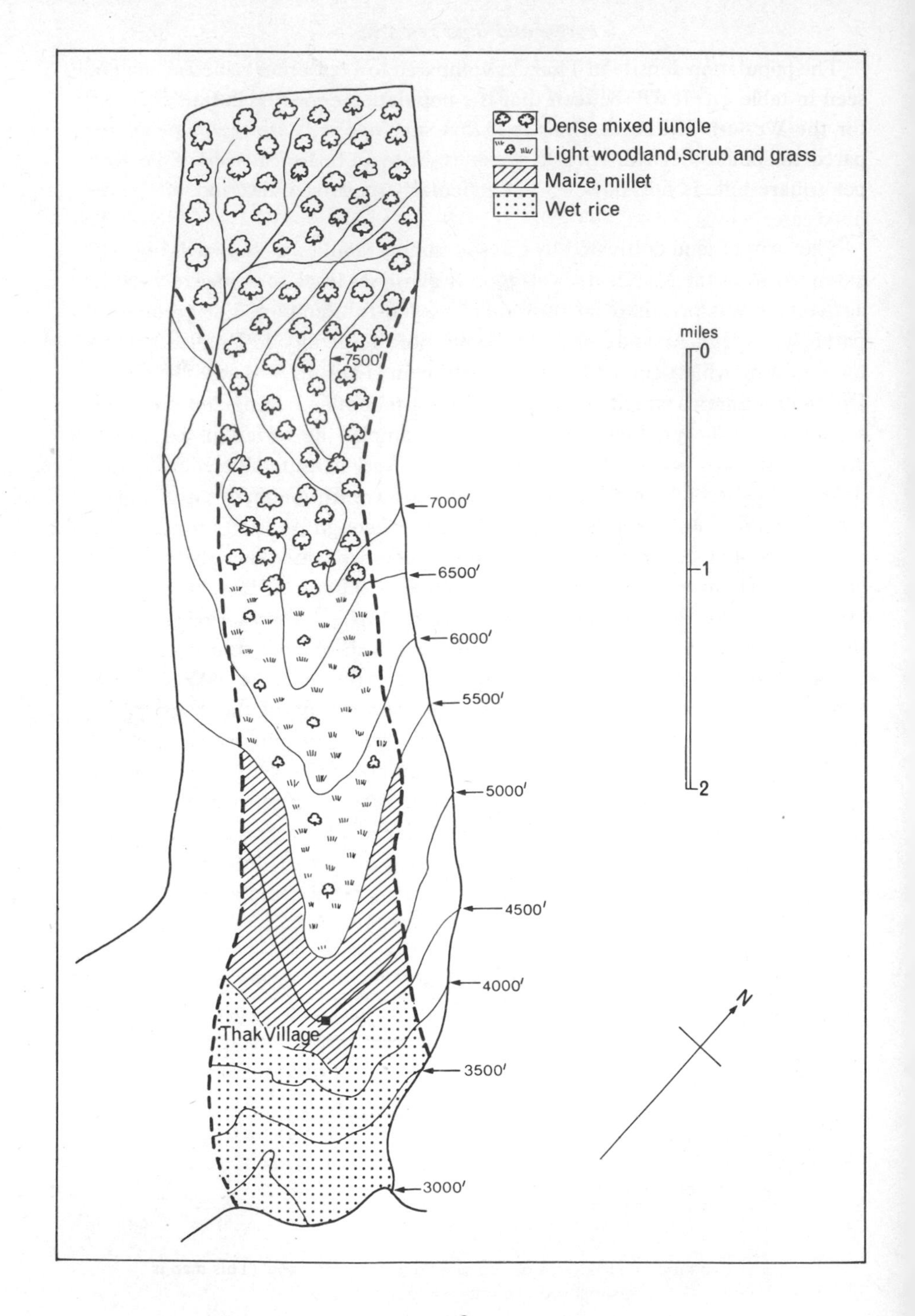
Dense mixed jungle
Light woodland, scrub and grass
Maize, millet
Wet rice
miles
0
1
2
7500′
7000′
6500′
6000′
5500′
5000′
4500′
4000′
3500′
3000′
Thak Village
N

The population density in Thak, as compared to a few other societies, may be seen in table 4.1. It will be seen that the population density is in line with that for the Western Hills as a whole, but that such densities are high when compared to some other third world societies, or to an historical society. Persons per square mile is not, however, a particularly sensitive index and will be refined later.

The strip of land cultivated by the 100 sample families, as shown in Fig. 4.2, extended from the Mahdi river at 3000 ft above sea level, to a ridge of 7500 ft; agriculture was practised on the side of a 4500-ft mountain. The gradient of parts of the *panchayat* is brought home more forcefully to English readers by Fig. 4.3, which compares the elevation in Thak to a slice of the Lake District mountains which include the highest mountain in England. The consequences of the gradient are many. For example, the variations in climate and hence crops between different levels was very considerable. There was a definite line beyond which wet rice was not grown. Although, of course, crops did not follow contour lines exactly, there was enough similarity to allow the areas to be divided as in Fig. 4.2. When we come to actual ownership, it will be seen that many areas within each crop area cannot, in fact, be used for farming because they are too steep and rocky. Fig. 4.2, therefore, is an oversimplified indication of crop regions, and does not show crops actually planted.

The steepest gradient occurs between the river and the village; some 2000 feet in a mile. It is on this slope that the majority of the cereal crops are grown. At about 5500 feet is the border between grazing and arable, though a little barley and some root vegetables are grown above this altitude. Above 5500 feet are scrubby bushes, patches of short-cropped, poor-quality, grass, and small trees: it is an area where forest has recently been cleared and now goats and buffaloes prevent anything of value from growing. The map gives the theoretical amount of land available for each crop, but the

TABLE 4.1 *Population density in Thak and other selected societies*[2]

Place	Persons per sq. mile
Thak *panchayat*	181
Thak 100 households	107
Nepal – Western Hills, 1961	174.7
Garos of Assam, 1951	77
Ndembu, Africa, 1952	6.13
England, seventeenth century	90

Fig. 4.2. Land use in Thak; area of 100 sample households, 1969. (This map is oversimplified and only roughly to scale.)

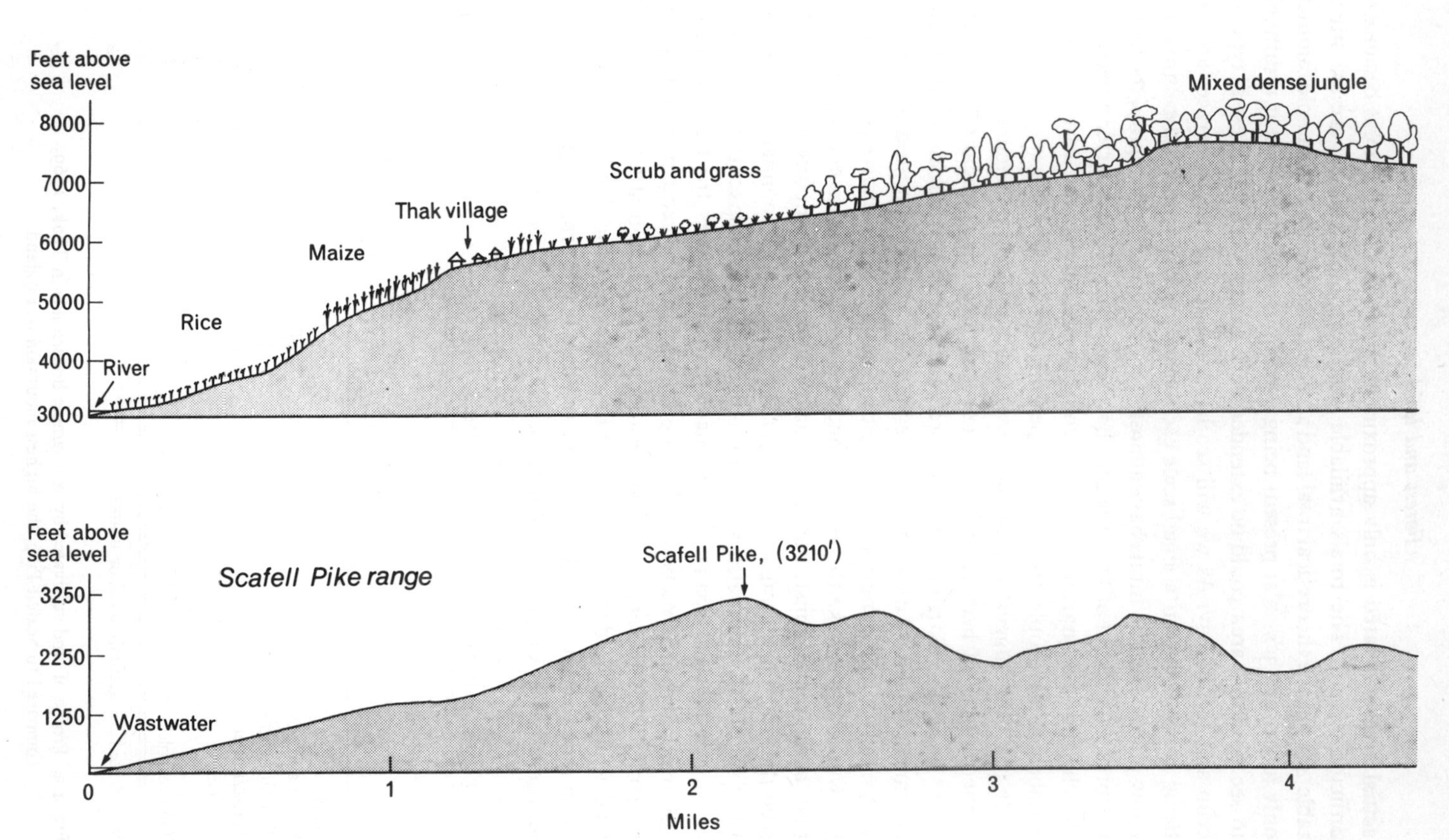

Feet above sea level
8000
7000
6000
5000
4000
3000
River
Rice
Maize
Thak village
Scrub and grass
Mixed dense jungle
Feet above sea level
Scafell Pike range
3250
2250
1250
Wastwater
Scafell Pike, (3210')
0
1
2
3
4
Miles

actual area cultivated is only approximately half the shaded areas because of difficult terrain. The totals available (in theory and practice) are set out in table 4.2. Of the theoretical total land area available to the 100 sample families, only just over 13 % is at present being used for arable crops. Yet it is difficult to see how this area could be extended very greatly with the present types of crop and technology. As we will see later, maize and millet terraces are still being constructed on a small scale each year, and rice could still be grown in a few places. But the limits have almost been reached. Very roughly, therefore, the present division of the area into half heavy forest, one quarter grazing and thatch, and one quarter arable, is probably not only dictated by the present number of the people but by what the land can be use for.

It has been suggested that the most accurate index of population density is the number of hectares of cultivated land/adult male engaged in agriculture.[3] Since the Gurungs depend more heavily than many societies on female agricultural labour, males being absent in the army, this would not be a fair assessment for Gurung villages. The problem, for comparative purposes, can be avoided if we make the assumption, as made for Indonesia in the table 4.3, that adult males constitute one quarter of the total population. It will be seen that the Thak sample is relatively prosperous by the standards of the area. Even so, the ha./man ratio is very low indeed: it is much closer to the very great density of Java or Japan[4] (0.7 ha./man) than the figures for European agriculture, where it is reckoned that 3.6 ha. agricultural land/man in Italy, for example, leads to very considerable unemployment, and at least 3.5 ha. total land would be needed to keep men fully employed.[5] Such high density can be maintained without double cropping, artificial fertilizers, etc. only because the village also has plenty of grazing, forest, and income from the army.

TABLE 4.2 *Area of land used for various purposes, Thak 1969*

Use	Total acreage	'Cultivated' acreage	Average acres of cultivated land per person
Heavy forest	1200	800	1.5
Scrub and grazing	530	350	0.66
Thatching grass	30	30	0.06
Maize/millet	240	120	0.23
Wet rice	400	200	0.38
Total arable	640	320	0.61

'Cultivated' = actually used or usable.

Fig. 4.3. Profile of land cultivated by 100 sample households in Thak, 1969, compared to Scafell Pike, the highest mountain in England.

TABLE 4.3 *Man/land ratios in various groups*

(Ha. agricultural land/man engaged in agriculture (assumed ¼ of total population))	
Thak, 100 households,	0.981
Western Hills of Nepal, 1961	0.364
West Java, *c.* 1959	0.63
Poland, 1950 (include pasture)	6.0
Italy, 1950 (include pasture)	3.6

Note: The figures for W. Nepal are computed from the figure cited in McDougall, *Village Economy*, p. 2, assuming that ¼ population = adult males. The figures for West Java and Poland/Italy are cited in Clark, *Subsistence Agriculture*, pp. 139, 143.

FOREST AND PASTURE

Wood and fodder flows from the high slopes above Thak, through the village where much of it is absorbed, down onto the cereal fields. This flow is shown in Fig. 4.4. On its way it produces many of the necessities of Gurung life; heat, housing material, protein, energy with which to work the fields, and manure with which to produce cereals (calories). It is because this chain is so very vital that present concern over deforestation and erosion is justified. Although erosion is not, as yet, a major problem in Thak, and the situation is much better than that in many neighbouring Gurung villages where the forest is already depleted, Thak makes a useful case study of the way in which forest and grazing resources are put under heavy pressure as population grows. It will also show the way in which the various parts of Gurung agriculture are interconnected.

The Gurungs cook on wood fires and keep such fires burning almost permanently. Consequently they use huge quantities of firewood. In the past, firewood was no problem, but continued prodigality in use does not suit an age of denuded mountains. Informants were asked how much wood they used per week, and the amount actually burnt was observed. A count was made of the number of bundles of wood stored up for the monsoon months when climate and work in the fields made cutting difficult. Wood is also needed for the framework of houses, and the villagers need considerable quantities of various bamboos for many types of tool such as baskets, ploughs, rakes and hoes. Table 4.4 shows approximate amount of wood consumed. The totals are very rough since it is extremely difficult to assess the average size and weight of a bundle of wood. The average weight of a load of wood as carried by the Gurungs was about 30 kg. The bundle is about 3 ft in length and 1½ ft in diameter, consisting of logs or sticks tied together. The weight per cubic foot of 'Empire

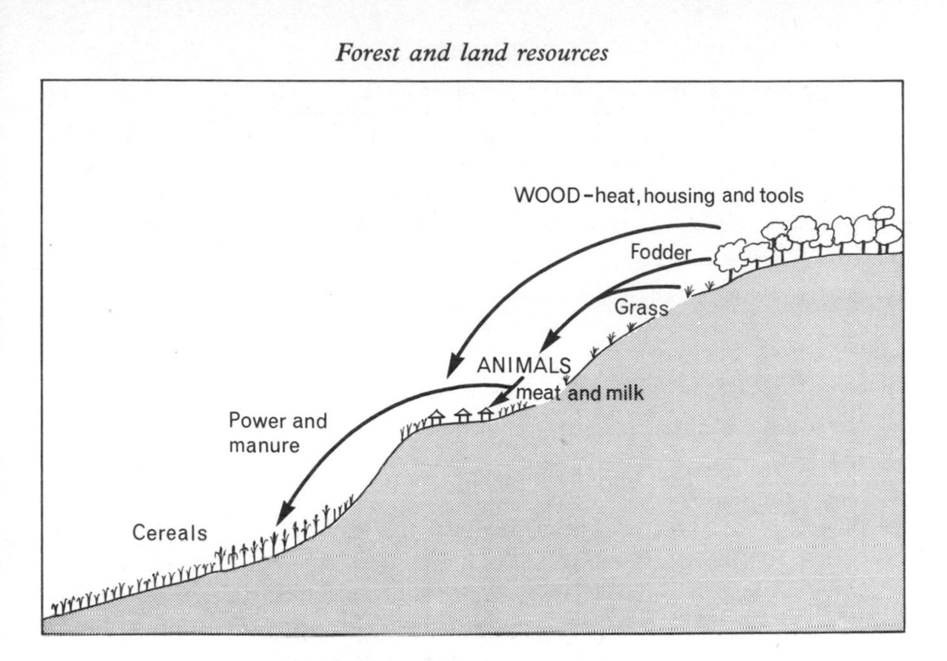

Fig. 4.4. Flow of resources through Thak.

TABLE 4.4 *Consumption of wood by 100 Thak households*

Type of wood	Bundles per house p.a.	Ave. size per bundle (cu. ft)	Total p.a. (cu.ft) 100 houses
Firewood	120	1.5	18,000
Building/tools	2	1.5	300
Bamboo	2	1.5	300
	124		18,600

Timbers' (at 15 % moisture content) is usually 35–55 lb per cubic ft.[6] If we accept a median figure of some 45 lb per cubic ft, then a 30-kg load would contain 1.5 cubic ft. On the above calculations each individual residing in the village in these 100 households would consume some 37 cubic ft p.a., or 1.05 cubic metres. It is worth noting that, despite the vital necessity of wood in the Gurung economy for building and burning, each individual consumes roughly only half the amount that a North American, on average, uses.[7] Given the above rate of consumption, when the population increases by 2 % in a group of some 500 individuals, an extra 370 cubic ft of wood is needed in the following year.

Guesswork is needed in order to estimate the total wood resources of these 100 households. It has already been suggested that they may have up to 800 acres of useable heavy forest at their disposal. In theory this should be more than enough to supply the households with wood. There are a number of estimates for the growth rates of wood in various climates; these vary from 1.1 to 58 cubic metres per hectare per year. Taking a median figure of 20, as does the compiler of the table,[8] we may calculate that these 800 acres should produce some 6475 cubic metres of wood a year. This would be nearly fourteen times the amount (467 cubic metres) calculated above as needed by the Thak 100 households. Theoretically, therefore, there would seem to be no problem.

Yet this illustrates the danger of abstract calculations *in vacuo*. A superficial glance at the scrubby landscape round the village of Thak shows that the forest cover has been rolled back rapidly over the last few years. This occurred when the population was smaller than it is at present. The forest has no chance to grow again with herds of goats grazing through it, and small trees are constantly lopped down for fodder. Older men told of how some two generations ago wild pig and other wild animals used to wander through the village from the surrounding forest. They remember when there was heavy forest at *Proree* (a mile north of the village) and just above the village on 'burial hill'. Medium-sized trees are now only to be found an hour's walk away, and the heavy monsoon jungle of huge trees festooned with creepers that once covered the whole area is now 1½ hours walk away. It is this heavy jungle that is yearly depleted in order to provide the great piles of logs for the monsoon months. It is impossible to be sure how fast such good forest is being used up. But it seems likely that, with growing pressure from neighbouring villages, the remaining good forest within Thak *panachayat* could be used up within 10–20 years. It is therefore not just a matter of harvesting annual wood growth, but of destroying the inherited capital of thousands of years. Within thirty years there will be nothing but scrub and small trees within 8 miles of Thak, which will mean that to fetch wood it will take some 5 hours just to walk to the forest and back.

Although the Thak *panchayat*, like others in Nepal, are making some attempt to prevent people from cutting down younger trees and green wood, there is little real hope that they will be able to make even a marginal impact on the problem, to judge from the past experience of other Gurung villages such as Siklis, which are surrounded by a huge treeless wilderness. There is no re-planting in Thak, and no real effort at conservation. In fact, given the huge demand for wood and the limited supplies, there is no easy solution. The problem which already faces bigger towns such as Pokhara, where the price of wood is very high, will soon afflict all Gurung villages. One of the solutions for Pokhara, cooking on kerosene stoves, is inhibited in the hills by extra transport costs. The present disastrous situation is found, of course, through most of the foothills of the Himalayas.[9] Even the present population is devouring non-renewable resources: if, as seems likely, population doubles in the next thirty years there is likely to be acute shortage.

There are various reasons why the actual position is much worse than an abstract account of demand and resources would suggest. One is that cutting is not controlled; nearer parts of the forest are destroyed, while further-off growth is left untouched. It is also possible that 20 cubic metres per hectare p.a. growth is too optimistic an estimate for the type of wood in this area. Furthermore, as stated before, other villages pay to use Thak facilities. But perhaps one of the most important reasons is that the remaining forests are subject to another pressure – the need for animal fodder. Hugh quantities of vegetation are consumed by village livestock, either roaming in the forest, or stalled in the village, and the cutting of large quantities of leaves off the trees undoubtedly inhibits growth.

Goats, cows and oxen are usually herded over the slopes above Thak and consume what they can find. Some buffaloes are also thus herded, but the best milking buffaloes are stalled in the village and are brought bundles of fodder. Cutting such fodder occupies much of the time of young adults and children. Each milking buffalo is brought one or two bundles of fodder each day, each bundle weighing up to 20 kg. The total demands for fodder of the livestock owned by the sample households is set out in table 4.5. The amount consumed per adult animal per day is probably a conservative estimate; it is not based on actual measured consumption, but on comparisons with the amount of fodder consumed by livestock elsewhere in the world.[10] The way in which the total livestock owned by the hundred sample families was converted into adult beast equivalents is described below.[11] It will be seen that the 350 acres of poor scrubby grazing has to support a very large number of animals, some 613. Even though such animals are small by European standards, this leads to overgrazing and necessitates recourse to other sources of food. One of these is the stubble and stalks from cereal crops. After the rice harvest the livestock (except goats) are pastured on the fields. They are also fed maize stalks and rice straw. But even this is not enough, so that expeditions have to be made to the forest

TABLE 4.5 *Amount of fodder consumed by livestock, Thak, 1969*

Type of animal	Approx. kg fodder per animal per day	Nos. adult animals	Total consumed p.a. (kg)
Buffalo	12	167	731,460
Oxen	8	135	394,200
Cows	8	64	186,880
Goats	4	247	360,620
			1,673,160

to cut leaves. Possibly up to a quarter of the fodder comes from trees; this would mean a demand for some 418,290 kg of vegetation, annually or roughly some 523 kg of fodder per acre if the load was distributed evenly. In fact, of course, parts of the forest are cut heavily, and other parts neglected.

If we average out the total demand for vegetation, each individual in the sample families consumes, by way of livestock, some 3346 kg of fodder per annum. It is not difficult to see the enormous strains a doubling of the population would put on grass and trees if it was felt necessary to double livestock also. The only alternative is either to improve the quality of the grazing, which is possible, but difficult to envisage, or to lower the ratio of livestock to persons – which would mean a drastic cut in proteins and manure. The further destruction of forest will thus affect not only the supply of wood, but also of protein and calories (*via* manure). Already the destruction has gone so far that two important food resources of the past, wild game, and wild fruit and vegetables, have been almost liquidated. It is also arguable that forest destruction will lessen the supply of another precious resource, water.[12]

ARABLE LAND

The fact that three-quarters of the total area upon which the sample households subsist is communally owned is important when we consider the distribution of capital in the community. The lower castes and poor Gurungs, with little arable land, still have free access, in theory, to the communal grazing and forest. In practice, however, it is the richer Gurungs who have the majority of the livestock and who thus reap the most from the communal resources. Nevertheless, the existence of the 'commons', as in pre-industrial England, is still an effective protection from absolute destitution. But, as in pre-industrial England, such common land is being diminished; the once communally owned maize land is now partitioned among households, and it is not difficult to forsee a time when grazing, and possibly even the remnants of forest, will be divided out – presumably among the wealthier families.

The total amount of land under the main cereal crops, worked out both from the map and from land records for individual households, is shown in table 4.6. Firstly, it will be seen that the area under various crops according to the two sources fits well, and suggests that the earlier guess that approximately half the available land is actually cultivated is a fairly accurate assessment. If we compare the above situation to other parts of Nepal, we find that the sample is favoured. It has been estimated that the arable land *per capita* for Nepal as a whole in 1962 was 0.47 acres;[13] for the Western Hills as a whole it was only 0.18 acres. Elsewhere it has been calculated that to provide a basic rice diet in India in the 1930s, or in Cambodia or Nepal in 1970, some 0.66 acres of rice

TABLE 4.6 *Arable land used by 100 households, Thak 1969*

Crop	Area on map (cultivated) acres	From land records acres	Acres per person (present)	Ha. per person (present)
Rice	200	182	0.4	0.162
Other	120	105	0.24	0.097
Total	320	287	0.64	0.259

Note: It is assumed that there has been some under-registration of land in the land records, and therefore the map areas are used to calculate the acres/ha. per person. Only those permanently in Thak are estimated in this sum.

land per person is needed.[14] The Gurungs reach this minimum, even without their subsidiary crops. Without intensifying agriculture, it is possible that the population could increase by nearly 100 % without people actually starving to death. But in practice it seems likely that starvation would begin before such a doubling was achieved since, for example, there are frequent harvest failures because of hail. Present surpluses help to tide villagers over these as well as providing a little over for livestock and luxury. Other villages do not have such ample reserves; we shall see that the rice and maize harvests per head in Mohoriya were far smaller than those in Thak.

The cereal resources measured in terms of grain produced, rather than acreage under various crops, show the same slight surplus. On the basis of what householders stated they had harvested from individual fields, checked against the totals for their whole farm, it appears that, though yields for different quality fields vary considerably, we can assume an average yield of 1½ *muri* of husked rice per *ropani*, and 2 *muri* of husked maize/millet per *ropani*.[15] These quantities are converted to kilograms and worked out, in table 4.7, for the whole area under cultivation. On these calculations there are over 500 kg *per capita* in grains. A number of comments, however, need to be made. On the one hand the table understates the quantity available; a number of other crops are grown, some grains,

TABLE 4.7 *Total production of main cereal crops, Thak, 1969*

Crop	Area under cultivation (*rops*)	Area under cultivation (acres)	Total prod'n (husked grain) (*muri*)	Total prod'n (husked grain) (kg)	Prod'n per head (resident) (kg)
Rice	1538	200	2050	140,630	281.3
Maize/millet	923	120	1846	119,990	239.9
Total	2461	320	3896	260,620	521.28

some root crops. These supplement the diet fairly considerably.[16] Secondly, the above is the average for *all* those resident, men, women, children, and infants. But if we were to work out the average per 'adult equivalent', it would be a good deal higher. Such a figure may be roughly estimated on the basis of later calculations of the number of consumption units (i.e. adult-equivalent consumers) in the sample households.[17] There are some 415 such adult-equivalent consumers, and if we exclude those away in the army in 1969 approximately 380. The total cereals divided between these units would allow 685 kg of cereal per adult.

On the other hand much of this cereal consists of millet and maize, both low in calories, and if we are measuring in rice or wheat equivalents this will have to be allowed for. Secondly, it is quite possible that the area under various crops has been overestimated: it has been assumed that the land records under-record by about 10 %. If this is not so, then the above totals would need to be adjusted accordingly. Finally, the above production is only achieved when both maize/millet and rice harvests are undamaged by hail. But in recent years either one or the other harvest has been seriously damaged once in every four or five years. In 1968, for example, the maize harvest was largely destroyed; in 1969 a few minutes of hail carried away over a quarter of the rice. We may therefore lower the above figures by some 10–20 % to allow for harvest losses. Probably another 5 % or more is lost to rodents while being stored.

It is difficult to balance these various factors accurately, but we would probably be safe to put the grain equivalent per person per year at between 400–500 kg, even allowing for harvest failure. This is well above minimum subsistence needs, if we accept Colin Clark's figures of 250–300 kg per person per year as roughly right.[18] If productivity and land use remained unchanged, the population could increase from between 50 % and 100 % before people were short of cereals, even if all livestock products dried up. In practice, however, it is likely that extreme malnutrition would occur before then, since people would be likely to be malnourished rather than give up certain 'luxury' goods such as cigarettes.

CAPITAL INVESTED IN LAND

We have considered some of the natural resources in the village. It is also necessary to consider the amount of capital invested in land by these hundred households in order to estimate their total personal resources. The price of arable land in Thak was climbing rapidly in the 1960s, another indication of population pressure. In 1969 we can say that 1 *muri* of maize/millet or rice land was, on average, worth 1000 rs. This is necessarily a rough figure since the value of individual pieces varies enormously with their relative quality. The

TABLE 4.8 *Total of cash invested in arable land*

Total land (*rops*) Rice/maize and millet land	Total invested by 100 households		Avge. per house		Avge. per person	
	(rs.)	(£)	(rs.)	(£)	(rs.)	(£)
2461	2,461,000	102,541	24,610	1025	4660	194

evidence upon which the assessment is made will be given below.[19] On this basis, the total amount of money at present locked up in the purchase price of cereal land (the forest and grazing is theoretically free) is as shown in table 4.8.

Thus over £100,000 is invested in the few hundred acres of arable land, in fact some £320 per acre. Each individual in the sample families, on average, has £194 worth of land. This does not, of course, reflect the productivity of the land, but rather the desire of returned army soldiers to buy it with their wages. The inflated prices can be seen if we compare the situation in Thak to that in a South Indian village, Wangala. In 1955 an average of 3636 Indian rs. per household was invested in arable land. Even if we estimate that one Indian rupee in 1955 was worth some four Nepalese rupees in 1969, Thak households have 24,000 or more rs. worth of arable land, on average, while Wangala households have only 14,544.[20] We may now turn to the actual distribution of arable land between individuals in the area of study.

5

Changes in the distribution of arable land

THE NATURE OF THE SOURCES

The great importance of learning how the population – land ratio and the distribution of wealth have changed over the last hundred years in a Gurung village is obvious. This makes it necessary to attempt to use records as difficult to interpret as the surveys (upon which land taxes were based). These *tiriges* (Nep. *tirij*: receipt given for payment of money; also *tirja*, authorization to collect taxes), as they are known in Thak, were compiled by village headmen (*kroh*). In Thak they were made in 1883 (Nepali calendar 1940) and 1933. They appear to exist for most or all Gurung villages, but vary in date from area to area. Thus Pignède referred to their existence, though he was unable to use them in the short time available to him.[1] In fact the Mohoriya records were kept in Pignède's informant's own house. They were made in the years 1899, 1906, 1942. There is also said to be one for 1868 at the Kusma *Mal* (Land Tax) Office. In Thak also, one copy is kept in the village and another in the local (Pokhara) taxation office.

The documents are written in ink on very coarse paper which has, in the village copy I used, been rolled into bundles. The difficulty my informants experienced in reading the old place names and script was increased by the frequently poor condition of the documents. There were, for Thak, documents written by twelve separate *kroh*, each one responsible for a dozen or more households. The description of the rice and maize fields took a different form and, in half the cases, each type of land was written on separate paper. Each piece of rice land was listed under the following general headings. Serial number (*mort*): Man's number (*mohi*): field number (*kitar*): details concerning field (see below): class of land (*doyam*)[2]: amount due per *muri* of land (*bali*): area of land in *muri* (*sa muri*): total tax due (*bali/tiro*): extra tax of 4 *paise* per plot of land (*kalo paise*): total due. The details concerning each field usually took the following form:

> Narbahadur Gurung became the owner of this land in the survey of 1933. In the survey of 1883 it was owned by Lakshman Gurung. In the survey of 1933 it became the land of Narbahadur, after the death of Lakshman. The

land is east from the forest, it is north from the path, south from the land of Daljid, west from the land of Lalbahadur. The name of the land is Kogon tari.

It will be seen that details are given concerning the 1933 and 1883 owner, the landmarks on all four sides, and the name of the field. Frequently the size of the land in 1883 is also given. Measurements for the 1933 survey were made by the *kroh* with a length of rope. A comparison of the figures from this survey and those in the recent very careful survey undertaken in connection with land reform is made in table 5.1. It suggests that usually the total in the *tiriges* is about one-third to one-quarter of the real amount of land as suggested by a recent survey. It is possible that in a number of cases the use of the holding has become more intensive since 1933. In other words new terraces may have been added on steeper areas which were not cultivated in 1933. This may account for a small part of the discrepancy, but since several of the fields compared were particularly flat and good ones, which are unlikely to have been enlarged by new terracing, this cannot be a large part of the explanation. It seems likely that sizes were deliberately minimized in order to lessen taxation.[3] But the important fact for our purposes is that the under-registration has been consistent: all but one of the pieces listed below vary between a quarter and a half of the presently assessed size. Therefore, in comparing land ownership over time, although total areas may be distorted, relative size of landholdings will be less unsure.

Another distortion that might arise is connected to the problem of owner-

TABLE 5.1 *Comparison of the size of certain holdings, as shown in tiriges and land reform survey (rice)*

	Area	
Field name	Tiriges (1933)	Land Reform Survey (1965)
	s.m. p. m.	s.m. p. m.
Bra taba	14. 12. 4	34. 15. 0
Lyju khet	10. 0. 0	44. 0. 0
Kargord	41. 11. 2	74. 15. 0
Tunibort	9. 12. 4	32. 11. 0
Cheemro	10. 0. 0	29. 10. 0
Kogu tari	14. 15. 0	36. 5. 0
Cheemro	18. 16. 6	40. 0. 0
Total	119. 8. 0	291. 16. 0

Note: The *tiriges* areas are given in *sa muri*, the survey areas were originally in *ropanis*. The latter have been converted to *sa muri m.* = *mana*, eight of which make one *pathi* (*p.*), twenty of which make one *sa muri* (*s.m.*), four of which equal one *ropani*.

ship. It is probable that in some cases a man who had sold his land was still credited with it in the survey, and that in others it was being worked by someone other than the owner. It seems unlikely that either of these factors will be very important in the Gurung context, to judge from the present-day situation. Even in 1969, with considerable land shortage, there was not a large amount of long-term leasing of land, and scarcely any mortgaging of land for security on loans. With rice land still fairly abundant in the past, there is likely to have been even less of this. Furthermore, it would seem likely that, when the surveys were made, the actual owner, rather than the previous one, was written down. Although the present payment of land taxes in the village shows that people seem prepared to go on paying taxes on pieces of land which they sold long ago, or are not working, it is likely that when the survey was made, some care was taken to work out actual ownership.

It is clear from the land records that rice terraces have been owned individually since at least 1883. As has already been described, maize and millet fields were less in demand and were only shared out individually during the years since about 1940. Before then, the patches of jungle were slashed and burnt by those who had the labour. The 1933 survey from which I worked did not refer to any earlier ownership of the plots of maize land; many of the entries state that tax has only been paid since the 1940s and 1950s. Some of the later documents specify the bordering lands, but mostly all that is given is the owner's name and that of the field. The quantity of seed it would take to sow the named area, also given, is clearly a standard estimate, bearing no relation to the actual area. The *tiriges* also list the uncultivated hillsides, which are owned collectively by groups of half a dozen or so Gurungs. Finally, a certain number of house sites are also listed, with their dates of occupation. The *tiriges* concentrate on the land near the central village of Thak; but some land owned by inhabitants of Thak to the north and south, on the borders of the *panchayat*, is also included as well as a few fields in the neighbouring *panchayat* of Moja.

The 1883 *tiriges* show a total of some 327 rice plots, held by some 113 persons. The vast majority of these landholders (89 of 113) held only one or two plots of rice land. Fifty years later new rice fields had been made, and one or two plots had been subdivided between heirs, so that now there were 478 plots held by 111 households. The distribution of the rice plots in 1883, 1933 and 1965 is seen most easily in Fig. 5.1. In 1883 the great majority of villagers had a small piece of rice land; possibly the abundance of land meant that every household had a plot. But few households had many plots; only seven households had ten or more plots, and only three had fifteen or more. The greatest single holding was 18 plots. By 1933 the clearing of new land, combined with the drop in the number of very small rice landholders, meant that a group of

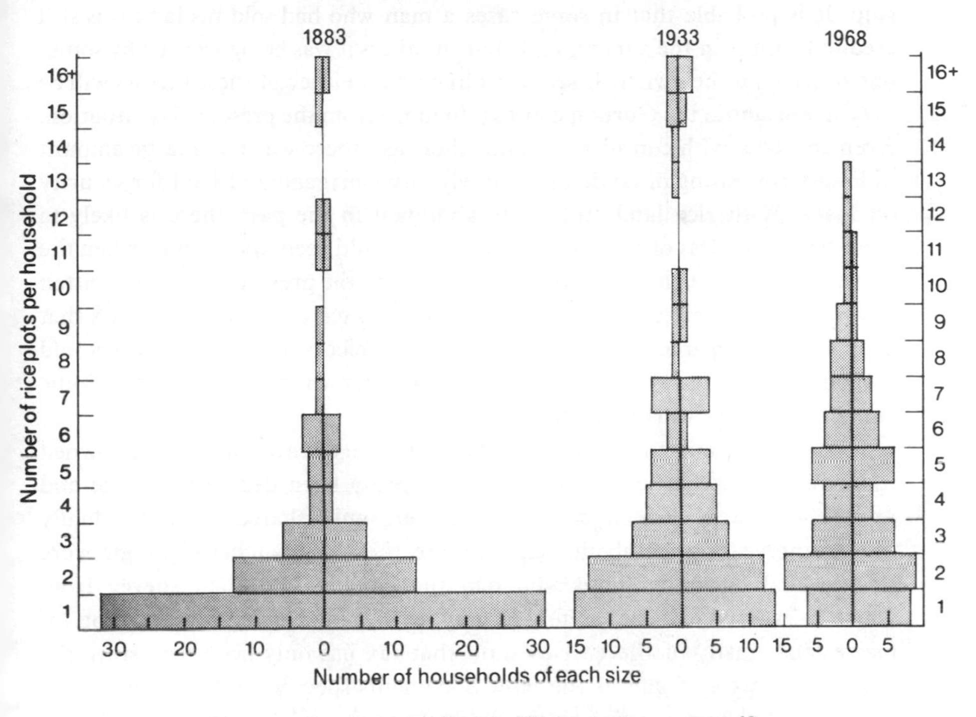

Fig. 5.1. Size of rice holdings in Thak in 1883, 1933, 1968.

middling and large landholders could emerge. This was perhaps the period of greatest inequality. At the top there were eleven rich households owning ten or more plots of rice land, seven of them owning fifteen plots each. The greatest number owned by a single household was 27 plots. Those lineages,[4] which had arrived first in the village, had now cleared most of the rice land which they claimed was theirs. The continuing dominance of the *carjat* perhaps enabled them to exact the labour to work this land. At this point, over half the rice land in the village was owned by 22 households. By the 1960s the position had again changed.

The expansion of army service in the Second World War had boosted some poorer families, while rising prices, divisions between inheriting sons, and land reform legislation had broken up the biggest estates. There are now (1968) no households with more than 13 plots of land, but a greater number with 5–8 plots. The number of very small rice holders has decreased.

A better comparison between the position in 1933 and 1968 is obtained if we just compare landholdings in our sample hundred households at these two dates, as in Fig. 5.2. This diagram eliminates outside owners from the 1933 calculations, particularly people living in Panigat and a number of Brahmins

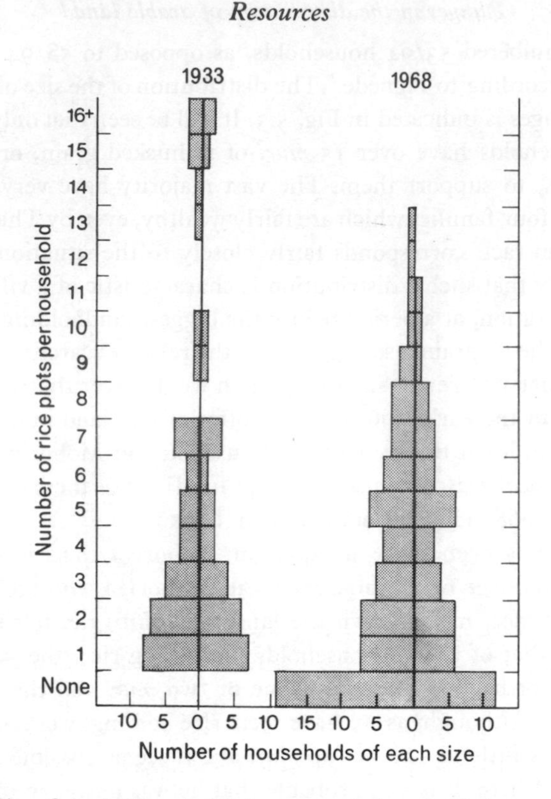

Fig. 5.2. Size of rice holdings in Thak 100 sample households in 1933 and 1968.

who often have one or two plots within the area covered by the land records, and thus emphasizes a double tendency. There is on the one hand a growing equalization of wealth among the Gurungs at about the 5-plot level; on the other hand there is growing inequality in that there are an increasing number of Blacksmiths, Tailors and non-Gurungs, as well as a few newly-arrived Gurungs, who have no rice land. Even though there are a growing group of those without rice land, such is the growth of population that the available rice land has also had to be split up among more households. Thus in 1933 there were 64 households with some rice land. In about 1965 there were some 81 such households. It must be stressed that the above figures, since they deal with numbers of plots, and the plots vary enormously in quality and size, give only a rough indication of the relative distribution of rice land. It is also likely that the pattern varies very much from village to village, and this may be checked by comparing Thak with Mohoriya.

I visited the village of Mohoriya in late 1969, and though I was unable to study the land records themselves, an extremely able informant gave me a list of how much unhusked rice was grown by each household in the village. The rice growers numbered 53/94 households, as opposed to 58/94 some eleven years before, according to Pignède.[5] The distribution of the size of rice harvest for the two villages is indicated in Fig. 5.3. It will be seen that only 7/53 of the Mohoriya households have over 15 *muri* of unhusked grain, or enough, by Thak standards, to support them. The vast majority have very small plots, while there are four families which are fairly wealthy, even by Thak standards. The diagram, in fact, corresponds fairly closely to the situation in Thak in 1883. It is likely that such a distribution is characteristic of a village roughly in its third generation, at a period before the biggest landholdings are split up between sons. The diagram also emphasizes the relative scarcity of rice land in Mohoriya, so that we are not surprised when we discover that 13 households left the village in the early 1960s on the offer of free land in the Terai. Nor is it surprising to learn that 2/3 of the households in Mohoriya had to buy millet from the *bacat kos* (compulsory savings fund) to tide them over before the new harvest in 1968. This did not occur in Thak.

The situation is even more unequal in Mohoriya than it looks in the diagram, for a number of the households in Mohoriya who are indicated as growing rice do not, in fact, own the land they cultivate, but sharecrop it. Pignède stated that of the 58 households harvesting rice 'the larger part of these these do not harvest more than one or two *muri* and the fields do not belong to them'.[6] Although, as we have seen, rice holdings were small in 1968, only 8/53 had as little as one or two *muri* and it seems possible that Pignède was misinformed here. It is also probable that he was mistaken in saying that over half the rice growers were sharecroppers. Although it is likely that I was not given the full figures, there seems to be too much of a gap between his estimate and the fact that only 4/53 of the 1969 rice-holders were specified to be sharecroppers. In Thak, as we have seen, only one family with no rice land of its own was able to join the ranks of rice-growers through sharecropping.

The diagram for Thak can only be a rough assessment since it is not based on recorded rice harvests, but on the amount of rice land owned, multiplied by a standard amount to give produce. The assumption is made that every *ropani* of rice land owned in the land survey records will produce 2 *muri* of unhusked rice. This is a conservative estimate, for earlier it was calculated that $2\frac{2}{3}$ *muri* are produced, on average per *ropani*; but taking such an estimate helps to allow for the fact that not all rice land is fully cultivated. Taking a standard conversion figure such as this also tends to understate the crops of the richer households: not only do such families have bigger holdings, but they tend to have the best quality land with a higher yield. The Thak diagram shows that only $\frac{24}{100}$ households have no rice lands, and $\frac{63}{100}$ have what would be considered to be large holdings producing over 15 *muri* of unhusked grain. It seems that Pignède was premature in saying that some 30 % of the population owning

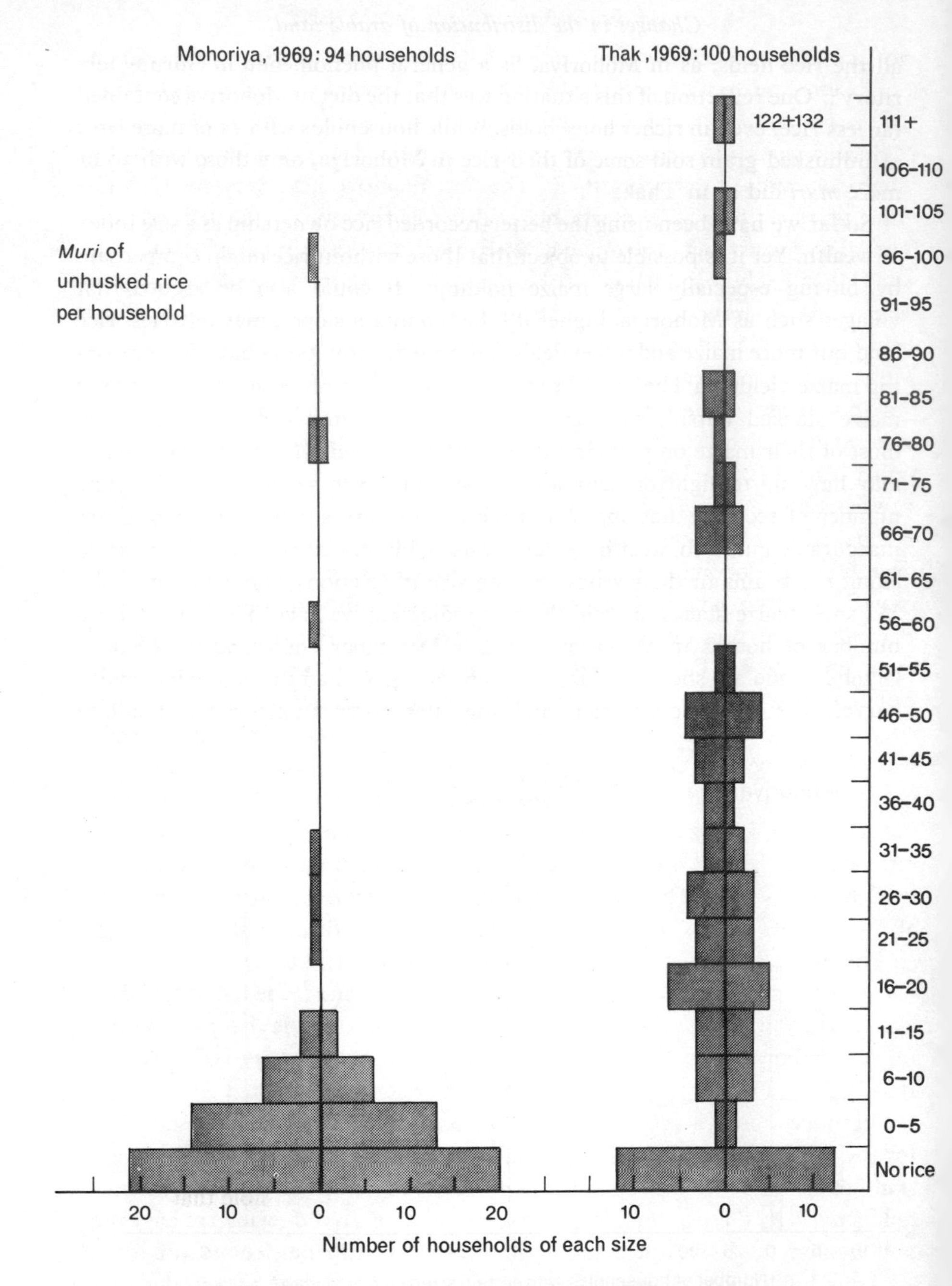

Fig. 5.3. Relative amounts of unhusked rice in two Gurung villages.

all the rice fields, as in Mohoriya, 'is a general phenomenon in Gurung territory'.[7] One reflection of this situation was that the diet in Mohoriya contained far less rice, even in richer households. While households with 11 or more *muri* of unhusked grain sold some of their rice in Mohoriya, only those with 30 or more *muri* did so in Thak.

So far we have been using the better-recorded rice ownership as a sole index of wealth. Yet it is possible to object that those without rice might compensate by having especially large maize holdings. It could also be argued that villages such as Mohoriya, higher up the mountain slopes, may have less rice land but more maize and millet fields. The only information I have for comparing maize yields, in Thak and Mohoriya comes from observing the amount of maize stacked outside various homes in the autumn. The Gurungs store most of their maize on poles in the courtyard (*mokhai suli*). A large landowner may have up to eight or more a poles, storing seven sections of maize. The number of sections that appear outside a house are a rough, but sometimes inaccurate, guide to wealth. A few households prefer to store their maize along the beams in their attics and the size of 'sections' varies considerably. Yet such maize stacks are still the best indication we have. The pattern for a number of houses in Mohoriya, noted in December 1969, and for Thak in October 1969 are shown in Fig. 5.4. Neither village had suffered a bad maize harvest the previous summer, and the later observation of the Mohoriya

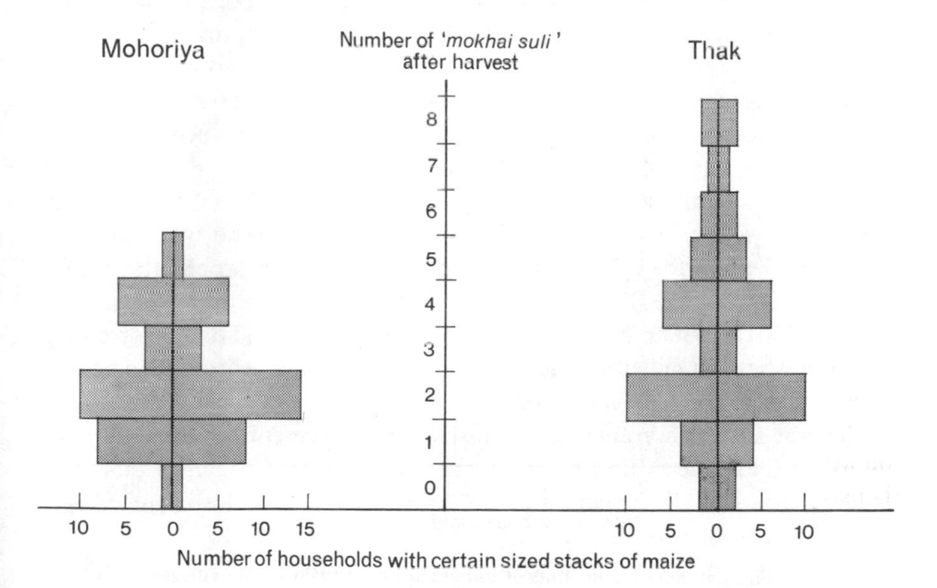

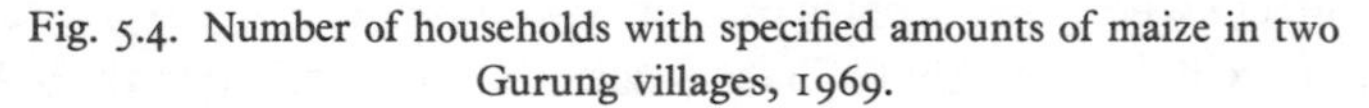
Fig. 5.4. Number of households with specified amounts of maize in two Gurung villages, 1969.

sample will make no difference since it is not until March or April of the following year that the maize stacks begin to be emptied. In both villages two 'sections' were the mode, but in Mohoriya only one-third of the households had three or more sections, whereas in Thak roughly half of the households had three or over. If anything, therefore, inhabitants of Thak have a greater amount of maize land, and such land is more unequally divided. It is also clear from the land records that, with the exception of Tamang/Magar families who tend to have large maize holdings, the distribution of maize/millet land is the same as that of rice land. It is the *carjat* Gurungs, owners of the majority of rice lands, who also own the larger part of the maize lands. In speaking of maize land, we have also included millet since the crops are grown in the same area of fields.

The above comparisons between the two villages are substantiatated by such general totals of crop production as we are able to obtain. In 1957, Pignède estimated a total production of 910 *muri* of (presumably unhusked) rice. The totals I was given for 1969 added up to 610 *muri* of unhusked rice. The drop of a third during the twelve years might be explained in a number of ways; fluctuations in the weather, mistaken observation by Pignède or myself, or a drop in the productivity of the land over twelve years as soil erosion and exhaustion grew. Whatever the reasons, it is clear that these 94 families have, on average, some 6–10 *muri* of unhusked rice per household. The 100 Thak households, at a conservative estimate, have some 28 *muri* of rice per household. As for maize, Pignède calculated that 449 *muri* were produced in 1957, or some 5 *muri* per household. Again taking a conservative estimate, there are approximately 12 *muri* per household in Thak. One interesting fact that emerges from this comparison is that, while the production of cereals in Thak is at least twice as high as it is in Mohoriya, this does not lead to the sale of surpluses; practically all of the grains are consumed in the village. Thus to double the yield of cereal grains in villages such as Mohoriya would not necessarily lead to the marketing of crops. The marginal propensity to consume is highly elastic. The relative affluence of Thak may, however, help to explain why the potato has not become widely popular and double-cropping (growing wheat or millet on the rice lands in the winter as is done in nearby villages) has not become common.

The way in which arable land is distributed at present between different groups in Thak, according to the Land Survey, may be seen in table 5.2. Three-quarters of all the land is owned by half the households in the village, the *carjat*. The Blacksmiths and Tailors have very little land indeed.

We may wonder how the situation in Thak compares with other villages nearby and elsewhere in Nepal. One set of comparative figures is shown in table 5.3. It will be seen that Thak is considerably wealthier than Armala;

TABLE 5.2 *Distribution of rice and maize land, Thak sample households*

Group	Total households for which totals are known (1965)	Total maize/millet land owned (*ropanis*)
Carjat Gg.	50	1622.12.3
Sorajat Gg.	21	433.00.3
Tamang/Magar	4	112.03.0
Blacksmith	11	28.01.2
Tailor	6	17.09.0

TABLE 5.3 *Distribution of holdings of various sizes*

Village	Size of holdings in *ropani*							Total households
	Below 1	1–2	2–3	3–5	5–10	10–20	20+	
Arghau[a]	0	3	2	3	11	14	30	63
Armala[a]	6	6	7	6	14	9	4	52
Thak	13	2	1	3	10	23	40	92

[a]The figures for Arghau and Armala (a partly Gurung village) are taken from B. P. Shreshta, *Report on Village Development in Pokhara* (1963) as reported in Shreshta, *Nepal Economy*, p. 55.

in Thak $\frac{40}{92}$ households have over 20 *ropanis* of land, in Armala only $\frac{4}{52}$. The proportion of landless is, however, fairly similar. Landlessness does not appear to be a problem, as yet, in Arghau. We need slightly different categories to compare the Thak figures to those collected by McDougall, for two areas in the Western Hills. (See table 5.4.) In both Sallyan and Doti there are a smaller proportion of landholders with 10+ *ropanis* of land, and the proportion of small landholders in Doti is very much higher than in Thak. On the whole, therefore, by Nepalese hill village standards, Thak is a moderately wealthy community.

CHANGE IN THE RELATIVE WEALTH OF LINEAGES, 1933–65

Unfortunately, informants were often unable to identify people named in the 1883 land survey, so that it is impossible to compare the position in 1883 with later estimates of land-ownership by lineage. It is certain, however, that

TABLE 5.4 *Thak compared to areas in the Western Hills*

Area	Size of holdings in *ropani*			Total households
	less than 5	5–9	10+	
Thak, 1965	19	10	63	92
Sallyan, 1967[a]	7	18	25	50
Doti, 1967[a]	22	13	15	50

[a]Figures for Sallyan and Doti are given in table 13, p. 27 of McDougall, *Village Economy*.

all of the eighteen households with five or more plots of land in 1883 belonged to *carjat* lineages. It is possible to make a rough comparison of the lands held by various lineages in 1933 and 1965. This is done in Fig. 5.5.

The 1933 position is based on the number of *sa muri* of rice land listed as owned by each lineage in 1933. All lineages, except the *konme*, have been shown as undivided. The *konme* have been divided into 8 lineages; probably some of these are sub-lineages, but they were recognized as distinct in 1968. Thus lineage 5, for example, comprised households 1, 28, 33A, who were fairly closely related to lineage 2. The *lamme* group, though in reality divided into several lineages, is shown undivided in the diagram. The overall impression of the situation in 1933 is of *konme* dominance. They owned over two-thirds of the rice land. The other third was split fairly evenly between the *lamme* and eight *sorajat* lineages. Within the *konme*, lineages 1 and 2 were dominant.

The 1965 situation is based on the more accurate totals of rice land ownership given by the land survey records of that year. The scale on the right of Fig. 5.5 has been chosen to make the total distribution as closely comparable as possible (visually). A number of changes since 1933 are immediately apparent. The *sorajat* have gained considerably, primarily at the expense of the *lamme* but also of the *konme*. There has been a particularly dramatic rise in the rice-owning by the *kebje* and *bucha* lineages. The Blacksmith/Tailor/Tamang/Magar increase is entirely due to land acquisition by Tamangs and Magars; the Blacksmiths and Tailors have less land than in 1933. The most conspicuous shrinking has been in the *lamme* and *konme*. Several of the smaller *sorajat* clans have also decreased, almost to the point of extinction. On the whole, however, the *konme* still retain their economic dominance in the village.

In order to analyse the way in which estates are built up and divided, four types of investigation will be made. Firstly the land position of particular lineages over time shows the way in which kinship and landholding intermingle. A different focus is given if we study particular field areas to see how the patterns of ownership fluctuate over time. A further perspective is given by seeing how the land of particular large landholders in the past has become divided among present households. Finally, we may look at the actual landholding patterns of households: two instances are taken.

A. PARTICULAR LINEAGES OVER TIME

The kebje lineage

One of the most successful groups over the last thirty years have been the *kebje*, represented in the village by two main lineages. The genealogy of what we will call *kebje 1* is shown in Fig. 5.6. According to a written list of ancestors

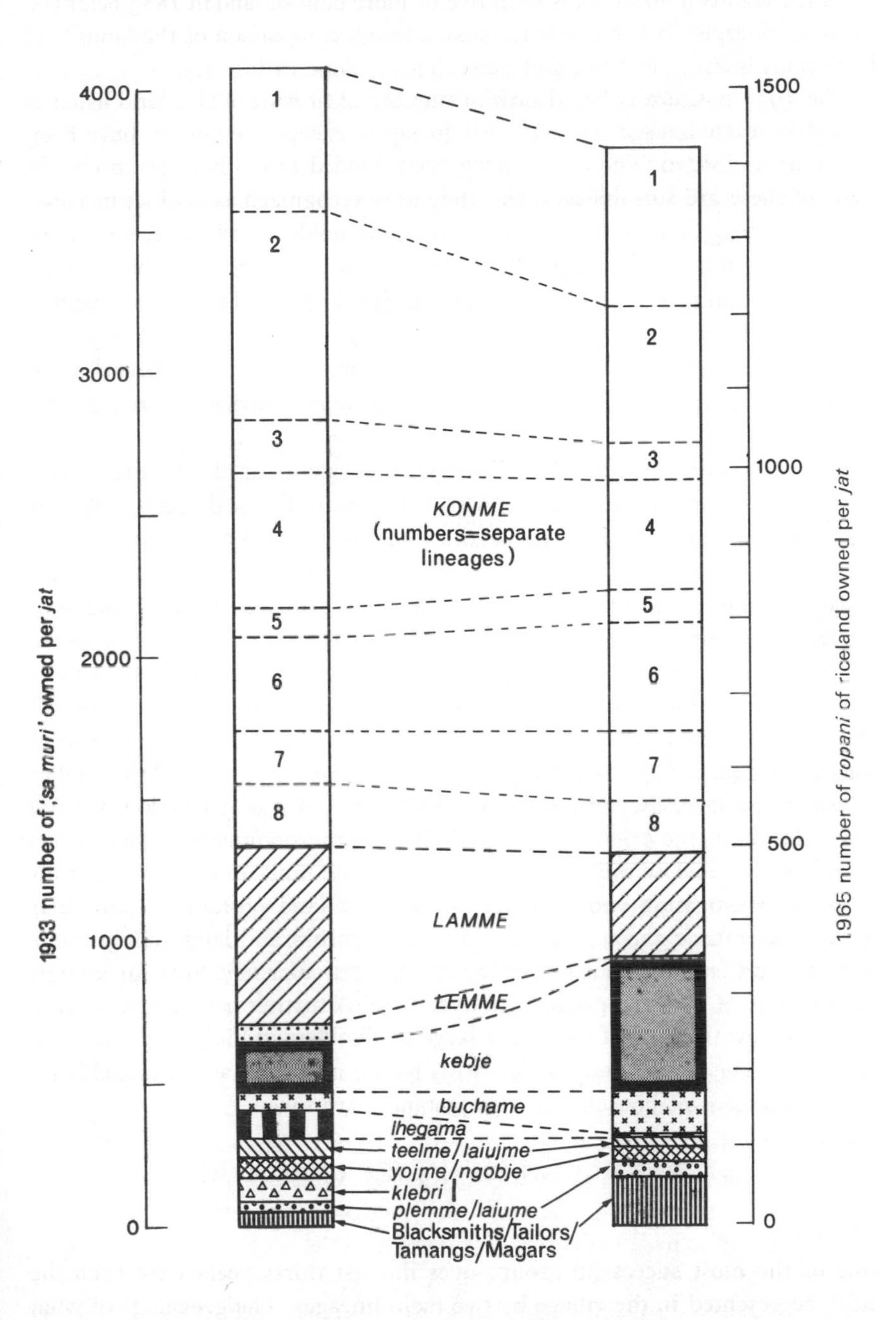

Fig. 5.5. Relative amount of land held by lineages and *jats*, 1933 and 1965.

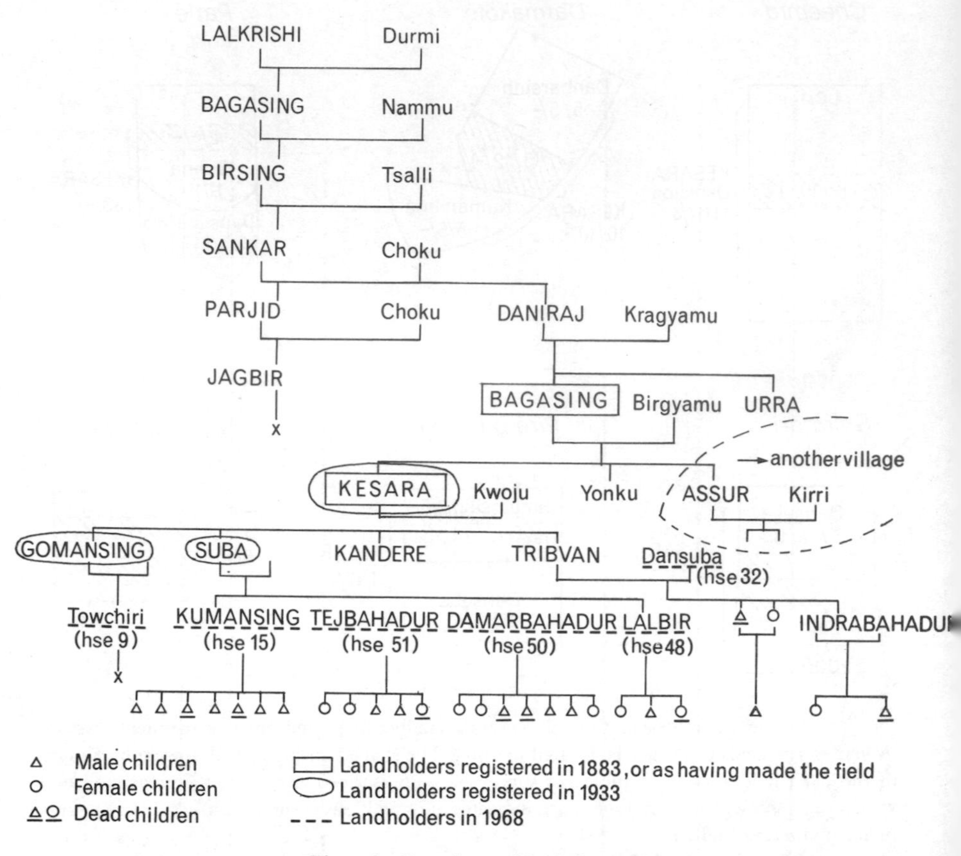

Fig. 5.6. Genealogy of *kebje* lineage I.

which I was shown, the founder came down to the village from Lamjung some eight generations ago, or in about 1730. But by the time of the 1883 land survey there was still only one household of this lineage in the village, represented by Kesara. This suggests that, although we know other branches had gone to other villages, the arrival of this lineage was probably more recent than the written genealogy would suggest. Rice land was comparatively plentiful in 1883 and Kesara was registered as owning seven strips, totalling 21.16.0 *sa muri* of rice land. These strips, and their later subdivisions, are shown in Fig. 5.7. Some fifty years later, in 1933, Kesara was still stated to be the owner of all these lands. By now, however, the land was fully utilized and the area under cultivation had quadrupled (assuming that the accuracy of measurement was equal at the two dates). In addition to this, his sons Suba and Gomansing had acquired, probably by purchase, three further pieces of land, as shown in Fig. 5.7. Thus by 1933 the lineage had accumulated some 133.13.0 *sa muri*

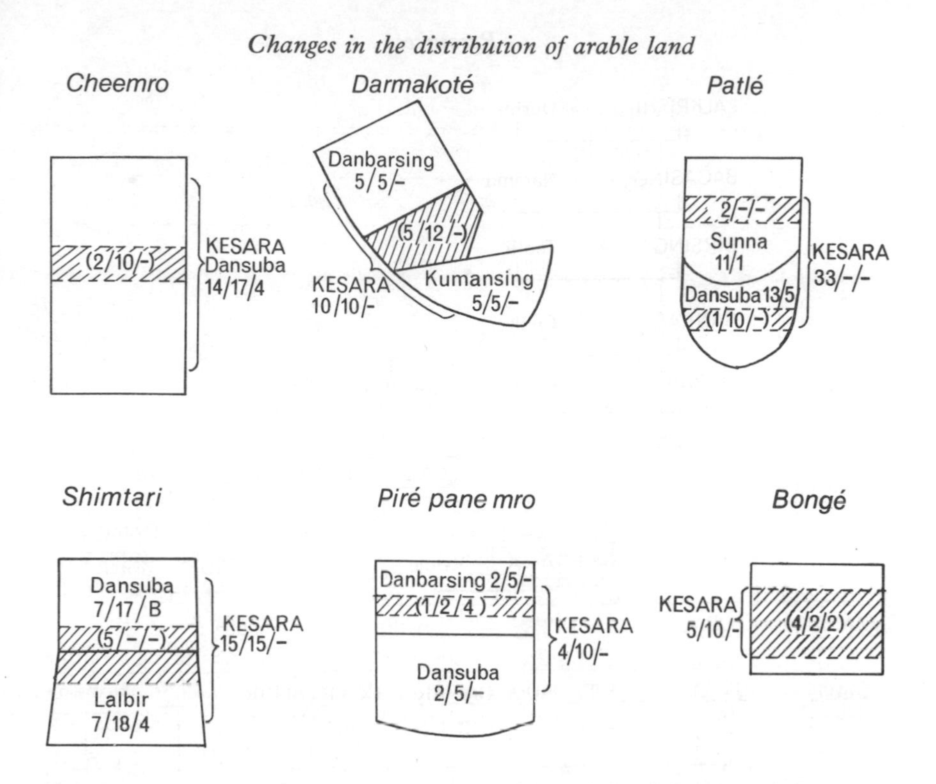

Fig. 5.7. Schematic representation of Kesara's landholdings and their subsequent owners. (*Notes*: *Bongé* fields could not be located in 1969. The shaded strips were all owned by Kesara in the 1883 land survey; in the 1933 survey he was described as owning the areas indicated KESARA. The present owners (1969) are indicated by small letters (thus, Dansuba). The figures indicate *sa muri* of land.)

of rice land in all. This then had to be divided out between the six heirs of Kesara. This was apportioned as shown in table 5.5. It will be seen that house 32 was the most fortunate, presumably because Dansuba's husband, being the same generation as Suba, inherited a large share from Kesara, whereas households 15, 51, 50, 48 had to share out Suba's inheritance. The land had by now been divided into 17 pieces between them. These households then proceeded to build up their landholdings. Allowing for what was earlier calculated to be an under-registration of up to two-thirds in the *tiriges*, the total area owned by this lineage had increased from 133 to 409 *sa muri*, or by a factor of three. This was achieved mainly through the pay from army service. In household 15 there are two sons in the British army and one in the Indian. Household heads in 48 and 50 spent over 18 years each in the British army, and the head of household 51 spent 20 years in the Indian army. Meanwhile household 32, headed by a widow, as well as substantial inherited land and a dead husband's pension, has had two sons in the British army, one of them now dead; the

TABLE 5.5 *Divisions of Kesara's holding between heirs (rice)*

	Inherited		Now has (1965 Survey)	
Household no.	*sa muri*	No. plots	*sa muri*	No. plots
15	9. 3.4	2	*c.* 100	7
48	19.18.4	2	*c.* 63	6
50	16. 9.2	4	*c.* 75	5
51	15.16.2	2	*c.* 60	4
9	16. 5.0	2	*c.* 11[a]	3
32	39. 7.0	5	*c.* 100	9

[a]This exceptional decrease was largely due to the washing away of a large field by the river. House 9 was also not a direct heir, and the heir, a woman, had been adopted into a *carjat* household.

second has just risen to the rank of Lieutenant. Only the woman adopted into household 9 has not prospered; her fields were washed away and she has no relative in the army.

In this conspicuously successful lineage, landholding has, so far, outstripped population increase. In 1883 there was one male landowner with 21 *sa muri* of rice land. In 1933 there were three with 133 *sa muri*, or 44 each. There are now six landholders with some 66 *sa muri* each. But it is difficult to see how this trend can continue into another generation. Probably the present number of living males is a roughly accurate indication of the number of parts into which the land will have to be divided, since deaths of living males will be more or less balanced by sons still to be born. Thus the land will have to be divided into 13 shares, which means that the lineage will have to double its present share of the village rice fields in order even to maintain its present position. This will mean depriving other households of some 400 *sa muri* of rice land. It seems almost certain that this cannot be achieved and that, although the total wealth of this now powerful lineage will increase, there will be less land per household for the twelve or more houses that will replace the present five.

An even more sensational rise to fortune, and one that has caused some envy and bitterness even among the generally tolerant and charitable Gurungs, is that of *kebje* lineage 2. Fig. 5.8 shows the genealogy of this lineage. It will be seen that in 1933 there was no male *kebje* landowner in the village; there was only Saguna, who had inherited 7.16.2. *sa muri* of rice land from her father of another lineage. Saguna's husband came into the village from the neighbouring village of Ianjacote, a landless man. Two of her sons then went into the British army, Indrajid serving for 17 years and reaching the rank of Staff-Sergeant, Bohansing serving for 24 years and reaching the rank of Lieutenant. Bohansing told me that when he left for the army, the family had a tiny house at the far

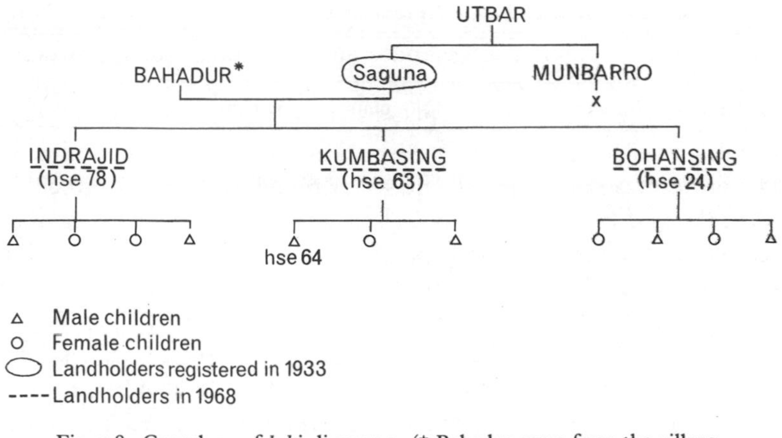

Fig. 5.8. Genealogy of *kebje* lineage 2. (* Bahadur came from the village of Ianjacote.)

end of the village and only 3–4 plots of land, including maize. Bohansing started at 18 Indian rupees per month, and ended up at approximately 1000 Nepali rupees per month. He did not smoke or drink, to save money, and spent approximately 18,500 rupees on land, and another 12,000 on buying the biggest and smartest house in the village to which he retired in 1967. Thus he fulfilled his early vow that he would 'one day be a top man in the village'. The way his lands were accumulated is shown in table 5.6. It will be seen that Bohansing had inherited four small bits of maize land, and one small rice field. The rest he had bought up over the years.

TABLE 5.6 *Bohansing's estate-building*

Name of field	Crop	Amount of crop (*muri*)	How acquired	From whom	When	Price (rs.)
Koshini	Maize[a]	2	Inherited	Father	1955	–
Tayikon	Maize	2	Inherited	Father	1955	–
Puje bari	Maize	2	Inherited	Father	1955	–
Chynoti	Rice	5	Inherited	Father	1955	–
Potecho	Maize	6	Inherited	Mother	1969	–
Mailo bari	Maize	4	Bought	Brikaras	1953	750
Chynoti	Rice	12	Bought	Brikaras	1956	3,500
Uli bari	Maize	6	Bought	Damarsing	1960	1,500
Kergot	Rice	15	Bought	Dilbahadur	1963	10,000
Puje	Maize	6	Bought	Gungabahadur	1968	2,000
Towli	Maize	6	Bought	Parmya	1969	750

[a] 'Maize' = maize and millet, and includes the yield of both.

Meanwhile his elder brother had followed the same course, on a slightly less spectacular scale, a few years before. His life pattern differed mainly in that he decided to build his own house down below the village. Also he was able to make some of his own rice fields from land as yet uncultivated. The middle brother did not leave the village and is consequently by far the poorest. Although one of his daughters has been adopted by Bohansing (because the middle brother remarried and the new wife found the teenager difficult), and he has inherited two small family houses and a little rice land made by his father, he is still very poor and spends most of his time down in the fields herding buffaloes. This is the usual recourse of poorer Gurung men. The total growth of land and households in this lineage can be briefly summarized in table 5.7. Again, although the lineage has been extremely successful, it is difficult to see how it can even maintain its present level of living for it will need to more than double the amount of land it owns in order to satisfy the seven present male heirs. If it succeeds, other lineages will lose land. Among those likely to suffer are the *lamme*, and to them we may now turn.

The lamme 1 lineage

By the time of the 1883 survey, *lamme* lineage 1 had already been present in the village for several generations. The genealogy since then is shown in Fig. 5.9. Karnasing was the registered landowner in 1883 and held eleven plots of rice land, five of which were passed on to his son Dambarsing and six others acquired by other villagers by 1933. Dambarsing appears to have been, at first at least, highly successful in acquiring land. By 1933 he was stated to hold 15 pieces of rice land, as well as the five he inherited. This made him the sixth largest landholder in the village. When we visited Thak some twenty-five years later his large two-storey house had been pulled down and a small one-storey house built nearby. In this small house lived his son Gomansing. According to the land survey of 1965, Gomansing had no rice land left, though according to the land-tax records and map of the village lands drawn for me, he still had one fairly substantial field. His case illustrates the way in which a family may in one generation drop from the wealthiest to the poorest rank, even without partition among sons (Gomansing was an

TABLE 5.7 *Amount of land and number of households,* kebje 2

Date	Amount of land (*sa muri*) (rice)	No. of landholders	Land per landholder
1933	7.15.4	1	7.15.4
1965	66. 0.0	3	22. 0.0

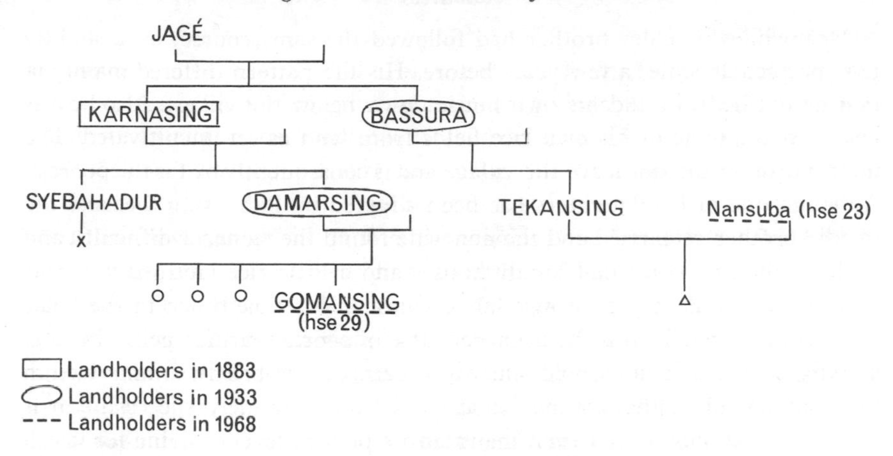

Fig. 5.9. Genealogy of *lamme* lineage 1.

only son), even in a supposedly stable agrarian society such as the Gurungs.

Unfortunately, I do not know how early the family lands began to be dispersed, though, as we have seen, even at Karnasing's generation a considerable amount of land went to people outside the family. Danbarsing himself sold off eight plots of land, six of them in the neighbouring *panchayat* of Moja. Nevertheless, there can be little doubt that the bulk of such sales have occurred during the last twenty years, and have been the result of Gomansing's actions. I was told that he was forced to sell because he had spent a number of unsuccessful years as a government contractor, helping with the construction of bridges, etc., in Pokhara. His failures had forced him to sell off his land and that of his wife. Now he has retired to the village, where he maintains a façade of power and importance, playing on the prestige which is still, to a certain extent, accorded to him by other villagers in recognition of his past eminence. But his son, only a Rifleman in the Indian army, has no chance of reviving the family fortune and will probably be regarded as among the lowest rank of Gurungs. Unfortunately, it was impossible to discover to whom he had sold all his land. In the ten cases where we can be certain, two pieces had gone to Bohansing (see above), and another to a group of Tamangs who have also been successfully acquiring land. Most of the rest has gone to *konme* lineage 1, and indeed Bohansing bought his land from a member of this lineage. This *konme* lineage had been particularly successful during the period 1933–65, largely because of the activity of one man. A brief study of this man provides a useful indication of the possibility of acquiring large fortunes even without the help of an army career.

Ranbahadur Gurung

The simplified genealogy of the *konme* to which Ranbahadur belonged is shown in Fig. 5.10. According to his surviving wife, Ranbahadur died in 1944, aged 44. Thus he was born at about the turn of the century. By the time of the 1933 land survey he was still a young man of about 33, yet even by that date he was the ninth richest landowner, with 152 *sa muri* of land. Nor had this land been inherited from his father Danbar. Study of the previous owners of his registered lands shows that only one plot had come from his grandfather Motilal, and none from Danbar. The rest had come from various *carjat* and *sorajat* families, including the *poju's* family, Tamangs, *lamme* and others. One informant estimated that his parents had contributed property worth 3000 rs., while, by his death, he was worth well over 100,000 rs. Another informant stated that though Ranbahadur's father was wealthy, before inheriting anything from him, Ranbahadur had built up a considerable estate. Unfortunately there is no way of knowing the size of the final estate since there is no further systematic survey for the eleven years after 1933. A rough estimate may be attempted by analysing the property owned by his heir in 1965. Of the total 172 *sa muri* owned in 1965 (inherited from Ranbahadur), only 94 *sa muri* had already been acquired by Ranbahadur by 1933. If this proportion bears any relation to his total acquisitions, he must have had considerably more than 250 *sa muri* of rice land by his death. This would have made him, by his death, the richest single landowner (for his rival Potamsing's land had been divided up by that time).

His wealth at his premature death (he was killed in his own tiger trap) was legendary. Though we may be sceptical of excessive claims, he certainly did own four houses (which still remain), and probably 30–40 buffaloes, about 70 cows, and about 100 goats. Yet he built up this wealth within the village, for there is no evidence that he ever went away to the army. Villagers said

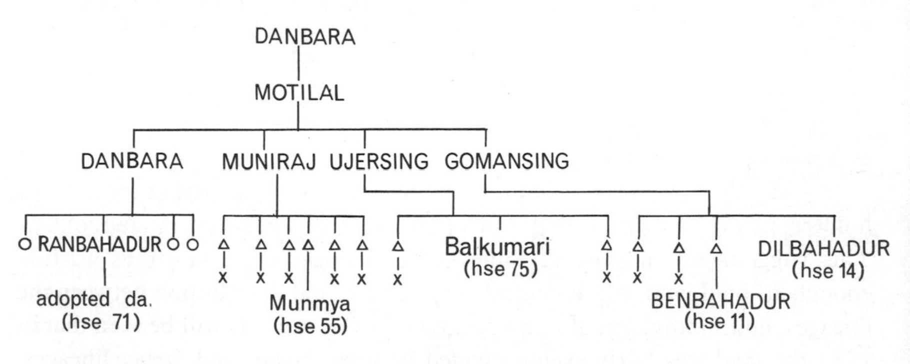

Fig. 5.10. Genealogy of *konme* lineage 1.

that with the money he acquired with his wife, he lent money to other villagers at interest. By the time of his death he was said to have 70,000 rs. out in such loans (or 'boons'); much of this could not be reclaimed. Although he married three times he had no children and since his death his wealth has melted away, though his adopted daughter still had 50 *ropanis* of rice land according to the land survey of 1965 and had married an extremely rich Gurung in another village. I was told that there still is one man in Siklis and one in Khilang, who, in 1969, are of the same stature as Ranbahadur. But in Thak, as we have seen, there is now more equality, at least among the Gurungs. Although Ranbahadur was generally spoken of with admiration by *konme* informants, I encountered subdued bitterness amongst some of the *sorajat* families who implied that he had been high-handed and had grabbed their land. His nephew, the ageing and almost blind Dilbahadur, who has continued Ranbahadur's money-lending tactics, is almost universally disliked and there have even been attempts to expel him from the village. Whether feeling ran so high in Ranbahadur's day it is impossible to say.

B. PARTICULAR FIELD AREAS OVER TIME

The land records make it possible to analyse the way in which particular fields have become colonized and subdivided. Two examples will be studied here; the first in the very heart of the best rice-growing area where the ground is flat and easily watered, another in the steep area to the north of the village where there is only medium-to-poor water and the hillsides are steeper.

Gedi/keyrbort field

In 1883 some 121 *s.m.* (*sa muri*) of this field were in use. By 1933 some 200 *s.m.* were used for rice. Thus, in the central and richest belt of rice land, some 6/10 of the land was already in use in 1883. Some of the smaller strips were already fully exploited in 1883: thus a strip given as 10 *s.m.* in 1883 was only 11 *s.m.* in 1933, another given as 5 *s.m.* was $5\frac{1}{2}$ *s.m.* some fifty years later. But most of the larger pieces were clearly not fully in use in 1883; thus a piece given as 20 *s.m.* in 1883 was reckoned to be 41 *s.m.* in 1933 and another of 20 *s.m.* as 35 *s.m.* at the later date. Taken as a whole, however, comparison of the two surveys suggests that the 1883 measurements were not much less accurate than those of 1933.

In 1883 the land was divided into nine plots, held by a total of seven landholders; in 1969 it was divided into 14 plots, divided between 11 landholders. This suggests an increase of some 50 % amongst those Gurungs wealthy enough to hold land in this central strip. The actual distribution between the lineages, and subdivision of strips is shown in Fig. 5.11. It will be seen that in 1883 the land was fairly evenly divided between *konme* and *lamme* lineages.

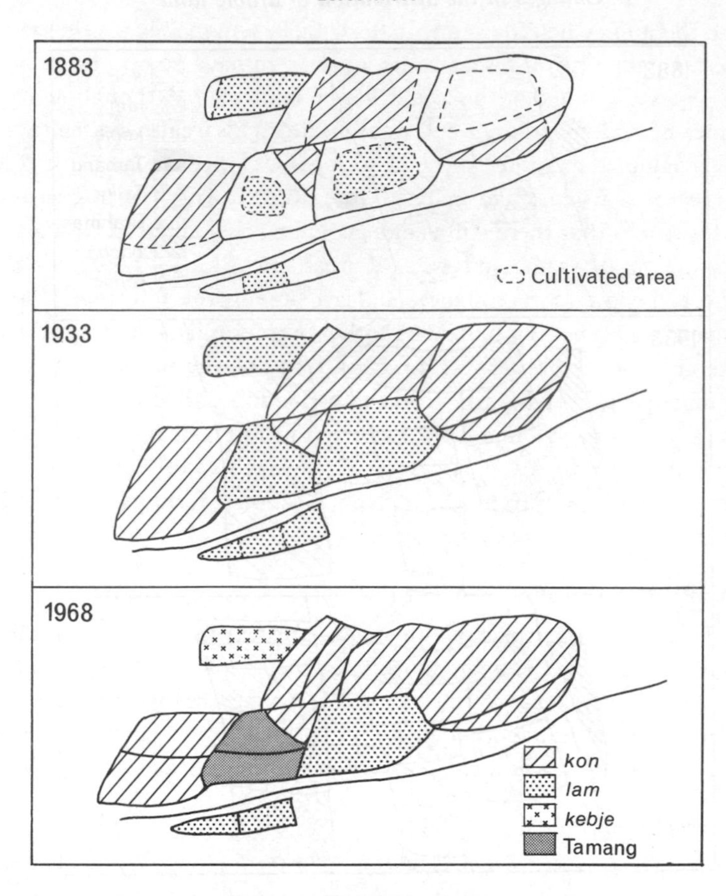

Fig. 5.11. *Gedi* field over time.

It remained in the same lineages some fifty years later, and the number of landholders was the same. The 50 % increase in landholders has thus occurred in the last twenty-five years. Part of this increase in number of landholders reflects the success of two groups in the village, the *kebje* and the Tamangs.

Patlé field

Here the situation differed in a number of ways. To begin with, as Fig. 5.12 illustrates, only a very small part of the field had been in use in 1883. In all, some 32 *s.m.* were under rice at that date. These same holdings measured 262 *s.m.* some fifty years later. This is some indication of the amount of terrace-making that was going on over this period, especially in lower quality rice lands. Completely new plots were also started, and this added a further 48 *s.m.* of rice land by 1933. Another difference, when compared to *Gedi*, was that even in 1883 other lineages than the *konme* and *lamme* were present.

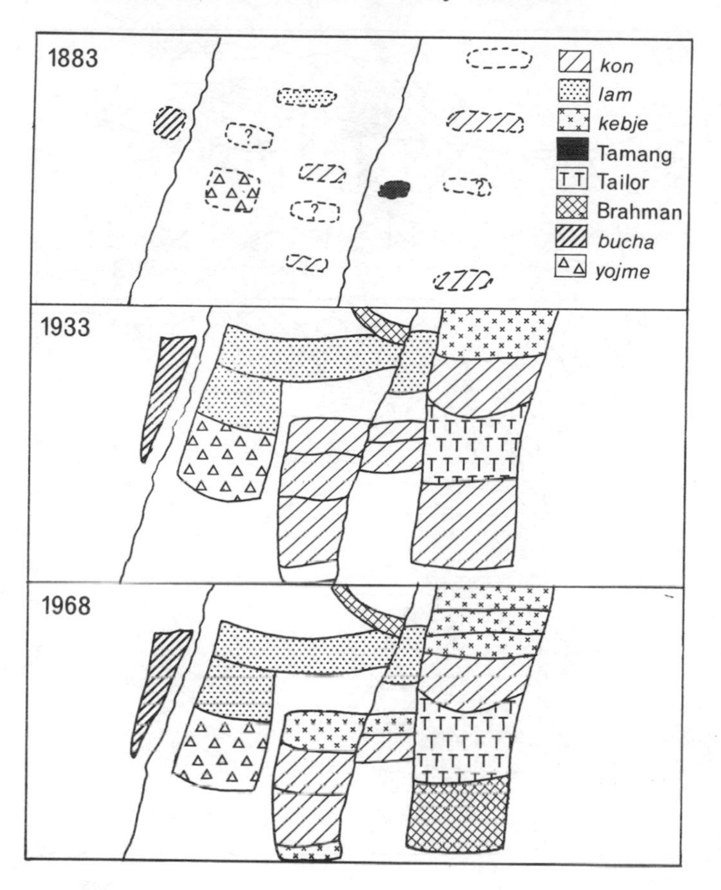

Fig. 5.12. *Patlé* field over time.

The ancestors of the *poju*, the *yojme*, *kebje* and Tamangs all had land. By 1933 the position was substantially the same, with the Tamangs gone, but there was a small Brahmin landholding and a larger Tailor plot. But the *konme* were, even at that date and in this area, dominant. By 1968 their dominance had been challenged by the *kebje* and the Brahmins had increased their holdings. There had not, however, been a significant increase in the number of landowners in this area, only one holding had been subdivided (into three parts) in the interval.

C. THE PRESENT DISTRIBUTION OF FORMER LARGE ESTATES

The distribution of lineage lands as a whole throughout the village is shown in Fig. 5.13. This shows the present distribution, which still reflects a considerable amount of grouping of lineage lands, despite the effects of inheritance and sale during the last forty years. This grouping is particularly obvious in

Fig. 5.13. Distribution of landholdings by lineages.

the case of the largest *konme* lineage who first claimed rice land in certain parts of the village and subsequently developed these. The process by which such early claims were distributed may most easily be illustrated if we follow the history of the land owned by three former landowners.

Parsing, ancester of house 70B (konme 2 lineage)

Parsing was one of the biggest rice landowners in 1883, listed as having eleven holdings, with a total area of approximately 170 *s.m.*[8] Eight of these eleven plots went to his direct descendants. This flow of property and the location (see Fig. 5.14) suggests that the very best land, just below pieces 28–30, had already been occupied. Parsing either came from a lineage which arrived slightly later than another *konme* lineage, or else he decided to develop virgin land. By the time of the 1933 survey his land had been divided between eight different landholders, only one of whom had more than two pieces. Consequently the pattern we see in the land map of 1968 is a very fragmented version of the 1883 position.

Motilal, ancestor of houses 11, 14 (konme lineage 1)

I was frequently told that the oldest house in the main part of the village was house 11, and that this and house 14 were the original settlement when the Gurungs first came down to the present village site. It is therefore of interest to look more closely at one of the richest ancestors of these two households, Motilal. In 1883 he was registered as owning 12 pieces of land, which even at that date measured some 104 *s.m.* (plus one small piece, area unspecified). The location and inheritance of this land is shown in Fig. 5.15. All but one piece went to direct descendants. It was divided, not exactly equally, between four sons. All the original rice land had been located in two areas. Ten pieces were down near the Modi river, undoubtedly the first area in the village to be planted with wet rice, and two pieces were up in the same area as Parsing's (mentioned above). This latter area was probably developed a little later. By 1933, however, this concentration had been split up between six landholders.

Potiram, ancestor of the lamme

From the placing of their houses in the village it is clear that the *lamme* arrived in the village after the main *konme* lineages had established themselves. They chose to build what is now termed '*lamme* village' (*lamme nasa*) on a steeper slope above the main village street. There are two main branches of this clan in the village. The first we have already discussed when analysing the

Fig. 5.14. Genealogy and map showing inheritance of Parsing's rice land. (Numbers = plot numbers in the land records; underlining = those dead.)

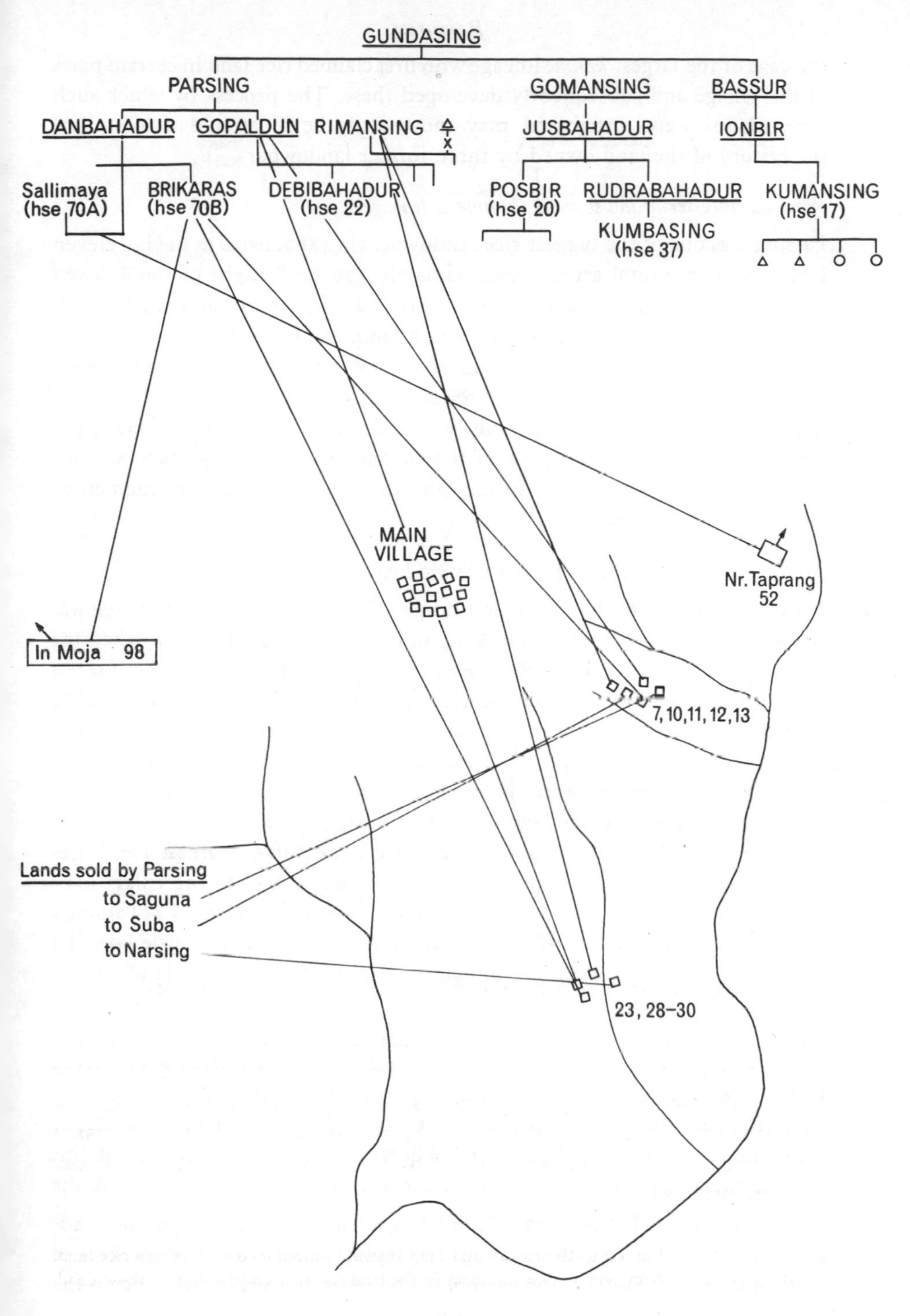

GUNDASING
PARSING
GOMANSING
BASSUR
DANBAHADUR
GOPALDUN
RIMANSING
JUSBAHADUR
IONBIR
Sallimaya (hse 70A)
BRIKARAS (hse 70B)
DEBIBAHADUR (hse 22)
POSBIR (hse 20)
RUDRABAHADUR
KUMANSING (hse 17)
KUMBASING (hse 37)
MAIN VILLAGE
Nr. Taprang 52
In Moja 98
7, 10, 11, 12, 13
Lands sold by Parsing
to Saguna
to Suba
to Narsing
23, 28–30

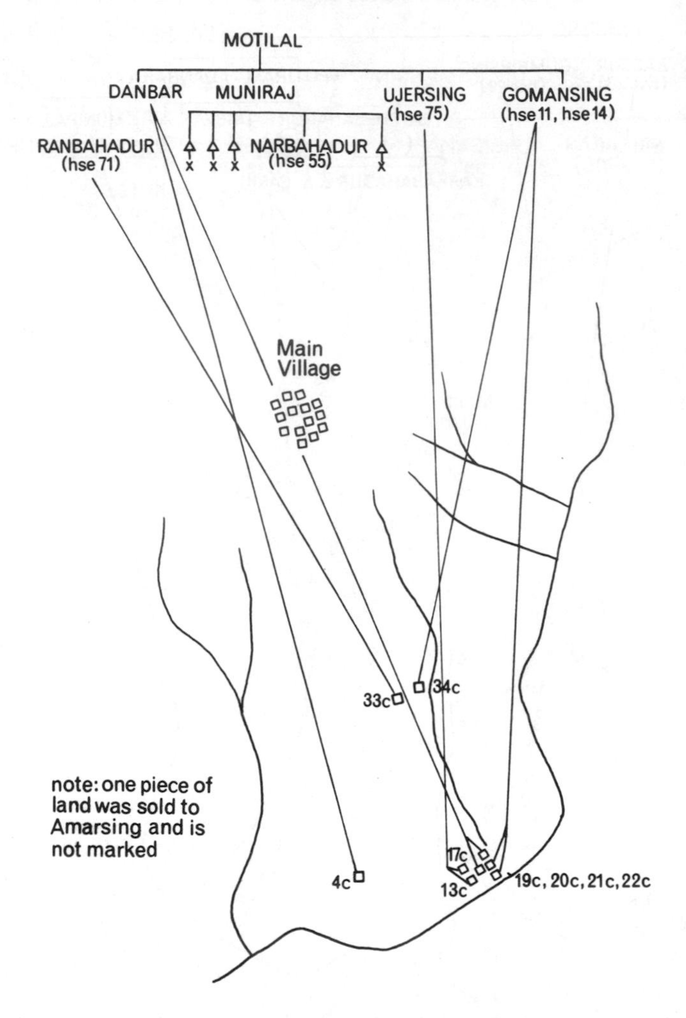

Fig. 5.15. Genealogy and map showing inheritance of Motilal's rice land.

declining fortunes of Karnasing and Gomansing. It is not clear in what way *lamme* 2, represented by Potiram in the 1883 survey, is related to the other branch. He may be a junior relative, or the oft-repeated (but unspecified) connection may be a later fabrication. At any rate, we may look at Potiram's landholdings in 1883 (Fig. 5.16) to see how they compare with the two *konme* cases studied above.

To begin with, Potiram was clearly less wealthy than the big *konme* landholders; he only had half the number of plots, and a third of the area of cultivated rice of Motilal, for example. The second obvious difference is the

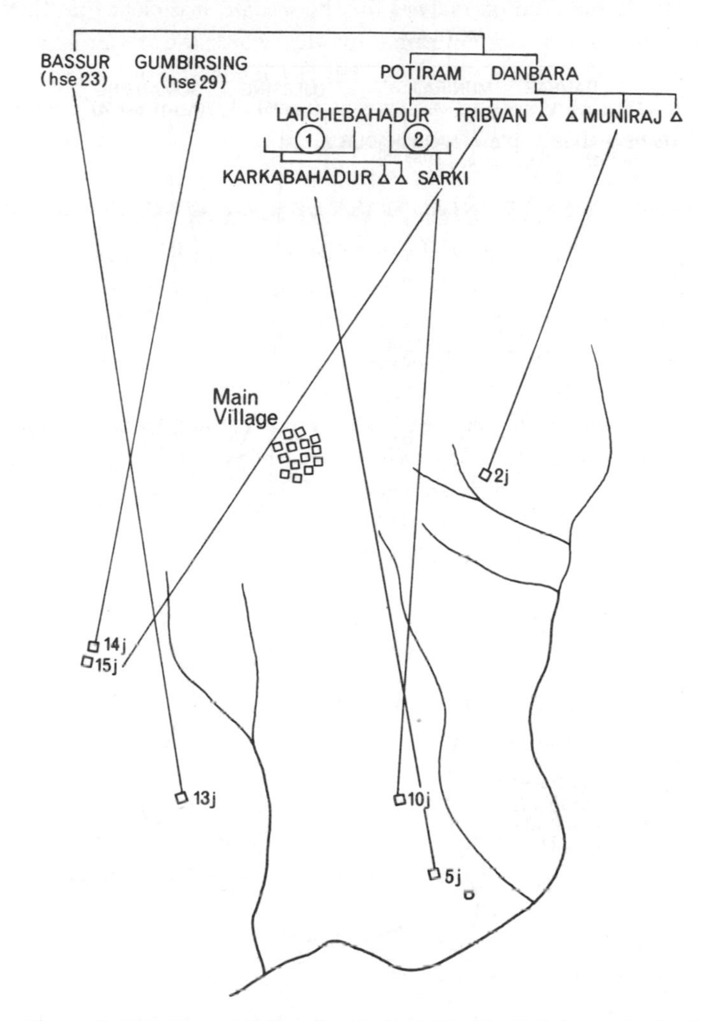

Fig. 5.16. Genealogy and map showing inheritance of Potiram's rice land.

distribution. Potiram's plots were spread all over the village rice fields, even in 1883. In only one field are there two plots. Either there had already been much subdivision or, as seems much more likely, Potiram or his father, having arrived after much of the land had been earmarked by the *konme*, obtained rice land on the margins of their territory. When the land came to be split up by inheritance, the plots were divided between six *lamme* landowners some fifty years later, four of them his direct descendants. Although the very few land-holdings held by the *sorajat* in 1883, and the difficulty of tracing the actual lineage of many of the smaller landholders in 1883, makes it impractical to carry out the same type of analysis for the *sorajat*, it is clear that they would show the same tendency as Potiram – in other words the scattering of holdings in single plots on the margins of the richer rice lands. It is only in the last thirty years that, as we have seen in the case of *Gedi* field, non-*carjat* Gurungs have managed to buy themselves into the best rice lands.

D. PRESENT LANDOWNING PATTERN OF TWO HOUSEHOLDS

The outcome of the splitting and sub-splitting may be illustrated by two of the households whose budgets we will examine in some detail in later chapters. The distribution of the maize and rice land of household 3B is shown in Fig. 5.17. It will be seen that the three plots of rice land are concentrated while the maize lands are spread out. The same is basically true of the larger landholding of household 17 (see Fig. 5.18). This reminds us that, though there has been much sub division of landholdings, many of the present landholders still have their rice land fairly concentrated since they now have smaller hold-

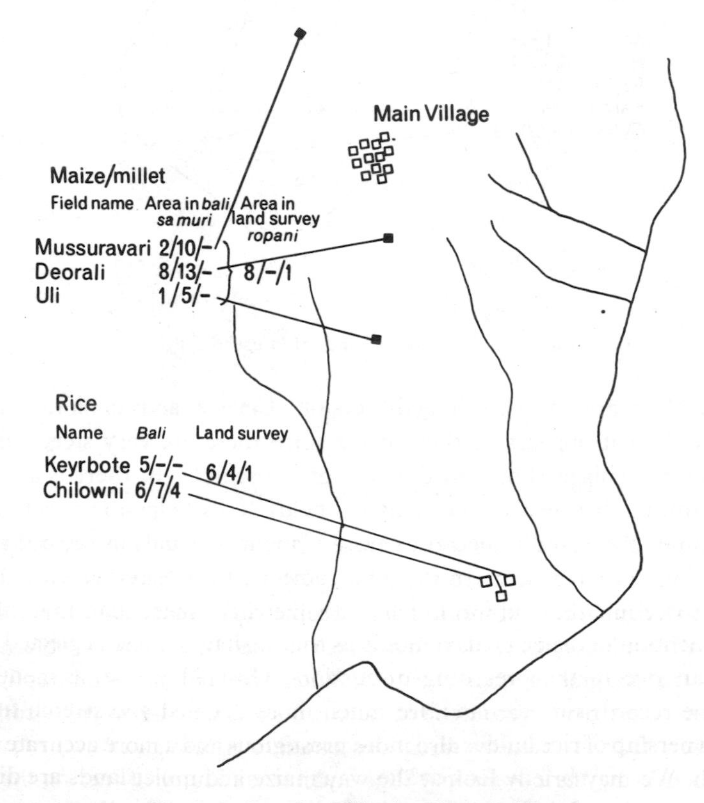

Fig. 5.17. Location of lands of household 3B.

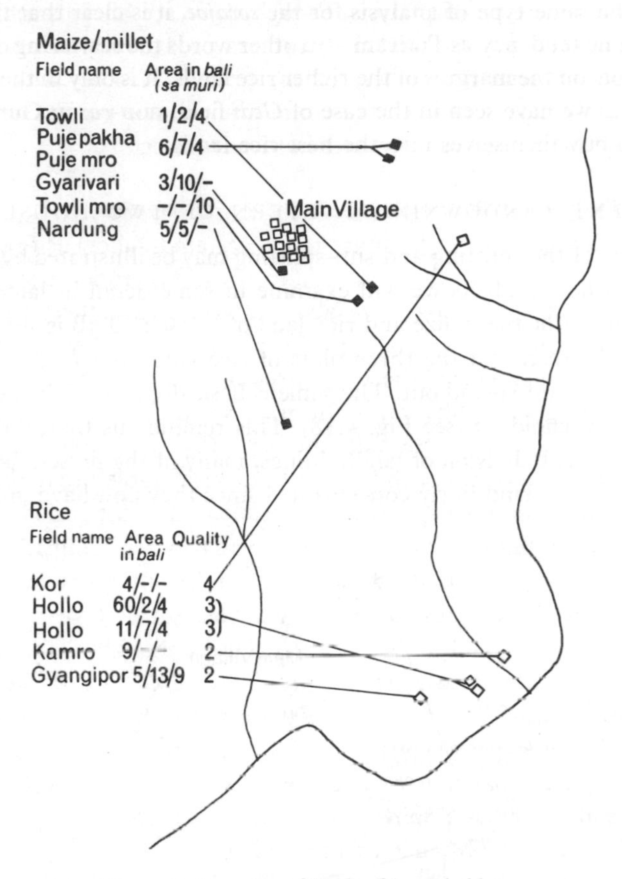

Fig. 5.18. Location of lands of household 17.

ings than their grandfathers. The dispersion of maize lands is more dramatic in reality than it appears in these maps since there are very steep hillsides just below the village. Thus, in the case of household 3B, there is a 1000-ft drop in altitude between *Deorali* and *Uli* fields. This helps to spread out the cultivation of maize and millet, thus easing labour demands in the one period of the year when labour is short. The same is, to a lesser extent, true of rice; thus rice in *Gedi* field would mature somewhat earlier than that in *Patlé*.

This mention of maize fields reminds us that we have almost neglected crops other than rice in the preceding discussion. This is because, as mentioned above, the records for rice land are much more detailed and stretch further back. Ownership of rice land is also more prestigious and a more accurate index of wealth. We may briefly look at the way maize and millet lands are divided at present to round off this account. The examples show how intermixed ownership is in these maize lands, though there are obvious indications, as in the case of *Uli* field, that land that once belonged to one household has been divided amongst several members of the lineage. Another way to view the distribution of maize and rice lands is to examine the process whereby both types of land have been brought into cultivation since 1933.

Extension of the area under cultivation; rice and maize

The figures for rice land in 1883 are too uncertain to allow us to compare the area under cultivation at that date and in 1933. But from the study of particular fields, such as *Gedi* and *Patlé* above, it is clear that there had been very considerable expansion, especially in the poorer areas. It would not seem an exaggeration to suggest that there had been more than a doubling of the area cultivated during those fifty years. In other words less than half the present rice lands in the village were cultivated in 1883. Since rice has never been sold in significant quantities, this suggests a considerable rise in the rice needs and labour force in the village. It is impossible to date the period of maximum rice-field making, but it seems likely that it was between about 1880 and 1925. One informant told me that all the good land, collectively known as *byasi* (Nep. = *bisi*, *besi*), was in use before he was born some 56 years ago, in other words by the time of the First World War. But he thought that a considerable amount of the poorer land to the north of the village was terraced after the War. By the time of the 1933 survey there was only a little good rice land uncultivated, of this he was the named owner. Since 1950 there has been no terracing of good rice land, except a little some distance from the village towards Taprang (by Brahmins and Chetris). His opinions on the situation since 1933 are given substance by the land records.

Since 1934 only 18 pieces of rice land have been recorded as being brought into cultivation. All of these pieces are classified as lowest grade land, and all except one piece are very small, one *ropani* or under. The one exception occurred in 1937 when a Brahmin opened up 50 *s.m.* of rice land some distance away from the village. Apart from this (which may be partly maize land), only 38 *s.m.* of rice land (approx. 9½ *ropanis*) has been recorded as being brought into cultivation during the 35 years before 1968. Of the small quantity newly cultivated, some 23 *s.m.* were opened up in the years 1934–40; since 1940 less than 4 *ropanis* are recorded as being newly used. Clearly the land records have missed some lands, the one important instance being a large field called Kamgaon which was terraced in the 1940s and now contains some 70 *s.m.* of fairly good rice land. In the 1933 survey it is described as *pakha* or an unused slope. But including this, and allowing another 30 *s.m.* for other unregistered land, we still have only approximately 140 *s.m.* (35 *rops*) brought into use since 1933. Even if we assume that the totals are only approximately one-third of the real area of the land, this represents only one-fifteenth of the total area under rice in 1965.

Fig. 5.19 showing the location of new terracing, indicates that the process since 1933 has been the last marginal filling in of potential rice-growing areas. Almost all the pieces are on the margins between already cultivated lands and unsuitable land. Even the pieces in the centre of Fig. 5.19 (49a, 53a) are on poor land bordering steep cliffs. No rice land was being brought into cultivation in the main part of Thak (though a little by Brahmins towards Taprang). It was clear to any observer that cultivation had now almost pushed to the extreme limits, and from the point of view of soil conservation possibly beyond safe limits.

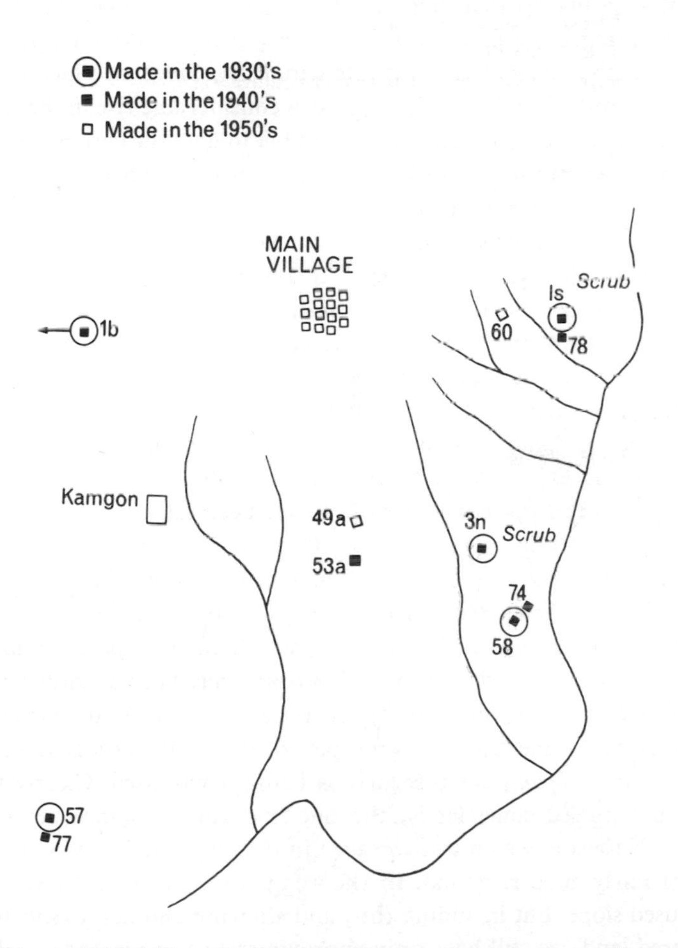

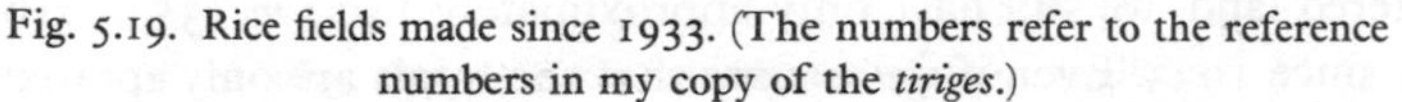
Fig. 5.19. Rice fields made since 1933. (The numbers refer to the reference numbers in my copy of the *tiriges*.)

Only two significant areas remain to be opened up. These are shown in Fig. 5.20. The 1933 land survey included *pakha* or uncultivated slopes. These were almost all stated to be owned by groups of *carjat* Gurungs, usually four or six of them. As can be seen in Fig. 5.20, only four areas lay below the rice-growing line. Of these *Kamgaon* has been cultivated, and *Shyallotti* is so rocky and the soil so bad that little more can be done with it. Steepness, lack of water, and rock outcrops have also helped to preserve *Tossim* and *Dorsiro pakha*, but they will probably be cultivated one day, perhaps when their present owner, householder 70B, divides out his estate. If we include *Shyallotti* and every other possible cultivable area on this map, another 50–100 *ropanis*

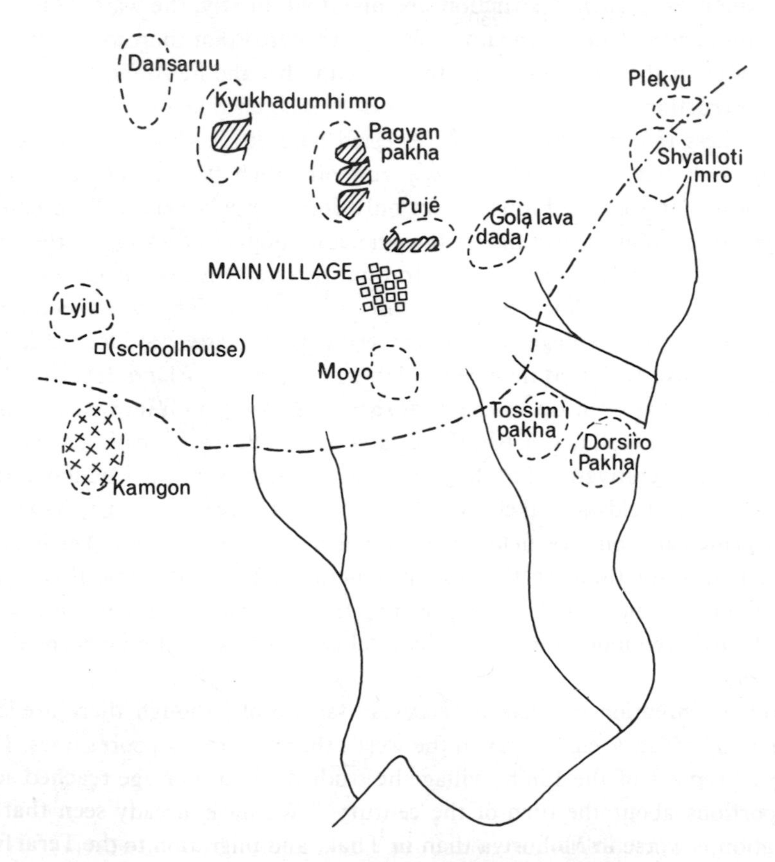

Fig. 5.20. Jointly registered unused slopes 1969.

of poor quality rice land might be squeezed from the hillsides. For practical purposes, therefore, we may say that the period of rapid expansion of rice land really ended in the 1920s; since then only a little poor quality land has been available. Even the small amount of poor land coming into cultivation since the 1930s has probably not balanced the effect of deterioration of land. Some notable fields, particularly *Lammaket*, have been swept away by the river, other fields suffer periodic landslides – for example *Balmorde* which had to be abandoned for ten years, and even then could not be fully repaired.

More difficult to estimate is longer-term deterioration resulting from leaching of the soil by rain, and constant re-use of land with little application of natural or artificial fertilizer. Informants admitted that the quality of land had deteriorated over the years, but unfortunately we have no quantitative evidence on this. The rice fields are also seriously, though indirectly, affected by the destruction over the last hundred years of the forest above Thak. The consequences of such destruction are manifold. Firstly, the water supply has been influenced. One informant in Mohoriya stated that there was now much less water in the monsoons than there used to be, and he connected this with the destruction of forest cover. Such a link could take one or both of two forms. Less rain may have fallen (forested land attracts more moisture than scrub) and that which did fall may run off much faster, not being stored temporarily in roots and foliage. Not only does a speedier run off increase the danger of erosion, it also makes the available supplies of water for the paddy field more erratic and briefer in duration. But water is not the only valuable resource that flows down from the hills above Thak. There is also manure. The overgrazing of village pastures and growing shortage of fodder reduces the number of livestock that may be available per acre of rice land. It is clear from the records that even up to the 1930s, parts of the land intermixed with the rice fields were used to graze buffaloes and cows. The bringing of this marginal land into rice cultivation has deprived the other strips of the benefit of animal manure. Rice fields are likely to suffer less than maize from this change, for it is principally on rice fields that animal manure is now put. Yet is is one more reason for thinking that rice production was higher some thirty years ago than it is now, and for suggesting that in another thirty years, when people are even more numerous, the total cereals produced may decrease still further.

Yet the situation in Thak is relatively favourable; though there are some richer hill villages (e.g. Atigar to the west), there are many poorer ones. Thus Caplan reports of the Limbu village he studied, 'land shortage reached acute proportions about the turn of the century'.[9] We have already seen that the situation is worse in Mohoriya than in Thak, and migration to the Terai from Siklis and other Gurung villages suggests that there, also, conditions are deteriorating. A change from abundance to scarcity seems to have occurred in the Modi valley, where Mohoriya is situated, even more swiftly than in Thak and neighbouring villages. Pignède stated that 'thirty or forty years ago a large number of the village fields in the Modi valley had not been distributed'.[10] But by the time of his visit to Mohoriya there was clearly little unused, but potentially cultivable, land still available. I was told that in the eleven years since Pignède's visit approximately 12 *ropani* of rice land had been brought into cultivation. Approximately half of this had been opened up by one household; the rest consisted of small fields of under one *ropani* each. I was told that there was possibly another 5 *ropani* or so of land that could be converted into rice fields. The migration of 13 households to Chitawan had temporarily relieved the pressure, but there is little prospect of expansion in the future.

The utilization of maize land

It has been assumed in the above discussion that only when tax began to be paid was rice land brought into cultivation. This seems a reasonable assumption in the case of rice, but it is not so certain when we discuss maize/millet land. It is quite possible that some of the land which is recorded as first being subject to taxation in the period after 1933 was already being partly cultivated, probably by shifting methods of slash-and-burn. But it was probably not under permanent cultivation and it is unlikely that manure was applied systematically. In the following discussion, therefore, it will be assumed that most of this recently taxed land *does* represent a real addition to the stock of maize land. In a number of cases, for instance in *Proree* field, it was possible to confirm the accuracy of land records by questioning and observation.

Whereas, as we have seen, there was very little rice land left to be developed by 1933, this does not seem to have been the case with maize. There are approximately 210 plots of maize land shown on the map of village landholdings (Fig. 5.4) in 1968. Yet between 1933 and 1960 some 110 maize plots are registered as paying tax for the first time. A few of these plots are outside the area of the map, but these are probably compensated for by the addition of a few plots since 1960 (after which date no more maize land is registered). Thus it seems that only approximately half the total number of maize plots were regularly cultivated by 1933. This may represent up to a doubling of the area under maize in the last forty years. Though recent plots are probably smaller and on worse land, some of the earlier plots have undoubtedly been extended in size, though such extension does not get noticed in tax records. It is not likely that total yield has doubled, however, for rich harvests must have been obtained from the earlier slash-and-burn techniques, and there was more abundant manure.

It is likely that the population of Thak found in the 1930s that its supply of rice land was failing to keep pace with numerical growth, and it was from then on that the cultivation of maize was pushed up the hillsides. A fairly close dating of this increase in maize cultivation can be made on the basis of the land records. In 1934–9, some ten pieces were registered to pay tax; 1940–9, three pieces; 1950–9, 98 pieces. Thus in the 1930s the demand was still fairly gradual; it would have taken 100 years to open up all the maize fields at this rate. Then, perhaps because of the War which reduced the labour force and the demand for food, hardly any maize land was opened up. The lull continued until 1949, as it seems to have done with rice land also. Then the rate picked up in 1950–5, when 15 pieces were registered. But it was during the years 1955–8 that there was a sudden burst of activity and some 82 pieces of maize

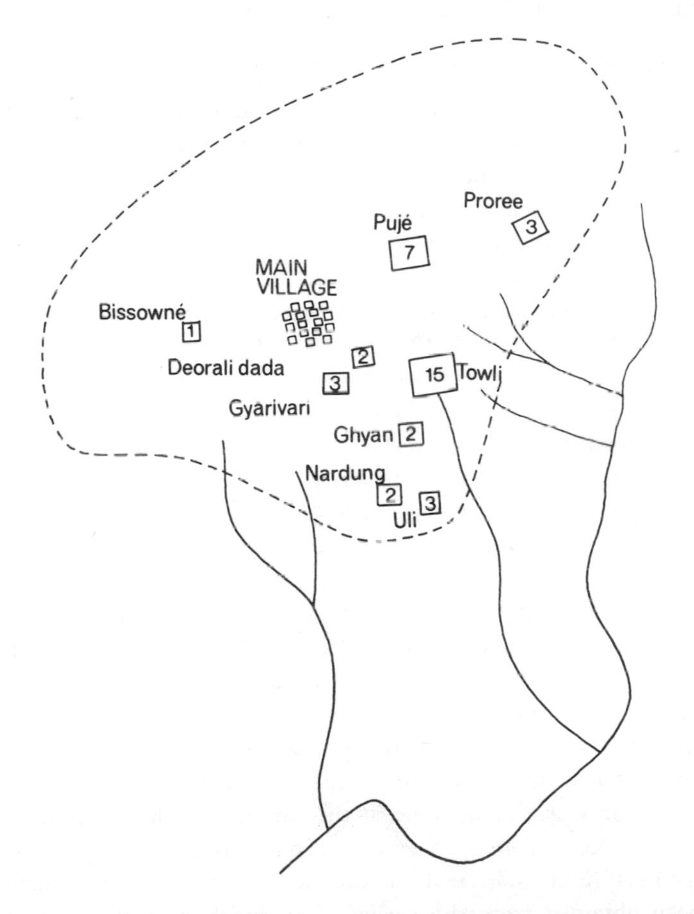

Fig. 5.21. Maize holdings registered since 1934. (*Note*: The numbers indicate the number of plots registered as opened up in a certain field. The broken line indicates the area of maize/millet growing.)

land were registered. In the peak year, 1958, some 28 pieces were registered, and only one less in 1956. It appears that this absorbed almost all the available maize land, for in 1959 there was only one piece registered. It is evident from inspection of the village fields, and comparison with known registrations (as

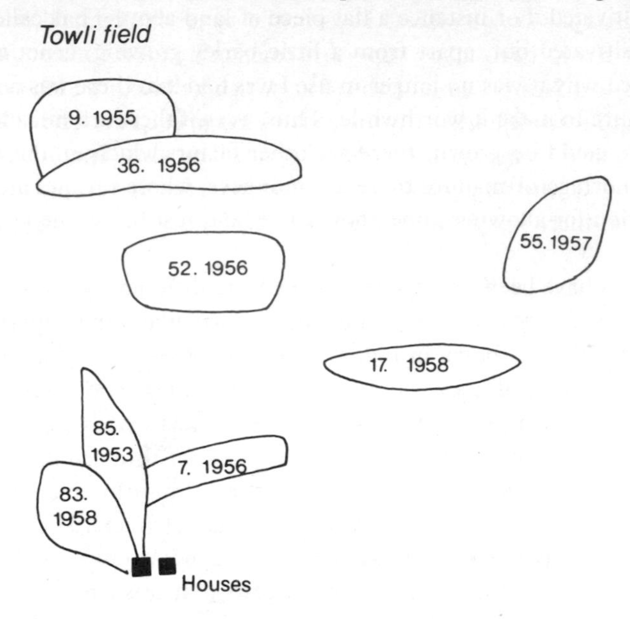

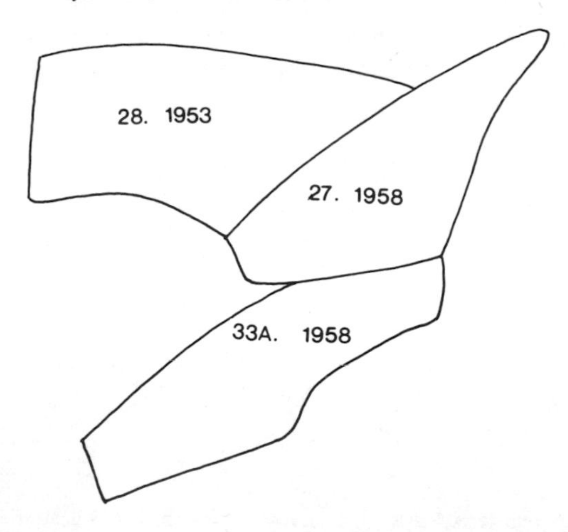

Fig. 5.22. Distribution of new maize holdings in two fields. (The figures in each plot indicate the household number of the registered owner and the date of registration.)

shown in Fig. 5.21), that hardly any maize land has been opened up in the 1960s. During our fifteen months in the village only a couple of small, rocky, and steep patches were being cleared. It would appear that the limits of maize cultivation have been reached. There are still one or two areas of land which could be cultivated. For instance a flat piece of land above Thak called *Garedi* was once cultivated but, apart from a little barley growing, is not now used. When I asked why it was no longer in use I was told that there was not enough animal manure to make it worthwhile. Thus, even if there are still a few slopes where maize could be grown, there are other factors which inhibit such use; as well as shortage of manure there are monkeys, whose ravages are given as an explanation for allowing some poor maize land just below the village to go out of use.

Maize plots have been opened up in over forty different parts of the village lands. Some of the areas nearer to the village, particularly the important fields of *Towli* and *Puje*, are shown in Fig. 5.21. It will be seen that there was still a considerable amount of maize land very near the village and unused in 1933. This was very different from the rice situation. Unfortunately it is not possible to place all the new maize holdings, but an attempt to do so in two fields is shown in Fig. 5.22. One of the most interesting things to emerge from this map occurs in the case of *Puje* field. The common characteristic of the three new landholdings is not kinship but neighbourhood; houses 27, 28 33A are near to each other in the village. This suggests that this land was once communally worked and owned by a group from these three households. When terraced it was divided between them. The same may be true of *Gyarivari*.

There are no land records dealing with arable lands in the forest where potatoes and other root crops are grown. Therefore the degree to which such cultivation has expanded cannot be studied in the same way as rice and maize fields.

6

Capital assets excluding land and forest

AGRICULTURAL CAPITAL

Apart from land, agricultural capital principally consists of livestock, tools and seed/unconsumed crops. All such capital lies within the *panchayat*. The most valuable category is livestock, for the Gurungs still depend very heavily on animals for milk, meat, manure and power. The distribution of animal ownership, based on figures collected during the household census, is shown in table 6.1. To convert the figures into the total value of capital invested in livestock we need to know the selling price of the various animals in Thak in 1969. On the basis of the figures in table 6.2 it will be assumed that the average price of adult animals in 1969 was as indicated in table 6.3, which also shows the average amount of capital per household, and the total amount in the 100 households. Thus, on average, each household had stock worth some 1285 rs., or just over £50. The *per capita* wealth invested in livestock is 296 rs., or just over £12. That this is a large investment by Nepalese standards may be seen if we compare the situation in Thak to that in the Far Western Hills and Terai, where the *per capita* totals were respectively 157 and 186 rs. Even allowing for up to 20 % depreciation in the value of currency since these surveys were carried out in 1967/8, it will be seen that an 'average' person in Thak has at least one-third more wealth invested in livestock than his compatriots in the Far Western Hills.[1]

The above figures are misleading, however, for livestock is not evenly divided between households. *Carjat* Gurungs, for example, own 156/166 of the cows collectively held by all the households, though such Gurungs constitute only just over half the households. The figures for distribution of animals by different groups in the population are shown in Table 6.4. These figures are for all animals owned, not adult equivalents. Inequality of ownership is especially shown in oxen and cows. Only 6/24 of the *sorajat* households, for example, have one or more oxen. This means that the others are dependent on hiring from their richer neighbours in order to plough. Only 17 of the 100 households have cows: all but four of these are *carjat* households. True ownership of larger livestock by lower castes, if we exclude the buffaloes looked after on a sharecropping basis, is practically absent.

TABLE 6.1 *Total livestock owned by 100 households, Thak 1969*

Animal	Total for 100 households	Total nos. of 'adult beasts'[a]	Avge. no. of 'adult beasts' per house
Buffalo	223	167	1.67
Cow	166	135	1.35
Ox	73	64	0.64
Goat	302	247	2.47
Chicken	*c.* 800	350	3.50

[a] In order to work out the value of all animals it is useful to convert young animals into 'adult beast equivalents'. To do this the following assumptions have been made. The proportions of young animals are as follows among each type of livestock: buffaloes, $\frac{1}{3}$; cows, $\frac{1}{4}$; oxen, $\frac{1}{6}$; goats, $\frac{1}{4}$; chickens, $\frac{3}{4}$. It is assumed that a young animal will be, on average, $\frac{1}{4}$ the value of an adult. The above assumptions are based on impressionistic observations.

TABLE 6.2 *Various estimates of price of adult livestock*

	Estimates of various informants			
Animal	Nansubar/Rudrab	The *poju*	Hse. 22	Prices paid by *gola* for animals
Buffalo	500–600 rs.	550 rs.	450 rs.	260 335 rs.
Ox	400 rs.	250–300 rs.	225 rs.	–
Cow	200 rs.	–	220–250 rs.	–
Goat	50 rs.	–	50 rs.	35–50 rs.

Note: The prices listed under the '*poju*' and the '*gola*' (a communal work party which invests its wages in buying meat) are actual prices paid in 1969.

TABLE 6.3 *Total livestock values, Thak, 1969 (in rs.)*

Animal	Number of adult animals	Value per adult	Total value	Value per household (average)
Buffalo	167	400	66,800	668
Ox	135	250	33,750	337.5
Cow	64	200	12,800	128
Goat	247	50	12,350	123.5
Chicken	350	8	2,800	28

Table 6.5 shows that few households have absolutely no livestock.[2] A comparison of Thak in 1969 with Mohoriya when Pignède visited it in 1958 is included. Thus we may see that there were over twice as many buffaloes per household in Thak, and also more oxen and goats; but Mohoriya households had a larger average number of cows. On the whole, the Thak households had considerably more wealth invested in livestock. I was not able to take a

TABLE 6.4 *Total livestock per household, various groups in Thak, 1969*

Group	Buffaloes	Oxen	Cows	Goats	Chickens	Total no. house-holds
Carjat Gurung	2.68	1.06	2.94	3.47	10.09	53
Sorajat Gurung	1.88	0.46	0.21	3.91	7.04	24
Blacksmiths	1.16[a]	0.17[a]	–	0.5	1.33	12
Tailors	1.2[a]	–	–	0.5	6.33	6
Tamangs/Magars	3.4	0.8	1	3	8.4	5

[a]The majority of these are '*adha*' buffaloes, in other words they are really owned by Gurungs, but are looked after and stabled by lower castes who give some of their produce to the Gurungs.

TABLE 6.5 *Total livestock, Thak and Mohoriya (livestock per household; all ages)*

Animal	Thak 1969	Mohoriya 1958[a]
Buffalo	2.23	1.05
Cow	1.66	2.27
Ox	0.73	0.68
Goat	3.02	1.47

[a]Figures are taken from *Gurungs*, p. 134.

complete livestock census at Mohoriya in 1969, but an intelligent informant gave me the following approximate figures for the number of animals he thought were owned by all the households (figures in brackets are numbers in 1958): buffaloes, 150 (99); cows, 150 (213); oxen, 54 (64); goats, 180 (138). The most significant change, if his guesses were right, was in the increase in buffaloes and also goats, and decrease in cows. Buffaloes produce more meat and milk but also consume more vegetation. Overall, there had been little change, though if the figures are exactly right, then there had been an average increase of value of 70 rs. per household in the intervening years.

Another major category of agricultural capital is tools. The agricultural technology of the Gurungs is extremely 'simple', in the sense that much of the power is provided by human labour and the tools are not elaborate. This has enormous effects on a whole range of Gurung activities and institutions, from the distribution of wealth to attitudes towards the environment. Pignède has already given a detailed description of the major techniques and instruments of Gurung agriculture.[3] It is therefore only necessary to list the types of tools owned by various Gurung households. The list also includes agricultural buildings, which are of two kinds. There are the small, stone, two-storey field houses down in the rice fields, where men and oxen rest during rice planting

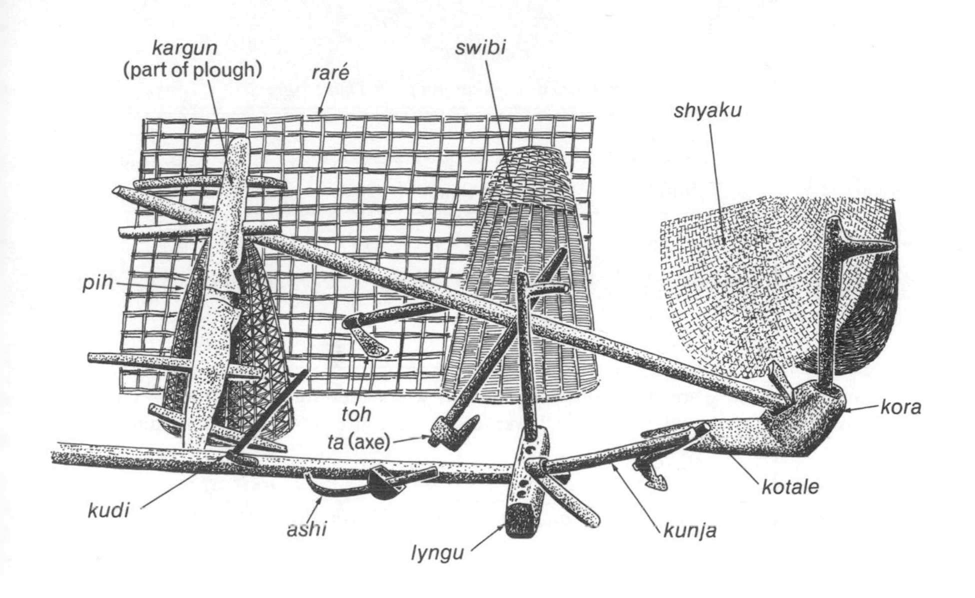

Fig. 6.1. Some agricultural tools.

TABLE 6.6 *Agricultural equipment owned by five households, Thak, 1969*

Purpose	Tool	Gurung name	Number of such tools owned					Stated average value per tool (rs.)
			Hse. 17 (rich)	Hse. 40 (rich)	Hse. 3B (medium . . .)	Hse. 19	Hse. 57 (poor)	
Arable	Hoe	*kotale* (Nep. *kodah*)	5	7	4	5	1	6
		toh	1	2	2	2	–	6
Work in the field		*kudi* (Nep. *kuti*)	0	0	2	2	–	?4
	Plough	*kora*	1	3	1	1	–	18
	Rake	*lyngu* (*lidko*)	1	1	1	1	–	5
	Fencing	*rare*	60 ft	90 ft	100 ft	60 ft	50 ft	1 (= 15 ft)
	Field house		1	1	½	½	–	300
	Total value (rs.)		363	419	216	227	9	
Arable	Drying mats	*pyoh*	4	5	3	3	–	8
		towni	–	–	1	2	1	3
Processing and storing	Winnowing tray	–	?1	?1	?1	?1	–	?2
	Sieving tray	–	?1	?1	?1	?1	–	?2
	Storage basket	*barkari* (Nep. *bhakan*)	6	6	7	5	–	5
		pih	2	4	4	4	–	2
	Quern	*rhendo*	–	1	1	2	1	6
	Rice pounder	*kuni*	–	–	1	–	–	?6
	Water mill		none					
	Total value		70	88	86	79	9	
Pastoral	Animal huts:		?					
	movable		?1	–	–	–	–	?30
	permanent		1	1	1	1	½	?50
	Milk storage jars		?3	?1	?1	?1	–	?10
	Churns		1	?1	1	?1	–	?10
	Total value		120	70	70	70	25	

Transport and carriage	Straps	*tobi*	4	8	5	4	1	1
	Basket	*pih*	4	2	4	4	2	2
		dowsa	1	2	1	1	–	3
	Total value		15	18	16	15	5	
Spinning and weaving	Wheel	*rara*	1	1	1	1	–	1
	Loom	*kwedo sada*	1	1	1	1	–	10
	Total value		11	11	11	11	–	
Wood and fodder	Knife	*ashi*	4	8	7	8	2	3
	Axe	*ta*	1	2	2	2	–	10
	Total value		22	44	41	44	6	
Metal and woodwork	Hammer and nails		–	–	1	1	1	3
	Blacksmith's tools		–	–	–	–	1	5
	Total value		–	–	3	3	8	
Overall value			601	650	440	446	62	

Notes: ? denotes a guess where figures were not collected. Obviously the value of articles vary considerably depending on their age, quality, etc. The figures in the last column, which represent roughly what it would cost to replace each tool in 1969, can only be an approximate guide. The first four families are Gurung, house 57 is a Blacksmith. Figures are based on inventories I took in the field.

and harvesting. Most Gurung families who own rice fields have one of these. Secondly, there are the animal sheds, bamboo or wooden constructions that are moved with the grazing animals, and the permanent cattle-sheds in the village. The latter are usually built next to the living house and shelter one or two buffaloes, oxen and goats. As regards other tools, the only digging instruments are the metal-tipped plough and the various-sized hoes. The major cereal processing tools are the *kuni* (or *Kunyu* (Nep.) = heap of grain) *donva* (Gg., to beat) or rice pounder, which is operated by foot, the hand-mill or quern, and the water mills. There are only two of the last within reach of Thak central village, about 1½ miles from the village to the north. They are only used for a portion of the maize grinding. Some tools, may be seen in Fig. 6.1. The total capital invested in the tools used for various agricultural tasks may be seen in table 6.6. Perhaps the most important feature of the list is the omissions, especially of any wheels (except the circular quern) or of any tools utilizing animal power, except ploughs and rakes. The ratio of capital invested in tools to the total amount invested in agriculture is very low: thus house 17 has some £1625 of arable land, which is worked with tools (excluding the rice house) worth only £2.46, and processed with tools worth £2.92. Transport of many tons of manure, fodder and cereals is undertaken with tools worth 63p (excluding animals). In every sphere, the consumption of labour is increased by the absence of tools. For instance, no families have hand-saws, which would substantially decrease the time spent felling trees. Yet this extremely labour-intensive technology makes sense where there is no shortage of labour and work is not unpleasant. A small diesel engine to pound the grains, and to lift grain and manure up and down the steep mountain, would immediately reduce the amount of work in the area by over a third – and do immense damage to the poorer sections of the community.

Another interesting feature is that the marginal demand for tools is not very elastic. Rich Gurung families have some £24–26 invested in tools and agricultural buildings, medium to poor households some £18. The difference is largely accounted for by buildings; the quantity of cultivating tools and equipment for storing/processing/carrying is almost identical in all the families. On the whole, the precipitous hillsides are cultivated with extremely light and simple tools; this gives great flexibility since they may be adapted to work on different crops at different altitudes. Most of the tools are multi-purpose ones. The storage system for grain, in large baskets which are constantly eaten through by mice and rats, is not efficient and inhibits the accumulation of large surpluses for more than one or two years. But methods of storage do not seem to be an obstacle to accurate budgeting, as they are said to be in an African society.[4] Gurung women usually know fairly exactly how much grain they have left.

There are three other types of agricultural capital which need to be dealt with if we are trying to assess the resources of an average family; fertilizer, seed, and unconsumed crops either in the field or in store. Expenditure on artificial fertilizer, can for the purposes of this account, be ignored; in Thak, 1969, only a few rupees' worth of Government-sponsored fertilizer was used. The value of the dung heaps produced by the stalled buffaloes is difficult to estimate and varies through the year. In order to allow for it, a small sum will be added onto the category of crops not yet consumed. It is impossible to estimate absolutely accurately the amount of capital locked away in seed for the following year, or in crops planted or in storage. Since the Gurungs do not suffer from a 'hunger gap', it seems safe to assume that, on average, there is more than one year's supply of crops either almost ready for harvesting, or in the houses. The seed to crop ratios, averaging out the statements of several informants, were as follows: maize, 1:40, millet, 1:60, rice, 1:70. If we add seed to standing and stored crops, and add in the value of lesser crops such as lentils and potatoes, it would seem reasonable to suggest that, on average, a household has approximately $1\frac{1}{2}$ times the value of a single year's cereal harvest invested in seed and crops.

The approximate amount so invested in five households, compared to the investment in other agricultural equipment, is set out in table 6.7. The table shows the relatively small amounts invested in tools and equipment, but the considerable amount of capital currently in crops, seed and manure. Poor families, such as the Blacksmith household 57, have less than £50 of agricultural capital. These figures are inflated by recent increases in the price of land. They are also distorted to a certain extent by the methods of calculating the value of land. Thus, on the assumption that 1 *ropani* of land is worth 1000 rs., house 17 has only 46,000 rs. of land, but crops and seed worth 18,150 rs.

TABLE 6.7 *Amount of capital invested in agriculture, five households, Thak, 1969 (rupees)*

	Hse. 17	Hse. 40	Hse. 3B	Hse. 19	Hse. 57
Arable land	46,500	63,500	12,750	17,500	500
Livestock	3140	1132	1447	1095	300
Tools, etc.	587	640	440	449	62
Seed/crops/manure	18,150	13,800	4525	5550	150
Total	68,377	79,072	19,162	24,594	1012
Total (£)	£2849.04	£3294.66	£798.42	£1024.75	£42.17

Note: The livestock under house 57, a Blacksmith household, consists mainly of a buffalo which they look after for a Gurung household. It has been assumed that they have a quarter share of the leased buffalo.

House 40, on the other hand, has 63,500 rs. of land on the same basis, but the crops and seed are worth only 13,800 rs. This is explained by the difference in the quality of their land. That of house 17 is very productive rice land, that of house 40, on the whole, lies in much steeper and less fertile fields.

NON-AGRICULTURAL CAPITAL WITHIN THE VILLAGE

We may now turn to non-agricultural capital assets, that is to say housing and household goods. As far as housing is concerned, Pignède has, once again, provided us with an excellent description, complete with photographs and diagrams.[5] He divides Gurung houses into two types: single-storey, wood and earth buildings with thatched roofs, and two-storey buildings made of stone with slate roofs. In Thak there were other variations of an intermediate type; the most common of these were wood/stone/mud in construction, with two storeys and a thatched roof. The distribution of the major types of housing are shown in Fig. 6.2.

Pignède also points out that large rectangular houses of stone and slate are replacing the smaller mud and thatch kind; the bigger houses become the symbol of success abroad. But he is probably wrong in thinking that the traditional Gurung house is the rectangular small one which he describes. Informants in both Thak and Mohoriya told me that some sixty years ago all houses in both villages were *round*. They were one storey high, made of wood, mud and thatch. Such has been the change that not one of this type remains in Thak, though there were still two examples in Mohoriya in 1969. One description of the Gurungs states that 'In Kaski & Lamjung, Gurungs live in small, round, oval or rectangular houses.'[6] The present style must be a copy of something the Gurungs have seen, either while serving in the Far East, or, as was suggested to me, in Assam. Their construction also reflects an altering ratio between the price of wood, stone, thatch and slate as the forest disappears.

The general shape of these round houses deserves description since they have now almost disappeared among the Gurungs I visited. One informant, who had lived in such a round house until he was about ten, described the lay-out in Fig. 6.3. Such houses are called *shur di* in Gurung (*di* = house) and *gola di* in Nepali (*gola* = round).

The increasing amount of capital invested in houses over the last two decades certainly indicates a period of prosperity in the region since the Second World War. It also reflects a certain tendency to conspicuous consumption. Instead of spending his saved capital on fertilizers or irrigation for his land, which would cost a few hundred rupees, a Gurung will spend up to 12,000 rs. on a new house. As with rice fields, the price of houses depends on

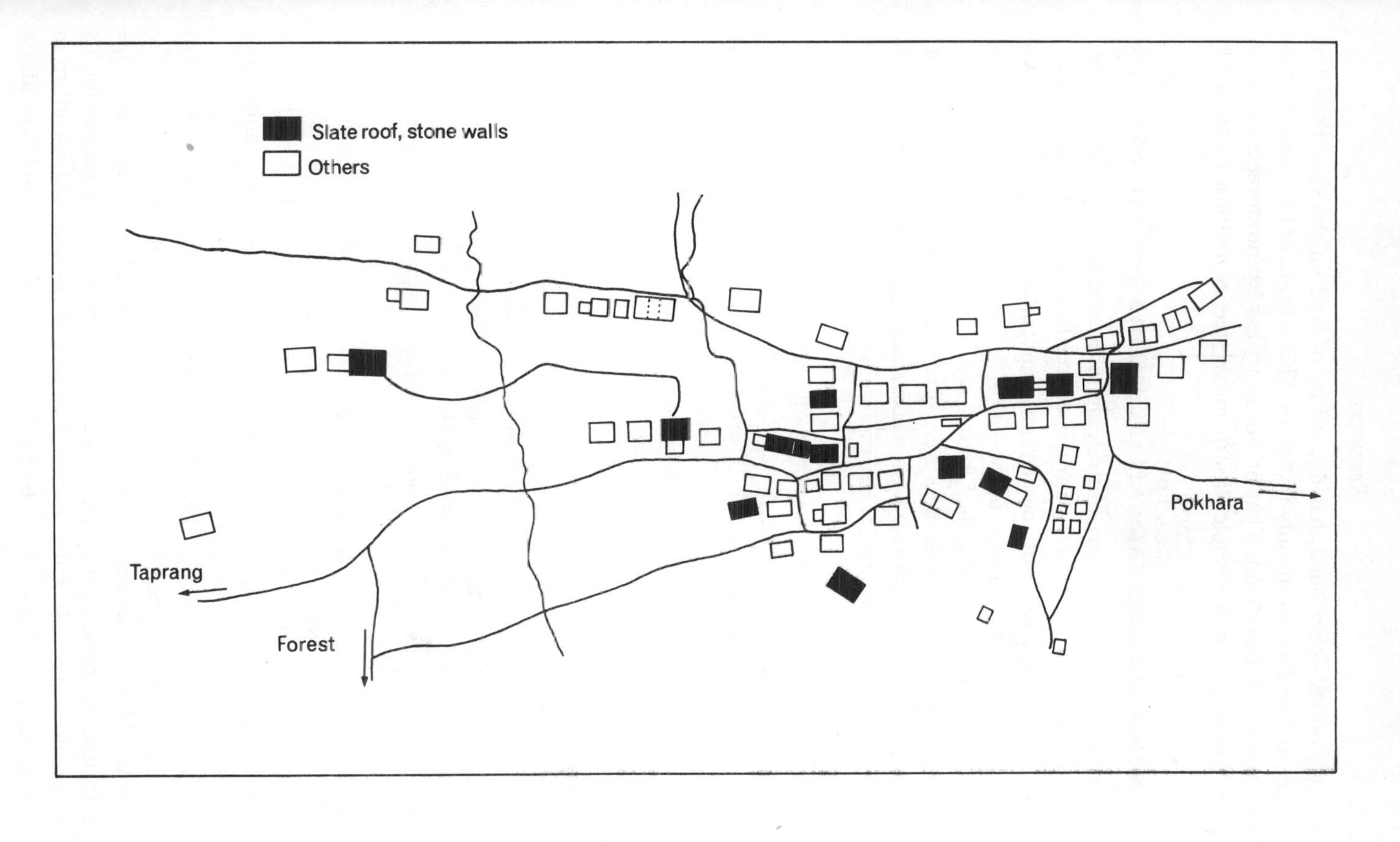

Fig. 6.2. Types of housing in main village of Thak.

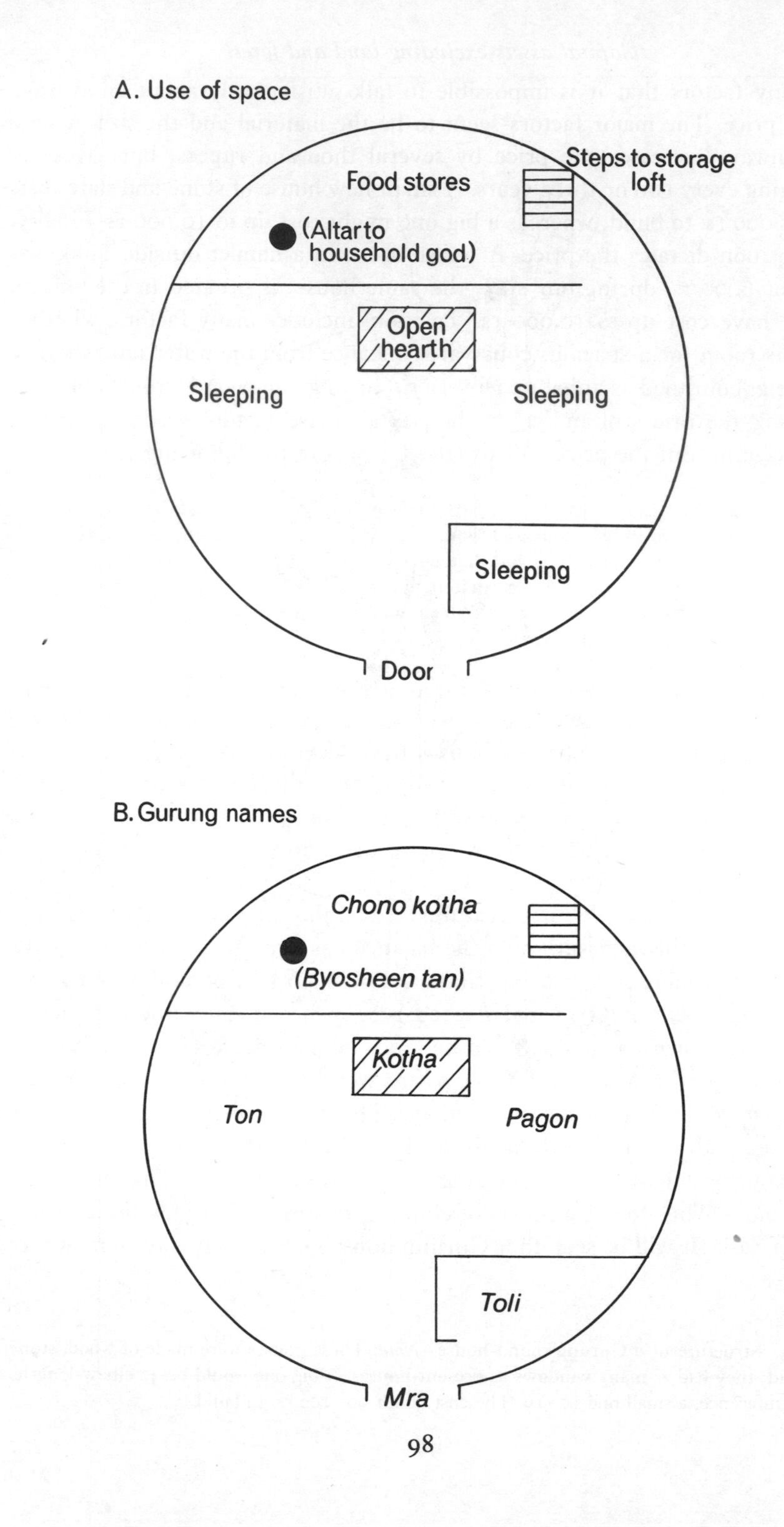
A. Use of space
Steps to storage loft
Food stores
(Altar to household god)
Open hearth
Sleeping
Sleeping
Sleeping
Door
B. Gurung names
Chono kotha
(Byosheen tan)
Kotha
Ton
Pagon
Toli
Mra

so many factors that it is impossible to talk satisfactorily about an average house price. The major factors seem to be the material and the size. A slate roof always increases the price by several thousand rupees, but saves re-thatching every two or three years. A small new house of stone and slate costs some 6000 rs. to build, whereas a big one might cost up to 10,000 rs. Finally, the position dictates the price. A house down in a hamlet outside Thak was sold for 6000 rs. during our stay; the same house, if situated in the village, would have cost up to 10,000 rs. 'Position' includes many factors; whether there is room for a spacious courtyard, distance from the water tap, whether the neighbourhood is inhabited by rich Gurungs or poor Untouchables. In assessing the prices of individual houses all these factors need to be taken into account. But the price will usually fall within the following range:

		As new (rupees)
Type A.	Two-storey, stone and slate	6000–12,000
Type B.	Two storey, stone and thatch	4000–10,000
Type C.	One-storey, stone and thatch	400–2000
Type D.	One storey, mud/wood walls, thatch roof; or bamboo matting walls and roof	100–500

In the following calculations, the value of each house will be assessed on its general state of repair, age, etc. as well as the above criteria. It will be noted on Fig. 2.4, that a number of houses have been divided in half, especially between brothers. Only one house (12B) in the village is rented – for a few rupees a year; the rest are owner-occupied. The value of the houses in the five sample households will be shown later in an inventory of all their possessions.

Pignède described the main features of clothing in a Gurung village.[7] His description is still valid, although the balance has swung even further towards shop-bought, more westernized, clothes. The main type of clothing in Thak, and the numbers of garments of each type owned in the same five sample families, is shown in table 6.8. Those kinds of clothing described by Pignède are indicated with a page reference to his work. It will be seen that very few of the articles are now made in the village. The sheep's wool cloak, listed as the last item under men's clothing, is made higher up the valley in Siklis and neighbouring villages where sheep are kept. The cobblers in Thak no longer make shoes. Thus the acquisition of clothing requires a considerable expenditure of cash. It will be seen that Gurung households usually have somewhere

Fig. 6.3. Structure of a Gurung round-house. (*Note*: These houses were made of wood, stone and mud; they had as many windows as present houses. A big one would be 32 elbow-lengths in circumference, a small one 17–19. The cost about 90–100 rs. to build.)

TABLE 6.8 *Clothing of five households in Thak, 1969.*

Article	Gurung or Nepal name	Page on which Pignède describes	Value of one article (rs.)	Number owned by				
				Hse. 17	Hse. 40	Hse. 3B	Hse. 19	Hse. 57
Men								
Hat/cap	*kulé*	75 ('*pulê*')	3	5	5	3	9	1
Vest/singlet	*vesta*		4	6	3[a]	3	2	–
Shirt	*chemise*		9	15	7	8	13	1
Shirt[c]	*bhoto*	76	5	2	5	1	–	–
Jacket	*jacket*		40	2	4	1	2	–
Sweater	*sweatera*		24	6	2	2	4	½
Linen over-shirt[c]	*renga*	76 (*rhangi*)	12	? 3	4	2	2	1
White cloak[c]	*phaki*	77 (*paki*)	25	? 1	1	–	–	–
Trousers/suit . . .			20	–	–	3	3[b]	–
Shorts	*habjagé*		3	6	3	7	4	–
Loincloth	*kot*		5	3	3	1	3	1
'Kilt' of linen	*kass*	76	8	7	4	4	4	2
Ordinary belt	*peti*		2	2	2	2	1	1
Ornamental belt	*peti*		30	1	2	2	1	–
Socks	*moza*		4	1	1	4	2	–
Shoes (women also)	*juta*		12	4	3	4	3	–
Woollen cloak	?	77 (*labru*)	50	? 1	? 1	? 1	? 1	–
Total value of men's clothing (rs.)				694	649	506	642	59
Women								
Rain shield (men also)[c]	*shyaku* (Nep) *kun* (Gg.)	77	4	6	7	5	5	1
Long skirt	*lungi*		9	5	2	1	3	–

Sari	*sari*		avge. 30	6	1	2	4	–
Headcloth	*kramu*	75	8	6	9	6	6	1
Buttoned blouse	*bundi*		3	2	2	3	1	–
Skirt (child's)	*skirt*		3	–	–	–	–	1
Blouse	*sola*	74(*colo*)	6	6	6	3	3	1
Frock (child's)	*parack*		7	4	1	6	2	–
Cummerbund	*pogi*	75	12	3	2	2	2	1
Blouse	*blousa*		4	4	2	3	2	–
Velvet overskirt	*tigissa*	75(*tiki*)	6	3	3	2	3	1
Petticoat	*petticoata*		8	–	2	3	2	–
Hair-braid	*dori*		8	3	3	4	2	–
Overskirt	*ngwi*	74(*ngue*)	11	6	5	2	2	–
Sandals (men also)	*chapal*		8	3	5	6	3	–
Total value of women's clothes				551	382	380	378	39
Total value of all clothes: rupees				1245	1031	886	1020	98
£				£51.88	£42.96	£36.92	£42.50	£4.08

Note: The values of various clothes are only very approximate. They are what I was told a new or almost new article would cost: the actual selling price of clothing would be much lower than the above. In the cases where an informant stated that a particular article was very much above or below average value, I allowed for this in the totals. In cases where I omitted to collect information, ? denotes a guess.

[a] Three articles were valued at 55 rs., because they included an expensive nylon singlet.

[b] One of the items was said to have cost 65 rs.

[c] Items still made in the village, now very few.

between £35 and £50 (replacement value) of clothing, divided between about 5–8 persons. Men's clothes are considerably more expensive. The amount invested per average household is roughly equal to the price of two and a half adult buffaloes, or one *ropani* of rice land. It is twice the sum invested in all agricultural tools. Despite such a stock of clothes, however, many of the villagers, especially the children, the old, and the poor, are inadequately dressed. More than half still do not wear shoes, which leads to damage of feet and illness, and during the cold weeks of January some of the less fortunate are numb with cold. House 57, the Blacksmith household, had less than £1 of clothing per person. On festive occasions, however, those of moderate wealth and above look splendid in their bright saris and velvets, the men in tightly-fitting suits or spotless *kass* and jacket. On these occasions it becomes abundantly clear that clothes are an important symbol of status, especially the wide 'Gurkha' ornamental belt.

Uncharacteristically, Pignède does not describe household furniture and utensils in any detail, merely referring to a few of the items in passing. The following list of household goods accounts, it is believed, for over 90 % of the items normally found in a Gurung house, though some important articles may well have been omitted. Very few items are nowadays constructed in the village. A considerably larger proportion must have been made in Thak even ten years ago. Now almost everything is available, for cash, in the Pokhara market. The estimated value of possessions is, once again, the approximate cost of a new or almost new replacement. Some of the items, of course, are old and not worth half the sum actually listed in the table.

Table 6.9 shows how much of a gap there is between a wealthy household, with nearly £136 of household goods, and a poor household, with less than £10. The major difference, however, lies in the amount of capital invested in bowls and water pots and storage flasks. The essential practical equipment does not vary much; all families sleep, sit, cook and eat with much the same equipment. It is obvious that with the absence of cash in the past, large pots and eating utensils were a useful way of storing wealth and displaying it. They were passed to sons and daughters at marriage or the division of the estate. As yet, luxury items have not replaced these traditional ways of displaying wealth. Thus household 17 had 1257 rs. in cooking and eating utensils, and only 139 rs. in 'luxury' goods. If, however, the younger son of the family, who is now in the army and the owner of a transistor radio, had been counted, the ratio would have been less extreme. Almost the first expenditure of young men in the army nowadays is on a watch, radio, and new clothes. Thus one boy returned to the village with a very high quality, 6-band, transistor radio; it had cost, including import duty, well over 2000 rupees: with that sum he could have bought 5 adult buffaloes. Another extremely expensive item is a

TABLE 6.9 *Household goods in five families, Thak, 1969*

Article	Local name	Value of one item (rs.)	Number of items in household				
			17	40	3B	19	57
Sleeping/sitting							
Cane stool[c]	*mora*	6	3	1	–	–	–
Bedstead[c]	*karda*	25	2	3	2	1	1
Mat, sleeping[c]	*gundri*	2	10	15	10	6	4
Mat, sitting[c]	*tsoury*	2	? 4	? 4	? 3	? 3	? 2
Wooden chair[c]	*kurchi*	10	–	1	–	–	–
Pillow	*krephung*	6	3	5	3	3	–
Blanket	*rari/shirga*	35	8	5	2	3	1
	Total value		394	334	164	166	72
Cooking/eating							
Jug with spout	*ankora*	10	3	8	–	–	–
Small brass bowl	*pela*	8	16	20	15	9	3
Medium brass bowl	*bahuna*	9	8	12[a]	1	4	1
Plates	*toli*	10	10	10	8	8	3
Spoon	*timsa*	1	3	1	1	2	–
Kitchen knife	*jaiku*	1	2	3	1	–	–
Ladle	*dodu*	1	3	3	3	3	1
Frying-pan	*tarbgya*	5	3	5	4	3	2
Kettle	*kilti*	5	–	2	1	1	–
Flat cooking pan	*korde*	10	–	–	–	1	–
Small-medium cauldron	*kassuri*	15	3	3	3[b]	7	1
Large cauldron	*kaia*	120	7	4	3	6	–
Firetongs	*chimta*	3	1	1	1	1	–
Cooking tripod	*jongo*	8	2	3	2	2	1
	Total value		1257	1083	683	1067	97

TABLE 6.9 (*contd.*)

Article	Local name	Value of one item (rs.)	Number of items in household				
			17	40	3B	19	57
Carriage/storing							
Small grain baskets	*dalo*						
Medium grain baskets	*thago*	4	11	15	10	11	–
Tin trunk	*boxa*	10	5	4	6	3	1
Wooden chest	*modusa*	20	3	3	1	1	1
Large water pot	*gowri*	30	7	14	4	6	1
Huge water pot	*roja*	300	2	1	–	–	–
Bucket	*baltina*	10	–	1	1	1	–
Wooden storage flask	*porru*	40	7	4	8	5	–
Shoulder bag	*jola*	2	4	5	3	4	–
	Total value		1252	1060	576	492	60
Miscellaneous							
Wick lamp	*boti*	10	2	2	1	1	–
Lock	*sanzo*	2	5	7	3	3	–
Medicine	*mae*	1	–	–	1	1	–
Comb	*kaia*	1	10	2	3	4	1
Thread	*ru*	1	–	–	1	1	–
Needles	*ta*	1	1	1	1	–	–
Mirror	*aina*	2	1	1	1	2	1
Razor and blades	*hspadaa di*	5	1	1	1	1	1
	Total value		48	44	29	31	8

Luxury items							
Gun and cartridges	*bundo*	1000	–	–	–	1	–
Radio	radio [*sic*]	300	–	1	–	–	–
Thermos flask	*garam bottle*	15	1	1	1	–	–
Wrist-watch	*gori*	150	–	1	1	–	–
Umbrella	*chata*	8	3	2	2	1	–
Torch	*bijili botti*	7	2	3	1	3	–
Books	*kidab*	3	20	70	20	15	–
Hurricane lamp	*laltina*	6	1	1	1	1	–
Pictures/photos	photo [*sic.*]	1	4	7	4	10	–
Pens/pencils	*pultina/pencina*	4	4	5	4	4	–
Scissors		3	–	–	1	–	–
	Total value		139	745	277	1106	0
Total value of all goods: rs.			3090	3266	1729	2862	237
			£128.75	£136.08	£72.04	£119.25	£9.86

[a] One of these was of silver, and was worth 50 rs.
[b] These three were worth 65 rs. in all.
[c] Items still made in the village.

gun, which combines prestige with utility. There are only four or five working guns in the village, and the same number of radios.

Among the interesting aspects of the list are the following: the almost complete absence of medical supplies; the simple sitting and sleeping arrangements; the considerable number of books (mainly for school). The importance of torches, another prestige object with great utility, in the nightly socializing carried out through the dark, stony, village streets, is also obvious.

One other type of property needs analysis, that is goods and ornaments. Until recently currency was little used in central Nepal; even now the total amount of cash in the Thak 100 households is probably not over 10,000 rs., or the value of one good house. Nor did any of the sample households have bank accounts. Therefore some medium for storing wealth is needed, especially the large sums that are saved by soldiers when serving abroad and sent home to the village. As we have seen, a certain amount is stored in household utensils; a good deal more is invested in golden ornaments. Gold is bought in Malaya or Hong Kong and brought back for wives and daughters. It is fashioned into one of the many beautiful ornaments worn by women, and conspicuously displayed. It can be easily used in an emergency and it is the major constituent in a girl's marriage portion. When given as such a portion it remains the girl's property and is hence an insurance for her and her children. The amount of gold which should, in theory, be given at a daughter's wedding, according to Thak informants in 1969, is shown in table 6.10. The table shows the ideal amount. A survey of the amount of gold owned by various households, as well as instances of how much was actually given in a number of cases shows that, nowadays at least, a little less is usually given. When I asked how much the eldest son of one of the richest men in the village would give to the bride, I was told some 10–12 *tolas*. This would be added on to what the girl received from her own family.

On the basis of this table, we would expect there to be some 2000–6000 rs. of gold per married woman in rich families, some 800–2000 in medium ones. This fits the actual inventories fairly well.

TABLE 6.10 *Gold to be given as marriage portions*

Wealth of family	Nos. of *tolas*[a]	Value (rs.)
Very rich	20–30	4000–6000
Medium rich	12–20	2,400–4000
Medium	4–12	800–2400
Poor	2–4	400–800

[a]The value, of course, depends on the quality of the gold; thus first quality gold is worth *c.* 250 rs. a *tola*, third quality gold only 150 rs. a *tola*.

Capital assets excluding land and forest

The items owned by the five sample families are shown in table 6.11; those ornaments which are described by Pignède are indicated, with page references.[8] As might be expected, the lower caste household, number 57, had no reserve of wealth in ornaments; gold is not a necessary part of lower caste weddings. Household 19, which is at present in a dire financial situation, mortgaging half its lands and heavily in debt, has obviously sold off much of its gold. It is possible that the other totals are underestimates. My informants were not very eager to talk about the amount of gold they had, and the omission of just one ornament could make a large difference when their value is so great. Even as it stands, however, it will be seen what a considerable proportion of Gurung

TABLE 6.11 *Ornaments and jewelry in five households, Thak 1969*

Article	Local name	Pignède page	Approx. value of one item (rs.)	Number of items in house				
				17	40	3B	19	57
Men								
Gold ring	*anguti*		300	1	1	1	–	–
Boy's ear-rings	*dalmar*		250(pr.)	–	1	–	–	–
Women								
Gold ring	*guname*	78(*ghanmai*)	125	–	1	–	–	–
Nose-ring	*puli*(*phuli*)		30	2	–	3	2	–
Ear-ring	*shirmundi,*		200	–	–	1	–	–
(Drop ear-rings	*ialim*		200	–	–	–	–	–)
Ear-ring	*maduli*		150	3	4	3	2	–
Small ear-ring	*dumri*		100	2	4	2	1	–
Large, loop ear-ring	*nagu*	78(*na-ku*)	250(pr.)	–	–	4	–	–
Ring: left hand	*asurphi*	78	250	2	–	2	–	–
Bar broach	*dodi*	78(*dhori*)	250(pr.)	2	–	2	–	–
Bracelet	*ryan*		c. 315	–	4[a]	–	–	–
Gold bangles	*mara tsura*		1000 +	1	2[b]	2	–	–
Gold clip	*kilip*	79(*khilip*)	250	–	2	–	–	–
Gold coin necklace	*hamil*	79(*hamel*)	2000 +	–	–	–	–	–)
(Gold headband	*mara tu*		1000 +	–	–	–	–	–)
	Total value (rs.)			3010	6015	5240	460	0
	Total value (£p)			125.42	250.63	218.33	19.17	0

Notes: Those items in brackets were found in the village of Thak, but not in the sample households. (pr.) = pair. In many instances the value of an article fluctuated very widely, depending on the weight, craftsmanship, etc. Thus 'the value of one item' can only be a very rough average.

[a] All four bracelets, together were worth some 1250 rs.

[b] The two gold bangles were worth some 2590 rs. altogether.

capital is stored in gold. When currency was not available and land too plentiful to have a high market value, as in the past, this would have made good sense. Now there is a feeling among some Gurungs that it would be better to invest such capital more productively in land or livestock. But the few individuals who feel this still conform to the strong social pressures around them. Also such investment would complicate the transmission of wealth, since it would increase the man's share at the expense of daughters who are now given gold. The importance of gold-giving at weddings in determining the age at marriage is obvious. Normally a family must raise several thousand rupees worth of gold before it can marry off a son or daughter. This would tend to delay marriage until after at least one trip to the army.

RELATIVE AND TOTAL INVESTMENT IN VARIOUS CAPITAL GOODS

It has frequently been pointed out by planners and others that the relative proportion of capital invested in productive and non-productive goods, as well as the total amount of capital available per producer, will have a very considerable influence on economic development and living standards. Such relative investment is also a useful preliminary index concerning priorities in the village. Table 6.12 indicates, on the basis of the foregoing statistics, the total amount invested in the five sample households. It will be seen that the proportion invested in non-agricultural goods is fairly low, varying between one-third and one-fifth of the total capital. As we would expect, the proportion grows higher as one moves towards poorer families. Nevertheless, as the table shows, there is a considerable expenditure on housing. The demand for tools seems to reach a ceiling at about 650 rs. Thus richer families do not attempt to increase their efficiency and production by procuring more equipment. Unfortunately there are not, as yet, any comparative figures for other parts of Nepal against which the table may be compared. It seems likely, however, that the amount of capital revealed here is higher than in most areas of the country. A *per capita* wealth of 3000–12,000 rupees, which would cover most Gurung families in Thak (£125–£500), is relatively high for an Asian society.

A detailed household inventory was taken for only seven village families, the five listed in table 6.12 and two others. Before we try to work out the total capital available in the village, it is necessary to see how the sample families compare in wealth to other households. Figures for landownership, livestock and housing were collected for all the 100 households and, since these constitute between 60 and 75 % of the total wealth of the sample households, it seems reasonable to assume that this is also true in other households. The distribution of all the households in Thak on a wealth scale, on the basis of land, livestock and housing, is shown in table 6.13. It will be seen that the

TABLE 6.12 *Total capital in five households, Thak, 1969 (rupees)*

	House 17		House 40		House 3B		House 19		House 57		5 Households	
Type	Total	*p.c.*	Total	*p.c.*	Total	*p.c.*	Total	*p.c.*	Total	*p.c.*	Total	*p.c.*
Agricultural												
Land	46,500		63,500		12,750		17,500		500		140,750	
Livestock	3,140		1,132		1,447		1,095		300		7,114	
Tools, etc.	587		640		440		449		62		2,178	
Seed and crops	18,150		13,800		4,525		5,550		150		42,175	
Total	68,377	7,597	79,072	8,786	19,162	2,737	24,594	2,733	1,102	253	192,217	5,058
Non-agricultural												
Housing	8,000		10,000		3,000		4,000		300		25,300	
Clothing	1,245		1,031		886		1,020		98		4,280	
Household goods	3,090		3,266		1,729		2,862		237		11,184	
Gold, etc.	3,010		6,015		5,240		460		0		14,725	
Cash	?500		?500		?300		?300		?50		1,650	
Total	15,845	1,761	20,812	2,312	11,155	1,594	8,642	960	685	171	57,139	1,504
Total	84,222	9,358	99,884	11,098	30,317	4,331	33,236	3,693	1,697	424	249,356	6,562

Notes: *p.c.* is *per capita*. There were 9 persons in houses 17, 40, 19 (including the one male away in the army), 7 in house 3B and 4 in house 57.

TABLE 6.13 *Wealth distribution of 100 households*

Rupees worth of land, livestock and housing combined	Household number in census
0–99	44A, 50A
100–199	11A, 12A, 27A
200–499	–
500–999	6A, 57A, 58, 61, 62
1,000–1,999	35, 57, 59
2,000–2,999	45
3,000–3,999	43
4,000–4,999	53
5,000–9,999	2, 12B, 33, 44, 46, 60, 64, 65, 74, 80B, 81
10,000–1,4999	3A, 63, 70A, 79, 80, 82
15,000–19,999	3B, 4, 7A, 13D, 18, 21, 31, 80A, 83A, 85
20,000–24,999	16, 19, 27, 29, 39, 77, 78, 83
25,000–29,999	1, 7, 20, 4
30,000–34,999	5A, 5B, 13A, 28, 38, 42, 42A, 48, 50, 51, 76, 84
35,000–39,999	23, 24, 36, 37
40,000–44,999	9, 10, 13, 25, 55, 56
45,000–49,999	22, 32, 72
50,000–54,999	–
55,000–59,999	17, 75
60,000–64,999	11
65,000–69,999	70B
70,000–74,999	40, 52, 73A
75,000–79,999	15
80,000–84,999	49
85,000–99,999	–
100,000 +	6, 14, 71, 73B

Note: The above table is based on the assumption that one *ropani* of land is worth 1000 rs.; only land actually owned (rather than rented) is counted. Livestock and housing prices are based on the values discussed in the pages above. Houses 66, 86–9 are omitted, since figures for landownership were not available for them. The five sample households are underlined.

five sample households are distributed fairly evenly over the various wealth grades, though no examples of the very wealthiest or very poorest were drawn. In fact, because of the assessment of 1 *ropani* of land being worth 1000 rs., table 6.13 somewhat distorts the real position; thus household 17 is, in fact, widely held to be wealthier than household 14, though the latter is listed above as having one hundred thousand rupees of property. The fields of number 17, though less in extent, are much better than those of 14.

The table shows wealth excluding household goods and gold. As already stated, the ratio in the sample households between land, etc. and total wealth, was approximately 6 or 7/10. In later calculations it will be assumed that, on average, in order to ascertain total wealth on the basis of land/livestock/housing, 35 % needs to be added.

HUMAN LABOUR AS A CAPITAL ASSET

In the forgoing discussion we have only dealt with the physical necessities of production; land, livestock, seed, etc. 'Human capital', labour and skills, also need detailed consideration. Given the simple tools and very difficult terrain of the Gurungs, this is especially important in their economy. Furthermore, since the problem of underemployment is now widely viewed as one of the major consequences of population growth in Asia, it is essential that a detailed analysis of available labour should be made.

It has been found useful in the study of household budgeting to employ a standard unit of measurement, the 'consumption unit'. In time and labour analyses we need an equivalent concept, the 'production unit'. This construct does not appear to have been utilized by anthropologists up to the present, though most writers in the field do make tacit assumptions about how much work various people do. The problem is to be able to turn the labour of persons of differing ages and both sexes into proportions of one 'production unit'. To work out, for example, how much the labour of children of various ages is worth. Thus it has been suggested for a south Indian village that the labour of boys aged 10–15 is worth half that of an adult male, and that 'in terms of wages paid and also roughly in terms of work performed one male labour day equals 2 female labour days'.[9] Among other assumptions that have been made, not entirely in accordance with the above figures, are that the average proportion of the family available for agricultural work in parts of New Guinea is some 60 % of the total household size, and that women's labour is worth 70 % that of men's in Yugoslavia.[10] The difficulty of assessing relative productivity is that it depends on so many different features of the particular society: for instance, if herding is the main occupation, children may be 100 % as efficient as adult men, whereas if portering is the way a living is made, they may be only 40 % as productive or even less. Likewise the traditional ideas about the division of labour between ages and sexes will influence the totals enormously. Where women are prohibited from doing fieldwork, or where children are supposed to start work only after completing secondary education, neither group may have much productive value. Then there is the problem of comparing different types of work: is the man who works for 5 hours at ploughing contributing more than the woman who does domestic work for 12 hours? Wages are not an adequate index; they may bear no relation to actual productivity, or expenditure of effort. Bearing in mind all these problems, we may turn our attention to the Gurungs.

There is very little division of labour among the Gurungs: most work is done in groups containing both men and women. There are very few tasks which may not be done by either sex. Pignède has provided a useful diagram (Fig. 6.4) which shows the division of labour, such as it is. In Thak, however, even his picture of a very flexible situation is somewhat too rigid, as may be seen by the modifications I have made to his figure. Even supposedly female activities such as cooking, or carrying water, may be done by men, though only in a minority of cases. The only male activities never undertaken by women in Thak were ploughing and basket-work, while men did everything performed by women except weaving and spinning. In practice, agricultural work is almost exactly shared. An analysis of the amount of agricultural labour said to be required for various crops will show that as many women-hours as man-hours are needed. Thak is in many ways similar to a 'commuter' community in the West; with 43 adult males away from the village from 100 households, it is not surprising that the remaining women, both married and unmarried, should have to perform most agricultural tasks. The division of labour in the family, based on Pignède's diagram, is shown in Fig. 6.4.

Observation of the actual amount of work done by women when collecting wood, planting, or weeding, suggests that, although their physical capacity is slightly less than that of men, in most tasks they do just as much work as men. Their labour is thought to be interchangeable with that of men in communal work parties, and for jobs such as carrying stones for housebuilding, or weeding, they are paid the same amount as adult men. Although it would be possible to assume, along with Caplan,[12] that an adult male and an adult female have an equivalent work value, a conservative estimate will be adopted whereby women are rated as 0.8 of a 'production unit' (i.e. adult male equivalent).

Pignède stated that children started to help with adult tasks from the age of 7 or 8.[13] For the next four or five years, however, their work value is slight. They can help with a little carrying, relieve adults of such tasks as animal-herding or monkey-scaring. But nowadays many of them do little to help the household until they leave primary school at 12 or 13. Thus a young girl of 12, whose household I observed closely for 6 months, only did a little work – minding the baby and occasionally herding a buffalo. From about 12 or 13, however, children start to collect water, wood, fodder, and to carry dung to the fields. Girls begin to help with agricultural work in earnest, sowing and weeding, at 15 or 16. They appear to be fully productive at the age of about 18. Boys do not start to plough until they are 16 or 17, and cannot carry full adult loads, unless they are early developers, until aged 19 or 20.

Both men and women among the Gurungs go on working until they die or are incapacitated by illness. Even the wealthiest in the village do not retire.

	Men	Women	Children
'loughing	●		
owing	○	●	
ransplanting	◌	◌	
e-digging the ground	○	●	
eaping	◌	◌	
hepherding near village (sheep/goats)	◌	○̲	◌̲ BG
hepherding in higher pastures	not done in Thak		
lerding cows	●		○̲ B
utting fodder for buffaloes	◌̲	◌̲	◌̲ BG
utting and fetching wood	◌̲	◌̲	
ooking, etc.	○̲	●	○ G
arrying water	○̲	●	○ G
arrying salt	no longer important in Thak		
tone, wood and basket-work	●		
pinning and weaving		●	
ooking after small children		◌	◌ G
amily religious activities	○	●	

Key

● Activity usually performed by this category of person

◌ Activity equally divided by the two

○ Activity secondarily undertaken by this category

○̲ Pignède's estimate where informants differed

B Boys G Girls

Fig. 6.4. Division of labour in the family. (Based on Pignède, *Gurungs*, fig. 25, p. 258.)

Old women in their seventies could still be seen carrying heavy loads of wood and water, and people in their eighties went on with basket-making and weaving. Full productivity for both men and women probably begins to decline in the mid forties, although both sexes continue to do heavy fieldwork, including ploughing for men, until at least 60 years of age. The amount of work done after the age of 45 depends, among other things, on the wealth of the family and the available amount of labour elsewhere. Thus one informant told me that a rich man aged over 50 would slacken down to some 40 % of his full effort, whereas a poverty-stricken man would work as hard as ever for a while.

I asked two informants to rate people on a five-point scale as to their value as workers, for both sexes and at various ages. They rated adult women as equal to adult men, which seems reasonable, but in view of the almost universal tendency of agricultural economists to rate female labour lower than that of males, we will stick to our conservative estimate. Their estimates were very similar, though not identical. Taking a man aged 30 as 1.00, their combined estimate was as shown in table 6.14 (where they disagreed a median figure was adopted). Later we will apply these multipliers to all the sample households, but first we may compare the results of using the above figures to those arrived at by multipliers employed by others. The Clark method gives too much labour to those with a large number of young children; in general, it would seem to be slightly too high a rating. Epstein's calculation, based on a low assessment of female labour, which is of particular importance among the Gurungs, underestimates the labour fund in this society.

TABLE 6.14 *Work capacity at various ages, males and females*

Age (years)	Male	Age (years)	Female
0–8	0	0–6	0
9–13	0.2	7–12	0.2
14–16	0.6	13–15	0.4
17–19	0.8	16–17	0.6
20–45	1.0	18–45	0.8
46–60	0.8	46–55	0.8
61–70	0.6	56–70	0.6
70 +[a]	0.2	70 +[a]	0.2

[a]For age 70 + I relied on my own estimate.

TABLE 6.15 *Various estimates of work capacity, arrived at by using various methods* (no. production units)

Hse. no.	Total persons	My estimate	Clark[a]	S-Epstein[b]
40	9	4.6	5.4	4.7
17	9	4.4	5.4	3.7
3B	7	4.2	4.2	3.4
19	9	4.6	5.4	4.5
57	4	2.0	2.4	1.75

[a]On the basis of Clark's reported figures (*Subsistence Agriculture*, p. 46), that available labour is 60 % of the total persons.

[b]S-Epstein (*Economic & Social Change*, pp. 78,49), on her assumption that a woman = half a man, and a male child of 10–15 also = half a man.

The Gurung working day naturally varies according to the task to be done. Its length also alters depending on whether one includes the walk to and from work, often taking up to 2 hours a day, as part of the labour. Pignède has given an account of the working day of a communal work group (*nogora*) in the rice fields. He rightly stresses how hard and well the Gurungs work, the task being lightened by singing, joking and conversation.[14] He suggests that workers usually set off at 7.30 a.m., have a break at 3 p.m. and, presumably, return to the village by 7 p.m. This is a long day's work, with 3 hours walking, 8 hours working, and an hour or so of rest. Sometimes the Gurungs in Thak worked even harder than this. For instance when harvesting rice, they would sleep in the fields, start work in the dark at about 4 a.m. and then, after breakfast, carry huge sacks of rice up the 2000 foot climb to the village, repeating the journey up to three times. The Gurungs like to work in bursts; they will work very hard for 3 days and then do nothing for a week, rather than spread the work out. During the two or three weeks of transplanting rice and the couple of weeks of rice harvest, they work extremely hard. The account above, however, gives a very distorted impression of the situation in the other weeks of the year. Even when they are fairly busy, for instance when cutting wood or bringing in the maize, the pace is relaxed. Although most people get up extremely early, the main work of the day does not begin until about 9.30 a.m. at which time, after the first main meal of the day, the workers leave for field or forest. There is a fair amount of resting on the way and at the job, and work ends about 5 p.m. Thus the actual amount of work done is, at the very most, 6 hours.

To illustrate the pattern of work in more detail, I asked my most accurate informant at the end of three separate days what he had done that day. Unfortunately I did not personally observe his actions on the particular days in question, but his descriptions fitted in well with what I had seen him doing on other days. All the accounts were taken during June–July; these are the two busiest agricultural months in the year, for they cover the transplanting of rice and the harvesting of maize. The informant was a young man of 21, perhaps a little more indolent than some, but a member of a wealthy household where there was much land to be worked. This is how he described his activities; the times are approximate, though he did have a watch.

Day 1. *Ploughing the fields for transplanting rice.*

5.30 a.m. Get up; urinate; go to nearby (5 mins.) Tailor's house to tell him that his services as a ploughman would be needed that day; drink tea; go to 'Blacksmith village' (2 mins.) to mend hoe, but no Blacksmiths there, so return home; visit village 'shop' for soap, but no one there.

8.30 a.m. Breakfast; go to fetch ox from house 15, told that there was not enough water in the fields; eat a snack of potatoes and drink milk; urinate; wash hands and face; fetch another ox; get together a plough and other equipment; take oxen and equipment down to field (20 mins.); urinate; hitch up oxen.

10.30 a.m. Plough one terrace; go to a nearby field; plough seven more terraces.

5.30 p.m. Unyoke oxen; rest for one hour, letting oxen graze, looking at view and singing; return to house; wash all over and drink water at water tap; eat supper; wash hands; milk buffalo.

8.00 p.m. Visit anthropologist's house.

It will be seen from the above account that it took some five hours before work actually commenced in the field, and that the ploughing lasted seven hours, with various interruptions. But the 'labour' involved in ploughing also included alerting another ploughman, getting together the oxen and taking them to the fields, grazing them, returning them. There was also the attempt to mend a hoe and the milking of the buffalo. Thus an eight-hour working day seems a minimum estimate, a ten-hour day is the maximum.

Day 2. *Preparing fields for transplanting of rice.*

(The informant slept in a shed in the fields)

5.30 a.m. Get up; smoke cigarette, drink tea, urinate; go to stream, start to make water channel to field; talk to a woman about seeds.

8.00 a.m. Cook some breakfast; wash; eat breakfast; smoke and rest for 15 mins.; work on fields (making six water channels and preparing eleven rice terraces).

4.30 p.m. Eat a snack; weed for half an hour; walk up to village, resting for half an hour on the way.

7.30 p.m. Eat supper.

Thus the informant had worked for at least eight or nine hours, and had then walked up to his house.

Day 3. *Fetching maize up to the village.*

(The maize was in a field some 500 ft below the village; it took about 15 mins. down and 30 mins. up.)

8.00 a.m. Get up – late because tired and it was raining; drink tea and smoke; wash and urinate; breakfast.

9.30 a.m. Set off down to maize field; defecate near path down to work; bring up a load of maize; drink some skimmed milk and vomit; go down to field again, stopping at a house on the way to have hair cut; bring back another load of maize; go down to fields again; shelter during a rain storm.

c. *6.00 p.m.* Return to house and supper.

Carrying large baskets up the steep slope is very tiring work and rests are certainly needed. Nevertheless, the informant was not pushing himself. He could have done the three journeys in 3 hours if he had been in a hurry to go off somewhere else. Thus the pace of work is adjusted to the amount that needs to be done. Often it will take someone a whole day to fetch a load of grass for the buffalo; on other occasions the same person will do the same job before breakfast and then set off to Pokhara. Parkinson's Law – that work expands to fill the time available for its completion – is of fundamental importance in understanding Gurung economics. All this suggests that the marignal returns on further labour input are low; the economy can only absorb a limited amount of labour. The same task may take one hour, or four hours.

The quality of the workers, if under pressure, is extremely high. Both Gurungs and other villagers, though physically small, are extremely strong, and they can walk great distances with huge loads. They work particularly well in teams, and most of the village work is done by groups. The women, especially are often very hard workers, grinding and pounding the grains deep into the night, scarcely ever idle. The men are fonder of gambling, drinking visiting Pokhara, or just sitting around talking, but they will work hard when there is work to do.

In assessing the quantity of labour or 'production units' available in the village, the calculations will be made in man-days. It will be assumed that the average amount of hours actually worked per day is six. This is based partly on the above accounts, where approximately 7, 8, and 3 hours work were done during the busiest months of the year; partly on general observation and by accompanying working parties on various jobs; and partly on one informant's statement that a normal working day for a communal work party was 10–6 in summer and 10–5 in winter, with 1–1½ hours rest during that time. This six-hour day is in line with assumptions about Gambia, and half an hour shorter than estimates for Africa as a whole.[15] Since our aim is to show that even with very considerable labour migration there is still considerable underemployment it is wise to take the lowest possible estimate of hours of work thought to constitute a full day's work. In this way the work available in the village will be estimated to spread over the maximum possible number of work-days. The number of days that can be worked per year could be taken to be anywhere in the range 260–300. Various studies have assumed the following number of work-days per year: south India, 300;[16] India, 300; Bulgaria, 290; South India, 260; Hungary, 300; Italy, 275.[17] Although 300 would seem a reasonable estimate of what, in theory, the Gurungs could work, since they do not have holy days when they may not work (though certain jobs may not be done for one day each month at full moon, when a person dies, etc.), again we will err on the conservative side and assume that 280 days per year constitutes 'full employment'. This gives each individual 85 days for illness and rest.

We may now turn to the available labour in various strata of the village. The people listed in the first half of table 6.16 will be omitted from the calculations because their disabilities made them incapable of anything but the very lightest work; those in the second half had their productive power, on average, halved by various other causes. On the basis of the rates in table 6.14, there was a loss of 4.6 production units through 'total disabilities' and 1.6 units from 'half disabilities'. This was approximately 1/50 of the total productive force of the 100 households.

If we stratify the production units by age, sex and caste, taking all 528 persons theoretically living in the Thak sample, and assessing their labour at the above rates, the productive capacity is as shown in table 6.17. Thus the males and females aged 0–16, in all, provided only 31.2 production units, or 9.4 % of the total of 294.4 units. Old men also provided little labour after the age of 61, but older women constitute quite an important fund of labour. Males, as a whole, provide only ten more units than females as a whole. If we multiply the above total by the previously assumed 280 man-days per year (as full employment), then there are 82,432 man-day-units to be employed in the 100 households – either in the village or in the army. Assuming a six-hour day, there are 494,592 man-hour-units to be so employed. The 528 persons provide some 294.4 production units; in other words the productive assets of the village represent 55.76 % of the total number of persons, which is a little less than the 60 % suggested by Colin Clark, as discussed above. Our task in the following chapter will be to see what proportion of this labour may be absorbed in the village.

TABLE 6.16 *Those with reduced work capacity in Thak*

House no.	Sex	Age	Disability
Totally incapacited			
6A	F	44	Mentally ill
9	M	15	Spastic
14	M	60	Almost blind
33A	M	89	Bedridden-dysentery
58	M	15	Mongol child
70B	M	56	Crippled
75	F	49	Very lame
Half incapacited			
13A	M	34	Had T.B. once
33	M	42	Had T.B. once
37	M	8	Mentally retarded
45	F	24	Deaf and dumb
85	F	69	Deaf and dumb
88	F	68	Partly blind

TABLE 6.17 *Distribution of production units in Thak, by age and caste*

Male (no. of production units)				Female			
Age	Gurungs	Tailors/ blacksmiths	Magars/ Tamangs	Age	Gurungs	Tailors/ Blacksmiths	Magars/ Tamangs
0–8	0	0	0	0–6	0	0	0
9–13	3.8	1	–	7–12	5.8	1.8	0.8
14–16	7.2	3	–	13–15	3.2	2.4	1.2
17–19	5.6	3	–	16–17	3.6	1.2	–
20–45	74	16	4	18–45	61.6	15.2	4.8
46–60	21.6	4.8	2.4	46–55	15.2	4.8	–
61–70	3	0	0.6	56–70	15	1.2	2.4
70 +	1.2	0.2	–	70 +	1.6	0	0.2
Total	116.4	29	7		106	26.6	9.4

In a later chapter a table of production units per household, as compared to consumption units, will be given in order to see which households are likely to have budgetary deficits. From that table it will be seen that the largest number of production units in a single household is 8.4 (in a Tailor joint household), while the smallest is 0 (in a house where only a mentally defective woman lives, begging off other villagers). The distribution by number of production units of the various households is shown in table 6.18. Thus, it will be seen that normally the number of production units per household is in the range 2–3.9; exactly 50 % of the sample households lay in this range with almost equal numbers above and below. Only 1/10 households have five or more production units. The above totals represent the potential numbers; in fact the production units available in the village are far fewer. Boys and girls who are away at school in Pokhara, and especially those away in the army, reduce the actual labour force for work in the fields. The number at work in the village (including school-children attending school there) is shown in table 6.19. The situation among non-Gurungs is the same, but the pattern among Gurungs has changed very considerably; army recruitment means that there are now usually only 1–2.9 production units per household working within the village – almost 50 % of the Gurung households fall within this range. Only three households now have five or more production units. It will be noticed that the army exodus emphasizes the larger average labour potential of non-Gurung households.

TABLE 6.18 *Distribution of total production units; 100 households*

Group	0–0.9	1–1.9	2–2.9	3–3.9	4–4.9	5–5.9	6+
Gurungs *carjat*	4	12	18	6	7	2	4
sorajat	2	4	10	4	3	0	1
	6	16	28	10	10	2	5
Blacksmith/Tailor	0	4	5	6	1	1	1
Tamang/Magar	0	0	0	1	3	1	0
Total (& %)	6	20	33	17	14	4	6

TABLE 6.19 *Distribution of production units of those working in the village*

Group	0–0.9	1–1.9	2–2.9	3–3.9	4–4.9	5–5.9	6+
Gurungs *carjat*	9	18	13	4	9	1	–
sorajat	5	6	6	5	1	–	–
	14	24	19	9	10	1	–
Blacksmith/Tailor	–	4	5	6	2	–	1
Tamang/Magar	1	–	–	2	1	1	–
Total (& %)	15	28	24	17	13	2	1

CAPITAL ASSETS OUTSIDE THE PANCHAYAT

So far we have only considered the capital resources within the *panchayat*. Since the Gurungs depend heavily on military service in the Indian and British armies, we also need to know the capital resources available per serviceman abroad. If all the inhabitants of the Western Hills were confined to their native area the standard of living there would drop very considerably. Thus the Gurungs may be seen, to a certain extent, as beneficiaries from the funds of British and Indian capitalists; their wealth comes indirectly and partly from British and Indian factories. Furthermore, it is necessary to see how much capital is available to the Gurungs within Nepal. Here we must consider not only the inherited amenities of the country, but also the very considerable inflow of foreign aid which has occurred during the last twenty years. Any investigation of such external capital resources poses very considerable problems for an anthropologist. Without a long investigation of the whole Indian, Nepalese, and British economies we can only obtain a very rough idea of the amount of capital – machinery, communications, personnel, etc. – upon which such labour migrants as the Gurungs operate. Necessarily, therefore, much of the following brief analysis will consist of guesswork, but guesswork justified, it is believed, by the importance of the topic.

The flow of foreign capital into Nepal and into the Hills in particular began in earnest with the opening up of Gurkha recruitment in the later nineteenth century. Before then the State under the Rajas had re-invested very little of the taxes they drew from the hill villages; they made practically no attempt to provide medical, educational, industrial or other facilities. There has been some change during the last twenty years, largely as a result of the considerable inflow of foreign capital which makes it possible to invest money in the Hills. This reaches the village in the form of services within the *panchayat*, and facilities at Pokhara and elsewhere. The main areas for investment are education, medicine, bridges, wireless and postal communications, local government, agricultural experiments. It is impossible to estimate exactly how much this is worth to an average Gurung household p.a. What *is* fairly certain is that it does not exceed the amount paid in taxation per household, roughly 50 rs. (£2) p.a. It seems likely that less than £2 p.a. is thus received per household per year in the form of services, and about that amount leaves the village households in taxes. As compared to the other source of external income, army service, the figures, as we shall see, are trivial.

As an alternative to writing a long analysis which examines British and Indian capital resources, an indirect, though rough, method of calculating resources available to Gurungs when they go outside Nepal will be adopted. Firstly, we will try to calculate the returns for labour invested in various types of activity, inside and outside Nepal; secondly, we will multiply this by the number of persons who are active in these various fields. Returns for labour are not, of course, an accurate index of the amount of capital available. They also reflect expectations, demand and supply, etc. Furthermore, calculations of this nature are, in fact, much more complex than represented below and simplification leads to distortion. If a fit male aged 20 in 1970 was contemplating the returns on investing his labour in various activities, the broad outline of the situation may be summarized in note form (all totals are given in Nepalese rupees).

1. If he was poor, with hardly any land, and laboured for others in the village (e.g. as a blacksmith/ploughman/building houses), his average income per day employed would be about 6 rs. ($3\frac{1}{2}$ rs. + two meals). Average number of days employed p.a. about 270; therefore his total earnings would be some 1620 rs.

2. If he had sufficient rice/maize land to absorb his labour (for example a middling to wealthy Gurung upwards), his average income from labouring on his land per day employed would be about 10 rs. The average number of days employed would be about 250. Thus total earnings of some 2500 rs.

3. As headmaster of the local primary school he would get 1800 rs. p.a.; as second or third schoolmaster some 1080 rs. In either case he would supplement this by agricultural or other work.

4. As a civilian or soldier in India he might expect to earn as follows: housing, food, clothing, provided – worth approx. 5 rs. per day or 1825 rs. per year; wages for one year, 2200 rs.; pension rights worth 720 rs.; a total of 4745 rs. p.a.

5. As a soldier in the British army, serving 15 years and rising to a middling rank, he might expect to earn as follows: housing, food, clothes worth 1825 rs. p.a.; wages at some 4400 rs. p.a.; pension rights worth 720 rs. The total earnings would be 6945 rs. p.a.

In the calculations leading to the total in options 4 and 5 it is assumed that the average recruit might expect to spend 10 years as a Rifleman, and 5 years as a Corporal and retire on a Corporal's pension. In fact, of course, he might remain a Rifleman all his time, or rise to a much better paid rank than Corporal. It is also assumed that he would live for 15 years after retiring and thus enjoy a pension for that time. The fact that ex-servicemen or their wives usually survive for a longer period that this makes the above calculations a conservative minimum.

Yet, even though they are conservative estimates, it will be seen that for the same amount of labour a man can earn almost twice as much in India as on his own fields, and in the British army he may earn three times as much or more. Since the demand for food and clothing is soon satisfied, much of this extra amount may be saved. Thus for the purposes of argument we may assume that the capital per person employed in India is twice that per person (male) in the village, and in the British army it is three times as much.

TOTAL CAPITAL OF 100 HOUSEHOLDS

Up to now we have been calculating on the basis of household units. This leads to distortion since household size and composition differs, and therefore it is necessary to allow for age and sex differences. We must use a more sensitive multiplier, namely the 'production unit' which assigns to persons of different ages and sexes a graded series of work abilities. The methodology for constructing such units within the Gurung economy has been discussed above; it is now time to apply the concept.

One further problem of a complex type faces us if we desire to know the total capital resources available to an adult male in our 100 sample families; this is the problem of communal resources. We have fairly adequate figures for the amount of private capital in the village, as indicated by the inventories, but it has been constantly stressed that the Gurungs depend heavily on supplies of forest and rough grazing. Without communal rights their whole economy would be immensely different and impoverished. Yet how are we to calculate the value of such communally owned capital? Some basis for an estimate is provided by the previous discussion of the amount of wood and fodder consumed per household and *per capita* in the 100 households. The problem is to decide how much capital resources this represents. Even to decide its monetary value is difficult; are we to assess it in terms of labour/time expenditure, or at what it would cost in Pokhara? A rough, highly questionable, guess will have to be made. It will be suggested that such communal resources are worth half that of the arable land owned by a household. The milk, meat, wild vegetables, fruit, manure, firewood, building wood, bamboos, thatching, which flow from the communally owned lands would seem to be worth at least this, although in terms of cash within the village they are not priced as high, or not priced at all. The ownership of such resources is in theory communal and equal: in fact, of course, those with large households and many animals, who also tend to be the richer households, make far greater use of such communal assets. This fact justifies us in varying the amount of such capital according to the arable land ownership of families. The 'per production unit' capital available to the 5 sample households is shown in table 6.20. We see that a rich family is calculated to utilize some 20,000–25,000 rs. worth of grazing and forest, a medium to poor family between 5000–10,000 rs worth. The average amount of capital per production unit varies from roughly 1000 to 28,000 rs. But, in fact, it is likely that the extremes would not be quite as

TABLE 6.20 *Capital per production unit in five households (rupees)*

Household no.	Capital			No. of prod'n. units	Avge. per prod'n. unit
	Private	Communal	Total		
40	99,884	31,750	131,634	4.6	28,616
17	84,222	23,250	107,472	4.4	24,425
3B	30,317	6,375	36,692	4.2	8,736
19	33,236	8,750	41,986	4.6	9,127
57	1,697	250	1,947	2.	974

[a] Private capital includes all goods, as well as arable land.

great as this since household 57 would undoubtedly use more than 250 rs. of communal resources.

From my personal observation, there appears to be a surplus of labour in households 3B and 19, whereas households 40 and 17 have to hire a little labour. It would therefore seem that to keep an adult male (one production unit) productively busy would require some 12,000 rs. or so of capital. If this estimate is correct, then the relative amount needed to produce the yields experienced outside the village would be as follows: employment in the village, 10,000–15,000 rs. per production unit; employment in India 20,000–30,000 rs. per production unit; employment in the British army, 30,000–45,000 rs. Of course this does not necessarily mean that the British army has this specified amount of capital per recruit. It merely means that if we express external capital in terms of the returns on capital in the village, this is the amount we arrive at.

TABLE 6.21 *Total capital reserves for 100 sample households, 1969*

Type	Total	Avge. per household	Avge. per prod'n. unit (294.4)
Internal: private	4,500,000	45,000	15,285
Internal: communal	1,230,500	12,305	4,180
External: army, etc.	1,195,000	11,950	4,059
	6,925,500	69,255	23,524

Note: The value of communal land has been assessed as half that of arable land. The private wealth has been based on the wealth of the 5 sample households, though a little has been deducted to allow for the fact that the sample was probably a little over the average in wealth.

One final problem remains: how many Gurungs in our sample area drew on these external sources of capital in India and the British army? Excluding for the moment pensioners, whose pensions have already been allowed for, those working abroad in 1969 (including those temporarily on leave) were as follows: India, civilian – 8, India, military – 27, British army – 8; total 43 persons. From this, on the basis of previous calculations, we may assess that those in India, at 25,000 rs. capital per adult, utilized some 875,000 rs. of capital; those in the British army, at 40,000 per adult, utilized some 320,000 rs. worth, or a total of 1,195,000 rs. This indicates the very large external resources of capital utilized. Its relative importance, in comparison with other types of capital, may be seen in table 6.21. It may thus be seen that army capital and communal resources are of about equal value on this reckoning. On average each household has some 69,255 rs. of capital (£2,885.63) and each production unit (adult male equivalent) some 23,524 rs. (£980.17). This is a large amount of capital for an Asian society.

7
The application of capital; input–output data

We now have some idea of the stocks of land, labour and other capital in a Gurung village. Given the simple technology and difficult terrain, how is this capital applied? The importance of the problems in this area have been recognized by various writers on Nepal. Thus there has been a Ministry of Economic Planning report on the subject, which provides interesting comparative data.[1] It has, furthermore, been argued generally of Nepal that 'the man/land ratio which has already grown high, is getting worse, with the result that the accumulation of idle man-power on land is mounting with the passage of time'.[2] A whole study has been devoted to the way in which labour surpluses in the Hills area of Nepal lead to labour migration to the Terai of India.[3] More generally, many studies of pre-industrial societies have shown that there is a huge problem of growing under- and un-employment; for example a study of India some twenty years ago calculated that, varying from district to district, only 53–81 % of the labour was actually employed, despite the labour-intensive and antiquated technology.[4] The situation among the Gurungs is of particular interest for two reasons. Firstly, it is clear that the very large-scale labour migration to the army must be linked to the labour situation in the village. Secondly, at first sight the Gurungs appear to be an exception to the above generalizations, for the predominant impression from reading Pignède's authoritative work is that there is, if anything, a labour shortage. Thus, for example, he writes that 'Agricultural work in a Gurung village is very arduous ... adult labour is insufficient because of the lack of men'. Even during the slack season, he believed, men and women were busy.[5] Another authority on the region also writes, 'Life in a Gurkha village is harsh and unrewarding: a matter of unremitting toil'.[6]

In the first part of this chapter we will examine each of the activities within the village, in order to see how much labour and other capital it absorbs. In the second half, the total amount of labour required in the village will be compared to that available and we will investigate whether there are certain groups, or certain periods, where there are particular shortages, or surpluses.

CEREAL GRAIN PRODUCTION

It is naturally extremely difficult to calculate the amount of labour and other capital input required to produce a given quantity of grain, or to till a given area of land. To talk of the 'average' amount we need to ignore many crucial variations – the size of the field, the quality of the soil, the distance from the village, the availability of water. Nevertheless, we need estimates so badly that over-simplifications will have to be made. The basis for the following calculations are as follows. I asked two informants to describe to me in detail the various processes involved in growing and harvesting rice, maize, millet, and other crops. I then asked them to think of a particular field they owned and to tell me how many men/women/oxen were employed for how many hours/days in order to complete the processes they had described. Some of the totals were checked with other informants, and others could be checked by observation. Both methods suggested that their descriptions were reasonably accurate. The two informant's estimates for each of the three main crops may be seen in table 7.1.

Most of the processes listed in the table are described in some detail by Pignède.[7] They include all the operations from the manuring of the fields up to cooking. (Ploughing with oxen is shown in Fig. 7.1.) It will be seen that the two informants estimates are close to each other, except in the case of millet, where the first informant calculated that a considerably longer time is necessary for threshing and grinding grain. The two most labour-consuming activities are weeding and grinding: between a quarter and one-third of the total labour needed for rice, for example, is used on these two processes. From the details of table 7.1 we can extract the labour needed per area of land, and compare this to the findings of a governmental report on the subject (see table 7.2). In the case of rice and maize the Thak estimates come somewhere in the middle between small and large holdings, but in the case of millet the estimate is lower than that even for large fields. This may be explained by the fact that millet is usually grown by the Gurungs on the fields where they also grow maize: therefore the preparation and manuring of the land, which is counted under the labour needed for maize cultivation, also serves for millet. But it should be noted that the Nepal totals do not include the time-consuming process of grinding. This makes the Gurung achievement on their small holdings even more impressive.

The amount of animal labour per area of land under the three main crops is as shown in table 7.3. Again it will be seen that the totals for this area are intermediate on the Nepalese scale. The degree of 'under-employment' of oxen will be considered later.

Finally we roughly calculate the amount of grain produced per man-day of labour in the fields. Table 7.4 includes all the processes up to the moment of

TABLE 7.1 *Physical input-output of main cereal crops*
Labour per *ropani*, in man-days (1 *ropani* = 0.051 ha. or 0.13 acres).
M = male, F = Female, M/F = either) underlined figures = oxen.
N.B.: yields are always in *unhusked* grain.

Activity	Informant one	Informant two
Rice		
Manure	0.11 M/F	0.18 M/F
Plough	0.11 M + 0.22	0.09 M/F + 0.18
Clean/weed	0.44	0.18 M/F
Break up lumps	0.33	0.45 F
Plough again / Rake / Plough	0.11 M + 0.22	0.09 M + 0.18
Water channels / Flattern earth / Sow / Scatter earth	0.67 M/F	0.55 M/F
Manure	–	–
Plough (1st)	0.44 M + 0.89	0.45 M + 0.91
Weeding/clean	2.22 M/F	1.64 M/F
Plough (2nd)	0.44 M + 0.89	0.45 M + 0.91
Rake / Transplant	2.78 F/M	1.82 F
Repair terraces		0.91 M
Put more water on	0.22 M	0.73 M
Weed	2.22 M/F	1.82 M/F
Weed ('*sungri*')	0.22 M/F	0.27 M/F
Cut	1.11 M/F	1.27 M/F
Collect/pile	0.44 M/F	0.64 M/F
Beat and thrash / Bring to house / Store	0.89 M/F + 0.56	1.73 M/F + 0.55
Dry	0.33 F	0.45 F
De-husk / Winnow	2.5 F	2.5 F
Total labour per *ropani*	15.58 + 2.78	16.22 + 2.73
Details of particular field:		
Yield per *ropani* (in *muri*)	2	1.82
Name of field	Patle	Kamgon
Quality (according to land records)	Medium	Good
Total area (according to land records)	9 *ropani*	11 *ropani*
Total production	18–20 *muri*	20 *muri*
Distance from house	15 mins	25 mins
Labour per *muri* yield	*c.* 7.5	*c.* 8.5
Maize		
Manure	4.29	2
Plough	0.29	

TABLE 7.1 (*cont.*)

Activity	Informant one	Informant two
Rake Re-plough	0.29 + 1.14	0.75 + 1.5
Edge and clean	3	2
Sow	0.57 + 0.57	0.5 + 1.0
1st weeding	1.14	2
2nd weeding	1.71	4
Harvest and to house	2	1.25
Cut off stalks	0.29	0.5
Store	1.43	1.75
Take off cob	0.29	0.75
Grind – at mill	0.57	0.5
– in house	3	1.5
Winnow	0.14	0.5
Total labour per *ropani*	19.01 + 1.71	18 + 2.5
Details of particular field:		
Yield per ropani (in *muri*)	1.75	2
Name of field	Uli	Uli
Quality	Good	Good
Total area	3½ *ropani*	4 *ropani*
Total production	6 *muri*	8 *muri*
Distance from house	25 mins.	1 min.
Labour per *muri* yield (man days)	11.08	9.0
Millet		
Prepare ground	3.43 M/F	1.25 M/F
Sow seed	0.57 M/F	0.5 F
Plough	0.57 M + 1.14	0.5 M + 1.0
Transplant (life)	1.71 M/F	1.25 M/F
Re-plant	6.29 M/F	5 F/M
Weed	2.0 F	3.0 F/M
Cut off heads Carry to house	3.43 M/F	2.5 F
Thrash	4.71 M/F	2.5 M/F
Grind – mill	0.25 M	0.5 M
– at house	2.0 F	1.5 F
Total labour per *ropani*	24.96 + 1.14	18.5 + 1.0
Details of particular field:		
Yield per *ropani*	1.14 *muri*	?
Name of field	Uli	Uli
Quality	Good	Good
Total area	3.5 *ropani*	4 *ropani*
Total production	4 *muri*	?
Distance from house	25 mins	1 min
Labour per *muri* yield (man days)	21.84	?

Fig. 7.1. Ploughing with oxen.

TABLE 7.2 *Labour needed per unit of land: Thak and Nepal compared*

Crop	Median man-days per crop; two Thak informants	Thak median in man-days per ha.	Nepal findings, per ha.	
			Small	Large
Rice	15.9	311.76	553	115
Maize	18.5	362.75	2883	188
Millet	21.73	426.08	6387	637

Note: Figures are taken from 'Physical Input–Output Characteristics of Cereal Grain Production', p. 46. The 'small" were holdings up to 0.5 ha. the 'large' were 1.0–2.0 ha. Both were in the 'Hills' region. Gurung holdings tend to approximate in size to the former rather than the latter.

TABLE 7.3 *Animal power needed per unit of land: Thak and Nepal compared*

Crop	Median ox-days per crop: two Thak informants	Thak, median in ox-days per ha.	Nepal, bullock-days per ha.	
			Small	Large
Rice	2.73	53.53	67	27
Maize	2.0	39.22	191	15
Millet	1.07	20.98	–	–

Note: Source for Nepalese figures, 'Input–Output Data', table 31.

TABLE 7.4 *Yield of husked grain per man-day of labour (median estimate of two Thak informants)*

Crop	Man-days per *muri*	Kg per working day
Rice	8	8.6
Maize	10	6.3
Millet	21.8	3.1

cooking. The number of working days needed to produce rice for various households will be analysed below.

OTHER CROPS

The Gurungs, of course, spend much time on activities other than cereal grain production. It is extremely difficult to calculate the amount of time on these other occupations, on animal husbandry, water and wood fetching, building, growing vegetables and other subsidiary crops. One author guessed that in a South Indian village 'the average farmer does not spend more than 30 labour days per year on his various subsidiary economic activities'.[8] This is likely to be too low an estimate in Thak where livestock are important and a considerable amount of time is spent on carrying wood and fodder. The following estimates are bound to be very rough. It is difficult, for example, for anyone to calculate how long they spend on feeding chickens, or fetching water. The problem is further complicated by the fact that, as previously observed, people fit the pace of the work to the amount of time they have in which to do it. Also it is extremely difficult to demarcate work/leisure in such a society, thus a somewhat arbitrary distinction has to be made between 'necessary' and unnecessary labour. A certain amount of the spinning and weaving and basket-work still performed is not 'necessary' economically, but it has useful social functions and occupies the time between more important agricultural work. In this study, which is primarily concerned with the amount of absolutely essential work, such activities will be considered as peripheral. The following account will describe the various agricultural processes in some detail since Pignède devoted less attention to minor crops than he did to the cultivation of rice, maize, and millet.

The Gurungs in Thak plant a number of crops in among the rice, or on the embankments of the rice terraces. The principal of these are called *masa* and *masyan*, varieties of lentils. The main processes in their cultivation and the time taken according to the same two informants who gave information about the main cereals is shown in table 7.5. Likewise planted in among other crops, usually among the maize, but also among rice, are *kwoia* or soya beans. Like *masa* this is of great importance nutritionally, and almost

TABLE 7.5 *Cultivation of* masa/masyan *(planted and harvested together)*

Activity	Labour to produce 1 *muri* of crop (Informant 1)	(Informant 2)
Sow	(10 F)	(10 F)
Weed	(10 F)	(10 F)
Cut	8 F	8 F
Beat	4 F	8 M/F
Grind	4 F	4 F
Total	16 F	20 M/F

Note: Figures in brackets need not be counted separately here since the labour expended on these processes has already been counted under rice cultivation, for *masa/masyan* are weeded at the same time as the rice, etc.

every family which has land harvests one or two *muri* of the two crops combined. The time taken in the cultivation of *kwoia* is shown in table 7.6. In among the millet is planted a crop called *toro* (a type of grain). Only about half the Gurung families in Thak grew this crop; where they did grow it, however, large quantities were planted, often equalling the amount of millet. The time spent in cultivation is shown in table 7.7.

On steep slopes or in high clearings in the forest are grown *alu* (potatoes) and *toyo* (yams). Potatoes have been grown by the Gurungs for many years, and in some villages they are an extremely important crop. In Thak, however, less than half the households grew them, and they are still only grown in small quantities. They are regarded as a vegetable, to be eaten as a relish with rice, rather than as a staple. The same is true of yams of which both leaves and roots are eaten. The cultivation of the two crops requires approximately the same time, so that we may look at *toyo* cultivation as representative of them both (see table 7.8). It will be seen that there is a considerable divergence between the two estimates, but whichever one we take this crop is far less labour-intensive than any that we have hitherto studied.

TABLE 7.6 *Cultivation of* kwoia *(man-days per* muri*)*

Activity	Informant 1	Informant 2
Plant	4	3
Weed	(counted in under main cereal)	
Cut/brought to house	4	4
Beaten	8	8
Total	16	15

TABLE 7.7 *Cultivation of* toro *(man-days per* muri *of produce)*

Activity	Informant 1	Informant 2
Manure	1.3 M/F	1.66 M/F
Plough	0.3 M	0.3 M
Weed/clean ground	1.66 M/F	1.66 M/F
Re-plough / Plant and gently rake	0.66 M	1.66 M
Weed	1.66 F	1.66 F
Weed and thin	1.66 F	1.66 F
Cut	1 M/F	1.66 F (Cut; Bring to house and de-stalk)
Bring to house and de-stalk	0.66 F	
Thresh with feet	1 M/F	1.66 F
Grind	2.5 F	2.66 F
	12.4	14.58

TABLE 7.8 *Cultivation of* toyo *(man-days per* muri*)*

Activity	Informant 1	Informant 2
Clear undergrowth/hoe and burn undergrowth	1.6	1.3
Plant	0.4	1
Weed	0.8	1
Prune, pluck lower leaves, cut off other leaves	0.6	2.25
Dig up, bring to house	1.2	2 (Dig up, bring to house; Put in baskets/break up)
Put in baskets/break up	0.2	
Total Labour	4.8	7.55

In a small, fenced-off, vegetable garden near the house most families grow a selection of vegetables, including *golbeda* (Nep. tomatoes), *shibi* (*sibi* (Nep. kidney beans)), *teme* (sweet potatoes), *khorsani* (Nep. chilli), *pasagi* (like spinach) and a number of others. The gardens are cultivated by both men and women, though predominantly by the latter. The work is done in spare hours, especially in the evening, and is neglected when the busy agricultural season is in progress. Informants stated that they would do an hour or two a week for about half the year, which would accumulate to about ten man-days a year. Another four or five man-days were devoted per adult to digging up, fetching and finding wild vegetables in the forest. Children shared in the latter activity, and collected wild fruit.

ANIMAL HUSBANDRY

The majority of livestock are herded by young children up to the age of 12, or by old men and women over 65. For instance, a group of four or five young children went out day after day with between sixty and one hundred goats, and an old man and his wife lived down in the fields pasturing fifteen or twenty cows and buffaloes. Often, however, there appears to be so little work to do that adult men will go off to the forest to herd only four or five buffaloes; this almost always happens when the adults concerned have no land. Given the low productive capacity of children and the fact that large numbers of animals may be herded by one person, animal husbandry need absorb little labour. If we work on the assumption that one child of 12 could herd 40 goats of all ages, it would appear that, ideally, one goat consumes 1/200 of an adult man-day per day. In practice, however, probably twice as much child labour as this is employed, so that an estimate of 3.65 man-days per goat per year is in order. If we then add in the other tasks connected with livestock keeping – repairing sheds, looking after the newly-born, milking, putting them away at night, it would seem reasonable to suggest that approximately twice this time is invested in each animal, or some 7 man-days per year. If we assume that an old man of 65 plus a young boy of 10 can look after eight buffaloes, then each buffalo consumes approximately 0.1 man-days of labour per day, or 36.5 p.a. Oxen and cows need approximately a third of the attention of buffaloes, and thus may be assessed at some 12 man-days p.a. each. Collecting fodder for stalled animals is the most time-consuming of all livestock tasks. Most households usually keep one female buffalo and a calf stalled in the village, to provide milk and manure. This buffalo and calf seem to consume as much as a girl of about 14 can cut and bring in a day, as much as would take an adult half a normal working day to cut and fetch. Thus such stalled animals may be rated at 0.5 man-days per day, or 182.5 p.a. The enormous investment of labour in such stalled buffaloes is emphasized if we remember that this amount of labour could till over 11 *ropanis* of rice land, which would feed a normal-sized family.

FIREWOOD

There are two major methods of collecting firewood. During the months from November until June, people go up to the forest day by day and cut small branches and trees, seldom more than 6 inches in diameter. This is done by people of almost any age and either sex. During the monsoon, however, the forest abounds with leeches and the wood is wet, also there is more work to be done in the fields. So people lay in a large store of wood, often between forty and seventy bundles. This is cut by teams of men, who axe down huge trees. They then split up the wood with the axes, leave it to dry for a month or two; then with the assistance of women, they carry it down in teams. We earlier estimated that an average household would use some 120 bundles of wood p.a. An adult man or woman could cut and fetch two such bundles a day, if pressed, though it is normal to spend almost the whole day fetching one bundle. In theory, therefore, such wood-fetching requires some sixty adult man-days p.a. Fetching bamboos and wood for other domestic purposes, such as making tools or house repairs, consumes another couple of days a year.

HOUSE BUILDING AND PATH REPAIRS

One or two new houses are being built every year in Thak. A medium sized house, such as house 13D which was built during our stay in the village, would require between 700 and 1000 man-days of labour, according to two informants. Pignède gave details for the building of a big stone and slate house, where a total of 1170 man-days was required.[9] Thus an average of some 1000 man-days per new house seems reasonable. If we assume an average of 1.5 new houses p.a. in the hundred sample households, then it is clear what a very large amount of labour is absorbed by building. This is especially important since it occurs during the idle winter months. Both men and women carry stone, but the building itself is done by men, particularly by members of the lower castes. It is easy to see how such building is a mechanism whereby the wealth that flows in with Gurung servicemen is spread out among the poorer members of the society.

Houses with thatched roofs, which comprise a little over half those in the village, need to be re-thatched. There are two kinds of thatching grass; the superior kind (*poi-ki*, *ki* = thatch) lasts some six or seven years, the normal kind (*solame-ki*) has to be changed alternate years. The majority of the houses appear to be thatched with the better quality thatch, so that the average period before re-thatching in the village may be taken as four years. To re-thatch an average sized house requires approximately 12 man-days of labour. A big house needs up to 18, a small one as little as 5. On average, we may say, each thatched house needs some 3 man-days of attention a year, and the animal byres next to them another day per household.

The steep rocky paths also need to be kept in repair and constant landslides have to be remedied. Each household is asked to contribute approximately 2 labour days (adult) per year for this purpose. In practice there is much shirking of this work, and it is unlikely that more than 100 man-days p.a. are spent on the upkeep of communal paths.

MARKET AND POLITICS

Certain commodities such as kerosene, sugar, cigarettes, iron, etc. have to be fetched from Pokhara. The journey to the market and back with a medium load, a matter of 25 miles and a total up and down climb of 5000 ft, can be done fairly easily in a day by a Gurung. But people often extend their visit, combining leisure with business. On average, a Gurung family needs three or four loads of commodities a year. The need to collect pensions, to visit the hospital, to register land sales or obtain licences, necessitate further visits. Probably some 6 man-days per household per year is a reasonable estimate for such necessary activities.

If we except the *Pradan Panch* (village headman), who is often busy, and also the heads of each ward, then there is not a great deal of local government work to be done. Three members of the *Panchayat* were from the 100 households; they meet once or twice a month for a few hours. Most of the men and some of the women attend the bi-annual village meeting. One of the lower caste men acts as town crier and messenger and goes round the village shouting out announcements. Each ward has two meetings a year, each lasting a few hours. The *Pradan Panch* has to visit Pokhara fairly frequently, and works hard at various jobs such as collecting land tax. He spends up to 50 man-days a year on his job. The three ward heads in our sample probably devote two full days a year, at the most, to local government.

DOMESTIC WORK

It is naturally impossible, without a most detailed time-and-motion study, to undertake a proper analysis of the amount of time devoted to such tasks as cleaning, cooking, fetching water, minding children. My observations were purely impressionistic. Nor is it easy to speak of averages. For example, all the water in the village has to be fetched from a central pipe, but the time this takes depends very much on its flow. The pipe is often blocked or broken and there is an enormous queue, so that fetching one *gowri* (large water pot), which would normally take 5 minutes, can take over an hour. A medium to small household uses approximately 2 *gowris* per day, a large household 3–4. If the family's oxen are drinking at the house, the quantities may have to be doubled. Informants thought that, on average, it would take half an hour to fetch and fill a *gowri*. If we assume an average need for 3 *gowris* per household per day, and take into consideration that about one-third of the water is fetched by children aged 10 upwards, an average family would consume 340 man-hours p.a. just fetching water; on a 6-hour day, this would be over 56 man-days p.a. With this amount of labour it would be possible to work over 3 *ropanis* of rice land.

I was told that it took 4 hours to cook the morning meal, and 3 hours for the evening one. This includes all the preparations; grinding the grain, fetching water and so on. From observation of the very careful way in which foodstuffs are prepared, it would seem reasonable to argue that in fact some

$1\frac{1}{2}$ hours is actually spent on cooking and clearing away. This would include the time spent on producing cheese and other milk by-products, but not millet beer. The latter is brewed every few weeks and needs several hours boiling and straining. Another hour a day is spent by women sweeping away dirt, re-plastering the floor (which is done every day with dung and earth) and in general tidying. Excluding child care, which is divided between mothers and the baby's siblings, it would therefore seem that, theoretically, a woman could do all the housework in about half a working day for 4 hours. She would thus have half the day free in which to fetch wood or fodder, to work in nearby fields, unless she had a young infant to look after. In practice, if there is urgent fieldwork to be done, women often work a full day in the fields, leaving a child of ten years or older to prepare the evening meal. But in the slack periods of the year, housework and gossip and a little weaving fill up the whole day. About three times a month people spend half a day washing clothes and hair at the village tap.

CRAFTS

The main articles made out of bamboo are carrying baskets, rain-shields, drying mats, fencing, and storage containers. The number of articles made per year, and the average length of time spent by two families on each article are shown in table 7.9. Over half the basket-work in informant 1's household was done by an old man of 85; if we take this into consideration, household 1 spent some 32 man-days p.a. on basket-work, household 2 spent some 83 p.a. The latter household was a poor one, where the man definitely made a few extra items, such as rain-shields, for sale. It must be emphasized that such work is used to fill in idle moments, and is almost a form of leisure activity. Examples of basket-work are shown in Figs. 7.2 and 7.3.

It is possible to argue that not all of the basket-work is vitally necessary.

TABLE 7.9 *Bamboo-work in two Gurung households*

	Number made p.a.		Man-days to make one	
Article	Informant 1	Informant 2	Informant 1	Informant 2
Carrying basket	10–12	12	1	0.5
Rain-shield	*c.* 14	*c.* 15	2	2
Drying mat	–	4–5	–	2
Fencing (section of)	15	10	0.25	0.25
Storage basket	4	3–4	2	1
Large sitting mat	*c.* 2	*c.* 2	*c.* 1	*c.* 1
Small sitting mat	*c.* 1	*c.* 1	*c.* 1	*c.* 1

Fig. 7.2. Making a rain-shield.

Fig. 7.3. Water-carrier.

This is even more true of the spinning and weaving. Up to some twenty years ago the Gurungs probably spun and wove most of their everyday clothes; now they may be obtained much more cheaply in Pokhara bazaar. Yet women, especially older ones, continue to spin and weave and this absorbs many hours, though the financial return is very small. The only garment made in Thak nowadays is the *renga* (man's over-shirt). The processes involved in turning the fibre from a certain tree into a garment which can be sold for a little over 50p are listed in table 7.10. Thus the returns per day of labour are less than 1 rs. The spinning wheels are taken out after the harvest is ended and much of the work is done round the fire in the evenings. There seems little doubt that if there was a heightened demand for the labour of middle-aged and elderly women, much of the remaining spinning and weaving would disappear.

LOWER CASTE ACTIVITIES

As with other village crafts, especially weaving, much of the former work of the village Blacksmiths, Tailors and Cobblers is no longer necessary because of the growing market for cheap tools and clothes at Pokhara. In practice, such lower-class groups have become landless agricultural labourers working for their Gurung patrons. Each Blacksmith family has between ten and twenty households for which he mends and makes a few agricultural tools; almost all cooking utensils come from Pokhara nowadays. Probably one day per household is the maximum of work a Blacksmith can expect: his yearly fee, partly irrespective of work done, is between three and ten *pothi* (Nep. = *pathi*) of rice. Thus there is probably something like 90 man-days of work to be shared out between the six practising Blacksmith households. The Tailors have even less caste work to do, they just sew and make a few children's clothes.

TABLE 7.10 *Making a* renga.

Process	Man-days per item
Fetching '*nangi*' or fibre	0.5
Twist and dry	0.5
Wash/boil/clean	0.5
Beat	0.5
Tease out	2
Spin	3
Weave (17 inches per day)	12
Sew into shape	1
	20 adult female days, or 16 'man-days'

One of the Gurung households has a sewing machine and others do a little stitching, which further reduces the work available to the Tailors. Probably less than 25 man-days of work p.a. is available to all six Tailor households combined. The Cobblers who live just outside the borders of our hundred sample households have no caste work to do at all. One of them has become the best village carpenter, however, and carves doors, makes furniture and similar jobs. He has become comparatively affluent by this means. In conclusion, it is certain that all the caste occupations left in the village provide less work than is needed to fetch fodder for one stalled buffalo.

CLEARING NEW LANDS AND MAKING TERRACES

One type of work which, until fairly recently, absorbed a good deal of labour, was clearing new land. For example, a man who had made a rice field measuring approximately 2 *ropani*, said that it took three men some 12 days to make the terraces. Thus 1 *ropani* took some 18 man-days. During the last few years the land available for making into rice terraces has run out. Now there are only a few steep, stony, slopes near to the village where meagre maize fields can still be made. During our two winters in Thak, the time when new land is normally cleared, less than 3 *ropanis* of land was opened up by the sample households. On the border of the *panchayat* to the north, woods were being felled and slopes being terraced by Brahmins, Chetris and some Gurungs; they were outside our sample area, however. Thus, during our stay, less than 25 man-days of labour p.a. were being used to clear land. If we assume that the total of 2461 *ropanis* of rice and of maize/millet land owned by the sample households have been opened up over the last two hundred years, this would have required approximately some 44,298 man-days of labour, or 221.49 p.a. over the two hundred years if the labour had been spread out. House building could thus be seen as an alternative to clearing new land.

LABOUR SUPPLY AND LABOUR DEMAND

The following analysis of the amount of labour theoretically needed to mobilize the Gurung economy is based on observation of the hundred sample families already described. It is bound to err in a number of ways, however. To begin with it is often impossible to be sure how long a job *ought* to take, or would take if there were other pressing demands on labour. Furthermore, many of the totals are based on an extrapolation from the half dozen families where detailed figures on hours spent on gathering firewood, visits to the village tap, etc. have been collected. They may not be representative. Finally, as we shall see, much of the 'labour' is fitted in during periods of rest, or two types of work may be done simultaneously.

The units of labour in theory required to perform certain tasks, and the number of such tasks per year, are set out in table 7.11. Army service is excluded. Although, of course, precise totals are impossible, there are some interesting relative proportions shown by this table. These are illustrated more clearly in Fig. 7.4. Over half the total effort goes into arable farming and gardening, and nearly another quarter into domestic work. Pastoral activities absorb relatively little labour, as do village crafts. A very large amount of labour is devoted to fetching wood and water – far more than is devoted to all the subsidiary crops.

Yet we need to be cautious about these totals, for if we check them against the total labour available in the village the two do not seem to fit, at least not absolutely. Some 88,473 man-days are needed, according to table 7.11; yet, if we subtract men while they are away in the army, then there were only 260 adult-equivalent labourers in the village. They would have had to work 340 days a year (at 6 hours a day) or some 255 days a year if they worked an eight-hour day. From my observation in the field it seems clear to me that adults and children are not nearly as busy as this. There are various ways of reconciling the facts.

Firstly, we have reckoned the total man-days of labour available on the basis that women only represent 0.8 of a man. For many jobs, however, they are easily equal to a man. This would put up the total of labour available. Secondly, people often work into the evenings and in leisure moments at lighter jobs. Thus an average woman's day, which consists of doing the cooking and housework, fetching a load of fodder, fetching the water, and doing a little weaving and spinning, constituted, on the above methods of reckoning, 1.25 work days. Often jobs are combined. Thus, those who herd the animals often bring back a load of wood or fodder when they return to the village. Drying grains, which is largely a matter of keeping animals away from the area, can be combined with other domestic work. Many jobs can be fitted into the evening after work – tending the garden, fetching water, grinding grains. A six or even an eight-hour work day is too short when it is considered that people rise at about five or six o'clock, and do not sleep until 11 p.m., and have little else to do except work or talk. Thus, much of the non-field or livestock work listed in the second half of the table 7.11 can be fitted around the essential farming tasks. It is therefore important to determine how much time is necessarily spent on staple crops and animals. In the former case the demands on labour are likely to be seasonal, and it is here, if anywhere, that labour shortages or surpluses will be felt.

It has been suggested in table 7.11 that some 48,726 man-days are required to cultivate the arable crops in the village. This includes the time spent on drying, storing and grinding the cereals. The 260 adult-equivalents

TABLE 7.11 *Total man-days spent on various tasks, 100 households*

Task	Man-days per task	Number of tasks p.a. in 100 fams	Number of man-days p.a.
Arable farming			
Growing/processing rice (per *rop.*)	15.9	1,538 *rops.*	24,454
Growing/processing maize/millet (per *rop.*)	20	923 *rops.*	18,460
Masa/masyan[a]	18	*c.* 70 *muri*	1,260
Kwoia[a]	15.5	*c.* 70 *muri*	1,085
Toro[a]	13.5	*c.* 180 *muri*	2,430
Toyo[a]	6.5	*c.* 20 *muri*	130
Alu[a]	6.5	*c.* 20 *muri*	130
Gardens and wild vegetables	15	*c.* 50 persons	750
Clearing/terracing 1 *rop.* of land	18	1.5 p.a.	27
		Total	48,726
Pastoral farming			
Feeding/tending one adult:			
buffalo	36.5	134	4,891
buffalo (stalled)	182.5	*c.* 33	6,022
ox or cow	12	200	2,400
goat	7	247	1,729
		Total	15,042
Domestic			
Cutting/fetching 1 bundle firewood	0.5	12,000	6,000
Fetching water	0.2	20,000	4,000
Cooking/cleaning	0.5	20,000	10,000
		Total	20,000

Crafts, etc.				
Bamboo work, per household active	35	50		1,750
Weaving/spinning, per *renga*	20	30		600
Blacksmith's work, per household	1	100		100
Tailor's work, per household	0.25	100		25
			Total	2,475
Miscellaneous				
House-building, per house	1,000	1.5		1,500
Visits to Pokhara market, etc.	6	80 houses		480
Path repairs, per household	1	100 houses		100
Village government, all activities	–			150
			Total	2,230
			Grand total	88,473

[a] Per *muri* of produce.

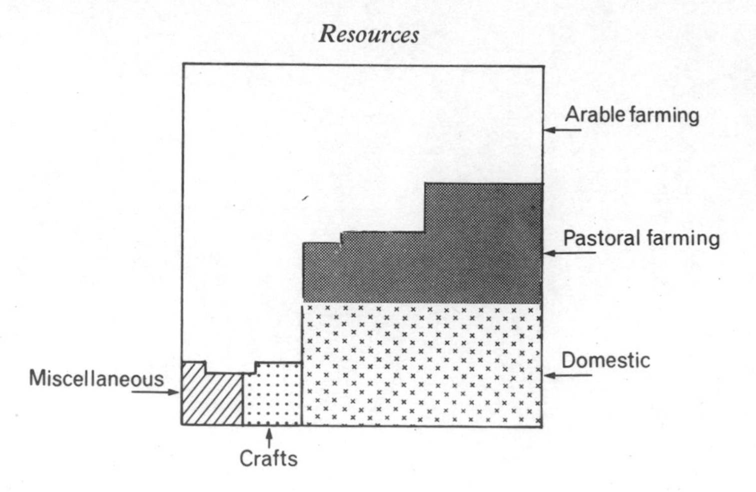

Fig. 7.4. Relative number of man-days spent on various tasks, 100 households.

would have to work for some 140 days per head to actually grow and harvest these crops, and a further 46 days in order to process them. These figures fit fairly well the finding of a South Indian village, where it was calculated that men would have to work 180 days a year, women 80 days, to cultivate the four major crops.[10] In Thak, if people worked continuously in the fields, the work could be done in just over four months at 6 hours a day. In actual fact, the agricultural season begins with the preparation of the maize fields in early April, and ends towards the end of November, when all the rice has been brought up to the house. Thus people are occupied a little over half the time during the busiest eight months.

Studies have been made by various agricultural economists of the relative degrees of employment per month in various societies.[11] Such an analysis for the Thak sample households can produce only a rough approximation to the situation. The outlines may be seen in Fig. 7.5. The diagram shows only specific tasks which occur periodically; other daily jobs, such as grinding grain, fetching water, domestic work, or cutting fodder for the animals are not shown. The diagram also needs to be smoothed out somewhat; for example, the first part of September is fairly busy, but there is almost nothing to do in the second half of the month. Nevertheless, general impressions are worth noting. In 4 months, less than a quarter of the potential labour force is employed; only in 2 months is more than half of it needed. Only in June is almost everyone busy. Thus, even with a large migration of adult males to the army, there is, for 9 months, considerable under-employment.

We may wonder how the situation appears to members of the culture. I asked one informant to tell me which months were busy, and which were times

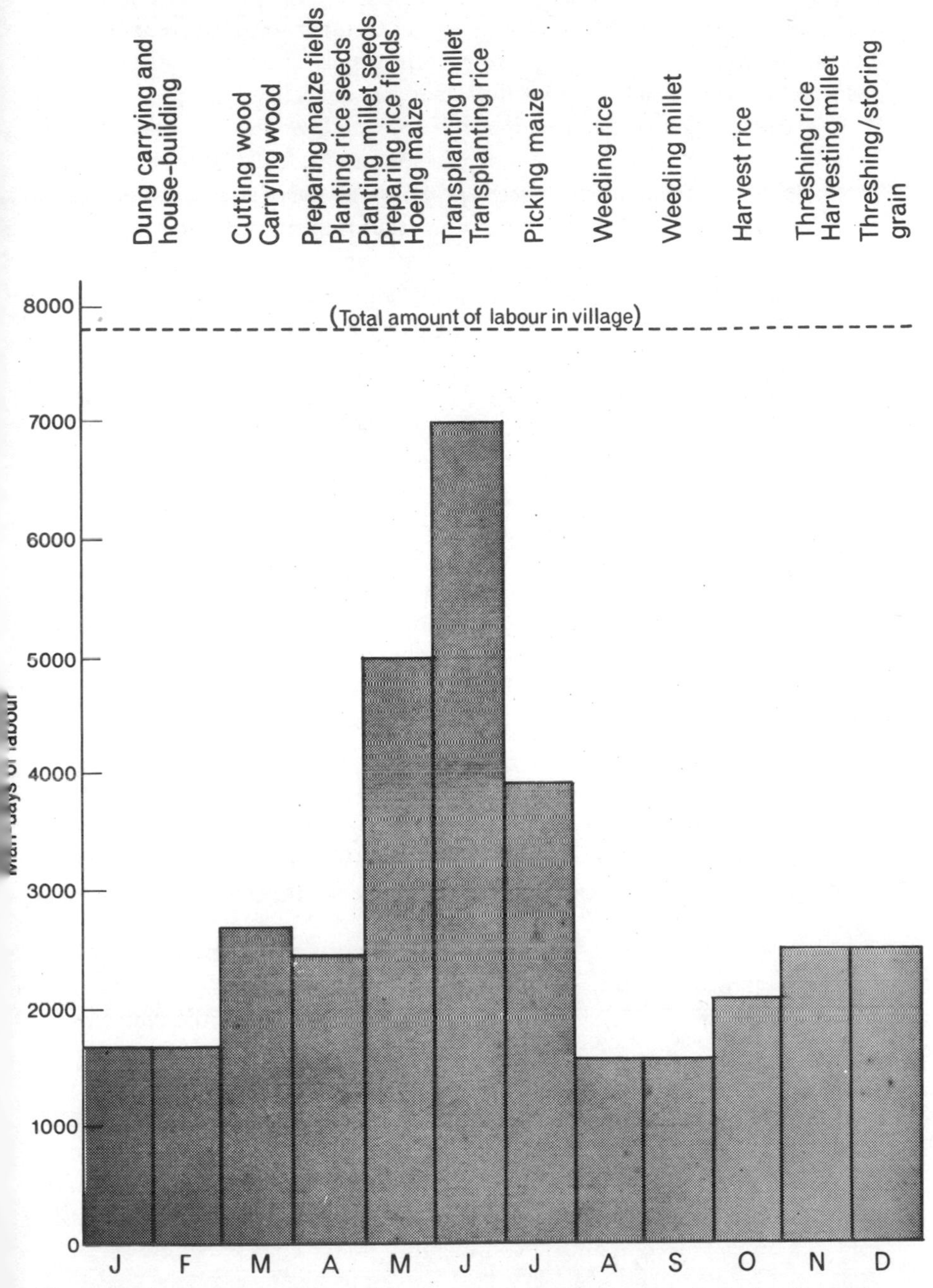

Fig. 7.5. Labour supply and demand in 100 sample households; major agricultural tasks, by months.

of leisure. He thought that December/January to January/February, March/April, and September/October to the end of October were leisure times. This fits the diagram exactly, though the way in which he described the situation made people sound much busier than they are in reality.

In order to examine the situation in more detail, we may turn again to our sample five households. Table 7.12 shows the amount of labour-units they had available, and the amount they needed during the busiest agricultural seasons in order to till their holdings. This shows that richer families have considerable labour deficits during these three months, while middling Gurung families almost balance their supplies of labour against their demands. The Blacksmith household had two-thirds of its labour resources free to work on other's land. From the above table it can be confirmed that the amount of land needed to keep an average-sized household busy during the three monsoon months is about 20 *ropanis* (2.6 acres) of mixed rice and maize/millet land. Yet the unequal distribution of land in the *panchayat* is to some extent evened out by the demands for labour; the lower castes, especially, benefit from the seasonality of demands. Without the labour shortages of the richer families, they would not be able to earn a share in the harvest.

The families which have a labour surplus or deficit during the three summer months of maximum activity are listed in appendix 2. The results, which are necessarily somewhat artificial, are summarized in table 7.13. It will be seen that there are, at present, theoretically some 29 households with a definite labour surplus, even in the busiest three months. These include all the Blacksmith and Tailor households and a few Gurung ones. The Tailors, for example, may be calculated to have about 14,440 surplus man-days of labour to offer to other households in the village during these three months. If those now away in the army were forced to return to the village for some reason, the situation would not, at first sight, change greatly. There would then be 51 instead of

TABLE 7.12 *Demand and supply of labour in five sample households*

Household number and units of labour available, May–July[a]		Units of labour needed for:		Surplus or deficit
		Rice and maize/millet	Domestic	
3B	315	210	45	+ 60
19	345	360	45	− 60
17	330	570	45	−285
40	345	600	45	−300
57	150	20	30	+100

[a] This is on the assumption that each individual would only be able to work 25 days a month, needing five or six days' rest.

TABLE 7.13 *Surplus and deficit of labour, May–July*

	At present (no. households)	If all absent men returned to village
Surplus	29	32
Balanced	9	10
Deficit	55	51
Unknown	7	7
	100	100

55 deficit households; not a great difference. But many of the households which still had a shortage would now need only small quantities of hired labour, instead of considerable amounts as at present. It seems likely that when the population has increased by 50 %, which it will do in the next twenty years or less, the majority of the households will have labour surpluses.

THE ACTUAL WORK PATTERN OF THREE HOUSEHOLDS

The previous general description needs to be supplemented by a more detailed analysis of what people actually did work at. I asked two young informants to report each day what each member of their household had done that day. Unfortunately, one of the informants left for the army after three months, so I chose another informant to report on another household for the rest of our stay in the village. Thus the periods for which I have work reports are as follows:

House 12A: 5 April – 6 July, 1969.
House 17: 6 April – 8 November, 1969.
House 3B: 8 July – 31 January, 1969–70.

House 12A consisted of almost the poorest Gurung family in the sample; the house was rented and the father had recently come to Thak, his wife's natal village. He had no maize or rice land of his own. But he had been able to obtain the lease of rice land producing some 26 *muri* of (unhusked) grain (from 20 *ropanis* of land) and 6 *muri* of millet (approx. 3 *ropanis*). He had to give half the produce on each type of land to the owner. He also grew a considerable amount of *toyo*, and some potatoes, *masa* and *kwoia*. His only livestock consisted of two goats and a few hens. He had five surviving children at home, three of them aged 14 or over. The family had 3.8 production units. Thus, at 280 man-days per production unit, he had 1064 man-days of labour available. The approximate amount of labour needed to run the holding was thus:

	Man-days
26 *muri* of rice, at 12 man-days per *muri*	312
6 *muri* of millet, at 22 man-days per *muri*	132
Other crops	*c.* 50
Livestock	*c.* 16
Firewood	*c.* 50
Water-fetching and housekeeping	*c* 240
Total	800

In fact, as we have earlier argued, if there has been an urgent need for labour, many of the above tasks could have been made shorter. The work could easily have been compressed into some 600 man-days – thus leaving some 464 free man-days. In order to find out what actually happens from month to month, we may study the reported activity of each member of the household (table 7.14).

The category 'other work' helps to explain how, despite labour surpluses, this family managed to remain fairly busy. Often the herding of animals, wood-fetching, etc. only took a couple of hours and the person concerned would spend the rest of the day in leisure. In table 7.14, however, this would be shown as an active day. The way this happened is well demonstrated by the family. They only had two goats, yet a boy of 9 and a girl of 14 spent respectively 26 and 58 days herding goats, and, occasionally, other people's buffaloes. Otherwise, both did hardly anything productive, while the little girl of 7 did not work. Thus the children aged 14 or under, who would be assessed as a total 0.8 of a production unit, contributed very little to the household labour supply, even in the three busiest months.

Father, mother and first son each worked an almost equal amount in the

TABLE 7.14 *Work undertaken in household 12A, 5 April–3 July 1969*[a]

Persons and age		Field labour	Other work[b]	Days spent on various activities				
				Pokhara	Rest	Ritual	Sick	Unknown
Father	55	45	15	5	2	1	0	9
Mother	49	42	22	4	1	2	1	5
Son	18	44	14	0	11	4	1	3
Da.	16	29	24	0	3	12[c]	0	9
Da.	14	3	58	0	2	1	0	13
Son	9	0	26	0	44[d]	0	0	7
Da.	7	0	0	0	77	0	0	0
Total		163	159	9	140	20	2	46

[a] I was away from the village 14–26 May, and did not record activities then.
[b] Includes domestic work, herding animals, etc.
[c] This girl was one of the two who performed the ritual *garda sheba* dance.
[d] Approximately half this time was spent at school.

fields – each of them working about 60 % of the available days at such work. Yet even in the busiest month of the agricultural year, June, the four eldest members of the family, who between them could have done at least 110 days in the fields, spent only 74 days on such work. None of them spent more than 20 days in that month on fieldwork. Even in the busiest of all months the head of the household could afford to go away to Pokhara for 4 days. He spent another four days sitting making rain-shields – a job which could easily have been done at another time. In April, also a busy month, the eldest daughter spent eight days dancing in the *garda sheba* or ceremonial dance. In view of this, it is not surprising that the eldest son asked if we would employ him, and that he was finally sent off by his family to seek a job in the Indian army. He set off on 4 July even though July is one of the busiest agricultural months.

After the above informant had left I started to record details of household 3B. In this household there was also a labour surplus, and again the eldest son left for the army after 3 months. Fortunately my informant was a younger son. The period studied includes the time of weeding and harvesting. The days spent on various activities by each member of the family is shown in table 7.15. Out of a total of 910 days in which the activities are known, only 364 were spent on work in the fields. The household in question had only a medium to small sized holding of 8 *ropanis* of maize/millet land and 6 *ropanis* of rice. This could be expected to provide them with some 232 days of work in all the year. But they also found an outlet for their labour in neighbouring households, for instance house 3A where the brother of the household head was away in the army. It will be seen from table 7.15 that the father and mother, the latter a good deal younger than the former, shared field work fairly equally,

TABLE 7.15 *Work undertaken in household 3B, 9 July 1969–7 January 1970*

		Days spent on various activities						
Persons	Age	Field labour	Other work	Pokhara	Rest	Ritual	Sick	Unknown
Father	59	65	57	17	25	9	5	6
Mother	42	66	92	2	13	7	0	4
Son[b]	21	34	45(38[a])	2	7	0	1	3
Da.	18	102	69	0	6	4	0	3
Son	15	97	123(26[a])	10	12	4	16	4
Da.	12	only a little baby-minding and buffalo herding)						
Total		364	386	31	63	24	22	20

[a] The figures in brackets are the number of days spent on schoolmastering, classified as 'other activity'.
[b] The eldest son was present for only half the total period of 184 days, since he left to go to the army.

but the main burden fell on their unmarried younger daughter who spent a considerable amount of time going out to work for other, richer, families in joint working parties. The father spent 17 days in Pokhara, and rested for 25 days. His daughter never went to Pokhara and rested for only 6 days. Sickness was of minor importance in reducing labour. The only one at all seriously impeded was the younger son, and his ailments were comparatively mild and would have been forgotten if there had been important work to do. Much of the 'other work' consisted of feeding the family buffalo and fetching wood. As in the village as a whole, work in this family varied very considerably from month to month. Thus, during the last 24 days of July when rice seedlings are transplanted, the family did 65 days of labour in the fields, while during the last 24 days of December they did none. The type and amount of work done in each month is best illustrated in the case of the third sample household.

As noted earlier, household 17 is one of the richest in the village and has a considerable labour shortage. It overcame this by hiring the labour of poorer Gurungs and service caste families. The amount and type of work done in each month in this family are shown in Fig. 7.6. The diagram shows that the peak of maize work actually carried out, occurred in June, rice in July, and millet in August – though the diagram may be a little unrepresentative since the monsoon rains were late in 1969. The diagram is also biased by the death of the grandfather in October, which added to the ritual necessary in that month. The greatest amount of fieldwork in any one month occurred in August, with 88 days. In October only 13 days of fieldwork were noted.

It has been a central theme of this analysis that the exodus of adult males to the army, rather than provoking a labour shortage, helps to ease an already considerable problem of under-employment. This is well illustrated by the activities of soldiers temporarily in the village, for instance the young soldier in this household. Although soldiers on leave are specifically ordered to take a rest and not to work too hard, it seems likely that if there was an urgent need for their labour, they would work. They have a stake in the farms at home, and would be likely to wish to make them prosper. But observation of the several army men who were on leave during our stay in Thak showed that they did practically no work during their months in the village, preferring to spend the time sleeping, lazing in the sun, or wandering to neighbouring villages. Household 17 provides a good example. As we have noted, it had a large area of land and a very considerable shortage of labour. In 1969, during the busiest period of the year (April to August) a young man from the British army returned on leave. He was at the peak of his strength at 22, and would soon be inheriting half the estate along with his brother. He was prepared to work if there was a real need; thus, when rice was being transplanted, he went down to the fields with the rest of the family and worked for 21 days. But this was

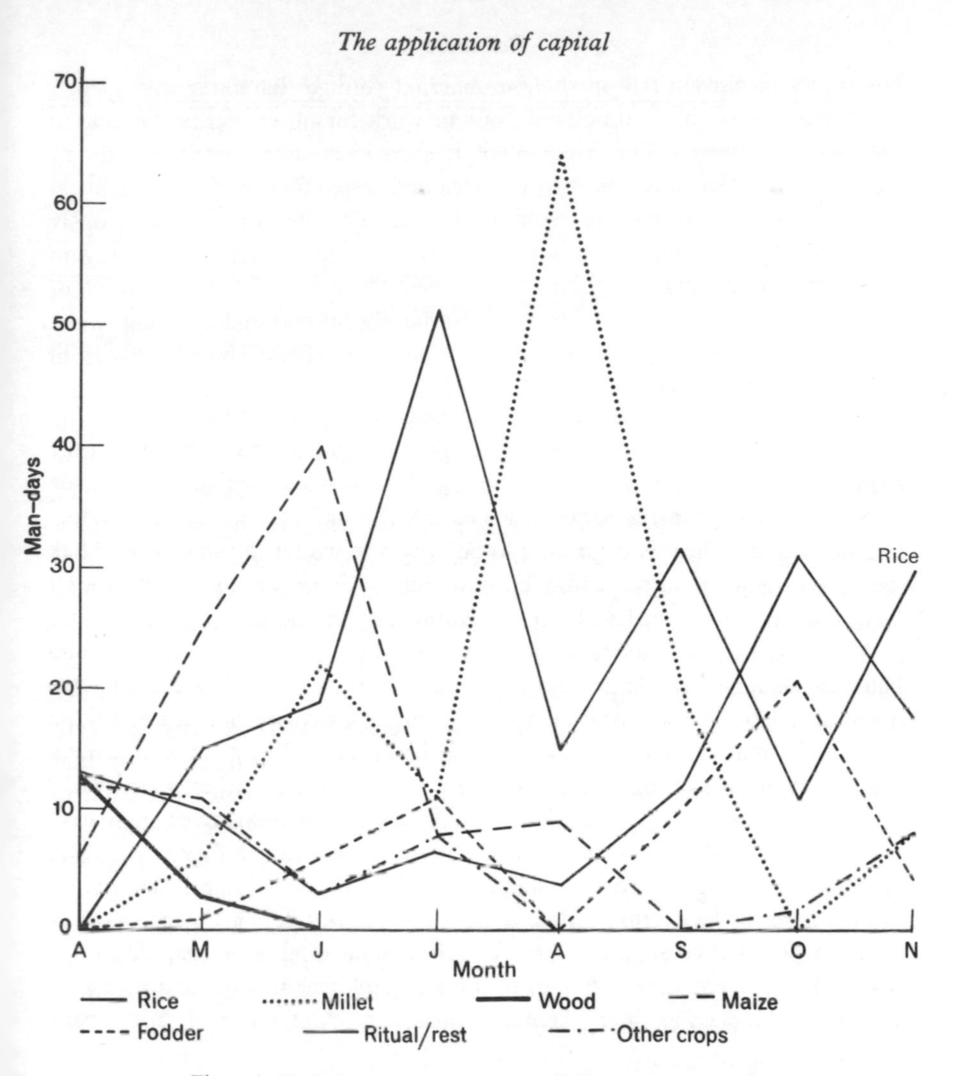

Fig. 7.6. Man-days spent on various activities, household 17.

practically all the work he did. His activities in each month are summarized in table 7.16. Thus in April he did not spend a single day in productive work, and very little in May or August. Of the 137 days for which there are records, he only spent 31 working in the fields. The rest, excluding three days making baskets, he spent listening to his transistor, gambling, going to other villages. That the second largest landowning household in Thak could afford to 'waste' 103 man-days of adult male labour in the busiest months of the year is a revealing fact. It is also revealing that this young Gurung was happy to sit and do nothing for day after day while his family worked round him. His status as

TABLE 7.16 *Activities of younger son of household 17, 6 April–23 August 1969*

	April	May	June	July	Aug.	Total
Leisure	24	22	20	16	21	103
Fieldwork	0	5	9	15	2	31
Other work	0	3	0	0	0	3
Not known	1	1	1	0	0	3

a returned serviceman, and his grandfather's favouritism, were a sufficient protection against work demands.

It is impossible to predict how fast unemployment will grow in the future. On the one hand continued population growth, and the cutting back of the British Gurkhas, could mean a doubling of the man/work-available ratio in the next thirty years. On the other, it is possible that cultivation may be intensified somewhat. Wheat is beginning to be grown in winter in some of the Thak fields, and more potatoes could be cultivated. Above all, the wider use of fertilizers and improved-yield seeds could have a significant effect. If we make the most generous estimates possible, then the use of fertilizers and better seeds might treble present crop yields. This would add a considerable amount of labour. For instance, it is possible to calculate that instead of an average 16 man-days per *ropani* of land being needed to grow and process grains, up to 28 man-days might be needed. This optimistic estimate would allow for up to 60 % population growth before unemployment increased, assuming that all other resources such as livestock and the forest could also expand. In fact, even with outstanding success in introducing new hybrid grains, it seems likely that all gains in that field will be swallowed up in 15 years of population growth. If more intensive farming is not rapidly introduced, the present barely-concealed under-employment will turn into very visible and damaging unemployment within the next ten to twenty years.

8

Income, consumption and expenditure

SOURCES OF INCOME

The Gurung economy has two major, overlapping, spheres. One consists of the basic foodstuffs which are produced within the village, and distributed without the use of cash. The other is a cash sector in which the men migrate to work, mainly in the army, and their pay and pensions are used to buy gold, clothing, and certain luxuries and necessities such as salt, cooking oil, cigarettes and sugar. The degree to which the village we studied was dependent on the inflow of foreign capital, and the ways in which such capital was distributed will be among the topics considered in this chapter. The following analysis will also make it possible to compare the domestic economy of the Gurungs with that of other Himalayan groups. Twenty years, or more, ago it would have been almost impossible to calculate the value of commodities in the subsistence sector. Nowadays certain foodstuffs, especially meat, rice and oil, are frequently purchased and assessments are easier. Yet there are still large areas where broad guesswork is needed, for instance in assessing family income from communally owned resources such as the forest. It should also be noted that the following account is a static analysis; it does not deal with the considerable fluctuations from year to year caused by good and bad harvests. Nor does it analyse the way in which household economies vary over the life cycle, domestic income increasing and decreasing with variations in the age and sex structure of the household.

The main types of income are illustrated if we look in detail at three households, rich, medium and poor. The total annual income from various sources at the time of our visit in these households was as shown in table 8.1. Some explanation of the way in which the totals were calculated is necessary. The first category, army service, is fairly obvious. Only one man in the three households was in the army. His pay and keep was worth more than twice the total income of household 57, though he was only a young man of 22 in the lowest ranks of the British army. The schoolmaster's wages as third master in the village primary school (90 rs. per month) are a little less than the Blacksmith gets from working as a labourer and ploughman. Household 3B earns a little from hiring out labour, but in the case of the Blacksmith household

TABLE 8.1 *The income of three households, 1969* (rs. p.a.).

Source of income	Household number 17	3B	57
Army: pay and keep	5,425	–	–
pension	–	420	–
Schoolmaster	–	1,080	–
Labour: building/agriculture	–	200	1,110
crafts	30	20	–
caste work	–	–	550
Farming: meat/milk/eggs	3,000	1,326	520
grains/vegetables	10,300	3,850	150
Forest products	700	565	260
Total	19,455	7,461	2,590
Total of production units	5.4	4.2	2.0

it is this occupation, and the hereditary caste payments, that constitute the major sources of income. I asked the head of household 57 to outline what work he did in a year and the rewards he received for such work; the results are set out in table 8.2.

It will be seen that the returns for working as a ploughman are about 10 rs. per day – which is about the same as that for a man working on his own land on other jobs. The rewards for Blacksmith's work are far higher, almost double in fact. It should be stressed that the above are only very approximate totals, and the number of days worked is especially uncertain. But if the returns on various types of labour are correct, the explanation appears fairly simple. Until a few years ago each Blacksmith and Tailor did a considerable amount of work for his client family and a fixed amount of grain, varying between 3–10 *pathi* (worth 20–70 rs. now) was paid for this, mostly after the harvest. This traditional amount is still paid; all those I asked saying that it is normal to give about 5 *pathi* of rice to the family Tailor

TABLE 8.2 *Sources of income in a Blacksmith household (57)*

Nature of work	Days employed p.a.	Cash equivt. of reward p.a.	Medium of payment
Work party, agricultural	*c.* 15	105	food/cash (½)
Work party, housebuilding	*c.* 30	210	food/cash (½)
Wife, casual work	*c.* 5	15	food
Ploughman (for hse 32)	*c.* 75	780	food/rice
Blacksmith's work	*c.* 30	550	rice
Total	*c.* 155	1660	

and the same amount to the Blacksmith. But the amount of work done, especially by Tailors, has decreased rapidly with the increased purchase of ready-made clothes and hardware at Pokhara. How long the Gurungs will be prepared to pay the old rates it is difficult to say. Probably as long as they have adequate supplies of grain for themselves, plus a small surplus for the service castes. Thus, when cereal shortages begin to occur, the service castes will soon lose up to a quarter of their total income.

The calculation of the next category of items is more complicated, since very little, if any, of such sources are turned into cash. Where necessary the calculation has been made on the basis of what the person would have had to pay to obtain such goods within the village. Thus, for example, we were informed that the right price for a bundle of firewood was about 3 rs., though in Pokhara it might cost up to double that sum. It is particularly difficult to calculate the value of foodstuffs obtained from communal land: fruit, wild vegetables, fish, wild animals. It is possible that this has been somewhat undervalued. The very considerable importance of forest land as a source of fodder is not included under 'forest products' since income from such fodder, when processed through buffaloes, is included in the value of milk/meat and the grains which are so heavily dependent on manure.

A number of points in table 8.1 are worth stressing. The ratio of income from arable as opposed to pastoral farming in the two Gurung families is 3.1. This probably reflects fairly accurately the degree to which the Gurung economy has become a settled cereal-producing one, having evolved from a predominantly nomadic and herding pattern. It will be seen that the difference between the earning power of a rich Gurung and that of a medium–poor Gurung is considerable, while that between the poorer Gurung and Blacksmith family is not so great. The actual gap is not as great as suggested in the table since household 17 has far greater expenses, especially that of hired labour. Finally, it should be noted that no allowance has been made in the calculations above for labour hired out by a household when an equal amount of labour from other households has had to be used on other occasions, in other words the exchange of labour common to Gurung society.

Now that we have some idea of the range of incomes of specific households we may turn to the income of the 100 households collectively. Although the calculations again require a considerable amount of guesswork, I believe that the overall proportions are of the right order. It should be noted that the pay to soldiers and civilians abroad, included under 'army' in the above table, includes their food and clothing, estimated to be worth 5 rs. per person per day. Such migrant labourers also spend some of their pay while abroad. Thus the above table does not represent the actual amount of money which flows into the village, but rather, total income.

TABLE 8.3 *Total income of 100 households, Thak, 1969*

Nature of resource[a]	rs. p.a.
Army: pay and keep (9 Br. army, 34 Ind. army)	189,960
pension (28 pensioners)	11,760
Schoolmasters (3 primary teachers)	3,960
[b]Agricultural: meat/milk/eggs	111,000
grains/vegetables	371,840
Forest: wood and food	50,000
	738,520

[a] When looking at single households, as in table 8.1, it was relevant to assess wage labour within the village, paid for by other villagers. But now that we are dealing with total sources of income for the 100 households, only sales of labour/craft products to persons outside the village need be included. Such sales do not amount to more than a couple of hundred rupees p.a. and, since they are balanced by similar purchases of such commodities by Thak villagers in nearby areas, they have been omitted here.

[b] The totals here were worked out on the basis of actual crops grown; they agree fairly well with the sample households in table 8.1.

Those now in army service, or working as civilians in India and Nepal, are as shown in table 8.4. Thus we see that there are currently nine persons in the British army, 26 in the Indian, and eight civilians. In keep and pay the British soldiers probably receive in the region of 59,400 rs. p.a; those in India, both army or civilians with para-military jobs, some 130,560 rs. Thus, of a total 294 production units in the village, the 43 units away from the village earn approximately one-quarter of the total income of the 100 households. This indicates how important migrant labour is.

Over one-quarter of the sample households were receiving an army pension in 1969. The grades of pension are indicated in table 8.5. The actual pensions

TABLE 8.4 *Those working abroad in 100 households, 1969*

Rank	Number in army civilian	
	Indian	British
Rifleman	18	5
Lance-Corporal	2	1
Corporal	3	1
Sergeant	1	2
Sgt.-Major	1	0
Major	1	–
Civilian (watchman/police)	7	–
Civilian – Nepal	1	

TABLE 8.5 *Pensions in 100 sample households*

Rank	Number of pensioners: Indian	British
Rifleman	10	4
Lance-Corporal		2
Corporal		1
Sergeant	1	4
Sgt.-Major	1	
Lieutenant	3	2

received by members of each rank may vary considerably, depending on injuries, service record and other factors. Thus one retired Lieutenant from the British army claimed to be getting only 25 rs. per month, while another, newly retired, was receiving six times that amount. Throughout the sample, the average (mean) pension is approximately 35 rs. per month.

The income from dairy and cereal products as stated in table 8.3 is again based on guesswork. In the case of meat/milk, the amount per household was estimated by comparing the three sample households to the figures for total livestock ownership in the village and multiplying by the relevant amount. In the case of grains and vegetables the calculation was made by working out the total production of grains in an average year, and then multiplying this by the cost of such grains if bought in the village in 1969. It will again be seen that dairy products are in the ratio of under 1 : 3 when compared to cereals. The proportion coming from the various major sources is most easily visualized by the help of Fig. 8.1. Almost exactly half the income comes from cereals, and the other half from labour services abroad and pastoral/forest produce. The diagram does not, however, do full justice to the crucial importance in the Gurung economy of the cash flowing from migrant labour. This can only be estimated when we have some idea of the proportion of a serviceman's wages which reaches the village.

Servicemen were not always willing to disclose how much money they brought back when returning on leave, but it is nevertheless possible to make fairly accurate estimates of how much is saved and brought home. The amount will, of course, vary with the rank and accumulative energies of the individual concerned. Colonel Langland, who has worked for many years as a recruiting officer with the Gurkhas, thought that a Rifleman from Malaya would take home about 3000 rs. after three years service. Men of higher rank would take around 5000 rs. Informants in the village, and the actual sums brought home by two young Riflemen during our stay, fitted with this estimate. About two-

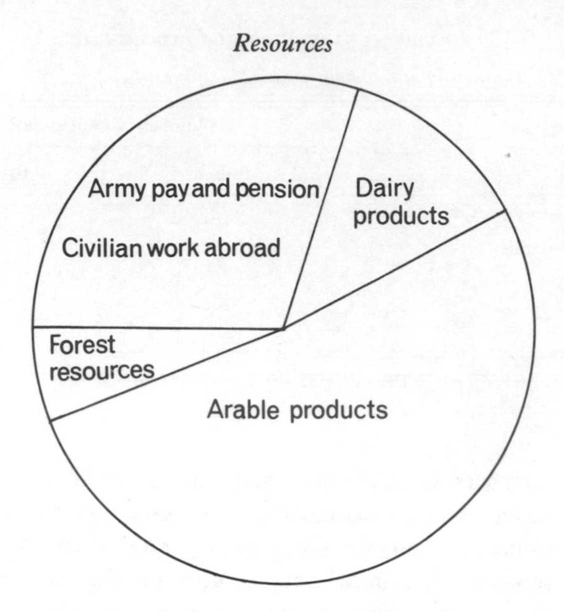

Fig. 8.1. Relative income from various major sources in 100 households.

thirds of the amount brought back is usually in cash, the rest is in gold, clothes, radios, watches, with gold as the predominant item. It seems probable that higher rank officers tend to accumulate cash and to bring it back at the end of their service career. Thus an outstandingly ambitious Gurung who reached the rank of Lieutenant in the British army was said to have brought back 50,000 rs. and 20 *tolas* of gold (worth about 200 rs. per *tola*). He also had to employ 24 porters to carry his other possessions up to the village; these possessions included chairs, hurricane lamps, a gramophone, shotgun, and a large sewing machine. In the Indian army, or as a civilian, more modest sums may be expected; thus one man who had served as a Rifleman in the Indian army and who hoped to be re-recruited said that 300–400 rs. in money, and 4–5 *tolas* of low-quality gold (at about 130 rs. per *tola*) plus a radio and some clothing for the women was normal after a three year period. A recently returned Corporal from the Indian army brought between two and three thousand rupees in money and gold during our stay. If we include clothing and utilitarian goods, but exclude non-essential goods such as radios and watches, it would seem reasonable to adopt the calculation of the amount of income flowing into the village from abroad set out in table 8.6. It will be seen that some 25,000 rs. or a little over is calculated to flow back into the village annually, or a mean average of 250 rs. per household. If we subtract the estimated cost of food and clothing for those abroad (some 78,000 rs. p.a.) then we are left with the fact that of their total pay of 111,485 rs. p.a., those abroad save and bring back a little

TABLE 8.6 *Flow of cash and utility goods from migrant labourers*

	Avge. saved per Rifleman[a]	No. of Riflemen	Avge. saved per officer	No. of officers	Total saved p.a.
British army	3000	5	5000	4	11,666
Indian army	1000	18	2000	8	11,333
Indian/civilian	1000	8			2,666
					25,665

[a]The totals of rupees *except* in the last column, are for three-year periods, the normal length of absence on one term of duty.

under a quarter. If we include the often expensive luxury items and the huge import duties paid on these, it would seem reasonable to estimate that soldiers abroad are saving approximately one third of their pay each month, or investing such pay in goods that will be taken home. This appears a low rate of saving if we compare it to the situation described for the Limbu of east Nepal, of whom it has been written that 'it can be assumed that about 60 % of a solder's pay eventually reached the Indreni settlements'.[1] The Limbu are often trying to buy back mortgaged land and are thus possibly more desperate to save. As will be shown, the cash sent back from the army is used primarily to buy land from other Gurungs, and to purchase goods at Pokhara. It could be argued that the village only needs a certain inflow of cash, and that men in the army are not expected to save more than that.

Finally we need to calculate the total cash income of the 100 sample households, however rough such a calculation must be. Table 8.7 indicates that the mean average of cash available per household is 460 rs. p.a., the bulk of which comes from army service. Practically no basket-ware or woven objects are sold outside the village nowadays; unlike Siklis, thick sheep's-wool blankets are not manufactured. A few carrying baskets and woven men's garments are sold and

TABLE 8.7 *Total cash income of 100 sample households, 1969*

Source	Total p.a.
From army wages	25,665
From pensions	11,760
Schoolmasters	3,960
Sale of craft products	200
Sale of agricultural products	4,500
	46,085

200 rs. per year is an outside estimate of what is earned from 'cottage industries'. Nor is there much sale of surplus agricultural crops. I was told that a large amount of cereals were sold from the neighbouring, richer, village of Taprang (predominantly populated by Brahmins) and that even within Thak the Brahmins were able to live far more economically and to sell their surpluses. But in the sample 100 households there was little surplus for sale. I was informed that in a good year perhaps 30–35 *muri* of rice, and about 10 *muri* of other grains, would be sold. During the year we lived in the village there were shortages due to hail the previous year and only some 4 or 5 *muri* of rice and the same quantity of *kwoia* had been sold to Pokhara. For the purpose of table 8.7, taking into consideration the frequency of poor harvests, I have reckoned that some 25 *muri* of rice and 10 *muri* of other grains are sold annually. This would produce the sum indicated in the table. It will be seen that less than 10 % of the total cash income comes from the sale of village products. For the cash to buy many of the necessities of life, therefore, these families are over 80 % dependent on cash coming from outside Nepal. Nor are improvements forseeable. There is now little land left for expansion and all attempts at intensifying agriculture will meet very great problems.

We have already analysed the distribution of land ownership, but to gain a total picture of relative incomes we need also to know which households receive cash from outside the village. Families with little land may still be prosperous if they have a son in the army. Bearing in mind that returns from service in the British army are considerably greater than other types of service, we may now look pictorially at the points at which cash flows into the village.

It will be seen from Fig. 8.2 that a majority (54/100) of the households have some source of extra-village income. A considerable number have several external sources. But only one lower caste household, a Tailor with a son in civilian work in India, has such an external income. Of the 77 Gurung households, some 50 have money flowing in from outside. One thing that emerges strikingly from the map is that it is the medium-poor Gurung households who have most access to army funds. These are predominantly *sorajat* households with insufficient lands on which to live in the village. The flow of cash from outside helps to balance them against the wealthier households which have had less incentive to send their sons away from the village. This predominance of *sorajats* in army service is shown both in the higher proportion (23/24) which have external income (as opposed to 44/53 *carjat* households), and also in the marked preference shown by the *sorajat* for the better paid but more demanding life of the British army. The figures are as set out in table 8.8. Thus the *sorajat* actually predominate as recipients of pay and pensions

Fig. 8.2. Flow of cash into 100 households.

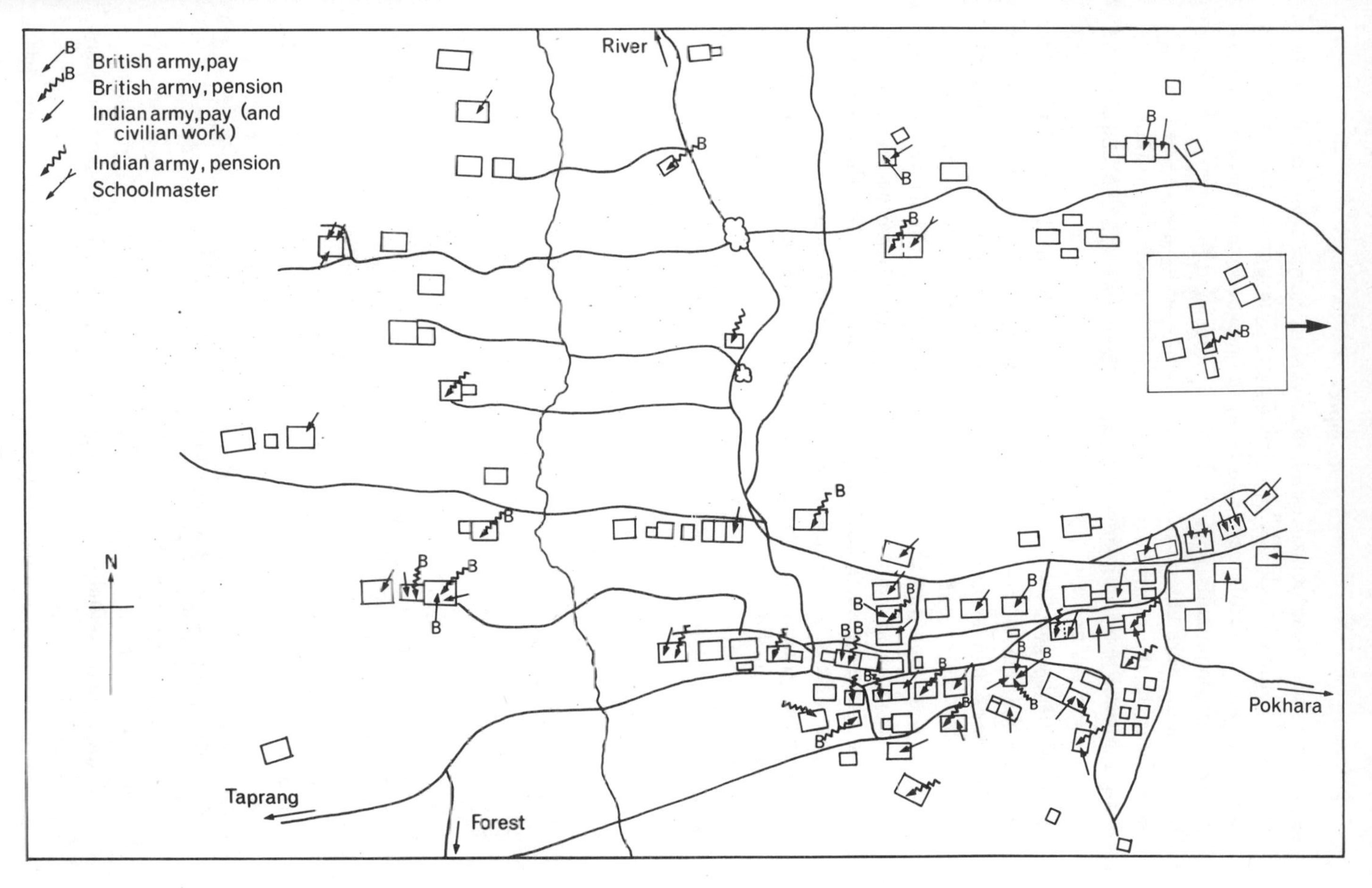
British army, pay
British army, pension
Indian army, pay (and civilian work)
Indian army, pension
Schoolmaster
N
River
Pokhara
Forest
Taprang
B

TABLE 8.8 Jat *recruitment into the British or Indian army*

	No. receiving pay		No. receiving pension	
Jat	British	Indian	British	Indian
Carjat	4	22	6	12
Sorajat	4	9	8	2

from the British army, while heavily outnumbered by the numerically superior *carjat* in the Indian army. The effects of this were recognized in the village; the upwardly mobile families, buying up land and building houses, or storing away wealth, were said to be households 15, 24, 32. All belonged to the same lineage of the *kebje* and all had close ties with the British army.

The wealth that flows in through the 54 households with outside connections is distributed along various channels throughout the community, benefiting Tailors and Blacksmiths as well as the recipient Gurung households. This process will be analysed after considering consumption and expenditure patterns.

CONSUMPTION AND EXPENDITURE

A theoretical framework for discussion: the 'consumption unit'

The need to construct 'consumption units' which enable one to take into account age and sex variations when comparing household budgets has been suggested by T. Scarlett Epstein.[2] Dr Epstein points out that Bailey considered 'all persons of fifteen years and over as full consumers, those from ten to fourteen as half-consumers, those from two to nine as quarter-consumers'. He ignored children under 2 years of age. Bailey's estimate is said to fit the situation in East Nepal, among the Limbus.[3] Dr Epstein herself 'accepted Lusk's coefficient' as follows:

Household members	*Consumption unit*
Males above 14 years	1.00
Females above 14 years	0.83
Males and Females of 10 years but below 14 years	0.83
Males and Females of 6 years but below 10 years	0.70
Males and Females of 1 year but below 6 years	0.50
Males and Females of below 1 year	Nil

One other study may be cited, that undertaken in Egypt and reported by Clark, where children under 13 were reckoned as 0.6 units; males 13–50 as 1.0 and then, over 50, as 0.8; females aged 13–50 as 0.7, then as 0.3.[4] Clearly the situation will vary from society to society and it will be worth seeing how the scales above fit with the Gurung situation.

Two methods of analysing the situation among the Gurungs were attempted. The first was to ask two informants to estimate in detail how much food both males and females of various ages would consume per day. Their answers are put on to a ten-point scale in table 8.9. It will be seen that men and women are believed by both informants to consume equally until the age of 15, and then one informant states that women never reach a higher rate than 75 % of male consumption. The peak period for men is between 20 and 60 according to informant A, and between 25 and 50 according to informant B. We may check the above observations against the actual food consumption as noted when I undertook a dietary survey of two Gurung households. During this the quantities eaten by various members of the household during a week were noted. The results are shown in table 8.10. The middle-aged father in family 2 is given the value '10'. These figures lend support to the estimates in table

TABLE 8.9 *Estimated consumption of food per day*

	Males		Females	
Age	Inft. A	Inft. B	Inft. A	Inft. B
3 months	None	None	Same as	Same as
6 months	1	None	males	males
9 months	$1\frac{1}{4}$	$1\frac{1}{4}$	until age	until age
1 year	$1\frac{1}{2}$	2	65 when	15
15 months	–	$2\frac{5}{8}$	they begin	
2 years	$2\frac{1}{2}$	4	to consume	
3 years	3	4	a little	
4 years	$3\frac{1}{2}$	4	less	
5 years	4	4		
6 years	–	4		
8 years	$4\frac{1}{2}$	$5\frac{3}{8}$		
11 years	5	$5\frac{3}{8}$		
13 years	5	6		
15 years	$5\frac{7}{8}$	$6\frac{5}{8}$		6
17 years	$7\frac{1}{2}$	$7\frac{3}{8}$		6
20 years	10	8		$6\frac{5}{8}$
25 years	10	10		$7\frac{3}{8}$
30 years	10	10		$7\frac{3}{8}$
40 years	10	10		$7\frac{3}{8}$
50 years	10	$9\frac{3}{8}$		$7\frac{3}{8}$
60 years	10	$9\frac{3}{8}$		$6\frac{3}{8}$
65 years	8	8		6
70 years	6	$7\frac{5}{8}$		6
80 years	6	$6\frac{5}{8}$		$5\frac{3}{8}$

8.9, for they are often identical. They confirm that women consume a little less than men when adult, and that full consumption begins for both sexes in the early 20s. We may compare the above estimates to those mentioned earlier by applying the various scales to our three sample households. The estimates in table 8.11 make the assumption that total consumption is in proportion to consumption of food. Thus all the earlier cited scales seem too high for the Gurung context, but Bailey's scale is only just too high and, on the whole, seems to be an accurate index. It therefore seems reasonable to adopt the Bailey scale and it will be used in the ensuing calculations about consumption units (see table 8.12). Some idea of the dependency ratio of young children will be obtained if we compare those aged under 15 to those over that age. The ratio is of the order of 1:7 (51.25/364) if we judge it in terms of consumption units. We may now turn to what is actually consumed.

Diet and nutrition

Food has a high symbolic value among the Gurungs and is much used in social and ritual activities. I spent a few days in three separate households watching the amount consumed. It would have been difficult to prolong the observation since those observed felt embarrassed and threatened by the procedure. The total amount consumed is set out in table 8.13. The various items on this table may be analysed individually.

Cereals

During the days of study the three households consumed the following quantities of grain: the 6.25 consumption units in house 17 ate $8\frac{2}{3}$, $9\frac{2}{3}$, $8\frac{2}{3}$ *manas* of husked grains in the 3 days of study; the 5.75 consumption units in house 3B ate $7\frac{2}{3}$, $8\frac{1}{3}$, and $7\frac{1}{3}$ respectively; household 57 ate the same quantity in proportion to its 2.75 consumption units, but all in maize. Thus approximately $1\frac{1}{2}$ *manas* of husked grain are consumed per consumption unit per day. This total agrees with Pignède's findings.[5] He noted that people stated that a man working hard is assumed to eat 2 *manas* of husked grain a day, but that, in fact, people seldom eat this much. The same assumption is made in Thak where, when land is being divided out between children, the ageing parents are allowed 9 *muri* of unhusked cereal p.a., which comes to just under 2 *manas* of husked grain per day. But observation of actual consumption shows that this is too high; some 550 *manas* of grain per consumption unit p.a. is more accurate. When I checked this with some informants they worked out in detail that the ideal of 9 *muri* per adult per year was far too high, and thought that 5–6 *muri* of unhusked grain per year was about average. If we allow a fairly generous estimate of 3 *muri* of husked grain per consumption unit per year, half of it in rice and half in millet or maize, this works out at approximately 195 kg of grain p.a. This is supplemented by cereals taken in the form of millet

TABLE 8.10 *Relative quantity actually consumed in two Gurung households in a week in 1969*

	Males household		Females household	
Age (years)	1	2	1	2
1½				2
4			2	
5				4
11	5			
12			4½	
13		6		
16	6			
18			9	
19				8½
21	10			
22		10		
26				8½
35				7½
36		10		
42			9	
59	10			
66		10		

TABLE 8.11 *Consumption units in three households*

	Household number		
Type of scale	17	3B	57
Bailey	6.25	5.75	2.75
Egyptian study	7.6	5.4	2.9
Epstein/Lusk	7.15	5.99	3.36
Table 17.1	5.75	5.00	2.65
Table 17.2	6.25	5.05	2.65

ABLE 8.12 *Consumption units, by age-groups, in 100 households*

		Gurungs		Non-Gurungs		Total	
ailey's multi-lier	Age group	Total persons[a]	Cons'n. units	Persons	Units	Persons	Units
.0	0–23 mth.	18	0	4	0	22	0
.25	2–9 yrs.	54	13.5	25	6.25	79	19.75
.5	10–14 yrs.	42	21	21	10.5	63	31.5
.0	15+	272	272	92	92	364	364
		386	306.5	142	108.75	528	415.25

All *de jure* members of the 100 households, including those temporarily away, are counted; but those temporarily present are not counted.

TABLE 8.13 *Diet in three Thak households*

Sex/age	Day 1 (August)						Day 2 (August)						Day 3 (August)						Day 4 (Nevember)					
	Rice[a]	*Toro*	Meat	Veg.	Milk	Etc.	Rice	*Toro*	Meat	Veg.	Milk	Etc.	Rice	Maize	Meat	Veg.	Milk	Etc.	Rice	*toro*	Meat	Veg.	Milk	Etc.
Hse. 17																								
66 M	5	1	$2\frac{1}{2}$	–	1		6	2	2	–	–		6	1	–	2	–							
36 M	–	6	2	–	1		–	6	2	–	–		–	6	–	2	–							
35 F	–	5	$1\frac{1}{2}$	–	1		–	4	2	–	–		–	4	–	2	–							
26 F	–	5	$1\frac{1}{2}$	–	1		–	4	$1\frac{1}{2}$	–	–		–	4	–	2	–							
22 M	6	–	2	–	1		6	–	2	–	–		6	–	–	2	–							
19 F	–	4	$1\frac{1}{2}$	–	1		–	6	2	–	–		–	6	–	2	–							
13 M	–	$4\frac{1}{2}$	1	–	1		–	4	1	–	1p		–	4	–	1	1p							
11 M	–	4	1	–	1		–	4	1	–	–		–	4	–	1	–							
10 M[b]	–	4	1	–	1		–	4	1	–	–		–	4	–	1	–							
5 F	–	$2\frac{1}{2}$	$\frac{1}{2}$	–	1		–	2	1	–	–		2	1	–	1	–							
$1\frac{1}{4}$ F	–	$\frac{1}{2}$	–	–	1		1	–	–	–	–		2	–	–	–	–							
Total	$2\frac{2}{3}$	6	$2\frac{1}{2}$	–	5	oil- 2	$3\frac{1}{2}$	$6\frac{1}{3}$	$2\frac{1}{2}$	–	1	a little	$3\frac{1}{3}$	$5\frac{1}{3}$	–	3	1	oil and						
	m.	*m.*	lb.		pts.	tble. s.	*m.*	*m.*	lb.		*p.*	oil	*m.*	*m.*		*m.*	*p.*	sugar						

Hse. 3B																					
59 M	$2\frac{1}{2}$	2	—	1	$\frac{1}{2}$		$2\frac{1}{2}$	2	2	2		$3\frac{1}{2}$	$4\frac{1}{2}$	3	3	2		Away in Pokhara				
42 F	1	2	—	$\frac{3}{4}$	$\frac{1}{4}$	a.m.	2	—	3	2		2	4	3	3	1		1	4	6		
21 M	$1\frac{1}{2}$	$1\frac{1}{2}$	—	1	$\frac{1}{4}$	only	2	—	3	3		3	3	3	3	2		2	4	8		
18 F	1	2	—	$\frac{3}{4}$	$\frac{1}{4}$	(*pela*)	2			2		2	4	4	4	1		1	4	6		
15 M	1	2	—	$\frac{3}{4}$	$\frac{1}{4}$		1		2	2		2	2	2	2	1		1	2	6		
12 F	1	1	—	$\frac{1}{2}$	$\frac{1}{6}$		$\frac{1}{2}$	—	1	1		2	1	2	2	1		1	1	4		
4 F	$\frac{1}{2}$	(breast/fd.)			$\frac{1}{6}$		$\frac{1}{2}$	—	2	1		2	—	1	1	1		1	—	2		
Total	$3\frac{1}{3}$	4	—	$6\frac{1}{2}$	5	oil	$1\frac{2}{3}$	$6\frac{2}{3}$	3	5	oil	$\frac{2}{3}$	4	1	$1\frac{1}{2}$	$2\frac{1}{2}$	oil	$3\frac{2}{3}$	$3\frac{2}{3}$	$\frac{1}{4}$	$2\frac{2}{3}$	5
	m.	*m.*		*m.*	pts.		*m.*	*m.*	*m.*	pts.		*m.*	*m.*	lb.	lb.	pts.		*m.*	*m.*	lb.	*m.*	pts.
Hse. 57		*Mze*					*Mze*						*Mze*									
39 M	—	20	—	2 cucumbs 1*m.* millet	2*m.* skimmed milk	— —	20	1 buffalo leg	—	1 pt. skimmed	1 pt. of millet gruel	—	20	tiny morsels	1 small cucumb.	2 *pelas* skimmed	2 *pelas* ground millet	—	Ground maize	—	Little raddish and soya beans	A little
35 F	—	20	—			— —	20		—			—	20					—		—		
11 F	—	10	—			— —	10		—			—	10					—		—		
6 M	—	10	—			— —	10		—			—	10					—		—		

[a] Units of measurement as follows; rice/maize or '*toro*' = the 'pct' or flat serving ladle, vegetables/meat the '*dodu*' (Nep. dāru) or ordinary ladle, likewise milk. *m.* = *mana* (approx 1 pt.). *p.* = *pela* or small bowl. tble *s.* = table spoon. *Mze* = number of maize cobs.

[b] This was a lower caste servant boy who worked for *hse.* 17.

beer, which is drunk in fairly large quantities. An approximate total of 210 kg of grain per consumption unit p.a. would seem reasonable.

The proportion of this total which is in the form of rice, and the proportion in other grains varies from family to family. Richer families eat more rice, but even they are forced onto other grains at certain times, as may be seen in table 8.13 where household 17, one of the wealthiest in the village, was consuming more *toro* than rice during August. Poor households, such as Blacksmith household 57, consume only maize for much of the year. To judge from the total amount of rice and other grains grown in the village, it would seem a fair estimate that in a medium-wealth household the diet is more or less equally divided between rice and other cereals. In wealthier households the ratio of rice to other cereals may be as high as 8:2, while in the poorest it may sink as low as 2:8. These poorer villagers have to depend for their rice on grain given in payment for services. Such payment is distributed in November after the rice harvest.

On the basis of the above discussion we may say that an adult male in an average Gurung family would consume approximately 105 kg of rice, and 105 kg of other grains (husked) p.a., or approximately 200 kg of 'wheat-equivalent' p.a.[6] A poor family would have less than 160 kg in wheat-equivalent per adult consumption unit, while a very rich household might have up to 240 kg per unit. We may make one comparison with the situation elsewhere, an average-wealth adult among the Gurungs consumes approximately 20 oz of wheat-equivalent per day, whereas the Bemba of Africa, when originally studied by Audrey Richards, consumed less than 12 oz of wheat-equivalent per day. The Bemba were on the brink of starvation; the Gurungs, at present, live well above the danger line. On the assumption that 'wheat-equivalent' has the same nutritional value as wholemeal flour, the above medium-wealth adult male among the Gurungs would eat cereal with the following nutritional value per day:[7]

Calories: 1820	Protein: 66 g	Fat: 10 g	Carbohydrate: 390 g
Calcium: 200 mg	Thiamine: 2.8 mg	Riboflavin: 0.6 mg	No vitamins A, C, D.

Rich and poor households would vary from this up to 25 % higher or lower.

Meat

Villagers eat mainly buffalo meat, which is supplemented on about one in four occasions by chicken, goat, fish or eggs (which will here be counted as 'meat' because of their high protein value). Up to recently this diet was supplemented by a considerable amount of wild game – deer, pig, jungle cock – and by mutton. Nowadays wild game has grown scarce and sheep are no longer kept. There are considerable reasons for believing that the amount of meat eaten per person is decreasing fairly rapidly year by year, and the same is true of milk. As with many societies, the Gurungs are being driven by the pressure of population from a protein-rich animal diet, to a carbohydrate-filled diet of cereals. At present they are at an intermediate state of transition, and are still in a better position than many of the neighbouring peoples to the south.

Meat is used for the relish to go with the rice or other cereal that is the real 'meal'. As a relish, it is interchangeable with vegetables. The Gurungs divide food up into three categories, *kae* (mainly rice, but also 'maize rice' when maize is ground up to resemble cooked rice), *pengo* (ground millet), and *ta* (relish). There is no rule that meat and vegetables should not be mixed or eaten at the same meal, and when entertaining visitors or feasting, both are prepared. But usually one or the other is eaten. Since this 'sauce', whether of meat or vegetables, provides much of the protein, and almost all the vitamins, in Gurung diet, it is essential to know how much is eaten and the way in which the distribution varies over the year.

To judge from the diet outlined in table 8.13, the normal amount of meat consumed by average Gurung households is about 1 or $1\frac{1}{4}$ lb of meat between 5.75 or 6.25 consumption units per day. This works out at about 3 oz per consumption unit per meal; thus a boy of twelve would only get about $1\frac{1}{2}$ oz of meat per meal. This includes skin and bone which are all chopped into the meal. If vegetables are being served as the relish, it would appear that some 3 *manas* (or approx. 3 pints) of vegetables are used per day. Again this provides roughly 3 oz per consumption unit per meal. We now need to find out how frequently meat is eaten, and what types of vegetables are consumed.

I asked two informants each evening for seven months what their families had eaten for 'sauce', and occasionally checked their reports by observation. No doubt there were lapses of memory, but not enough to alter the general impression which may be studied from Fig. 8.3. The two Gurung households are shown for each month. If we look at the meat consumption at the bottom of the diagram, it will be seen that only once does it (just) rise above 25 % of the total meals per month. Normally it is in the range 8–12 meals per month. To judge from these seven months (which include the period of most intense work and hence maximum protein intake), household 3B averaged just over 10 meat meals per month, or about 12 per month if we allow for days when I failed to record the meal. Assuming, as evidence from January seems to suggest, that the rate in the other five months is lower, then an average of 10 meat meals per month throughout the year would seem reasonable. This would provide some 360 oz of meat per consumption unit p.a., or 1 oz per day (including skin and bone). Making the generous estimate that the meat was of the quality

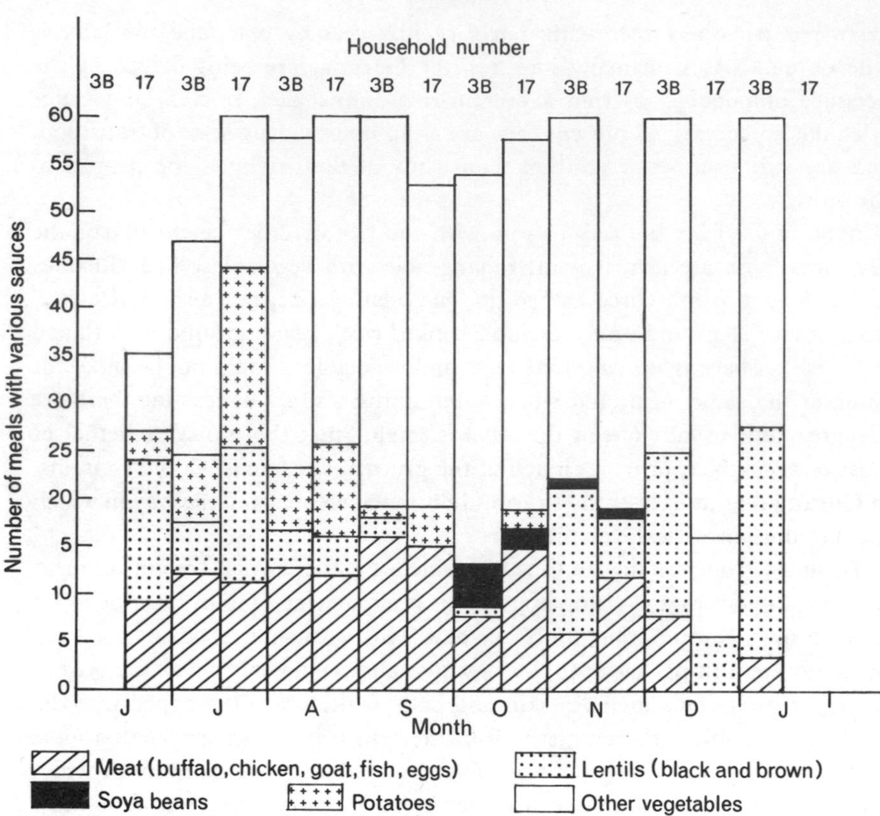

Fig. 8.3. Diet in two Gurung households, June 1969 to January 1970.

of stewing steak (beef), this would provide the following nutritional factors:

Calories: 62 Protein: 4.8 g Fat: 4.5 g Calcium: 3 mg Iron: 1.1 mg
Thiamine: 0.02 Riboflavin: 0.06 No carbohydrate or vitamins.

In household 17 there was a slightly higher meat consumption, as one might expect with the second richest household in the village, and a household that owned a sizeable herd of buffaloes. In the six months from June to November, they had 73 recorded meat meals. The average per day per consumption unit would thus probably be about 1.25 oz. The figures for house 3B represent a middling Gurung household. A very poor household, such as the Blacksmigh household studied earlier, only obtains meat occasionally; even when it does have meat, it tends to be the skin and bones from a carcase. Nor would such a household eat many eggs, chickens, fish or other high-protein foods. Their consumption of meat is probably in line with that of the Bemba of Africa, who averaged 0.25 oz per day.[8]

Vegetables

Fig. 8.3 also shows the consumption of various types of vegetable and pulse. The most important single item is lentils. They are grown in among the rice and, like soya beans, are extremely nutritious. They are consumed throughout the year. Over the six months July–December, household 3B had the following number of relishes of various vegetables: lentils ($44\frac{1}{2}$); potatoes ($14\frac{1}{2}$); soya beans ($5\frac{1}{2}$); other vegetable (210). It is likely that the ratio of lentils to other vegetables is higher in the six unrecorded months. The period under examination included the monsoon season when most of the green vegetables such as beans, cucumber and tomato grow. Beans and spinach are especially nutritious, but the cucumbers and radishes which make up at least half the 'other vegetables' category have little nutritive value.

On the assumption that the half year recorded above is roughly equal to the half of the year not recorded, a generous assumption as we have seen, then the following rough estimate of the intake of one consumption unit, or adult man, per day, from all the relishes eaten with cereals is as shown in table 8.14. Especially worthy of note is the fact that lentils/soya beans provide more protein in the diet than does meat. The table is based on only one household, and we may wonder how representative this was. If we compare household 17 to household 3B we get the figures shown in table 8.15. Thus the proportion of lentils to other vegetables is fairly similar.

Milk

The final major form of foodstuff is milk and its by-products, especially oil. It is impossible to obtain exact figures of milk consumption per family, since this depends entirely on fluctuations in the state of the family buffalo. Thus we may see from table 8.13 that house 3B had milk every day, while house 57 had a little milk each day and house 17 only had milk on one of the three observation days. Since all villagers are very fond of milk and will drink it when they can obtain it, the problem is one of supply.

Although goats and cows give a little milk, over 90 % of the milk consumed in the sample households came from buffaloes. The following analysis will, therefore, be confined to buffaloes. It is reckoned that, when in milk, an average female buffalo will give roughly 6 pints of milk a day. Since they produce milk for approximately half of each year only (on average some 9 months after calving, another nine months being needed to produce another calf), we can assume a rough average of 3 pints of milk per day per adult female buffalo. The periodicity of the supply is minimized by inter-family borrowing. When a family's buffalo is in calf, the household goes to neighbours for *kola* or skimmed milk; it then returns the favour when neighbours are in need. Milk is consumed in a variety of ways; it is drunk when boiled up,

TABLE 8.14 *Average nutritive value of 'relishes' per consumption unit*

Foodstuff	Amount (oz)	Calories	Protein (g)	Fat (g)	Carbohydr (g)	Calcium (mg)	Iron (mg)	Vitamin A, C, D (i.u. mg)	Thiamine (mg)	Riboflavin (mg)
Lentils Soya beans	1	84	6.8	0	15.1	11	2.2	0	0.14	0.07
Potatoes Other veg.	4	40	1.9	0	8.6	47	0.9	A = *c.* 610 C = 33 D = 0	0.08	0.05
Meat	1	62	4.8	4.5	0	3	1.1	0	0.02	0.06
Total	6	186	13.5	4.5	23.7	61	4.2	as above	0.24	0.18

Note: Conversions are based on the figures in *Manual of Nutrition* Appendix A. Meat, as before, is reckoned to be equivalent to stewing steak, and 'other veg.' as equivalent to a compound of cabbage, lettuce, potato and turnip.

TABLE 8.15 *Consumption of 'vegetables', two households*

Vegetable	Household 17 (June–Nov.)	Household 3B (July–Dec.)
Lentils/soya	43	50
Potato/other veg.	185	225
Not known	60	20

made into a kind of cottage cheese, or a type of yoghurt (Nep. *dahi*), or made into cooking oil (*chugu*). Earlier we saw that the 100 households had 223 buffaloes. If we allow for young and male buffaloes, there are still approximately a maximum of 150 adult females. This means that on average each of the 100 households should receive 4½ pints of milk products per day, or approximately a pint per consumption unit per day. Naturally enough, some people with larger herds, and particularly those living out in the forest or fields minding the buffaloes, drink far more milk. Others, especially lower caste households without a buffalo, consume far less. But a middling Gurung family probably consumes at about the above rate. A child of 13 would, unless especially favoured, expect to receive less than half a pint a day.

Other foodstuffs

In the summer there are considerable supplies of wild fruit, mostly berries, in the woods above the village. These are predominantly eaten by children. Occasionally the fruit diet is supplemented by oranges, bananas and fruit bought from other parts of the *panchayat* or from Pokhara. But though fruit would grow well in the village, little attempt is made to cultivate it. As yet it is not a large item in local diet, though it provides some additional and vital vitamins, especially for children. For the purposes of later calculation it will be guessed, on the basis of observation, that an adult male would consume about half a pound of fresh fruit a month, or ¼ oz per day. It is probable that, with the destruction of the forest, less fresh fruit is available each year. The only other product of any importance is honey (*kudu*), which is produced either in hives in the houses, or sought in woods and cliffs. Nowadays it is increasingly replaced as a sweetener by sugar from Pokhara market. Probably no more than 5 pints of honey are consumed annually (mean average) per household p.a., while roughly 20 lb of sugar is the average per middling household p.a. It may therefore be roughly estimated that an adult would consume about 6 lb of sugar-equivalent p.a., or about ¼ oz per day. This is a generous estimate. Sweets, biscuits, herbs and other special treats from Pokhara, as well as the essential salt, have no significant nutritional influence (except as a possible source of iodine in the case of salt).

On the basis of the above description we may make a very rough analysis of the nutritional value of the diet of an adult male Gurung in a family of middling wealth in 1969 (table 8.16). To estimate that of a woman, child or old person, or to calculate that of the very poor or very rich it would be necessary to multiply the following totals by the fractions already suggested.

It has been estimated that, for S.E. Asia, a sedentary adult male aged 20–29 needs some 1829 calories per day, with an extra 155 extra calories for each hour of labour. The above diet would sustain an adult Gurung for less than 3 hours work per day.[9] Figures published for other S.E. Asian countries in the early 1960s, collected by F.A.O., are as follows (cals. per day): Pakistan, 2030; India, 2050; Burma, 2150; Thailand, 2185.[10] Thus the Gurungs appear to be relatively a little better off nutritionally than neighbouring societies, largely because of their large consumption of milk.

As for protein requirements per day, there is considerable argument about the amount of protein needed per day to prevent malnutrition; estimates vary from 35 to 68 grams per day as a minimum.[11] But there can be little doubt that 88 grams a day is well above the safety level; this is again largely due to milk, and also soya beans/lentils. The above level is much higher than that of many societies that hover on the brink of starvation; for example the Zande in the 1940s had an average protein intake that fluctuated between 33 and 60 grams/day over the year.[12] It would seem that there are sufficient quantities of calcium (again milk is vital here), but vitamin B deficiency diseases were noted in a medical survey of Thak.

The results of table 8.16 may be compared to the levels recommended by the Ministry of Agriculture and Fisheries for a moderately active British woman.[13] No comparable figures for fat and vitamin C are given for the British woman, but in both cases it appears that the Thak level is a good deal lower than that likely to be recommended. It should also be remembered that the diet of many of the poorer households in Thak would be considerably worse than that taken as a sample above.

The only published figures I have been able to find for other Nepalese villages are those based on a 24-hour recall dietary survey undertaken by the Dooley foundation. They found a wide range of diets, with from 1923 to 3554 calories per day, and from 45.4 to 98.0 grams of protein per day. Especially deficient in most areas were vegetables, fruit, meat and eggs. If we compare the Thak findings to the table of the situation in a number of villages,[14] we find that it is about average for the western mountain region, but that 'the higher altitude, western mountain villages seem consistently better off with regard to both calories and proteins than does any other region'.[15] None of the villages surveyed by Worth had a consumption of vegetables, fruit, meat and eggs above the WHO long-term target, and only 11 % had the required level for fats and oils.[16]

TABLE 8.16 *The diet of a middling-wealth adult Gurung (per day)*

Foodstuff	Quantity (oz)	Cals.	Protein (g)	Fat (g)	Carbohydr. (g)	Calcium (mg)	Iron (mg)	Vit. A. (i.u.)	Thiam. (mg)	Ribofl. (mg)	Vits. C (mg)	Vits. D (i.u.)
Cereals	20	1820	66	10	390	200	22	–	2.8	0.6	–	–
Lentils/soya	1	84	6.8	–	15.1	11	2.2	–	0.14	0.07	–	–
Meat	1	62	4.8	4.5	–	3	1.1	–	0.02	0.06	–	–
Vegetables	4	40	1.9	–	8.6	47	0.9	*c.* 610	0.08	0.05	33	–
Milk	10	190	9.0	11	14	340	–	*c.* 400	0.1	0.4	6	4
Fruit[a]	$\frac{1}{4}$	2.5	0.05	–	0.6	3	0.02	*c.* 5	0.01	0.0025	3.5	–
Sugar/honey	$\frac{1}{4}$	28	–	–	9.5	–	–	–	–	–	–	–
Total	36.5	2226.5	88.55	25.5	437.8	604	26.2	*c.* 1015	3.15	1.183	42.5	4

[a] Fruit is assumed to be at the nutritional level of oranges.

By western standards many of the Gurungs are malnourished. Thus Morris wrote of the situation before the Second World War, 'I was able to observe many thousands of Gurkhas of all sorts, and most of them were undernourished.'[17] But if we compare the diet level to that elsewhere in India or Nepal, we are soon aware that there is far less protein or calorie deficiency than in most of Asia. Undoubtedly the considerable supply of milk and lentils makes a great difference. Nor is there a 'hunger gap' before the main harvest as in many agricultural societies. Planning, reasonable storage facilities, a mixed economy which combines several main cereal crops (so that if one is destroyed people may fall back on the other), plus the still abundant grazing and forest which enables pastoral farming – all these factors help to stabilize the diet. Income from the army adds the possibility of small luxuries. Although there were many recorded harvest failures in the past, I was only informed of one serious famine in living memory. Informants disagree as to whether there had been any starvation deaths from this, but starvation was certainly not given as a cause of death in my census.

Attitudes to food

As in most societies, food plays a vital part in religious symbolism and in all social relationships. Stages in a person's life are marked out by the types of food consumed, and gifts of blood and rice are central to almost all attempts to communicate with the spirit world. The normal greeting on the villages paths is 'Have you eaten?' (*kae tsae wa*). Yet, if we compare the Gurungs to a really food-obsessed society such as the Bemba of Africa,[18] we realize that food plays a less important part in Gurung conversation than it might. When I tried to carry out a food questionnaire, asking people which foodstuffs they preferred, and which they thought the most nutritious, they showed no interest in the topic and almost immediately changed the subject. There was no consensus on which foods were most tasty, though egg omelettes, rice-milk and potatoes were generally favoured. Nor was there unanimity about which foods were strength-giving. One informant suggested that maize was more nutritious than rice; another thought that millet and lentils were most nutritious, fol-

TABLE 8.17 *Recommended diet for British women, and diet of adult male in Thak*

	Calories	Protein (g)	Fat (g)	Calcium (mg)	Iron (mg)	Vit. A. (iu)	Thiam. (mg)	Ribofl. (mg)
British woman	2500	70	?	800	12	5000	1.0	1.5
Thak, adult male	2226	88.6	25.5	604	26.2	1015	3.15	1.182

lowed by meat, then rice, maize, milk. When a mother is recovering from childbirth and needs strength, she is fed with oil made from purified milk, and chicken meat. This suggests that assessment of food values is fairly accurate. Some attempt is made to teach a few basic nutritional ideas in the English-reading lessons at school: but the text, which recommends lots of green vegetables, eggs and meat, speaks of an ideal world so far from village reality that it makes no impression. Many of the men have eaten strange foods in the army and this may help to make the Gurungs flexible in their attitudes. Nor are they hidebound by caste ideas; in the past they used to eat domestic pig, and will still do so in the army, though not in the village. Otherwise they will eat practically anything at any time of the year. The only prohibition appears to be in the case of the magician or *poju*, whose family may not eat buffalo meat. As for drink, they are very fond of home-brewed millet beer, but there are few habitual drunkards.

Consumables purchased with cash

Some of the items consumed by the Gurungs have already been described at some length and do not need to be re-analysed here: the amount of wood and fodder from the forest, the amount of food grown in the village. There are a number of other goods, particularly those for which cash needs to be spent, which also merit attention.

I asked nine informants what items they purchased with cash and how much they spent on each of these in a year, and also the quantities of each item consumed. Clearly it would have been more satisfactory to have checked each time that a person went to Pokhara and asked him what he bought, and likewise after each purchase in the village. For various reasons this was not practicable. The following amounts are therefore only rough totals; probably in some items, such as various foodstuffs, the quantity has been understated, while in others, such as clothes, prestige may dictate an inflation of the sums. Thus household 12A, a poor and practically landless family, appears to have exaggerated throughout, for instance in its estimates of expenditure on cooking utensils and domestic rituals. This exaggeration is also shown in the fact that the totals reached from adding up individual items is much higher than the amount which informants gave as a grand total when asked to estimate their whole year's expenses.

Another difficulty is that certain items only occur once every few years; for instance this is the case with very expensive large cooking utensils. Consequently they have been averaged out over the years in table 8.18.

The table shows a huge gap between the expenditure of the Gurung households and the one lower caste family (no. 57). The Blacksmith family only bought tiny quantities of various foodstuffs and no clothes. Over half of its

TABLE 8.18 *Annual household expenditure (in Nepalese rs.) in 5 village households*

House no	Informant's estimate of total expenditure	Kerosene	Salt	Metal	Sugar	Flour	Chile	Mixed herbs	Biscuits	Condensed milk	Tea	Cartridges	Oranges and lemons	Potatoes	Sweets	Hair oil	Other fruit (bananas, etc.)	Onions	Soap	Letters & writing material	Cigarettes	Matches	Kitchen utensils	Batteries and torch	Clothes and shoes	Medicine	Books	Carriage from market	Oil	Honey	Domestic rituals	Taxation
17	600	35	40	45	112	–	60	36	30	36	30	–	20	30	20	10	40	30	45	75	300	12	100	30	600	40	25	20	200	60	70	180
40	–	52	30	35	32	10	40	36	10	20	20	–	10	25	5	30	12	6	15	30	100	15	120	45	250	50	5	10	150	60	10	135
3B	600	35	26	20	40	–	40	39	10	–	20	45	30	17	20	–	10	5	36	10	162	10	60	18	300	5	10	15	150	5	60	66
12A	6–800	35	20	15	8	–	45	24	6	20	10	10	10	20	12	12	25	6	30	20	162	16	125	33	300	10	8	–	75	25	200	50
57	–	2	10	–	2	–	–	3	$\frac{1}{2}$	–	–	–	1	–	–	3	1	1	2	–	1	–	–	–	–	–	–	–	6	–	30	15
Quantity bought for a certain sum																																
quantity[a]		1 tin	1 *p.*	1 *d.*	1 *d.*	1 *d.*	1 *p.*	1 m.		tin				1 *d.*		btle.					bdl.							load	tin	1 *m.*		
rupees		35	2	5	8	10	5	3		4				$2\frac{1}{2}$		3					14							5	50	6		

[a] d. = *dharni* = *c.* 6lb
p. = *pathi* = *c.* 8 pints
m = *mana* = *c.* 1 pint
btle. = bottle, bdl. = bundle

Note: Drink (millet beer) and cereals are also bought and sold to a certain extent within the village. These have been omitted in the above totals. In the case of millet beer, most households sell about as much as they buy, and thus there is no cash drain. In the case of cereals it was impossible to learn how much each family was forced to buy: all the households in the table below 3B bought cereals; households 17, 40 sold them – but the quantities were not great. Meat purchases are also difficult to calculate and have been omitted, but here again there would be a drain from poorer families (e.g. house 12A is reckoned to spend some 200 rs. a year on meat).

Household 40 is that of the village magician or *poju*, hence lack of expenses under 'domestic rituals'.

Under 'informant's estimate of total expenditure', the total for household 17 did not include clothes, that for 3B and 12A was said to include clothes.

TABLE 8.19 *Annual expenditure on certain items* (Nep. rs.)

	Thak, 1969		W. Nepal 1967–8[a]		E. Nepal 1964–5[b]	
Item	Hse. 17	Hse. 3B	Doti	Sallyan	Hse. A	Hse. B
Clothes	600	250	438	320	60	160
Salt	40	26	15	11	10	16
Metal	45	20	10	10	10	12
Gur or sugar	112	40	35	37	?	?
Kerosene	35	35	24	28	20	52
Soap	45	36	31	26	3	4
Total	877	407	553	432	103 +	244

[a] Figures from McDougall, *Village Economy* p. 40.
[b] Figures from Caplan, *Land and Social Change*, p. 80.

total expenditure was on ritual and taxation, whereas these are relatively unimportant items for Gurungs. It is necessary for such poor households to beg from the Gurungs such small luxuries as tea and spices.

The most expensive items in Gurung budgets were, in order of expense, clothes, cigarettes, oil, taxation, kitchen utensils. Of the other foodstuffs, sugar and salt were the most costly. Medicine and 'domestic rituals' (hiring a priest) were not of importance, except in household 12A, which appears to be a mistake. The father in this household was himself a part-time practising ritual expert (*poju*) and the son may have confused income with expenditure. It will be seen that there is enough cash for a certain number of luxuries; sweets, biscuits, hair oil, and, of course cigarettes.

It is of interest to compare the above totals with figures for other parts of the Nepal hills region. This is done for selected items in table 8.19. Although we have to take into account a considerable depreciation in the value of the rupee since 1964–5, there can be no doubt that the Gurungs spend more on the selected goods than do the Limbus of E. Nepal. On the other hand, it would seem that they spend about the same amount as an average Sallyan household, and less than an average Doti one.

The average expenditure on household and village ceremonies appears to be similar for the Gurungs and those living in Sallyan district, about 50 rs. per household p.a. That for Doti district is above double this amount.[19]

There are a number of other expenses which are much harder to calculate. One of these is the running cost of the farm – seed, depreciation of capital equipment, hired labour, etc. These agricultural items do not normally require cash, except where wealthier families hire labour. It is unlikely that such hired labour requires more than 50 rs. p.a. per family, on average; the total for

Sallyan district is about 66 rs. p.a.[20] Likewise, most of the payments to Tailors or Blacksmiths are still made in grains.

Extraordinary expenditure: marriages, funerals, houses

Most households have three or four children whose marriages must be paid for. This requires considerable expenditure in cash or gold, expenditure which varies with the wealth of the parents. The actual wedding ceremony in a Gurung village is held at the groom's house, and will cost about 300 rs. for an 'average-wealth' family. The money is spent on feasting and presents. Probably a little less than one quarter of this will be retrieved from presents of money given by kin. Thus an average of 250 rs. per son, and about half that for each daughter is necessary. In the latter case the new groom and his friends go to spend a few days at the bride's village just after the wedding ceremony and have to be entertained.

It is also customary for the bride to be given gold and other goods, both by her own parents and her future husband. This gold, clothes, cooking utensils, and occasionally livestock, are her own property. She may retain them if her husband dies or there is a divorce. In fact it is a form of insurance for her children and herself. The situation is illustrated in Fig. 8.4. Wealth does not flow from one group to the other, but from parents to the next generation. In other words it is a form of inheritance. For example, mother's gold acquired at marriage is often handed over to daughters at this point. In a number of cases I recorded, nothing was given by the husband and his family, and it was stated

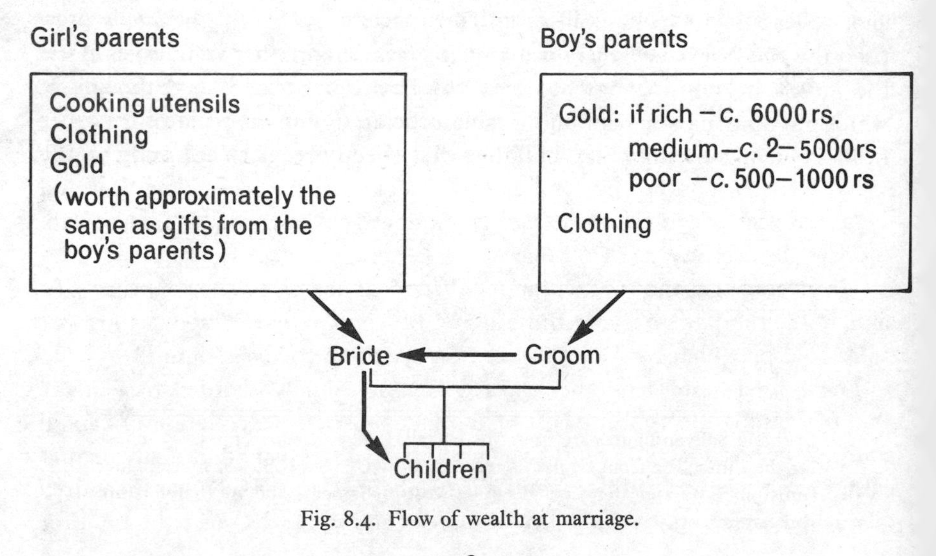

Fig. 8.4. Flow of wealth at marriage.

by some informants that in the case of cross-cousin marriage it was not necessary to give gold. But actual instances suggest that gold may be given in such marriages; it depends on the wealth and inclination of those marrying. It is important to be aware that marriage payments are an inheritance mechanism, for it means that we must not count the full cost of such payments under 'expenditure'. Since they are a transmission of wealth within the family, it is only the actual expenditure on hospitality at the wedding ceremony that needs to be counted here.

From a comparison with other Napalese hill peoples, the Gurungs appear to spend a good deal less than others on the actual wedding festivities. It is for them a far less elaborate rite than that associated with death, an emphasis that contrasts with the situation in the other districts listed in table 8.20. For the purposes of analysis, it will be assumed that an average Gurung family has to marry one son and two daughters (or two sons) every twenty-five years. This would mean an average annual expenditure of 20 rs.

The most important of all Gurung ceremonies is the *pae* or ritual for guiding the wandering soul of the dead person to the land of the dead. This should be performed between 3 and 49 days after the death, but it is often put off for a number of years so that enough money can be raised to perform it. The poorer Gurung families cannot afford to undertake individual *pae*, and join with others in celebrating a joint one. Sometimes, as in one probably exceptional instance mentioned to me, as many as 26 households may join together to honour their ancestors. Non-Gurungs celebrate different rites; in the case of the Blacksmiths and Tailors the Hindu rite of the *kyrie*, which is much less costly than the *pae*, is used. Even the Gurungs are divided. Up to a few years ago, at least in the Siklis valley, all Gurung lineages except the *lamme* practised the *pae*. Nowadays there is a growing fashion for other *jat* lineages to join the *lamme* in substituting the *chemphar*. This is a rite of Tibetan origin, in which no animals are slain and a lama officiates. Thus it replaces the specifically Gurung *pae* in which buffaloes and sheep are sacrificed and the *poju*

TABLE 8.20 *Cost of marriage ceremony in various places*

Place[a]	Son	Daughter (rs.)
Gurung, average, 1969	250	125
Doti, 1967/8	1189	652
Sallyan, 1967/8	811	573
Limbu, 1964/5	*c.* 600	?

[a] Doti and Sallyan figures are from McDougall, *Village Economy*, pp. 52–3. Those for the Limbu are from Caplan, *Land and Social Change*, p. 88 (the much higher sums on p. 90 appear to include bride-wealth payments and are therefore not comparable).

and *klevri* officiate. As yet, however, only one or two families in Thak have turned to the *chemphar*, a much cheaper rite which costs approximately half the amount spent on a *pae*. I was told by several informants that the *pae* of a rich person would cost about 3000 rs., that of a medium-wealth person 2000, and that of a moderately poor person 1000. Pignède was told that funerals cost 300–1500 rs. Given the doubling in prices in the ten years intervening, his figures for Mohoriya agree with those for Thak.[21]

Most of the expense lies in providing food and drink for the numerous guests, though kinsmen of the deceased are expected to contribute some rice and money. In the past they were expected to bring two *pathi* of unhusked rice, and ½ rupee; nowadays they give one *pathi* and one rupee. At the most, such contributions might cut the total cost by about one-fifth. Such *pae* are celebrated for both males and females aged over about 14. They are separate from the actual burial or cremation, which occurs shortly after death and which is a much smaller ritual. Cremation is reckoned to be far more expensive, and was usually undertaken by *carjat* households. The expenses of hospitality at such a cremation or funeral are probably about one tenth of those for a *pae*. Table 8.21 gives the comparative cost of mortuary rites in various tribal groups and shows how very high the expenditure among the Gurungs is. Omitting the very small amount spent at birth (in purchasing an astrological prediction) we may add the cost of all *rites de passage*. If we do this, we find that the Gurungs spend a little less than the inhabitants of Doti district, but considerably more than the Limbu, on average. Although the expenditure on funerals, mainly consisting of meat and rice, usually comes back to a family over a lifetime through the free hospitality they receive at other *pae*, it has been decided to count the cost of such *pae* in the total of family expenses. It will also be assessed in cash, though a wealthier family would be able to

TABLE 8.21 *Cost of mortuary rites; Gurungs and others*

Group	Cost (rs.)
Gurung, 1969[a]	1800
Limbu, 1964/5[b]	250
Doti, 1967/8[c]	105
Sallyan, 1967/8[c]	141

[a] For a Gurung household of average wealth: the cost of the actual burial/cremation *c.* 200 rs., that of the *pae* (after deducting presents from kin) 1600 rs.

[b] Source for Limbu, Caplan, *Land and Social Change*, p. 83.

[c] Source for Doti/Sallyan districts, McDougall, *Village Economy*, p. 53.

provide at least some of the rice and livestock from its own estate. If we assume that each household has to perform one set of mortuary rites every ten years, then the average annual expenditure would be 100 rs.

If a person has more than one son a separate house will finally have to be built for the older son at or after his marriage. The original house will require repairing and periodic rebuilding, and frequent re-thatching if it has not a slate roof. Such building may be paid for in cash, as seems usually to be the case in Thak, or by providing labour to a joint house-building group as Pignède describes. In either case, the cost of a reasonable stone and slate house, of the type built by a family of average wealth in Thak in 1969, would be about 6000 rs. If we assume that two new houses are being built each year in our hundred households, this means that roughly 12,000 rs. (or 120 rs. per household) is being spent in this way. If we add the cost of labour for re-thatching and repairs to houses, the sum would be on average at least 130 rs. p.a. per household. Of course, poorer households would not spend such a sum; house-building is a way in which cash flows from richer to poorer families, especially to Blacksmith and Tailor groups who provide labour. Also, those who have no sons or only one, have to spend less.

Other items of expenditure

We have, so far, only considered expenditure in the village or at Pokhara. The money spent by soldiers and their wives when serving in India or Nepal has not been considered, except where the goods, for instance gold and clothing, are brought into the village. Other goods, transistor radios, watches, guns, Thermos flasks and the other items listed in the inventories in chapter 6, were also brought in, usually after the payment of considerable customs duties. In the five inventories analysed above, the average value of such goods, including those bought in local markets, was about 350 rs. If we include customs duties, and gun and radio licences, there is a probable annual expenditure of some 500 rs. per household p.a. Again there will be very considerable fluctuations per family and per year.

Finally, the servicing of debts requires cash. Although this may be an important item in the finances of a particular family, the majority of Gurung households are not in debt, and when they are it is usually for small sums to other members of the village. In a discussion of the flow of wealth within a village such debts would obviously have to be considered. But here, where our major purpose is to work out an average cash expenditure, we will for simplicity's sake omit this item, just as we omitted debt repayments in the discussion of household income in the previous chapter.

Total expenditure and comsumption

Most analyses of Nepalese domestic budgeting have been confined to cash expenditure. The discussion of the Gurungs above enables us to look at both total consumption, and the proportion of this which requires cash. The results are tabulated in table 8.22. It will be seen that less than one-third of the consumption requires cash. Of the 1500 rupees of cash spent, almost exactly half is spent outside the village, in Pokhara or abroad.

It should be stressed that table 8.22 is not an actual budget, nor is it a mean average of all family budgets. It is, rather, a composite budget estimated for a Gurung family of five consumption units and from a middling economic level. Thus the consumption per 'consumption unit' is just under 1000 rs. p.a. in total, and some 300 rs. if cash only is counted. The relative proportion spent on various items may be seen more clearly from Fig. 8.5. Thus we can see that food constitutes approximately $\frac{3}{5}$ of the total consumption needs, fuel roughly $\frac{1}{4}$, clothing about $\frac{1}{6}$, and other consumer goods about $\frac{1}{10}$.

The proportion spent on non-food items would suggest that the Gurungs are well above the subsistence level. We may contrast them, for example, with the overseas Chinese in Sarawak who spend some 82 % of their income on food.[22] On the other hand the 60 % they spend on food is a little higher than the 54 % spent on food in Thailand, 1930–1.[23] It has been suggested for East Africa that 'Food consumption tends to stabilize when it has reached a level of

TABLE 8.22 *Average annual consumption and cash expenditure of a middling Gurung household, 1969*

Item	Total consumed (value in rs.)	Total cash expenditure (rs.)
Food	3025	250
Clothes	300	300
Housing	130	130
Fuel – wood	360	–
– kerosene	35	35
Consumer goods	455	455
Taxes (and savings)	75	75
Medicine	15	15
Domestic/village ritual	75	25
Rites of passage	205	205
Agric. (seeds, etc.)	150	–
Caste services (incl. hired labour)	150	10
Total	4975	1500

Note: The hiring of Gurung labour, usually on an exchange basis, is not included; nor, as stated above, are the servicing of debts or the cost of goods consumed abroad.

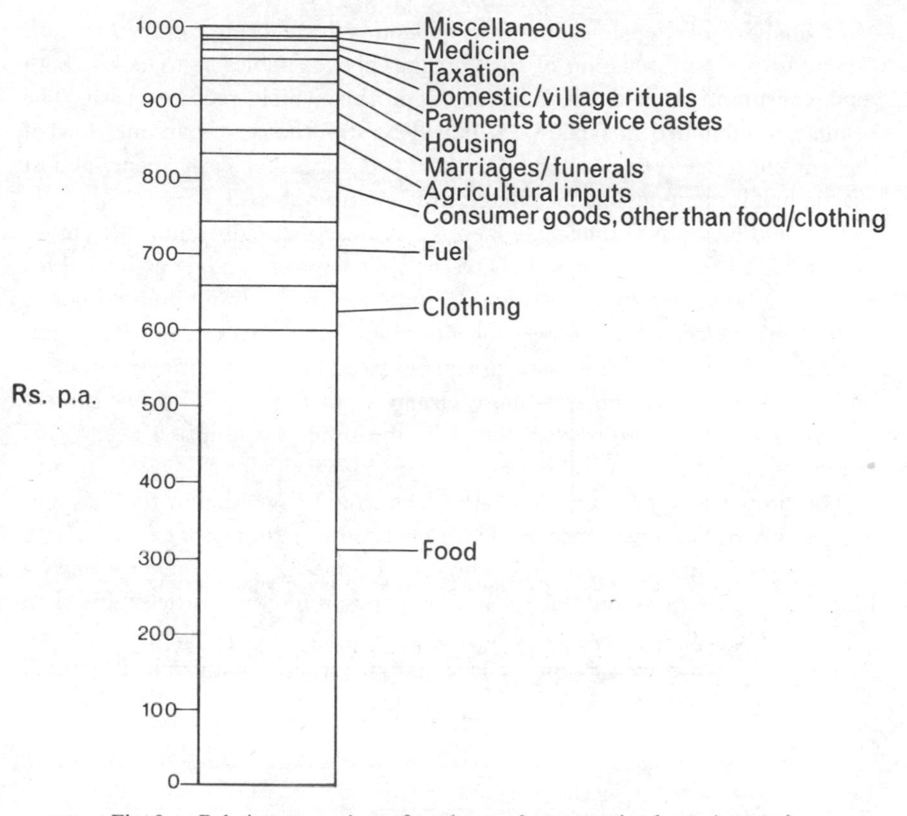

Fig. 8.5. Relative proportions of total annual consumption by an 'average' adult Gurung.

about £28/person/year',[24] while in Thak, in this middle-range hypothetical household, it has reached a level of about £25/person/year. It is likely that the importance of fuel as an item is likely to increase as wood supplies dwindle. It is easy to envisage a situation where a growing proportion of the family budget, including cash now used for other consumer goods, will have to be paid out to obtain fuel, as kerosene replaces wood.

The actual cash expenditure on various items for this 'typical' Gurung household is illustrated in Fig. 8.6. Food constitutes about $\frac{1}{6}$, clothing $\frac{1}{5}$, and other consumer goods between $\frac{1}{3}$ and $\frac{1}{4}$, of the total monetary expenditure. The cash needed for periodic weddings and funerals is also important.

In table 8.23 the total cash expenditure for various groups in Nepal is again compared to that for the Gurungs.

Allowing for depreciation of currency, cash expenditure is considerably higher among the Gurungs than the Limbus, though it is slightly less than

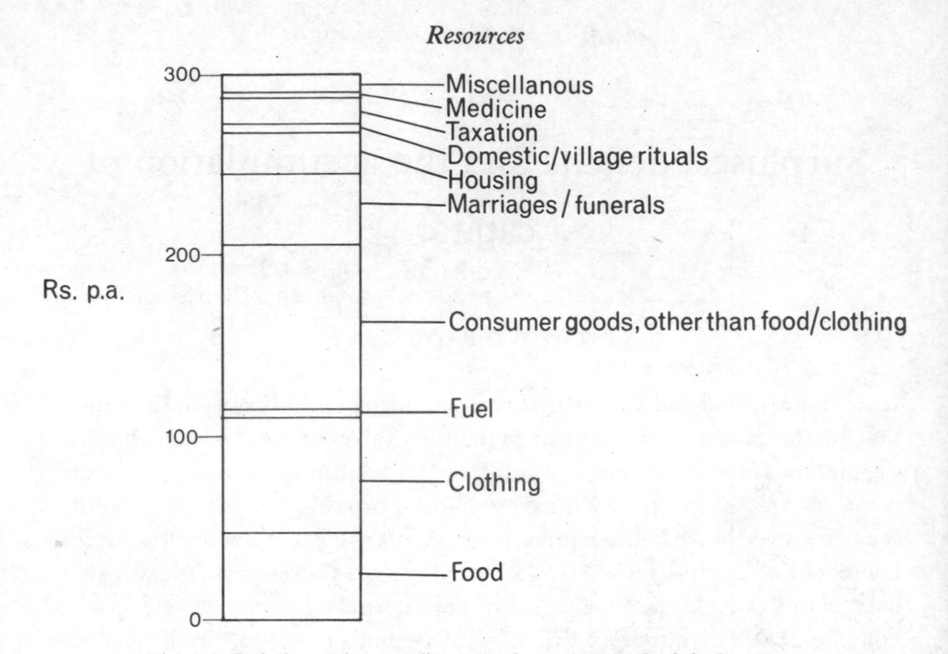

Fig. 8.6. Relative cash expenditure p.a. by an 'average' adult Gurung.

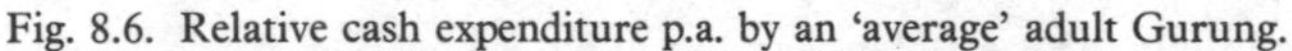

TABLE 8.23 *Cash expenditure in various groups*

Group, date	Rs.
Gurung, average, 1969[a]	1295
Limbu, 1964/5; household A	314
household B	634
Doti district, 1967/8	1123
Sallyan district, 1967/8	986

[a] This figure does not include expenditure on marriages/funerals since this is omitted in the calculations for other groups also. The Limbu figures are from Caplan, *Land and Social Change*, p. 80; those for Doti and Sallyan from McDougall, *Village Economy*, p. 44.

that in Doti district, and about the same as that in Sallyan. There is thus, as in W. Nepal, a great need for cash in order to purchase various goods. As indicated earlier, none of this is generated by the local economy. All of it must flow from the south, principally in the form of army wages and pensions.

9

Surpluses, deficits and the accumulation of capital

AT THE VILLAGE LEVEL

It seems very doubtful whether there is a tendency towards capital accumulation in the village as a whole at present. In table 8.7 we saw that the total cash inflow from all sources, excluding capital projects financed by the government, is 46,000 rs. p.a. With development projects and all other sources somehow over-looked, this cannot reach 50,000 rs. p.a. Meanwhile a 'typical' household was seen (table 8.19) to spend some 1500 rs. p.a. in cash, about half of this outside the village. Even if we entirely omit the twenty poorest households in our hundred, who may be assumed to spend very little indeed outside the village, this still leaves us with a total cash expenditure of 66,160 rs. p.a. Sales of village forest-cutting rights, and of village lands to outsiders are probably short-term attempts to meet this deficit. But in view of a sizeable shortage, all attempts at long-term capital accumulation in the village appear doomed.

We have only spoken of cash spent outside the village in this context since we are considering the budgetary situation of the whole village as if it were a separate island. The buying of land, expenditure on ritual, food and other objects within the village merely circulates cash within the unit. The situation is demonstrated in Fig. 9.1. We can see how the inflowing cash is reallocated. The most obvious instance of this process is the payment of lower caste families.

After the last war a very considerable amount of wealth poured into the village in the form of pensions and wages. An improved diet and a burst of house building swallowed this money up. At the period of our visit it is likely that the situation was changing rapidly. The war boom had spent itself and mounting population, plus declining recruitment into the British army, was beginning to have serious effects. The earlier wealth had been partly used to open up the remaining, poor quality, virgin land, but none of it had been used to improve communications or agricultural productivity. Without any scope for investing in better tools, most of it was spent, or stored in housing and gold. The merchants of Pokhara, and the Gurungs, who enjoyed a temporary rise in living standards, were the main beneficiaries. Now the chances of saving decline day by day.

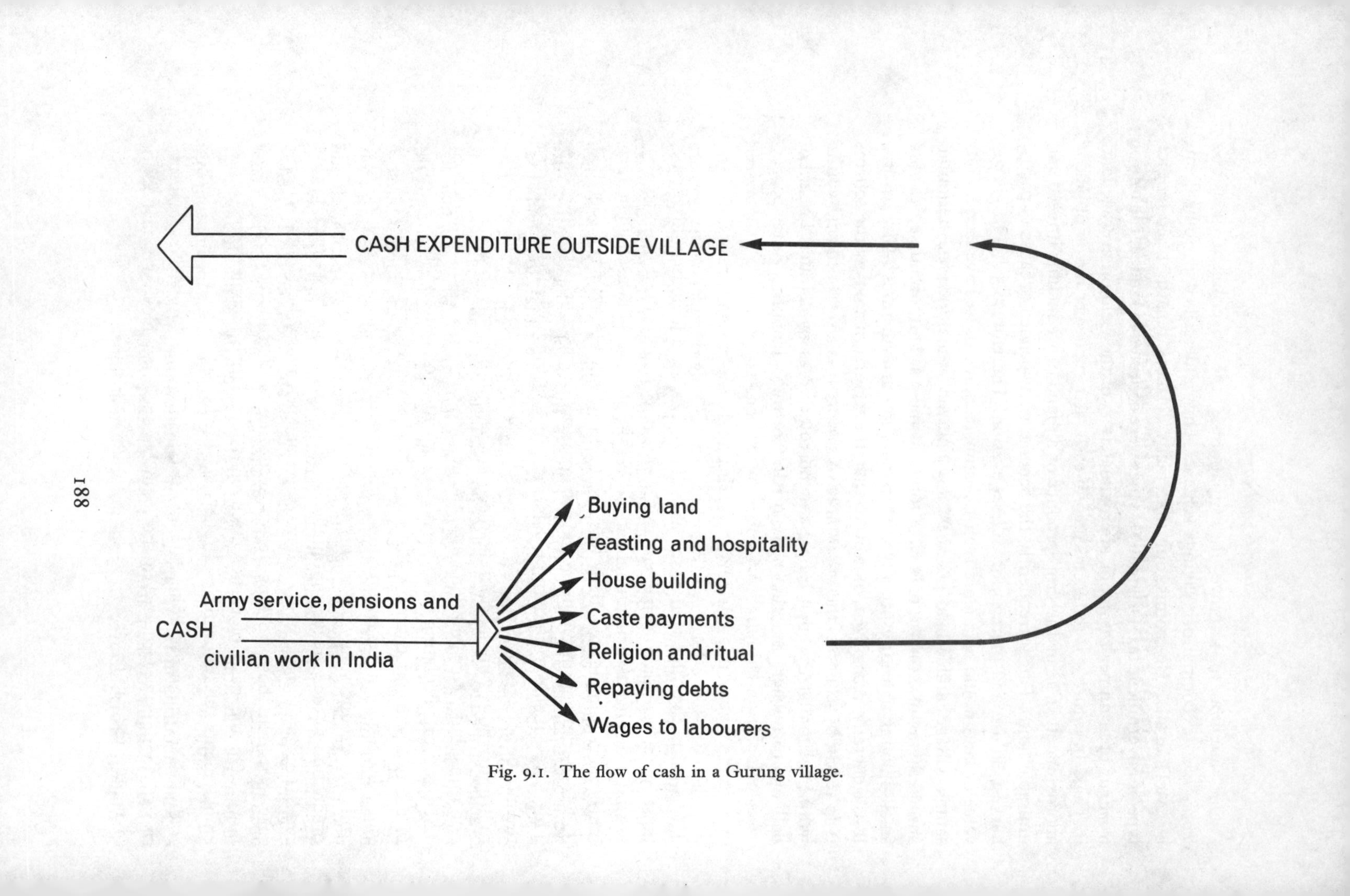

Fig. 9.1. The flow of cash in a Gurung village.

One attempt to improve the situation is the government-sponsored '*bacat kos*' or compulsory savings scheme. This is described in some detail by McDougall.[1] He points out that many farmers regard it as another type of government tax. Originally savings were collected in kind, at the rate of 6 *manas* of grain per *ropani*, or approximately $\frac{1}{80}$ of the yield on average land in Thak. In future it is to be collected in cash, at 1 rupee per *ropani* of land – approximately 1 % of the crop produce of all land (if we include unused and unusable land). Fairly frequently the scheme is suspended because of partial harvest failure and there is, of course, evasion. Therefore 0.5 % of the crop value of land would be a more realistic estimate. Since, as we have seen for our sample village, arable land provides only half the annual income, there is an annual saving of, at most, 0.25 % of total income p.a. This, of course, is a very small amount indeed, especially with population growth rates of 1–2 % p.a. It is generally recognized, however, that the main function of the scheme is to teach, by example, the importance of saving. It is also hoped that a fund will be accumulated so that people may borrow at reasonable rates. I heard of only one case where a person had actually borrowed from this fund.

AT THE HOUSEHOLD LEVEL

The wealth that flows in from abroad reaches certain households first – those with pensions or men in the army. It is largely these families that exhibit a surplus in their annual budget. Yet the question of household budgeting is more complicated than this; proper answers require a very detailed, daily recording of consumption and expenditure in each of the 100 households. This I was unable to undertake, and the best that can be done is to compare the number of production units in each household to the number of consumption units. For example, household 57, a Blacksmith family, has 1.4 production units, but 2 consumption units, and hence is classed as a deficit household. The basis for calculating production and consumption units has been outlined in the two previous chapters, but one added refinement is necessary. In previous discussions it has been assumed that an adult female is one consumption unit, but produces only 0.8 of this amount in the local economy. The level of production in the village is not high enough to finance consumption at normal rates. The gap is made up by foreign wages and pensions. Therefore it is necessary to weight those working abroad according to their increased productive power. On the basis of earlier discussions of relative income from various employments the following multipliers are used:

Man labouring in the village = 1.0 production unit.
Man in India (civilian/army) = 3.0 production units.
Man in British army = 4.0 production units.

Thus, for example, if all the members of household 17 worked in the village, it would be rated as 5.4 production units: but the fact that one of the sons is in the British army raises the level to 8.4. There is thus a small surplus over the 7.25 consumption units in this household. The rating for all households, showing the number of units and whether there is a total surplus or deficit, is given as appendix 2 below.

It will be seen from the appendix that there is only one household (no. 16) where there is a man in the army, yet the family still has a deficit. Otherwise, when we discover that there are 65 deficit households and 35 surplus ones, it is not surprising to find that there are 64 households with no man earning wages abroad. Now this is not the same as saying that all the deficit households are the poorer households, while surplus ones are the rich. The present wealth distribution in the village is the result of many factors over the last hundred years, particularly the number of sons at each generation and the amount of previous military service. But it does seem that those who now have a surplus are gaining on their neighbours. Thus household 15, one of three sons of a *sorajat* Gurung, did not start life well placed, nor did the fact that he had five sons appear to offer him much chance of advancement, since his small landholding would have to be minutely subdivided. Three of his sons are now in the army, however, so that, allowing for their increased productivity, he has a household with 13.2 production units, and only 7.5 consumption units. He is thus able to accumulate property at a rapid rate. Household 6, on the other hand, is a deficit household, but the richest in the village. There are seven daughters and no-one in the army. Yet it seems probable that this widow's lands are large enough, and the demand for land to rent at 50 % of crop value so high, that she is able to turn an apparent deficit into a surplus. It seems likely that at least fifteen of the other supposedly 'deficit' households have enough land to do this.[2] From this it would appear that, in fact, exactly 50 % of the households have a surplus in their annual budgets, and the other 50 % a deficit. In almost all cases the gap is under two units either way, but there are a few cases where the gap is wider.

The following households may be regarded as potentially conspicuous savers or spenders, having a surplus or deficit of over two units:

	Gurungs	*Tailors*
Households with 2.1 +(surplus)	15, 18, 20, 49, 84	
Households with 2.1 −(deficit)	3B, 40, 56 (Magar)	43

Some comments may be made about these families. Household 15 we have already discussed above. Household 49 had just been rebuilt on a large scale. The eldest brother was Pradan Panch of the village and had been given his portion of land on retirement from the army. House 20, although it may now be improving its position, has been visibly sinking over the last few years, selling off its land in considerable quantities. The fact that there are four unmarried daughters aged 19 to 35 suggests that there are still difficulties. House 84 is reckoned to be investing surpluses in increasing its very large herds of livestock. As for those at the bottom, house 3B has been selling off land, and the son had been forced to leave the village (where he was an assistant schoolmaster) in order to find a more lucrative job. Even if he found a job in India there would still be problems. House 40 was the wealthy household which contained the *poju*; he managed to bridge the gap by the grain and money which he obtained for his magical services. The head of the household was the only son of an only son and his lands were extensive; only a very large and young family and the inability of his son to get into the army had pulled him down. House 56 was a recently settled Magar family; the husband was always lamenting about how poor he was becoming. Household 43 was a Tailor joint household where a father lived with his two married sons. If each of the three nuclear families had lived separately, they would have shown the normal lower caste feature, a deficit of 0–2 units per household, but their united deficit was considerable.

We may compare the above tentative budgets with some for other Nepalese groups. Hitchcock, writing of the Magars, makes the general point that a number of families are not economically viable, but he has not, as yet, given any statistics.[3] Caplan reports of the Limbus that 64.4 % produce less food than they require, but does not give any figures to show whether total budgets balance or not.[4] McDougall notes that, on average, in the Doti sample, the average cash expenditure exceeds the cash income by 84 rs., and in Sallyan by 43 rs.[5] But he does not show what proportion of households have a deficit/surplus. The best comparative figures come for two south Indian villages, where, in the 1950s, it was reported that '42 % of Dalena's sample households and only 38 % of Wangala's households have a deficit in their current budget'.[6] In Thak, as we have seen, the proportion is higher, at about 50 %.

THE CIRCULATION AND DISTRIBUTION OF WEALTH

While only some families have cash coming in from abroad, almost every household needs money to buy consumer goods such as kerosene and salt. Likewise, while only some families own land, all need cereals. We may wonder how the flow of wealth is achieved. One of the difficulties of discussing this and other related problems, particularly the degree to which wealth differences between groups in the village are growing, is that even in the five years preceding 1969 the situation had changed a great deal. An increased supply of consumer goods and an increasing pressure of population on land is even now rapidly altering the situation so that few generalizations account for both the earlier and the present patterns.

Pressures towards the equalization of wealth

Of major importance here is the periodic shortage of labour in Gurung agriculture. The concentration of most agricultural work into the monsoon months means that even now, when there are over-all labour surpluses, there are certain months when every hand is needed to plant and reap the harvest. Poorer families can earn good wages, either in cash or crops, by contributing their labour, for it is a scarce resource. This puts them in a good bargaining position, which is reflected in the general Gurung attitude to lower caste workers. They were regarded in Thak as tricky and awkward workmen, likely to back out of an agreement at any time, and to go and work for another household. We have seen from the study of one Blacksmith's income that they were rewarded well for their labour, receiving almost as much profit from their work per hour as a man working in his own field. Many factors have contributed to this labour shortage in the past. The very primitive technology combined with steep gradients has made agriculture enormously labour-intensive. There has traditionally been a vast area of virgin land to be used; labour has been the limiting factor in production. Added to this is the adult migration to the army, often depriving the village of up to 50 % of those males at their working prime. This shortage of labour has had many effects. For example it has been difficult to draw much profit from owning more than a limited amount of arable land. The problem has been to recruit labour, not to own land. Those families who were drawing money from abroad had to spend a large part of it on paying for their village lands to be cultivated.

Another vital pressure which has contributed to producing the fairly egalitarian situation in Thak has been the absence of a cash crop. There has been no way of converting the produce of land into a commodity which could then be re-converted into buying further land. The situation is illustrated in Fig. 9.2, which contrasts the situation in a cash-crop economy with that in an economy such as Thak. Those who have a large surplus of rice or other cereals cannot use this to further increase their economic lead; an abundance of land in the village, and no outside market, means that there is little demand for a man's surplus. Hence surpluses are distributed or destroyed, in order to gain social or ritual power, rather than being sold in order to gain cash with which one may buy more land. Many stories were told in Thak of very rich men in the past who had, at their deaths, destroyed vast quantities of rice, oil, and livestock by having them thrown on a fire or distributed to holy men. The costly funeral *pae*

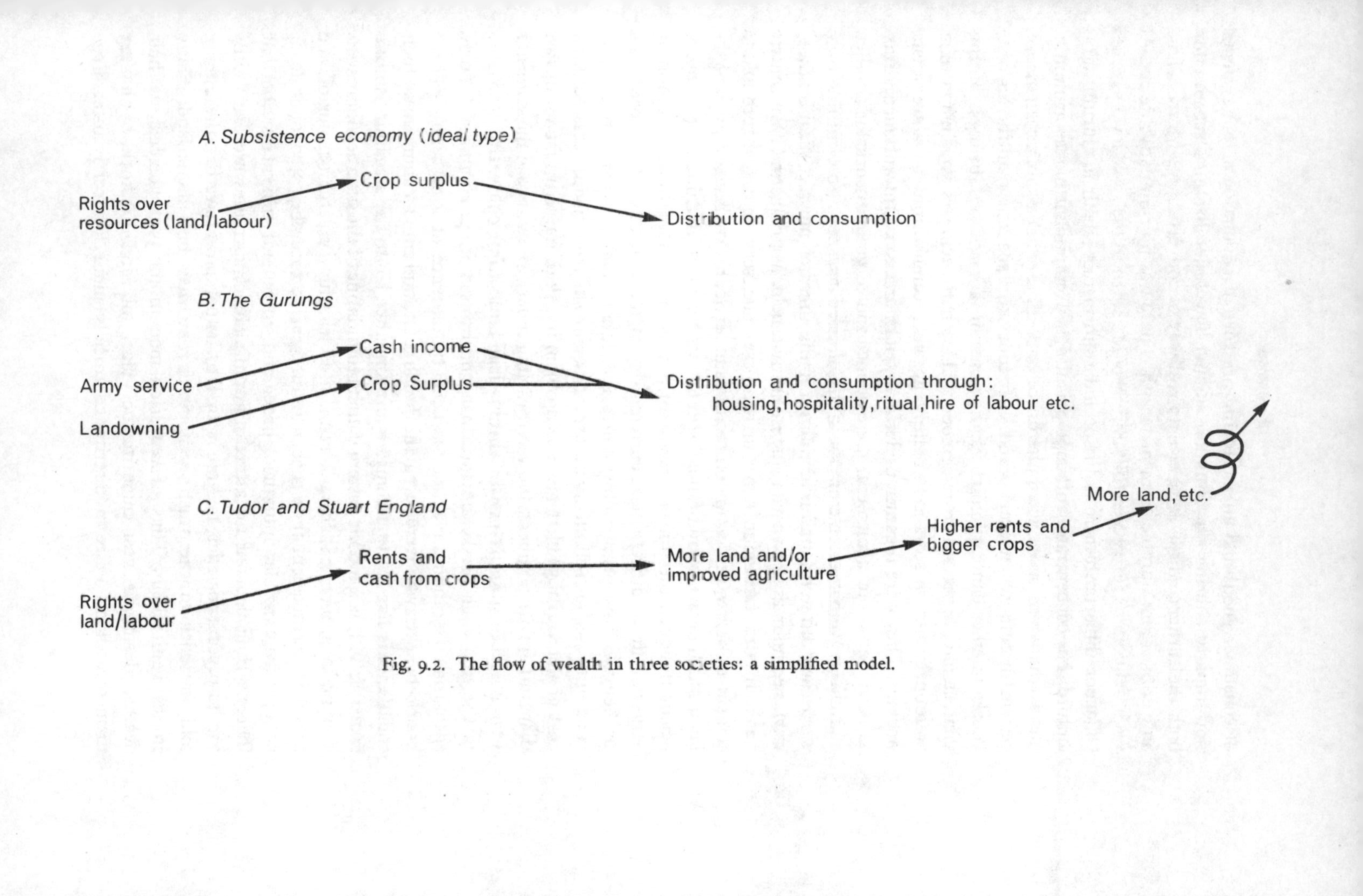

Fig. 9.2. The flow of wealth in three societies: a simplified model.

partakes of this distributive function. A man used surpluses to buy merit and prestige at his death: there was no way he could transfer such subsistence wealth. In other words there was no real way of converting wealth from land into some more durable form of wealth. There was no cumulative device. At each generation the successful family would return to the same level as other villagers. This problem of storing and re-investing wealth is crucial: it has been discussed by many anthropologists. For example Barth's description of the way in which nomadic peoples find it impossible to rise above a certain level of wealth before they are forced either to become sedentary cultivators or to break up their lands, illuminates the situation among the Gurungs.[7] In this context it is important to remember that even thirty years ago the Gurungs were primarily pastoralists, merely growing cereal crops as a subsidiary activity. They were thus still under many of the pressures towards an egalitarian distribution of wealth that are evident in most pastoral societies.

Another important factor which has tended to keep the Gurungs from rigid class differentiation is their multiple sources of income. Wealth flowed from several major channels; pastoral activities, arable crops and army service have all been important. A person who was successful in one sphere had to use his resources to obtain commodities in another. Furthermore, two of the three major occupations tend, by their nature, to inhibit long-term capital accumulation; livestock rearing, for the reasons suggested above, and army service. The qualifications necessary for a successful army career could not be bought. Even the poorest Gurung could enlist, provided his physical condition was suitable; it was a career open to talent. Indeed, it is arguable that poorer Gurungs were more likely to enlist, since it is they who were more desperate for employment and money.[8] In a sense, we might see the army as a negative feed-back mechanism, automatically smoothing out wealth disparities in the village. In Thak, the wealthier land-holders of the 1920s did not send their sons into the army; there was plenty for them to do at home. But the poorer families who were recruited then have now profited and increased their wealth. This has led to a considerable amount of bitterness against the *nouveaux riche*. It is a mobile system which reminds one of the situation in western Europe. A number of channels of mobility leads to a much more flexible and balanced arrangement than that in most agrarian societies.

A more intangible, but crucial, pressure is the general 'ethic of distribution'. There is the characteristic dislike of hoarding and meanness which we usually find in peasant societies, and the normal social pressures towards consumption and distribution rather than saving. Such pressure is most obviously displayed in the institution of the *garda sheba* dance, which is performed in Thak. Whenever a rich visitor comes to the village, or a child is born, or an army man comes home on leave or retires, a dance is held. For this the dancers must be paid. This is a polite ritual way of extracting money from the individual concerned, money that is consumed by the community as a whole. Nor are the sums always trivial; medium-wealth families would give 30–40 rs. each year, when such dances are held at their house. Others sometimes give over 100 rs. for a single dance. On a smaller scale, whenever a person is lucky in a particular way, for example out hunting, or in the birth of a new buffalo calf, he is expected to share such good fortune with others by the distribution of meat or milk. Any piece of expensive property, as we soon discovered with our pressure lamp, is considered to belong to the village and to be permanently available for borrowing. Likewise it is expected that the poorest families of untouchables will constantly come round asking for scraps of soap, herbs, or foodstuffs. There are, in fact, a thousand ways in which people are forced and expected to share, not least at their funerals. The wealthier a person becomes, the stronger the pressures grow.

On the other hand, the situation does not appear to be as oppressive as in some wholly agrarian societies. There does not appear to be a strong prevalence of the ethic of 'limited good', in which envy is believed to be rife, and the success of one family is seen as a direct threat to all others. People who had risen to outstanding success in the past were regarded with admiration; families of declining wealth were not generally feared to be envious. People were not afraid to praise babies, or to build expensive houses, or to wear new imported clothes. It is tempting to relate this to the fact that, unlike the agrarian societies where the 'limited good' ethic normally prevails,[9] the economic situation means that resources, for the Gurungs, are *not* limited. Wealth has been flowing in, in considerable quantities, from outside. It is neither economically nor psychologically appropriate to consider that the increase in wealth of one family is necessarily paid for by the loss of another. The cake is, or has been, expanding fast enough for everyone to have a large slice. How people will feel if, as seems likely, the economy begins to contract (with population pressure mounting and recruitment declining) it is difficult to predict. We may expect a simultaneous hostility to those who try to accumulate, and a growing tendency towards such accumulation and economic differentiation. It is a paradox that at present, by encouraging conspicuous consumption of wealth in housing and clothes, a relaxed attitude prevents the accumulation of land which would destroy the present egalitarian system. If there is a growing hostility to the symbols of wealth differentiation, more wealth will, in the end, be deflected from consumption into investment, and thus the problem of inequality will be exacerbated.

An important mechanism whereby wealth is distributed throughout the village is the rising price of land and the cost of housing. At present, land and housing absorb most of the wealth that flows into the village. Unlike the case of the Limbus, however, the land is not being bought back from another set of landowners to whom it has been mortgaged.[10] It is bought from other Gurungs. In other words, cash from abroad is used to alter the land-owning pattern at each generation. But so far, because of the factors listed above, as well as others, such land sales have not resulted in permanent class divisions. Rather, the very high prices paid for not particularly productive land are a means of dispersing wealth. It is a process somewhat similar to that whereby seventeenth century English businessmen bought estates from declining landed families and thus suffused the countryside with new capital. One difference in the situation is obvious, however. In England some of this new wealth was used to increase the productivity of land by improving agricultural technology. Such improvements helped to destroy the vestiges of the small independent yeomanry and to create a large landless labouring class. Neither the technological nor social revolution have occurred in the Gurung village I studied. The technology is almost unchanged, and almost all Gurungs own land. But in the previous discussion of land distribution we saw some signs of a long-term trend towards a greater inequality, an inequality that is reported to be growing among the Magars, Limbus, Lepchas, and Gurungs elsewhere.[11]

One final pressure towards equality is especially important; this is the way in which wealth is transmitted between the generations. Such transmission does not occur only at death; education and marriage payments are often as important as the wealth actually handed over at the parent's death. Among the Gurungs there has been little scope, until recently, for wealthier persons to give their children a better start in life by educating them. This was partly because there were few formal educational facilities, and partly because there were no obvious ways in which education gave a person any advantage in the absence of bureaucracy, commerce and the professions. A group of wealthier families living just below the main village of Thak had hired a tutor in the late 1940s to teach their children. This was before the village school was founded. But the recipients of this early education have found it to be of little advantage. One is the head-master of the local school, for which he receives far less pay than he would as a rifleman in the army. Another wanders around, bored, yet unwilling or unable to leave the agricultural life of the village. A number of other families have invested considerable sums to have their children educated to a secondary level at Pokhara, but it is unlikely that they will be able to obtain well-paid jobs if we consider the huge quantity of school leavers competing for jobs in a small bureaucracy. Western-style education gives no advantage in village cultivation or recruitment to the army. Thus one valuable mechanism, whereby superior wealth in one generation can ensure superior wealth in the next, cannot operate.

The transmission of wealth at marriage and death among the Gurungs is such that all children benefit, though sons receive larger portions than daughters. Such partible inheritance between all sons is another mechanism whereby capital accumulation in certain families is checked. A large landholding, such as that of house 17, may well be broken into pieces too small to sustain individual families within a couple of generations. Rich families are also expected to give away a considerable amount of wealth with their daughters. Thus their wealth is being distributed between all the children. This is a significant contrast to the systems of primogeniture which helped to preserve the European class divisions of the seventeenth and eighteenth centuries, at the expense of younger sons who were de-classed. The cumulative effect of partible inheritance is that, at each generation, the number of holdings will increase dramatically. Some families may be forced right off the landowning map, as occurred during our stay in Thak when a man from an illegitimate branch of a *carjat* lineage was forced to sell off his last piece of rice land and went to try to live off his buffaloes in the forest. Those forced out provide land for those with cash from the army. But the overall effect is likely to be a village where land is fairly evenly divided between a large number of peasant proprietors, all other things being equal.

Pressures towards accumulation of wealth in a few hands

It has frequently been pointed out that the penetration of cash into a subsistence economy breaks up old relationships, and provides the mechanism whereby an accumulation of wealth may occur which encourages a growing inequality. That cash, of itself, does not necessarily have this disruptive effect is shown by the history of the Gurungs. Ever since the First World War, large quantities of cash have been paid to recruits, but in the absence of labour that could be bought with such cash, of consumer goods, and a market economy, this inflow was minimally disruptive. There was difficulty in spending army wages in the village because other Gurungs did not want or need large amounts of money. There was nothing to buy with it. Hence much of the army pay was turned into non-productive goods with little exchange value; gold, clothes and other goods from Malaya. Land was widely available, people were not forced to sell much of their labour. Cash was an alien element in a subsistence economy. Recently the situation has changed dramatically. Much of this is due to the factors listed below.

As population grows and land becomes scarce, it becomes a 'good' which it is worth investing money in. Land has, of course, been bought and sold for many years. But now it is becoming more and more obvious that the wealthy persons in the village are those who own land. Also it is becoming more difficult to hold on to land. When land was plentiful in relation to people, anyone with sufficient labour could work enough land to feed himself; now it is only possible to hold on to land if one is making a profit in annual budgeting, in other words if one is not part of a 'deficit' household. The weaker are forced off the land in the increasingly competitive struggle for an obviously limited resource. At the same time, a shift towards a surplus of labour on the land means two things. Firstly, people are prepared to hire out their labour to others for cash returns, rather than to live off their own or be idle. Secondly, such returns, both in cash and kind, though at present fixed by 'conventional' standards to a certain extent, are likely to decrease as a proportion of the real productive value of the labour. In other words, the bargaining power of labour will also decline. There will also be less and less work for people to do, so that the annual income of those who do depend on wage labour will decline. The same amount of land will have to provide work and crops for a growing number of people and there will be less and less to go round.

Such a tendency will be exacerbated by improved agricultural technology without greatly increased yields. Any use of labour-saving devices, such as the new plough and spaced crops (to make non-human weeding possible), as suggested for the Trisuli development area in the *Wye Valley Report*,[12] would have an enormous effect in reducing the demand for labour, as would the use of automatic grinding and de-husking machines suggested in the same report. Such improvements would mean, in effect, that larger land-owners could accumulate more land and be less dependent on a labour force rapidly becoming redundant. It is not surprising, therefore, that the same report argues that such developments must be accompanied by the re-settlement of a large part of the village population. In Thak and many other Nepalese villages such resettlement is now out of the question, and indeed the population is rapidly becoming more dense. What is needed are methods of making agriculture both more productive and also labour intensive. Double cropping and the use of improved seeds and fertilizers spring to mind here, but there are many difficulties in their adaptation to hill conditions. One social difficulty is that those with spare capital for such improvements are likely to be the rich. For example, as Caplan has pointed out,[13] it is only those who have a large herd of livestock and hence much manure who can afford to grow wheat in the dry season. Thus wealth differences in the village would be accentuated. It is also not yet clear whether the cost of fetching fertilizer to the village and carrying crops down to Pokhara will make it possible to compete with areas nearer the market. For domestic consumption, such use of fertilizer, if it could be combined with regulation of livestock grazing and improved water supplies, would help to feed and occupy the growing population for a few years longer. But behind this are all the dangerous concomitants of the 'Green Revolution'. The disease and pest dangers of a monoculture, the very serious ecological side-effects of fertilizers and pesticides already make it difficult to recommend their use at all. It is a terrible choice – poisoning one's environment or going hungry. But it is a choice which the Gurungs, like all people's throughout the world, will increasingly have to face.

The mechanism whereby certain families are forced down and others up is the budgetary surplus or deficit. A combination of favourable conditions has led the Gurungs to expect a higher standard of living over the last twenty years. The expenditure on what are now considered 'necessaries' such as cigarettes, sugar and kerosene has increased considerably. Yet such expenditure demands an income which many families do not have. They are forced to sell capital, gold and land, or go into debt. At the same time the reserves of good new land have come to an end and each generation sees the present fields subdivided between an increasing number of children. More and more families find it impossible to balance their income and expenditure; it is far easier to expand than contract expenses. This process has, I believe, only just started to be apparent in a comparatively wealthy and new village like Thak: in poorer or older villages such as Mohoriya or Siklis it has been obvious for some time. The problem has also been delayed by army money; the poorer households have remade their fortunes by sending a son abroad. Yet the problem is likely to grow. Such deficits are the way in which an increasing split between a class of small peasant proprietors and a landless group comprising up to half of the village, could occur during the next twenty years.

One of the correlated phenomena which may well emerge during this period is increased indebtedness and rural moneylending. According to the law, all debts had to be registered in the year 1966, or else they were without legal force. Although it is certain that a good many debts were not so registered, an examination of the Land Reform records for Thak confirmed the impression gained from informal questioning that most families are, at present, solvent. Even the eleven Gurungs who were stated to be borrowing money usually borrowed small sums, normally from other Gurungs and within the village. There is also borrowing from the affluent village of Khilang, some ten miles to the north, but no registered borrowing from Brahmins or town moneylenders. In comparison to many other communities, for example that studied in Eastern Nepal by Caplan, the Gurungs of Thak seem to be relatively unencumbered by debts. Mortgaging of land and large-scale borrowing are, however, likely to be the mechanism by which increasing inequality occurs as population presses on resources.

Such a tendency to more permanent class differentiation will be exacerbated by the evaporation of communal resources. Where there are rich resources of wood, fodder, fish, wild fruit and vegetables and wild game, this will be of especial benefit to poorer families. Though they do not have the guns to kill larger game, they can draw on the 'commons' to overcome food deficits, and for free fuel and building material. The deterioration in the state of the woods and rivers around Thak has already been indicated. It seems likely that within twenty years there will be little of value left. Much of it is being cleared for individual landholdings, particularly towards Taprang. Thus both the quantity and quality is being rapidly eroded. Whether anything equivalent to the enclosure of the commons (which in pre-industrial England both symbolized and caused the destruction of small-holders and hence helped create a landless proletariat), will occur in Thak, it is difficult to predict. But certainly one important cause and sign of equality will soon be merely a shadow of its former self. The poor will suffer most. They, for instance, will not have the cash to buy the fuel needed to supplement the rapidly vanishing supply of free wood.

Another essential prerequisite for the growth of economic inequality is a market economy. As argued earlier, only if people can convert their surpluses into a fund for buying more productive power is an accumulative spiral possible. Otherwise small economic advantages are not transformed into permanent and growing ones. Such a market economy is the dream of development experts. For example the experimental farm at Lumley, where Gurungs are trained (under British Aid auspices) to grow cash crops such as fruit and nuts, hopes to develop widespread cash-cropping. As yet it is not certain whether there will be a market. At present hardly anything produced in Gurung villages is sold outside, which is another reason for their comparatively egalitarian structure.

In this brief sketch of some of the mechanisms whereby a landless labouring class is likely to be created in Thak a somewhat 'ideal type' model society has been drawn and predictions have been made on the basis of this. It is, however, likely that many other factors, for instance general price changes, as well as changes in the whole situation in Nepal and India over the next twenty years, will alter the outcome. Nevertheless it does seem worth suggesting the following hypothesis. When any landholding gets below a certain viable size, the owner is forced into debt and then into selling his capital. Holdings will tend to be concentrated into fewer and fewer hands, though perhaps let out to tenants at a high rent. Such renting of land has only just started in Thak. It awaits the development of a cash crop and market, a final depletion of communal resources, and a growing build-up of population before it becomes a major form of landholding. If it does happen, as it happened in pre-industrial and industrializing England, and in India, there will be the same problem of a rural, landless, workless, heavily-indebted proletariat. It is doubtful whether such people will find room in a tiny industrial and bureaucratic sector. The problems India faces now, Nepal will face during the next two decades. The demographic aspects of this prediction will be examined empirically in the following chapters and at the theoretical level in the final chapter.

PART II
POPULATION

10

Population growth in Nepal

GENERAL FEATURES OF NEPALESE POPULATION STRUCTURE

The sources for the study of Nepal's population are extremely restricted in quantity and quality. All calculations are therefore extremely uncertain. Yet a number of features of the population are now clearly established. Firstly, Nepal is an almost entirely rural and agricultural country: in the 1952–4 Census, 94 % of the population gave their primary occupation as agriculture, only 2 % as manufacturing, and there has been little change since.[1] The population lives predominantly in small settlements: in 1952–4 'nearly three-fourths of the population live in villages with fewer than 1000 inhabitants, whereas only 3 per cent of the population live in the 10 largest cities.'[2] On the whole, people still work their own land: in 1952–4, 78 % of the active male workers claimed to be either self-employed or unpaid family workers.[3] These farming communities show many of the features which we associate with what is termed 'stage one' of demographic development; high fertility, high mortality, a large number of young people dependent on adults, and a moderate to high population growth rate.[4]

The overall changes in Nepal's population from 1911–1971, as indicated in the censuses, may be seen in table 10.1. The decline to 1920 is ascribed by Shreshta to First World War casualties and the influenza outbreak of 1918, though there was probably also under-enumeration in 1920. The 1930 census was vitiated by a threat of war with Tibet, which meant that people thought that the census might be used for conscription purposes, and hence there is considerable under-registration. The 1941 census was affected by the large numbers recruited for the Second World War, and the casualties in an earthquake in 1934 also lowered the numbers. Shreshta summarizes the growth rates up to 1954 as follows, 'The average rate of growth during the period of 43 years from 1911 was 1.2 % a year. It was 2.2 % over the period of 24 years from 1930 to 1954 and 2.9 % over 13 years from 1941 to 1954'.[5] The population in 1971 was 11,289,000. By 1975 it is estimated that it will be between 11,750,000 and 13,100,000 according to U.N. estimates, though even the latter figure may be too low.[6] The Government Family Planning office unofficially calculated in 1969 that, if family planning is not successful (and as

TABLE 10.1 *Growth of population 1911–61*[a]

Year	Population	Percentage change
1911	5,638,749	—
1920	5,573,788	−1.2
1930	5,532,574	−0.8
1941	6,283,649	+13.5
1954[b]	8,661,853	+37.8
1961	9,753,378	+12.6
1971[c]	11,289,000	+15.7

[a] Adapted from B. P. Shreshta, *The Economy of Nepal* (Bombay, 1967), p. 34.
[b] The total for 1954 is adjusted from the census of 1952–4.
[c] This is a provisional estimate, kindly supplied by the Royal Nepalese Embassy in London.

yet there are few signs that it will be), by 1995 there will be approximately 25,700,000 people in Nepal. In the 84 years since 1911 the population will have increased nearly five-fold. From the various community studies to be considered shortly, it seems that the population of many villages increased roughly five-fold between 1850–1950. If we allow a generous margin, and assume that only a three-fold increase occurred throughout Nepal, then the population of Nepal in 1850 was, at the very most, 3 million. Thus in the 150 years after 1850 the population is predicted to increase by a factor of ten. This enormous rate of growth is illustrated in Fig. 10.1. In order to illustrate how dramatic is this rise in an almost purely agrarian country, with little initial capital, the graph has been compared to that for a period in pre-industrial England when that country may fairly be considered already to have been economically and socially more advanced than Nepal in 1950.

Much guesswork is involved in working out the probable present growth-rate of Nepal's population. Between 1954 and 1961 it was calculated to be 1.8 % p.a., and this was a widely accepted figure. Then a detailed medical and demographic survey of some 5011 people, carried out by the Dooley Foundation and Hawaii University, produced the much higher growth rate of 2.7 % p.a. for the years 1965–6.[7] It is possible that the growth rate was already rising as health improved, but it is more probable that the more intensive survey collected information on children missed in the national census. The Government Family Planning office accepted this figure in 1967, but in 1969 went back to an intermediate figure of 2.03 % p.a.[8] Even with this lower figure, population will double in less than 35 years. This is a particularly high rate of growth when we consider that it is achieved against a background of continued

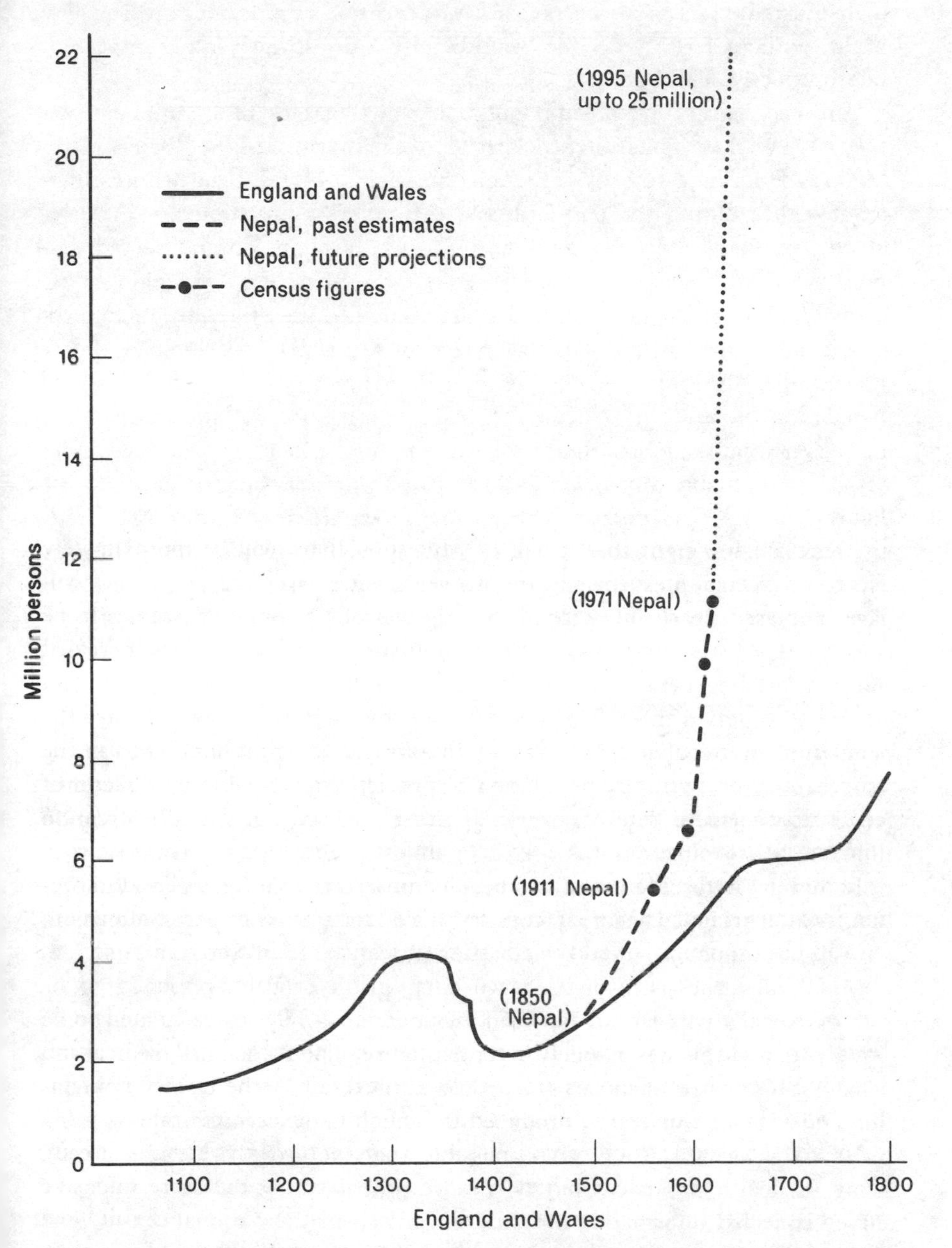

Fig. 10.1. Population of Nepal (1850–2000), compared to that of England and Wales (A.D. 1000–1800). (** Adapted from E. A. Wrigley, *Population and History* (London, 1969), p. 78.)

high mortality. As has been pointed out, a major improvement in Nepalese health without fertility decline 'would cause a disastrously rapid increase in non-productive children'.[9]

Anthropologists have noted population growth in most of the areas in which they have worked. Thus Hitchcock writes of the Magar village of 'Banyan Hill', 'Figures from land records (although they are to be relied on with caution) suggest that during the past century, the *thum*'s population has increased about fivefold'.[10] Since the *thum* now consists of about 600 households,[11] it must then have consisted of about 120. Of the Sherpas we are told that 'the great increase of the last hundred years coincided with the introduction and spread of the potato. In 1836 there were in the whole of Khumbu only 169 households, compared with the 596 households in 1957'.[12] In other words the population increased $3\frac{1}{2}$-fold in 120 years. If this rate continued there would be over a thousand households by the end of the century. For the Limbu, Caplan was unable to provide any of his own figures, but he quotes census figures for the Ilam district which show an approximate 40 % increase in population between 1920 and 1961, a rate he believes applies to the Limbus. He records that 'pressure on land was recognized as the principal cause of emigration as early as the 1890s'.[13]

GENERAL CONSEQUENCES OF POPULATION GROWTH IN NEPAL

The causes of population growth and high fertility rates have hardly been discussed by those writing on Nepal. The probable consequences of continued or even accelerated population growth have received a little more attention, though anthropologists tend to refer to some of the effects – increased pressure on land leading to the splitting of holdings and emigration – without going into much detail. The effects on work opportunities and unemployment, on capital accumulation and the distribution of wealth in the community, on diet and maternal health, on the rate of destruction of natural resources, on the availability of social services such as education, on family structure, and on the whole area which may loosely be termed 'religion and thought', have hardly been mentioned. Economists have shown interest in some of the problems. B. P. Shreshta of Kathmandu points out the following features of the Nepalese economy. The age-structure consequent on very high fertility is such that there is 'heavy youth dependency'. About 40 % of the population in Nepal is aged fifteen or under. He continues, 'the decline in the level of fertility can alone be an effective solution to the problem of huge waste of scarce resources on account of maintaining the growing army of children in countries like Nepal'.[14] The present population growth rates have a disastrous effect on any chance of economic growth. For example, there will be in the next few years a huge growth in the labour force, anything up to 2 million extra persons in the period 1955–75. He calculates that 'The magnitude of investment required to absorb the annually growing labour force in the non-agricultural sector may not probably be less than Rs. 400 million a year – the amount which is almost twice as much as the total outlay on the Five Year Plan financed largely from external resources in the form of outright grants!' He continues by saying that 'the prospect for initiating a fairly high rate of economic growth in Nepal in the face of mounting pressure of population is very bleak'.[15] Put at the very simplest level, that of feeding the extra mouths, in order to keep the (very inadequate) 1961 standard of consumption and export of cereals, cereal production would have to be increased by about 42 % by 1975, merely to keep pace with population.[16] Though it could be argued that this could be achieved by the increased use of new hybrid seeds and fertilizers, the already acute shortage of protein and vitamins would still be exacerbated. As population pressure forces the use of more and more pasture land for cereal growing, the nutritional situation will deteriorate, even if absolute starvation were warded off temporarily.[17] Likewise the already over-grazed and over-cut lands, suffering increasing erosion, will deteriorate rapidly. After a very detailed study of the economics, soil, grass, cereals, livestock of an area to the north of Kathmandu, the investigating team came to the conclusion that the only possible solution to an already serious situation was that some of the present cereal land must be taken out of production, and thus 'A policy of resettlement of the population is recommended'.[18]

As the percentage and absolute number of unemployed is likely to rise considerably, the trickle to the towns will turn into a flood. In the villages the mutilated forests will finally be cleared to the ground. Meanwhile the attempt to improve social services will find it increasingly difficult to cope with the rising numbers. For instance, the Government Family Planning office informed me that universal education, planned for 5–11 year olds by 1985, cannot possibly be achieved. By 1995, they calculate, there will be nearly 5 million children aged 5–11, if present population trends continue; a number which equals half the total population of Nepal in 1960. Perhaps the most alarming feature of all is that this growth rate is being achieved *before* the very high mortality rate has really been affected by western medical and hygienic measures. Nepal has one of the highest mortality rates in the world, approximately 27 per 1000 is the crude rate, and 150 per 1000 for infants.[19] Such a high rate is not surprising since in the 1960s Nepal had the lowest health expenditure per head of any country in the world, and the second lowest doctor-to-patient ratio in the world.[20] The results of the rapidly growing public water, anti-malaria, and anti-tuberculosis campaigns will therefore be enormous. Without a corresponding effective control of births, the population growth rate could rise to nearly 4 % p.a. in the next ten years, or a doubling of the population in as little as twenty years.

Rapid population growth is influencing the whole social and economic structures of the communities studied by anthropologists. This alone justifies us in taking demography as a central theme for anthropological analysis. Another justification is that through the analysis of demographic factors, which are principally a series of events over time, the inevitable tendency of anthropological accounts to be static cross-sections of a society and to give a false sense of equilibrium may be partially corrected.

POPULATION CHANGE AMONG THE GURUNGS

There are four principal sources for the study of Gurung population; a nineteenth-century land tax on the whole of Nepal copied out by Brian Hodgson, official censuses since 1911, army recruitment records, and land tax records for particular villages. Each has great deficiencies and must be used with the utmost caution. The first rough estimate of the number of Gurungs was made at the beginning of the nineteenth century by Buchanan, who wrote that in Kaski district 'the Gurungs remain in these parts in great numbers' while in Parbat district 'In the whole country it is supposed that there are 100000 families, of whom three fourths are Gurungs'.[21] It is important to be certain of the area of which Buchanan was speaking. Modern Parbat in the 1952–4 census, only had some 164,962 inhabitants, or approximately 33,000 families at five to a family. Either Buchanan was speaking of a wider area or, as seems likely, he was accepting grossly exaggerated totals.

Not until the 1952–4 census were Gurungs (Fig. 10.2) distinguished from other ethnic groups: they then constituted some 2 % of the total population of Nepal.[22] The only index the census enumerators could use of 'Gurunghood' is the fact that people speak Gurung as their 'mother tongue'. The total number of persons claiming to do so in censuses since 1952–4 is shown in table 10.2. It would appear, at first sight, as if Gurung population declined during the 1960s. But it is more likely that these figures merely show more people speaking and/or claiming Nepali as their mother tongue, especially among more isolated groups of Gurungs. This phenomenon was noted long ago in the *Linguistic Survey of India*, where it was shown that, for example in Sikkim, Gurungs were abandoning their old dialect in favour of what was then known as 'Khas'.[23] A more detailed analysis of the distribution of Gurung speakers is given in table 10.3. The overwhelming majority of Gurungs live in the Western Hills area, but, as Pignède has explained,[24] the number of erstwhile Gurungs, who have often lost their language but not all their customs, is probably much greater in the Eastern Hills than indicated in the table.

Fig. 10.2. A family group.

TABLE 10.2 *Number of Gurung speakers in national census, present in Nepal*

Date	Number
1952–4	162,192
1961	157,178

Even in the areas where Gurungs are congregated, they only form a minority of the population: in the Western Hills area in 1954, for example, they constituted only 4.7 % of the total population.[25] Even in an area such as Kaski district, one of the longest-inhabited Gurung regions, there were only 21,413 resident Gurung speakers in a total resident population of 127,515 in 1961.[26] Furthermore, we have already seen that in a particular Gurung village, Thak,

TABLE 10.3 *Distribution of Gurung speakers present in national census*

	1952–4	1961
Eastern Hills	9,147	6,915
East Inner Terai	13	23
Eastern Terai	233	524
Kathmandu Valley	505	589
Western Hills[a]	149,554	147,499
Centre Inner Terai	2,511	1,157
West Inner Terai	30	1
Mid Western Terai	189	469
Far Western Terai	10	1
	162,192	157,178

[a]The two areas of 'Western Hills' and 'Far Western Hills' in the 1961 census have been amalgamated to compare them with the 1952–4 divisions.

less than half the total of households were Gurung. This means, among other things, that it is difficult to infer too much from a general rise in population in areas where Gurungs are concentrated. Nevertheless it is worth examining the changes in population in the Kaski district as a whole (see table 10.4). The 1952–4 and 1961 figures are based on the censuses of those years. The 1820–1 figure is based on Brian Hodgson's manuscripts where there is a transcript of the 'returns of the tax called *Sawani-phagu*' collected in the year 1877–8 (Nepal style; western dating 1820–1).[27] This lists, village by village, the number of households and the amount of tax paid per village. It occasionally gives the type of landowners, number of widows heading households and other details. It is impossible to be sure of its accuracy, but the marginal notes and comparison of the names of villages with later censuses suggest that it may well be fairly reliable. From the table we can see that between 1821 and 1961 the number of households increased between five and six-fold. This seems to fit well with what we know of the expansion of the individual villages of Thak and Mohoriya. The households in 1821 were distributed in 47 named villages. The 1952–4 census showed nearly five times the total of households, but the number of villages had only increased by 13 to a total of 60.[28] Though it is impossible to

TABLE 10.4 *Population change in Kaski district, 1820–1961*

Date	No. of households
1820–1	5,318
1952–4	23,982
1961	27,882

be sure that they are speaking of the same area when they refer to the same named village, a comparison of the situation in selected villages is interesting (see table 10.5). Thus some villages, for example Mouja, a village very near to Thak, increased six-fold, while others, such as Harpan, less than three-fold.

From 1850 Gurungs were officially recruited for the British army. During the four recruiting seasons 1914–15 to 1917–18 approximately 7000 Gurungs were recruited from West Nepal into the regular battalions. Many more were enlisted in other capacities.[29] Assuming that men were usually between 15 and 29 when recruited and that up to 75 % of the males in this age group *were* recruited, and that the sex–age structure was similar to that for the Kaski district of Nepal in 1961, there must have been at least 100,000 Gurungs of all ages, male and female, in Western Nepal in about 1914.

GROWTH OF TWO GURUNG VILLAGES: MOHORIYA AND THAK

From genealogies, Pignède calculated that the village of Mohoriya was founded in about 1815–20. Some thirty years later there are said to have been 12 houses.[30] A list of those paying taxes for maize and millet land which I saw during my visit to Mohoriya gave a total of 69 households; it was undated but was probably compiled in about 1940. In June 1958, at Pignède's census, there were 98 households; the total population, including those absent, was 496. Thus the number of households had increased eight-fold in the hundred years after 1850. This very great increase was undoubtedly caused partly by migration from other villages, especially from Dansing to the south. Between 1958 and December 1969, when I undertook a census of Mohoriya, the population had only increased by twelve persons.[31] But this, in fact, conceals a con-

TABLE 10.5 *Comparison of selected villages*

	Total number of persons	
Name (as in 1820–1)	1820–1[a]	1952–4
Armalla	384	2,248
Arva	504	1,719
Bijaypoor	318	1,229
Galel	930	2,540
Ghachock	894	2,214
Harpan	498	1,353
Mouja	306	1,817

[a]The 1820 figures are only for households. It has been assumed that there were six persons per household. This is probably a generously large estimate, but allows for any decrease in size over the last 130 years down to the present size of about 5 per household (according to the censuses).

siderable natural growth in the intervening $11\frac{1}{2}$ years. Comparing the censuses we find that there had been 115 births (52 male and 63 female) to families present in both enumerations. Another 21 girls had come in as wives from other villages. Against this total influx of 136, some 30 males and 43 females had disappeared from the village either through death or marriage out. Thus there had been a natural increase of 63 persons on a total population of 418.[32] Assuming that roughly the same number of girls married out as into the village, this is a growth of just over 15 % in $11\frac{1}{2}$ years, which suggests a natural rate of growth of a little over 1 % p.a. This, as we have seen, is lower than that for Nepal as a whole, and it may also be unnaturally low for a Gurung village due to the distortion created by emigration.

In 1963 some twelve Gurung households and one Sunwar family left the village, in order to take the free land in the Terai being opened up as a result of malaria eradication. These were more than averagely large households, and prolific ones (one, for example, is known to have had seven children since it left the village). They have only been replaced by some 30 immigrants, so that the natural increase of 63 persons is offset by a net outflow of 48.[33]

Evidence of house-building in Thak and Morhoriya provides a rough but valuable index of population growth.[34] In about 1920 in Thak central area there seem to have been about fifty houses; by 1969 there were some 97 houses, with 103 households in them. The growth was even more rapid in Mohoriya. In 1920 there were approximately 22 houses, while in 1958 there were over ninety. Such rapid growth was the result of both natural increase and immigration. The housing records support the impression of increasing pressure on space derived from land records and genealogies. Increases in prices also suggest considerable population growth. The price of rice land has probably doubled in both Thak and Mohoriya in the last ten years. Thirty years ago the price was sometimes as low as 3 % of the 1970 price. Other commodities have also increased very greatly in price.[35]

The strictly demographic records confirm the impression of considerable growth. The figures from recent censuses for the *panchayat* of Thak are given in table 10.6. Although it seems likely that the boundary was not changed with the introduction of the *panchayat* system in the early 1960s, I was unable to confirm this. Assuming that there has been no change in boundary, then the total resident population has risen from 1113 in 1954 to 1733 in 1971. Thus in the seven years after 1954 the population appears to have risen by less than 10 % (though the absentee population grew much faster than this), while in the ten years after 1961 the total resident population increased by at least 40 %. It is impossible to know the reasons for this apparent change. Improvement in public health (a piped water supply was installed in the main village of Thak in *c.* 1960), or increased immigration from the south are obvious hypotheses.

TABLE 10.6 *Population change in Thak, 1954–71*

	No. of houses	Households	Total persons (present)	Male	Female	Absent
1954 Thak	174	174	898	438	460	68
N.D.[a]	36	36	215	109	106	27
Total[b]	210	210	1113	547	566	95
1961 Thak	201	206	1000	444	556	121
N.D.	39	41	214	103	111	47
Total	240	247	1214	547	667	168
1971 Total	?	?	1733	828	905	?

[a] *Naule danda*, a hamlet to the south of the main village.
[b] Totals are based on the respective censuses of those years.

The overall impression is that while Gurung population is growing less rapidly than that of Nepal as a whole, it is nevertheless growing fast enough, at present rates, to double in well under forty years. The constituent elements of this growth, and some of the social correlates of fertility, will be the themes for subsequent chapters.

11

Social structure and fertility I: intercourse variables

The titles of this and the following chapters, as well as their arrangement, are based on the 'Analytic Framework' proposed by Kingsley Davis and Judith Blake in an important article.[1] Although their model does not overtly deal with every possible factor, it provides an extremely useful way of organizing the material. Davis and Blake divide their framework into three parts: factors affecting exposure to intercourse ('Intercourse Variables'), those affecting exposure to conception ('Conception Variables'), and those affecting gestation and successful parturition ('Gestation Variables'). This chapter will deal with the former, the next chapter the latter two. 'Intercourse variables' are divided into two parts: the former concerns features 'governing the formation and dissolution of unions in the reproductive period', the latter 'those governing exposure to intercourse within unions'.

FACTORS GOVERNING THE FORMATION AND DISSOLUTION OF UNIONS IN THE REPRODUCTIVE PERIOD

The first of the factors listed under 'intercourse variables' is 'Age of entry into sexual unions'. This is the most complex and important of all the variables which influence fertility in human societies: in most societies throughout the history of the world it has been the major mechanism for regulating fertility, because a few years delay in entering upon sexual union may have a profound effect on fertility. For example the fact that pre-industrial Europeans usually married, (at least in Western Europe after about 1500) at the age of roughly 25 or more and disapproved of pre-marital intercourse, whereas many non-European societies have married their children off at puberty or shortly afterwards, is one of the most significant reasons for the present differences between East and West.[2]

Age at entry into sexual unions

It seems likely that the age at which Gurungs normally enter sexual relations has risen during the last twenty years in most Gurung villages. This is due to a change in the attitude to pre-marital sexual intercourse and not to any change in the age at onset of puberty. There is no evidence that physical maturation occurs earlier now than it used to. Gurung children still look much younger for their years than their western counterparts. Boys of 17 or 18 often have unbroken voices, girls of 14 or 15 look like girls of 8 or 9 in our society. The first sign of the swelling of breasts usually occurs in girls at the age of 12 or 13, but some of 14 still have no sign of such swelling. There is no indication of any belief to parallel that of the Lepchas that sexual intercourse is needed to stimulate the onset of puberty,[3] nor is there evidence of sexual relations before puberty. It is thought that the age of procreation for boys is 15–16, girls 12–13, and that intercourse is, theoretically, permissable from then on. It seems likely that premarital sexual relations were once normal and not greatly disapproved of; marriage and sexual intercourse were not linked. The institutional setting for this, the *rodi* or communal houses, has been described in considerable detail by a number of authors; they bear a striking resèmblance to the young people's dormitories of Assam and India.[4] Basically, they seem to have been girl's dormitories, to which boys were invited in the evening to joke and sing. There is some dispute about the amount of sexual licence allowed in the past, but stories and genealogies suggest that this was considerable. Although the *rodi* still flourish in certain areas, they have practically been extinguished in Thak, possibly as a result of Hindu disapproval. From the evidence we have, it seems likely that until recently sexual relations among the Gurungs would start at the age of 17–18 for both sexes, either in the *rodi* or in fields and forest.[5] The men would then marry some 3–5 years later, the women 2–4 years later. We might, therefore, expect a considerable number of illegitimate births, as is said to happen at Siklis. More recently the Gurungs have come under pressure from their Hinduized neighbours to the south to wait until marriage before commencing sexual relations.

It is impossible to tell accurately how many women in Thak have conceived before marriage. In some cases the fact was concealed from me, in others a subsequent marriage between the two partners covered the event, in still others the foetus or newborn child was destroyed. I was told that the only occasion on which people would attempt to procure an abortion (Gg. *pasi* (child) *waba* (discard, throw away)), apart from when a lower caste women conceived by a Gurung man or *vice versa*, was when an unmarried woman became pregnant after intercourse in the *rodi*. Women are also said to go off to the forest to have their child, which their clothing allows them to bear without being noticed, and there to strangle it at birth. How often either abortion or infanticide occurs it is impossible to say; I only heard of one case of each occurring in the village during the last five years. Such practices do suggest, however, that while intercourse may have been accepted, to become pregnant was shameful. At the present generation I encountered five women who have had pre-marital livebirths, in one case, two separate infants. Their age at first delivery was 18, 19 and three at 21, which suggests that, even allowing for the period of reduced fertility after menarche, it is likely that few women start sexual intercourse before the age of 17. Such illegitimate children are known as *pregya* (Gg. ?).

It is difficult to say whether the mothers of illegitimate children suffer as a consequence, since the situation is probably changing. One informant said their chance of marriage was lessened, and pointed out a woman who had remained unmarried to the age of 36, and then married a very poor man, after having an illegitimate child. This case, however, could also be explained by the evil reputation of the woman's mother, and the general decline in the family's position in the village. In the other case where a mother of an illegitimate child had remained unmarried, possibly no one had wanted to take on the spastic son, and the mother herself was needed to look after the woman who had adopted her as her daughter. In another case a woman had remarried several times, and was not in the least ashamed that her first child was illegitimate (it had subsequently died). She was from Siklis, where older Gurung attitudes appear to remain. At Siklis, and in the past, the situation may have been close to that among the Lepchas where 'the production of a bastard is no drawback on the girl's subsequent marriage; on the contrary the fact that she has shown herself fertile makes her if anything more desirable'.[6] Certainly there was no stress on marital virginity as a particular virtue, no testing of the unbroken hymen or emphasis on chastity as a religious virtue. As with the Lepchas, there appears to be no specific word in Gurung meaning 'virgin'.[7] 'Bastard' or its equivalent was not used as a term of abuse and several informants spoke fondly and proudly of their past illegitimate offspring.

As to the legal treatment of bastards, there appears to be some divergence of opinion. Pignède states quite categorically that male bastards inherit a full share of goods and lands from their putative fathers.[8] This is certainly not the case in Thak or Siklis, however. Informants in Thak were adamant that illegitimate sons were not given a full *ansha* (Nep., share) and the current poverty of the poorest *konme* families in the village was explained by the fact that one or two generations ago the male heir had been an illegitimate son and was hence only given a small portion of the land. The amount given depends on a number of factors. An informant from Siklis said that village pressure would be put on the father, if he were reluctant, to give the illegitimate son enough to live on. The division would, as in all *ansha* making, be decided between the father and a group of village elders. Although they were the 'unwanted men in the society' according to this young informant, they would inherit in preference to a father's brother if there was no legitimate son, and he thought that a bastard and daughter would inherit equally in a similar case.

If a woman is found to be pregnant before marriage, we were told, she would be shouted at and occasionally hit by her parents, but she would not be turned out of the house. She would be forced to admit who was responsible. If the man was eligible for marriage, then the pair should marry, and if either party refused he or she would have to pay a fine of the same size as in a divorce case. Eighty rupees to be paid by the woman, forty rupees by a man are the basic sums, though they might be much higher if one partner was really eager to marry. If the partners were respectively from *sora* and *carjat*, theoretically endogamous, they should still marry. If they were from the same clan, for example *lamme*, then they would have to pay a very heavy fine, depending on their means, and going up to several thousand rupees. This is partly punishment, partly a bribe to the village elders to keep quiet about the incident since, by the national law, the culprits should be imprisoned. One case of the latter occurred, but I was unable to discover how, in actual practice, a case of premarital pregnancy is treated by a family.

It thus seems likely that, until recently, most people would commence sexual intercourse at about 17 or 18 years of age, and that fairly frequently this would lead to marriage. Pignède, however, believed that sexual relations before marriage were 'rare', mainly because there was little time in which they could occur. Men, he argued, went away to the army when they were physically mature, at about 19, and girls were married at between 15–18.[9] In fact Pignède's own statistics suggest that over half the girls in Mohoriya married at 18 years or over[10] and this is also true of Thak. Likewise, both in Thak and Mohoriya men often did not go to the army until the age of 20 or over, although this was over the official age for recruitment. Thus in both sexes there was a gap of up to five years between puberty and marriage/departure. My informants agreed, however, that engaged couples seldom had sexual relations before marriage, although there would have been no social condemnation if they had done so.[11] Pignède stated that a young couple might be teased by their friends if caught *in flagrente delicto*, a teasing which suggests at least a measure of tolerance. He goes on to argue that there would be no condemnation of the boy, but that the girl would be reprimanded by her parents.[12] Such a rigid 'double standard' does not seem to have been held in Thak, at least in theory, and in cases where intercourse led to pregnancy. Although the girl might receive the worse scolding, as we have seen, strenuous efforts would be made to find the man responsible and make him marry her or pay a fine. Several informants said that the man was as much to blame as the girl.

The first overt sexual experience of most Gurung boys is homosexual. From about the age of 12 until 16 or 17, boys will masturbate, either individually or in groups when out working in the forest.[13] This is known in Gurung as *ngyoh laba* (*laba* = to do/make; *ngyoh* = ? possibly 'oneself') as opposed to *mrih laba* which is ordinary intercourse with a woman (Gr. *mrih* = wife). I was told that if boys were seen doing this they would be shouted at, but not otherwise punished. The activity does not appear to bring guilt or shame. In later years grown men who, as boys, masturbated together will sometimes jokingly reminisce about their shared enjoyment. Girls are believed occasionally to masturbate themselves with their fingers, and a story is told of a girl (not Gurung) in south Nepal who became ill when she lost the egg-plant (Nep. *bhendā*) she was using for this purpose inside her. I found no trace of intercourse with girls before puberty, nor of the sexual initiation of boys by elder married women, both characteristic of other Himalayan tribal societies.[14] I did not ask a specific question in the census as to age at first intercourse or with whom it first occurred, but it was clearly not a topic of central interest as it was among the Lepchas.

Age at marriage. Although marriage-age and child-bearing are not as closely linked among the Gurungs as among, for example, western Europeans, fertility is still considerably affected by marital habits. The ideal age for Gurungs to marry, for both men and women, is said to be between 15 and 25. Several informants in Thak agreed that men should marry from the age of 20 on, women from the age of 15. One informant, who had himself been married at 18 and felt strongly that this had been too young, argued that marriage was best delayed for both sexes until they were about 23–4 because it would stop people from having too many children. This was the only occasion when informants drew a connection between age at marriage and control of birth and since this informant knew of my views on the subject, may have been said partly to please me. I was told that the relative ages of bride and groom do not matter as long as they are within seven years of each other and their astrological positions relative to each other are satisfactory. It does not matter if the man is a few years the younger. If the girl is too young, there is some disapproval, as in a recent case where a man had married a girl of 12 and made her pregnant a year later. Some of the villagers are aware of a recent Nepalese law which forbids the marriage of women under 14 and of men under 18 years of age. Such a law has undoubtedly had little effect on the Gurungs, who very seldom married under this age even before the law. The institution the law *might* affect is childhood betrothal. Very occasionally (only one case was reported to me for Thak in recent years) a boy and girl, often cross-cousins, would be betrothed between the ages of 6 and 10. Usually just a verbal agreement would be made, but if there is a ceremony it is said to be the same as the ordinary wedding ceremony. It is called *Kanyadhan* (Nep., a small girl given). Such a betrothal cannot be broken without a divorce, and the partner who instigates such a rupture has to pay a fine as in a normal divorce. When either partner remarries another person there is not a full wedding ceremony.

In the one reported case in Thak such a divorce had occurred because the girl refused to cohabit with her betrothed husband.

It has long been known that the hill peoples of Nepal tend to marry later than those dwelling to the south of them. The 1952–4 census showed that while half the girls and a little over a quarter of the boys aged 10–14 living in the Terai were married, only 22 % of the girls and 7 % of the boys in the hills area were so married.[15] It is suggested by some authorities that this late marriage has not always been the case, at least among the Gurungs. In a textbook on the Gurkhas, referring to the Gurungs in the 1920s, it is stated that marriage 'usually takes place at about the age of fifteen'.[16] one of the authors has recently repeated that among the Gurkhas (including Gurungs), 'Marriage usually takes place at about the age of sixteen for boys, fourteen for girls'.[17] Since one of the older men in Thak stated that there had been no change in the age at which people had married during his lifetime it is necessary to look at this question in some detail.

The evidence for Mohoriya, as analysed by Pignède, is set out in table 11.1 (the table refers to women only). In commenting on the table he states that in all the 13 cases where a woman was said to have been 13–14 at marriage, the woman was now aged 30 or over. Nowadays the marriage of very young girls is rare. He suggests that this is because many of the soldiers who come back to the village have picked up the idea that marriages with young girls are wrong. In Thak, however, in two of the rare cases where a very young girl was married it was to a serviceman on leave; indeed, if they are serving in India, they are likely to see much *earlier* marriages than they are used to. It could as well be argued that such pressures as there are in the opposite direction. For further evidence let us look at the situation in Thak.

The figures in table 11.2 are based on the household census of Thak, and although there is likely to be a small margin of error, especially among the older women, there is unlikely to be very much distortion.[18] Three-quarters of the

TABLE 11.1 *Age at first marriage (237 cases at Mohoriya)*

Age group	No. of cases	%
13–14 years	13	6
15–18	114	48
19–22	92	39
23–26	10	4
27–30	3	1
31–34	2	1
35–38	3	1

Source: Pignède, *Les Gurungs*, p. 234.

TABLE 11.2 *Age at first marriage of Gurung women in Thak*

Age at marriage	Present age of women									
	15–19	20–4	25–9	30–4	35–9	40–4	45–9	50–9	60–9	Total
11–12	1	1		1			1	1		5
13										0
14										0
15			1						1	2
16							1			1
17		1		2	2	1				6
18			2				2	1	1	6
19					1	1	1		2	5
20		1	2	1	1			1	1	7
21		2		1		1		1		5
22							1			1
23										0
24										0
25									1	1
26										0
27				1						1
28						1			1	2
29				1					1	2
										44

marriages (29/44) have occurred at between 17 and 21 years. The mode is 20, the mean average just over 19. Only 8/44 women married at under 17 years of age. This gives a different emphasis to that put on the Mohoriya figures by Pignède, though it seems likely that if his figures were analysed as in this table the results would be very similar. Given the difference in the size of the total sample, there is a greater proportion of very early marriage in Thak (up to age 14) than in Mohoriya; yet this does not alter the general impression that Gurung women tend to marry from the age of 17 years onwards. Nor do the figures indicate any obvious change during the last thirty years since Morris wrote. Although the figures are too small for any statistical certainty, those now aged forty and over seem to have married at almost exactly the same ages as those now aged 15–40. Nor do the number of marriages of very young girls seem to have decreased. It is possible that the Gurungs marry at a later age than the Magars, and that the military authorities confused the two groups. Thus we are told of the Magars 'It is customary for girls to be married before they have passed very far into their teens'.[19]

We have no ready analysis for Mohoriya, but we may look at the age of first marriage for men in Thak. Table 11.3 shows that only $\frac{1}{43}$ Gurung men is recorded as having married under the age of 17. It is difficult to reconcile this

TABLE 11.3 *Age at first marriage of Gurung men in Thak*

Age at marriage	Present age of men					
	20–9	30–9	40–9	50–9	60–9	Total
15				1		1
16						0
17				1		1
18	1	2				3
19	1	1	2			4
20		2				2
21	1	3	1	2		7
22			1			1
23		2	1	3	1	7
24			2			2
25		2		2		4
26		1	2			3
27						0
28		2	1			3
29			1			1
30		1	1		1	3
31			1			1
						43

with the previously quoted remarks by army officers that Gurung men marry at 15 or 16. The mode is divided between 21 and 23. Less than one-quarter of the men marry at under the age of 20, and less than a quarter over the age of 26. Nor does the table suggest any significant changes during the last forty years; marriages for men throughout that period have normally taken place between the ages of 19 and 30. During the last thirty years many Gurungs have not married until they are much older than the norm for Nepal.

Factors affecting the age at marriage. The first and most crucial factor is the degree to which marriage is the point at which the transfer of wealth and authority between generations occurs. If marriage is the occasion when land is passed on, when the new couple gain independence and a separate house, becoming a distinct economic, ritual, jural and social unit, then we may expect marriage age to be high. If, however, the young couple remain within the parental household, still subject to the father's discipline and contributing to a joint estate, then there is no forced transfer of resources and marriage can occur at a very young age. There is a third intermediate situation. In this the young couple still set up a separate household as in our nuclear family system, but as in the joint household system, they do not require that the older generation hand over their inheritance as a lump sum at marriage. Migrant labour, such as that practised by many Gurungs who go to the army, is an obvious example of such a middle way.

The Gurungs, in fact, exhibit a pattern which lies between two extremes. On the one hand, as examination of the household structure has shown, they do not live in joint households. Two married couples scarcely ever live together permanently in one house, though there is perhaps not as strong an antipathy to such an arrangement as, for example, in England at present. Thus marriage does alter the pattern, but not radically or straight away. A tabular analysis is given in appendix 6 to show to what degree marriage, inheritance of property and the death of parents is correlated in Thak. It shows that only in $\frac{3}{35}$ cases was the *ansha* (division of the property) made at the first marriage of a son. The normal pattern is to wait for a few years until all the sons are married and have children or more than one has returned home permanently from the army. The property is treated as a joint estate until then. Nor, as we have argued, is there an immediate change in social and ritual status at marriage. Young married people do not change their clothes, their groups of friends, or gain any new authority in financial, ritual, or other decisions. Since this is so, it is not surprising to find from the table just referred to that there is no correlation between death of parents and age at marriage. The young do not have to wait for their parents to retire or to die. Neither the reported dates of death of mother or of father are correlated with statements about when the *ansha* was made. As stated before, the pattern is an intermediate one. While it is expected that a family should have accumulated enough capital to build a separate house for a son a few years after his marriage, and hence must wait until he is fairly old before marrying him, there is no real threat to the parents implied in marriage, and therefore it can occur when they are still far from senile.

Not only the timing of inheritance, but the way it is distributed between children is crucial in determining age at marriage. Where inheritance is impartible, we may expect considerable differences in age between inheriting and non-inheriting children. Among the Gurungs, however, where all sons inherit equally, with the youngest getting the house and looking after the aged parents as long as they live, we find little difference between first, second, third and other sons, in their age at marriage, nor between daughters. The first son does not marry later than the others; he is not forced to wait for his father to leave him the farm, as in many peasant communities.

Another variable determining age at marriage in all societies is the amount of capital believed to be needed at marriage – housing, land, agricultural equipment, livestock, and a small reserve for illness and children. Related to this is the amount of time it takes, given the technology and social institutions, to accumulate this necessary quantity. The age at marriage can thus be affected by any one of these. If, for example, there is a shortage of housing space or materials, this can put up the age at marriage. As Malthus remarked, 'One of the most salutary and least pernicious checks to the frequency of early marriages in this country [i.e. eighteenth century England] is the difficulty of procuring a cottage'.[20] Where the amount of capital needed is low, or where individuals expect to be able to earn considerable sums for the rest of their lives with little inherited capital, for example where rich land is freely available, the fishing is good, or industrial jobs plentify, then marriage age is likely to be low. Again the Gurungs are in a middling position. All except the youngest brother will have to build a solid, fairly expensive house. It is expected that both men and women bring several thousand rupees worth of gold and other possessions to the marriage as a form of insurance for the future.[21] But against the fairly high costs of marriage, there has been, until recently, the widespread availability of rich resources of forest and land. The decline in such resources over the last thirty years has been temporarily compensated for by large-scale employment in the army. Outside agents, Britain and India, provided the capital to set young Gurung men to work. By village standards they could earn large sums, and finally ensure themselves a pension. Some of the money undoubtedly went to buy gold and housing which were the basis of their marriages.

The size of the unit which pays for each marriage will also determine the age at marriage. In general, the smaller the unit is, the later marriage is likely to be. In societies where marriages are arranged between two kinship groups, and corporately financed by them, then the young couple are, at marriage, drawing on the reserves of a much wider and wealthier group. They need not wait until they and their parents have accumulated a specified amount, but they can borrow in advance, a loan which will be repaid over the years as they finance other weddings of kin. The Gurungs appear to be nearer to a Western pattern, largely depending on the individual nuclear family rather than the lineage to finance marriages. Although relatives contribute rice and a token amount of money at the wedding celebrations, this only partly covers the cost of the actual celebrations. The expense of dowry and brideprice and housing is almost entirely borne by the particular household.

Another important factor influencing, and influenced by, age at marriage is the way in which a marriage is arranged. It seems to be generally true that where the choice is made by the young couple, attracted to each other by personality and physical appearance as well as wealth, this will preclude both a very young or very old age at marriage. The norm is likely to be in the range 18–23 for men, 17–22 for women. The arrangement of marriage by groups of kin makes it possible to marry off the partners at or near puberty. But arrangement by parents may hold up marriage and force it very late. What is crucial, is that the 'romantic love complex' effectively weakens the link between the economic structure and age at marriage. Whereas marriage is primarily determined by economic, political and social considerations in the 'ideal type' arranged marriage, now powerful private emotional factors intrude. Age at marriage takes on a momentum of its own, unrelated to the purely economic situation, and subject to many of the pressures of other fashions. Traditionally, the Gurungs appear to have maintained an ethic of romance and love among girls and boys who flirted together, alongside a fairly formal arranging of marriages by parents. In several cases we heard of, or witnessed, the bride and groom were only informed that they were to be married, and told who their prospective spouse was to be, a few hours before the wedding. It was generally agreed, however, that if, after the wedding, either partner maintained a steady objection to the other, the parents would finally give in to their pressure. As well as this negative veto, some young people, though probably a small proportion, elope to marry. After a while they are usually accepted back into their family, though, as in one case we witnessed, the battle of wills may go on for many months.[22]

There are many other factors which would have to be considered in any more general study of age at marriage. The general standard of living, the fluctuations in the real income of various groups, both will often lead to fluctuations of age at marriage. Changes in technology and the availability of land, or changes in the point at which men may be expected to reach maximum earning power, all have a profound influence. Again, the sex ratio, especially in small communities, may have a great effect. If there is a shortage of men, for example, the age of women at marriage may soar. Then there are the equally important cultural factors. The attitude to the danger inherent in being an unmarried post-pubertal woman; the necessity to ensure a male heir to pray at one's funeral; the concepts of when a girl is 'mature' and ready to be a wife, these are only three out of many fundamental attitudes which influence age at marriage. Lacking the detailed statistics over time with which to test these hypotheses on the Gurungs, it does not seem worth while taking up too much space on them here. It may be observed, however, that Gurung sexual and religious attitudes do not put pressure on them to marry children off at puberty. It is not necessary to have a son for the funeral ritual,[23] and there is no 'honour and shame' culture, either in its Hindu or Mediterranean version, to make unmarried post-pubertal girls a threat to their brothers or other kin. In conclusion it may be said that social attitudes, like social and economic structure, allow considerable flexibility and would lead us to expect a situation lying somewhere between that in traditional Hindu India and post-famine Ireland, representing neither the pre-puberty marriages of the former, nor men and women waiting until their late twenties or early thirties before they could marry.

Gurung age at marriage is high in comparison to many other Nepalese societies. Thus the mean average age of the mother at the birth of her first child in Thak over the last few years is 23, while for a sample throughout Nepal the average at first birth is between 18 and 20.[24] The difference is partly due to later marriage, partly to the greater average gap between marriage and first conception among the Gurungs. It means that an average of a little over one livebirth per marriage is lost among the Gurungs as compared to the Nepalese average. The Gurung situation is entirely different, for example, from that in pre-industrial England where the age at marriage was sometimes as high as 27 for women, which effectively reduced their fertility by 3–4 livebirths. It is thus not difficult to see how the Gurungs have a high completed fertility rate of 5–6 live-births per married woman, although they marry at a mean average age of over 19, whereas the Lepchas of Sikkim, for example, who used to start intercourse before puberty and whose girls were all married by 14, usually produced no more than three or four children.[25] Indeed it could be argued that by waiting until girls are stronger and at their fertility peak (and by inadvertently spacing their children because their husbands are away in the army) the Gurungs have achieved considerably higher fertility than many of those groups who so urgently stress child-bearing.

Permanent celibacy: the proportion of women never entering sexual unions

Whereas in parts of pre-industrial Europe it was common for up to 20 % of the adults never to marry, the normal pattern in Asia and Nepal is for almost 100 % of those who reach the age of 35 to be married.[26] Thus the 1952–4 census for Nepal showed that less than one per cent 'go through life in Nepal without ever having been married'.[27] Yet some of the Bhoteas, with whom the Gurungs have affinities, have a different pattern incorporating a large number of never-marrying women.[28] This fact, and the suggestion that many of the pressures which make the Gurung age at marriage higher than that in Nepal as a whole may also be expected to be at work here, makes it important to see what results the statistics yield. Although the proportion never marrying is scarcely ever as important a factor as age at marriage in lowering fertility,[29] it could still have appreciable effects on population growth.

Pignède's evidence suggests that the Gurungs conform to the general Nepalese pattern. He found no cases of men or women aged over 40 who had never married. He reported, furthermore, that Gurungs think that an adult who never marries is an abnormal being. The villagers, he wrote, were astonished at the fact that he was not married, and so he concluded that 'Marriage, alone, gives an adult his full status'.[30] My brief census of Mohoriya confirms Pignède's statistics: there was only one woman in the whole village aged over 25 who had not married and she was a girl of 27 who was looking after her old widowed mother. There were also two men aged over 33 who were not married, both of them looking after an aged mother. Such exceptions do not modify Pignède's picture of almost total adult marriage.

The situation in Thak, however, appears to be quite different, both statistically and in attitudes. I never heard any expression of the idea that to remain unmarried is peculiar, or that unmarried people have anything less than full adult status. I asked several people whether not marrying is in any way odd, or whether the older unmarried people in the village are in any way deviant, and they said not. Only one informant, from Siklis, said that in a quarrel one might use such a fact as a jibe. As already stated, marriage does not appear to be an important turning point, economically, ritually or socially. A person is not looked on as incomplete if he or she has no spouse or children. Unmarried girls in Thak are as confident and respected as married ones. One of the most respected and forceful women in the village is a woman of 49 who, because she is crippled, has never married. This tolerance is undoubtedly linked to the presence in Thak of a particular group of young, never-to-be-married, women.

It seems likely that in the past, in Thak as in Mohoriya, almost all Gurungs married. The only three women aged over 40 who had not married were the cripple already mentioned and two sisters, one of them deaf and dumb, the other looking after her.[31] Almost all men get married. There are only three men aged over 30 who are not married, the two aged 30 and 32, both away in the army, will probably do so fairly soon. The only man unlikely to marry is a man of 34, who claims that the T.B., for which he was discharged from the army, prevents him from supporting a wife. It is also possible that he is influenced by the survival of his old mother whom he looks after. The situation of the young women in the village, however, is quite different. There are 36 Gurung women aged between 26–40 whose normal home is in Thak; of these, 10 are not married. It is possible that the two aged under 30 will get married, but it is unlikely that any of the other eight will do so. One striking characteristic of this group is that all but one belong to *carjat* families, indeed eight belong to a single clan, the *konme*. Thus of the 27 upper *jat* women aged 36–39 in the village, one-third are not married and unlikely to be so. The only *sorajat* woman is an adopted daughter, who had been adopted to look after a widowed woman. By now it will have become obvious that looking after a single widowed parent (usually the mother) is a frequent correlate of non-marriage. It was present in at least five of the cases where a girl had not married. Another common feature is that where there are a large number of daughters, not all of them may marry. Thus a wealthy woman who had had seven daughters and no sons had not married off her third daughter, who is now 32. In another case there are five daughters aged 35, 26, 24 and 19, of whom only the eldest is married. Marriages of daughters are expensive and it may be better to reserve their labour for the family holding. There does not appear to be resentment among the girls who are doomed to spinsterdom. Marriage, which drags a girl off to an unknown man and unknown set of kin, is not necessarily attractive. There is no criticism of the girls or their parents in the village, indeed the girls who realize they will not marry seem to have formed a special friendship group. When I talked to one of them about marrying she said, possibly a little defensively, that she never wanted to marry and that four of her friends had decided not to marry also.

It is possible to suggest a number of reasons why this group of never-to-be-married girls has arisen. It could be partly connected to higher-than-normal male mortality in the last war, which is now having a delayed effect. Since I do not have the figures for neighbouring villages this cannot be tested. The fact that the incidence is largely within the *konme* clan may mean that they have increased disproportionately in relation to other clans with whom they marry. A shortage of *lamme* or *plemme* men in neighbouring villages could leave this village without brides. The *sorajat*, whose inter-clan regulations are, as we have seen, less restrictive, might avoid such instances. Whatever the cause, it is interesting to see that up to 30 % female non-marriage can occur, even if very locally, in the midst of a country such as Nepal. I have no evidence that non-marriage leads to any particular frustration, sexual or otherwise.

Amount of reproductive period spent after or between unions

When unions are broken by divorce, separation or desertion. In Nepal generally, very few people were reported in the 1952–4 census to be living apart from their spouses; some 0.4 % of the males and 0.3 % of the females.[32] This suggests that the loss of reproductive unions is small. The situation seems similar among the Gurungs. Although divorces are frequent, their type means that they have practically no effect on fertility. The total number of persons who had been married more than once in Mohoriya was analysed in detail by Pignède. With reference to 220 women, he found 36 divorces; 29 first marriages were broken by divorce, 36 by the death of the husband. Though these figures seem low, in combination they mean that in almost half of all Gurung marriages, one of the partners has been married to someone else previously. In Thak, of 75 couples heading households, in 36 cases one or both of the partners had been previously married. Table 11.4 shows that only a little over a quarter of the women had married more than once. Apart from the death of a spouse, which accounts for over half the re-marriages, there are two principal reasons for the break-up of a marriage, divorce for sterility and divorce for incompatibility. Adultery was never given as grounds for an actual divorce, though it is possible that with so many males away so much of the time it is not uncommon.[33]

TABLE 11.4 *Number of times married, Gurungs in Thak, as at 1969*

Marriage	Men	Women
1st	43	54
2nd	18	16
3rd	4	3
4th	1	—
Not known	9	2
	75	75

The main cause for men divorcing their wives is the supposed sterility of the woman. The alternative to divorce, bringing in another woman as a second wife, is the more frequent solution. Such a type of divorce will have a minimal effect on fertility; in fact it may even add to overall fertility by releasing fertile women from sterile men. The other major type of divorce is linked with the nature of Gurung marriage. During the first few years, before a child is born, marriages are often precarious. The girl frequently still spends most of her time in her own village and only visits her husband's home occasionally. If, as often occurs, he has left for three years service in the army soon after the wedding, the tendency for the marriage to lapse is considerable. The girl still associates with her old friends, and is likely to have affairs with other men. Often the first visit to the groom's home during the wedding rites is enough to convince the girl that she does not like her prospective husband or in-laws. Sexual intercourse, I was told, seldom occurs on this first visit so that another visit is necessary before there is a possibility that the girl may conceive. If she is adamant in her refusal to visit her in-laws again, it is almost impossible for her family to make her do so. A fine may be paid; a basic 80 rs. if the woman instigates the divorce, 40 rs. if it is the man. The sums may be much higher if those concerned are wealthy and one partner is loath to lose the other. Thus one man in Thak, who wished to divorce his daughter from the man with whom she had eloped, had to pay over 500 rs. in fines, which are distributed between the injured spouse's family and her or his village. I came across a considerable number of arranged marriages which have just faded away in this manner. It is even said that if both partners agree, as they often do, then no fine need be paid and there is no official rupture. They may just remarry, though usually without any ceremony.[34] It is likely that a considerable proportion of the women who are recorded as having married several times belong to this category, and that although army service has perhaps slightly exacerbated the tendency, there has always been a fairly high rate of dissolution of marriages during the first few years.[35] Risley, some eighty years ago, noted of the

Gurungs that in their attitude to divorce there was 'great license . . . on repayment of the bride-price to the woman's father'.[36] Although such divorces delay the establishing of permanent unions, they have only a very slight effect on fertility. Indeed the lost years of child-bearing are probably more than recompensed by the flexibility which such an institution allows. The improved happiness and adjustment may add to the chances of successful intercourse. Nor is there evidence of any stigma on women who have been divorced, or divorced others. There is no evidence that they find it more difficult than others to remarry, or of long gaps between divorce and re-marriage.

When unions are broken by the death of a spouse. In most societies with pre-industrial demographic characteristics, the break-up of marriage through the death of a spouse is statistically far more important than divorce and separation. Among the Gurungs a combination of low adult mortality and high divorce rate has brought the figures closer than they often are; thus, as we have noted for Mohoriya, 36 first marriages were ended by death, 29 by divorce. There is an added interest in studying the Gurung situation. Normally, the majority of marriages are broken by the death of women in labour, whereas, as we shall see in a later chapter, such female mortality is low in Thak, whereas the level of male mortality has been raised by army service. The possible seriousness of widowhood as a cause of lowered fertility is suggested in the 1952–4 Nepal census, which reported that 41 % of the women aged 45–64 in the Hills region were widows, and 60 % in the Terai.[37]

At first sight the statistics from Thak would also seem to indicate that widowhood is a considerable phenomenon among Gurungs and will have a lowering effect on fertility. In the 100 census households there were 25 widows and four widowers; thus 25/117 of the women aged over 20 were widows without husbands. From this we might have concluded that women are left abandoned far more often than men and that the problem is quite serious. Further analysis, however, alters the picture somewhat and shows considerable regional variation. Thus Pignède concluded that a higher proportion of men remained widowed than women, suggesting that it was more difficult for a man to re-marry than for a woman.[38] This is partly related to the temporary age-structure. There were many more old women than men in Thak, whereas the position was reversed in Mohoriya.

Widows and widowers are usually older persons who have lost their spouse towards the end of their childbearing period or after the end of it. If the spouse dies when they are still young they tend to remarry. Table 11.5 shows that in only 5/21 known cases did a woman lose her husband at the age of less than 40 and not re-marry. Only in these cases, which represent some 6 % of all the Thak marriages, would there be any appreciable effect on fertil-

TABLE 11.5 *Age at which women now widows in Thak (1969) lost their husbands*

Age at loss	Number of cases
Under 30	1
30–9	4
40–5	7
46+	9
Unknown	4
	25

ity. At present, in the 100 households, there is no widowed woman aged under 56, and no widowed man under 66.

If we turn to those who were widowed young, two things strike the observer. The first is that, except in one case where a woman widowed at 27 had not subsequently remarried, permanent widowhood always occurred after the mother had borne a considerable number of children. Of one woman we do not have full details, but the other three had a total of 13–15 live-births, an average of up to 5 each, which almost puts them in line with normal, uninterrupted, fertility. Thus, even in the exceptional cases where a woman was widowed young, this has had little effect on fertility. Secondly, it is clear that there is less pressure to re-marry after a husband has been killed in war. The three war-widows in Thak are all women who have remained widows from an unusually young age; at 27, 37, 40. It thus seems highly likely that widows who receive an army pension because of their husband's death have less incentive to remarry. The one informant I asked about this admitted that the increased security such a pension gave would lessen the likelihood of another marriage. On re-marriage the pension is forfeited, he said; and since a person would normally report to the authorities if she re-married (for honesty's sake, and because gossip would probably reach official ears in any case) the inconvenience of another marriage might be accompanied by no financial gain.

In Thak the loss through widowhood has been of no great consequence to fertility levels. It has meant the loss of about 30 woman-years up to the age of 39, and 40 woman-years thereafter, a total which might have produced up to some 12 livebirths. As a proportion of the approximate total of 180–200 livebirths during the last forty years to women still living and aged over 40, this is only a small fraction.

One of the major reasons why fertility is scarcely affected by widowhood is the tolerant attitude to widow re-marriage. As noted above, this occurs in most cases where the woman is young; a year is considered a decent time for mourning before a new marriage is made. Two possibly interlinked factors determining the attitude to widow re-marriage are suggested by Davis and Blake. They suggest that re-marriage is usually most tolerated in societies 'practicing a shifting cultivation, hunting, or pastoral pursuits' and where there is a 'strong clan or lineage organization'. In these societies, they argue, marriage is a contract between groups, and once a lineage has acquired, often at considerable expense, a new member, it will treat her as a permanent possession. If her husband dies she will be inherited by a kinsman of the husband. When the economy becomes more advanced and stable, they continue, and the household gains power at the expense of the lineage, then marriage of the widow to a close relative of the deceased husband is frowned on. It may even be felt that the widow should never remarry.[39] The model works fairly well for the Gurungs who have, until recently at least, been mainly hunters and pastoralists with a fairly strongly developed clan and lineage system. There should also be evidence of a changing attitude as the Gurungs settle down, their economy and social system changing rapidly. This also we find.

There is evidence that, like the Bhoteas whom they resemble in a number of ways,[40] the Gurungs once practised fraternal widow-inheritance from elder to younger brothers. In 1891 it was stated by Risley that the widow 'may live with a man, especially with her late husband's younger brother (but not the elder) as his concubine'.[41] I only asked one informant about this, who stated that it does sometimes still occur, but there is no general rule that it *ought* to happen, and in most cases the widow marries elsewhere. Sometimes the woman may be added to a previous marriage to form a polygynous household. He thought it was not a good idea if the age-gap was too great, since the elder brother's wife often tended to be regarded as a maternal figure by the younger brother. If she marries out of the family she loses her husband's land, but will probably take the gold given to her by her husband. It seems likely that if this custom had been still common in Thak and Mohoriya either Pignède or I would have come across cases in the genealogies and censuses we took. The nearest to such a case in Thak was that of a widow who was living next door to her dead husband's younger brother. Her husband had been killed in war when she was 27 and she had never remarried. I have no evidence that she is officially married to, or has ever cohabited with, her brother-in-law, though it is perhaps significant that his wife has gone off to live in Pokhara, which is tantamount to separation. Future fieldwork could well clear up the problem of whether there is now growing opposition to re-marriage with close kin. It could also confirm or destroy Risley's, and later Northey and Morris', observations which state that in such a re-marriage there is no ceremony.[42] What is certain is that both men and women who lose their spouse fairly early in life normally set up a new union, usually within a year or two, though not necessarily, or even usually, with another widowed person.[43]

FACTORS GOVERNING THE EXPOSURE TO INTERCOURSE WITHIN UNIONS

Voluntary abstinence

There are four principal types of voluntary abstinence not dictated by a conscious desire to limit fertility, as suggested by Davis and Blake: post-partum abstinence after the birth of a child, 'occasional' abstinence principally for ritual occasions, abstinence during the gestation period, and during menstruation. As these authors point out, only the first two can have a lowering effect on fertility; the latter will, if anything, raise fertility if adhered to. Undoubtedly the greatest potential influence on fertility consists of post-partum abstinence, which often lasts until weaning at the age of two or three years. Such prolonged abstinence is not a custom among the Gurungs. Although they do not go to the other extreme, as do the Lepchas who practise ritual copulation 3, 7 or 21 days after childbirth,[44] sexual relations commence fairly soon. I was told by several informants, including mothers, that intercourse normally commences some two or three months after childbirth. There is no ban on intercourse during breast-feeding. Since, as Davis and Blake point out and is well known, fertility is very low indeed during the first two months after birth, there can be little doubt that Gurung fertility is only very minimally affected by post-partum abstinence.

Nor is 'occasional abstinence' of any real significance. Even where, as in India, ritual taboos are frequent, only some 24 or so days are said to be lost in certain rural areas and the effect on fertility is negligible.[45] Among the Gurungs the loss is much less. Although one informant stated that couples are meant to abstain from intercourse if there is going to be a really important *puja* the following day, such abstention can only mean the loss of four or five days per year per couple, at the very most. The man who has to abstain most is the *poju*, who is not meant to have intercourse before certain of his domestic and village rites. This would, in theory, mean abstention for up to two weeks a year, at the most. Yet even he had not had his reproductive powers much hampered; he had had eleven children and at least one illegitimately. Thus we may conclude that voluntary abstinence of these types has no real effect on fertility.

Pignède correctly reported that sexual relations among the Gurungs continue until the sixth or seventh month of gestation;[46] a number of Thak informants were agreed on this. I did not come across any beliefs that such continued intercourse was necessary for the growth of the foetus nor, on the other hand, that it was dangerous. There did not seem to be any special rules about intercourse during menstruation. The position seems to be, as Morris observes,[47] that although it is considered undesirable to have intercourse during the three or four menstrual days, in practice people sometimes do so without fearing any evil consequences. Such intercourse seems to be regarded as messy, but not polluting; an attitude very similar to that in England today. This fits in with the generally relaxed attitude towards menstruation. Although a woman should not cook during this period, she often does, in fact, do so. Although informants were aware of the belief that menstrual women are polluting, this is hardly reflected in everyday life. The nearest they come to such action is the custom whereby women wash their hair and their clothes (which have anyway often been soiled in the absence of any form of sanitary towel) after their menstruation has ended. The reasons why some societies have firm rules enjoining sexual abstinence on certain ritual occasions and during various periods of the female sexual cycle are too complicated for analysis here. It is sufficient to say that the Gurungs seem to have few rules and these are interpreted in a relaxed way. Sexual intercourse does not seem to be highly charged, full of dangerous power which needs to be controlled and which may threaten men. As yet, Hindu attitudes on this subject do not seem to have made much impact.

Involuntary abstinence (from impotence, illness, unavoidable but temporary separations)

I heard of no cases of impotence in Thak, and there were no special rituals in the *poju*'s armoury of weapons against evil to deal with this ailment. It seems unlikely that it has any significant effect on Gurung fertility. Nor does the medical survey, reported on in chapter 14, suggest that much time is lost to married couples on account of illness. Serious illness of the kind that would inhibit sexual intercourse, especially leprosy and venereal disease is, as we shall see, very uncommon. I did not encounter any cases where husband and wife were even temporarily not cohabiting because of disease.

'Unavoidable but temporary separations' is obviously a category of great importance for the Gurungs with their pattern of migration to the army. The degree to which army service lowers fertility by reducing the period when a couple cohabit, or raises it by spacing births and hence improving maternal health, will be discussed, with statistics, below.[48] A comparison of couples where the husband did army service, with those where the man stayed almost permanently in the village, as well as an examination of the fertility histories of various couples, suggests that army recruitment has very little general effect in lowering Gurung fertility. Indeed, it can be argued that the improvements in maternal health and standards of living which it brings about help to explain why the Gurungs have one of the highest average fertility rates in Nepal.

The other major cause of temporary absence for males arises from the agricultural system of the Gurungs. Shepherds are needed to look after livestock. It is possible that when the Gurungs were predominantly pastoralists, herding huge flocks of cows and sheep high up on the Himalayan slopes, the men would be absent for up to half the year.[49] For the last twenty or thirty years, however, the flocks have dwindled and so has male absence. In Thak, half a dozen men at the most would be engaged in looking after cows and buffaloes either in the rice fields after the harvest, or up in the forest while the crops are growing. Much of the herding is left to old men and women, widowers and others who are anyway infertile. There is unlikely to be more than a minimal effect on fertility.

It has already been observed, in connection with divorce, that it is common for there to be a considerable gap between marriage and first sexual intercourse, and between marriage and first conception. Pignède noted this phenomenon, suggesting that often a young couple were too shy to have intercourse regularly to begin with, so that when the husband went away to the army he left his wife childless. She then had to wait three years for another chance of impregnation.[50] Although there is evidence that women married to soldiers tend to spend two or three years before conceiving, it has already been argued that the total effect of army service is very slight. Even those whose marriage is not disturbed by army migration may not start procreation for some time because of the reluctance with which many newly-weds start intercourse. There seems nothing equivalent to the pressurized love-making characteristic of parts of pre-industrial Europe. The decision to cohabit after marriage depends among the Gurungs on a number of factors which may be illustrated by two cases from Thak. In one, a pair of cross-cousins had been married, at the age of 20 and 18 respectively, one year before. I was told that they had not commenced to sleep together and they continued to live in their own houses in the village. They did not feel physically attracted to each other and would, I was told, finally have to be pushed into cohabiting by their respective families in two or three years. There was no particular hurry as the boy did not intend to go to the army. Thus we can see that army service may, in fact, precipitate, rather than delay, conception. In a contrasted case, a young man on leave from the army and aged over 25 married a girl slightly younger than himself from another village whom he had previously never seen. I was told that within two months of their wedding they would probably cohabit, since they found each other physically attractive. When teasingly asked by his friends if he had had intercourse, the boy would, with great embarrassment, deny this. He would be returning to Malaya shortly.

Coital frequency (excluding periods of abstinence)

There is some evidence that coital frequency may have a significant effect on fertility.[51] The data for the Gurungs is very impressionistic. Probably Morris exaggerates when he states that intercourse 'generally takes place once, or more rarely twice, every night'.[52] The frequency depends on a number of factors and though informants agreed that such intercourse often occurs daily between young people during the first few years of their marriage, the average for all couples of fertile age, taking into consideration age and the inconvenience of communal sleeping, is unlikely to be higher than nine or ten times per month. One young informant put the average lower, stating that more than once a night very seldom occurred, while the average was about once a week. Usually the couple lie down separately and wait until everyone is supposedly asleep, in other words about half an hour, and then one of them goes to join the other. Pignède states that this is always the woman,[53] but my informants said it might be either partner. The woman usually sleeps fully dressed and just lifts her long skirt. Occasionally, if possible, the young couple sleep elsewhere, upstairs or on the verandah. When they sleep with other members of the family, and hence lie down in different parts of the room, no pre-arrangement to have intercourse is made. Thus the sleeping arrangements and need for secrecy probably inhibit very frequent intercourse. The high fertility of the Gurungs, however, make it plain that sexual relations are frequent enough to have little influence on general reproductive patterns.

12

Social structure and fertility II: conception and gestation variables

FACTORS AFFECTING EXPOSURE TO CONCEPTION

Fecundity or infecundity, as affected by involuntary causes

We may distinguish five main involuntary causes affecting fecundity: health, diet, psychological state and working conditions of women, and length of breast-feeding. The general health of women, and particularly the prevalence of venereal disease and other genito-urinary infections may be important in lowering fecundity among some Himalayan groups. It may help to account for the fact that Gorer found that of 56 married women aged over 20, 18 were completely sterile.[1] We shall argue below, however, there is little evidence that such disease is at all widespread among the Gurungs among whom I lived. It is likewise possible that fecundity is lowered in some societies by dietary deficiency.[2] The Gurungs eat better than most other Nepalese societies and this may possibly improve the health and fecundity of the women. In any case, it seems unlikely that fecundity is adversely affected, for high rates have been achieved in human groups with a far lower standard of diet. If it is true, as Davis and Blake suggest, that Western fecundity may be lowered by 'nervous tension' and 'artificial modes of life' induced by industrial society, then this third variable would undoubtedly favour the Gurungs.[3] By most standards the Gurungs lead a very relaxed and 'adjusted' life, with very little apparent stress and tension. If, as seems likely, psycho-somatic factors can affect the physiological process of conception, such factors are likely to be minimal where, as among the Gurungs, there is little worry about the ability to bear children or the danger and pain of childbirth.

Another variable suggested by Davis and Blake is the working conditions of women; it is possible that the hard physical labour often undertaken by women in pre-industrial or industrializing societies weakens or strains them, and hence lowers their fecundity. It seems likely that the effects, if there are any, will be more powerful in causing high foetal mortality and difficult childbirth, rather than in lowering the rate of conception. As far as can be seen, foetal deaths and deaths at childbirth are rare among Gurung women. This suggests that although they virtually farm the difficult mountain slopes in the absence of their husbands, carrying very heavy loads of dung, wood and fodder, and doing all the bending work of weeding and transplanting, this has little effect on their health. Since it is difficult to conceive of their physical life being much more difficult, this is an interesting negative finding. It is possible, however, that there is a little truth in the observation of a mission doctor who works in a Magar village to the north-west of Pokhara. She noticed several cases of prolapse of the womb, which she ascribed to the practice of carrying very heavy loads on the back and the custom, shared by Gurungs, whereby women tie a tight cummerbund round the waist. She thought that tying this downwards would force down the uterus. It would be worth testing whether such damage is widespread. No indication of such harmful effects was noticed in any records of heavy maternal mortality or foetal deaths in Thak.

The final factor is the reduced fecundity induced by breast-feeding. It is known that lactation reduces the chance of conception by about 25 % after the first few months, and it seems likely that this relative infecundity helps to widen the gap between conceptions in some societies.[4] Gurung breast-feeding customs would make it likely that such a factor would work to the full. The normal Gurung practice in Thak is to continue to breast-feed a child until the mother becomes pregnant again. When a new pregnancy is recognized the previous child is weaned, although it has for some time been having some solid food. Himalayan tribes seem to wean late; Gorer noted that Lepcha children sometimes continued to breast-feed up to the age of 10, and Morris also noted a belief that this occurred in Nepal up to the same age.[5] I never noticed cases of Gurung infants being fed beyond the age of 5, though one informant said they might be breast-fed up to 7 or 8, and an old woman said she had fed her child thus until he was 9 or 10. The normal length of time is about 3 years, which is also the average time before the birth of the next child. Only one mother reported that she had stopped breast-feeding at one year, because her milk had dried up, and another stated that she had ended after 2 years for the same reason. I heard of no cases where the mother was entirely unable to breast-feed any of her children through failure to lactate. Like the Lepchas, the Gurungs appear to lactate easily and for a long time. Undoubtedly this slightly lowers their fecundity. If it reduced fecundity by the absolute maximum of 25 %, which is very unlikely, it could be argued that such a custom might reduce fertility by about two conceptions per woman of completed fertility. It could well be argued, however, that its general effect is to *raise* fertility, even if it slightly lowers fecundity. By giving women a little rest between childbearing, and by decreasing the number of infant deaths caused by food infections, it may have the total effect of raising the number of surviving children per mother.

Use or non-use of contraception

Up to 1967, knowledge and use of mechanical or chemical methods of contraception were virtually non-existent among the Gurungs. A number of pre-industrial societies attempt to prevent conception by inserting various articles into the vagina,[6] but the eight Gurungs I asked on this subject were agreed that they had used no type of contraceptive technique, and several were sure that no such methods were known in the village.[7] During the two years preceding our visit in 1969 Radio Nepal had begun to give an almost daily exhortation to practise birth-control and there had been some description of the methods which were available. Another source of information is the retired soldiers who have spent many years in India or Malaya. Most of those I questioned said they had not encountered birth-control propaganda or methods while abroad, but one recently retired officer proudly showed me a small stock of condoms which he had brought back from Malaya. Both Indian and British army officers concerned with Gurkha rehabilitation claimed that returning soldiers are given a lecture on birth-control methods, and stated that facilities for birth-control are available in the army for those who want them. I was also told that a government team had visited the village the previous year to demonstrate birth-control methods. The nearest contraceptive facilities are in Pokhara; the government hospital provides a month's supply of pills for half a rupee, and fifteen condoms for the same price. Vasectomies and loop insertions are free. What is clear, however, is that despite a considerable official barrage of information, absolutely nothing was being done in the village about actually using these techniques. Not a single person had visited the government hospital to obtain either more information or technology, nor had people, as far as I could ascertain, attempted to buy condoms from the bazaar where, at far higher prices, they are beginning to be sold. As will be seen shortly, this cannot be explained away by saying that the Gurungs want many children, or that they object, in principle, to any of the contraceptive devices.

Coitus interruptus and other non-mechanical methods of avoiding conception are more widespread in non-industrial societies than are mechanical methods. Yet these, also, appear to be unused among the Gurungs. Several informants were convinced that *coitus interruptus* is 'unknown', and likewise any other similar methods. Nor did I encounter the deliberate and conscious extension of breast-feeding as a means of preventing conception, which Morris states in a characteristic of some 'Nepalese'.[8] In fact, no deliberate attempt to limit population or births appears to have been traditional among the Gurungs. If we turn to the economic situation we can see some of the reasons why this should have been so.

It seems likely that there has been a considerable shift in the desire to have children, even during the last few years. Until approximately one generation ago, the pressure of population on land could hardly have been felt amongst the Gurungs, except in long-established villages such as Siklis. Resources of forest and cultivable land must have seemed limitless, and local pressure could be relieved by moving off and clearing a new site for a village. The details of what happened in Thak during this stage have been examined in previous chapters. The chronic land shortage which has characterized some Himalayan peoples from at least the beginning of this century was absent among the Gurungs.[9] Each generation did not see the family land divided into several parts. Each man had as much land as he could clear. Labour was valuable, and many children were no burden. Indeed, with the characteristic mortality patterns of such a society, there was no question of needing or wanting to limit the number of births. The population could be allowed to expand to fill the ample resources. We might expect the attitude to be similar to that among the Magars in the 1950s where, we are told, 'Parents hope for as many children as possible'.[10] Women, who bear the brunt of high fertility, were not able to limit conception even if they had wanted to.

It is impossible to date the realization that resources are limited, and that instead of contributing to the wealth and prestige of a family, many children are a burden. Certainly, however, such an attitude was present by the time we arrived in Thak, though it was undoubtedly fostered by the discussions we encouraged. It is doubtful whether this change had much to do with formal birth-control propaganda, though it is possible that people now became aware of the important fact that it *is* possible to control the environment in this manner. Two economic phenomena may have helped to alter attitudes. The first is the recession of the forest; every year it takes markedly longer to fetch wood and fodder. The second is the shortage of good agricultural land. The price of such land has risen rapidly, and it is now widely observed that families which were once wealthy are now only moderately well off because inheritance has split a large estate between several sons. Many Gurungs linked the poverty of the lower castes to their supposedly large numbers of children.

A general survey discovered that the number of surviving children desired throughout Nepal is between four and five.[11] This is a good deal higher than the actual average number which *do* survive at present (about three) and helps to confirm the hypothesis that successful family planning, based on individual decisions, could only have a very minor effect on population growth rates in a country such as Nepal.[12] It seems likely that the average number desired by Gurung women is lower than this. The most popular number in Thak was two surviving sons and two surviving daughters, almost as popular was two sons and one daughter. Several informants specifically stated that two of each were needed in case one of them died. Several informants, especially young men and women, said that one son and one daughter were enough. It seems likely that if they could ensure that one of each sex would survive, many parents would be prepared to stop at that. Those who wanted only one of each sex were especially articulate about the cost in clothing, food, and the effort of having many children. On the whole, therefore, it would seem that these Gurungs would be prepared to limit their families after having three or four children, though their experience of infant and child mortality would make them reject any birth control method which is irreversible until they have more than this number.

Another feature which, in practice, would raise the average number of children is the fact that people do not usually get an equal number of children of each sex. Although there does not seem to be a great necessity to have sons, for ritual or social reasons, it is clear that parents would, on the whole, like to have a son and heir in much the same way as this is true in England today. I therefore asked how many girls a mother would be prepared to have before she gave up the attempt to have a son. I was given totals of between three and five daughters. As one woman pointed out, one could afford to have many daughters because they did not divide the family land but went to another family, although they needed gold. In theory, therefore, people would appear to be likely to consider contraception when they felt that three or four children, whatever their sex, would survive. With the present patterns of mortality, this is, in fact, precisely what occurs.

Yet there may be a considerable gap between what people say they will do, and what they actually do, especially in such a highly-charged area as sexual relations. When, we may ask, do people actually feel impelled to attempt birth-control among the Gurungs? During my stay in Thak, and on my visit to Mohoriya, I let it be known that I had *pasi a'peeba mae* (Gg., *pasi* = child; *a'peeba* = give (negative); *mae* = medicine), in other words that I had pills and condoms. Some sixteen people asked me for some 'medicine'. In about two-thirds of the cases it was the woman who came to ask, probably reflecting their greater feelings on the topic. Half were Gurungs; the others included a Magar, Tamang, Brahmin, and three service castes. Since I was on both occasions centred on a predominantly Gurung village, this suggests that other ethnic groups in the area would also be ready to accept contraceptives, if they were locally and cheaply (we gave them out free) available. Some other facts about the recipients are set out in table 12.1.

The mean age of the mothers in the table is approximately 36. Thus they had already completed their most fecund years. Nevertheless, effective control

TABLE 12.1 *Ages and number of living children of women who desired (or whose husbands desired) contraceptives: Thak and Mohoriya*

	Present age of mothers	Number of living children		
		Male	Female	Total
Thak	40	6	3	9
	38	2	1	3
	27	4	3	7
	32	3	2	5
	40	3	1	4
	35	2	3	5
	29	1	2	3
	40	5	4	9
	?	?	?	5
	35	3	?	3+
	36	7	1	8
Mohoriya	38	2	4	6
	38	5	1	6
	41	3	4	7
	32	1	4	5
	45	6	6	12
		53+	39+	97+

of the last eight or nine years before the menopause would still probably prevent an average of up to two births per woman, or 32 children to these mothers. Obviously it would also have been of immense value to the health of the women concerned. The woman aged 27, for example, was a very poor leatherworker's wife. She suffered from very heavy menstrual bleeding and further childbearing might well mean her death. She already had seven living children. Such birth-control would also have saved the life of a Tailor woman who died in labour at the age of 45, giving birth to her tenth child. The mean average number of children already born and still surviving to Thak mothers desiring contraception is over 5, and for Mohoriya is over 7. This indicates that even with entirely successful contraception, these families would still be large. Generation replacement only requires between two and three surviving children per couple. Only in four cases did women seek contraception when they had less than five surviving children. In the fifteen cases where we know the number of surviving sons, the mean average was approximately 3.5 per mother. It is worth noting, however, that in two cases women were prepared to consider contraception when they had only one surviving son.

The attitude to family planning among the Gurungs seems to be very favourable. Most informants are aware of the dangers of overcrowding and poverty, and they showed no particular objection to birth control in principle. Yet it seems likely that family planning will be ineffective in seriously reducing the birth rate for many years to come. We may wonder why this is. Firstly, and quite naturally, the recent years of medium mortality among infants and children make people reluctant to use the cheap, effective, but irreversible methods such as vasectomy. Likewise they are even less keen to have loop insertions. The official and impersonal aura of hospital, and possibly some rumours concerning lack of hygiene, would be enough to quench most villagers' desire to have such an operation. It seems likely that if a travelling team, which included a Gurung nurse and doctor, visited the villages, spending a few days getting to know the inhabitants, and consulting the village leaders as to who might be interested, they could do many such operations and possibly even loop insertions, in the security of the villagers' own homes. It would certainly be worth experimenting.

As it is, the initiative is left entirely to villagers, and scarcely anything is being achieved. When I visited it in 1969, the government hospital at Pokhara, the second largest town in Nepal and the regional and medical centre for several million Nepalese, was keeping approximately 35 people supplied with condoms and pills, and doing approximately 1 loop insertion or vasectomy a week. At the very most, therefore, they would be preventing some 50–100 births p.a. With an average population increase of say, 2–3 % p.a., the two million people dependent on Pokhara are adding to their numbers by between 40,000 and 60,000 p.a. The present effort in the Pokhara region would thus have to be increased by 1000-fold before it kept population steady, even with present high mortality rates. There can be little doubt that when public health and medicine really succeed in Nepal, any chance of stemming the flood on present lines will be completely destroyed. Already the installation of one new water pipe to half a dozen hill villages undoubtedly saves more infant lives every year than are prevented by the whole family planning campaign outside the Kathmandu valley.[13]

Yet even if touring teams, well equipped and trusted, visited every Nepalese village once a year, providing free facilities, could this deal with the situation? If my experience in one Gurung village is anything to go by, it could not. I spent over a year in Thak, learnt Gurung, and spent many hours talking to people. I announced at the village meeting that I had pills and condoms which could be obtained free from my wife or myself, and the head of the *panchayat* explained their purpose and encouraged people to use them. I gave him instructions and asked him to distribute some contraceptives, which he was happy to do. I also kept a supply for distribution. I talked to many people about the need for birth-control, and undertook a questionnaire on the subject. Two coloured posters advocating birth control and written in Nepali were put up at strategic places. A few dozen small booklets were distributed. Here, then, was a village comparatively inundated by birth-control propaganda, but not so flooded that there was a counter-reaction. Most of the influential members of the village, the *Pradan Panch*, local headmaster, *poju*, retired army officers, were in favour of the idea. What was the response?

In our sample hundred households there were eighteen women who had four or more living children and were aged under 44 at the time of our census, and hence still able to reproduce. Of these, only three came to us to ask about contraception. Thus only one-sixth of those who have enough children to ensure that at least one survives took the decision to attempt contraception. Two of these three cases were mothers of 7 and 9 still-living children. Of mothers with 4–6 children, only one of 16 asked for contraceptives. Since most Gurung families fall in the range 4–6, it can be seen that less than 7 % appear to be sufficiently interested. This suggests that even where contraceptive devices are locally available, distributed by a trusted villager, free, in a setting where there is a widely discussed pressure on land and forest, only a very small percentage even of those with over four children still living will avail themselves of such facilities. The only negative factor was that our supplies would last a maximum of six months. For further condoms and pills, or for more permanent contraceptives, villagers would have to visit the government hospital. Since this was not stated in the propaganda, and could only be learnt when people came to ask for contraceptives, it seems unlikely that this had a very great negative effect.

The very small effect our distribution of contraceptives might have, even if those who asked for contraceptives used them successfully, can be seen from comparing the reproductive years left to all married women in our census with those for contraceptive seekers. Assuming reproduction ended in their forty-fifth year, the four Thak women from the census population to whom we gave devices would, if they continued to use such devices for the rest of their years until the age of 45, cancel out some 26 reproductive years (years of lowered fecundity at the end of the reproductive cycle). The potential reproductive years left to the married women in the census was 434. Thus, even supposing 100 % of success, only approximately 1/17 woman years would be affected, and these the less fecund ones.

Yet we cannot assume that even those who asked for such contraceptives used them, or, if they used them, used them correctly. People did not seem to find it difficult to understand, theoretically, how to use condoms and pills, but there is some indication that they soon gave up their use, if they ever started at all. At least five of the pill supplies we distributed were timed to run out before we left the village, and I told those to whom they were given to come back for more when their suppliers were running out, before we left the village. None did so, and it seems unlikely that they preferred to make a special journey to Pokhara and to pay money, rather than to get them from us in the village, free. In one case I know that a woman stopped taking them after a few days; she developed a bad sore throat and I was nervously asked whether the pills could have caused this. It is easy to see how any latent objection to using contraceptives could be buttressed by suggesting that they caused one of the many ailments which constantly occurred in the village. A few notorious cases of such a connection being made, and an early receptive attitude could turn into general hostility. This is rumoured to have occurred in Pokhara where gossip has spread that a number of women have suffered serious disorders after the insertion of loops: it is quite possible that there is a factual basis for such rumours in this case. The loop-insertion rate in Pokhara has fallen swiftly after the first few months.

Thus the total effect of our attempt to provide contraceptive facilities was probably negligible. It did show, however, that there is a considerable interest in contraception, though such enthusiasm as there is cannot be tapped by the present method of providing cheap contraceptives in government dispensaries and hospitals.[14] Furthermore, it suggests that mobile teams, even if they attempt to gain the confidence of the people with whom they work, and provide free facilities, will not achieve very much. Only a combination of such teams with some form of penalty for those who continue to produce more than a set number of children, bonuses to those who abstain, and other inducements and sanctions can *begin* to tackle the problem. Something on the lines of the malaria eradication and smallpox vaccination campaigns, but much more organized, is needed. Unless this is done within a few years there can be no chance that even the modest aims of the Nepal Family Planning Federation, which, 'hopes to keep the country's growth rate to below 2 % and to reduce it to 1 % by 1985', will be achieved.

Fecundity or infecundity, as affected by voluntary causes (sterilization, subincision, medical treatment, etc.)

As yet, this variable has no appreciable effect on the Gurungs. Subincision is unknown, and I heard of no Gurungs who had been sterilized. Although some facilities for male sterilization are available in Pokhara, as far as I know, female sterilizations are not yet carried out.

FACTORS AFFECTING GESTATION AND SUCCESSFUL PARTURITION

Foetal mortality from involutanry causes

In the absence of accurate records of miscarriages and stillbirths it is impossible to be certain, but it seems highly likely that the Gurungs do not suffer greatly from unintentional foetal mortality. The regular spacing of births at two and three-yearly intervals which will be noted in the next chapter and the scarcity of reported miscarriages, point to this conclusion, as does the absence of the genito-urinary diseases which might cause such mortality.

Foetal mortality from voluntary causes

It is well known that abortion is a more widespread method of controlling population than is contraception. Consequently a number of societies which have no contraceptive techniques do use abortion.[15] The Gurungs are in this category, for they have no native contraceptive methods, but do practice abortion and infanticide.[16] As with the Lepchas,[17] the actual techniques for inducing abortion appear to be somewhat half-hearted: tampering with the foetus by physical means does not appear to be practised. I was told that eating certain mixtures, sugar cane juice, a mixture of certain vegetables (*garda ta*) and honey might be successful. Other informants said that there were no effective abortifacients in the village, but that people sometimes purchase 'medicine' in the bazaar at Pokhara. The fact that two women in Thak came to us asking for medicine to rid them of an unwanted foetus (Gg. *pasi* (infant) *waba* (throw away)) indicates both the desire for such abortifacients, and their absence in the village.

Pignède stated that Gurungs feel great repugnance towards abortion (and presumably infanticide).[18] I did not notice such a feeling among the several men and women with whom I discussed the subject. Their tone implied no particular criticism of the practice; it depended on the particular situation as to whether it was a justified measure. They all thought that the only occasion when such methods would be used would be when a child had been conceived outside the normal marital relationship. When a lower caste woman has conceived by a Gurung, or two people of the same clan have had a productive intercourse, then, unless the infant is destroyed before or after birth, there will be a great scandal and expense. Most Gurungs would probably admit that a person who tried an abortion in this situation would only be doing the sensible thing. There does not seem to be a feeling that life before birth is sacred, and that such abortion is tantamount to murder. Likewise, as in one case of which we heard, a woman who has been made pregnant while her husband is away in the army may try to find some potion to cause an abortion. I asked my informant on this case whether women used such methods to get rid of unwanted legitimate babies. He said they did not do so because it was 'sinful' (*pap kaba: pap* (Nep.) = sin; *kaba* (Gg.) comes). The implication was that sinfulness is more than outweighted by social necessity in certain cases.

It is impossible to be certain as to how many children are killed in the womb or strangled at birth. One informant said that 'many' were so dealt with, but I only heard of two cases. The clothing of women makes it possible for them to conceal pregnancies right up to birth. Thus they can, if necessary, go off to the forest alone and kill the newborn infant. Given the tolerant attitude prevailing in the past towards pre-marital sexual relations, however, it seems unlikely that many infants were destroyed because they were illegitimate. There is no evidence that children born in wedlock have ever been killed or allowed to die. It thus seems likely that only an occasional infant, conceived in a highly forbidden union, is killed. This would not significantly alter the overall fertility rates.

CONCLUSION: THE OVERALL RATING OF GURUNG FERTILITY

Overall fertility among the Gurungs is moderately high, as we shall see. The way in which this is achieved, as compared to the model devised for pre-industrial societies by Davis and Blake, is set out in table 12.2.[19]

From the table it will be seen that the Gurungs deviate in many ways from the simple model of a pre-industrial society. In four out of the six predictions about a 'usually high' or 'usually low' value, they do not fit the prediction. Thus, as with many other features of their society such as literacy, mortality,

TABLE 12.2 *Intermediate variables affecting fertility*

Usual values in pre-industrial societies	Gurungs
Usually high values[a]	
1. Age of entry into unions	Medium
2. Permanent celibacy	Normally high
8. Contraception	High
9. Sterilization, etc.	High
Usually low values	
4. Voluntary abstinence	Medium to high
10. Foetal mortality – involuntary	Medium to high
High or low values	
3a. Time between unstable unions	High
3b. Post-widowhood celibacy	High
11. Foetal mortality – voluntary	Medium to high
Indeterminate	
5. Involuntary abstinence	Low
6. Frequency of coitus	Medium
7. Involuntary sterility	High

[a] A 'high' value, means that this will tend to encourage high fertility, not that the incidence is high.

and other rates, they need to be placed near the middle of the continuum which runs from technologically simple to technologically sophisticated societies. Probably their manner of life is in many ways closer to that of pre-industrial Europe than it is to that of India, or even other parts of Nepal. Most interestingly, however, the study of Gurung society shows how a high reproduction rate can be achieved alongside many factors which might be thought to inhibit this. Pensions to help deal with the problem of old age, a moderately high age at marriage, army service which takes most adult men away from the village for up to fifteen years, the absence of an ancestor cult and need to produce sons, all these might have made one predict that Gurung fertility would be low. Furthermore, there is no special emphasis on fertility or virility in the society, and there is no great opposition to contraceptives and abortions in themselves. Despite all this, Gurung population has been growing fairly fast and fertility rates have been moderately high. This suggests that those planners who place their faith in such things as old-age insurance, or raising the age at marriage by law, as solutions to the population explosion will have to rethink their position. Likewise, those who blame high fertility on religious or cultural factors are oversimplifying the situation.

13

The demographic consequences of social structure: fertility statistics

Now that we have examined some of the factors affecting fertility, we may turn to the actual reproductive rates, particularly in the sample Gurung communities of Mohoriya and Thak. This task has an especial importance since very little is known concerning the demography of Himalayan communities. Nor is very much known concerning fertility patterns at the national level in Nepal. Even the crude birth rate (CBR) of the population as a whole, the simplest of all measures, is in dispute. Thus the Family Planning Office informed me that they had reckoned it to be 43/1000 in 1961, in 1965 their estimate jumped to 54, in 1969 it was 48; meanwhile the official figure for 1969, in the U.N.[1] publication of that year, was given as 41 per 1000. The only detailed study of fertility in the country found, on the basis of urine tests and current pregnancy history, a CBR of 57 per 1000. This latter report concluded that 'fertility in Nepal is about as high as could be observed anywhere in the world, with a crude annual birth rate in the neighbourhood of 50 to 55 per 1000 population, and an annual fertility rate of about 220 births per 1000 women aged 15–49'.[2] The same survey also contains some study of age-specific and other fertility rates, and this will be cited when we come to deal with particular fertility analyses for the Gurungs. A recent re-analysis of the 1952/4 and 1961 censuses leads the authors to suggest a CBR of 47.[3] Anthropological research into fertility is, so far, sketchy. Hitchcock writes of the Magars that 'Since there is no taboo on sexual relations once the mother has recovered from the birth, children can follow each other in almost yearly succession', but no figures are given to show whether they do.[4] If we re-work the figures of Gorer for the Lepchas of Sikkim, we find that the number of live-born children to women aged 50–69 is extremely low. Even if we assume that there has been a complete omission of female children who died young, the 13 women only had an average of 3–4 children each,[5] though allowing for the four who said they had never had any, this rises to about 4.75 each. The study by Kihara of a Bhotea village suffers from the same defects as Gorer's analysis, especially the inadequate size of the sample. It, also, gives an impression of low fertility. If we take those aged 50–69, we find that some 14 women bore 46 children (now dead or alive). This gives a rate very similar to Gorer's, but loss of memory among older informants probably lowers such a rate considerably. The reason why the rate in both Lepcha and Bhotea cases is lower than that for Nepal as a whole seems fairly clear. It lies in the age at giving birth to the first child. Thus the Nepalese population as a whole usually give birth to their first child at between 18–20,[6] while the Lepchas usually do so between 20–22 (only 3/23 reported a birth at the age of under 20),[7] and, according to Kihara, the average age of the forty-three Bhotea women at first childbirth was 27.1, though he thinks that 'the actual age (was) ... probably about 25–26 years old'.[8] Why childbirths should occur so late, especially since, as among the Lepchas, marriage occurs young, is a far more difficult problem.

Thus there are indications of two different patterns of marriage in Nepal, with upland tribal groups showing lower fertility than the lowland areas.[9] We may now turn to the Gurungs to see how they compare with the brief figures given above.

The following account is based on two very small samples. In 1958, Pignède recorded the fertility histories of 102 women in the village of Mohoriya. He seems to have excluded women who had had no children.[10] He does not state the present age of the women, but it is likely that they were of all ages – in other words many of them had not yet completed their childbearing. In the village of Thak I recorded all the births which took place within a sample of 100 households. I also undertook a questionnaire/census which included retrospective questions on fertility. These questions are listed in Appendix 1. Usually, but not always, it was possible to get the woman concerned to answer the questions. As will become clear, there was definitely omission of foetal deaths, miscarriages and stillbirths. The main defects, however, were the very small size of the sample, the fact that it was impossible to make it a 'random sample' since nothing was known about Gurung fertility as a whole and therefore this village may not be representative of Gurung villages, and, finally, that not all women within the sample were questioned. On the first point, this makes many of the statistics too small for significance. On the second, though there is nothing to suggest that Thak is atypical, and a comparison with Mohoriya makes a partial check, it should be stressed that the situation may, indeed, vary very much between different villages. On the third, it is necessary to state precisely how the women within the sample were selected.

When I took the census of a household, I recorded the full fertility history of the oldest female in that household, provided she did not appear to be senile. At the time of the census there were a total of 185 women aged 15 or over, including those temporarily present and those temporarily absent. Of these, some 47 were still unmarried. Of those who had been married at least once, I recorded the fertility history of 105 (of all ages) and omitted that of 33 women who were the second woman in a household. It is possible that such a selection will bias the following calculations. For example, those selected tended to be older women and thus we do not have a fair age-distribution.[11] If the sample were bigger and more carefully drawn, it might have been worthwhile to work out some statistical procedures for overcoming this bias. As it is, all the following figures are highly impressionistic and do not merit the application of highly refined corrective techniques.

CRUDE BIRTH RATE

In Thak village in 1969 there were some 9 live-births in a total *de facto* population of 496. This gives a crude birth rate (live-births per thousand population) of 18.1 for Thak in the year 1969. If we include those temporarily absent, mainly husbands whose wives are living in the village, then the rate is 17. These are extremely low rates for a pre-industrial society and are more in line with modern Western patterns. Since they are based on a very small sample for only one year they may be totally unrepresentative. A tentative attempt may be made to widen the base by adding together all the reported live-births, to mothers now living in Thak, for the last five years. Since there is not very great female geographical mobility, it is unlikely that many women have left the village in that time. In the total are included children now dead, who died in infancy. A total of 47 livebirths are recorded over the five-year period 1965–9. If we assume that the base population was approximately 515 in 1967,[12] then the annual CBR was 18.3 – which is remarkably close to the estimate for 1969. Yet even this seems far too low and is probably the result of particular features of the age-structure. Thus, for example, if we take the births in another five-year period, 1957–61, some 73 children born during that period are still alive and another 18 are known to have been born and died. Thus, even if we assume that no other children have been forgotten, and that the base population in 1959 was 65 less than 1967 (i.e. 450) the annual CBR was 40.4. This is much closer to the Nepal figures. Looking at the age structure, it would seem that 1957–61 witnessed a bulge in births, while 1965–9 saw less than normal. Probably the CBR lies somewhere between the two extremes – perhaps at around 30/1000. This is substantially lower than Nepal as a whole. But the inadequacies of the evidence make it imperative that we look to other types of measure.

FERTILITY RATIOS

The Survey of Nepal Health found that the general fertility rate (number of livebirths in a year divided by total women aged 15–49 × 1000) for their sample was 257 or 219, according to two different methods.[13] For Thak in 1969 the rate for Gurungs and service castes (Tamangs/Magars and those only temporarily present were omitted) was 72.6 (9 births to 124 women aged 15–49). This very low figure, based on the same tiny sample as the CBR, is probably not representative. A slightly more satisfactory rate is the fertility ratio (proportion of surviving children under 5 to women 15–50).[14] For Gurungs/service castes in Thak, 1969, the rate was 335 (42 surviving children to 125 women). This is in line with European nations in the 1930s (Czechoslovakia, 1930 = 352; Norway, 1930–1 = 322) rather than that of developing countries (Chile, 1930–2 = 574; Yao in Africa, 1956 = 738).[15] Again it is based on too small a sample to be reliable, and its unrepresentative nature can be seen if we look at figures for another Gurung village, Mohoriya. On the basis of Pignède's census in 1958, it appears that the fertility ratio at that date was approximately 675. Eleven years later I took a census of the same village and found a fertility ratio of 496.[16] Both totals are substantially higher than Thak, and suggest a level somewhere between the European and African levels of fertility.

TOTAL COMPLETED FAMILY SIZE

The Nepal Health Survey discovered that the sample of women aged 50 or over throughout Nepal reported a mean average of 6.0 live-births. The mean average of surviving children to 249 women aged 50+ was 3.02.[17] These figures undoubtedly under-represent completed fertility, since older women tend to forget children who die young. Nevertheless we may wonder how the figures compare to those for the Gurungs. This particular index of fertility will be explored in some detail because it is somewhat more satisfactory for a small village analysis than the previous rates discussed. Being based on live-births over the last fifty or so years it tends to overcome the temporary fluctuations which were seen to undermine previous rates. It will therefore be used to make a preliminary analysis of differential fertility among various groups in Thak and Mohoriya. In order to make the basis for analysis larger, it has been decided to analyse all women aged 40 and over, instead of the traditional 45 or even 50 and over. In Thak, for example, this means that instead of the reproductive histories of 24 married women aged 50+, one has that of 53 women aged 40+. The disadvantage, of course, is that one is no longer dealing with completed families; women may still bear one or more children over the age of 40. Of sixteen Gurung women in Thak, aged 50+, whose age at last child-birth is recorded, five had children at between 40 and 43. This suggests that roughly one-third of Gurung women will have a child at over the age of 40. Fourteen women aged 40–4 are included in the following statistics; given the fact that they are distributed over all the years to 44 and hence may, for example, have had a birth at 42 or 43, it seems likely that only approximately between one and three live-births will have been missed by including women from age 40. This will hardly alter the following statistics, and the same is likely to be true of Mohoriya.

One other defect of the Thak material must be mentioned. As far as possible, retrospective fertility histories of women within the sample (as defined above) covered *all* their marriages. It is likely, however, that if a woman had been married several times, a live-birth by a former husband might be overlooked. Thus the mean average of children born to women aged 40 + (Gurungs) still on their first marriage, was 6.0; while the same average for women married more than once (11/53 women) was only 4.6. The difference may be wholly or partly accounted for by lowered fertility due to disturbance of marriage. It may also be partly due to omitted births. If we assume that these eleven women failed to record an average of just under 0.5 live-births each – a generous estimate – then subsequent figures need to be adjusted upwards by another 5 live-births to obtain true fertility. Finally, the following calculations omit four women who had married and had no livebirths, three women who had not married, a mentally unbalanced woman, and an old woman who could not remember how many of her children had died. Thus we are discussing the marital fertility rate of a small sample. The figures for Thak may be seen in table 13.1. Thus the average completed family size for all the women was 5.2. If we allow for two children not yet born to the women aged 40–4, 5 children unrecorded by women who were several times married, and another 10 children forgotten by old people, then we have a rate of 5.5. The Gurung rate is on average one child lower than that for Nepal as a whole, and even allowing for under-recording, it is probably a little below the mode of six for a representative selection of societies.[18]

In order to see whether Thak is exceptional we may look at the evidence for another Gurung village. Pignède stated that among women of all ages there was a mean average of about 4 pregnancies in the village of Mohoriya.[19] Using his unpublished census notes we can refine this further; table 13.2 is comparable to that for Thak. The most striking thing is that the mean average size is almost exactly similar for each group and for the total population as that for Thak. This gives further confidence in both sets of

TABLE 13.1 *'Completed family size', women aged 40 +, Thak, 1969*

	Total births	Total women	Mean average
Gurungs	171	34	5.0
Tailors/Blacksmiths	66	12	5.5
Total	237	46	5.2

TABLE 13.2 *'Completed family size', women aged 40+, Mohoriya, 1958*

	Total births	Total women[b]	Mean average
Gurungs[a]	205	40	5.1
Tailors, etc.	22	4	5.5
Total	227	44	5.2

[a]The Magars in Mohoriya are included under Gurungs in this table.
[b]Women with no children, omitted.

figures, and in the accuracy of reproductive histories. It also encourages one to use this type of index to test various hypotheses concerning the distribution of fertility.

The first hypothesis we might test is whether there has been any obvious change in the size of completed families, in other words a change in overall fertility. The simplified results may be seen in table 13.3. It will immediately be seen that the trend is entirely different in these two sets of figures. In Mohoriya the complete family size appears to have been getting smaller up to the present, while in Thak the opposite is true. No obvious explanations, except poor recall among older Thak informants, can be given, but we will return to this problem later. Meanwhile another possible explanation could be changes in the proportion of men away doing army service.

It may seem likely, at first glance, that if men are away for fifteen or so years of their adult lives even though they come home on leave at least every three years, this will lower fertility. Yet it has been suggested that military service, or other forms of migrant labour, may, in fact, *increase* fertility, for example by spacing births and hence improving maternal health.[20] We may therefore look with interest at what happens among the Gurungs. The figures for the two villages are summarized in table 13.4. In Mohoriya the difference is almost 2 livebirths per women, in Thak it is only 0.3 per woman. Therefore it is impossible, as yet, to state confidently that army service has a substantial

TABLE 13.3 *Mean average number of live births to women of various ages*

	Women aged		
	40–9	50–9	60+
Mohoriya, 1958	4.3(17)	5.9(14)	7.1(11)
Thak, 1969	5.1(27)	5.5(10)	3.9(9)[a]

[a]This rate is only for Thak women aged 60–9, since those over 70 appear to have forgotten many live-births. The table is only for women who have had one or more live-births. Figures in brackets indicate the number of women upon which the averages are based.

TABLE 13.4 *Army service and mean average number of live-births per woman aged 40 +*

	Husbands 10 + years away from village	Less than 10 years
Mohoriya, 1958	4(12)	5.9(18)
Thak, 1969	5.3(16)	5.6(12)

Note: All the above were Gurungs. Only those with one or more live-births were counted. Figures in brackets indicate the number of women.

effect in all Gurung villages, though it may have in some. It does seem likely, however, that the fact that the Gurung completed family size is lower than that in Nepal as a whole is largely due to migrant labour in the army. Again we will consider this further below.

The Gurungs are split into two 'classes', the *carjat* and the *sorajat*. In both Thak and Mohoriya the major part of the village fields are controlled by the former, earlier established, *carjat* families. Although the correlation with wealth is not absolute, to compare the completed fertility of the two *jats* is a useful preliminary way to see whether wealth and fertility are related, especially in view of Pignède's remark that part of the reason for *carjat* dominance has been their larger families.[21] Gurungs in the two villages, classified on the basis of this division, are analysed in table 13.5. The position in the two villages is different; in Mohoriya the *sorajat* had fractionally more children, in Thak, the *carjat* had a higher average. The difference is not big enough to suggest that there is a different fertility pattern in the two groups either because of different ethnic origin, or because the wealthier marry younger/older etc.

In tables 13.1 and 13.2 evidence was presented to show that the poorest inhabitants of two Gurung villages, the 'untouchable' castes of Tailors, Blacksmiths and Goldsmiths had slightly larger completed families than the Gurungs, on average 0.5 more livebirths. This lends further support to the

TABLE 13.5 Jat *membership and average number of livebirths per woman aged 40 + (with one or more children)*

	Carjat	*Sorajat*
Mohoriya, 1958	5.4(16)	5.5(22)
Thak, 1969	5.3(23)	5.0(10)

Note: Pun Magars in Mohoriya have been counted in under '*sorajat*'. Figures in brackets indicate the number of women on which average is based.

argument that wealth does not necessarily become correlated with large families. Further evidence for Thak may be obtained by comparing groups within the Gurung population, stratified by wealth. The way in which the population was divided into five economic groups is discussed elsewhere and can only be a rough division in such a society.[22] Of the five groupings, only the middle three had enough women aged over 40 to produce any kind of meaningful statistics. The figures are given in table 13.6. (Nothing similar could be computed from Pignède's notes on Mohoriya.) It will be seen that middling Gurungs had the largest number of children, followed by poor Gurungs, then the rich. In fact, it is likely that there is very little difference caused by relative wealth, and that the above figures mainly reflect differences in age structure. We saw earlier that younger women in Thak record a higher number of live-births than older ones, either because of better memories, or because of a real change in fertility. Now it happens that at present in Thak the rich, class II, also happen to be the oldest group of women (only $\frac{2}{7}$ were under 60), whereas in class IV, $\frac{6}{11}$ of the women were aged under 60. Thus we would expect class IV to have a larger number of live-births, merely on account of their age. Yet the table certainly does not provide support for the thesis that fertility and 'class' are correlated.

AGE-SPECIFIC FERTILITY RATES

In the absence of accurate registration of births it is extremely difficult to compile satisfactory age specific fertility rates. Yet this is such an important measure that some attempt to calculate it must be made. The following analysis is based on recalled reproductive histories in two Gurung villages, one set collected by myself, the other from the unpublished notes collected by Pignède. It was not possible to include 17 married women in Mohoriya, since Pignède's notes did not give full details concerning marriage and fertility, and likewise in Thak the data was found to be inadequate for eleven women.[23] It is possible that the women omitted had had somewhat more disturbed marriages than those included and that therefore their fertility would be slightly lower than that of the sample analysed below. Married women who had had no live-births are included below; there were five in Thak and three in Mohoriya. Nine women in Pignède's Mohoriya census who had died before the taking of

TABLE 13.6 *Wealth and average number of live-births to Gurung women aged 40–79, Thak, 1969*

	Rich(II)	Medium(III)	Poor(IV)
Average livebirths	4(7)	5.8(15)	5.5(11)

Note: Figures in brackets = number of women.

the later census in 1969 are omitted in the following analysis, although reproductive histories are available for them, for their inclusion would confuse the issue.[24] All those inhabiting the two villages, Gurungs, Pun Magars and lower caste, are included together in most of the analysis, but 2 households of Magars and 2 of Tamangs in Thak are omitted. Stillbirths have been counted as ordinary births, but the very occasional reported miscarriage has been omitted. Twins have been counted as one birth.

The figures for the two villages, and for a general Nepalese sample, are summarized in Table 13.7. It will be seen that in all groups, the rates are highest in the 20–4 age-group, and that in both Gurung samples each age-group that follows has a lower rate than the previous one. The contrasts with other societies, as well as the difference between two villages, is shown in Fig. 13.1. Both villages exhibit very high rates, but the two patterns are different. In Mohoriya there is very high fertility in all the age-groups up to 34, then rates are low. In Thak the distribution is more even, with consistently high average rates, maintained until age 39. These may seem improbably high rates, but if we compare them to an English village before the industrial revolution, where marriage was even later than in Thak, it will be seen that they are not so extraordinary (see table 13.8). The very low rate in Thak at age 15–19 is probably accounted for by the custom whereby men and women do not cohabit much during the first few years, the man going off to the army, or the women returning to her home village for long periods. It is especially interesting to compare the above figures since the English rates, higher though they were through all ages 15–35, were achieved at a time when it is believed that birth control was practised.

Although the samples are really too small for statistical significance, it still seems worthwhile to try to add to our slender information about the demo-

TABLE 13.7 *Age-specific fertility rates, three samples*

	Women aged (rates per 1000)						
	15–19	20–4	25–9	30–4	35–9	40–4	Total (avge.)
Mohoriya, 1958[a]	230	365	317	251	120	42	246
Thak, 1969	90	297	278	260	216	101	230
Nepal, 1965[b] (approx.)	145	340	240	250	100	110	–

[a] These are, in fact, *marital* fertility rates, being based on the number of 'married women years' lived.

[b] This is deduced from fig. 3, Worth, *Nepal Health*, p. 25, which is based on urine tests of a sample of 1006 women in all. Worth states that the figures for those aged 35 + are too small for reliability.

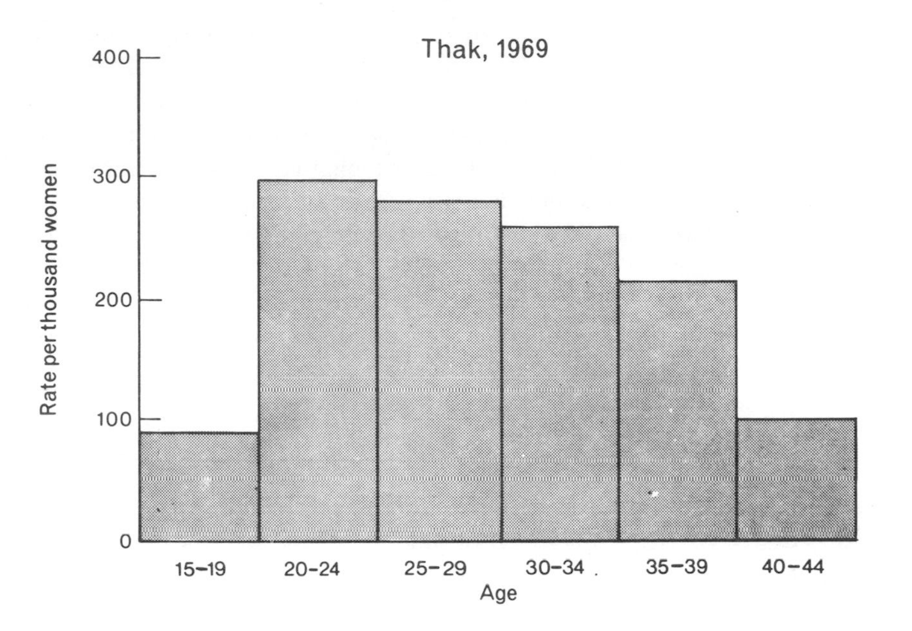

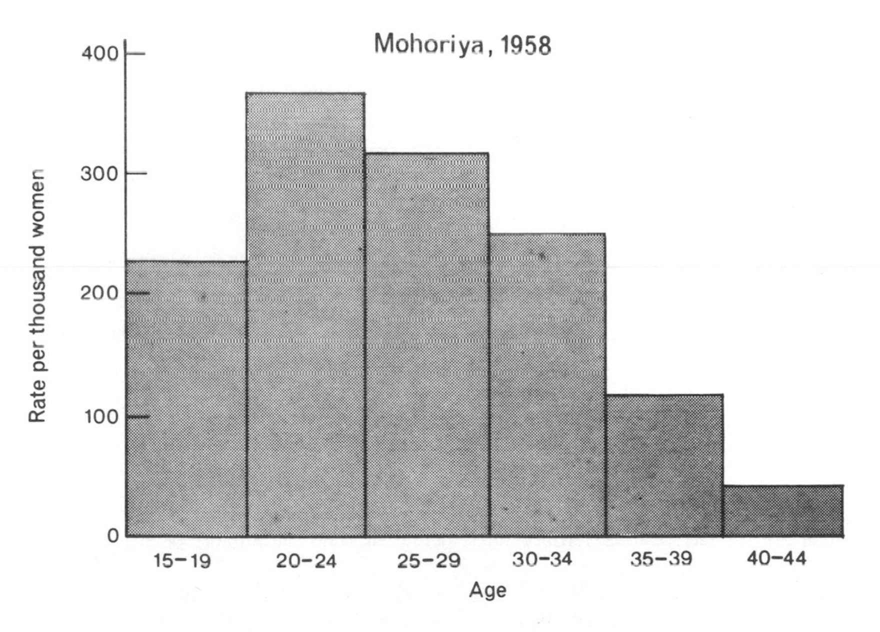

Fig. 13.1. Age-specific marital fertility rates.

TABLE 13.8 *Age-specific marital fertility rates compared*

	15–19	20–4	25–9	30–4	35–9	40–4
Thak, 1969	90	297	278	260	216	101
Colyton, 1647–1719[a]	500	346	395	272	182	104

[a] From Wrigley, 'Family Limitation', p. 89.

graphy of small tribal societies by breaking down the age-specific marital fertility rates somewhat further. The figures for the two villages of Thak and Mohoriya, with the number of married woman years upon which they are based, may be seen in table 13.9. None of the rates are really based on sufficient women years for certainty, and those where the figure falls below 50 or thereabouts become subject to large random fluctuations. Nevertheless, some tentative hypotheses can be drawn. If we compare the different cohorts in Mohoriya, for example, we find different patterns from group to group. Thus the fertility rates for cohorts aged 30–9 and 50–9 are much higher than those for those aged 40–9. In Thak, however, the rates have declined as one moves backwards in time from those aged 30–9, though the youngest cohort also has a low rate. The highest rate was achieved by Mohoriya women now (1958) aged 50–9 when in the age group 20–4 – a rate of 467. It is possible that the very high rate for Thak women now aged 50–9 during the years 15–19 (based on a tiny sample), reflects a higher frequency of pre-marital pregnancies in the past.

A comparison of the rates of Gurungs as opposed to Tailors/Blacksmiths in Thak showed no great differences. The over-all level was slightly lower for the Gurungs, and while Gurungs reached their highest fertility in the age-group 20–4, the Blacksmiths and Tailors did so in the age-group 25–9. But the figures are really much too small to be depended upon.

AGE AT BEARING CHILDREN AND BIRTH INTERVALS

The normal age at bearing a first child varies considerably throughout Nepal. While the Nepal Health Survey discovered that nearly half of their sample had given birth to a first child by the age of 18,[25] the author of a brief study of Bhotea fertility concludes that the average age at giving birth to a first child is probably 'about 25–26 years old'.[26] Pignède published some figures for the village of Mohoriya, which showed that in only 15/102 cases did the first birth occur at under the age of 19; 19–22 was the most common age for such births.[27] The situation in Thak, for once-married Gurung women now aged 30+, may be seen in Fig. 13.2. The mode of this very small group is 20, the mean average 23. If we compare this to the situation for Mohoriya, shown on

TABLE 13.9 *Age-specific marital fertility; two Gurung villages*

Present age[a]		Women aged						
		15–19	20–4	25–9	30–4	35–9	40–4	Average
20–9	T	62(16)	257(35)	166(18)	–	–	–	188(69)
	M	233(60)	426(101)	156(45)				310(206)
30–9	T	37(27)	355(76)	313(83)	222(72)	142(14)	–	265(272)
	M	348(23)	420(69)	418(91)	339(59)	83(12)	–	378(254)
40–9	T	94(32)	282(85)	280(107)	289(128)	224(125)	137(102)	235(579)
	M	148(27)	209(67)	256(82)	179(90)	64(78)	15(65)	149(409)
50–9	T	333(9)	345(29)	244(41)	256(39)	191(42)	67(45)	215(205)
	M	148(27)	467(45)	388(67)	267(75)	127(71)	34(59)	238(344)
60–9	T	– –	167(24)	286(35)	239(46)	260(27)	50(40)	192(177)
	M	363(11)	214(28)	265(34)	257(35)	231(39)	100(40)	219(187)

[a] 'Present age' was the age of the woman at the time of the Census; Thak, 1969 = T, and Mohoriya, 1958 = M. Thus a woman aged 30–9 in the Mohoriya Census of 1958 would be in the 40–9 group by the time of the Thak Census. The number of 'married woman years at risk' is given in brackets. This was computed by finding out how many women lived (being married) through a certain group of years; if they died, married, separated, or reached a certain age as the census was taken, in each case this was counted as a $\frac{1}{2}$ year. Although in some cases such events would happen near the beginning or end of the year, over a number of cases they ought to even out.

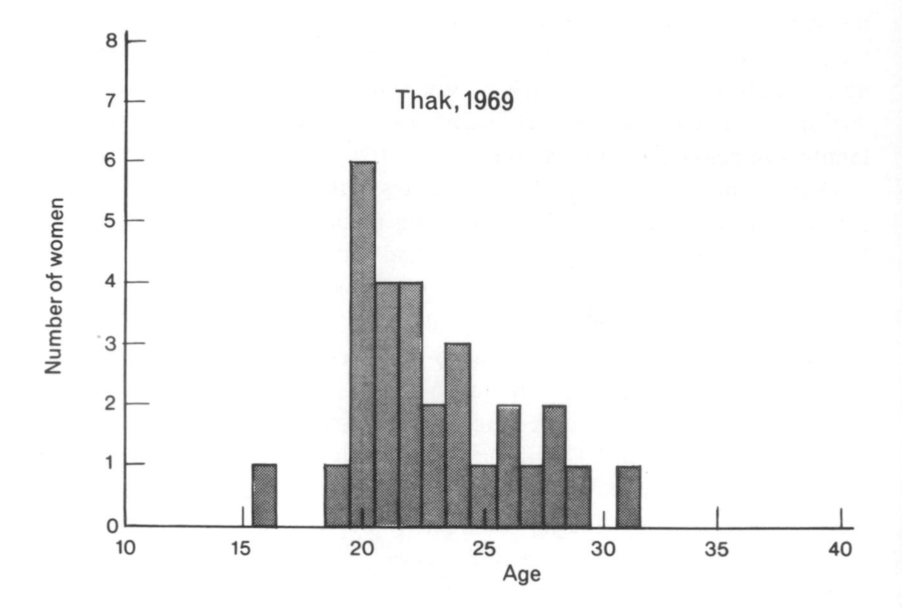

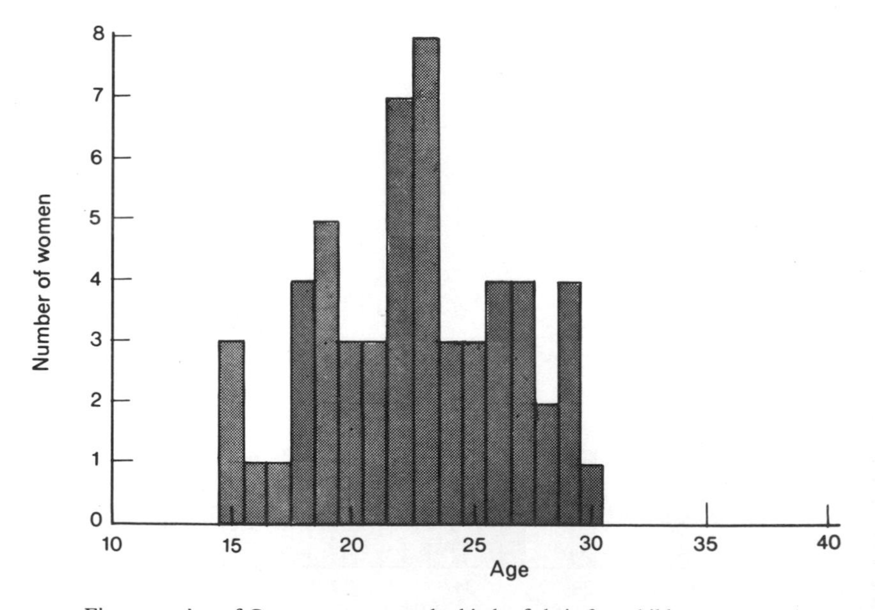

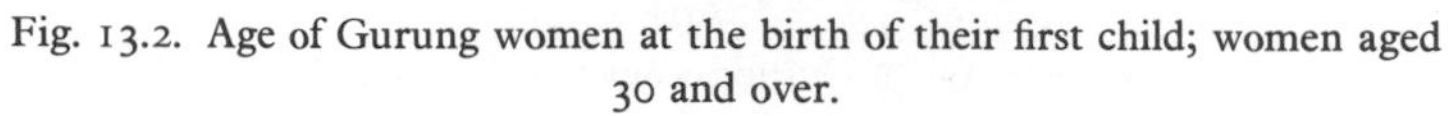
Fig. 13.2. Age of Gurung women at the birth of their first child; women aged 30 and over.

the same diagram and based on Pignède's original census, it will be seen that the peak comes at an older age, the mode being 23. This relatively high age at first childbirth is undoubtedly of great importance in lowering Gurung fertility; in spite of high marital fertility rates, the Gurungs have a completed family size below the national average.

Despite their Hindu origins, lower castes in Thak and Mohoriya appear to exhibit the same age at first childbearing as the Gurungs. In Thak only $\frac{2}{12}$ Blacksmith/Tailor women aged over 30 had had a child at under the age of 18; in Mohoriya exactly the same figures are found – $\frac{2}{12}$. In both, the majority have their first child at between 20 and 23.

The Nepal Health Survey included a diagram of age at final pregnancy of women aged 50 or more. The mean age was 36.6 years, the mode was 39. This fairly early cessation of fertility also seems to occur among the Gurungs. Pignède calculated that 88 % of the births in his sample occurred in the group aged between 19 and 38 years.[28] The situation in Mohoriya and Thak may be seen more clearly in Fig. 13.3; that for Mohoriya is based on Pignède's field notes. The mode in Thak was split between 32 and 41, in Mohoriya it was 36. The mean in Thak was 35.8, in Mohoriya 37. Thus, despite the fact that Gurungs start their childbearing comparatively late, they also finish fairly

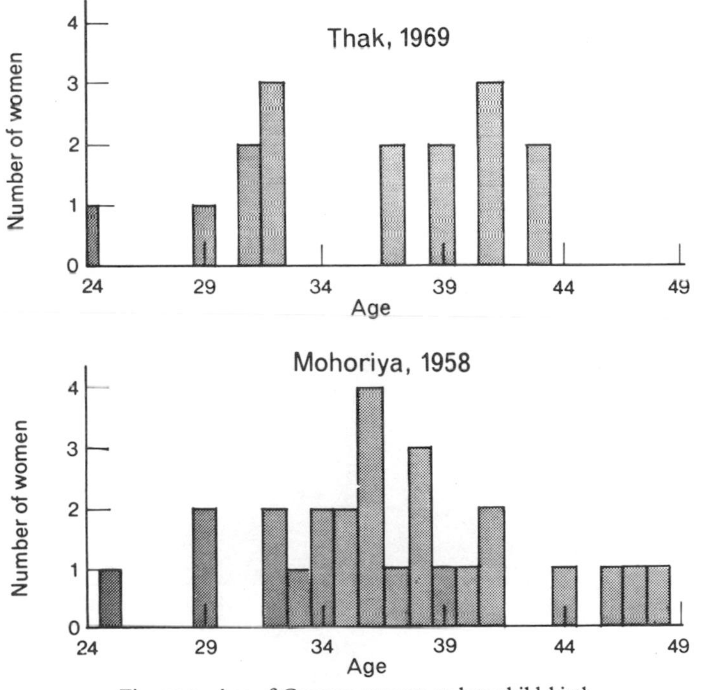

Fig. 13.3. Age of Gurung women at last child-birth.

early. It is not possible, however, to draw the conclusion that Pignède did from this, namely that 'the menopause seems to occur quite early'.[29] It is well known that there may be a long gap between the average age at last birth and the menopause; thus, for example, in a sample of 93 Bengali women the average age at last birth was 35.1, while the age at menopause was 47.5.[30] The Gurung mean age at menopause almost certainly falls within the normal range 44–49 years, but social factors intervene to inhibit pregnancies during the last few years of marriage.

We may now look at the culmination of the foregoing rates, the actual age at which women bore children. Pignède published figures which showed peaks in the age groups 19–22, 23–26, 27–30, all roughly equal.[31] The situation among the Gurungs in Thak is shown in Fig. 13.4. The individual peak was at age 28, with high levels for most of the period between 21 and 41. The numbers are too small however to make any definite conclusions.

Pignède remarks that 'three or four years separate each pregnancy. This

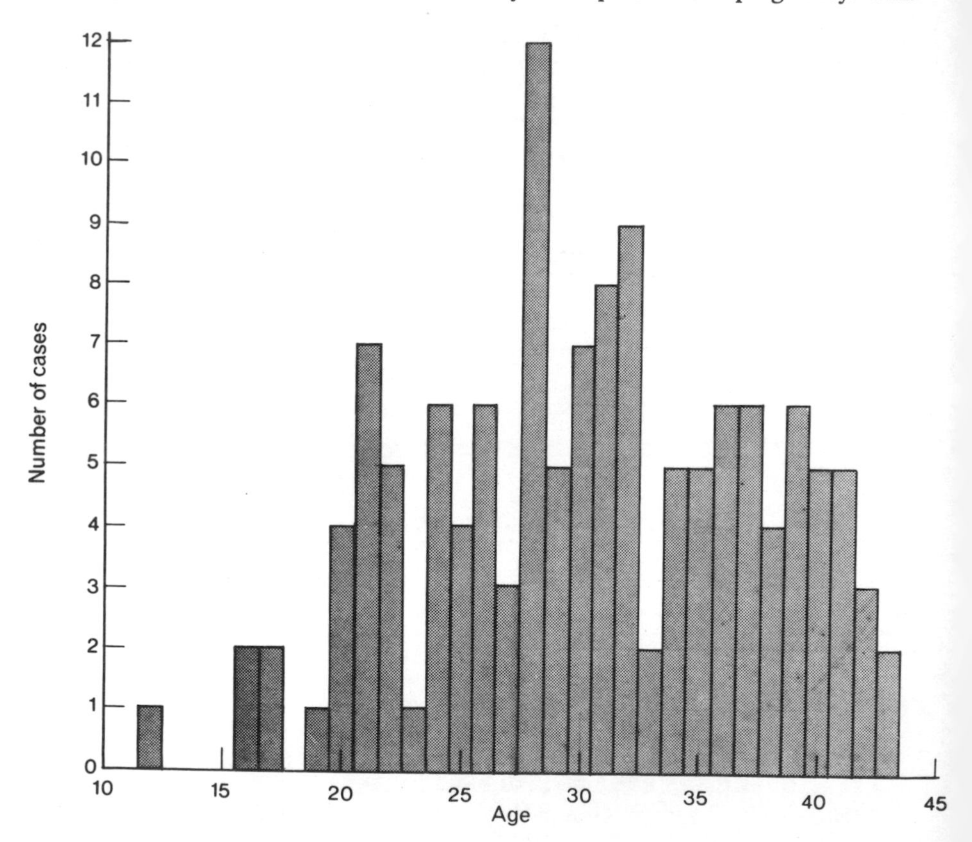

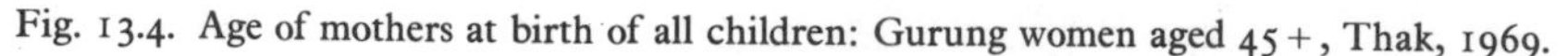

Fig. 13.4. Age of mothers at birth of all children: Gurung women aged 45+, Thak, 1969.

interval corresponds to the time during which the husband is absent (in the army)'.[32] Since he does not give any actual examples, we may be permitted to examine this contention a little further, since spacing of births is indeed a good index of the influence of army service on fertility. Again diagramatic presentation is the easiest method of seeing the situation; Fig. 13.5 compares five Gurung men who have served ten or more years in the army with five who have not served at all, or, at the most, a couple of years. It will be seen that those who served in the army tend to marry later and hence they begin to

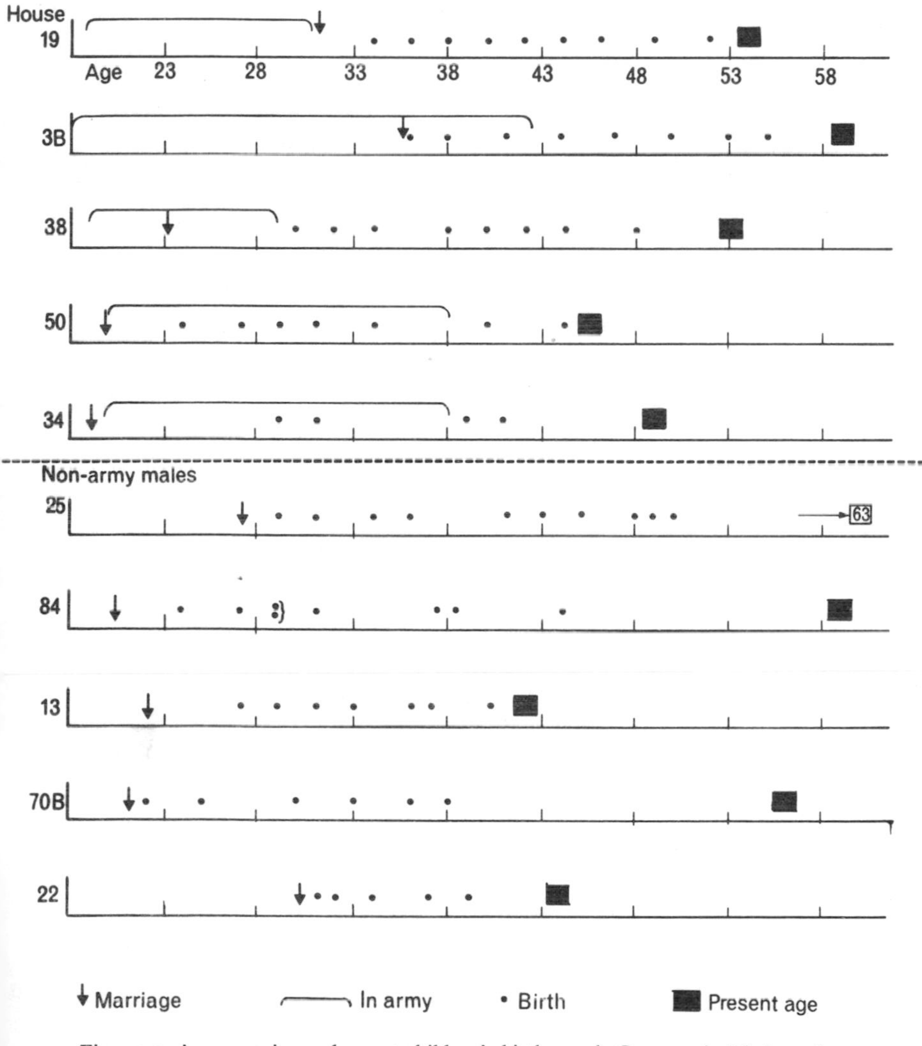

Fig. 13.5. Army service and age at children's births; male Gurungs in Thak, 1969.

produce children later. There is also a tendency for most births to occur after early service is over. This does not necessarily inhibit the creation of large families; thus household 19 produced nine children, though the man was 34 when his wife gave birth to her first child. House 50 illustrates how births may occur during army service, and at less than three-year intervals. Indeed the gaps are by no means regularly three years, and those not serving in the army appear to produce children at the same intervals as those who are away in the army. The overall impression is that, as noted from other statistics, army service does lower fertility a little, but its effect is probably mainly indirect, by raising living standards and encouraging men to wait a little longer until they marry. One direct influence, however, is on the gap between marriage and first birth; there is often a long interval between these two events for soldiers, a good deal longer on average than that for non-soldiers.

The data from two Gurung villages suggests that fertility may be high enough to lead to rapid population increase despite a number of factors which have traditionally been thought to inhibit such growth. The Gurungs are migrant labourers, with a relatively high standard of living, a pension system (for ex-army employees) and a relatively late age at marriage. They have no great cultural stress on fertility or the need for sons. Yet their completed family size is approximately 5.5, only 0.5 lower than that for Nepal as a whole. Only a high mortality rate could prevent such a reproductive figure from leading to rapid population growth.

14
Social structure and mortality

SOME CAUSES OF DEATH

Virtually nothing is known about the incidence of various diseases as causes of death in Nepal.[1] The few health surveys of the country confine themselves to analysing the present prevalence of illness, and the meagre statistics which can be culled from hospital records clearly give a very distorted picture of the pattern in rural areas. Yet huge vaccination and other public health campaigns are launched on the basis of very little knowledge of local conditions. For an anthropologist, the only way to gather information on causes of death, in the absence of any coroner's examinations and medical certificates or even of simple vital registration of deaths, is by retrospective questioning. This was carried out on the 100 sample households in Thak during the taking of the census. Informants were asked the cause of death of all infants and children stated to have died, and also the date and cause of death of parents, and one other near relative who had died recently. Naturally, answers came in the form of descriptions of symptoms; for example a person was said to have died of a 'lump in the stomach' or 'fever'. This could describe a number of ailments, and checking through with a doctor from the neighbouring hospital at Pokhara left many such cases unclassified. Furthermore, there is likely to be loss of memory. Finally, the figures are too small for any statistical significance to be attached to them. Yet they do show certain broad features of the situation, for example the low rate of mortality at child-birth, the absence of certain epidemic diseases and the importance of dysentery/gastro-enteritis and T.B. For this reason, and those stated above, it seems worth recording the findings. Nor are the categories much cruder than those now available for such countries as Ceylon, which include, for example 'Convulsions of children under 5 years' as a cause of death.[2]

The major causes of death, according to replies to the census, are set out in table 14.1.

Although too much weight cannot be attached to the relative incidence of various causes, it is clear that dysentery/gastro-enteritis, tuberculosis, and chest infections are high on the list. Deaths from fighting in foreign armies

TABLE 14.1 *Stated causes/symptoms of death in Thak census, Gurungs and others, 1969*

Cause	Infancy	1–9 years	10–49	50+	Total	%
Dysentery/enteritis	5	16	3	15	39	19.5
Tuberculosis	–	7	13	7	27	13.5
'Cancer' (lump)[a]	–	–	9	13	22	11
'Fever' (typhoid, etc.)[a]	–	6	2	8	16	8
Swollen body (heart/kidney)	–	–	2	12	14	7
Pneumonia/bronchitis	7	5	–	1	13	6.5
Typhoid	–	1	6	5	12	6
Accidents (falls/burns)	2	3	5	2	12	6
Warfare	–	–	10	–	10	5
'Stomach painful'[a]	–	3	2	1	6	3
Childbirth (mothers)	–	–	4	–	4	2
Infant at childbirth	4	–	–	–	4	2
Ulcers/'body wounds'[a]	–	–	2	2	4	2
Malaria	–	–	4	–	4	2
Meningitis	1	–	1	–	2	1
Measles	–	2	–	–	2	1
Malnutrition – infant	2	–	–	–	2	1
Epilepsy/insanity	–	–	1	1	2	1
Quinsy/tonsular abscess	–	1	–	–	1	0.5
Leprosy	–	–	1	–	1	0.5
Lockjaw (tetanus)	–	–	1	–	1	0.5
Nephritis	–	–	1	–	1	0.5
Goitre	–	–	–	1	1	0.5
	21	44	67	68	200	100

[a]The possible diseases which these broad symptoms may refer to will be discussed below. But since it is impossible to classify many deaths, the table does not give an accurate index of certain diseases – for example typhoid may appear under several of the headings above.

accounted for ten men, the second highest cause of mortality among those aged 10–49, but only 5 % of all deaths. Maternal mortality only accounted for 2 % of the total 200 cases. Perhaps even more interesting than the high figures are the omissions; though a few cases may be concealed under 'fever', etc. there are no reported cases of cholera, smallpox, bubonic or pneumonic plague, and only two cases of measles. Over the last sixty years Thak seems to have avoided any serious epidemics. If we look at the separate age groups, we get some idea of the major cause of mortality at each stage. Pneumonia and dysentery/gastro-enteritis account for over half the infant deaths; accidents and complications at birth account for less than one third. In the years 1–9, gastro-enteritis/dysentery is the greatest killer. In the age group 10–49, one-fifth were believed to be caused by T.B. and one-sixth by warfare. Typhoid and malaria also reached their peak in this stage. The last period, when 16 people were merely described as dying of 'old age' (not included in this table) again saw a predominance of 'dysentery' and 'lumps in the stomach'.

It is a commonplace observation that mortality varies with the seasons. For example, Gorer suggested that many poorer Lepchas died of dysentery in June.[3] The incidence of those deaths where I was given the month when death occurred are shown in Fig. 14.1. It will be seen that almost all infant deaths occur in the summer months, and the same is true of children and adults. Mortality, however, is just as high before the onset of the monsoons in *Asar* as it is when the village is flooded and dank. Nor do the few weeks of cold weather, often bringing frost and snow to Thak and leaving the lightly-dressed villagers shivering, seem to raise the mortality; mid-January to mid-March is one of the least dangerous periods.[4]

There appears to have been in the recent past a complete absence of the typical Malthusian checks on population growth. There are no traces of epidemics of any kind, in the Thak records. There were no smallpox scars in Thak, although it has been found that this disease is fairly prevalent (between 3–27 % of those aged 10–29 examined had scars) in Nepal, and especially in the Western Mountains.[5] Nor were there any reported deaths from this cause, although there is a Gurung name for it (*pro*) which suggests that there has been some encounter with it in the past. I was told that some six or seven years previously, three or four people had died of this disease in the neighbouring village of Taprang, but no one in Thak had been affected. The likelihood of future epidemics is slightly lessened by government innoculation campaigns. I was told that the innoculators had visited Thak some fifteen years ago, and then not again until three years ago. They again visited the village while we were present. Partly due to insufficient warning being given, partly due to the absence of any exhortation, explanation, or inducements/sanctions, a large number of people were missed on the visit during our presence. As in Nepal generally, the situation is alarming.[6]

There is no evidence of bubonic or other types of plague, of cholera, of influenza, of scarlet fever, mumps or polio epidemics. The situation is very different from that in the Terai where, up to recently anyway, it was reported that there were 'frequent epidemics of cholera, plague and smallpox . . . usually in the spring and early summer'.[7] Although rabid dogs occasionally reach the village, the prompt slaughter of all the village dogs (as occurred in Thak some three or four years previous to our visit) helps to prevent the spreading of the disease, and no deaths from rabies are reported from Thak. A large number of other potential afflictions are also omitted from the list of diseases above, notable among them leprosy and syphilis.

The second Malthusian check, after plague, is famine. There are no recorded deaths from famine in the Thak records, though it is, of course,

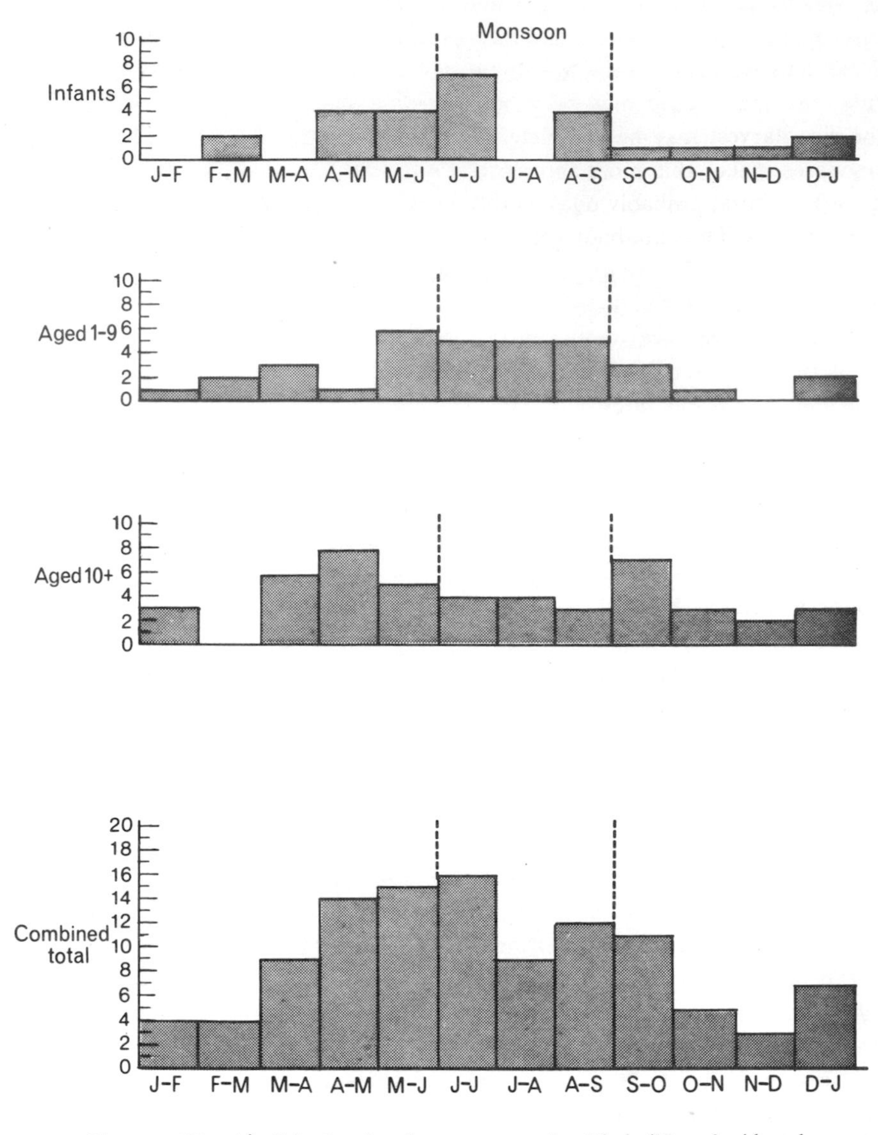

Fig. 14.1. Months of deaths of various age categories, Thak. (*Note*: Accidental deaths and deaths in child-birth are omitted.)

possible that some of the deaths from other listed causes were precipitated by malnutrition after harvest failure. Nor do we know whether famine was a serious cause of mortality among the Gurungs in the nineteenth century. It seems likely, however, that their diversified agriculture, part pastoral, part arable, as well as the abundant forest resources of plants and animals would have sustained them through difficult years. As the Gurungs become more and more dependent on grain crops the threat of famine increases. If there is hail in July, the maize crop may be destroyed; if it hails in September–October, the rice harvest may be completely lost. The decline in livestock and forest resources makes this more and more of a threat. Such hail, furthermore, frequently occurs; probably one or other harvest is seriously damaged every five years or less. Thus in about 1964 the maize crop in Thak was destroyed, and some of the rice also. In 1968 most of the maize was lost, and the rest had to be used for seed for the following year. In 1969 five minutes of hail in the autumn destroyed over a quarter of the rice harvest.

At present, even if both crops are completely destroyed, absolute starvation would probably not occur. The rich families have considerable reserves of grain from the previous year and other nearby villages usually provide a surplus which may be bought at Pokhara (the hail usually has a very localized distribution, just sweeping up one or two valleys). On the occasion when both maize and some of the rice failed some five years ago the richer families had no need to buy grain, though the middling to poor had to purchase it from Pokhara at nearly twice the normal price. Some of these less wealthy villagers had to sell off some of their capital possessions, land, gold, cooking vessels, or to borrow from richer villagers. No one died of hunger however. Some twenty-five years ago, I was told, the rice and maize crops were both completely destroyed. One young man, just born at the time, said that a number of people died of hunger, but there is no evidence of this in the replies to the census and another older man stated that there were no deaths, for grain was obtainable from other villages. It seems unlikely that this check to population growth will operate for a few years until population pressure on resources increases beyond its present level. It is quite possible that it will begin to take effect, in combination with epidemic disease, well before the end of the century.

We have already seen how the third of Malthus' natural checks, warfare, has at present ceased to play any real part in controlling population. It seems unlikely that the Gurungs will ever again be involved in a large-scale conventional war. Even if they were, and casualties were on the same scale as previous World Wars, deaths would not curb population growth effectively – though it would temporarily limit fertility.

Although the statistics on cause of death are extremely flimsy, it seems likely that the two main impressions from this discussion are correct. The first is that water-borne faecal diseases (dysentery, gastro-enteritis, typhoid) and tuberculosis are the two major causes of death in Thak. The second is that both causes are likely to decline rapidly in the next few years, and indeed have already commenced to do so. In the case of water-borne diseases, the installation of a water-pipe some twelve years ago has lowered mortality quite considerably. There are plans to extend and improve such piped water facilities, and similar piped water is spreading in other villages, for example Mohoriya, Pignède's village. Furthermore, it now seems likely that the government and/or private bodies will initiate serious B.C.G. campaigns against tuberculosis in this area in the near future. This will have a similar effect to the malaria campaign in the Terai. A combination of these two public health measures will mean that the crude death rate could be cut in half among the Gurungs between 1960 and 1975. Without a comparable reduction in births this will have enormous effects on the whole economic, social and mental life of the Gurungs.

MORTALITY STATISTICS

As with the fertility statistics, the following figures are rendered less significant by three main types of flaw. Firstly, the 100 households chosen for detailed observation in Thak were not a random sample, based on proper sampling technique. Although we can often compare them to those for another community, Mohoriya, and this helps to make it less likely that findings will be entirely exceptional, we can by no means generalize safely from the following figures. Secondly, the area covered is too small for statistical significance. We are dealing with a total population of only about 500 persons, which is often broken down into half that number, or less, for certain purposes. Figures based on such small numbers cannot be tested for statistical significance, and are hardly more than impressionistic. Thirdly, the quality of the data available to the anthropologist is not satisfactory. No records were available except those gathered by myself; for example there is no vital registration of deaths except in the year I was present in the area. This makes it extremely difficult to compute even the simplest of figures such as the crude death rate. In fact, the following chapter may be seen more as an attempt to see how one can possibly arrive at a general impression concerning mortality patterns from inadequate data. The data is basically of four kinds. For the village of Mohoriya we have two censuses, made in 1958 and 1969. These may be compared to see who had died in the interval, and thus we may establish survival rates. Secondly, there is the census of Thak in 1969. This includes retrospective questions about mortality, which are the third source. As stated above, I asked for the births and deaths of all infants and children of selected women[8] in the past, and also for the age and date of death of parents of the head of each household and his wife. Also asked for was the date of death of the most recent near relative to have died, other than parents. Finally, I recorded all births, marriages and deaths during the year 1969. My general impression is that the census data is pretty accurate and that not a large number of infant and child deaths were missed. A number of respondents were not able, however, to fill in the names or dates of their parents' death or that of a near relative. The chief defect of the information for Thak is obvious. While there is a reasonable coverage for the year 1969, retrospective questions tend to concentrate on the young and the old; middle-aged people who died are likely to be missed.

CRUDE DEATH RATE

The 1952–4 Census makers guessed at a crude death rate (CDR) in Nepal of some 30/1000.[9] This very high figure has been supported by the medical survey of Nepal in 1965, which reported a figure of 27/1000, and a recent reanalysis of the 1952–4 and 1969 Censuses which suggests an even higher rate of 32.[10] This would make it one of the highest crude rates in the world.[11] We may wonder how the predominantly Gurung village of Thak compares with this figure. In 1969 there were 480 persons actually resident in the village at mid-year. During the whole year some 13 people died. This gives a rate of 27/1000, exactly in line with the Nepal average. There are, however, reasons for thinking that this is a good deal too high. We could properly add in all those temporarily away in the army and elsewhere; if they had died their deaths would have been considered a loss to the village. If we do this we have a rate of approximately 25/1000. Yet this is still likely to be far too high. The difficulty is that, as is well known, a rate based on one year, especially for such a small population is subject to very large fluctuations. The fact that of the 13 deaths in 1969 some 9 were of adults, immediately suggests that, given what we know about the high infant and child mortality rates in such a society, it was a somewhat exceptional year. To construct a more satisfactory rate requires several assumptions. If we take the period 1965–9, it will be assumed that since the population (including temporarily absent) in 1969 was 528, and since it was known to have been increasing by at least 1 % p.a., then the mid-period population in 1967 may be assumed to be about 515 persons. The retrospective questions in the Census for this period gave the deaths of 36 persons. This probably represents most of the children to the age of 10 and adults over 50 who died. If we make the assumption that some four persons aged 10–50 also died, but were not recorded, then we have an average CDR of 15.5 over the five years. Given what we know about the Gurungs, their relatively high standard of living and uncrowded villages, it seems likely that such a CDR is of the right order for recent years.

INFANT AND CHILD MORTALITY

The Nepal Health survey showed that infant mortality ratios, based on various different types of evidence, varied between 130 and 208/1000. A national rate of about 150/1000 is therefore quite likely.[12] The figures for child mortality are even vaguer. The same health survey discovered a mean number of 6.0 live-births to women now aged 50 + but the mean average of children still alive to such women was only 3.02, which suggests that only approximately 50 % of live-born infants survive to adulthood.[13] This is a figure paralleled by Gorer's observation that 9/19 of the males born to women aged 50–69 at his visit had died.[14] For the Gurung village of Mohoriya, Pignède stated that of the 380 last infants born at Mohoriya, some 30 % had died before reaching the age of 17.[15] This immediately suggests that Gurung rates may be lower than those for Nepal as a whole.

With only one year of registration for a population of just over 500, it is not worth even stating the infant death rate for Thak in 1969, since one or two added deaths will make such a huge difference to the figures. We will therefore have to approach the problem in an indirect way. One such method, similar to that noted above, is to find the proportion of children stated to have been live-born in the census and who have subsequently died. The detailed figures for Thak are set out in table 14.2. The general conclusion is that some 33 % of the children of women now aged over 40 are dead. The overall rate does not vary very much between Gurungs and untouchable castes, but while Gurung males have a much higher mortality in infancy and childhood than females (a normal characteristic since females are usually stronger), among Tailors and Blacksmiths female infant and child mortality is twice as high as that of males. This suggests some form of discrimination, presumably in feeding. The fact that the ratio of male to female births is 122:115 gives some confidence as to the accuracy of recall since this is exactly the ratio one would expect given normal births. The figure also fits with the 30 % mortality by age 17 suggested by Pignède, but it contradicts his suggestion that there is a higher infant/child mortality among girls as a whole than among boys, a hypothesis which he based on arguments concerning the sex/age structure.[16]

The proportion of children who survive may be used to test a number of other hypotheses, crude index though it is. One of these is that there is, as Pignède suggested for the Gurungs, a higher child and infant mortality among poorer villagers than among the richer.[17] Evidence contradicting this hypo-

TABLE 14.2 *Proportion of children died to women aged 40 + in 1969*

	Males			Females			Total		
	Total born	Now dead	%	Born	Dead	%	Born	Dead	%
Gurungs	91	35	38.5	80	22	27.5	171	57	33.3
Tailors and Blacksmiths	31	7	22.6	35	14	40	66	21	31.8
Total	122	42	34.4	115	36	31.3	237	78	32.9

thesis has already been provided by table 14.2. Gurungs are, on average, much wealthier than the service castes but, as shown in the table, 33.3 % of their children had died and only 31.8 % of the Tailors and Blacksmiths. Not too much weight can be placed on this since it may be affected by the different age-structure of the two groups and, possibly, by their relative interest in recalling births and deaths. But corroboration comes from other sources. Taking *carjat* and *sorajat* Gurungs separately, we find that (to women now aged 40 +) 34.2 % of the *carjat* children had already died and only 31.4 % of the *sorajat* (the total of children born to each group were 120 and 51 respectively). Now the *carjat* are, on the whole, wealthier than the *sorajat*, yet they suffered higher infant/child mortality. One final figure can be given to bear out this conclusion. The population of Thak was stratified into five classes during fieldwork, on the basis of wealth.[18] In class II, who are prosperous villagers, 10/27 or 37 % of the children of Gurung women aged 40 + in 1969 had died; in class III, middling in wealth, some 31.3 % (26/83) had died; in class IV, poor Gurungs, some 35.4 % had died. The Tailors and Blacksmiths, we have seen, suffered 31.8 % mortality. In other words the richest Gurungs suffered the highest mortality, followed by the poor. Middling wealth Gurungs were the healthiest on this index. The range, however, is not very great. Why this should be so, if it really does reflect differences in mortality rather than differences in age-structure, it is at this stage impossible to say.

Another negative conclusion is that army service has no direct effect on infant/child mortality. Indirectly it may help by raising living standards throughout the village, but there is no real difference between specific individuals depending on whether the father has been in the army or not. Women aged 40 + whose husbands had been in the army for ten or more years had lost 26/84 (31 %) of their children, while those whose husbands had not served, or served for only short periods, had lost 22/84 (32.3 %) of theirs.[19]

One other way of measuring infant and child mortality is by comparing the two censuses of Mohoriya. Thus we may find out what proportion of those listed in 1958 was still present in 1969. The families which emigrated are known and can be excluded. Girls aged 6 years or over in the earlier listing are also difficult since their absence in 1969 may well be due to marriage into another village rather than death. If we confine ourselves to those aged 0–4 years in the earlier listing, of 47 children only 6 had died (12.7 %); mortality was higher among boys than girls, 4/35 of the former, 2/22 of the latter. This suggests a fairly low rate of infant/child mortality by Nepalese standards. Of the 64 males aged from 0–16 in 1958, only 10, or 15.6 %, had disappeared; it is possible that one or two of these had gone abroad and not been noted as being absent. If anything, mortality was a good deal higher among Gurungs; 9/47 Gurungs had disappeared by the second listing, and only 1/17 of the service caste males aged 1–16. This may have been distorted a little by the above mentioned migration to the army, but cannot be entirely explained by that phonomenon. Of the 15 babies said to be up to one year old in 1958, some 20 % had disappeared. The general impression is that, as in Thak, the mortality was not high by Nepalese standards.

Another way to look at infant and child mortality, based on the Thak census, is to tabulate the age at death of all children born to mothers now aged 20+. This is done in table 14.3 One fact that emerges from the table is that older informants, especially those aged over 60, appear to have forgotten deaths of children aged under 6 months; it cannot be likely that no infants under that age died to women now aged 60+. Therefore for accurate information we will have to confine ourselves to those aged up to 55 years of age. Another impression is that the worst periods are during the first week and years 1–3. Some twelve infants are recorded as dying in the first week and mortality continued at a relatively high level until the end of the third year. A striking feature, to be examined in more detail, is the contrast between the

TABLE 14.3 *Age at death of all children to mothers aged 20+, Thak, 1969*

	Age of mother in 1969 (all women)									
Age at death	20–4	25–9	30–4	35–9	40–4	45–9	50–4	55–9	60–4	65–74
Birth		1		1		1[a]	1	1		
1–7 days						5	1			
8–14 days							1			
15–30 days					3	3	1			
2–3 mths.					1					
4–6 mths.				2		1				
7–11 mths.		1			2	1	1	1	1	
1st year		1			4	3		3		2
2nd year				1	2	1	1	2		
3rd year					3	3		2	3	
4th year				1	1	1	1			
5th year					1	4		1	1	2
6th year										
7th year							1			
8th year										1
9th year					1	1			1	
10th year					1		1			
11th–13th year						2	1			
14th –16th year						1	1			
17th +						1(22)	1(25+)	1(29)	1(27)	6[b]

[a] Also three stillbirths.

[b] Aged 32, 20, 21, 27, 36, 36 years.

mothers now aged 20–34, who have lost hardly any infants, and those aged 40–54 who lost many.

Another interesting feature of the table is the infrequency of death within 24 hours of childbirth. Of the total 187 live-births recorded for mothers now aged 20–54, only 3 are recorded as dying at birth; this low rate is confirmed by observation and villager's comments. It seems to contrast with a small sample for the whole of Nepal, where 11/63 infant deaths had occurred on the first day after birth.[20]

Another way of looking at the Thak material from the census is to analyse the age-specific mortality of young children up to the age of 10. This is done in table 14.4, showing the results as deaths per 1000 infant/child years lived, for Gurungs. The table is divided by age of mother (in 1969) so that we may see if there has been any change in recent years. The first feature worth drawing attention to is the infant death rate in column one. For all women it is 86/1000 live-births. This is much lower than the probable 150/1000 for Nepal as a whole which we noted earlier; for younger mothers the rate is 71/1000, which is even better. Mortality rates from the second year on are half those for the first year, but they remain moderately high until the fifth year. There is some evidence of a dip in the mortality rate at age two; probably, if this is correct, this would be a safe period when the child was still benefiting from parental milk, but strong enough to survive many infant infections. Another interesting feature is the contrast between younger and older women. We have already noted that infant mortality is a good deal lower among women aged under 39, and mortality is lower at all other ages except year 4. The average mortality of infants/children from age 1–5 is thus 39/1000 for younger mothers, 47/1000 for the older. Since, if anything, we would expect younger mothers to recall deaths of young infants better than older women, it is very doubtful whether this reflects a difference in memory. It suggests that there has been a considerable improvement in infant/child health sometime during the last 10–20 years. It is probable that this is related to the installation of a water-pipe in the village some ten or more years ago whose influence on the pattern of illness can be seen elsewhere.

ADULT MORTALITY

The assessment of adult mortality among the Gurungs is even more difficult than that of infant and child mortality since a census, however the questions are framed, is unlikely to give as complete a coverage of adult deaths as of young children. Three methods will be used in order to try to establish approximate mortality patterns, but it should be emphasized that the results must be very tentative until an adequate registration system is set up in Nepal.

TABLE 14.4 *Age-specific mortality of children at various ages, to Gurung women in Thak, 1969*

Women now aged	Age of children[a]						
	0–11 mths.	12–23 mths.	Age 2	Age 3	Age 4	Age 5	Avge. 1–5
20–39	71.4	41.7	22.2	–	54.1	–	39.8
	(56)	(48)	(45)	(40)	(37)	(32)	(258)
40–54	93.2	47.2	30.0	41.2	11.4	47.0	47.1
	(118)	(106)	(100)	(97)	(88)	(85)	(594)
All women (including above)	86.2	45.4	27.6	29.2	11.5	34.2	45.12

[a]The top figures are rates per 1000 child-years lived; the figures underneath, in brackets, are the number of completed child-years upon which the rates are based. Those who are at present aged 3, for example, are only counted as having completed the categories up to the end of age 2 and are *not* counted as 'at risk' in 'Age 3' since they may die before they leave the year. This means that the rates are a little too high since they are based on too few 'at risk' children in reality.

One method is to compare the two censuses of Mohoriya, and to see what proportion of those in certain age categories in the first census had died by the time of the second one, eleven years later. If we omit the families which have moved out of the area in the intervening period we are left with the figures shown in table 14.5. It is likely that some of those who have 'disappeared' have not, in fact, died. Several of the younger men and women had undoubtedly either married out or merely emigrated; this is likely to affect females aged 17–29 most of all. Unfortunately I did not have a copy of Pignède's original census with me in Mohoriya and so could not actually ask whether individuals had died in the meantime. Thus all the rates above are undoubtedly too high. Nevertheless, there are some interesting features. Firstly, it will be seen that the total rates for the two sexes are almost equal, the slightly higher female rate probably being more than accounted for by marriages out of the village. Secondly, the rate for males and females aged 50–69 is very low by most standards, and is almost exactly equal for the two sexes. Where women do seem to have heavier mortality, probably, as we shall later see, because of deaths at the menopause, is in the age-group 30–49, which is the age of lowest mortality among men. Those aged over 70 in 1958 have not been included since all but one of the 10 persons (half of them aged 80 or over) were dead eleven years later. This very heavy rate at old age fits in with the lower levels in middle age and is surprisingly like the modern Western pattern. A comparison of Gurungs with lower castes (both included in the above tables) did not show any significant difference; if anything, the lower castes seemed to suffer less mortality in the age group 17–49 than the Gurungs; thus of 15 lower caste women, only one disappeared in the eleven years between the censuses (and she was aged 20 and may have married out), while 14/68 of the Gurung women were no longer present at the later date.

TABLE 14.5 *Mortality in Mohoriya between 1958 and 1969*

	Males (aged)			
	17–29	30–49	50–69	Total
No. present in 1958	41	41	29	111
No. missing in 1969	8	5	7	20
Rate per 1000 p.a. (11 yrs.)	17.7	11.1	21.9	16.4
	Females (aged)			
	17–29	30–49	50–69	Total
No. present in 1958	39	44	25	108
No. missing in 1969	6	9	6	21
Rate per 1000 p.a. (11 yrs.)	13.9	18.6	21.8	17.6

Another method sometimes employed by demographers when mortality data is lacking, is to analyse the number of marriages broken by the death of husband or wife.[21] Unfortunately I was unable to ascertain in all cases whether a person had married again because the first spouse had died, or after divorce. Therefore I cannot provide concrete statistics on this problem. The general impression from the census, however, is that the majority of people were still on their first marriage and that few marriages had been broken by the death of a spouse. When widowhood occurred, it was usually late in life. Thus no marriages of women aged under 55 in 1969 had been broken by the death of a husband.

In the census of Thak, informants were asked to state the age of both their parents at death, as well as those of their spouse, and how long ago the death had occurred. Since roughly three-quarters of the households had a man and wife as heads of household, this should have produced the age at death of some 500 to 600 adults (given the fact that parents overlapped between different families in the village). Often, however, one of the partners was absent and the other one knew nothing about his or her absent partner's parent. Sometimes an informant could not hazard a guess at his or her own parent's age at death. I was able to ascertain the age at death of some 153 parents, and these may be seen analysed in table 14.6. There is no reason to think that the ages are biased in any particular way, except that there was 'heaping' at the deccenial points. Occasionally informants said that their parents were 'about 60' etc. at death. Informants usually knew how many years ago the death occurred.

A number of interesting conclusions emerge from table 14.6. Above all, it shows the great change that appears to have occurred in recent years. If we look at the Gurung males, then we see that during the period 0–9 years ago, only $\frac{1}{15}$ deaths have been of men aged under 60, whereas among these who died 20+ years ago, $\frac{20}{33}$ died aged under 60. Those who died during the 10–19 years ago period are between these two extremes. Thus it appears that Gurung men are now living longer. If we compare Gurungs with service castes, although an equal proportion of each reached the age of 60, Gurungs then seemed to survive into the seventies and eighties in a larger number of cases.

If we turn to females we will see the same features, if anything more pronounced. During the period 0–9 years ago, $\frac{8}{11}$ Gurung parents died at the age of 70 or over, while in the period 20+ years ago only $\frac{3}{24}$ are reported to have died at 70 or over. In the period before 1960, there was a very high mortality of women aged under 50. Some $\frac{21}{39}$ of the women who died before 1960 were aged under 50, whereas in the period 0–9 years ago only $\frac{1}{11}$ was under 50. If the earlier pattern is associated with the female disorders related to the menopause, it is difficult to see why there should have been such

TABLE 14.6 *Parental age at death in Thak*

	Male					
	Years ago (Gurung)					
Age at death	0–9	10–19	20 +	Unknown	Service caste[a]	Total
To 40	–	–	3	–	1	4
40–49	–	4	8	–	4	16
50–59	1	4	9	2	–	16
60–69	4	5	5	4	5	23
70–79	5	4	8	–	1	18
80–89	5	1	–	–	1	7
Total	15	18	33	6	12	84

	Female					
	Years ago (Gurung)					
Age at death	0–9	10–19	20 +	Unknown	Service caste	Total
To 40	–	–	3	1	1	5
40–49	1	7	11	–	4	23
50–59	1	3	4	3	1	12
60–69	1	3	3	2	4	13
70–79	4	2	2	–	2	10
80–89	4	–	1	1	–	6
Total	11	15	24	7	12	69

[a] All dates.

a considerable change during the last few years. The fact that caste women tend to show a better survival than Gurung women is largely explained by the relative age of the two groups; most of the caste deaths about which we have information have occurred during the last fifteen years and this seems to have been the period when health has improved.

The table also tends to corroborate earlier suggestions that mortality of men and women during the earlier years of marriage is low. Of the 139 Gurung parents whose age at death we know, only 7 were aged under 40. Only a very few Gurungs lost either parent when they were still young, a fact that distinguishes them from many other societies with higher mortality rates. The 3 male parents who died young were aged 30, 34, and about 36; the four females, only one of whom was said to have died in childbirth, were aged 20, 25, 28, 30. That only $\frac{4}{57}$ mothers whose age at death we know should have died under the age of 40 does suggest that the maternal mortality rate is not high. At present the highest mortality rates for both men and women are over the age of 70; in the past the peak for women appears to have been 40–9 and for men 50–9.

We may briefly restate the main findings, tentative as they must be. Firstly, there appears to have been a considerable decline in all mortality rates, except of the very old, during the last ten or fifteen years. Secondly, the pattern for two Gurung villages, Thak and Mohoriya, appears fairly similar. Thirdly, there appears to be no obvious difference between the experience of sub-groups, stratified either by wealth or caste. Fourthly, the Gurungs appear to have lower mortality rates than many of the other groups living elsewhere in Nepal. This offsets their slightly lower fertility rates.

15
The age and sex structure of the Gurung population

The previously analysed patterns of fertility and mortality plus migration result in a specific age and sex structure for the Gurung population. This structure, for example the number of men or women of a certian age present in the region, will, as we have seen, influence patterns of production and consumption. Thus the age/sex structure is the mediator between demographic trends and the current economic and social situation in a community. Analysis of such structures is particularly important in societies, such as the Gurungs, where we have no registration of births and deaths and little information about past fluctuations in population. There are a number of problems, however, in even the simplest analysis of sex and age structures. Often it is impossible to obtain accurate ages in non-literate societies, but this problem is absent among the Gurungs because everyone knows the year in which he was born in a twelve-year cycle of years or '*lho*'.[1] The Gurungs' exceptional nature in this respect makes a thorough analysis of demographic structure all the more worthwhile. Nevertheless there is still some inaccuracy concerning very young children. In the ensuing tables and graphs, children aged up to one year are probably under-represented, partly because of the omission of very young infants which characterizes many non-literate societies, partly because of the difficulties of interpreting the *lho* system. This defect, however, is unlikely to affect the first five-year age group of young children as a whole, or later ages, to any significant extent. Another difficulty is whether to count those temporarily absent in the army or elsewhere as part of a Gurung village or not; in other words whether to analyse the *de jure* or *de facto* structure. For certain purposes their existence is the significant fact, for instance when we work out the total productive assets of the village, either economic or demographic, whereas for other analyses, as in the way in which the land is worked and the supply of labour, it is their absence or non-existence that is important. For this reason it is necessary to give an analysis of both *de jure* and *de facto* populations.

For purposes of analysis we will divide the discussion into 'age structure' and 'sex structure' although, in fact, the two are too interlinked to be really divisible. We may also adopt an over-simple, but useful, classification of age-structures originally suggested by Sundbarg and summarized as follows: 'He identified three types of population: (*a*) *progressive*, having a high proportion of children and a high rate of growth; (*b*) *stationary*, having moderate proportions of children and aged persons with slow growth or stationary numbers; (*c*) *regressive*, having a high proportion of aged persons and declining number'.[2] Most non-industrial societies exhibit pattern (*a*) in having a high proportion of children, but not necessarily in having a high growth rate. It will be one of the tasks of this chapter to see to what extent the Gurungs fit into this simple model, and to see how their age and sex structure differs from other technologically comparable societies. In the final section there will be a brief discussion of the other crucial demographic variable, migration.

AGE STRUCTURE

The stated ages of the members of 100 households in Thak, 1969, are shown in pictorial form as part of Fig. 15.1. The first, and most general, point, is that the shape of the diagram is half-way between the 'ideal-type' shape of pre- and post-industrial populations. It lacks the wide base and very sharply tapering pyramid of a rapidly expanding population, or the bell-shape of some modern Western countries such as Sweden.[3] Another way to illustrate this intermediate position is to look at the proportion of the total population in various age-groups. It is characteristic of many developing countries that up to 50 % of the population is aged under twenty; thus Ceylon in 1955 had 50.4 % of its population under this age. On the other hand, so-called 'developed' countries characteristically have 20–30 % of their population under this age; thus England and Wales in 1958 had 29 %, whereas in 1821 it had had 49 %.[4] Of the total 386 Gurungs in Thak, some 153 or 39.64 % were aged under 20. This is almost exactly half-way between England and Ceylon. If we turn to the non-Gurungs, however, we find that $\frac{71}{142}$, or exactly 50 % were aged 19 or less. The latter figure is much closer to the national average for Nepal; for example, in 1969 the proportion under 20 in the Kaski district as a whole, in which Thak is situated, was 48.87 %.[5] For Nepal as a whole it was 50 %.[6]

Another way of analysing the data makes it possible to work out the proportion of the population who are too young or too old to be maximum economic producers. We may compare the figures to those for two other societies, a tribal group in Africa, and a Western society. (See table 15.1.) It will be seen that the Gurungs on their own have a pattern which is nearest to that for Sweden, with less young people, over 50 % in the range 15–49, and a considerable number of people aged over 50. As far as economic productivity is concerned, this would appear to be a reasonably favourable balance.

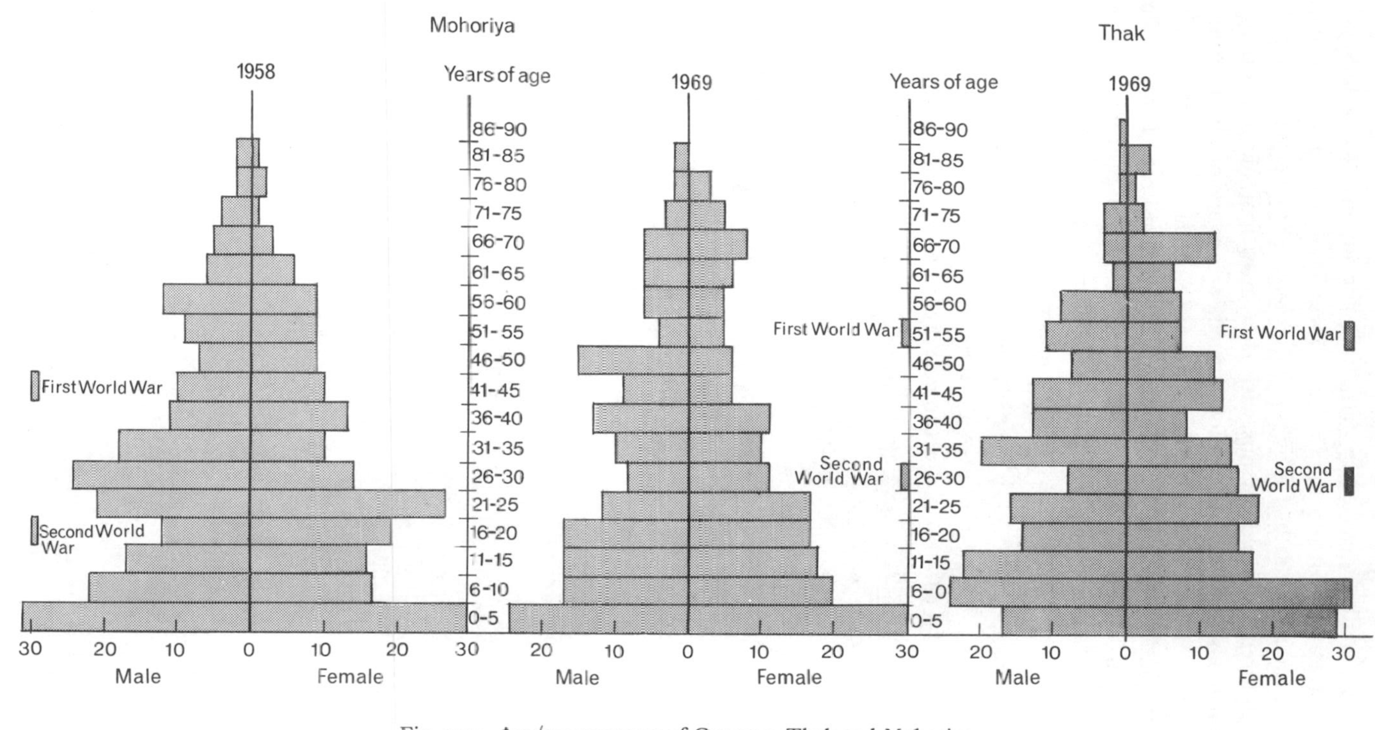

Fig. 15.1. Age/sex structure of Gurungs, Thak and Mohoriya.

TABLE 15.1 *Thak and other groups compared: Sundbarg's age-divisions*

Group	Year	Youth, 0–15	Middle age 15–49	Old age over 50
Thak, total	1969	33.7	49.4	16.9
Thak (Gurungs only)	1969	31.4	50.3	18.4
Yao (with absentees)	1946	42.6	47.4	10.0
Sweden	1940	20.4	54.8	24.6

Note: The figures for Yao and Sweden and the general layout of the table are taken from J. C. Mitchell, 'An Estimate of Yao Fertility' *Africa*, xix (1949), no. 4, p. 301.

It could be objected that an analysis based on only one (very small) sample is not very convincing and that we need to know whether the Thak age structure is typical of the Gurungs. Fortunately we have figures for another Gurung village, Mohoriya, in a different valley, obtained at two points in time, in 1958 and 1969. The age–sex structure of that village at these two dates and that of Thak in 1969 are shown in Fig. 15.1. There are considerable differences between the three pyramids. If we look at those in the 0–5 year age-group we find a much smaller proportion in Thak than in Mohoriya. This may be related to the fact that there seem to have been less males born in Thak during the Second World War than in Mohoriya. If we look at the diagrams as a whole their shape is very alike, neither particularly steeply graduated nor having the characteristic 'bell-like' shape of an ageing population. The situation in the two villages in 1969 is particularly alike; nor is it possible to see a very great change over time in the single village of Mohoriya. Particular features have undoubtedly changed. Thus the large number of girls aged 21–5 in the earlier census has disappeared by the later date, presumably through marrying out of the village since, as we have seen, maternal mortality is not high among the Gurungs. It is possible, however, to note one major change; the latter pyramid is getting steeper, the bulge at middle age of earlier days is disappearing, and one is perhaps moving towards a situation of increasing youth-dependence. To investigate this and other differences further we need to break the diagrams down into figures.

In table 15.2 we compare the proportion of Gurungs in three age categories. The most striking similarity is in the proportion aged 51 + years; all three fall within an amazingly narrow range. There is also considerable similarity between the situation in Thak in 1969, and that in Mohoriya in 1958. Between 1958 and 1969 however, the situation in Mohoriya changed considerably and the ratio of those 0–15:16–50 changed from 32:50 to 36:46. It is probable that the reason for this change was the migration of a number of Gurung families, containing a larger than average number of young adults, down to

TABLE 15.2 *Percentage of Gurungs in three age categories*

Place, year	% aged 0–15	16–50	51 +
Thak, 1969	33.7	48.4	17.9
Mohoriya, 1958	32.5	50.1	17.4
Mohoriya, 1969	36.1	46.4	17.5

newly-opened lands in South Nepal. This migration will be discussed later in the chapter. Allowing for such migration, the situation in Thak appears to be normal, unless the Gurungs in Mohoriya are also, for some reason, exceptional.

The Gurungs themselves are divided into two strata or *jats* as we have seen in an earlier chapter. The *carjat*, who are normally wealthier, probably arrived earlier in Thak and Mohoriya than the *sorajat* and we might therefore expect there to be a difference in their respective age-structures, with more old people among the former. That this is, in fact, so may be seen from table 15.3. While the proportion aged 16–50 is almost identical, the *sorajat* have a considerably higher proportion of young members and fewer old people. We have seen that this cannot be accounted for by higher mortality rates amoung the *sorajat*, nor is it due to different emigration rates. It must therefore be due to differences in immigration or fertility. For example a larger number of *sorajat* households have come into the village fairly recently and have not had time to grow old.

Table 15.1, where Gurungs and all those living in Thak were compared, has already suggested that Gurungs and non-Gurungs in Thak exhibit different age-structures. This can be seen more precisely in table 15.4. By 'Non-Gurungs' in this context we are, in fact, largely talking about Blacksmith and Tailor castes who represent $\frac{18}{23}$ of the families involved. The most striking fact about these predominantly lower caste families is that here, for the first time,

TABLE 15.3 *Percentage of Gurungs of the two* jats *in each age group, Thak, 1969*

Jat	% aged 0–15	16–50	51 +	Total persons
Sorajat	39	48.3	12.7	118
Carjat	31.3	48.5	20.1	268

TABLE 15.4 *Percentage of Gurungs and non-Gurungs in each age group, Thak, 1969*

	% aged 0–15	16–50	51 +	Total persons
Gurungs	33.7	48.4	17.9	386
Non-Gurungs	44.4	43.7	11.9	142

we find a higher proportion aged 0–15 than 16–50. Thus the economically weakest group, who own little land, also have to support a higher child-dependency ratio. However, if we break down the figures still further we find that the situation is more complex than this; the Tailors have only 34.2 % of their members aged under 16, which is similar to the Gurungs, whereas the Blacksmiths have 45.8 % of their members aged under 16 and the same percentage aged 16–50. Unfortunately, we are beginning to get into such small numbers with these sub-groups that very small fluctuations can make a huge percentage difference. If we turn to Mohoriya in 1969, the situation of non-Gurungs can be seen in Fig. 15.2, which shows the large proportion aged under 16 and the rapidly narrowing pyramid characteristic of a group whose population is increasing fast. I am unable to explain the curious difference between the males and females under ten years of age; the numbers are so small that it could be due to chance.

Finally, we may look at Fig. 15.1 again to see whether it provides any evidence concerning particular features of mortality or fertility in the past. This is an extremely complicated operation since a bulge or gap in certain age groups may as easily represent features of the fertility history of a previous generation as a certain mortality pattern at the time of the bulge/gap. Another complication, that of in-marrying girls from other villages adding

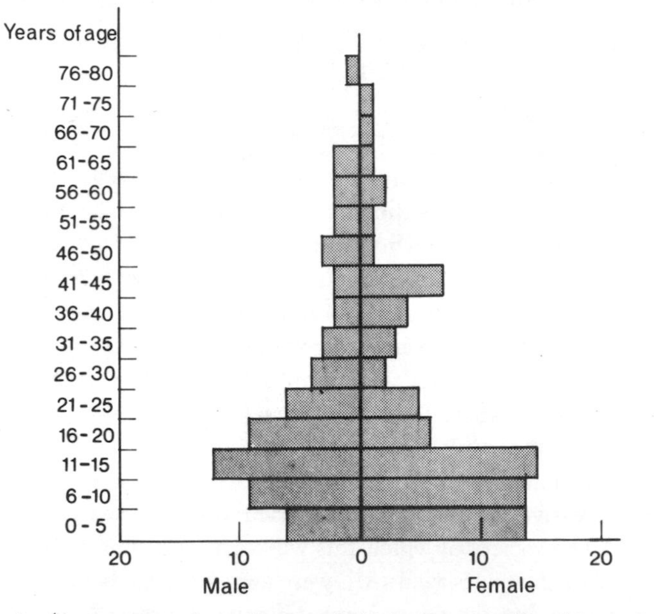

Fig. 15.2. Age/sex structure of non-Gurungs in Mohoriya, 1969 (Pun Magars have not been included here, but under Gurungs).

to the female side of the diagrams from the age of 20 on, means that over that age we have to restrict ourselves to males only. The diagrams show when the First and Second World Wars occurred, both in relation to people being born and to those aged 20–5 at the time (the fit is only approximate since the wars did not exactly overlap with the five-year age-groupings). It is noticeable that in all three groupings, during both wars, there is a considerable indentation in the male births during the war (except in Thak for the First World War). It is hardly likely that all these cases can be accounted for by a shortage of young males or females in the previous generation and indeed we can see that this is not so in several cases. Therefore it seems that we can accept the suggestion made by Pignède that the mass exodus of men during the Wars led to a low number of conceptions in certain villages.[7]

If we assume that those aged 20–5 at the time were the most likely to be killed during the wars we may test the effect of war-time mortality on the male age structure. The diagrams do not show any striking correlation, though there may be slight traces of a relationship in the Mohoriya, 1958, diagram. For Thak there seems no obvious effect, a fact which fits well with previous analysis of causes of death which showed that deaths during war have not been a major cause of mortality, and were, in any case, spread out over men aged 20–40.

Although the evidence is not conclusive, there is no obvious sign of a really serious epidemic or famine in the past in either village. This negative suggestion is corroborated by villager's statements in Thak and by the previous analysis of the actual dates when deaths occurred.

SEX-RATIO

The question of sex-ratio must be divided into two when speaking of a people such as the Gurungs where there is very considerable labour migration. There is the sex-ratio of all those who are *de jure* members of a Gurung community, and there is the ratio of those actually (*de facto*) living in such a community at a point in time. Both are important facts, and may influence many other features of social life, for example age and economic transactions at marriage, relations between the sexes, the organization of labour. It has been suggested of another society where the males migrate to work that 'the abnormally low masculinity of the adult Reserve population, which is mainly the result of labour migration, is conducive to problems such as adultery, prostitution and the excessive dependence of married women on their matrilineal male relatives'.[8] The society of which this was written was one where between 46.8 and 69.3 % of the males aged 18 + were away on wage labour.[9] This is remarkably similar to the figure in many Gurung villages. When Pignède visited one such village, some 62 % of the men aged 19 to 45 were away from the village on wage labour in the army or elsewhere.[10] We may wonder, therefore, how the situation with regard to morals and economics compares to that in other migrant labour situations.

Pignède found that when he visited Mohoriya there were more males than females (220:198) if all those temporarily absent were counted in. He then goes on to argue that this is a general phenomenon in Gurung villages: 'In all the villages one encounters more men than women in the under 65 age group' and 'I have noted this fact in all Gurung territory'. Having decided that this is so, he suggested possible reasons; 'It seems that infant mortality among girls is higher than among boys. But above all, women die in childbirth'.[11] Impressions, however, are not the same as censuses and it is fatal to generalize from too small a sample. The ratio I discovered among Gurungs when in Thak and re-visiting Mohoriya is shown in table 15.5. It will be seen that in both villages, both in those aged under 65 and in all ages combined, females outnumbered males. Thus, if Pignède had visited his village ten years later he would have come to a different conclusion. It has earlier been argued that maternal mortality is relatively low among the Gurungs and the above figures support this conclusion rather than Pignède's arguments about high female mortality. In fact the ratio of females to males may be *higher* in Gurung villages than in Nepal as a whole, where in 1954 it was calculated that there were 99 females to 100 males.[12] Until we have more studies it would be foolish to generalize from a sample almost as inadequate as Pignède's.

TEMPORARY MIGRATION

From before the beginning of the present century, but more intensively since the First World War, the Gurungs have been a society based on migrant labour. Almost all those leaving the village have enlisted in the British or, since partition, Indian armies and they serve between three and twenty-five years (normally between ten and fifteen) in India or the Far East. The proportion of Gurungs in Thak in 1969 who had spent a year or more in the army (including police, and civilian work at army camps)[13] is shown in Fig. 15.3. It will be seen that a majority in each five-year period from 21 to 55 have been in the army. Of 109 Gurung men in Thak aged 21 or over, some 74 (67.9 %) are, or

TABLE 15.5 *Sex-ratio of Gurungs in two villages*

	Aged to 65		All ages	
	Male	Female	Male	Female
Thak, 1969	177	182	186	200
Mohoriya, 1969	158	162	171	178

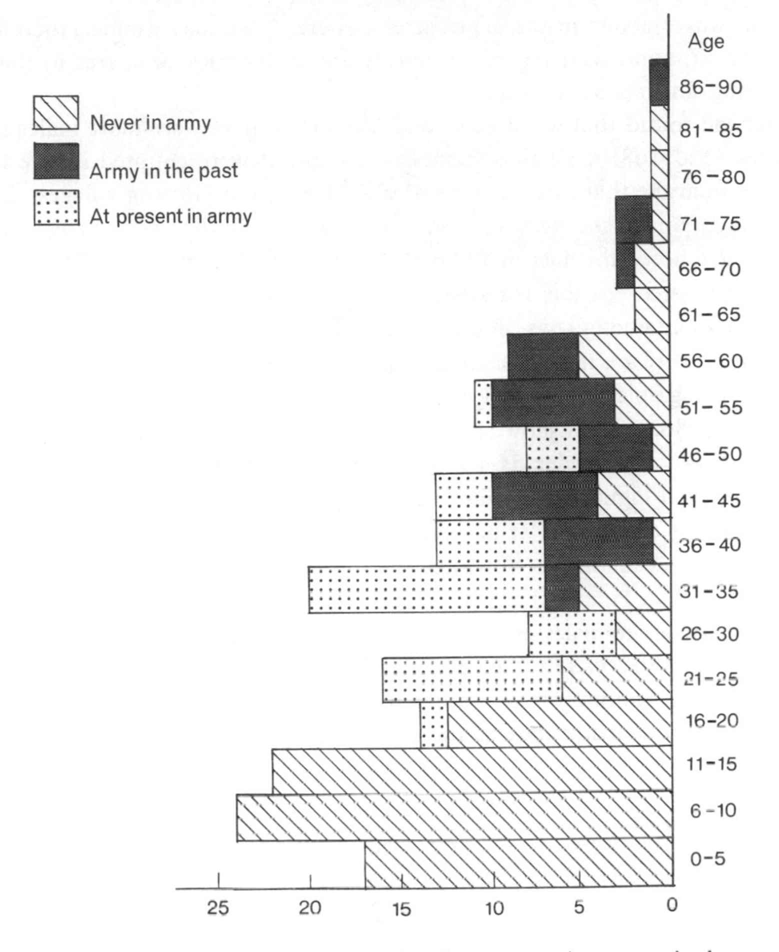

Fig. 15.3. Proportion of Gurung men undergoing army service, now or in the past, Thak, 1969.

have been, in the army. The diagram distinguishes past and present service, and shows that in 1969, of 57 men aged 21–40, some 34 or 59.6 % were serving in the army. Another eight had already completed a spell of army service. The effect of the absence of up to 60 % of the males at the peak of their productive labour on village agriculture has already been discussed. As Pignède rightly emphasized, we are looking at a society 'in demographic disequilibrium, composed of children, women, old people and a small number of men aged over 30 years'.[14] Thus he found that in Mohoriya, $\frac{20}{24}$ of the young men aged between 19 and 25 (Gurungs only) were soldiers.

The effect of this on the sex ratio is demonstrated in Fig. 15.4. The lop-sided

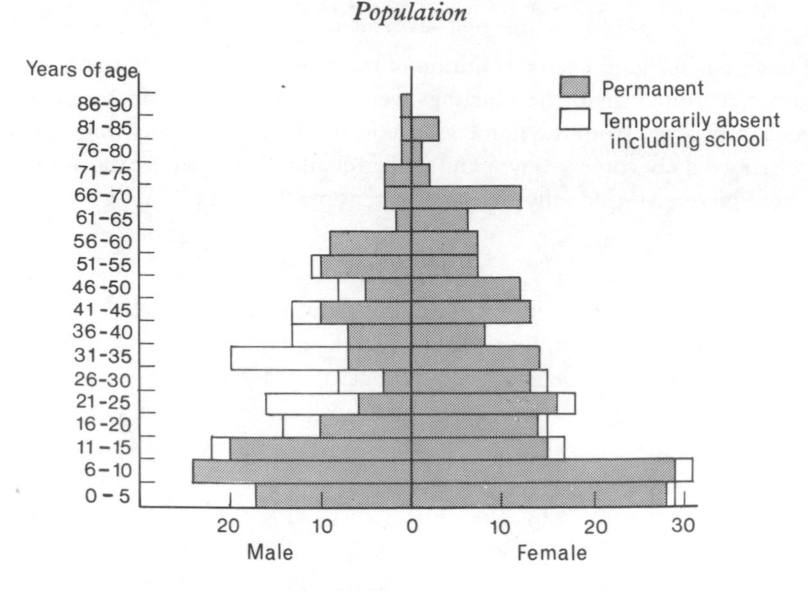

Fig. 15.4. Age/sex structure of Gurungs present full-time in Thak, 1969.

figure which emerges if we only count those actually present full-time in Thak is easily seen. The result was that there were 139:191 males to females permanently in the village, and in the important economic group 21–50 there were 38:76, or exactly two females for every male. In the earlier discussion of labour requirements we have seen how young men from the untouchable castes, particularly Blacksmiths and Tailors, replace this absent labour force. Thus of a total labour force of 67 males aged 16–45 in Thak, some 24, or just over one-third, were lower caste. The 39 absent Gurungs, earning relatively high wages in the army, were replaced by some 24 lower caste men aged 16–45.

It is likely, however, that the pattern is beginning to change, and traces of this may be seen in the age-group 21–5 in Thak, 1969. Some $\frac{6}{16}$ of the males in this age-group were unable to obtain a military job, although most of them wanted to do so. The British army has been drastically cutting down its recruitment of Gurkhas and it is quite possible that the Indian army will do likewise. The problem now and in the future will probably not be labour shortage and imbalance in the sex-ratio, but labour surplus and too many males in the village. The effect on village life and attitudes will have to be dealt with elsewhere. It will, for example, be necessary to explain why, while one anthropologist has described another society where there is extensive male labour migration as accompanied by 'an atmosphere of decay and frustration... granaries and huts (are) neglected, the women lustreless, the gardens poor',[15] the same has not happened in Thak. On the contrary the women are cheerful and the men scarcely seem to be missed. One reason for this could well be that there has for long been a tradition of male labour migration. Even before the army recruited men, the Gurungs were traders and herdsmen and were consequently away from the home village for long periods. Thus wage labour in the army did not come as a new and sudden change; furthermore the numbers recruited increased gradually over half a century.[16]

PERMANENT MIGRATION

In the past the Gurungs were to a certain extent nomadic hunters, and there is still considerable geographical mobility as population pressure builds up in the older-established settlements. Both Thak and Mohoriya saw a very considerable influx of settlers during the nineteenth century and early twentieth century, and their arrival is analysed below.[17] Here we will deal briefly with migration out of these villages in recent years. In Thak there has been scarcely any permanent emigration during recent years, at least in the sample census area. One soldier, instead of retiring to the village, remained near Bhairuwa, and one woman has set up a boarding house in Pokhara. Yet there is very little evidence of the sometimes widespread tendency not to return to the village after military service. Nor was there any migration from Thak when free land was offered near Chitwan in the early 1960s (after the malaria eradication compaign). While other villages in the same valley were affected, for example Siklis is said to have had an exodus of at least one hundred persons, pressure in Thak was not great enough to force people to move.

In Mohoriya, however, the man–resources ratio was much worse even when Pignède visited it, and in between his visit in 1958 and my census in 1969 members of 16 households had disappeared, all but three of them to near Chitwan, the other three to India. Some 78 persons left the village, out of a total population of 496 or some 15.7 % of the census population. The majority of the families were of the poorer *sorajat*. Four were upper *jat* and there was one Gharti and one Brahmin. The *jat* of those who left, as well as the size of the houses that still stand, once occupied by them, suggest, not surprisingly, that it was poorer villagers who left to take advantage of the new land. In the case of the *konme* families (3), however, the husbands were in the army and may have found life in India attractive. The sexes were not equally represented; 48 of the 78 who emigrated were men. Although there are exceptions, more than half of the emigrating families consisted of young married couples with one or two children, classic 'settler' material. In several cases it was stated that subsequently the emigrants had had large families, having left the village with only one or two children.

16

Resources and population: some general models

The population of Nepal has more than trebled in the years between 1850 and 1960, from a base of between three and four million. It is predicted that it will reach a total of about 25 million by the year 2000. This growth has occurred despite the absence of significant medical improvements before 1960.* It appears that the Gurungs have also trebled in numbers during the last century, but in some villages the growth has been much greater. In Mohoriya, for instance, there was an eight-fold increase during the hundred years after 1850. Between 1961 and 1971, according to the censuses for those years, the population of Thak has increased by 40 %. At this rate there would be a doubling of the population every twenty years. This seems to be a more rapid growth than in the period up to 1960. Characteristically the Gurungs appear to have population rates which are somewhat lower than those for Nepal and Asian societies as a whole. While the Crude Birth Rate for Nepal is probably about 50 per 1000, that for the Gurungs is below 40 per 1000. The completed family size for Nepal as a whole is probably six children or more; that for the sample villages is approximately 5.5. Turning to mortality, while the Crude Death Rate for Nepal is between 27 and 32 per 100, that for the sample communities is under 20 per 1000. Likewise, infant mortality is substantially lower among the Gurungs. While about half of the Nepalese population taken together die before they reach the age of 20, in Thak less than one-third of the Gurungs die before that age. The vital rates are reflected in their age and sex structure which is intermediate between that typical for slow-growing Western nations and the steeply tapering pyramid often found in rapidly expanding populations.

There are strong reasons for believing that the Gurung population will grow faster in the future, replacing a rate which has led to a trebling every century by one in which a ten-fold increase each century would occur. This can be seen from the numbers of houses being built in the central part of Thak. If the trend of the last twenty years was projected into the future, there would be 1600 households by the year 2100, in an area which supported less than 50 in 1920. Moderate population growth has occurred without medical change, but it is public health measures which are turning this moderate growth into a rapid rise. Water-borne diseases, particularly those associated with faecal matter, such as dysentery, gastro-enteritis and typhoid, are the main causes of death among the Gurungs, as well as tuberculosis. Both types of mortality are likely to decline rapidly in the next few years under the impact of improved water supplies and the B.C.G. campaign. The mortality rate could be cut in half in a decade. Epidemic disease, unimportant in the recent past among the Gurungs, can be kept at bay by inoculation campaigns. It is difficult to see how fertility will be lowered to counterbalance this reduction. The Gurungs maintain moderately high fertility despite the absence of many adult males in India and Malaya and despite an age at marriage which is several years higher than for Nepal as a whole. There are no signs that contraception will be practised on a scale sufficient to influence fertility. Traditionally, contraception has not been used among the Gurungs and despite considerable advertising by the government there is no indication from the work I carried out that birth-control methods will be widely used for a number of years to come.

It seems clear that the population growth of the last hundred years has had enormous effects on their economy and social structure. For many centuries the Gurungs were wandering bands of shepherds who also practised hunting and a certain amount of slash and burn agriculture. By the middle of the nineteenth century they were also traders over the mountain passes to the north and beginning to be famed as army recruits. During the following century, population pressure forced them to establish villages lower down the slopes, where wet rice could be grown, but herds and flocks could no longer be grazed. They now have permanent fields which they plough instead of hoeing. Although they still provide a dwindling number of army recruits, the other occupations have virtually ceased in many villages. The agricultural technology remains extremely simple and labour intensive on the mountainous rocky slopes, yet there are increasing signs of a transition from a society where there was a surplus of land and other resources and a shortage of human labour, to the reverse situation. Yet the Gurungs are still fortunate in relation to the rest of the Nepalese. In Thak, there was nearly one hectare of all types of land per man engaged in agriculture, compared to an average of just over one-third of a hectare for the Western Hills as a whole; there are 0.64 acres *per capita* of cultivated arable land, as opposed to an average of only 0.18 acres *per capita* in the Western Hills generally. Likewise, the forest in Thak is renowned for its luxuriance and size. The relative affluence can be seen in their housing, personal possessions, clothing and diet. This analysis has not focused on an extreme case, but rather on a village which is relatively affluent by Nepalese standards.

It is difficult to be certain, but it would appear that population growth is now pressing on natural resources even in this community. An obvious index are the forests. The woods in Thak will be destroyed over the next generation. There is not enough to supply the demand, not only for 620 kg of wood per person per year for fuel, but the 3000 kg of vegetation per year which each individual consumes through his livestock. A 2 % p.a. population growth, which is probably the current rate, would mean that in the year 1969–70, the hundred sample households in Thak required an extra 6000 kg of wood and 30,000 kg of vegetation just to maintain present standards. As the vegetation is crucial in order to produce manure as well as milk and meat, it seems likely that there will be a deterioration in diet, the familiar change from high-protein to carbohydrate foods. There is also likely to be growing under-employment. The Gurungs have succeeded in producing all their major foodstuffs on extraordinarily difficult terrain, using few tools and with a large proportion of the adult males absent. An examination of labour input suggests that just over 4 months work at 6 hours a day would be enough to grow and process all the crops in Thak.[9] There is already considerable 'leisure'. It is possible that the introduction of new agricultural methods, especially artificial fertilizer and high-yield grains, could increase the labour demand. At present population growth rates this would only put off the problem of widescale unemployment for a few years. The first to suffer from growing unemployment will be the lower castes whose labour replaces the absent Gurung males.

It is also likely that cash will grow scarcer. At present, in Thak, three-quarters of the income of the villagers is from the army, either in pay or pensions. Very little village produce is sold. Without army pay there would only be an average of about 70 rs. per household for cash purchases instead of the present 460 rs. Yet the British army is drastically cutting back recruitment and the Indian army may follow suit. Neither army is likely to be able to double the present number of recruits every thirty years. Those males unable to find service abroad will not find new lands to open up in the *panchayat*. The supply of unused land which was suitable for rice ran out in the 1930s, that suitable for maize or millet was almost all allocated by the mid 1960s. It is possible that a little more land could be squeezed from the hills and that increased use could be made by double cropping. It is unlikely that such additions would do more than compensate for the annual deterioration in the quality of the resources.

All guesses about the future of Thak, for the Gurungs generally, or for Nepal as a whole, depend on so many political and other variables that they can have little predictive value. Furthermore, the implications of the data on resources and population which has been examined in the previous pages will depend entirely on the underlying models of the interrelation between economics and demography which we choose to apply. General theories as to why population continues to grow will influence any predictions as to what is likely to occur in Nepal. It is therefore necessary to make explicit the possible population models to which the Gurung data can be compared. It is also necessary to examine demographic theory if we wish to answer two particular queries which arise out of the data for central Nepal. Firstly, population is known to have grown fairly rapidly well before the arrival of any medical or sanitary improvements. The frequently repeated assertions that the 'population explosion' is the result of technological changes in medical and para-medical services does not fit. Secondly, population grew despite an absence of any obvious resource expansion, caused either by technical improvements in farming or the chance discovery of a particular resource. Thus it would seem that the argument that population rises as a response to resource growth is of little relevance here. It becomes necessary to re-examine conventional theories relating to population and resources and to modify these in order to accommodate the Gurung and Nepalese data.

One major hypothesis concerning the interrelation between resources and population is represented by the work of Malthus. As somewhat over-simplified by his critics, Malthus' position appears to be a variety of Parkinson's Law: population expands to absorb the food resources available, and a little bit over. Certainly this is *one* of the arguments put forward by Malthus. He stated that 'population has this constant tendency to increase beyond the means of subsistence'.[1] He also argued that 'population invariably increases when the means of subsistence increase', unless halted by one of the three 'preventive checks' of moral restraint, vice or misery.[2] Furthermore, he did see the chain of causation to be one which led from physical resources, particularly food, to population. Thus he wrote that 'agriculture may with more propriety be termed the efficient cause of population, than population of agriculture . . .' Yet the determinism is not as simple as it may seem, for he continues the passage by stating that 'they certainly re-act upon each other, and are mutually necessary to each other's support'.[3] Malthus did not merely see population growth as a reaction to increases in food production, it had a momentum of its own. Thus he wrote:

> We will suppose the means of subsistence in any country just equal to the easy support of its inhabitants. The constant effort towards population, which is found to act even in the most vicious societies, increases the number of people before the means of subsistence are increased. The food, therefore, which before supported eleven millions, must now be divided among eleven millions and a half.[4]

To this extent population growth is an independent variable. But what Malthus is unwilling to concede is that such growth will *necessarily* have beneficial effects on agriculture. Since his argument on this subject anticipates the major counter-thesis put forward since his time, it is worth quoting the passage in full. He writes:

> That an increase of population, when it follows in its natural order, is both a great positive good in itself, and absolutely necessary to a further increase in the annual produce of the land and labour of any country, I should be the last to deny. The only question is, what is the order of its progress? In this point Sir James Steuart . . . appears to me to have fallen into an error. He determines, that multiplication is the efficient cause of agriculture, and not agriculture of multiplication. But though it may be allowed, that the increase of people, beyond what could easily subsist on the natural fruits of the earth, first prompted man to till the ground; and that the view of maintaining a family, or of obtaining some valuable consideration in exchange for the products of agriculture, still operates as the principal stimulus to cultivation ... We know, that a multiplication of births has in numberless instances taken place which has produced no effect upon agriculture, and has merely been followed by an increase of diseases; but perhaps there is no instance where a permanent increase of agriculture has not effected a permanent increase of population somewhere or other.[5]

Here Malthus agrees with those who argue that population growth stimulates agricultural growth. He goes on to say, however, that there is no inevitability about this causal chain. Population *may* grow autonomously *without* leading to agricultural growth. If so, there will be disaster. We will see that Malthus is fairly close to his later critics in this view. He also shares their basic psychological premise concerning man, namely that he is lazy and uninventive, or, put in another way, that he places leisure above every other good. Thus Malthus speaks of 'the natural indolence of man' and argues that 'A state of sloth, and not of restlessness and activity, seems evidently to be the natural state of man'.[6]

Malthus' four main propositions can conveniently be summarized as follows.

A. Population growth *sometimes* leads to agricultural growth.
B. Resource growth *always* leads to population growth (though he later qualified this).
C. Population will always grow, unless curbed by moral restraint, vice or misery.
D. Population grows geometrically (exponentially), resources grow arithmetically.

There are a number of major criticisms that can be made of these propositions, some of which are based on evidence which has been accumulated since Malthus wrote. There is little disagreement with Proposition A, indeed it is the central tenet, in a strengthened form, of those who criticize him most forcefully. The second proposition can be shown to be invalid as a universal generalization, even though many agricultural historians would agree with Slicher van Bath that 'In an agricultural society, favourable economic conditions almost inevitably lead to an increase of population'.[7] It is ironic that it is English history, in the century before his birth, that provides one of the best negative examples to this thesis. It is generally agreed that between about 1650 and 1730 the population of England remained static, despite considerable improvements in agriculture and communications and hence a growing gross national product and per capita income.[8] Increased wages 'instead of occasioning an increase of population exclusively, were so expended as to occasion a decided elevation in the standard of their comforts and conveniences'.[9] Another type of counter-argument has emerged from the study of what happens after a sudden high mortality. It appears to be a logical extension of Proposition B that if resources become more abundant, then population will grow quickly to absorb them, whatever the cause of resource increase. It would seem to be predicted that if an epidemic or famine significantly reduced population, without destroying the resource base, fertility would increase or expectation of life improve, so that the newly vacant resources would quickly become absorbed. This is found to be the case in certain societies, for example seventeenth century France,[10] but England is again a negative instance. In the high mortality of the 1630s, for example, the crisis was succeeded not by a rapid spate of marriages and births but the reverse.[11] Likewise, after the Black Death in England, population continued to decline for another century. The sum of all this is that Proposition B is false; increased resources do not *always* lead to an immediate expansion of population.

Proposition C is also untrue. Even in the absence of 'vice, misery and moral restraint' population does not necessarily grow. A good example of this negative finding seems to be Tibet, whose population appears to have been declining since it reached its peak between A.D. 600 and 800. There are no obvious ecological or economic reasons to explain this; resources have been plentiful. Social and psychological factors have intervened.[12] Studies of animal behaviour support this negative conclusion. It is impossible to explain fluctuations in animal numbers merely in terms of food resources or to assume that numbers will always rise if there are resources available. Quite the opposite is true.

> All the animal populations which have been the subject of observation have been found to suffer periodic declines in numbers which are not

generally the result of starvation. These declines often continue in successive generations under conditions in which there could be no question of a shortage of food, and yet may result in the near-annihilation of a local population.[13]

It is, of course, just possible to reconcile these findings with Malthus's argument by defining 'vice' and 'moral restraint' very widely so that they include territoriality, the selective neglect of the young and the old, animal migrations, delayed marriage. Restated in this more general way the proposition would be 'Population will always grow unless there are physical or cultural checks which prevent it growing'. Although this appears to be a tautology, it does contain one central and crucial truth, namely, that, unimpeded, population always grows rapidly. If maximum fertility is allowed and there are no checks, there will be a huge expansion of any population. Given this premise, the problem is to analyse the checks. This would appear to be a more helpful way to look at problems than to assume that populations are normally in equilibrium, loss of which is the problem.

The final proposition concerns the speed of growth; exponential growth of population as opposed to arithmetical growth of food resources. With figures for world population in our mind there is no need to emphasize Malthus' prescience. Technological growth however has made the growth of resources appear to be exponential also. This, for example, is the background to the remark by Gellner that 'one is tempted to invert Malthus and observe that technological advance makes resources grow geometrically, whilst population growth becomes at most arithmetical'.[14] This is one of the cases where changes have occurred since Malthus' time which have made his analysis over-simple. The other enormous change, which in many ways only reinforces his warnings, has been in death control. Public health measures and anti-biotics have added a new element to the debate, especially as they are not necessarily related to social and economic developments of other kinds.[15] Malthus' argument is based on changes in fertility, for this alone was really within the control of man when he wrote. The problem as he envisaged it was that fertility rose to absorb an increase in resources. What he could not have forseen was that there would be huge decreases in the death rate, not only in wealthy countries but in materially poor countries. To take but one example, in Jamaica the deaths per thousand dropped from 26.9 in 1916–20 to 9.5 in 1956, while over the same period the births per thousand *increased* marginally from 36.4 to 37.3.[16] The other major advance since Malthus' day has been in what he would have termed 'vice', namely contraceptive technology. Although, so far, birth control has proved immeasurably weaker than death control, there is a new element in the various equations.

As Malthus stated, the causal chain between population growth and resource growth is the 'hinge' on which the whole argument turns. If he is right, the picture is extremely pessimistic. Although population *may* grow autonomously, it will *certainly* grow as a result of any technological advance. Mankind is trapped; he quotes approvingly the remark that 'distress and poverty multiply in proportion to the funds created to relieve them'.[17] It follows from this position that the only way to break out of the vicious spiral is to control population rather than to increase resources; as he wrote, 'Finding, therefore, that from the laws of nature we could not proportion the food to the population, our next attempt should naturally be to proportion the population to the food'.[18] It is not surprising that such a hypothesis should have many critics. Here we will consider the most powerful of these anti-Malthusian attacks, that put forward most cogently by Boserup[19] and given statistical backing by Clark[20] and historical and anthropological support by Dumond and Wilkinson.[21]

The basic aim of what we shall call the Boserup thesis is to turn Malthus on his head, in other words to return to the position of Sir James Steuart and the eighteenth century agriculturalists. Boserup states that 'population growth is here regarded as the independent variable which in its turn is a major factor determining agricultural developments'.[22] Or, as Clark puts it, 'population increase generally comes first, and then, usually with great reluctance, people adopt technically more efficient methods because they have to provide for the increased population'.[23] As Boserup admits, the historical and anthropological evidence for such a thesis is really too thin to prove that the chain of causation runs one way or the other. She therefore argues from *a priori* grounds as follows.

Proposition A. People prefer leisure to all other goods.

Proposition B. The intensification of production, for example the move from hunting and gathering to swidden cultivation and then from swidden to settled multi-cropping, always brings more work for less rewards.

Proposition C. The only force strong enough to force people to intensify production is increased population.

Proposition D. Since population growth can no longer be explained by growth in resources (since the chain works the other way) some other cause of such growth must be suggested, apart from improved living standards. The suggestion is that this is a purely technical improvement in health due to medical and sanitary developments.

Proposition E. Given the above propositions, population growth is not an evil, indeed it is necessary. For example, it is true to assert, as Boserup does, that 'primitive communities with sustained population growth have a better chance to get into a process of genuine economic development than primitive communities with stagnant or declining population'.[24]

Proposition F. Population growth is not only a *necessary* cause of economic development, it is also implicit that it is a *sufficient* cause. It will, except in exceptional circumstances, trigger off such development. When this supposedly automatic development does not occur it is explained away as a 'special case' rather than dismantling the whole model. For example, Clark cites a number of cases of 'extreme congestion' or 'rural overpopulation' from all over the world and then explains that they 'represent an unhappy by-road from the normal course of economic development'. Yet he remains puzzled and concludes that 'It is hard to give any generalized reason as to why this state of affairs should come about. On the whole we must seek for political and historical rather than for narrowly economic reasons. Historically, some deficiency in the political order often prevented or impeded the development of towns and of commercial activities. . . .'[25] Since it is basically in this last proposition that the emotional appeal of the model lies, we will return to it later.

The assertion that people prefer leisure to all other goods, though echoing Malthus, seems untenable as a universal generalization, as any anthropologist could show. Status and prestige, power, material wealth, merit or other religious rewards, all these and other goods are frequently desired more than leisure. People may be inventive or work harder in pursuit of such goods irrespective of population growth. Once this is accepted, much of the rest of the model evaporates. The second proposition, that the intensification of production always brings more work for less rewards, has a considerable measure of truth. No longer is it possible to assert that the more primitive the means of production, the harder people have to work. For example the !Kung bushmen, who are hunters and gatherers, have been calculated to have a working week that varies from 1.2 to 3.2 working days per adult: Lee concludes that 'hunters may actually enjoy more leisure time per capita than do peoples engaged in other subsistence activities'.[26] But while there is much truth in the proposition, it is not universally valid. Ethnographic evidence can be brought against it, for example Waddell in a detailed study of a New Guinea Society concludes by arguing that there is 'little to suggest that extensive systems are inherently more productive than intensive ones' per unit of labour input.[27] Another complication explains a certain ambivalence in the use of this argument. Boserup and Clark are not merely prepared to accept that economic development automatically leads to less and less productive labour. They hope to show that at a certain point 'cultural and social' development will also occur, which requires growing leisure. Their case would hardly be a strong one if mankind were on a treadmill, working ever harder to feed more mouths. Thus it is necessary for Boserup to argue that 'a period of sustained population growth would first have the effect of lowering output per man-hour in agriculture, but in the long run the effect might be to raise labour productivity in other activities and eventually to raise output per man-hour also in agriculture'.[28] This appears to contradict Proposition B, and the reason why advanced industry should be able to free mankind from drudgery while advanced agriculture can not do so is not made clear.

The third proposition, that the only force strong enough to force people to intensify production is increased population, is linked with Proposition A, the leisure hypothesis, which has already been disputed. Counter-evidence of a historical nature can also be adduced. There is evidence for a considerable 'agricultural revolution' in England during the period 1650–1730, yet this occurred in a period of static population in this country. Surpluses were produced to export and to raise the standard of ostentation of the rich and the standard of living of the middling, *not* merely as a response to threatened starvation. In fact the whole Weber–Tawney thesis of 'acquisitive capitalism' is centred on the attempt to show how certain societies pursue economic growth apparently for its own sake, pushed on by the 'work ethic' beyond customary targets.

Proposition D states that since population growth is not the result of growth in resources, some other external cause must be found and that this is medical improvement in the widest sense. Thus the emphasis is on a decline in mortality rather than, as Malthus argued, a rise in fertility. Although this is not a subject of central importance to Boserup for, as she says, 'our inquiry is concerned with the effects of population changes on agriculture and not with the causes of these population changes',[29] yet it is rather essential that some alternative to agricultural growth as the cause of population growth be offered. Thus Colin Clark saw England's population growth during the late eighteenth century and onwards as due to a fall in mortality owing to the disappearance of plague and in the nineteenth century as due to the elimination of smallpox and discoveries such as anaesthetics.[30] Boserup also assumes that, 'medical invention and some other factors', other than food production, explain population growth.[31] Clark realized that finding such an explanation 'may seem to some trivial or irrelevant. But it is not. Here we find the underlying cause, for better or worse, of the increase in the rate of world population growth which has been going on . . . since the middle of the eighteenth century'.[32] Recent studies of demographic history suggest that Clark's interpretation is over-simple and mostly incorrect. Medical improvement and a decline in the death rate do not seem to have been the causes of population growth. A detailed comparison of two English communities based on the technique of family reconstitution has shown that it was a lowering in the age at marriage and hence a rise in fertility, as Malthus argued, that caused population growth, rather than a decline in mortality.[33] More generally, as we have noted, the data from Nepal and other parts of the world shows that rapid increases in population have often occurred long before any medical improvements can have been effective. Thus Proposition F is also incorrect.

If the previous propositions had been correct, it could be argued, as in Proposition E, that population growth is not an evil, in fact it is a *necessary* cause of economic growth. Since the causal chain has been disputed at every point, the proposition has little force. It is further weakened by a large number of studies which tend to show that population growth makes economic growth more difficult, rather than easier.[34] Having rejected the earlier propositions, it is even more difficult to accept the final proposition, namely that population growth is not only a necessary but also a sufficient cause of economic growth. Although this is not stated to be an iron law by Boserup, her message is essentially optimistic. She argues that 'the scope for additional food production in response to population growth is larger than usually assumed' and dismisses the negative examples that could be brought forward as follows. 'Growing populations may in the past have destroyed more land than they improved, but it makes little sense to project past trends into the future, since we know more and more about methods of land preservation and are able, by means of modern methods, to reclaim much land, which our ancestors have made sterile'.[35] Yet Boserup admits that there is no inevitability of a technological advance occurring after population growth. 'If it is true . . . that certain types of technical change will occur only when a certain density of population has been reached, it of course does not follow, conversely, that this technical change will occur whenever the demographic prerequisite is present.'[36] This nod in the direction of the many great famines which have afflicted most of the great civilizations, India, China, France, has an implicit optimism and belief in 'technology' behind it. This was perhaps understandable in 1965 before Bihar and Sahel and the growing starvation of the last few years.

While the emotional appeal of the Malthusian and counter-Malthusian arguments lies in rigid predictions which are not likely to be true, there is a principle which lies behind both positions which has very great implications for social anthropology. This is that while there is a two-way link between population and agriculture and social structure, population growth is, in itself, an important force for change. This is more explicitly recognized by Boserup and her followers. By asserting that population growth is the independent variable, mainly the result of forces outside the control of individuals, they let loose a chain of causation which is powerful enough to explain much of what anthropologists observe. Population is an independent variable, restructuring the world as we know it, altering institutions and modes of thought inexorably, if practically invisibly. If this is true, then it is patently the concern of the anthropologist. Yet this conception of population growth as the prime-mover lies embedded in Malthus also. We have seen that he admitted the possibility that population growth could occur autonomously. In a sense, expansion of resources does not *cause* population growth, it *permits* it. Such resource growth merely relaxes for a while the vicious controls which normally hold back the operation of this immensely powerful 'natural law'. The 'natural law' of population growth to which he subscribes is that the superfluous fecundity of human beings which arises from the 'passions of mankind', is independent of all human institutions. Population expansion is more powerful than political and social systems; only death, from disease, famine, or war, can hold it in check. Arguing against the Utopian Godwin, Malthus wrote that 'though human institutions appear to be, and indeed often are, the obvious and obtrusive causes of much mischief to society, they are, in reality, light and superficial in comparison with those deeper-seated causes of evil which result from the laws of nature and the passions of mankind'.[37] The accidental amelioration of the environment by expansion of resources only allows such laws to operate to their full. Without committing oneself to a full Malthusian position, it is easy to see that both Malthus and his critics present a strong case for believing that population trends, rather than economic changes, provide a framework for understanding the current world. It certainly appears to justify the method adopted in this treatment of a Nepalese community where population growth has been taken to be the determining variable, while resources and social structure are treated as dependent.

In order to be convincing, however, we do not need merely to know *why* population grows, but also *how* it grows and how it is held in check. We need, therefore, to investigate actual models of population change. The search for such models led to the growth of what has been called 'transition theory', that is an attempt to correlate demographic patterns with the major social transformation since Malthus' day, namely industrialization. The model is a fairly simple one. It divides population situations into three kinds as follows:

1. That in which neither mortality nor natality is under reasonably secure control and where the potential growth is large despite a possible current low rate of increase.
2. That in which, while both natality and mortality are declining, natality decreases at first less rapidly and then more rapidly than mortality, and the population grows until it reaches the third stage;
3. That in which natality and mortality are low and under secure control, and the population is stationary or in a state of insipient decline.[38]

This is illustrated in Fig. 16.1. Superficially such a model seems to fit with historical experience in the West fairly well. It also has the comforting virtue of predicting that all will be well in the end. Furthermore it offers some hope of fitting demographic change with stages of economic and social growth.[39] It goes further in that it also suggests reasons for the changes from stage to stage. These have been summarized as follows:

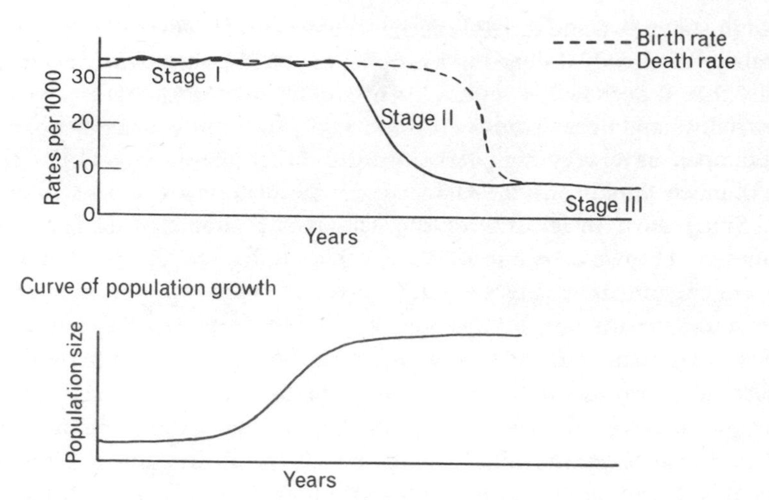

Fig. 16.1. The demographic transition; classic model.

> Transition theory assumes that premodern populations maintain stability of numbers by balancing high, though fluctuating, death rates with high birth rates. As they begin to experience the effects of modernization, improvements in nutritional and health standards reduce mortality while fertility remains high and rapid growth ensues. Later, urbanization and other social changes associated with the more 'mature' stages of industrialism create pressures favoring smaller families, and the birth rate falls, once again approaching balance.[40]

This theory is anti-Malthusian in that population growth is the dependent variable, medical changes and life styles the moving forces.

A number of powerful criticism can and have been made of this model. At the general level it fails to separate causal from descriptive propositions. It generalizes from the historical pattern of population growth followed by western Europe in the past three centuries, but such generalizations, even if they were based on much sounder historical evidence, would not necessarily apply to the rest of the world. Even as a descriptive model, however, recent evidence from a variety of sources casts doubt on its empirical accuracy. Three major criticisms are as follows. Firstly, there is no parallel between Europe before the industrial revolution and the *contemporary* Third World. It appears that fertility in Europe was much lower than in Asia and Africa and that population densities were not as high as in the main paddy areas today. Nor, as we have seen, is it clear that it was a drop in mortality that caused population growth in the late eighteenth century; a rise in fertility may have been just as important. Crucial differences between the West and the contemporary Third

World in stages two and three of the model have become obvious. For example, mortality has already declined in a number of non-Western countries far more rapidly than it declined in western Europe in the nineteenth century. Nor does industrialism and urbanism always bring a drop in fertility; a number of cities, for example, have very high fertility rates.[41]. Yet the stereotype lies at the back of much thinking on the subject and is therefore worth a closer examination. Since most social anthropologists have traditionally worked within societies which would be classified as in 'Stage One', or 'Stage Two', it is at these traditional patterns that we will look.

The major characteristic of 'Stage One' or what we will call 'Traditional' societies, according to the above thesis, is that there is little population growth because of high death rates which cancel out high birth rates. According to Boserup, for example, 'until recently rates of population growth were low or very low in most pre-industrial communities'.[42] The logic behind the argument seems cogent and has been stated by Warren Thompson.

> There is mathematical proof that birth and death rates must have been at about the same level, on the average, throughout most of human history. This proof is quite simple. If population grows steadily at any given rate, even a very low rate, it will double in a given period of time . . . Man has had a high death rate until rather recently because of what Malthus called the positive checks to population growth – disease, famine, and war.[43]

Such a hypothesis has several important implications. It suggests that the main control on population has been perennial malnutrition and everyday disease. It also seems to suggest that fertility is high *because* mortality is high; in other words, people see that they have to breed in order that the race survive. It would then seem logical to argue that 'One hard-headed argument for continuing efforts to lower mortality rates is that fertility is unlikely to be brought down very much until mortality rates are lowered'.[44]

A closer look at both data and logic suggests many flaws in this hypothesis. While it may be true that *on the average* human population has grown at an extremely low rate over long periods, this may conceal an entirely different short-term pattern than that implied above. This pattern has been well outlined by Kunstadter as follows.

> A more nearly accurate model of demographic conditions in the small hunting and gathering or agricultural communities within which most non-modern men have lived may have been high fertility (beyond the level needed for replacement in normal years) with low-to-medium death rate, with occasional or periodic variations in death rates due to natural disasters (floods, earthquakes, climatic fluctuations disrupting the normal environ-

> mental relations, insect plagues, crop failures . . . etc.), and probably more recently, epidemic diseases. Chronic food-shortages must also have been a limiting factor on population growth.[45]

This alternative pattern, which we may term a 'crisis' model in accordance with its description by French historical demographers, may be understood more easily by way of Fig. 16.2, which contrast it with the original model implicit in the demographic transition hypothesis.

Although we have no long-term data for hunting and gathering communities, it is possible to examine the history of various agrarian societies. Diagrammatic evidence for Chinese population 500–1953,[46] for Egyptian population 700 B.C.–1966,[47] and for French seventeenth-century parishes,[48] all show a pattern similar to that suggested by the 'crisis' model. In normal years there is a fairly rapid growth, which is cut back periodically by massive disasters of various kinds. The important consequence of establishing this alternative traditional pattern is that it throws open again the whole question of why population growth has recently been occurring in many parts of the world. It is no longer satisfactory to explain it in terms of lowering of everyday very high mortality as a result of medical improvements or an improved standard of living. It is more profitable to look at the elimination of periodic crises. This is especially important for the study of Nepalese demographic history since it

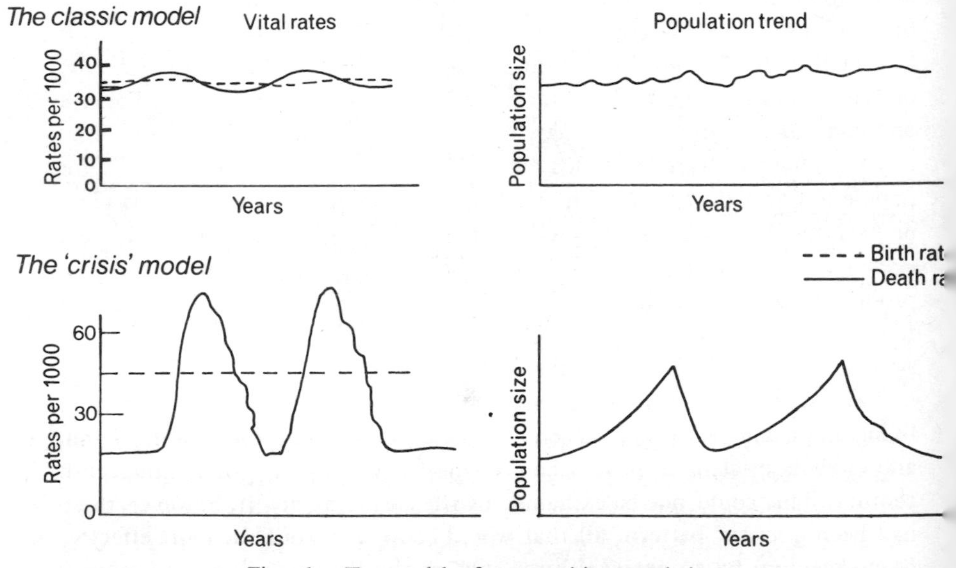

Fig. 16.2. Two models of pre-transition populations.

appears likely that, like most societies, those in Nepal fitted the 'crisis' pattern. To explain the growth of population from at least 1850, therefore, we need to look to the elimination of crises.

Of what nature, we may wonder, were such crises. If we look at the eight events which are believed to have led to massive declines in Egyptian population, it appears that five were conquests, in other words 'war'. Many of the Chinese declines were also caused by conquest; the invasions and devastations of the Mongols are thought to have reduced Chinese population to half its former level within fifty years, over 60 million people dying or failing to be replaced.[49] One of the results of the conquest of Central Mexico by the Spanish was the appalling drop in the population from about 25 million in 1519 to 2½ million in 1608.[50] The Thirty Years War, on a cautious estimate is reckoned to have lowered the population of Germany from 21 to 13.5 million.[51] But warfare, with its major side-effects of starvation and plague, has declined as a major check during this century. The two World Wars together are estimated to have led to the death of up to 60 million persons – a little more than the Mongol conquest of one nation, China.[52] The demographic impact of war, the localized famines and epidemics it brings, have been minimized and the percentage of world population destroyed by it this century will probably, on present levels, be the lowest for many centuries.

While war has evidently been a major check to the growth of large agricultural civilizations, the same is probably true in many of the smaller hunting and gathering societies studied by anthropologists, of whom the Gurungs, until recently, were an example. The lack of historical records makes it difficult to establish this fact but Brookfield and Brown, in their study of the Chimbu of New Guinea, argue that warfare and epidemics were common in the past and continued until the early part of the present century.[53] The elimination of such endemic warfare under external pressure is among the reasons for population growth. It is easy to see that the same may be true in many parts of Asia and Africa. In societies which are small and close to subsistence level, even a small skirmish at the wrong time of year can have disastrous effects on production and lead to high mortality. The effects of such mortality may last for several generations. If this second model is correct it helps to explain the previous puzzle of why population growth in many parts of the world seems to have started well before any medical advances or rise in the standard of living. For example, the population of Nepal, Java, Ceylon, Northern Thailand, and elsewhere seems to have been growing from at least the early nineteenth century. This could not be explained by the earlier model. If, however, there had been a 'crisis' pattern, all that would be needed would be more effective peace-keeping, by an external force such as the British in India, to prevent periodic wars. This explanation fits well with the hypothesis developed by Vayda and others that warfare is often developed, or acts, as a form of population control.[54]

The improvements in communications and agriculture which prevent localized famines have also helped to allow natural growth to occur. This is a complex phenomenon since technological changes are only a part of the explanation. As Kunstadter has put it:

> With regard to famine as a limit of population, perhaps as important as the introduction of new food technologies has been the introduction of social changes. The effect of these is to cushion the temporary fluctuations in availability of foods. Money, credit, markets, and wage-labour opportunities have meant the expansion of economic activities far beyond the bounds of primitive community ecosystems.[55]

Again, what has probably happened is not that yearly production has been increased dramatically, but rather that the periodic crises caused by bad weather, pests, or other phenomena which might reverse a generation's population increase in one year, have been eliminated. This process has been observed at work in eighteenth-century Europe and probably helped to eliminate the crisis pattern, in France.[56] This may not be such an important factor in some Third World countries since, as Wilkinson has observed, 'starvation appears to have been a rarity before the disruptive effects of European contact'.[57] Yet, during the last century, such changes have been important in allowing continued population growth.

It is also difficult to estimate the importance of the eradication of disease. As a correlate of warfare, epidemics have taken a huge toll. It is worth reminding ourselves, as a recent author has pointed out, that although pestilence and malnutrition are often assumed to have 'always been a feature of human existence until . . . the advances of medicine in the past half century'. 'In fact, for well over 90 per cent of man's time on earth, before the Neolithic development, neither pestilence nor malnutrition is likely to have been a common cause of ill-health or death'.[58] The major virus diseases of today, cholera, dysentery, plague, tuberculosis, typhoid, are all dependent on high human densities and can therefore have been prevalent only in fairly recent times.[59] Like warfare, they appear to have been a phase through which world societies passed when a certain density occurred. Like warfare and localized famine, however, they appear to have been temporarily eliminated on a large scale. The influenza epidemic in India in 1918–19 was the last great mortality; up to twenty million lives were lost.[60] As a proportion of the total population of India today, some 50 million deaths would be the equivalent. Even the current tragedies in Bangladesh, Sahel, Bihar and elsewhere are not, as yet, on this scale.

The model above suggests that population growth is the normal condition of mankind, only held back by periodic crises. This view has been held by a number of historians and anthropologists.[61] It helps to explain much of the data we have, for though there clearly have been some societies with the classic features of perennial high mortality and high fertility, probably a greater number have followed the 'crisis' pattern. Yet these two models do not account for all the pre-transition populations of which we know. A third model that needs to be developed is one where there is a homeostatic adjustment between births and deaths which keeps fertility below its maximum. Here the check is not mortality, but social controls on fertility. We shall call this third model the 'homeostatic' pattern.

This pattern has been observed in England between the fifteenth and eighteenth centuries, in France during the later eighteenth century and in Norway at the same date.[62] In the latter two countries it developed out of an earlier 'crisis' pattern. The 'crisis' and 'homeostatic' patterns are illustrated in Fig. 16.3. Perhaps the best example of the homeostatic pattern in action is in England during the period 1650–1730 when population was kept level, not by very high mortality rates, but by keeping fertility below its maximum. Here England was strongly contrasted with France with its 'crisis' pattern.[63] In England it was marriage patterns and, possibly, the use of contraception which

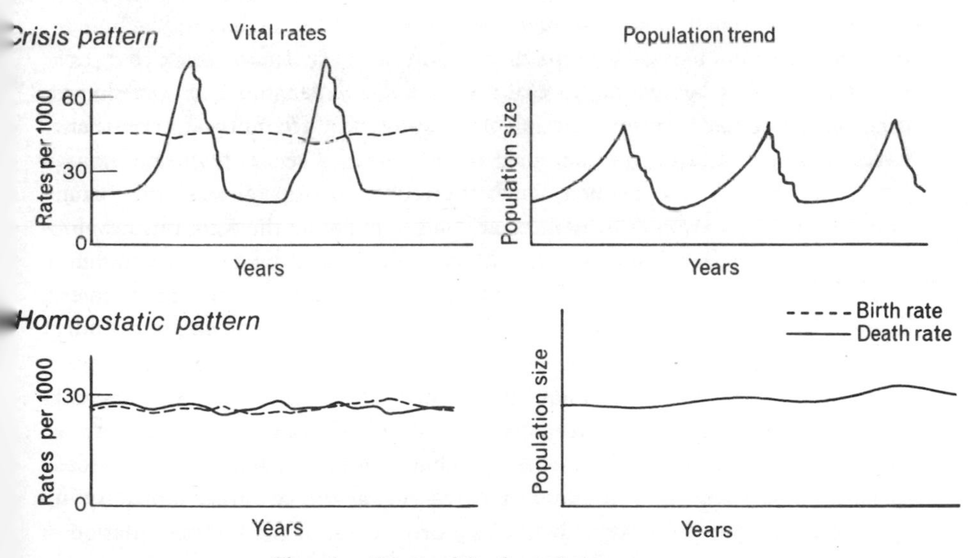

Fig. 16.3. Two models of population patterns.

kept population level with resources. In England this pattern even allowed resources to increase while population was static.

Interestingly, animal populations also appear to exhibit both 'crisis' patterns and 'homeostatic' ones. The 'crisis' pattern is very similar to that described above. Here is one description of the process.

> Some of them (i.e. animals) accept crowding and violence as a recurrent situation, and populations of these animals have regular cycles of rise and decline, with crises that cut them down to size every four or five generations. These species include voles ... and muskrats.... At the beginning of the cycle, the population builds up rapidly, in an uncontrolled way. When a certain density is reached the animals become extremely aggressive ... many pairs are forced into poor feeding-grounds; but this reduction in density is only attained at the cost of savage fighting, including lethal attacks on the young ... The after-effects of violence ... persist after the density has been lowered, and it takes some time before the population recovers and begins a new cycle of growth.[64]

This description of war and violence appears to be a good account of the situation in some of the societies we have examined. But there is another, homeostatic, pattern, especially among birds. The data and the thesis to explain it is particularly associated with the work of Wynne-Edwards. The argument is that what dictates fertility is not physical resources, in other words food and shelter as Malthus tended to argue, but social resources, particularly the availability of 'social space'. Though the food supply may increase, the population of some animals will remain constant because social space has not expanded. Mating behaviour, care of the young, and many other crucial determinants of population growth are all affected by the availability of terrritories. Large numbers of birds, for example, will not breed if there are no territories. Hierarchy is also a mechanism which intervenes to stop the easy flow from resources to population. Some of the animals dominate, others are pushed out. Animals and birds exhibiting this pattern rarely breed up to a point where they starve to death. On the other hand these 'social controls' are often vicious. There is often a very high infant mortality rate arising from infanticide, abortions, neglect. Among some small songbirds up to 90 % of the eggs never produce chicks which grow to adulthood. One author has argued that 'Animal populations would seem to be adapted to their food resources by a variety of built-in physiological and instinctive mechanisms rather than by starvation, and these come into play in response to signals of incipient over-crowding in advance of serious shortage of food'.[65]

Although, as Benedict has pointed out,[66] territorial and hierarchical behaviour among humans has 'conspiciously not led to a control of population' in many societies, and it is necessary to add many other cultural factors to the rather simple model of animal behaviour, the homeostatic model is a useful one. It helps us to understand certain population patterns, for instance that of England, and it is possible that there are a number of societies, particularly, perhaps, those inhabiting confined areas such as islands, which have kept their fertility well below maximum in this way. Where this homeostatic pattern is present the explanation of sudden population growth is more likely to be a decline in the controls over fertility than in the elimination of perennial or crisis mortality. It is perhaps not a coincidence that Malthus, living in one of the first large-scale civilizations known to exhibit this pattern, should have concentrated on fertility changes as the major determinant of population growth.

The model which appears to fit the Gurung case best is the second one, though the evidence is very scanty. It seems unlikely that their present medium to low mortality is solely the result of modern medical improvements. Thus they are unlikely to have had their population over the last few hundred years held in check by perennial disease and high infant mortality. Nor is there evidence that they have controlled population by maintaining a homeostatic control of fertility, either through contraception, high age at marriage, or very considerable use of abortion and infanticide. This leaves the middle pattern. Their subsistence life and the frequent wars of pre-nineteenth-century Nepal make this at the least a plausible explanation. If this hypothesis is correct it has several important implications. As far as the resources and population argument is concerned, it suggests that both Malthus and Boserup are both right and wrong. Malthus is right in arguing that population will expand to fill the resources available to it, but wrong if taken rather over-simply to mean that resources expand first in time, to be followed quickly by population growth. On this issue Boserup is probably correct to believe that, in the absence of crises, population was the propelling force, driving the Gurungs into settled arable farming, for example. She was wrong, however, to believe that the cause of population growth was medical change. Peace and order were enough.

The practical implications of accepting this model are extremely grave. There are reasonable grounds for believing that as the moderately high mortality rates are cut back further, population will grow even faster than at present. There are only three ways in which an inevitable equilibrium will be reached. Firstly, there is the prospect of day to day mortality rising steeply to balance high fertility, perhaps with a rapid rise in infant deaths. Secondly, there could be a return to the 'crisis' pattern from which, for a short time, Nepal and the Gurungs have escaped. Thirdly, there is the possibility of establishing a control of fertility by a very considerable rise in the age at marriage combined with use of contraception on a scale beyond the dreams of family planners. The alternatives to this third solution are bleak. The growing unemployment, inequality, landlessness, malnutrition, soil erosion and other effects of population growth which have been discussed in the account of Gurung agriculture in the first half of this work are likely to accelerate rapidly. Finally, population will be stabilized by a rise in the death rate.

Appendix 1
Census schedule utilized

Section one. De facto census.
(*a*) How many people slept in your house last night?
(*b*) What are their names starting with the eldest and including informant?
(*c*) Are they male or female?
(*d*) What is their *lho* (animal year)? How old are they now?
(*e*) What is their relationship to the informant?
(*f*) How many years have they lived in Thak?
(*g*) Where else, including residence abroad, and rank if in army, have they lived, and where were they born?
(*h*) What is their *jat* (lineage)?
(*i*) Have they been to school, if so, for how many years?
(*j*) Can they read or write?

Section two. De jure census.
(*a*) How many members of the family who normally sleep in the house were temporarily absent (up to one month) last night?
(*b*) Questions continue as in (*b*)–(*j*) above.

Section three. Semi-permanent absence.
(*a*) Have you any close relatives (parents, brothers, sisters, husband, wife or children) who are permanently abroad (over one month), away at school, living in another village, etc?
(*b*) Questions continue as in (*b*)–(*j*) above, except that instead of (*f*) and (*g*) above substitute the following.
(*c*) How many years or months ago did the person leave?
(*d*) When do you expect him/her to return to the village permanently?
(*e*) Where are they now living?
(*f*) What are they doing away from the village? If in the army, their rank?

Section four. Marital history.
(Fill in the names of all married persons in sections one to three above and then ask the following questions).
(*a*) What age was the man when he was married?
(*b*) How old was the woman when she was married?
(*c*) How many years ago did they marry?
(*d*) Where did the man live before they married?
(*e*) Where did the woman live before they married?

(*f*) What is the *jat* of the man, and that of the woman before she married?
(*g*) Were they related by family ties in any way before marrying?
(*h*) How did the marriage end, if it has ended? (By death/divorce/separation.)
(*i*) How long ago did it end, and have either of the partners remarried?

Section five. Fertility history of one central woman (if possible, the oldest married woman).
(*a*) How many conceptions (including children born dead) has woman experienced?
(*b*) How many of the above conceptions ended in the birth of a live child?
(*c*) What are the names of those who were born (alive), and of those who have subsequently died? (In order of birth, indicating those dead before being named, i.e. still-births and miscarriages).
(*d*) In what month and what *lho* was each product of conception delivered?
(*e*) What is the present age of those still alive?
(*f*) In what month and year (*lho*) did those children who have died, die?
(*g*) How many years ago did that happen? (i.e. did child die.)
(*h*) Was the child able to walk, no longer breast-fed, when it died?
(*i*) If the child was dead when born, how long had it been conceived? (i.e. was it a miscarriage or a still-birth).
(*j*) If the child has died, what was the cause of death?

Section six. Details of parents.
(*a*) What is the name of the father and mother of the two eldest members?
(*b*) If alive, where do they live? If dead, where did they die?
(*c*) If alive, what is their age? If dead, how old were they when they died and how many years ago did this occur?
(*d*) What was the cause of death of those dead?
(*e*) If the cause of death was illness, how long were they ill?
(*f*) Was the deceased cremated or buried?

Section seven. Previous two deaths in the family, excluding those above.
(*a*) What were the names of the last two persons in the family who died, excluding those mentioned above?
(*b*) Proceed with questions as in section six above.

Section eight. Various questions.
(*a*) How long ago was the house you live in built? (Which member of the family built it?)
(*b*) How long has your family lived in this house?
(*c*) How many years ago were the family lands last divided?
(*d*) Were they divided when parents died, when a son married, or at what point?
(*e*) Are there any permanently ill persons in the household? If so, from what are they suffering?
(*f*) How far from Thak has the informant been – the furthest point reached – and how often?

Appendix 2

Production and consumption units per household

TABLE A2

House no.	Total of prodn. units	Total prodn. units in village	Army-weighted units**	Total of consumptn. units	Deficit or surplus	May–July, deficit or surplus	May–July, if absent men returned
1	4	3	6	5.5	+	–	=
2	2.4	1.4	4.4	4	+	=	+
3A	2.6	1.6	4.6	3.5	+	–	–
3B	4.2	4.2	5.2[c]	5.75	–	+	+
4	2.4	1.4	3.4	3	+	–	+
5A	2.6	1.6	4.6	3.25	+	–	–
5B	2.4	1.4	4.4	3	+	–	–
6	4.2	4.2	4.2	6.0	–	–	–
6A	0	0	0	1[a]	+	+	+
7	3.2	1.6	5.2	4.75	+	–	–
7A	2.4	2.4	2.4	3	–	–	–
9	1.4	1.4	1.4	3	–	–	–
10	2.5	1.8	4.6	3.5	+	–	–
11	2.8	1.8	4.8	3	+	–	–
11A	1.2	1.2	1.2	2.25	–	+	+
12A	3.8	3.8	3.8	5	–	+	+
12B	2.6	1.6	4.6	3.5	+	+	+
13	2.4	2.4	2.4	3.75	–	–	–
13A	2.9	1.1	4.9	4.5	+	–	–
13D	2.8	1.2	4.8	4.25	+	=	–
14	2	2	2	3.25	–	–	–
15	6.2	3.2	13.2	7.5	+	–	=
16	1.2	0.2	3.2	5	–	–	=
17	5.4	4.4	8.4	7.25	+	–	–
18	2.8	0.8	4.8	2.5	+	–	–
19	4.6	4.6	4.6	6	–	+	+
20	7.2	4.4	11.2	9	+	+	+
21	2.4	2.4	2.4	3.25	–	–	–
22	4.6	2.8	6.6	6.5	+	–	–
23	4.2	4.2	4.2	5	–	=	=
24	4.6	3.6	6.6	6.25	+	–	–
25	5	3.4	7	6.5	+	–	–
27	1.8	0.8	2.8	2.25	+	–	–
27A	0.2	0.2	0.2	0.75	–	=	=

TABLE A2

House no.	Total of prodn. units	Total prodn. units in village	Army-weighted units**	Total of consumptn. units	Deficit or surplus	May–July, deficit or surplus	May–July, if absent men returned
28	3.4	2.8	4.4[c]	4.75	—	—	—
29	2.4	1.4	4.4	3	+	—	—
31	0.6	0.6	0.6	0.75	—	—	—
32	3.2	2.2	6.2	4.25	+	—	—
33	1.3	1.3	1.3	2.5	—	+	+
33A	0.2	0.2	0.2	1.5	—	—	—
34	2	2	2	2.75	—	=	=
35	1.6	1.6	1.6	2	—	+	+
36	1.4	1.4	1.4	2	—	—	—
37	2.8	1.8	4.8	3.25	+	—	—
38	3	3	3	4.5	—	—	—
39	2.6	2.6	2.6	4.25	—	—	=
40	4.6	4.6	4.6	7.25	—	—	—
41	2.4	2.4	2.4	3.5	—	—	—
42	1.8	1.8	1.8	2	—	—	—
42A	4.6	2.8	6.6	5.25	+	—	—
43	8.4	7.4	7.4	10.5	—	+	+
44	3.4	3.4	3.4	4.5	—	+	+
44A	1	1	1	1.25	—	+	+
45	5.4	4.4	4.4	6.0	—	+	+
46	4.4	4.4	4.4	5	—	+	+
48	2.4	1.4	4.4	3	+	—	—
49	6	4	11	7.25	+	—	—
50	3.6	3.6	3.6	4.75	—	+	+
50A	3.2	3.2	3.2	4.25	—	+	+
51	2.8	2.0	4.8	4	+	—	—
52	4.2	4.2	4.2	5.75	—	—	—
53	1.8	0.8	3.8	2	+	=	—
55	2.4	2.4	2.4	3	—	—	—
56	4.0	4.0	4.0	6.25	—	—	—
57	2	2	2	2.75	—	+	+
57A	1.4	1.4	1.4	2	—	+	+
58	2.8	2.8	2.8	4.5	—	+	+
59	3.2	3.2	3.2	4.25	—	+	+
60	3.8	3.8	3.8	4.75	—	+	+
61	1.8	1.8	1.8	3.5	—	+	+
62	3.8	3.8	3.8	5	—	+	+
63	2.8	0.8	4.8	3	+	?	?
64	1.8	0.8	3.8	2.25	+	?	?
65	2.4	2.4	2.4	3.25	—	+	+
66	2.8	2.8	2.8	3.5	—	?	?
70A	0.6	0.6	0.6	1	—	—	—
70B	2.6	1	3.6[c]	4	—	—	—

TABLE A2

House no.	Total of prodn. units	Total prodn. units in village	Army-weighted units**	Total of consumptn. units	Deficit or surplus	May–July, deficit or surplus	May–July, if absent men returned
71	1.4	1.4	1.4	3	−	−	−
72	3.0	2.0	3.0	4	−	−	−
73A	3.8	2.8	6.8	5.25	+	−	−
73B	6.2	5.4	8.2	7	+	−	−
74	2.8	2.8	2.8	4.5	−	=	=
75	0	0	0[b]	1	−	−	−
76	4	0.8	6	4.75	+	−	−
77	3.4	3.4	3.4	4.75	−	=	=
78	3.4	3.4	3.4	5	−	+	+
79	1.8	1.8	1.8	2	−	−	−
80	2.6	2.6	2.6	3.25	−	=	=
80A	4.6	3.6	6.6	5.75	+	+	+
80B	2.6	2.6	2.6	3.75	−	+	+
81	3.6	3.6	3.6	4.75	−	+	+
82	3.4	3.4	3.4	4.5	−	+	+
83	0.8	0.8	0.8	1.75	−	−	−
83A	1.8	1.8	1.8	2.75	−	−	−
84	7.8	4.8	13.8	9	+	−	+
85	1.1	1.1	1.1	2	−	−	−
86	2	2	2	3	−	not known	
87	2	2	2.5	2.5	−		
88	1.1	1.1	1.1	2	−		
89	5.0	5.0	5.0	7	−		
Totals: deficit = 65							
surplus = 35							

Symbols: + – surplus, – = deficit, = = balanced.

[a] A mentally defective woman.

[b] A crippled woman.

[c] Schoolmasters in the village.

Notes:

Estimates of production units are based on table 6.14 (p. 114 above) and the discussion there; consumption units are calculated on Bailey's weighting, as discussed on ch. 8, p. 162.

The third column indicates the number of producers residing permanently in the village so that those away in the army/at school/ only temporarily present are not counted.

**'army-weighted units' takes into account the fact that those working away in the army produce much more than those at home. The following rate has been adopted: man labouring in the village, 1 unit; man labouring in India, 3 units; man in British army, 4 units. Schoolmasters both receive a salary and are able to do agricultural work at busy times, and have therefore been calculated as 2 units, see ch. 9 for further details.

'Deficit or Surplus' in column 6 compares the totals in columns 4 and 5.

The significance of columns 7 and 8, which refer to the overall labour supply and demand during the busiest agricultural season, are discussed in ch. 7.

Appendix 3

Growth in the number of houses in Thak and Mohoriya

There are a number of difficulties in using housing as an index of population growth. Until about 1950 the simple mud, wood and thatch houses could quickly disappear without a trace if uninhabited for a few years. It seems certain that a number of such houses have completely disappeared; for instance there was once a house where the new night school stands. Possibly up to half a dozen or so small huts have disappeared without trace. The following maps of house construction are based on two types of information. For the period before 1935 we have to rely on answers I obtained during the village census. I asked each informant whether he knew who had built the present house, when it was believed to have been built, whether there had been a house there before and, if so, when the earlier house had been built. For the period 1935–60 such replies can be checked, for from that date when a house site was developed, tax started to be paid on it and this was entered in the land tax records (*tiriges*). Thus an entry reads 'From 1948 (2005 in the Nepali calendar), Manseram, Blacksmith, made a house in the field in front of the path, where the Blacksmith's forge is'. Sometimes the entries are not as detailed as this, just giving name and date. Such records appear to have been made in certain years, rather than every year. Thus almost all the houses registered fall under the year 1948 or 1957, whereas it is highly probable that they were more spread out over the years.

Some 30 new house sites are recorded in this manner in the land records. Of these, 11 lie just outside the area covered by the census, and it is therefore impossible to check their dates against replies in the census. What is significant about these outside houses, as will be seen from Fig. A3.1 is that almost all were built by Brahmins or Tamangs. Before these households arrived there were few, if any, Brahmins in the area. It is thus clear that while the Gurungs arrived in the area and cleared land over two hundred years ago, the Brahmins arrived in the 1940s and 1950s, and similarly the Tamangs. Some instances of the accumulation of rice lands by both groups have been described here.

A number of points may be made about the area of intensive study. We may first check informant's statements about the age of their houses against taxation records in order to check their mutual accuracy.

It will be seen that more-recently-built houses are remembered fairly accurately, both by Gurungs and Blacksmiths, while there is a margin of error of up to about ten years for those said to be built between 30 and 50 years ago. Houses were undoubtedly built in different years, not in two blocks as the taxation records suggest. For the purposes of the following analysis, all houses registered for tax in 1948 and 1957 will be assumed to have been built in the time period 1940–59. There may, of course, be one or two exceptional cases where the house was built before 1940, though not registered until 1948.

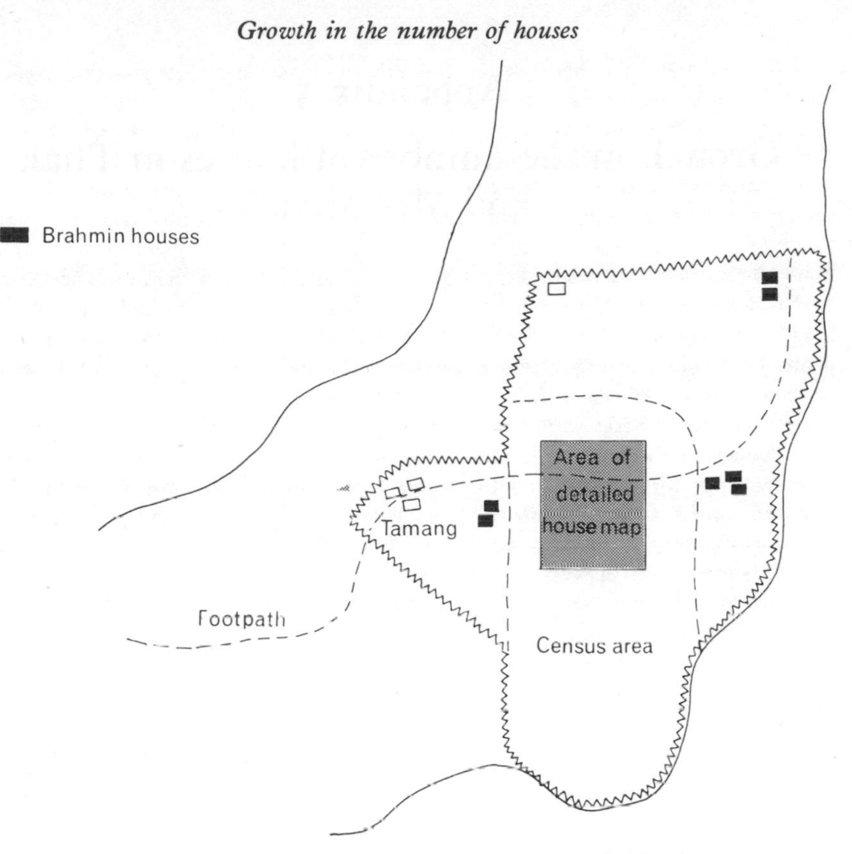

Fig. A3.1. Houses built near area of detailed observation, as recorded for the years 1940–59 in the land records for Thak. (*Note*: Other houses were also undoubtedly built, e.g. by the Tamangs at Mailo. Before 1940 it is unlikely that there were more than two or three households in the area demarcated by the wavy line.)

TABLE A3.1 *Date of housebuilding*

House number	*Jat*	Date given in census	Date given in tax records
57	Blacksmith	50 years ago	1948
56	Magar	45 years ago	1948
41	Gurung	40 years ago	1948
45	Tailor	35 years ago	1948
46	Tailor	33 years ago	1948
61	Blacksmith	17 years ago	1948
79	Gurung	17 years ago	1957
38	Gurung	16 years ago	1957
74	Blacksmith	16 years ago	1957
55	Gurung	13 years ago	1957
78	Gurung	12 years ago	1957
37	Gurung	12 years ago	1957

Figs. A3.2 and A3.3 therefore, are probably fairly accurate. As stated above, the information for the period up to 1940 and after 1960 came from replies to the census. The situation in about 1920 was as shown in Fig. A3.2. There were then some 47 houses, if we include three now derelict or vanished houses to allow for those that have now disappeared without trace. In 1969 there were some 97 houses, some of which had been subdivided so that there were 103 households. Over fifty years, therefore, the number of houses approximately doubled. In the 1920s the great majority of the houses were on the flat ridge where the central village still stands. The presence of only two Tailor and two Blacksmith houses suggests that such groups had not been very long in the area. The three separate *lamme* groups (as indicated in the map) were also probably of comparatively recent origin, possibly dating from the earlier nineteenth century. Two of the *konme* lineages had six houses each, which, if we assume a 50 % growth at each generation (or two sons surviving each alternate generation) would take them back about five generations, in other words to the late eighteenth century. The tendency for lineages to group their houses together is also noticeable. The fourteen *sorajat* households already included at least six different *jats*, of which *yojme*, *lhega*, *kebje* were each represented by two houses.

The houses built between 1920 and 1939 were as shown in Fig. A3.3. If we allow for two houses that were built and then disappeared without trace, some 16 houses were added during this period, an increase of 33 % in twenty years. Not all of this occurred

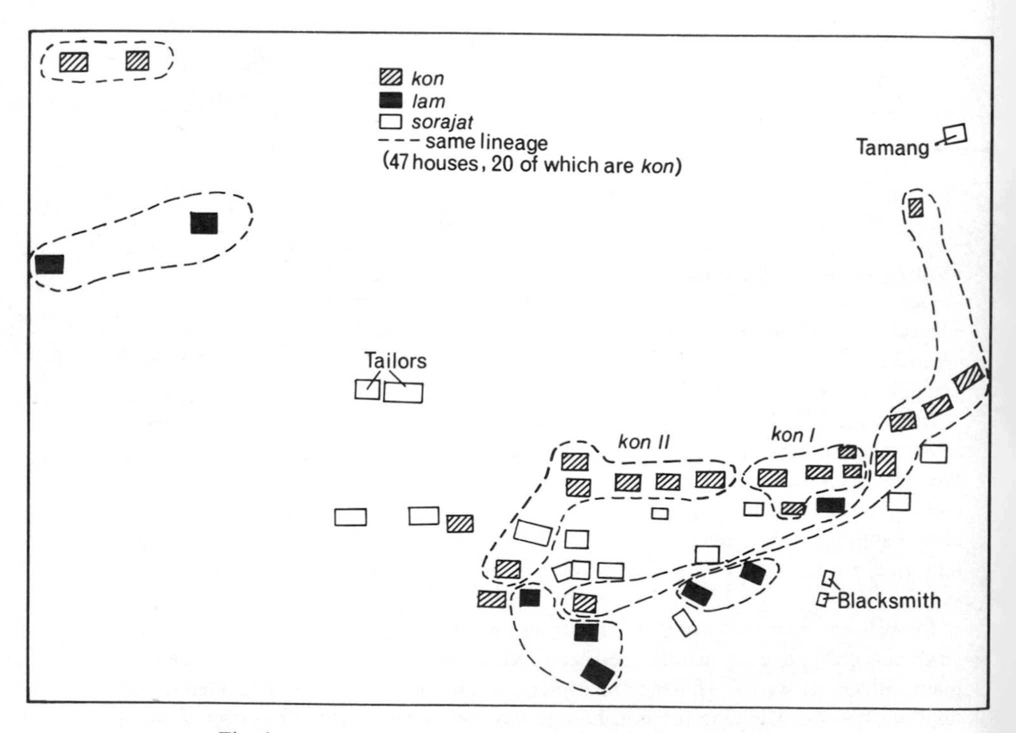

Fig. A3.2. Houses probably present in Thak main village in 1920.

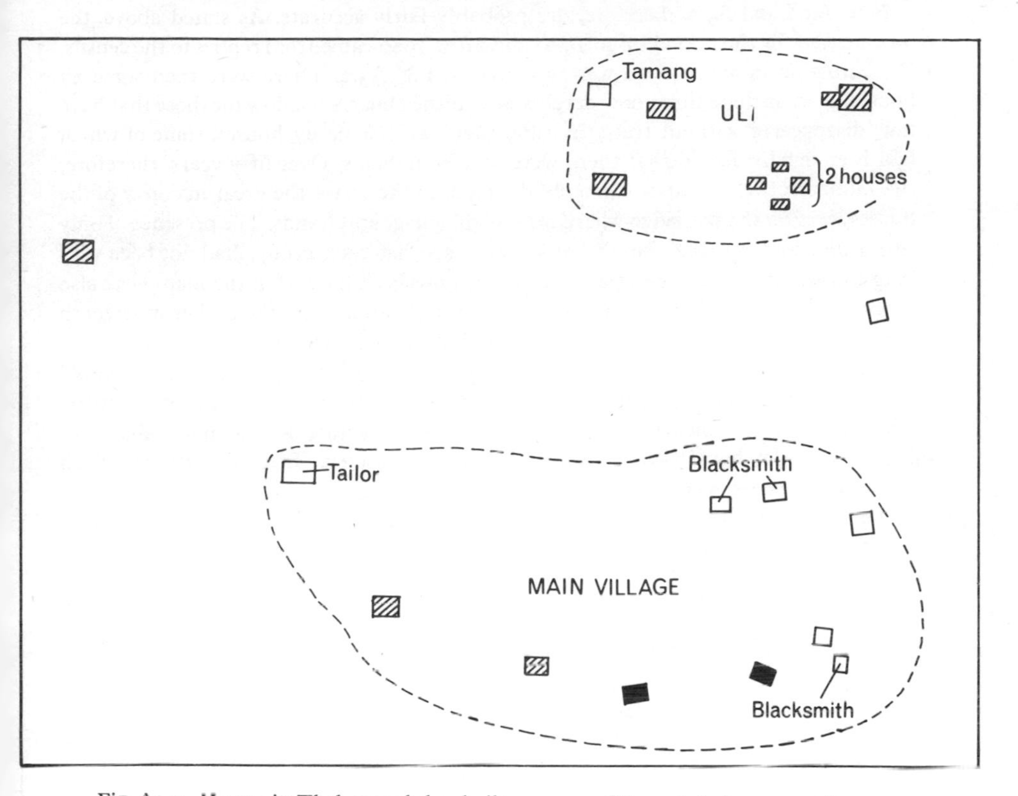

Fig. A3.3. Houses in Thak recorded as built 1920–39. (*Note*: circled areas are the two main settlements.)

through natural population growth within the village. Certainly the Tamang, one of the *lamme*, and probably two of the Blacksmiths came in from other areas. Thus a 20 % natural growth rate, well under 1 % p.a. seems likely. Nearly half the buildings were erected outside the main village, for the richer *konme* moved several of their households down a thousand feet to found the hamlets of *Powlo* and *Uli* in about 1930.

In the following two decades, 1940–59, there was a greater expansion of houses, some 23 in all, or an average of more than one a year. We know that the two Magars, the two Blacksmiths and four Gurung (*sorajat*) households migrated into the area, these being indicated in Fig. A3.4 by arrows. Those persons building in the area with cross-hatching were forced to live on very steep and rocky lands. Excluding such migrants, we are left with a total growth of between 20 and 25 % over these twenty years.

Finally, in the period 1960–9, the situation was as shown in Fig. A3.5. In this ten years not only have 12 new houses been built, but growing pressure on space in the main village, as well as shortage of capital, has led to five new units added by subdividing houses. Allowing for two houses that are derelict, there has been a growth of some 15 household units in this period, of 1.5 p.a. Given the fact that four of the

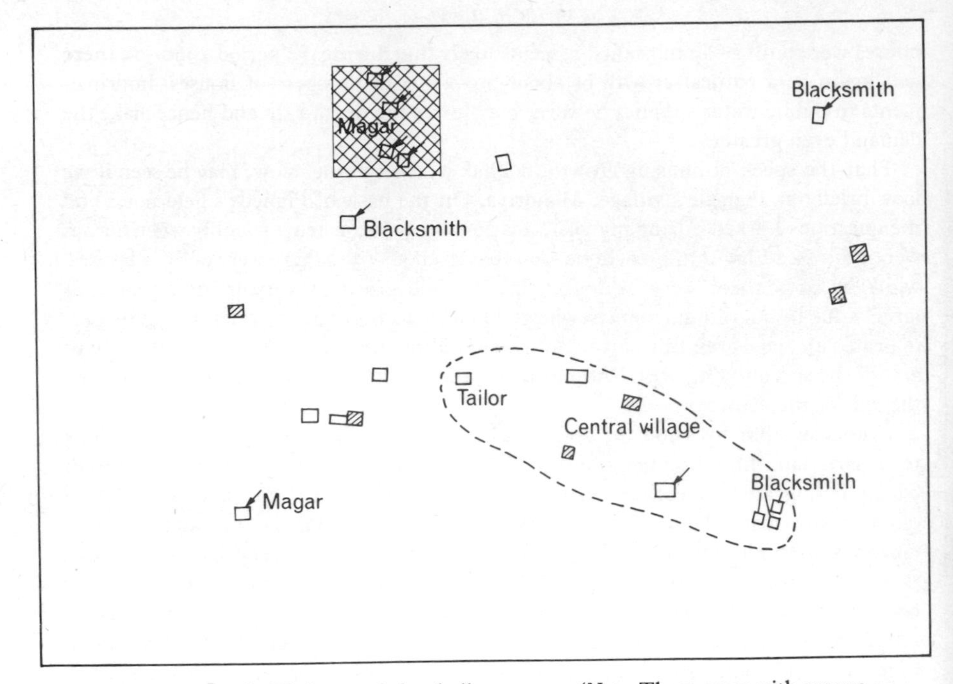

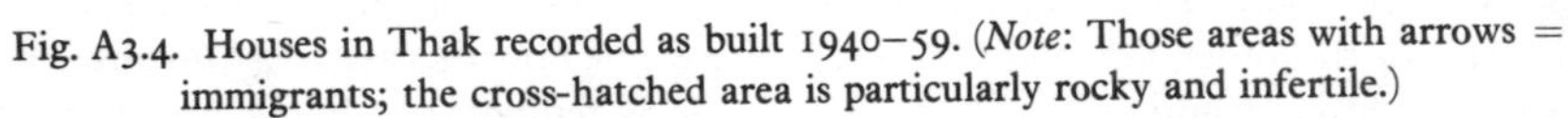
Fig. A3.4. Houses in Thak recorded as built 1940–59. (*Note*: Those areas with arrows = immigrants; the cross-hatched area is particularly rocky and infertile.)

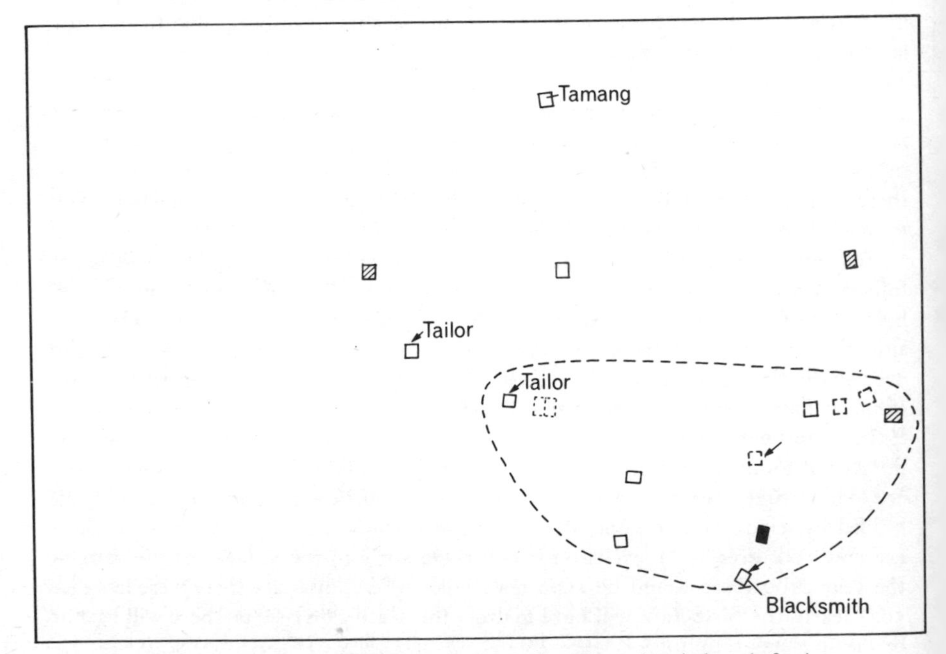

Fig. A3.5. Houses in Thak recorded as built 1960–9 (symbols as before).

houses were built by immigrants, it seems likely that during the period 1960–79 there will again be a natural growth of about 20–25 % in numbers of houses. Improvements in public water supplies however may lower the death rate and hence make the demand even greater.

That the speed of housing growth in Thak is, if anything, slow, may be seen if we look briefly at Pignède's village, Mohoriya. On the basis of Pignède's field notes and the questions I asked during my visit, it is possible to reconstruct roughly when houses were built (see Fig. A3.6). It will be seen that in about 1920 there were only 22 houses, while in 1958 there were over 90. This fourfold growth in under forty years was largely due to migration from elsewhere. Then there was a pause when 13 households migrated to the Terai. But now pressure is building up again, both within the village and in the surrounding area. Without relief, the whole region will be very crowded by the end of the century.

It appears that by 1960 the ability of even the relatively rich *panchayat* of Thak to absorb land-hungry immigrants had almost vanished. Most of the households which immigrated in earlier periods now own a little rice land and considerable quantities of maize land. There was then still room for Magars, Tamangs and new Gurungs to build up landholdings. In this there is a considerable contrast with those who came into the village in 1965–9. None of the latest immigrants have been able to build proper houses: the three Tailor or Blacksmith households, retreating from areas where there is even greater unemployment and overpopulation, have all built small wood and bamboo shacks, primitive structures when compared to the other Gurung or caste houses. The fourth case is a Gurung who is also retreating from Sikhs in the north. He is temporarily living in a part of his wife's natal house. None of these four immigrants have been able to buy any land of their own, and none has been given to them. This corroborates the evidence from the study of land-use, namely that with the present technology and even with resources and employment abroad, this part of the Hills region has reached population saturation point. What will happen when population doubles in the next thirty-five or so years is difficult to predict. What is certain is that there will be a demand for twice as much food, twice as much grazing land, twice as much fuel and twice as many houses.

The future demands for housing within the village may be roughly calculated as follows. There are, at present, some 67 males aged 41–80 in our 100 sample households. The rest of the households are headed by younger males or widows. There are also in these households some 183 males aged 0–40. If we assume that all those aged over 40 die during the next thirty years and that roughly 50 of the younger generation of males have died by the end of thirty years (both are generous estimates, especially if there are further public health measures), then there would be roughly double the number of adult males aged over 40 in thirty years time. Given the fact that few of them are able to find alternative villages to live in and that the proportion of households headed by widows is the same, there would have to be 200 households where there are now 100, even if we exclude further migration into the village. At this rate, by the year 2100 there would be 1600 households where, in 1920, there were less than 50. Clearly the birth rate will have to drop, the death rate rise, or there will have to be massive emigration.

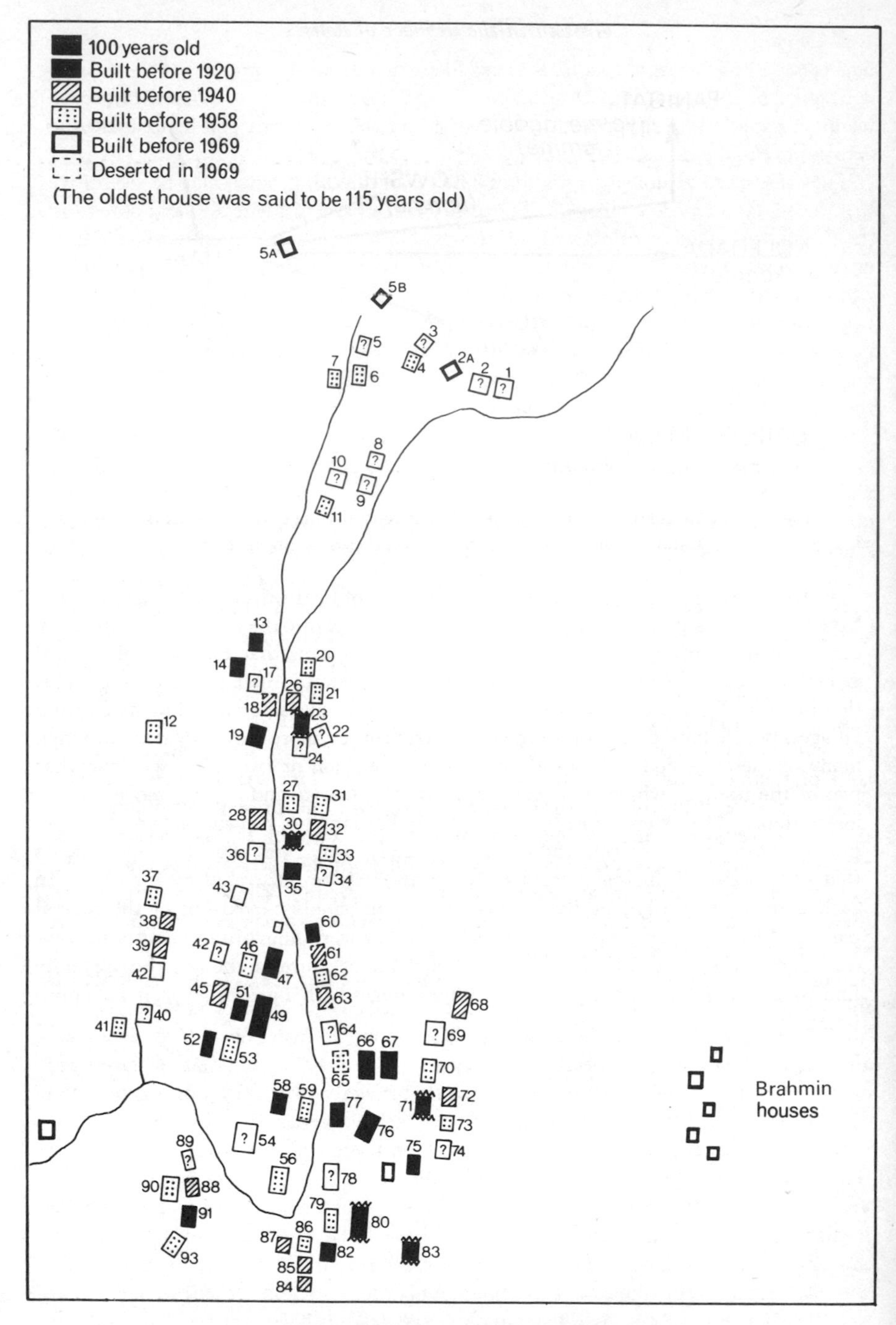

Fig. A3.6. Housebuilding in Mohoriya.

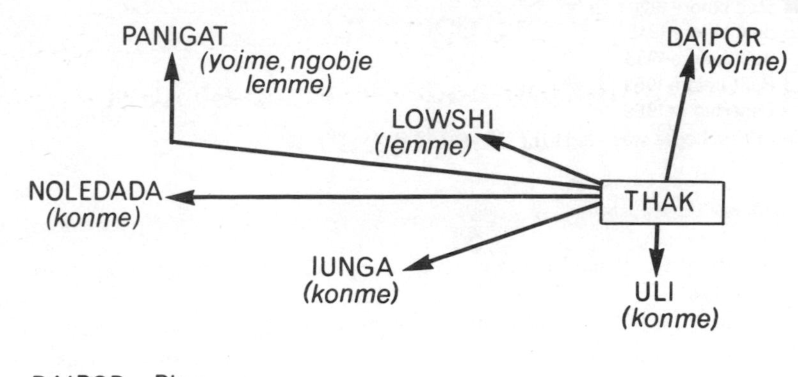

Fig. A3.7. Movement of lineages out of Thak central village over the last 80 years (capitals = places; small type in parentheses = lineages/*jats*).

In the past, those people produced by surpluses of births over deaths within Thak have found it possible to move out of the central village into the surrounding virtually uninhabited countryside. Among other things this means that estimates of natural growth based merely on the central village tend to underestimate the speed of population increase. What has happened in Thak is probably characteristic of many Gurung villages; people flowed down into the village from other, more crowded, areas and then many of their descendants moved on after a generation or two. Thus we know that two of the lineages which first reached Thak, the *Lemme* and *Ngobje*, moved out to lower slopes. They were represented in the earlier land tax records of 1883, but had practically disappeared from the central village area by 1969. The main movements that have occurred during the last eighty years may be illustrated by Fig. A3.7. In each case of migration, probably only a few households moved out of the central part of Thak, but by 1969 *Panigat* and *Noledada* were flourishing villages in their own right. Yet the possibility of future relief for pressure at the centre is severely limited. All round Thak there are now other villages with a growing surplus of population.

Appendix 4
Population and the price of land and other goods

Although the price of land is not just a simple reflection of population pressure, it is still a useful index of when land began to become scarce among the Gurungs. A really comprehensive treatment would require a long study of the unsorted documents in the land registration (*Mal*) office in Pokhara. It would have taken an enormous amount of time to find Thak individuals, since people are not indexed under *panchayats*. Instead, ten household heads in Thak were presented with a list of their landholdings derived from the land tax records and asked to value them at present. They were also asked to state, if possible, how much money had been paid for pieces purchased in the past. This information, combined with the known acreage and yield, is the basis for the following analysis.

The price of land varies not only with its supposed crop, but its liability to suffer erosion, distance from the village, and a number of other factors. Where everything has to be carried on the back, a difference of one thousand feet in altitude will have a great influence on prices. This helps to explain the considerable variations in value shown in Fig. A4.1. Informants' estimates of how much their various fields were

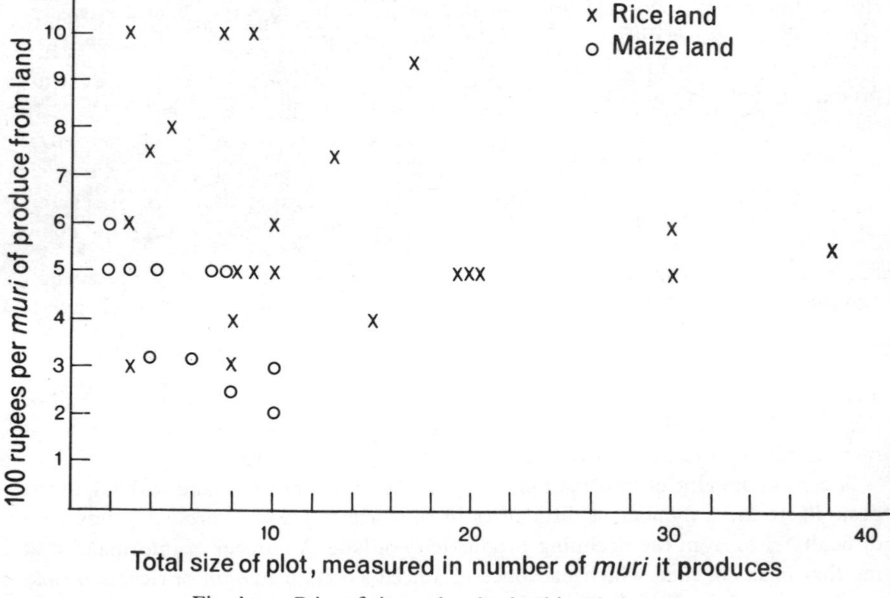

Fig. A4.1. Price of rice and maize land in Thak, 1969.

worth in 1969 are reduced to a common denominator, the number of Nepalese rupees per *muri* of unhusked rice produced. This was the way villagers themselves calculated the price of land. Thus I was told by one informant that for every *muri* of rice produced by a piece of land, one thousand rs. would have to be paid; for every two *muri* of maize/millet a similar price would be paid. Another informant thought that 800–900 rs. would be the right sum for such quantities, if the land were not too far from the village. Thus he reckoned that a piece of rice land producing 10 *muri* of rice would cost some 7000–8000 rs. According to Thak villagers, prices were higher in Thak than in neighbouring villages, for instance Mauja and Taprang; they were also about 20 % higher than in Mohoriya at the same time. Since land is still more abundant in Thak than in these other villages, it is clear that prices are determined by other factors also, for example the number of soldiers who are trying to buy land in their home village at the time. The actual valuation of land in Thak, 1969, is as shown in Fig. A4.1.

It will be seen that rice land varied between 300 and 1000 rs. per *muri*, and maize land between 200 and 600 rs. The average was about 600 and 400 rs. respectively. The actual selling prices of land is probably about one-third higher than this, however. Many of the informants had not sold land for some time, and were not aware of the steep rise in demand. Furthermore, when they valued their land for me, it was not for the purpose of sale. They had no desire to sell, and would not have done so at the prices indicated in the diagram. If we allow for the other grains grown with rice, the selling price of rice land in Thak was approximately ten times the annual value of the crop. This is only a general total, and there are wide variations. For example, a piece of land owned by household 40 and producing some 9–10 *muri* of unhusked rice was valued at only 4000–5000 rs., while a nearby field producing only half that amount of rice was valued at 4000 rs. I was told that the former field was difficult to irrigate, very steep and hence difficult to work, and only produced a low quality 'yellow' rice, and no *kwoia* or *masyan*. Thus not only do we have to allow for the quantity of the produce, but also the quality; not only for the steepness of the climb to the village, but the steepness of the actual terraces.

Pignède was told that land producing one *muri* of unhusked maize would cost 200–300 rs., and the same quantity of unhusked rice, 300–500 rs.[1] Ten years later the prices were reckoned to be twice this. There has, however, been a considerable devaluation in the real value of the Nepalese rupee during the period. There are no figures available for the area where Mohoriya is situated, but figures for Kathmandu and the Terai worked out by U.S. AID, indicate the following general price changes:[2]

1957–70; 1959–72; 1961–78; 1963–86; 1965–111; 1967–110; 1968–125.

Thus in the period 1957–67, prices rose by nearly 60 per cent; possibly up to half of this was due to currency devaluation; it seems likely that land in Mohoriya has increased its real value by between 50 and 70 % in the last ten years.

A certain amount of information was gathered on the price of land in Thak in the past. There are a number of difficulties in comparing this with present prices. One difficulty rises from the declining productivity of land. A number of informants told me that pieces of land which had once produced a certain amount of rice, now only produced about 75 % of that quantity. To allow for this possible deterioration in crop, since estimates of the crops a field would produce in the past were based on present yield, the present value of rice and maize land has been adjusted upwards a little, from 800–900 rs. per *muri* produced, to 1000 rs.

If we chart the recorded price of maize and rice land sold in the past as a percentage of its value if sold now, we have the trend shown in Fig. A4.2. If we overlooked for the moment the devaluation of the currency, we could estimate that the price of rice land has increased by a factor of ten in the last 25–30 years. In certain cases, the price thirty years ago was as low as 2–3 % of its present price. It appears that the sharp rise in land prices began soon after the Second World War, perhaps with the return of a large number of pensioned army recruits who wanted land. The rise in maize prices may have started a little later, for until the 1950s such land was relatively plentiful. The figures are extremely rough, but they do suggest a doubling in prices during the last ten years, as in Mohoriya. Such price changes appear to have been common throughout Nepal. Thus we are told that in eastern Nepal the price of paddy increased fourteen-fold in the 50 years after 1914.[3] Between 1934/5 and 1962, it has been estimated that the price of rice land in Kathmandu valley went up nearly eight-fold; that of maize land went up about the same amount.[4]

The comparisons over time are complicated in Thak by the fact, that until recently, despite trade and army service, the economy of the Gurungs was still mainly a subsistence one, in which *specia* was looked on with suspicion, especially paper money.[5] The following statements about changes in prices of various commodities in Thak are based on the observations of one extremely intelligent, but young, man. They should thus be treated with caution. He first stated how much had been paid for certain

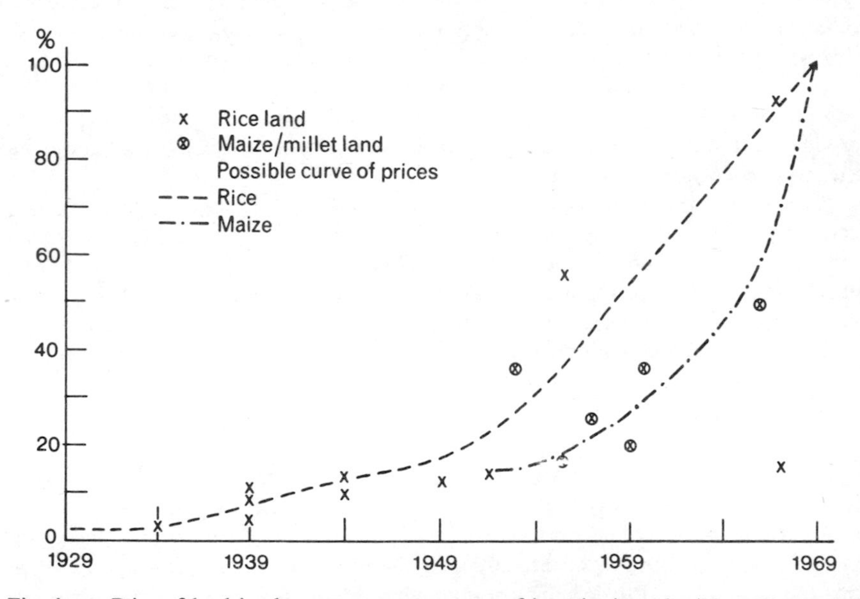

Fig. A4.2. Price of land in the past as a percentage of its price in 1969. (*Note*: The marked discrepancy between rice prices two years ago can be accounted for by the fact that one plot was sold cheaply within the lineage, while the other was sold to a lower caste Leather-worker.)

articles when his grandfather, still alive and active at 85, was a young man – in other words about 60–70 years before. Then he gave some of the prices when he himself was a boy, some fifteen years before, and then the present prices (table A4.1). Thus we see that the price of a milking buffalo has increased some ten-fold or more, oil some 12 to 14 times, since before the First World War. This is a more accurate indication of price changes than the 56-fold rise in rice prices, or 87-fold rise in ordinary wages. The latter are influenced by the subsistence nature of the economy. Labour would hardly ever be paid in cash; usually work was done on an exchange basis. During the last ten to fifteen years there appears to have been a doubling or trebling of rice and oil prices. This fits with the changes noted for Mohoriya. It also fits with the fact that a buffalo in 1957 cost about 120–200 rs. according to Pignède,[6] while in 1969 a buffalo bought for the same purpose cost some 350–400 rs.

TABLE A4.1 *Changes in prices in Thak* (in rs. and paise: 100 paise = 1 rs.)

Commodity	*c.* 1900–10	*c.* 1955–60	1969
Day's labour	4 paise + food	75 paise + food	3½ rs. + food
Plate of meat at Pokhara	2 paise	?	2 rs.
Rice (1 *poti*)	6 paise	1¼ rs.	3½ rs.
Oil (1 *mana*)	50 paise	3 rs.	6–7 rs.
Good milking buffalo	60–70 rs.	?	600–800 rs.

Appendix 5
Household and family structure among the Gurungs

The Kaski district, within which Thak is located, has one of the lowest mean average household sizes in Nepal, some 4.6 persons per household, according to the 1961 census. The mode is four persons per household.[1] This suggests that most families will be of the nuclear variety. There has been, as yet, little analysis of other groups in Nepal in relation to household structure, but the Limbus have simple households also. Only 9.4 % of Limbu households in the sample analysed by Caplan were of the joint-type; 43/85 families lived in nuclear family households.[2] The household unit is of very considerable importance among the Gurungs. There is no local term for the nuclear family by itself; a group consisting of just parents and children is not distinguished. The only unit smaller than the lineage (*santan* or *khalak*, Nep.) or kin generally (*ista mitra*, Nep.; *rajamajame*, Gg.) is the household (*Jahan* or *pariwar*, Nep.). Any person sharing the same part of a house and, therefore, eating from the same hearth, is part of a specific *jahan*. This household unit has important functions as a labour, ritual, commensual, and child-rearing group. All members, except servants, also have property rights in the joint estate. In the very fluid social structure of the Gurungs, this smallest atom of the social world has a very great significance in daily life. We may thus wonder what such households are constructed of.

The household structure in two Gurung villages is elaborated in the two tables below. The categories are based on those initially devised by Donald Pitkin and used in Banfield's, *Moral Basis of a Backward Society*.[3] As with all classifications, there are unsatisfactory features and it has also been necessary to add one extra category to make the analysis fit the Gurung situation. This addition arises out of the general problem of how one is to define a 'joint-family'. A common feature of Gurung villages is the situation where there would normally be a joint household, with several married brothers living with one or both of their parents. But with army service, there is often only one married son and his wife actually residing in the parental house. The other brothers are away for most of the time on army service, though their wives may be living in their husband's household. This is a rather unusual structure and it has been decided to give it a special term, widely in use in the analysis of European household structures,[4] but not so common in Indian anthropology, namely to call this a 'stem' family. One of the most extreme examples of this is household 49 in Thak. The eldest brother has already built a separate house and works his own share of the land. The other three brothers, all of whom are married and whose wives live together, still hold their property in common and have no other house than that in which their mother lives. At first sight this might appear to be a typical joint household. But only one brother, recently retired from the army, is permanently resident, the younger ones are away in the forces for most of the time. There were three such situations in Mohoriya when I visited it. In one sense they are joint households, but in actual residential terms they are not. Another example of the theoretical problems caused by labour migration is in the analysis of nuclear families. The second most frequent type of household structure in Thak was the broken nuclear family; mother and children living alone, with the father away in the army. For convenience sake this has been classed with normal nuclear households, but for certain purposes it could be distinguished. The household structure in Thak is best shown in tabular form (see table A5.1).

Before commenting on the table we may look at a simplified version (table A5.2) for another Gurung village, Mohoriya, in order to see whether the figures in table A5.1 are likely to be typical of the Gurungs. A comparison of my census taken in 1969 with Pignède's observations in 1958 will also enable us to see if there have been any obvious change in household structure during the last 10 years.

It will be obvious from the tables that the majority of those living in Gurung villages. Gurungs and non-Gurungs alike, live in nuclear households; over 60 % in both villages. If we define 'joint' households as permanently co-residing siblings (married), then there is only one case in each of the samples.[5] Even if we adopt the broader definition employed by Caplan, including cases where a widower living in the same house as his married son, there are still only a very few cases, five households in all. It is possible that, as with the Limbus,[6] the incidence of joint households has declined over the last few years. John Morris, on the basis of observations made some forty years ago, notes that 'A Gurkha village is more a series of extended family groups than a collection of unrelated individuals' and that the 'extended-joint-family' is the common ideal, though it usually breaks up fairly quickly.[7] One of my older informants in Thak said that some fifty or so years ago each household was bigger than it is now and usually contained a joint family of all the brothers and their children. He thought households often consisted of 20–25 persons. The economy was much more pastoral then, he explained, so that at least one of the brothers would be away grazing large flocks of sheep or herds of cows. That this is both an idealized picture, and also refers mainly to the richer households, is obvious. It is possible, however, that the shift from a primarily pastoral to an arable economy has led to a decline in the proportion of fraternal joint households.[8] This is a tendency reinforced by large-scale army recruitment which has enabled sons to set up separate households before their father's death or decision to transmit their share of the property. Army pay helps them to finance the building of a new house. Army service may, on the other hand, also delay the splitting of *de jure* joint households since adult male brothers are seldom home on leave together. Comparison of the 1969 census of Mohoriya with Pignède's 1958 census notes, shows that there has been no decrease in the size of households or in the proportion of joint households. If anything, households were larger in 1969 than they had been in 1958; in each census there way only one fraternal joint household.

It does seem certain that the 'extended' family, that is those families where some more distant relative or relatives are resident, have always been rare among the Gurungs. There were no cases of such households in either Thak or Mohoriya in 1969. Nor, for demographic reasons, can the percentage of 'stem' families, those with three or more generations simultaneously present, ever have been much greater than it is now. It has been calculated for another non-industrial society that, given the prevailing mortality and nuptiality rates, three-generation households were only possible in up to one third of the cases, at the most. Although there have been some

TABLE A5.1 *Structure of 100 households in Thak, 1969*

Type of household	No. of such households				No. of such persons		
	Gurung Class[a] 1–3	Gurung Class[a] 4–5	Non-Gurung	%	Gurung	Non-Gurung	%
Nuclear: fa/mo. and unmarried children and unmarried siblings. Also 'broken' nuclear families where a parent is dead or abroad	23	21	18	62	215	101	61.
Stem: either, fa. and/or mo. + children + one married child and spouse, or, fa./mo. + children and more than one married child, but only one couple present, i.e. other husbands away abroad[b]	14	6	4	24	131	24	30.
Extended: elementary family, plus some other relative other than parents or married siblings	–	–	–	–	–	–	–
Joint: married brothers or sisters living together	–	–	1	1	–	13	2.5
Others:							
two sisters unmarried	1	–	–	1	2	–	0.4
single	2	3	–	5	5	–	1
fa., fa. wife, children and divorced son	1	–	–	1	6	–	1.2
parents and children, son's wife and wife's fa.	1	–	–	1	9	–	1.7
informant, stepdada, broda. and dadada	1	–	–	1	4	–	0.8
grandmo and granda	1	–	–	1	2	–	0.4
mo. da. and da's illeg. son.	1	1	–	2	3	–	0.6
bro. and sister (unmarried)	1	–	–	1	2	–	0.4
	46	51	23	100	379	138	100%

[a] As described in appendix 7 below, the hundred households were stratified into five economic groups by three informants. Thus classes 1–3 are the middling to rich Gurungs, 4–5 the poorer to very poor.

[b] The reasons for adding this category are described on p. 330. Only three Gurung households, nos. 22, 49, 73B, fall into it.

fluctuations in both mortality and age-at-marriage rates among the Gurungs, these have probably not been great enough, as yet, to alter household composition very greatly. The situation is probably long established; some two-thirds of the population live in two-generation households, and approximately one third in three-generation ones. This is largely because only in approximately one in three cases do parents live long enough to see their own children produce offspring. Thus 24 % of the Thak sample and 19.5 % of the Mohoriya households in 1969 were three generation ones. One of the probable long-term consequences of improved health in Nepal will be a movement towards the recent European phenomenon. In seventeenth-century England there were usually only two generations alive simultaneously, now in England there are often four generations overlapping. Naturally such a demographic change will have immense consequences for the structure of the household unit.

It has frequently been suggested that the size and structure of households is correlated with the absolute wealth of the community. The structure will also differ with the varying economic levels within the community. Thus we are told that the greater the food supply, the larger the household size; the extended family will only occur where the supply is large.[9] It has also been shown that in a number of societies, the larger the family estate, the larger the household.[10] In Nepal, Caplan has noted for the Limbus that the wealthiest families split up the latest.[11] There appears to be only a slight correlation, if any, between wealth and household size in Thak. If we compare the wealthier *carjat* to the *sorajat* households, the mean average household sizes are 5.01 and 4.92 respectively. This is hardly a marked difference. If we look at the structure of the households, as analysed in table A5.1 it will be seen that the poorest families in the village, the non-Gurungs, almost all live in nuclear households. Likewise the poorer Gurungs, in classes 4–5, have a significantly lower proportion of persons living in stem households than the wealthier Gurungs. Furthermore, the stem households of the wealthier group are, on average, considerably larger than those of groups 4–5; the former average over seven persons per household, the poorer households, some five per household. A relatively large estate appears to hold sons and daughters together longer, perhaps because their labour is more valuable. We may therefore expect that as estates are increasingly subdivided in the next few years, household units will shrink in size. It is possible that this will continue a process which has been in operation over the last 30 years as population has pressed on land resources. It does not appear in the comparison between the 1969 and 1958 censuses for Mohoriya because considerable emigration from the village in the intervening years kept the total population static and momentarily halted subdivision of land.

TABLE A5.2 *Structure of 87 households in Mohoriya, 1969*

Type of household	No. of households	% of households
Nuclear	59	67.9
Stem	25	28.8
Extended	–	–
Joint	1	1.1
Other	2	2.2
	87	

Appendix 6

TABLE A6 *Marriage, inheritance and death of parents in Thak*

House no.	Years since division	Man's age at	Who between	Years since marriage	Years since death of father	Years since death of mother	Stated cause of division
3A	*c.* 10	35	Brothers	22	32	47	–
3B	*c.* 10	49	Brothers	23	32	47	–
2	*c.* 10	27	Brothers	*c.* 16	32	47	–
7A	*c.* 80	Unborn	?	*c.* 18	3	Not dead	–
11	*c.* 17	7	?	*c.* 17	*c.* 17	17	Father's death
12A	23	32	Brothers	32	15	?	At father's marr'ge
13	*c.* 10	32	Brothers	20	39	Not dead	(Wives quarrel?)
13D	*c.* 10	34	Brothers	18	39	Not dead	(Wives quarrel?)
14	*c.* 20	40	Brothers	41	?	?	After marriage
15	12 +	33	Brothers	37	19	4	All brothers were
50	12 +	36	Brothers	24	19	4	married and had
48	12 +	28	Brothers	14	19	4	many children
17	this year[a]	36	Brothers	18	Not dead	8	Fa. old, yo. son wants
20	13	55	Bro's son	45	40	14	Younger man's mge.
37	13	20	Uncle	12	17	15	At marriage
21	8	37	Brothers	21	?	?	–

24	13+	29	Brothers	26	24	Not dead	Because all
78	13+	40	Brothers	29	24	Not dead	their families
63	13+	36	Brothers	34	34	Not dead	getting big
25	*c.* 25	*c.* 38	Brothers	36	?	?	All bro. married[b]
28	23	29	Brothers	27	23	Not dead	Fathers's death
32	41	*c.* 25	Brothers	43	?	?	All bro's married[b]
33	48	?	?	48	?	?	At marriage
33A	56	34	?	56	?	?	At third marriage
34	*c.* 10	39	One bro.	31	24	Not dead	Eldest brother
49		26	Takes up his	7	24	Not dead	had married, and
49	*c.* 10	21	Claim from	5	24	Not dead	retired, with
49		14	The rest	Not married	24	Not dead	children
38	*c.* 15	38	Brothers	31	*c.* 9	*c.* 9	–
39	*c.* 15	33	Brothers	19	*c.* 9	*c.* 9	–
72	*c.* 25	37	Brothers	39	56	7	Each had a family
83	?	?	Brothers	45	50	70	*before* marriage
83A	4	37	Father/son	11	Alive	Alive	A quarrel fa./son
86	12	32	Brothers	16	38	Alive	Each brother
87	12	27	Brothers	11	38	Alive	had a family

[a] This was an attempted division during 1969; it was not accepted by one of the brothers. The younger brother wished to retain the money he was earning in the army, rather than invest it in a communal estate with his elder brother.

[b] And had several children.

Appendix 7

Estimates of relative wealth by three Gurungs

I asked three young Gurungs to place each household on a five-point scale of wealth. I gave no guidelines as to how wealth was to be assessed beyond stating that category 1 = 'very rich', 2 = 'rich', 3 = 'middling', 4 = 'poor' and 5 = 'very poor'. It will be seen that the three informants largely agreed on their assessments, though informant 3, the one *carjat* assessor, tended to see his fellow *carjat* villagers as richer than they appeared to the other informants. The estimates were as follows.

TABLE A7

House no.	Informant 1	Informant 2	Informant 3	House no.	Informant 1	Informant 2	Informant 3
1	4	4	3	18	4	4	4
2	4	5	3	19	4	–	4
3A	4	4	3	20	4	3	2
3B	4	4	3	21	4	4	3/4
4	4	4	3	22	3	2	2
4A	4	–	–	23	2	–	2
5A	4	4	3	24	3	3	2
5B	4	4	3	25	3	3	3
6	1	1	1	26	4	4	4
6A	4	5	5	27A	4	4	4/5
7	3	3	3	28	3	3	2
7A	4	4	3/4	29	4	3	2
8	5	5	4	31	4	3	3
9	3	3	3	32	2	2	1/2
10	3	2	2	33	4	5	4
11	2	2	2	33A	3	3	2
11A	5	–	5	34	3	4	3
12A	4	4	3/4	35	5	5	5
12B	4	4	3/4	36	2	–	2
13A	4	4	3	37	3	2	3
13C	3	–	–	38	3	3	3
13D	–	4	3	39	3	3	3
13	4	–	3	40	2/3	2	2
14	3	2	2	41	4	3	3/4
15	3	3	3	42	3	2	3
16	4	3	3				
17	2	2	1				

TABLE 7 (*cont.*)

House no.	Informant 1	2	3	House no.	Informant 1	2	3
42A	4	5	4	67	5	5	5
43	5	5	5	70A	3	2	3
44	5	5	5	70B	2	2	2
44A	5	5	5	71	2	1	1
46	5	4	5	72	2	2	3
47	4	5	5	73A	1	1	2
48	3	3	3	73B	1	1	2
49	2	2	3	74	4	4	5
50A	–	–	5	75	2	2	2
50	3	3	3	76	3	2	4
51	3	3	3	77	3	3	3/4
52	2	2	2/3	78	3	3	3
53	4	3	3	79	4	4	4/5
54	5	5	–	80	4	4	4/5
55	3	3	3	80A	4	4	4
56	3	3	4	80B	4	4	4
57	4	5	5	81	4	4	5
57A	5	–	5	82	4	4	5
58	4	5	5	83	2	2	3
59	4	5	5	83A	2	2	3
60	4	5	5	84	2	3	3
61	5	5	5	85	3	3	3
62	4	5	5	86	1	2	2
63	4	4	3/4	87	1	2	2
64	4	4	3/4	88	1	2	2
65	5	–	5	89	3	3	4
66	5	4	5	90	4	4	5

Notes

(Full titles for abbreviated references are contained in the select bibliography, p. 354 below.)

1. DEMOGRAPHY AND ANTHROPOLOGY

1. Ehrlich, *Population*, p. 1.
2. McNamara, 'Address', p. 1.
3. Myrdal, *Asian Drama*, i, p. 114.
4. Wrigley, *Population and History*, p. 14; Ford (ed.), *Social Demography*, p. 374.
5. Thompson, *Population and Progress*, p. 347.
6. Stone in the preface to Tawney, *Agrarian Problem*, p. xi.
7. For example the figure in Wrigley, *Population and History*, p. 78.
8. Myrdal, *Asian Drama*, iii, p. 1608.
9. Hawthorn, *Sociology of Fertility*, p. 23.
10. In Harrison & Boyce (eds.), *Structure of Populations*, p. 73.
11. Summarized in Macfarlane, 'Population crisis'.
12. 6th edn. (1951), p. 58.
13. John Beattie, *Other Cultures* (1964); Godfrey Lienhardt, *Social Anthropology* (Oxford, 1964).
14. Hauser & Duncan (eds.), *Study of Population.*
15. In Harrison & Boyce (eds.), *Structure of Populations*, p. 283.
16. Obeyesekere, *Land Tenure.*
17. Stirling, *Turkish Village*, p. 23.
18. Bailey, *Caste*, pp. 9, 219–20.
19. Barth, *Nomads*, p. 114; Southall (ed.), *Social Change*, p. 5; Ardener, *Divorce and Fertility*, pp. v, vii.
20. Forde, 'Population data'.
21. Krzywicki, *Primitive Society.*
22. Lorimer (ed.), *Human Fertility.*
23. Firth, Borrie & Spillius, 'Population of Tikopia', pp. 229–52.
24. Mitchell, 'Yao fertility'.
25. Roberts, 'Demographic study'.
26. Nag, *Factors Affecting Human Fertility.*
27. Ardener, *Divorce and Fertility.*
28. Douglas, 'Population control'.
29. Allison (ed.), *Population Control.*
30. Mamdani, *Myth of Population Control.*
31. Baker & Sanders 'Demographic studies in anthropology'; Nag, 'Anthropology and population'.
32. *Structure of Populations.* Chagnon and his associates are particularly concerned with the collection of demographic data and their methodology is of wide interest; see, for example, Chagnon, *Fierce People* and *Studying the Yąnomamö.*
33. Goody, 'Inheritance, property, and marriage'; 'Sideways or downwards?'; 'Strategies of heirship'.

34. Geertz, *Agricultural Involution.*
35. Rappaport, *Pigs for the Ancestors*; Clarke, *Place and People*; Waddell, *Mound Builders*; Brookfield & Brown, *Struggle for Land.*
36. Vayda (ed.), *Environment and Cultural Behaviour.*
37. Spooner (ed.), *Population Growth.*
38. *New Guinea Research Bulletin.*
39. Recent developments are well summarized in Wrigley, *Population and History.*
40. Some of the recent work in this field is summarized in Harrison & Boyce (eds.), *Structure of Populations*, chs. 1, 8, 9, 13.
41. Well surveyed in Hawthorn, *Sociology of Fertility.*
42. An introductory set of readings is provided in Allison (ed.), *Population Control*, in chapters by Perrins, Brown and Calhoun, which suggest further reading.
43. An excellent survey is Ehrlich, *Population.*
44. 'Sociology and demography', pp. 833–4, 838, 842.
45. The absence of historical depth has often been lamented by social anthropologists. Among the best discussions are those in Evans-Pritchard, *Essays in Social Anthropology*, chs. 1, 3.
46. Moore, 'Sociology and demography, pp. 838, 842.
47. The methodology is set out by T. S. Epstein in Epstein (ed.), *Craft of Social Anthropology*, pp. 153–80.
48. This difficulty is discussed by Gallin, *Hsin Hsing, Taiwan*, p. 35.
49. Employed by Firth *et al.*, 'Population of Tikopia', p. 409; Mitchell, 'Yao fertility', p. 295.
50. Forde, 'Population data', p. 149.
51. Lorimer (ed.), *Human Fertility*, p. 363.
52. Carrier & Koblenzer, 'Rungus Dusun', p. 275.
53. Gorer, *Himalayan Village*, p. 433.
54. Carrier & Koblenzer, 'Rungus Dusun'.
55. Nash & Nash, 'Marriage ... in Upper Burma', p. 265.

2. THE GURUNGS OF NEPAL

1. *Census of Nepal*, 1961, pp. 2, 15.
2. Pignède, *Gurungs*, ch. 1, provides a thorough description of the geography, flora and fauna of the area mainly inhabited by Gurungs.
3. There is a detailed description of the meaning of the various terms, as well as further analysis for Thak, in appendix 5.
4. Pignède, *Gurungs*, chs. 5 and 6 gives a detailed and definitive account of Gurung clan and lineage systems. Part of this account in available in English in *Contributions to Indian Sociology*, vi (1962), pp. 102–19. This may be supplemented for specialist readers by Macfarlane, 'Gurungs of Nepal', pp. 32–40; Messerschmidt, 'Social status ... in a Gurung community', *passim*; Allen, 'Ethnography of Nepal', pp. 138–51.
5. As reported in Messerschmidt, 'Social status ... in a Gurung community', p. 73.
6. Pignède, *Gurungs*, p. 64.
7. *Gurungs*, part 2.
8. *Gurungs*, p. 189.
9. The detailed evidence upon which the generalizations in the text are based is to be found in Macfarlane, 'Gurungs of Nepal', pp. 40–9.

3. LONG-TERM CHANGE IN THE GURUNG ECONOMY

1. Buchanan, *Account of Nepal*, pp. 27, 28, 274.
2. Hodgson MSS., vol. 5, pp. 10–11, 44, 77.
3. McDougall, *Village Economy*, p. 48.
4. *Gurungs*, p. 151.
5. *Peoples of Nepal Himalaya*, iii, p. 17.
6. *Gurungs*, p. 113.
7. Pelzer; quoted in Clark, *Subsistence Agriculture*, p. 35.
8. E.g. the description in Gorer, *Himalayan Village*, pp. 69–70, 92; and more generally, Clark, *Subsistence Agriculture*, ch. 3.
9. Hodgson MSS., vol. 5, pp. 51, 52, 57, 58.
10. Though it is impossible to be certain whether the 'ploughing' was done with animals or hoes.
11. *Gurungs*, pp. 104, 149.
12. *Gurungs*, p. 39.
13. Morris, *Gurkhas*, p. 63: and, as Dr Allen pointed out to me, was probably out of date by the 1930s.
14. Pignède, *Gurungs*, p. 142 indicates that the change had already largely occurred in the late 1950s.
15. Morris, 'Thesis on Central Nepal', p. 90; since this was based on hearsay rather than observation, the 'westernization' of villages was probably exaggerated.
16. Pignède, *Gurungs*, p. 32.
17. *Gurungs*, pp. 134–8.
18. Clark, *Subsistence Agriculture*, p. 38.
19. Clark, *Subsistence Agriculture*, pp. 47–9, summarizes findings.
20. Clark, *Subsistence Agriculture*, pp. 35–6.

4. FOREST AND LAND RESOURCES

1. It is assumed in these calculations that actual acreage is that on Fig. 4.1, plus an added $\frac{1}{4}$ to allow for the steep gradient. (Dr. N. Allen pointed out to me that merely to allow for the gradient one needs to add only $\frac{1}{30}$ rather than $\frac{1}{4}$. Therefore, even allowing for the considerable irregularities on the surface this is a very generous estimate. Since I hope to prove that land resources are strained even at present, it seems best to start with an estimate on the optimistic side.)
2. The sources for this table are as follows: Nepal, Western Hills, 1961 (McDougall, *Village Economy*, p. 2 on the basis of the 1961 census); Garos (Burling, *Rengsanggri*, p. 21); Ndembu (Turner, *Schism & Continuity*, p. 17); England, seventeenth century (*Daedulus*, p. 435).
3. Clark, *Subsistence Agriculture*, p. 136.
4. *Ibid.*, p. 139.
5. *Ibid.*, p. 146.
6. Desch, *Timber*, p. 114.
7. Clark, *Population Growth*, p. 150.
8. *Ibid.*, p. 151.
9. It is commented on, e.g. in McDougall, *Village Economy*, pp. 3, 37; Pignède, *Gurungs*, pp. 28, 152; Pant, *Social Economy of the Himalayas*, p. 86.
10. This consumption is equivalent to the consumption of dry matter per day of the following live weights of bullocks:
    buffalo = 10–12 cwt. bullock

oxen	= 6	cwt. bullock
cows	= 6	cwt. bullock
goats	= 2–3	cwt. bullock or 30–40 lb sheep.

Source: Evans, *Rations for Livestock*, p. 47, table 1 and p. 74, table 8.

11. See p. 89.
12. See pp. 83.
13. Shreshta, *Nepal Economy*, p. 51.
14. Clark, *Subsistence Agriculture*, p. 88.
15. For the detailed calculations on which this is based see pp. 128–9.
16. The quantities are discussed on p. 132.
17. See pp. 190 for the statistics.
18. As described in Clark, *Subsistence Agriculture*, p. 60.
19. See p. 326.
20. Epstein, *Economic and Social Change*, p. 27 gives the amount of cultivated land; p. 90 the value per acre; p. 24 the number of households.

5. CHANGES IN THE DISTRIBUTION OF ARABLE LAND

1. *Gurungs*, p. 153.
2. Dr L. Caplan kindly pointed out to me that properly *mohi* means tenant or cultivator, not serial number, and that *doyam* is a class of land (of which there are four *abal, doyam, sim, chahar*) and is not the term for class. Since, however, the Gurungs who translated the documents for me used these terms and gave the translations I have appended, I have left them in the text. Clearly the original words have changed meaning.
3. For various criticisms of the accuracy of land records see Regmi, *Land Tenure In Nepal*, i, p. 159.
4. For a full discussion of Gurung lineages and the *carjat* and *sorajat*, see Pignède, 'Clan organization'.
5. *Gurungs*, pp. 156–7.
6. *Gurungs*, p. 156.
7. *Gurungs*, p. 157.
8. The 1883 figures, with frequent totals of 40 s.m. for lands which were later less than half that total, seem to be inaccurate in this case: possibly they are those of a joint holding, later split up.
9. Caplan, *Land and Social Change*, p. 45.
10. *Gurungs*, p. 153.

6. CAPITAL ASSETS EXCLUDING LAND AND FOREST

1. McDougall, *Village Economy*, p. 100.
2. See table 6.7.
3. *Gurungs*, pp. 94–105.
4. Richards, *Land & Labour*, pp. 87–90.
5. *Gurungs*, pp. 80ff.
6. Bista, *People of Nepal*, p. 77; Morris, *Winter in Nepal*, p. 108, also states that Nepalese houses are often round or oval. See also *Peoples of Nepal Himalaya*, iii, p. 30.
7. *Gurungs*, pp. 74ff.
8. He also describes other kinds (*Gurungs*, pp. 77–9) which were not observed in Thak.

9. Epstein, *Economic & Social Change*, pp. 78, 49.
10. Clark, *Subsistence Agriculture*, pp. 46, 144.
11. *Gurungs*, p. 259.
12. Caplan, *Land and Social Change*, p. 108, where he speaks only of adults, not differentiating males and females.
13. *Gurungs*, p. 259. Hitchcock, *Magars*, pp. 51–2, says that children among the Magars start work when about 8, and when they are 12 they 'can do almost all adult tasks & can be genuine assets to the household'. Kawakita estimated, *Peoples of Nepal Hamalaya*, iii, p. 315, that boys of 8–15 were worth half a man.
14. *Gurungs*, p. 129. The *nogora* or communal work groups of the Gurungs, recruited on neighbourhood lines and undoubtedly adding to the pleasure and hence efficiency of the work, are described in Pignède, *Gurungs*, pp. 127–9, and Macfarlane, 'Gurungs of Nepal', pp. 53–5.
15. Clark, *Subsistence Agriculture*, pp. 91, 95; Epstein, *Economic and Social Change*, p. 78, assumes an eight-hour working day.
16. Epstein, *Economic and Social Change*, pp. 78, 225.
17. Clark, *Subsistence Agriculture*, pp. 143–5.

7. THE APPLICATION OF CAPITAL; INPUT-OUTPUT DATA

1. Nepal Govt., *Physical Input–Output in Agriculture, passim.*
2. Shreshta, *Nepal Economy*, p. 63; the whole chapter is devoted to this problem.
3. McDougall, *Village Economy*, *passim* and esp. pp. 64ff.
4. Clark, *Subsistence Agriculture*, p. 143.
5. *Gurungs*, p. 126; though Pignède does recognize that poorer families do not have enough land to work (p. 125).
6. Morris, *Winter in Nepal*, p. 135.
7. *Gurungs*, ch. 3.
8. Epstein, *Economic and Social Change*, p. 78.
9. *Gurungs*, p. 84.
10. Epstein, *Economic and Social Change*, p. 78.
11. A useful summary of figures is given in Clark, *Subsistence Agriculture*, pp. 146–56; *Wye College Report*, 'Crop production report' gives comparative figures for another part of Nepal.

8. INCOME, CONSUMPTION AND EXPENDITURE

1. Caplan, *Land and Social Change*, p. 117.
2. Epstein (ed.), *Craft of Social Anthropology*, p. 160.
3. Caplan, *Land and Social Change*, p. 77.
4. Clark, *Subsistence Agriculture*, p. 172.
5. *Gurungs*, p. 140.
6. The conversion is made on the basis of the table in Clark, *Subsistence Agriculture*, p. 222.
7. Conversion based on *Manual of Nutrition*, p. 68.
8. Richards, *Land and Labour*, p. 40.
9. Clark, *Subsistence Agriculture*, p. 15, table.
10. Reported in *ibid.*, p. 19.
11. Some of the figures summarized in *ibid.*, ch. 1. and p. 54.
12. Culwick's figures, cited in Clark, *Subsistence Agriculture*, p. 20.

13. *Manual of Nutrition*, p. 40.
14. Worth, *Nepal Health*, table 5, pp. 44–5.
15. *Ibid.*, pp. 42–3.
16. *Ibid.*, table 10, p. 52.
17. Morris, *Winter in Nepal*, p. 96.
18. Richards, *Land and Labour*, ch. 3.
19. McDougall, *Village Economy*, p. 43.
20. *Ibid.* p. 44.
21. Pignède, *Gurungs*, p. 140.
22. Clark, *Subsistence Agriculture*, p. 164.
23. *Ibid.*, p. 168.
24. *Ibid.*, p. 169.

9. SURPLUSES, DEFICITS, AND THE ACCUMULATION OF CAPITAL

1. McDougall, *Village Economy*, pp. 55–6. I gather that this scheme has now been suspended indefinitely (1971).
2. They are houses 6, 14, 23, 40, 52, 55, 70A, 70B, 71, 72, 83, 83A, 86, 87, 88.
3. Hitchcock, *Magars*, p. 105.
4. Caplan, *Land and Social Change*, p. 77.
5. McDougall, *Village Economy*, pp. 45–6. (Thus the total deficit for 100 Sallyan households would be 8000, approx. half that calculated for Thak).
6. Epstein, *Social and Economic Change*, p. 267.
7. Barth, *Nomads of South Persia*, pp. 106–11.
8. This does not seem to be universally true, for Messerschmidt, 'Social status . . . in a Gurung community', pp. 55–6, notes for another Gurung village that it is the richer who migrate to the army, while the poorer stay in the village.
9. Foster, 'Image of limited good', outlines the ethic.
10. Caplan, *Land and Social Change*, ch. 5.
11. Hitchcock, *Magars*, pp. 105, 108; Caplan, *Land and Social Change*, p. 170; Gorer, *Himalayan Village*, p. 87; Pignède, *Gurungs*, p. 144.
12. *Wye Valley Report*, 'Crop production'.
13. Caplan, *Land and Social Change*, p. 13.

10. POPULATION GROWTH IN NEPAL

1. *1952–4 Census*, p. xv and table 17, p. 69.
2. *Ibid.*, p. viii.
3. *1952–4 Census*, p. xiv and table 17.
4. For a description of these 'stages', now somewhat discredited but still a useful preliminary typology, see U.N., *Determinants and Consequences of Population Trends*, p. 44.
5. Shreshta, *Nepal Economy*, p. 36. (Krotki & Thakur 'Population of Nepal', give strong evidence for thinking that there has been considerable under-enumeration in the 1952–4 and 1961 censuses.)
6. *Ibid.*, p. 37 cites the U.N. figures. The Nepal Central Bureau of Statistics, in its 1968 'Population projections for Nepal, 1961–81', p. 4, gives an estimate of 12,392,794 for the year 1976.
7. Worth, *Nepal Health*, p. 31.

8. Figures were given informally in an interview. Krotki & Thakur, 'Population size . . . in Nepal', p. 21 estimate a growth rate of 15 per thousand by subtracting death rates from birth rates.
9. Worth, *Nepal Health*, p. 31.
10. Hitchcock, *Magars*, p. 104.
11. *Ibid.*, p. 14.
12. Fürer-Haimendorf, *Sherpas*, p. 10.
13. Caplan, *Land and Social Change*, pp. 55, 6.
14. Shreshta, *Nepal Economy*, p. 40.
15. *Ibid.*, p. 30.
16. *Ibid.*, p. 84.
17. The already serious deficiencies are shown in Worth, *Nepal Health*, ch. 5, esp. p. 52, table 10. While 100 % of the villages had, by W.H.O. standards, enough cereals, under 40 % had enough beans/nuts, milk and only 11 % enough fats and oils. 0 % had enough vegetables, fruit, meat, fish or poultry.
18. *Wye College Report*, unfortunately unpaginated; 'Recommendations' of 'Crop production' report.
19. Figures for mortality are given in Worth, *Nepal Health*, p. 28 and are discussed in more detail in ch. 8 above. An even higher rate of 32 per thousand is suggested by Krotki & Thakur, 'Population size . . . in Nepal', p. 91.
20. King (ed.), *Medical Care in Developing Countries, 1:1.*
21. Buchanan, *Account of Nepal*, pp. 27, 374.
22. *1952–4 Census*, p. 46.
23. Grierson, *Linguistic Survey of India*, p. 182.
24. *Gurungs*, p. 47. It is also worth noting that 1/9 of the Gurungs recruited during the 1914–18 War came from East Nepal, whereas by the 1952–4 Census, only 1/16 of the 'Gurungs' were shown as coming from E. Nepal.
25. *1952–4 Census*, p. 46. It is not made clear whether this refers only to those present at the time of the census, or includes those absent. From the previous table it is probably the former.
26. *1961 Census*, tables 7, 8.
27. The document is in the India Office library, Hodson MSS., vol. 3, fol. 139ff. I am grateful to Dr N. Allen for help with its dating.
28. *1952–4 Census*, table 3.
29. Northey & Morris, *The Gurkhas*, p. 267. The statistics for Gurung recruits are taken from C. J. Morris, *Handbooks for the Indian army. Gurkhas* (Delhi, 1933), appdx. 6.
30. *Gurungs*, p. 62.
31. Four Brahmin and one Leather-worker families, numbering 21 persons in all, who had settled in the fields below Mohoriya have not been included in my calculations, partly because they were outside the area studied by Pignède, partly because I was unable to obtain full details concerning them.
32. Since 78 persons, out of Pignède's original 496, emigrated out, we only have figures for the 418 who did not leave.
33. There is some difficulty in matching the censuses. This accounts for the discrepancy of three persons which is left after we add the recorded population increase of twelve persons.
34. For details of house construction and an outline of sources and problems in their interpretation, see appendix 3.
35. The sources upon which these totals are based are given in appendix 4, which contains a more extensive analysis of price changes.

11. SOCIAL STRUCTURE AND FERTILITY I: INTERCOURSE VARIABLES

1. Kingsley Davis & Judith Blake, 'Social structure and fertility: an analytic framework', *Econ. Devt. & Cultural Change*, 4, no. 3 (Apr. 1956), pp. 211–35.
2. The classic discussion of the western pattern is by John Hajnal in D. V. Glass & D. E. C. Eversley (eds), *Population in History* (1965) ch. 6. Also see Spengler in *Deadulus*, Spring 1968, p. 433.
3. Gorer, *Himalayan Village*, p. 315.
4. There is an excellent description of a flourishing *rodi* organization in Messerschmidt, 'Social status ... in a Gurung community', pp. 64–72. There are also descriptions of the phenomenon in Pignède, *Gurungs*, p. 260 and Macfarlane, 'Gurungs of Nepal', pp. 55–9. The classic description of the Indian system is V. Elwin, *The Muria and their Ghotul* (Bombay, 1947), chs. 16, 17.
5. *Gurungs*, p. 216 alludes to intercourse in the fields. Morris, 'Thesis on Nepal', p. 132 noted that there is no specific word for a 'bastard' in Nepali, though the word meaning 'child of a co-wife' (*jharkolo*) is often used. The one Gurung I asked about this said that *pregya* was a Gurung term. Morris, 'Thesis on Nepal', p. 127, thought that intercourse usually commenced at puberty among Gurungs, but this was on hearsay.
6. Gorer, *Himalayan Village*, p. 174.
7. *Ibid.*, p. 236.
8. *Gurungs*, p. 268.
9. *Ibid.*, p. 218.
10. See p. 219. Of the 48 % aged 15–18, it seems certain that at least one-third, or 16 %, were married at 18, which would make the ratio of those married at under 18 to those married at 18 + of the order of 40:60.
11. Pignède, *Gurungs*, p. 218, makes the same point.
12. *Gurungs*, p. 216.
13. This phase is described by Morris, *Winter in Nepal*, p. 127.
14. For the Lepchas, see Gorer, *Himalayan Village*, ch. 12; the Bhoteas are described in *Peoples of Nepal Himalaya*, iii, p. 256.
15. 1952–4 Census, p. x. and table 7.
16. Northey & Morris, *The Gurkhas*, p. 194.
17. Morris, *Winter in Nepal*, p. 122. In fact statistics in his own 'Thesis on Nepal', p. 165 contradict Morris' own arguments. Only 5/54 of the men aged 29 or under said they had married at age 16 or under.
18. When the census of Thak was taken, a number of older informants could not remember how old they were when they married. In these cases my translator tended to assume that marriage occurred two years before the birth of the first child. This may distort some of the information for older age-groups, but it seems likely that informants would have remembered if they had been married at a very early age.
19. Hitchock, *Magars*, p. 40.
20. Malthus, *Essay on Population*, ii, p. 250.
21. There are figures for the cost of marriage on pp. 181.
22. Pignède, *Gurungs*, pp. 222ff. discusses the arrangement of marriage.
23. Though it is now said by a few informants that it is necessary to have a son to put fire in one's death in order to go to heaven; clearly this is an example of Hindu influence.
24. For a discussion of the statistics for Thak, see p. 258; for Nepal, see Worth, *Nepal Health*, p. 19.

25. Gorer, *Himalayan Village*, p. 435.
26. For Europe the evidence is summarized by Hajnal in *Population in History*, pp. 101ff. On p. 104 of the same there is a summary of some of the evidence for Africa and Asia.
27. 1952–4 Census, p. x and table 7.
28. *Peoples of Nepal Himalaya*, iii, pp. 259, 280
29. Davis & Blake, 'Social structure and fertility', p. 218 show that this factor never lowers fertility more than 25 %, and in western Europe (e.g. Switzerland) has only one-third as strong an effect on fertility as compared to the influence of age at marriage.
30. *Gurungs*, p. 234.
31. I was told that the sisters had taken a vow of chastity to earn religious merit; I do not know at what age this was taken, nor to what extent they were making a virtue of necessity.
32. 1952–4 Census, p. x and table 7: there is likely to be considerable reporting of absence, however.
33. Pignède, *Gurungs*, p. 265 argued that adultery is 'not frequent' and I noted no anxiety or gossip about adultery. Morris, 'Thesis on Nepal', p. 150 thought adultery *was* frequent, however.
34. One informant, from Siklis, stated that there might be a ceremony at remarriage, this would be up to the man. Risley (*Tribes and Castes*, p. 304) noted that 'Divorced women may marry again by the full ceremony'.
35. Pignède, *Gurungs*, p. 52 noted 'several cases' and on p. 265 he discusses the effect of the army on marital stability.
36. Risley, *Tribes and Castes*, p. 304. Pignède, p. 266, states that usually the woman takes back her goods, the man retains his, at divorce. Sometimes a little gold is given to the woman if she keeps the children.
37. 1952–4 Census, p. x.
38. *Gurungs*, p. 50. But in 1969, in the census which I took, there were 23 widows and only 5 widowers and it seems unlikely that the proportions can have changed so very much.
39. Davis & Blake, 'Social sturcture and fertility', pp. 227–8.
40. *Peoples of Nepal Himalaya*, iii, pp. 266–7.
41. Risley, *Tribes and Castes*, p. 305.
42. *Idem.*, and Northey & Morris, *The Gurkhas*, p. 198.
43. Among the Lepchas, however, it was fairly common for widows to marry widowers (Gorer, *Himalayan Village*, p. 160).
44. Gorer, *Himalayan Village*, p. 292.
45. Davis & Blake, 'Social structure and fertility', p. 232.
46. Pignède, *Gurungs*, p. 213.
47. Morris, *Winter in Nepal*, p. 126.
48. See p. 263.
49. See p. 27.
50. *Gurungs*, p. 52.
51. As Davis & Blake, 'Social structure and fertility', p. 233 point out, available statistics on this subject are extremely unsatisfactory, but most of what there is, is summarized in Hawthorn, *Sociology of Fertility*, pp. 10–14.
52. Morris, *Winter in Nepal*, p. 126.
53. *Gurungs*, p. 245.

12. SOCIAL STRUCTURE AND FERTILITY II: CONCEPTION AND GESTATION VARIABLES

1. Gorer, *Himalayan Village*, p. 174.
2. The somewhat inconclusive evidence is summarized in Nag, *Factors Affecting Human Fertility*, pp. 115–6, 207.
3. Davis & Blake, p. 234.
4. Nag, *Factors Affecting Human Fertility*, pp. 78–9.
5. Gorer, *Himalayan Village*, p. 294; Morris, *Winter in Nepal*, p. 75.
6. Norman E. Himes, *Medical History of Contraception* (London, 1936) contains a useful survey of contraceptive methods in many societies.
7. Gorer, *Himalayan Village*, p. 173, stated that the Lepchas had 'no known method of avoiding conception'. Morris, 'Thesis on Nepal', p. 129 wrote that 'There is, however, no doubt that any form of contraception is quite unknown, nor is *coitus interruptus* practiced in any form'.
8. Morris, *Winter in Nepal*, p. 75.
9. For example, the shortage among the Limbus, Caplan, *Land and Social Change*, p. 6.
10. Hitchcock, *Magars*, p. 49.
11. Worth, *Nepal Health*, p. 32 and Fig. 9, p. 33.
12. For the classic discussion of this problem, see Kingsley Davis in *Science*, 158. no. 3802, 1967, pp. 730–9.
13. The Britain–Nepal Medical Trust hospital at Biratnagar in the Terai laid special emphasis on birth-control among its prospective aims. In a letter of 24 December 1970 Dr Cunningham informed me that 'Loops are very unpopular and we do about one insertion per fortnight as compared to approximately twelve new "Pill" patients per fortnight and ten vasectomies'. The hospital had been in operation for less than two years and it will be interesting if it can keep up a rate which is far higher than that achieved by Pokhara hospital. We, also, found that people preferred reversible, non-clinical, methods, such as pills and condoms.
14. The likelihood of people being supplied from the hospital is rendered even less by a regulation which forbids the distribution of more than three months supply of pills or condoms at a time. This means that the majority of the population who live at least a day's walk or more from Pokhara will have to tramp long distances every 3 months (especially difficult during the monsoon months) in order to re-stock.
15. Nag, *Human Fertility*, pp. 136–7.
16. Although conceptually different, infanticide and abortion are similar in their effects, and are treated together here.
17. Gorer, *Himalayan Village*, p. 173 described the only kind of Lepcha abortion as 'bathing in hot sulphorous streams'.
18. *Gurungs*, p. 52.
19. Cf. Davis & Blake, p. 214.

13. THE DEMOGRAPHIC CONSEQUENCES OF SOCIAL STRUCTURE: FERTILITY STATISTICS

1. The Family Planning figures were given in a private communication. The figure from the U.N. population data sheet for 1969 was taken from Ehrlich, *Population*, p. 331.

2. Worth, *Nepal Health*, pp. 24, 19. The report does point out that it did not cover the mid-western and high altitude areas where late age at marriage would probably lower the fertility rate.
3. Krotki & Thakur, 'Population size ... in Nepal' p. 11.
4. Hitchcock, *Magars*, p. 49.
5. Gorer, *Himalayan Village*, pp. 435–6; for comparative figures showing the normal range between 4.5–6.5 for completed fertility, see Nag, *Factors Affecting Fertility*, pp. 169–170.
6. Worth, *Nepal Health*, pp. 19, 20 Fig. 1.
7. Gorer, *Himalayan Village*, pp. 435 6.
8. *Peoples of Nepal Himalaya*, iii, p. 236. Among a Sherpa group recently studied, the mean average age at first birth was 23–5 years (Lang, 'Kunde Hospital', p. 14).
9. This is suggested by Worth, *Nepal Health*, p. 19.
10. *Gurungs*, p. 53.
11. The necessity for formal training in demography for social anthropologists about to do fieldwork is emphasized by such an omission.
12. In 1969 there was a *de jure* population of 528, which had been increasing annually.
13. Worth, *Nepal Health*, p. 23 (table 2).
14. I have followed the method adopted by Mitchell, 'Yao fertility', pp. 301–2, where comparative rates may be found.
15. Figures are from Mitchell, 'Yao fertility', table 7, p. 302.
16. The calculations were made as follows. According to the table on p. 48 of *Gurungs*, there were, in 1958, 81 children aged 0–5 and 115 women aged 16–50. If we adjust these (subtracting $\frac{1}{8}$ of 10 children at age 5, and adding 5 women for age 15) we then have an approximate rate of children aged 0–4 to women aged 15–50. From my census for 1969 I was able to work out the figures exactly; there were 59 children aged 0–4, and 119 women aged 15–50.
17. Worth, *Nepal Health*, pp. 21, 25.
18. Nag, *Factors Affecting Fertility*, pp. 169–70 runs from an average of 10.4 (Hutterites) to 2.6 (some Pacific groups).
19. *Gurungs*, p. 53.
20. Myrdal, *Asian Drama*, ii, p. 1435, note 1, cites a modern study of labour migration which shows its heightening effect on fertility.
21. Pignède *Gurungs*, p. 54, in fact, did not suggest that the *carjat* were more fertile, but that they suffered a lower mortality rate; that he was wrong in thinking this is suggested on p. 272.
22. See appendix 7.
23. Women omitted in Mohoriya were (according to Pignède's census) 3, 12, 14, 18, 19B, 28, 34, 36, 45A, 47B, 52, 66, 68A, 75A, 83C, 84A, 89. In Thak there were 6A, 9, 11A, 38, 35, 36, 43C, 44A, 53, 57A, 80B.
24. Because, in fact, they would belong to an older cohort than their age at death would suggest, since they had died some time before.
25. Worth, *Nepal Health*, p. 20, Fig. I. There appears to be some discrepancy between this figure, which shows that a little over half the total married under the age of 18, and the comment on p. 20, which states that 'most' marriages took place over the age of 18.
26. *Peoples of Nepal Himalaya*, iii (ed. Kihara) p. 236.
27. *Gurungs*, p. 51.
28. *Gurungs*, p. 52.
29. *Idem.*

30. Cited in Nag, *Factors Affecting Fertility*, p. 114.
31. *Gurungs*, p. 53.
32. *Idem.*

14. SOCIAL STRUCTURE AND MORTALITY

1. The most detailed study of incidence of disease in Nepal is contained in chs. 5–10 of Worth, *Nepal Health*, where a number of comparative statistics are to be found: also Taylor, *Medical Survey of Kali Gandak.*
2. Cited in Myrdal, *Asian Drama*, ii, p. 1416.
3. Gorer, *Himalayan Village*, pp. 52–3.
4. A detailed analysis of each type of symptom, and of the minor illnesses and healing system of the Gurungs is given in Macfarlane, 'Gurungs of Nepal', pp. 182–240. It is hoped to publish this separately.
5. Worth, *Nepal Health*, pp. 69–70.
6. *Ibid.*, p. 71.
7. Taylor, *Medical Survey of Kali Gandak*, p. 427.
8. For a description of how the women were selected see p. 249.
9. *1952–4 Census*, p. xvii.
10. Worth, *Nepal Health*, p. 29; Krotki & Thakur, 'Population size in Nepal', p. 91.
11. E.g. India in 1969 had a rate of 18, Pakistan, 19. (Figures from Ehrlich, *Population*, p. 331).
12. Worth, *Nepal Health*, p. 29. No figures for Nepal were given in the 1969 U.N. data sheet. In the same year the rate for India was 139, for Pakistan, 142. A recent survey of the Sherpas suggested an infant mortality rate of 158/1000 livebirths (Lang, 'Kunde Hospital', p. 4).
13. Worth, *Nepal Health*, p. 21.
14. Gorer, *Himalayan Village*, pp. 434–6, re. the Lepchas of Sikkim.
15. *Gurungs*, p. 54; presumably the 300 % is a misprint for 30 %. For the Sherpas, a loss of 25 % by the age of twelve years is suggested (Lang, 'Kunde Hospital', p. 4).
16. *Gurungs*, p. 50. For a discussion of the atypical age-structure, see p. 282.
17. *Gurungs*, p. 54.
18. For a discussion of this see appendix 7.
19. It is not known whether the husbands of women who between them had nineteen live-births were away in the army or not; they have been omitted.
20. Worth, *Nepal Health*, p. 27, Fig. 2, though the two ratios are not, of course, directly comparable.
21. Koblenzer & Carrier, 'Rungus Dusun', p. 272, for example, found that $\frac{6}{13}$ of the married women aged over 45 had been widowed.

15. THE AGE AND SEX-STRUCTURE OF THE GURUNG POPULATION

1. The *lho* system is discussed fully in Pignède, *Gurungs*, pp. 315–19.
2. U.N. *Determinants . . . , p. 141.*
3. There are diagrams of both the 'ideal type' and actual age-structures for example, in Wrigley, *Population in History*, pp. 24–5.
4. The figures for Ceylon and for England and Wales have been taken from the table on p. 103 of Laslett, *World we have lost.*

5. Calculated from the Nepal *1961 Census*, vol. i, table 1.
6. Worth, *Nepal Health*, p. 30.
7. *Gurungs*, p. 51.
8. Marwick, *Sorcery in its Social Setting*, p. 50.
9. Ibid., p. 48.
10. *Gurungs*, p. 56. In another Gurung village, in Lamjung, the proportion of the total population in the army was almost identical to that in Thak according to Messerschmidt, 'Social status . . . in a Gurung community', p. 54.
11. *Gurungs*, p. 50.
12. *1954 Census*, p. ix.
13. These three kinds of wage-labour connected to the army have been amalgamated; in fact, over 90 % of those from Thak were serving in the military ranks, rather than as civilians or in Indian or Assam police.
14. *Gurungs*, p. 56.
15. Gluckman, 'Review of land and labour', p. 71.
16. M. Mead (ed.) *Cultural Patterns . . .*, p. 248, has pointed out that an earlier pattern will soften the effects of migrant labour.
17. See pp. 318ff.

16. RESOURCES AND POPULATION: SOME GENERAL MODELS

1. Malthus, *Population*, i, p. 6.
2. Malthus, *Population*, i, pp. 314–15 and also p. 304.
3. *Population*, ii, p. 144.
4. *Population*, i, p. 15.
5. *Population*, ii, p. 144.
6. *Population*, ii. p. 25 and i, p. 59.
7. Slicher Van Bath, *Agrarian History*, p. 314.
8. The evidence concerning population, wages and cost of living is conveniently summarized in Wilkinson, *Poverty and Progress*, p. 71.
9. Flinn, *Industrial Revolution*, p. 66 is here quoting Malthus; the same point is made by Chambers, *Population and Society*, p. 59.
10. Graphs 18–20 in the supplement to Goubert, *Beauvais*, show that baptisms, marriages and deaths moved together until the middle of the eighteenth century.
11. Wrigley, *Population and History*, figure 3:4.
12. Ekvall in Spooner (ed.), *Population Growth*, p. 269.
13. Stott in Vayda (ed.), *Environment and Cultural Behavior*, p. 91.
14. Gellner, *Thought and Change*, p. 118; Wrigley, *Population and History*, p. 53, makes a similar point.
15. As Lord Balogh, among others, has pointed out in the preface to Dumont & Rosier, *Hungry Future*, p. 10.
16. Blake, *Family Structure in Jamaica*, pp. 7, 8. These crude rates do not take into account changing age structure and are therefore only a very rough index.
17. *Population*, i, p. 274.
18. *Population*, ii, p. 172.
19. *Conditions of Agricultural Growth* (hereafter cited as *Conditions*).
20. *Economics of Subsistence Agriculture* with Margaret Haswell; *Population Growth and Land Use.* Geoffrey Hawthorn has pointed out to me that Boserup and

Clark are proposing crucially distinct theses; the former applying to the transition from hunting and gathering, through swidden, to settled agriculture, the latter to all socio-economic systems. It is therefore only at the most general level that the two can be bracketed together. He also rightly suggested that some of Boserup's theses can be saved by re-formulating them and limiting them strictly to hunting and gathering or swidden systems.

21. Dumond, 'Population growth', was published in the same year as Boserup's work, yet the two seem to have had no influence on each other. Dumond's argument (especially on pp. 313, 318) that population growth is often a cause of economic growth is identical to Boserup's. Wilkinson, *Poverty and Progress.*
22. *Conditions*, p. 11.
23. Allison (ed.), *Population Control*, p. 231.
24. *Conditions*, p. 118.
25. *Economics of Subsistence Agriculture*, pp. 159, 162.
26. Lee in Vayda (ed.), *Environment and Cultural Behavior*, pp. 62, 74. A general summary of the data is contained in Sahlins, *Stone Age Economics*, ch. 1.
27. Waddell, *Mound Builders*, p. 218.
28. *Conditions*, p. 118.
29. *Conditions*, p. 14.
30. *Population Growth and Land Use*, pp. 50–1.
31. *Conditions*, pp. 11–12.
32. *Population Growth and Land Use*, p. 53.
33. McKeown and Brown, 'Medical evidence' in Glass & Eversley (eds.), *Population in History*. David Levine, 'The demographic implications of rural industrialization' (Cambridge Univ., Ph. D., 1974).
34. Major studies by Coale & Hoover, Hoover & Perlman, Ruprecht, Enke, Newman & Allen, are discussed by Jones 'Population growth' in the *New Guinea Research Bulletin*, no. 42. All the studies show that per capita income will increase faster with lower fertility. A less dramatic conclusion is reached in the survey of the problem by Easterlin in Ford (ed.), *Social Demography*, p. 273.
35. *Conditions*, p. 43.
36. *Conditions*, p. 41.
37. *Population*, ii, p. 12.
38. From U.N., *Determinants*, p. 44.
39. For example those suggested by Ryder and summarized in Hawthorn, *Sociology of Fertility*, p. 70.
40. Wrong, *Population and Society*, pp. 18–19.
41. Some of the evidence is summarized by Boyden in Harrison and Boyce (eds.), *Structure of Populations*, p. 426.
42. *Conditions*, p. 56.
43. Thompson, *Population and Progress*, p. 16.
44. Jones, 'Population growth' in *New Guinea Research Bulletin*.
45. In Harrison & Boyce (eds.), *Structure of Populations*, p. 315.
46. Clark, *Population Growth and Land Use*, p. 72.
47. Hollingsworth, *Historical Demography*, p. 311.
48. Goubert, *Beauvais*, p. 45. The concept (and term) 'crisis' has been adopted from the work of the French historical demographers.
49. Clark, *Population Growth and Land Use*, p. 72.
50. Hollingsworth, *Historical Demography*, p. 135.
51. Russell, *Violence*, p. 182. Dr Wrigley pointed out that the type of disease

circulated by the Spanish invasion of Mexico (external) and by the armies in the Thirty Years War (internal) were very different.

52. The figures are from Russell, *Violence*, p. 9.
53. Brookfield & Brown, *Struggle for Land*, p. 73.
54. Vayda (ed.), *Environment and Cultural Behavior*, ch. 10. Some striking evidence from medieval Europe and from China, as well as a similar argument to that in the preceding paragraphs, is presented in Dumond, 'Population growth', pp. 304–7.
55. In Harrison & Boyce (eds.), *Structure of Populations*, p. 328.
56. Goubert, *Beauvais*, ch. 3.
57. Wilkinson, *Poverty and Progress*, p. 23.
58. Boyden in Harrison & Boyce (eds.), *Structure of Populations*, p. 415.
59. *Idem.*
60. Quoted in Thompson, *Population and Progress*, p. 125.
61. For instance Helleiner, 'Vital revolution' in Glass & Eversley (eds.), *Population in History*, pp. 79–86; Kunstadter in Harrison & Boyce (eds.), *Structure of Populations*, p. 348.
62. Wrigley, *Population and History*, ch. 3; Drake, *Population in Norway*, p. 39.
63. The various patterns are well described in Wrigley, *Population and History*, especially ch. 3.
64. Russell, *Violence*, p. 158.
65. Scott in Vayda (ed.), *Environment and Cultural Behavior*, p. 113. There is, as one might expect, considerable disagreement about 'animal' population dynamics and this is consequently an over-simplification. One good summary of different views is in the appendix to Lack, *Population Studies of Birds*. I owe this reference to Geoffrey Hawthorn.
66. In Harrison & Boyce (eds.), *Structure of Populations*, p. 82.

APPENDIX 4. POPULATION AND THE PRICE OF LAND AND OTHER GOODS

1. *Gurungs*, p. 155.
2. U.S. AID, Economic Data Paper, vol. 11, no. 1. Aug. 1969, p. 1. (U.S. AID, Nepal).
3. Caplan, *Land and Social Change*, p. 39.
4. Shresta, *Economy of Nepal*, p. 116.
5. As Pignède, *Gurungs*, p. 151, points out.
6. *Gurungs*, p. 103.

APPENDIX 5. HOUSEHOLD AND FAMILY STRUCTURE AMONG THE GURUNGS

1. *Census of Nepal*, 1961, pp. 2, 15.
2. Caplan, *Land and Social Change*, p. 33.
3. Paperback edn., p. 174.
4. See for example the discussion of its use in Laslett (ed.), *Household and Family Structure*, pp. 28–32.
5. The one Mohoriya case is doubtful. The head of the household was away in Bhairuwa, though his wife still lived in the village, as did his brother and father.
6. Caplan, *Land and Social Change*, p. 33.
7. Morris, *Winter in Nepal*, pp. 99, 103, 104.

8. Iijima, 'Ecology, economy and social system', p. 102, suggests on the contrary that arable farming is correlated with extended households, pastoral with nuclear ones.
9. There is a suggestion to this effect in Wolf, *Peasants*, p. 65.
10. Examples are south India (Epstein, *Economic and Social Change*, p. 178) and seventeenth century England (Laslett, *World we have lost*, p. 46).
11. Caplan, *Land and Social Change*, p. 34.

Select bibliography

(Place of publication is London, unless otherwise specified.)

Allen, N. J., 'Some problems in the ethnography of the peoples of Nepal and their neighbours' (Oxford Univ. B.Litt. thesis, 1968).

Allison, A. (ed.), *Population Control* (1970).

Ardener, E., *Divorce and Fertility* (Oxford, 1962).

Aspin, J., 'Tuberculosis among the Gurkhas', *Tubercle*, xxviii, nos. 7 and 8 (1947).

Bailey, F. G., *Caste and the Economic Frontier* (Manchester, 1967).

Baker, P. T. & Sanders, W. T., 'Demographic Studies in Anthropology', in *Annual Review of Anthropology*, i (1972) ed. B. J. Siegel.

Banfield, E. C., *Moral Basis of a Backward Society* (New York, 1958).

Barth, F., *Nomads of South Persia* (1964).

Benedict, B., 'Population regulation in primitive societies', in *Population Control*, (1970) ed. A. Allison.

Bista, D. B., *People of Nepal* (Kathmandu, 1967).

Blake, J., *Family Structure in Jamaica* (New York, 1961).

Brookfield, H. C. & Brown, P., *Struggle for Land* (Melbourne, 1963).

Boserup, E., *Conditions of Agricultural Growth* (1965).

Buchanan, F., *An Account of the Kingdom of Nepal* (Edinburgh, 1819).

Burling, R., *Rengsanggri, Family and Kinship in a Garo Village* (Philadelphia, 1963).

Caplan, L., *Land and Social Change in East Nepal* (1970).

Carrier, N. H. & Koblenzer, P. J., 'Fertility, mortality and nuptiality of the Rungus Dusun', *Population Studies*, xiii, no. 3 (March, 1960).

Census of Nepal, 1952–4, Report.

Census of Nepal, 1961, Report.

Chagnon, N., *Yąnomamö, The Fierce People* (New York, 1968).

Chagnon, N., *Studying the Yąnomamö* (New York, 1974).

Chambers, J. D., *Population, Economy, and Society in Pre-Industrial England* (Oxford, 1972).

Clark, C. & Haswell, M., *Economics of Subsistence Agriculture* (3rd edn., 1967).

Clark, C., *Population Growth and Land Use* (1968).

Clarke, W. C., *Place and People. An Ecology of a New Guinea Community* (Los Angeles, 1971).

Daedulus, Spring 1968 issue on 'Historical population studies'.

Davis, K., 'Population policy: will current programs succeed?', *Science*, 158, no. 3802 (November 1967).

Davis, K. and Blake, J., 'Social structure and fertility: an analytic framework', *Economic Devt. and Cultural Change*, 4, no. 3 (1956).

Desch, H. E., *Timber, Its Structure and Properties* (3rd edn., 1962).

Douglas, M., 'Population control in primitive groups', *Brit. Jnl. Sociology*, xvii, no. 3 (Sept. 1966).

Drake, M., *Population and Society in Norway 1735–1865* (Cambridge, 1969).

Dumond, D. E., 'Population growth and cultural change', *South Western Jnl. of Anthropology*, 21 (1965).

Dumont, R. & Rosier, B., *The Hungry Future* (1969).

Ehrlich, P. & A., *Population, Resources, Environment* (San Francisco, 1970).

Epstein, A. L. (ed.), *Craft of Social Anthropology* (1967).

Epstein, T. S., *Economic Development and Social Change in South India* (Manchester, 1962).

Evans, R. E., *Rations for Livestock* (H.M.S.O., 1960).

Evans-Pritchard, E. E., *Essays in Social Anthropology* (1962).

Firth, R., Borrie, W. D. & Spillius, J., 'The population of Tikopia, 1929 and 1952', *Population Studies*, x, no. 3 (March 1957).

Flinn, M. W., *Origins of the Industrial Revolution* (1966).

Ford, R. (ed.), *Social Demography* (New Jersey, 1970).

Forde, D. & Charles, E., 'Notes on some population data from a Southern Nigerian village', *Sociological Review*, xxx, no. 2 (April 1938).

Foster, G. M., 'Peasant society and the image of limited good', *American Anthropologist*, 67, no. 2 (April 1965).

Freedman, R., 'Sociology of human fertility', *Current Sociology*, x/xi, no. 2 (1961–2).

Fürer-Haimendorf, C. von., *Sherpas of Nepal* (1964).

(ed.), *The Anthropology of Nepal* (1974).

Gallin, B., *Hsin Hsing, Taiwan: A Chinese Village in Change* (Berkeley, 1966).

Geertz, C., 'Form and variation in Balinese village structure', *American Anthropologist*, 61 (1959).

Geertz, C., *Agricultural Involution* (Berkeley, 1968).

Gellner, E., *Thought and Change* (1964).

Glass, D. V. & Eversley, D. E. C. (eds.), *Population in History* (1965).

Glover, J. R., 'Structure and function in the Gurung interrogative', *Jnl. of Tribhuvan Univ.*, (Special Linguistics number, no date).

Glover, W. W., 'Three Gurung equivalents of English Be', *Jnl. of Tribhuvan Univ.*, (Special Linguistics number, no date).

Gluckman, M., 'How the Bemba make their living', *Rhodes–Livingstone Institute Jnl.*, June 1945.

Goode, W. J., *World Revolution and Family Patterns* (New York, 1963).

Goody, J., 'Inheritance, property, and marriage in Africa and Eurasia', *Sociology*, 3, no. 1 (Jan. 1969).

Goody, J., 'Sideways or downwards? Lateral and vertical succession, inheritance and descent in Africa and Eurasia', *Man*, 5, no. 4 (December 1970).

Goody, J., 'Strategies of heirship', *Comparative Studies in Society and History*, 15, no. 1 (Jan. 1973).

Gorer, G., *Himalayan Village, An Account of the Lepchas of Sikkim* (2nd edn., 1967).

Goubert, P., *Beauvais et le Beauvaisis de 1600 à 1730* (Paris, 1960).

Gurung, H. B., 'Pokhara Valley, Nepal Himalaya' (Edinburgh Univ. Ph.D. thesis, 1965).

Hajnal, J., 'European marriage patterns in perspective' in *Population in History*, eds. D. V. Glass and D. E. C. Eversley (1965).
Harrison, G. A. & Boyce, A. J., *The Structure of Human Populations* (Oxford, 1972).
Hauser, P. M. & Duncan, O. D. (eds.), *The Study of Population: an Inventory and Appraisal* (Chicago, 1959).
Hawthorn, G., *Sociology of Fertility* (1970).
Himes, N. E., *Medical History of Contraception* (1936).
Hitchcock, J. T., 'Some effects of recent change in rural Nepal', *Human Organization*, 22, no. 1 (Spring 1963).
Hitchcock, J. T., *Magars of Banyan Hill* (New York, 1966).
Hodgson, B. H., Collection of MS., India Office Library, London.
Hodgson, B. H., *Essays on the Language, Literature and Religion of Nepal and Tibet* (1874), 2 vols.
Hollingsworth, T. H., *Historical Demography* (1969).
Iijima, S., 'Ecology, economy and social system in the Nepal Himalayas', *The Developing Economies*, ii, no. 1 (March 1964).
Karan, P. K. & Jenkins, W. M., 'Population, land utilisation and possible expansion of cultivated area in Nepal', *Pacific Viewpoint*, 2, no. 1 (March 1961).
Karan, P. K. & Jenkins, W. M., *The Himalayan Kingdoms* (New Jersey, 1963).
Kihara, H. (ed.), *Peoples of Nepal Himalaya*, vol. iii (Kyoto Univ., 1957).
King, M. (ed.), *Medical Care in Developing Countries* (Nairobi, 1966).
Krotki, K. J. & Thakur, H. N., 'Estimates of population size and growth from the 1952–4 and 1961 censuses of the Kingdom of Nepal', *Population Studies*, 25 no. 1 (1971).
Krzywicki, L., *Primitive Society and Its Vital Statistics* (1934).
Lack, D., *Population Studies of Birds* (Oxford, 1966).
Lang, S. D. R. & Lang, A., 'Kunde Hospital and a demographic survey of the Upper Khumbu, Nepal', *New Zealand Medical Jnl.*, 74, no. 470 (July 1971).
Laslett, P., *World we have lost* (1965).
Laslett, P. (ed.), *Household and Family in Past Time* (Cambridge, 1972).
Lorimer, F. (ed.), *Culture and Human Fertility* (U.N.E.S.C.O., 1954).
Mcdougall, C., *Village and Household Economy in Far Western Nepal* (Kirtipur, Nepal, no date, *c.* 1969).
Macfarlane, A., 'Population crisis: anthropology's failure', *New Society*, 10 October, 1968.
Macfarlane, A. D. J., 'Population and economy in Central Nepal: a study of the Gurungs' (London Univ. Ph.D., 1972).
McNamara, R. S., 'Address to the University of Notre Dame', 1 May, 1969.
Malthus, T. R., *An Essay on the Principles of Population* (Everyman edn., no date), 2 volumes.
Mamdani, M., *The Myth of Population Control; Family, Caste, and Class in an Indian Village* (New York, 1972).
Manual of Nutrition (H.M.S.O., Ministry of Agric. Fish & Food, 1961).
Marwick, M. G., *Sorcery in its Social Setting* (Manchester, 1965).
Mead, M. (ed.), *Cultural Patterns and Technical Change* (New York, 1955).

Messerschmidt, D. A., 'Social status, conflict and change in a Gurung community of Nepal' (Oregon Univ. Ph.D., 1974).

Messerschmidt, D. A. & Gurung, N. J., 'Parallel trade and innovation in Central Nepal', in *The Anthropology of Nepal*, ed. C. von Fürer-Haimendorf (1974).

Mihaly, E. B., *Foreign Aid and Politics in Nepal* (Oxford, 1965).

Mitchell, J. C., 'An estimate of Yao fertility', *Africa*, xix, no. 4 (Oct. 1949).

Moore, W. E., 'Sociology and demography' from *The Study of Population: an Inventory and Appraisal* eds. P. M. Hauser and O. D. Duncan (Chicago, 1959).

Morris, C. J., *Gurkhas* (Delhi, 1933).

Morris, J., 'Social life in Central Nepal' (Cambridge Univ. M. Sc. thesis, 1935).

Morris, J., *A Winter in Nepal* (1963).

Myrdal, G., *Asian Drama* (1968), 3 vols.

Nag, M., *Factors Affecting Human Fertility in Non-industrial Societies* (New Haven, 1962).

Nag, M., 'Anthropology and population', *Population Studies*, 27, no. 1 (March 1973).

Nash, J. & Nash, M., 'Marriage, family, and population growth in Upper Burma', *South Western Jnl. of Anthropology*, 19 (1963).

Nepal, Ministry of Economic Planning, *Physical Input–Output Characteristics of Cereal Grain Production . . . Nepal 1965/6* (mimeo).

Nepal, Central Bureau of Statistics, *Population Projections for Nepal, 1961–1981* (1968). (mimeo).

Nepal and the Gurkhas (H.M.S.O., 1965).

Nepali, G. S., *The Newars* (Bombay, 1965).

New Guinea Research Bulletin, No. 42, 'Population growth and socio-economic change' (Australian National Univ., Canberra, 1971).

Northey, W. B. & Morris, C. J., *The Gurkhas* (1928).

Obeyesekere, G., *Land Tenure in Village Ceylon* (Cambridge, 1967).

Okada, F. E., 'Ritual brotherhood: A cohesive factor in Nepalese society', *South Western Jnl. of Anthropology*, 13 (1957).

Pant, S. D., *Social Economy of the Himalayas* (1935).

Pignède, B., 'Clan organization and hierarchy among the Gurungs', *Contributions to Indian Sociology*, vi (1962).

Pignède, B., *Les Gurungs: une population himalayenne du Népal* (Paris, 1966).

Platt, Lord & Parkes, A. S. (eds.), *Social and Genetic Influences on Life and Death* (Edinburgh, 1967).

Rappaport, R. A., *Pigs for the Ancestors* (Yale, 1971).

Regmi, M. C., *Land Tenure and Taxation in Nepal* (Berkeley, 1963–5), 3 vols.

Richards, A. I., *Land, Labour & Diet in Northern Rhodesia* (Oxford, 1939).

Risley, H. H., *Tribes and Castes of Bengal* (Calcutta, 1891).

Roberts, D. F., 'A demographic study of a Dinka village', *Human Biology* 28 (1956).

Russell, C. & W. M. S., *Violence, Monkeys and Man* (1968).

Sagant, P., 'Les Marchés en Pays Limbu', *L'Ethnographie*, 1968–9.

Sahlins, M., *Stone Age Economics* (Chicago, 1972).

Shreshta, B. P., *The Economy of Nepal* (Bombay, 1967).

Slicher van Bath, B. H., *Agrarian History of Western Europe A.D. 500–1850* (1963).

Stirling, P., *Turkish Village* (Paper edn., New York, 1965).
Southall, A. (ed.), *Social Change in Modern Africa* (Oxford, 1961).
Spooner, B. (ed.), *Population Growth: Anthropological Implications* (Cambridge Mass., 1972).
Tawney, R. H., *The Agrarian Problem in the Sixteenth Century* (Harper Torchbook edn., New York, 1967).
Tawney, R. H., *Equality* (Unwin paper edn., 1964).
Taylor, C. E., 'A medical survey of the Kali Gandak and Pokhara Valley of Central Nepal', *Geographical Review*, 41 (July–Oct., 1951).
Thompson, W. S., *Population and Progress in the Far East* (Chicago, 1969).
Turner, V. M., *Schism and Continuity in an African Society* (Manchester, 1957).
United Nations, *Determinants and Consequences of Population Trends* (New York, 1953).
U.S. AID/Nepal, *Economic Data Paper*, 11 no. 1 (August 1969).
Vayda, A. P. (ed.), *Environment and Cultural Behavior* (New York, 1969).
Waddell, E., *The Mound Builders* (Seattle, 1972).
Wilkinson, R. G., *Poverty and Progress* (1973).
Wolf, E. R., *Peasants* (New Jersey, 1966).
Worth, R. M. & Shah, N. K., *Nepal Health Survey* (Univ. of Hawaii Press, Honolulu, 1969).
Wrigley, E. A., 'Family limitation in pre-industrial England', *Economic History Review*, 2nd series, xix, no. 1 (1966).
Wrigley, E. A., *Population and History* (1969).
Wrong, D. H., *Population and Society* (New York, 1956).
Wye College (University of London), *Nepal Project, 1969* (mimeo).

Index